THE COLLECTED STORIES OF

Hortense Calisher

THE COLLECTED
STORIES OF
Hortense Calisher

New York

FOR RICHARD HOWARD

Contents

❧ I ☙

❧ II ☙

CONTENTS

A STORY is an apocalypse, served in a very small cup. Still, it wants to be considered in its own company only. The presence of neighbors changes it. Worlds meant to be compacted only to themselves, bump. Their very sequence can do them violence. Even when all the stories are by the same hand.

Here are thirty-six, covering almost two decades, and combining three prior collections. *In the Absence of Angels*, here entire, was my first book as well; it is full of beginnings. Yet it too was a selection. By the time it went to press there were more stories available, and I continued to write them. Three years on, however, I began a novel which was to take another seven years to complete. After its publication came *Tale for the Mirror, A Novella and Other Stories* —a selection from among the shorter works written during that eleven-year interim. A second novel was followed by *Extreme Magic* —again a novella with stories. The two title novellas are here omitted. All the stories are here, plus one which is new to book form. Since all three collections are only weakly chronological and follow no other natural order, I have felt free to desert their tables of contents for another arrangement entirely.

What I have done is to try for what a conductor asks of a program, or a composer would hope for if he had the concertizing of his own work—to sustain and pleasure the natural rhythms of an audience. These rhythms—the rise and fall of interest, the need to go from frivol to gloom, from dark to light, from female to male to the general, and from an untrustworthy reality to a joyously recognizable fantasy—I take to be much the same as my own.

One group of stories, those centered around the Hester-Kinny

ix

Elkin family, are related. They are indeed, my relations. Yet, in all quasi-autobiography, as one exorcises the family world the mere facts begin to disappear, in favor of the mere truth. Hester was certainly me. But Kinny, the boy in "A Box of Ginger," was also. When I found that out (in answer to a canny question from William Maxwell), I was the one surprised. I was to find this knowledge useful and comforting whenever I wrote of men and boys. There is no reason why they should not be our Bovarys.

Even so, Kinny in "The Gulf Between" is my real brother, as a sibling seen. And by the time the young man in "The Sound of Waiting" and the young wife in "The Rabbi's Daughter" come along, it no longer matters that they are aspects of me; they are youth revolving before the prospect of the world and not yet aware who they are; he doesn't yet know that as a valet to memory only, he will sink back, as those parts of oneself do; she, whose feminism scarcely has a name, doesn't know that she will revolt. As for the Father and Mother, as I have just this moment seen, they do not change; they remain like the *ushabti*, the statuettes placed in the tomb so that its owner, dead or dreaming, may be served by them. In such stories, only the children mutate. And grow up to write them.

I had intended to do more about the Elkins. They were to be a grand first novel, of many story-chapters centering out like the spokes of a wheel. Gradually I saw that this wheel might be turning all my life. And that though I might at any time return with another spoke, I must now leave at once. When I did return, the tone ("Time, Gentlemen!" and "Songs My Mother Taught Me") had altogether changed. Few of this group were written chronologically, none toward that end, and none of course came really from behind the eye of a child. So there was no obligation to begin the book with them. I put them in its center, where they may radiate.

I begin rather with the story in which I deserted the literal world forever, for the imaginary one. "In Greenwich There Are Many Gravelled Walks" was also the story after whose appearance the press began poking the idea of novels at me, as if on my own I might never have thought of them. My answer at the time—made with that hauteur which is the other side of fright—was: If a tale can be told in seven thousand words, why use seventy? I still believe that. And

I still feel that same respectful scare—at the thought of all the tales, long some of them, which wait to be told.

Meanwhile, scanning this table of contents, of course I see many connections with the novels that were to come. (And with some yet to come.) Sometimes a novel-in-progress may erupt a story sideways, as with "May-ry," written while I was on the section of *False Entry* that takes place in the Southern United States (I had to give myself a guilty permission to delay the longer concentration: I've lost many stories by not doing so.) Conversely, I can see, if I'm not careful, that whoever wrote "The Watchers" might well write a novel narrated by "the heart doomed to watch itself feel," that Spanner in "One of the Chosen" faintly anticipates the Judge in *The New Yorkers*, as the young Peter Birge in "In Greenwich There Are Many Gravelled Walks" is very close, in the writer's sympathies, to the hero of *Eagle Eye*. (As the "rabbi's daughter" and her baby are kin to the young mother-and-child in *Textures of Life*.) I can see now why the young beauties who are just pulling off their blouses in "Songs My Mother Taught Me" will end up in *Queenie* in the buff. (Alongside Queenie's political ancestress, "Ginevra Leake.") And why, if one doesn't strain at swallowing newts à la "Heartburn," one may someday open one's jaws wide enough to accommodate an eight-foot ellipse, swum in from the Elsewhere that only the uninitiate still call science-fiction, and as human a noncharacter as you ever wrote—of whom your English publisher will ask "Tell me. I have to know. W*as* he a Lesbian?"

To which you must close ears, eyes, and quickest—mouth. In case you were about to quip "No. She was Gulliver." Analogies are everywhere—afterward. And though you would rather not, you can see them sharper than anybody.

I do see, more gladly, a certain temperament in the story form. Its very duration, too brief to make a new mode in, verges it always toward that classical corner where sits the human figure. And perhaps the genre flourishes best during those periods of life—both for authors and eras—when the human drama is easier accepted as the main one going. Whenever we lose this sense of ourselves as a train of people and gear, plodding eternally down the ages or purposefully up, we tend to dissipate into style—in every genre. The novel, that deceptively ragged cave, can take more echoing. For a time. And maybe more gear. But a loss of the humanist spirit will show up earliest in the shorter form, not because it is any more conservative, but because there is no space where that loss may hide. A story can have only one heart at a time, and it must palpitate visibly.

So doing, it can animate any idea, in any shape. A story may float like an orb, spread like a fan or strike its parallels ceaselessly on the page—as long as all its clues cohere. Language itself may *be* the idea. Many stories now being written are about the imperfect clueing between language and life. Or about the ugliness of shape. Often, after an upsurge in any art—such as we have had here in the past fifty years of the short story—artists tire of symmetry, of conclusiveness, and even of the very authority that such a renaissance brings. This is natural. The old avant-garde is coming back. Hail! In literature one need never say farewell.

I've grown to think that any art form is avant-garde to begin with, by having hurtled itself over and through our animal and psychic barriers to become—itself. How extraordinary of a statue not to be a stone—and for thousands upon thousands of quiet gazers to know this—at once. How odd of a story to be never only conversation, yet neither a poem nor a song.

I go to the short-story world most perhaps for the multiplicity of its voices, which crowd in, endearingly intimate, approachable, from across terra firma whose scale one can almost see. For the writer, that world is as fell—in the sense of a knockdown blow—as any other. It's the world where once I learned, and learn again laboriously, that a writer's own voice may clap in many tongues, all the while the single meaning keeps chanting its Gregorian. Staring at these stories, I know that they have already arranged themselves. The stories of an individual writer are already a collective; that is *their* nature. Between the written ones—these rows of tumuli that I visit so rarely—and those other motes still searing toward me from the wide lens of the unwritten, a membership has been forming from the beginning. At any moment another may join them. Looking forward is looking back.

—H. C.

I

In Greenwich There Are Many Gravelled Walks

ᵉᵍ O N A N afternoon in early August, Peter Birge, just returned from driving his mother to the Greenwich sanitarium she had to frequent at intervals, sat down heavily on a furbelowed sofa in the small apartment he and she had shared ever since his return from the Army a year ago. He was thinking that his usually competent solitude had become more than he could bear. He was a tall, well-built young man of about twenty-three, with a pleasant face whose even, standardized look was the effect of proper food, a good dentist, the best schools, and a brush haircut. The heat, which bored steadily into the room through a Venetian blind lowered over a half-open window, made his white T shirt cling to his chest and arms, which were still brown from a week's sailing in July at a cousin's place on the Sound. The family of cousins, one cut according to the pattern of a two-car-and-country-club suburbia, had always looked with distaste on his precocious childhood with his mother in the Village and, the few times he had been farmed out to them during those early years, had received his healthy normality with ill-concealed surprise, as if they had clearly expected to have to fatten up what they undoubtedly referred to in private as "poor Anne's boy." He had only gone there at all, this time, when it became certain that the money saved up for a summer abroad, where his Army stint had not sent him, would have to be spent on one of his mother's trips to Greenwich, leaving barely enough, as it was, for his next, and final, year at the School of Journalism. Half out of disheartenment over his collapsed summer, half to provide himself with a credible "out" for the too jovially pressing cousins at Rye, he had registered for some courses at the Columbia summer session. Now these were almost over, too, leaving a gap before the fall semester began. He had cut this morning's classes in order to drive his mother up to the place in Connecticut.

He stepped to the window and looked through the blind at the convertible parked below, on West Tenth Street. He ought to call the garage for the pickup man, or else, until he thought of someplace to go, he ought to hop down and put up the top. Otherwise, baking there in the hot sun, the car would be like a griddle when he went to use it, and the leather seats were cracking badly anyway.

It had been cool when he and his mother started, just after dawn that morning, and the air of the well-ordered countryside had had that almost speaking freshness of early day. With her head bound in a silk scarf and her chubby little chin tucked into the cardigan which he had buttoned on her without forcing her arms into the sleeves, his mother, peering up at him with the near-gaiety born of relief, had had the exhausted charm of a child who has just been promised the thing for which it has nagged. Anyone looking at the shingled hair, the feet in small brogues—anyone not close enough to see how drawn and beakish her nose looked in the middle of her little, round face, which never reddened much with drink but at the worst times took on a sagging, quilted whiteness—might have thought the two of them were a couple, any couple, just off for a day in the country. No one would have thought that only a few hours before, some time after two, he had been awakened, pounded straight up on his feet, by the sharp, familiar cry and then the agonized susurrus of prattling that went on and on and on, that was different from her everyday, artlessly confidential prattle only in that now she could not stop, she could not stop, *she could not stop*, and above the small, working mouth with its eliding, spinning voice, the glazed button eyes opened wider and wider, as if she were trying to breathe through them. Later, after the triple bromide, the warm bath, and the crooning, practiced soothing he administered so well, she had hiccuped into crying, then into stillness at last, and had fallen asleep on his breast. Later still, she had awakened him, for he must have fallen asleep there in the big chair with her, and with the weak, humiliated goodness which always followed these times she had even tried to help him with the preparations for the journey—preparations which, without a word between them, they had set about at once. There'd been no doubt, of course, that she would have to go. There never was.

He left the window and sat down again in the big chair, and smoked one cigarette after another. Actually, for a drunkard—or an alcoholic, as people preferred to say these days—his mother was the least troublesome of any. He had thought of it while he packed the pairs of daintily kept shoes, the sweet-smelling blouses and froufrou underwear, the tiny, perfect dresses—of what a comfort it was that she had never grown raddled or blowzy. Years ago, she had perfected the routine within which she could feel safe for months at a time. It had gone on for longer than he could remember: from before the death of his father, a Swedish engineer, on the income of whose patents they had always been able to live fairly comfortably; probably even during her life with that other long-dead man, the painter whose model and mistress she had been in the years before she married his father. There would be the long, drugged sleep of the morning, then the unsteady hours when she manicured herself back into cleanliness and reality. Then, at about four or five in the afternoon, she and the dog (for there was always a dog) would make their short pilgrimage to the clubby, cozy little hangout where she would be a fixture until far into the morning, where she had been a fixture for the last twenty years.

Once, while he was at boarding school, she had made a supreme effort to get herself out of the routine—for his sake, no doubt—and he had returned at Easter to a new apartment, uptown, on Central Park West. All that this had resulted in was inordinate taxi fares and the repetitious nightmare evenings when she had gotten lost and he had found her, a small, untidy heap, in front of their old place. After a few months, they had moved back to the Village, to those few important blocks where she felt safe and known and loved. For they all knew her there, or got to know her—the aging painters, the newcomer poets, the omniscient news hacks, the military spinsters who bred dogs, the anomalous, sandalled young men. And they accepted her, this dainty hanger-on who neither painted nor wrote but hung their paintings on her walls, faithfully read their parti-colored magazines, and knew them all—their shibboleths, their feuds, the whole vocabulary of their disintegration, and, in a mild, occasional manner, their beds.

Even this, he could not remember not knowing. At ten, he had been an expert compounder of remedies for hangover, and of an evening, standing sleepily in his pajamas to be admired by the

5

friends his mother sometimes brought home, he could have predicted accurately whether the party would end in a brawl or in a murmurous coupling in the dark.

It was curious, he supposed now, stubbing out a final cigarette, that he had never judged resentfully either his mother or her world. By the accepted standards, his mother had done her best; he had been well housed, well schooled, even better loved than some of the familied boys he had known. Wisely, too, she had kept out of his other life, so that he had never had to be embarrassed there except once, and this when he was grown, when she had visited his Army camp. Watching her at a post party for visitors, poised there, so chic, so distinctive, he had suddenly seen it begin: the fear, the scare, then the compulsive talking, which always started so innocently that only he would have noticed at first—that warm, excited, buttery flow of harmless little lies and pretensions which gathered its dreadful speed and content and ended then, after he had whipped her away, just as it had ended this morning.

On the way up this morning, he had been too clever to subject her to a restaurant, but at a drive-in place he was able to get her to take some coffee. How grateful they had both been for the coffee, she looking up at him, tremulous, her lips pecking at the cup, he blessing the coffee as it went down her! And afterward, as they flew onward, he could feel her straining like a homing pigeon toward their destination, toward the place where she felt safest of all, where she would gladly have stayed forever if she had just had enough money for it, if they would only let her stay. For there the pretty little woman and her dog—a poodle, this time—would be received like the honored guest that she was, so trusted and docile a guest, who asked only to hide there during the season of her discomfort, who was surely the least troublesome of them all.

He had no complaints, then, he assured himself as he sat on the burning front seat of the convertible trying to think of somewhere to go. It was just that while others of his age still shared a communal wonder at what life might hold, he had long since been solitary in his knowledge of what life was.

Up in a sky as honestly blue as a flag, an airplane droned smartly toward Jersey. Out at Rye, the younger crowd at the club would be commandeering the hot blue day, the sand, and the water, as if these were all extensions of themselves. They would use the evening

6

this way, too, disappearing from the veranda after a dance, exploring each other's rhythm-and-whiskey-whetted appetites in the backs of cars. They all thought themselves a pretty sophisticated bunch, the young men who had graduated not into a war but into its hung-over peace, the young girls attending junior colleges so modern that the deans had to spend all their time declaring that their girls were being trained for the family and the community. But when Peter looked close and saw how academic their sophistication was, how their undamaged eyes were still starry with expectancy, their lips still avidly open for what life would surely bring, then he became envious and awkward with them, like a guest at a party to whose members he carried bad news he had no right to know, no right to tell.

He turned on the ignition and let the humming motor prod him into a decision. He would drop in at Robert Vielum's, where he had dropped in quite often until recently, for the same reason that others stopped by at Vielum's—because there was always likely to be somebody there. The door of Robert's old-fashioned apartment, on Claremont Avenue, almost always opened on a heartening jangle of conversation and music, which meant that others had gathered there, too, to help themselves over the pauses so endemic to university life —the life of the mind—and there were usually several members of Robert's large acquaintance among the sub-literary, quasi-artistic, who had strayed in, ostensibly en route somewhere, and who lingered on hopefully on the chance that in each other's company they might find out what that somewhere was.

Robert was a perennial taker of courses—one of those nonmatriculated students of indefinable age and income, some of whom pursued, with monkish zeal and no apparent regard for time, this or that freakishly peripheral research project of their own conception, and others of whom, like Robert, seemed to derive a Ponce de León sustenance from the young. Robert himself, a large man of between forty and fifty, whose small features were somewhat cramped together in a wide face, never seemed bothered by his own lack of direction, implying rather that this was really the catholic approach of the "whole man," alongside of which the serious pursuit of a degree was somehow foolish, possibly vulgar. Rumor connected him with a rich Boston family that had remittanced him at least as far as New York, but he never spoke about himself, although he was extraordinarily alert to gossip. Whatever income he had he supplemented by renting his extra room to a series of young men students. The one opulence among his dun-colored, perhaps consciously Spartan effects was a really fine record-player, which he kept going at all hours with selections from his massive collection. Occasionally he annotated the music, or the advance copy novel that lay on his table, with foreign-language tags drawn from the wide, if obscure, latitudes of his travels, and it was his magic talent for assuming that his young friends, too, had known, had experienced, that, more than anything, kept them enthralled.

"*Fabelhaft!* Isn't it?" he would say of the Mozart. "Remember how they did it that last time at Salzburg!" and they would all sit there, included, belonging, headily remembering the Salzburg to which they had never been. Or he would pick up the novel and lay it down again. "*La plume de mon oncle*, I'm afraid. *La plume de mon oncle Gide. Eheu*, poor Gide!"—and they would each make note of the fact that one need not read that particular book, that even, possibly, it was no longer necessary to read Gide.

Peter parked the car and walked into the entrance of Robert's apartment house, smiling to himself, lightened by the prospect of company. After all, he had been weaned on the salon talk of such circles; these self-fancying little bohemias at least made him feel at home. And Robert was cleverer than most—it was amusing to watch him. For just as soon as his satellites thought themselves secure on the promontory of some "trend" he had pointed out to them, they would find that he had deserted them, had gone on to another trend, another eminence, from which he beckoned, cocksure and just faintly malicious. He harmed no one permanently. And if he concealed some skeleton of a weakness, some closeted Difference with the Authorities, he kept it decently interred.

As Peter stood in the dark, soiled hallway and rang the bell of Robert's apartment, he found himself as suddenly depressed again, unaccountably reminded of his mother. There were so many of them, and they affected you so, these charmers who, if they could not offer you the large strength, could still atone for the lack with so many small decencies. It was admirable, surely, the way they managed this. And surely, after all, they harmed no one.

Robert opened the door. "Why, hello—Why, hello, Peter!" He seemed surprised, almost relieved. "Greetings!" he added, in a voice whose boom was more in the manner than the substance. "Come in, Pietro, come in!" He wore white linen shorts, a zebra-striped beach shirt, and huaraches, in which he moved easily, leading the way down the dark hall of the apartment, past the two bedrooms, into the living room. All of the apartment was on a court, but on the top floor, so it received a medium, dingy light from above. The living room, long and pleasant, with an old white mantel, a gas log, and many books, always came as a surprise after the rest of the place, and at any time of day Robert kept a few lamps lit, which rouged the room with an evening excitement.

As they entered, Robert reached over in passing and turned on the record-player. Music filled the room, muted but insistent, as if he wanted it to patch up some lull he had left behind. Two young men sat in front of the dead gas log. Between them was a table littered with maps, an open atlas, travel folders, glass beer steins. Vince, the current roomer, had his head on his clenched fists. The other man, a stranger, indolently raised a dark, handsome head as they entered.

"Vince!" Robert spoke sharply. "You know Peter Birge. And this is Mario Osti. Peter Birge."

The dark young man nodded and smiled, lounging in his chair. Vince nodded. His red-rimmed eyes looked beyond Peter into some distance he seemed to prefer.

"God, isn't it but hot!" Robert said. "I'll get you a beer." He bent over Mario with an inquiring look, a caressing hand on the empty glass in front of him.

Mario stretched back on the chair, smiled upward at Robert, and shook his head sleepily. "Only makes me hotter." He yawned, spread his arms languorously, and let them fall. He had the animal self-possession of the very handsome; it was almost a shock to hear him speak.

Robert bustled off to the kitchen.

"Robert!" Vince called, in his light, pouting voice. "Get me a drink. Not a beer. A drink." He scratched at the blond stubble on his cheek with a nervous, pointed nail. On his round head and retroussé face, the stubble produced the illusion of a desiccated baby, until, looking closer, one imagined that he might never have been one, but might have been spawned at the age he was, to mummify perhaps but not to grow. He wore white shorts exactly like Robert's,

9

and his blue-and-white striped shirt was a smaller version of Robert's brown-and-white, so that the two of them made an ensemble, like the twin outfits the children wore on the beach at Rye.

"You know I don't keep whiskey here." Robert held three steins deftly balanced, his heavy hips neatly avoiding the small tables which scattered the room. "You've had enough, wherever you got it." It was true, Peter remembered, that Robert was fonder of drinks with a flutter of ceremony about them—*café brûlé* perhaps, or, in the spring, a *Maibowle*, over which he could chant the triumphant details of his pursuit of the necessary woodruff. But actually one tippled here on the exhilarating effect of wearing one's newest façade, in the fit company of others similarly attired.

Peter picked up his stein. "You and Vince all set for Morocco, I gather."

"Morocco?" Robert took a long pull at his beer. "No. No, that's been changed. I forgot you hadn't been around. Mario's been brushing up my Italian. He and I are off for Rome the day after tomorrow."

The last record on the changer ended in an archaic battery of horns. In the silence while Robert slid on a new batch of records, Peter heard Vince's nail scrape, scrape along his cheek. Still leaning back, Mario shaped smoke with his lips. Large and facilely drawn, they looked, more than anything, accessible—to a stream of smoke, of food, to another mouth, to any plum that might drop.

"You going to study over there?" Peter said to him.

"Paint." Mario shaped and let drift another corolla of smoke.

"No," Robert said, clicking on the record arm. "I'm afraid Africa's démodé." A harpsichord began to play, its dwarf notes hollow and perfect. Robert raised his voice a shade above the music. "Full of fashion photographers. And little come-lately writers." He sucked in his cheeks and made a face. "Trying out their passions under the beeg, bad sun."

"*Eheu*, poor Africa?" said Peter.

Robert laughed. Vince stared at him out of wizened eyes. Not drink, so much, after all, Peter decided, looking professionally at the mottled cherub face before he realized that he was comparing it with another face, but lately left. He looked away.

"Weren't you going over, Peter?" Robert leaned against the machine.

"Not this year." Carefully Peter kept out of his voice the knell the words made in his mind. In Greenwich, there were many gravelled walks, unshrubbed except for the nurses who dotted them, silent and attitudinized as trees. "Isn't that Landowska playing?"

"Hmm. Nice and cooling on a hot day. Or a fevered brow." Robert fiddled with the volume control. The music became louder, then lowered. "Vince wrote a poem about that once. About the Mozart, really, wasn't it, Vince? 'A lovely clock between ourselves and time.' " He enunciated daintily, pushing the words away from him with his tongue.

"Turn it off!" Vince stood up, his small fists clenched, hanging at his sides.

"No, let her finish." Robert turned deliberately and closed the lid of the machine, so that the faint hiss of the needle vanished from the frail, metronomic notes. He smiled. "What a time-obsessed crowd writers are. Now Mario doesn't have to bother with that dimension."

"Not unless I paint portraits," Mario said. His parted lips exposed his teeth, like some white, unexpected flint of intelligence.

"*Dolce far niente*," Robert said softly. He repeated the phrase dreamily, so that half-known Italian words—"*loggia*," the "Ponte Vecchio," the "Lungarno"—imprinted themselves one by one on Peter's mind, and he saw the two of them, Mario and Roberto now, already in the frayed-gold light of Florence, in the umber dusk of half-imagined towns.

A word, muffled, came out of Vince's throat. He lunged for the record-player. Robert seized his wrist and held it down on the lid. They were locked that way, staring at each other, when the doorbell rang.

"That must be Susan," Robert said. He released Vince and looked down, watching the blood return to his fingers, flexing his palm.

With a second choked sound, Vince flung out his fist in an awkward attempt at a punch. It grazed Robert's cheek, clawing downward. A thin line of red appeared on Robert's cheek. Fist to mouth, Vince stood a moment; then he rushed from the room. They heard the nearer bedroom door slam and the lock click. The bell rang again, a short, hesitant burr.

Robert clapped his hand to his cheek, shrugged, and left the room.

Mario got up out of his chair for the first time. "Aren't you going to ask who Susan is?"

"Should I?" Peter leaned away from the face bent confidentially near, curly with glee.

"His daughter," Mario whispered. "He said he was expecting his *daughter*. Can you imagine? *Robert!*"

Peter moved farther away from the mobile, pressing face and, standing at the window, studied the gritty details of the courtyard. A vertical line of lighted windows, each with a glimpse of stair, marked the hallways on each of the five floors. Most of the other windows were dim and closed, or opened just a few inches above their white ledges, and the yard was quiet. People would be away or out in the sun, or in their brighter front rooms dressing for dinner, all of them avoiding this dark shaft that connected the backs of their lives. Or, here and there, was there someone sitting in the fading light, someone lying on a bed with his face pressed to a pillow? The window a few feet to the right, around the corner of the court, must be the window of the room into which Vince had gone. There was no light in it.

Robert returned, a Kleenex held against his cheek. With him was a pretty, ruffle-headed girl in a navy-blue dress with a red arrow at each shoulder. He switched on another lamp. For the next arrival, Peter thought, surely he will tug back a velvet curtain or break out with a heraldic flourish of drums, recorded by Red Seal. Or perhaps the musty wardrobe was opening at last and was this the skeleton—this girl who had just shaken hands with Mario, and now extended her hand toward Peter, tentatively, timidly, as if she did not habitually shake hands but today would observe every custom she could.

"How do you do?"

"How do you do?" Peter said. The hand he held for a moment was small and childish, the nails unpainted, but the rest of her was very correct for the eye of the beholder, like the young models one sees in magazines, sitting or standing against a column, always in three-quarter view, so that the picture, the ensemble, will not be marred by the human glance. Mario took from her a red dressing case that she held in her free hand, bent to pick up a pair of white gloves that she had dropped, and returned them with an avid interest which overbalanced, like a waiter's gallantry. She sat down, brushing at the gloves.

"The train was awfully dusty—and crowded." She smiled tightly at Robert, looked hastily and obliquely at each of the other two, and bent over the gloves, brushing earnestly, stopping as if someone had said something, and, when no one did, brushing again.

"Well, well, well," Robert said. His manners, always good, were never so to the point of clichés, which would be for him what nervous *gaffes* were for other people. He coughed, rubbed his cheek with the back of his hand, looked at the hand, and stuffed the Kleenex into the pocket of his shorts. "How was camp?"

Mario's eyebrows went up. The girl was twenty, surely, Peter thought.

"All right," she said. She gave Robert the stiff smile again and looked down into her lap. "I like helping children. They can use it." Her hands folded on top of the gloves, then inched under and hid beneath them.

"Susan's been counselling at a camp which broke up early because of a polio scare," Robert said as he sat down. "She's going to use Vince's room while I'm away, until college opens."

"Oh—" She looked up at Peter. "Then you aren't Vince?"

"No. I just dropped in. I'm Peter Birge."

She gave him a neat nod of acknowledgment. "I'm glad, because I certainly wouldn't want to inconvenience—"

"Did you get hold of your mother in Reno?" Robert asked quickly.

"Not yet. But she couldn't break up her residence term anyway. And Arthur must have closed up the house here. The phone was disconnected."

"Arthur's Susan's stepfather," Robert explained with a little laugh. "Number three, I think. Or is it *four*, Sue?"

Without moving, she seemed to retreat, so that again there was nothing left for the observer except the girl against the column, any one of a dozen with the short, anonymous nose, the capped hair, the foot arched in the trim shoe, and half an iris glossed with an expertly aimed photoflood. "Three," she said. Then one of the hidden hands stole out from under the gloves, and she began to munch evenly on a fingernail.

"Heavens, you haven't still got that *habit!*" Robert said.

"What a heavy papa you make, Roberto," Mario said.

She flushed, and put the hand back in her lap, tucking the fingers under. She looked from Peter to Mario and back again. "Then you're not Vince," she said. "I didn't think you were."

The darkness increased around the lamps. Behind Peter, the court had become brisk with lights, windows sliding up, and the sound of taps running.

"Guess Vince fell asleep. I'd better get him up and send him on his way." Robert shrugged, and rose.

"Oh, don't! I wouldn't want to be an inconvenience," the girl said, with a polite terror which suggested she might often have been one.

"On the contrary." Robert spread his palms, with a smile, and walked down the hall. They heard him knocking on a door, then his indistinct voice.

In the triangular silence, Mario stepped past Peter and slid the window up softly. He leaned out to listen, peering sidewise at the window to the right. As he was pulling himself back in, he looked down. His hands stiffened on the ledge. Very slowly he pulled himself all the way in and stood up. Behind him a tin ventilator clattered inward and fell to the floor. In the shadowy lamplight his too classic face was like marble which moved numbly. He swayed a little, as if with vertigo.

"I'd better get out of here!"

They heard his heavy breath as he dashed from the room. The slam of the outer door blended with Robert's battering, louder now, on the door down the hall.

"What's down there?" She was beside Peter, otherwise he could not have heard her. They took hands, like strangers met on a narrow footbridge or on one of those steep places where people cling together more for anchorage against their own impulse than for balance. Carefully they leaned out over the sill. Yes—it was down there, the shirt, zebra-striped, just decipherable on the merged shadow of the courtyard below.

Carefully, as if they were made of eggshell, as if by some guarded movement they could still rescue themselves from disaster, they drew back and straightened up. Robert, his face askew with the impossible question, was behind them.

After this, there was the hubbub—the ambulance from St. Luke's, the prowl car, the two detectives from the precinct station house, and finally the "super," a vague man with the grub pallor and shamble of those who live in basements. He pawed over the keys on the thong around his wrist and, after several tries, opened the bedroom door. It was a quiet, unviolent room with a tossed bed and an open window, with a stagy significance acquired only momentarily in the minds of those who gathered in a group at its door.

Much later, after midnight, Peter and Susan sat in the bald glare of an all-night restaurant. With hysterical eagerness, Robert had gone on to the station house with the two detectives to register the salient facts, to help ferret out the relatives in Ohio, to arrange, in fact, anything that might still be arrangeable about Vince. Almost without noticing, he had acquiesced in Peter's proposal to look after Susan. Susan herself, after silently watching the gratuitous burbling of her father, as if it were a phenomenon she could neither believe nor leave, had followed Peter without comment. At his suggestion, they had stopped off at the restaurant on their way to her stepfather's house, for which she had a key.

"Thanks. I was starved." She leaned back and pushed at the short bang of hair on her forehead.

"Hadn't you eaten at all?"

"Just those pasty sandwiches they sell on the train. There wasn't any dinner."

"Smoke?"

"I do, but I'm just too tired. I can get into a hotel all right, don't you think? If I can't get in at Arthur's?"

"I know the manager of a small one near us," Peter said. "But if you don't mind coming to my place, you can use my mother's room for tonight. Or for as long as you need, probably."

"What about your mother?"

"She's away. She'll be away for quite a while."

"Not in Reno, by any chance?" There was a roughness, almost a coarseness, in her tone, like that in the overdone camaraderie of the shy.

"No. My father died when I was eight. Why?"

"Oh, something in the way you spoke. And then you're so competent. Does she work?"

"No. My father left something. Does yours?"

She stood up and picked up her bedraggled gloves. "No," she

said, and her voice was suddenly distant and delicate again. "She marries." She turned and walked out ahead of him.

He paid, rushed out of the restaurant, and caught up with her.

"Thought maybe you'd run out on me," he said.

She got in the car without answering.

They drove through the Park, toward the address in the East Seventies that she had given him. A weak smell of grass underlay the gas-blended air, but the Park seemed limp and worn, as if the strain of the day's effluvia had been too much for it. At the Seventy-second Street stop signal, the blank light of a street lamp invaded the car.

"Thought you might be feeling Mrs. Grundyish at my suggesting the apartment," Peter said.

"Mrs. Grundy wasn't around much when I grew up." The signal changed and they moved ahead.

They stopped in a street which had almost no lights along its smartly converted house fronts. This was one of the streets, still sequestered by money, whose houses came alive only under the accelerated, febrile glitter of winter and would dream through the gross summer days, their interiors deadened with muslin or stirred faintly with the subterranean clinkings of caretakers. No. 4 was dark.

"I would rather stay over at your place, if I have to," the girl said. Her voice was offhand and prim. "I hate hotels. We always stopped at them in between."

"Let's get out and see."

They stepped down into the areaway in front of the entrance, the car door banging hollowly behind them. She fumbled in her purse and took out a key, although it was already obvious that it would not be usable. In his childhood, he had often hung around in the areaways of old brownstones such as this had been. In the corners there had always been a soft, decaying smell, and the ironwork, bent and smeared, always hung loose and broken-toothed. The areaway of this house had been repaved with slippery flag; even in the humid night there was no smell. Black-tongued grillwork, with an oily shine and padlocked, secured the windows and the smooth door. Fastened on the grillwork in front of the door was the neat, square proclamation of a protection agency.

"You don't have a key for the padlocks, do you?"

16

"No." She stood on the curb, looking up at the house. "It was a nice room I had there. Nicest one I ever did have, really." She crossed to the car and got in.

He followed her over to the car and got in beside her. She had her head in her hands.

"Don't worry. We'll get in touch with somebody in the morning."

"I don't. I don't care about any of it, really." She sat up, her face averted. "My parents, or any of the people they tangle with." She wound the lever on the door slowly, then reversed it. "Robert, or my mother, or Arthur," she said, "although he was always pleasant enough. Even Vince—even if I'd known him."

"He was just a screwed-up kid. It could have been anybody's window."

"No." Suddenly she turned and faced him. "I should think it would be the best privilege there is, though. To care, I mean."

When he did not immediately reply, she gave him a little pat on the arm and sat back. "Excuse it, please. I guess I'm groggy." She turned around and put her head on the crook of her arm. Her words came faintly through it. "Wake me when we get there."

She was asleep by the time they reached his street. He parked the car as quietly as possible beneath his own windows. He himself had never felt more awake in his life. He could have sat there until morning with her sleep-secured beside him. He sat thinking of how different it would be at Rye, or anywhere, with her along, with someone along who was the same age. For they were the same age, whatever that was, whatever the age was of people like them. There was nothing he would be unable to tell her.

To the north, above the rooftops, the electric mauve of midtown blanked out any auguries in the sky, but he wasn't looking for anything like that. Tomorrow he would take her for a drive—whatever the weather. There were a lot of good roads around Greenwich.

Heartburn

&§ THE LIGHT, gritty wind of a spring morning blew in on the doctor's shining, cleared desk, and on the tall buttonhook of a man who leaned agitatedly toward him.

"I have some kind of small animal lodged in my chest," said the man. He coughed, a slight, hollow apologia to his ailment, and sank back in his chair.

"Animal?" said the doctor, after a pause which had the unfortunate quality of comment. His voice, however, was practiced, deft, colored only with the careful suspension of judgment.

"Probably a form of newt or toad," answered the man, speaking with clipped distaste, as if he would disassociate himself from the idea as far as possible. His face quirked with sad foreknowledge. "Of course, you don't believe me."

The doctor looked at him noncommittally. Paraphrased, an old refrain of the poker table leapt erratically in his mind. "Nits"—no—"newts and gnats and one-eyed jacks," he thought. But already the anecdote was shaping itself, trim and perfect, for display at the clinic luncheon table. "Go on," he said.

"Why won't any of you come right out and say what you think!" the man said angrily. Then he flushed, not hectically, the doctor noted, but with the well-bred embarrassment of the normally reserved. "Sorry. I didn't mean to be rude."

"You've already had an examination?" The doctor was a neurologist, and most of his patients were referrals.

"My family doctor. I live up in Boston."

"Did you tell him—er . . . ?" The doctor sought gingerly for a phrase.

One corner of the man's mouth lifted, as if he had watched others in the same dilemma. "I went through the routine first. Fluoroscope, metabolism, cardiograph. Even gastroscopy." He spoke, the doctor noted, with the regrettable glibness of the patient who has shopped around.

"And—the findings?" said the doctor, already sure of the answer.

The man leaned forward, holding the doctor's glance with his own. A faint smile riffled his mouth. "Positive."

"Positive!"

"Well," said the man, "machines have to be interpreted after all, don't they?" He attempted a shrug, but the quick eye of the doctor saw that the movement masked a slight contortion within his tweed suit, as if the man writhed away from himself but concealed it quickly, as one masks a hiccup with a cough. "A curious flutter in the cardiograph, a strange variation in the metabolism, an alien shadow under the fluoroscope." He coughed again and put a genteel hand over his mouth, but this time the doctor saw it clearly—the slight, cringing motion.

"You see," added the man, his eyes helpless and apologetic above the polite covering hand. "It's alive. It *travels.*"

"Yes. Yes, of course," said the doctor, soothingly now. In his mind hung the word, ovoid and perfect as a drop of water about to fall. Obsession. A beautiful case. He thought again of the luncheon table.

"What did your doctor recommend?" he said.

"A place with more resources, like the Mayo Clinic. It was then that I told him I knew what it was, as I've told you. And how I acquired it." The visitor paused. "Then, of course, he was forced to pretend he believed me."

"Forced?" said the doctor.

"Well," said the visitor, "actually, I think he did believe me. People tend to believe anything these days. All this mass media information gives them the habit. It takes a strong individual to disbelieve evidence."

The doctor was confused and annoyed. Well, "What then?" he said peremptorily, ready to rise from his desk in dismissal.

Again came the fleeting bodily grimace and the quick cough. "He —er . . . he gave me a prescription."

The doctor raised his eyebrows, in a gesture he was swift to retract as unprofessional.

"For heartburn, I think it was," added his visitor demurely.

Tipping back in his chair, the doctor tapped a pencil on the edge of the desk. "Did he suggest you seek help—on another level?"

"Many have suggested it," said the man.

"But I'm not a psychiatrist!" said the doctor irritably.

"Oh, I know that. You see, I came to you because I had the luck to hear one of your lectures at the Academy. The one on 'Overemphasis on the Non-somatic Causes of Nervous Disorder.' It takes a strong man to go against the tide like that. A disbeliever. And that's what I sorely need." The visitor shuddered, this time letting the *frisson* pass uncontrolled. "You see," he added, thrusting his clasped hands forward on the desk, and looking ruefully at the doctor, as if he would cushion him against his next remark, "you see—I am a psychiatrist."

The doctor sat still in his chair.

"Ah, I can't help knowing what you are thinking," said the man. "I would think the same. A streamlined version of the Napoleonic delusion." He reached into his breast pocket, drew out a wallet, and fanned papers from it on the desk.

"Never mind. I believe you!" said the doctor hastily.

"Already?" said the man sadly.

Reddening, the doctor hastily looked over the collection of letters, cards of membership in professional societies, licenses, and so on—very much the same sort of thing he himself would have had to amass, had he been under the same necessity of proving his identity. Sanity, of course, was another matter. The documents were all issued to Dr. Curtis Retz at a Boston address. Stolen, possibly, but something in the man's manner, in fact everything in it except his unfortunate hallucination, made the doctor think otherwise. Poor guy, he thought. Occupational fatigue, perhaps. But what a form! The Boston variant, possibly. "Suppose you start from the beginning," he said benevolently.

"If you can spare the time . . ."

"I have no more appointments until lunch." And what a lunch that'll be, the doctor thought, already cherishing the pop-eyed scene —Travis the clinic's director (that plethoric Nestor), and young Gruenberg (all of whose cases were unique), his hairy nostrils dilated for once in a *mise-en-scène* which he did not dominate.

Holding his hands pressed formally against his chest, almost in

20

the attitude of one of the minor placatory figures in a *Pietà*, the visitor went on. "I have the usual private practice," he said, "and clinic affiliations. As a favor to an old friend of mine, headmaster of a boys' school nearby, I've acted as guidance consultant there for some years. The school caters to boys of above average intelligence and is run along progressive lines. Nothing's ever cropped up except run-of-the-mill adolescent problems, colored a little, perhaps, by the type of parents who tend to send their children to a school like that —people who are—well—one might say, almost tediously aware of their commitments as parents."

The doctor grunted. He was that kind of parent himself.

"Shortly after the second term began, the head asked me to come down. He was worried over a sharp drop of morale which seemed to extend over the whole school—general inattention in classes, excited note-passing, nightly disturbances in the dorms—all pointing, he had thought at first, to the existence of some fancier than usual form of hazing, or to one of those secret societies, sometimes laughable, sometimes with overtones of the corrupt, with which all schools are familiar. Except for one thing. One after the other, a long list of boys had been sent to the infirmary by the various teachers who presided in the dining room. Each of the boys had shown a marked debility, and what the resident doctor called 'All the stigmata of pure fright. Complete unwillingness to confide.' Each of the boys pleaded stubbornly for his own release, and a few broke out of their own accord. The interesting thing was that each child did recover shortly after his own release, and it was only after this that another boy was seen to fall ill. No two were afflicted at the same time."

"Check the food?" said the doctor.

"All done before I got there. According to my friend, all the trouble seemed to have started with the advent of one boy, John Hallowell, a kid of about fifteen, who had come to the school late in the term with a history of having run away from four other schools. Records at these classed him as very bright, but made oblique references to 'personality difficulties' which were not defined. My friend's school, ordinarily pretty independent, had taken the boy at the insistence of old Simon Hallowell, the boy's uncle, who is a trustee. His brother, the boy's father, is well known for his marital exploits which have nourished the tabloids for years. The mother lives mostly in France and South America. One of these perennial dryads, apparently, with a youthfulness maintained by money and a yearly immersion in the fountains of American plastic surgery. Only time she sees the boy . . . Well, you can imagine. What the feature articles call a Broken Home."

The doctor shifted in his chair and lit a cigarette.

"I won't keep you much longer," said the visitor. "I saw the boy." A violent fit of coughing interrupted him. This time his curious writhing motion went frankly unconcealed. He got up from his chair and stood at the window, gripping the sill and breathing heavily until he had regained control, and went on, one hand pulling unconsciously at his collar. "Or, at least, I think I saw him. On my way to visit him in his room I bumped into a tall red-headed boy in a football sweater, hurrying down the hall with a windbreaker and a poncho slung over his shoulder. I asked for Hallowell's room; he jerked a thumb over his shoulder at the door just behind him, and continued past me. It never occurred to me . . . I was expecting some adenoidal gangler with acne . . . or one of these sinister little angel faces, full of neurotic sensibility.

"The room was empty. Except for its finicky neatness, and a rather large amount of livestock, there was nothing unusual about it. The school, according to the current trend, is run like a farm, with the boys doing the chores, and pets are encouraged. There was a tank with a couple of turtles near the window, beside it another, full of newts, and in one corner a large cage of well-tended, brisk white mice. Glass cases, with carefully mounted series of lepidoptera and hymenoptera, showing the metamorphic stages, hung on the walls, and on a drawing board there was a daintily executed study of Branchippus, the 'fairy shrimp.'

"While I paced the room, trying to look as if I wasn't prying, a greenish little wretch, holding himself together as if he had an imaginary shawl draped around him, slunk into the half-dark room and squeaked 'Hallowell?' When he saw me he started to duck, but I detained him and found that he had had an appointment with Hallowell too. When it was clear, from his description, that Hallowell must have been the redhead I'd seen leaving, the poor urchin burst into tears.

" 'I'll never get rid of it now!' he wailed. From then on it wasn't hard to get the whole maudlin story. It seems that shortly after Hallowell's arrival at school he acquired a reputation for unusual proficiency with animals and for out-of-the way lore which would impress the ingenuous. He circulated the rumor that he could swallow small animals and regurgitate them at will. No one actually saw him swallow anything, but it seems that in some mumbo-jumbo with another boy who had shown cynicism about the whole thing, it was claimed that Hallowell had, well, divested himself of something, and passed it on to the other boy, with the statement that the latter would only be able to get rid of his cargo when he in turn found a boy who would disbelieve *him*."

The visitor paused, calmer now, and leaving the window sat down again in the chair opposite the doctor, regarding him with such fixity that the doctor shifted uneasily, with the apprehension of one who is about to be asked for a loan.

"My mind turned to the elementary sort of thing we've all done at times. You know, circle of kids in the dark, piece of cooked cauliflower passed from hand to hand with the statement that the stuff is the fresh brains of some neophyte who hadn't taken his initiation seriously. My young informer, Moulton his name was, swore however that this hysteria (for of course, that's what I thought it) was passed on singly, from boy to boy, without any such séances. He'd been home to visit his family, who are missionaries on leave, and had been infected by his roommate on his return to school, unaware that by this time the whole school had protectively turned believers, en masse. His own terror came, not only from his conviction that he was possessed, but from his inability to find anybody who would take his dare. And so he'd finally come to Hallowell. . . .

"By this time the room was getting really dark and I snapped on the light to get a better look at Moulton. Except for an occasional shudder, like a bodily tic, which I took to be the aftereffects of hard crying, he looked like a healthy enough boy who'd been scared out of his wits. I remember that a neat little monograph was already forming itself in my mind, a group study on mass psychosis, perhaps, with effective anthropological references to certain savage tribes whose dances include a rite known as 'eating evil.'

"The kid was looking at me. 'Do you believe me?' he said suddenly. 'Sir?' he added, with a naive cunning which tickled me.

" 'Of course,' I said, patting his shoulder absently. 'In a way.'

"His shoulder slumped under my hand. I felt its tremor, direct misery palpitating between my fingers.

" 'I thought . . . maybe for a man . . . it wouldn't be . . .' His voice trailed off.

" 'Be the same? . . . I don't know,' I said slowly, for of course, I was answering, not his actual question, but the overtone of some cockcrow of meaning that evaded me.

"He raised his head and petitioned me silently with his eyes. Was it guile, or simplicity, in his look, and was it for conviction, or the lack of it, that he arraigned me? I don't know. I've gone back over what I did then, again and again, using all my own knowledge of the mechanics of decision, and I know that it wasn't just sympathy, or a pragmatic reversal of therapy, but something intimately important for me, that made me shout with all my strength—'Of course I don't believe you!'

"Moulton, his face contorted, fell forward on me so suddenly that I stumbled backwards, sending the tank of newts crashing to the floor. Supporting him with my arms, I hung on to him while he heaved, face downwards. At the same time I felt a tickling, sliding sensation in my own ear, and an inordinate desire to follow it with my finger, but both my hands were busy. It wasn't a minute 'til I'd gotten him onto the couch, where he drooped, a little white about the mouth, but with that chastened, purified look of the physically relieved, although he hadn't actually upchucked.

"Still watching him, I stooped to clear up the debris, but he bounded from the couch with amazing resilience.

" 'I'll do it,' he said.

" 'Feel better?'

"He nodded, clearly abashed, and we gathered up the remains of the tank in a sort of mutual embarrassment. I can't remember that either of us said a word, and neither of us made more than a half-hearted attempt to search for the scattered pests which had apparently sought crannies in the room. At the door we parted, muttering as formal a goodnight as possible between a grown man and a small boy. It wasn't until I reached my own room and sat down that I realized, not only my own extraordinary behavior, but that Moulton, standing, as I suddenly recalled, for the first time quite straight, had sent after me a look of pity and speculation.

"Out of habit, I reached into my breast pocket for my pencil, in order to take notes as fresh as possible. And then I felt it . . . a skittering, sidling motion, almost beneath my hand. I opened my jacket and shook myself, thinking that I'd picked up something in the other room . . . but nothing. I sat quite still, gripping the pencil, and after an interval it came again—an inchoate creeping, a twitter of movement almost *lackadaisical*, as of something inching itself lazily along—but this time on my other side. In a frenzy, I peeled off my clothes, inspected myself wildly, and enumerating to myself a reassuring abracadabra of explanation—skipped heartbeat, intercostal pressure of gas—I sat there naked, waiting. And after a moment, it came again, that wandering, aquatic motion, as if something had flipped itself over just enough to make me aware, and then settled itself, this time under the sternum, with a nudge like that of some inconceivable foetus. I jumped up and shook myself again, and as I did so I caught a glimpse of myself in the mirror in the closet door. My face, my own face, was ajar with fright, and I was standing there, hooked over, as if I were wearing an imaginary shawl."

In the silence after his visitor's voice stopped, the doctor sat there in the painful embarrassment of the listener who has played confessor, and whose expected comment is a responsibility he wishes he had evaded. The breeze from the open window fluttered the papers on the desk. Glancing out at the clean, regular façade of the hospital wing opposite, at whose evenly shaded windows the white shapes of orderlies and nurses flickered in consoling routine, the doctor wished petulantly that he had fended off the man and all his papers in the beginning. What right had the man to arraign *him?* Surprised at his own inner vehemence, he pulled himself together. "How long ago?" he said at last.

"Four months."

"And since?"

"It's never stopped." The visitor now seemed brimming with a tentative excitement, like a colleague discussing a mutually puzzling case. "Everything's been tried. Sedatives do obtain some sleep, but that's all. Purgatives. Even emetics." He laughed slightly, almost with pride. "Nothing like that works," he continued, shaking his head with the doting fondness of a patient for some symptom which has confounded the best of them. "It's too cagey for that."

With his use of the word "it," the doctor was propelled back into that shapely sense of reality which had gone admittedly askew during the man's recital. To admit the category of "it," to dip even a slightly co-operative finger in another's fantasy, was to risk one's own equilibrium. Better not to become involved in argument with the possessed, lest one's own apertures of belief be found to have been left ajar.

"I am afraid," the doctor said blandly, "that your case is outside my field."

"As a doctor?" said his visitor. "Or as a man?"

"Let's not discuss me, if you please."

The visitor leaned intently across the desk. "Then you admit that to a certain extent, we *have* been—?"

"I admit nothing!" said the doctor, stiffening.

"Well," said the man disparagingly, "of course, that too is a kind of stand. The commonest, I've found." He sighed, pressing one hand against his collarbone. "I suppose you have a prescription too, or a recommendation. Most of them do."

The doctor did not enjoy being judged. "Why don't you hunt up young Hallowell?" he said, with malice.

"Disappeared. Don't you think I tried?" said his vis-à-vis ruefully. Something furtive, hope, perhaps, spread its guileful corruption over his face. "That means you do give a certain credence—"

"Nothing of the sort!"

"Well then," said his interrogator, turning his palms upward.

The doctor leaned forward, measuring his words with exasperation. "Do you mean you *want* me to tell you you're crazy!"

"In my spot," answered his visitor meekly, "which would you prefer?"

Badgered to the point of commitment, the doctor stared back at his inconvenient Diogenes. Swollen with irritation, he was only half conscious of an uneasy, vestigial twitching of his ear muscles, which contracted now as they sometimes did when he listened to atonal music.

"O.K., O.K. . . !" he shouted suddenly, slapping his hand down on the desk and thrusting his chin forward. "Have it your way then! I don't believe you!"

Rigid, the man looked back at him cataleptically, seeming, for a moment, all eye. Then, his mouth stretching in that medieval grimace, risorial and equivocal, whose mask appears sometimes on one side of the stage, sometimes on the other, he fell forward on the desk, with a long, mewing sigh.

Before the doctor could reach him, he had raised himself on his arms and their foreheads touched. They recoiled, staring downward. Between them on the desk, as if one of its mahogany shadows had become animate, something seemed to move—small, seal-colored, and ambiguous. For a moment it filmed back and forth, arching in a crude, primordial inquiry; then, homing straight for the doctor, whose jaw hung down in a rictus of shock, it disappeared from view.

Sputtering, the doctor beat the air and his own person wildly with his hands, and staggered upward from his chair. The breeze blew hypnotically, and the stranger gazed back at him with such perverse calm that already he felt an assailing doubt of the lightning, untoward event. He fumbled back over his sensations of the minute before, but already piecemeal and chimerical, they eluded him now, as they might forever.

"It's unbelievable," he said weakly.

His visitor put up a warding hand, shaking it fastidiously. "*Au contraire!*" he replied daintily, as though by the use of another language he would remove himself still further from commitment. Reaching forward, he gathered up his papers into a sheaf, and stood up, stretching himself straight with an all-over bodily yawn of physical ease that was like an affront. He looked down at the doctor, one hand fingering his wallet. "No," he said reflectively, "guess not." He tucked the papers away. "Shall we leave it on the basis of—er—professional courtesy?" he inquired delicately.

Choking on the sludge of his rage, the doctor looked back at him, inarticulate.

Moving toward the door, the visitor paused. "After all," he said, "with your connections . . . try to think of it as a temporary inconvenience." Regretfully, happily, he closed the door behind him.

The doctor sat at his desk, humped forward. His hands crept to his chest and crossed. He swallowed, experimentally. He hoped it was rage. He sat there, waiting. He was thinking of the luncheon table.

The Night Club in the Woods

WE FIRST saw her, Mrs. Hawthorn, sitting alone, the first one down in the tender that waited to take us off the Bermuda boat. She was wearing a quilted taffeta suit, expensively flared at shoulder and hip, and a matching hat—one of those deep, real hats we were all wearing in the fall of 1935—and her arms were full, crammed full of tea roses. Under a city marquee, she would have had an enviable chic, but on the white deck of the tender, in the buttery Bermuda sun, she looked outlandishly urban for that travel-folder scene. As the rest of us climbed down into the tender, she made room for us with an apologetic shifting of the roses, but one could see, as she nestled her long, rouge-assisted face into the buds, that she was pleased with them.

Later on, in the week that followed, we saw her at our hotel, and Luke and I, drifting in the ambience of our honeymooners' table, idly watched her dinner entrances. Each evening, appearing late but consciously unflurried, in a different gown—one always too dominantly colorful and sparkling for the off-season crowd—she crossed to the table reserved for her and her companion, a dark, pear-shaped man, shorter than she, who received her with an anxious, hesitant courtesy.

On the first evening, Luke, nudging me, had pointed to the single bird-of-paradise bud with which the hotel kept the tables adorned, each beaked bloom soaring from its coarse glass holder like an immoderately hued bird, and every evening thereafter, the analogy had kept us amused. One evening, however, as she passed us, her tall, haggard figure sheathed in green sequins that boomeranged the light, a child at a nearby table cried out: "Look, Mommy! Christmas tree!" As she stopped, and bent toward the child, the sequins not

2 8

quite concealing the middle-aged line from breast to hip, we heard her say, in a mellow voice, as if she were indulgently amused at both the child and herself—"Yes, darling! Christmas tree!"—and we felt ashamed, and liked her.

We met the two of them again, as we were all herded docilely into one of the glass-bottomed sightseeing boats, and she told us her name. The little man, tentative and deferential in the background, was one of those hovering people whose names one never catches, and we never did, although she told us it too. Again we saw her, alone on the beach in front of the hotel, in a maillot that was still somewhat scandalous for that time. We were a little embarrassed for her, not at the suit, but at its cruel, sagging revelation, and I remember that both of us, looking away with the instinctive distaste of the young for the fading, glanced down with satisfaction at our own bodies. One of her arms was covered almost from wrist to elbow with diamond and sapphire bracelets, and she must have seen me staring at them, or trying not to. She laughed, on the same mellow note.

"I'd feel naked without them." She turned, and slid into the water. She swam well, better than either of us, her long, water-sallowed face, which once must have been very handsome, sinking deep into the fervid blue of the water, the one mailed arm flashing in the sun.

In those days, the thing to do was to go down on the *Monarch* and come back on the *Queen*. The little stenographers squandering their vacation on off-season rates, an "interchangeable" wardrobe, and one shattering evening dress, the honeymooners, intent on seeming otherwise, all said it airily: "We came down on the *Monarch* and will go back on the *Queen*." On the return voyage, we met Mrs. Hawthorn and her vague companion again. The ship had run into bad weather, the usual October storms of the Caribbean, and at dinnertime, the little stenographers had been unable to appear in their evening dresses after all.

Luke had been affected too, although I was not. After dinner alone, I wandered into one of the ornate lounges that hollowed the ship. Seated in one of the gold chairs, her lamé gown blending so well that at first I did not see her, was Mrs. Hawthorn. She beckoned to me.

"I see you're a good sailor, too," she said. "I never get sick. Dave —the friend who is traveling with me—is down in his cabin." There was the slightest emphasis on "his." "Women are the stronger sex, I always say. You two are newlyweds, aren't you?"

"Yes."

"Look," she said. "Why don't you and your husband come up to my stateroom and have champagne. It's the best thing in the world for seasickness—and after all we really should celebrate for you two. Yes, do! We really must!"

I went down to our cabin, and roused Luke. "You think you're inveigling me," he said. "But it's really Mrs. Hawthorn who intrigues me."

We climbed the ladders from D deck to A. Up there, with no feel of more ship above us, the ocean, silhouetted against the looming slant of the stacks, seemed to shift its dark obliques more pervasively near us.

"The water seems more intimate up here with the rich, doesn't it?" I said.

"Hmmm," said Luke, "but it's not an intimacy I care to develop at the moment." I giggled, and lurching together, hip to hip, half with love, half with the movement of the deck, we entered Mrs. Hawthorn's stateroom.

The room was banked with flowers. Mrs. Hawthorn and her companion were waiting for us, sitting stiffly in the center of the blooms like unintroduced visitors in the anteroom of a funeral chapel. Wedged behind a coffee table blocked with bottles, Mrs. Hawthorn did not rise, but we greeted each other with that air of confederate gaiety adopted by hostess and guest at parties of whose success neither is sure. Across from her, behind an imitation hearth, a gas log burned insolently, as if a fireplace burning in the middle of the sea might serve to keep the elements in their place.

"Life on the hypotenuse," said Luke. He retrieved a bunch of gladioli, and set them back on the erring horizontal of a table.

Mrs. Hawthorn shifted her bracelets. "Dave is the florist in our home town—Hawthornton, Connecticut. I needed a rest, so Dave came down with me. Senator Hawthorn couldn't get away. He's the senator from there, you know."

Luke and I nodded, eager to let her see that we took her explanation at its face value, unwilling to appear abashed at the malpractices of the rich and worn. I imagined her life—the idle, probably childless woman, burdened with an exuberance no longer matched by her exterior, drawing toward her, with the sequins of wealth and difference, the self-conscious little man who was doggedly trying to fill the gap between them with the only largesse at his command— his abracadabra of flowers. Luke and I exchanged looks across the flowers, secure in our cocoon of beginnings, seeing before us an itinerary that repudiated compromise, and made no concessions to the temporal.

As we drank, the fraudulent solidity of the room was displaced now and again by a deep, visceral sway that drained the chair arms from beneath our digging fingers, and the wine seemed only to accentuate the irrationality of the four of us so transiently, so unsuitably met. At one point, Mrs. Hawthorn told the blond, mild-featured Luke that he had a "sulphurous" look, which roused us all to unsteady laughter, and again I remember her asking, with the gaucherie so denied by her appearance, if he were a "college man."

Then, suddenly, with an incredulous look on his face, Dave, the little man, stood up. Edging backwards, he felt for the doorknob, caught it, and disappeared around it. Ignoring his defection, the three of us sat on; then Luke, with a wild look at me, lurched through the flapping door and was gone.

Mrs. Hawthorn and I sat on for a moment, united in that smug matriarchy which joins women whose men have acted similarly and disgracefully. The heat from the burning log brought out the reek of the flowers, until it seemed to me that I had drunk perfume instead of champagne. Slowly the log up-ended and pointed toward the ceiling, but this too had slid far to the right, so that the room hung in a momentary armistice with the storm, the implacable hearth still glowing in its center. I stood up, and moved toward the door. It sidled toward me, and I achieved the corridor, but not before I had caught a last glimpse of Mrs. Hawthorn. She was sitting there like one of those children one often sees at dusk in the playground or the corner lot, still concentrated in fierce, solitary energy on the spinning top or the chalked squares of the deserted game, unwilling to admit the default of the others who have wilted, conceded in the afternoon's end, and acquiescently gone home.

By the time Luke and I had made our separate ways to the cabin, the ship had ridden out the storm area and was running smoothly.

We would dock next morning in New York Harbor. We greeted each other, and slid limply into bed. Luke put his arms around me with a protectiveness tinged, I could not help thinking, with a relief that I had not proved so indomitable after all. For a second, I held him at arm's length. "Tell me first," I said. "Are you a college man?" Then we nestled together, in the excluding, sure laughter of the young.

At the docking the next day, we got through the lines early, without seeing anyone we knew. We had exchanged addresses with Mrs. Hawthorn, never really expecting to see her again, and in the busy weeks after, during which we returned to our jobs and our life together, we forgot her completely.

About a month later, sometime in November, we got a note from her, written in a large, wasteful hand on highly colored, expensive notepaper, and followed, when we did not immediately answer, by a phone call, during which her voice came over the wire as gaily insistent as before. Would we come up for dinner and stay the night? We accepted without particular consideration, partly out of a reawakened interest in her and what she would be like at home with the Senator, and partly because it was a place to go with the Chevvie—and no sense of the stringency of time had led us as yet to a carping evaluation of the people with whom we spent it.

On the way up that Saturday, a run of about seventy miles, we drove steadily through a long, umber autumn afternoon. At our left the sun dropped slowly, a red disc without penumbra. Along the country roads, the escarpments of pines and firs were black-green, with the somber deadness of a tyro's painting of Italy. Lights popped up in the soiled gray backs of towns, and a presage of winter tingled in our minds, its remembered icicle sliding down our spines. I was twenty-two, free, still catching up with a childhood where hot dogs had been forbidden. I made Luke stop for them twice. After that we drove silently, my head on Luke's shoulder. Inside the chugging little car, the heater warmed us; we were each with the one necessary person; we had made love the night before.

At seven, when we were expected, we were still twenty miles away. Luke stopped to phone. He came back to the car. "She says dinner will wait for us, not to rush. We're to go on to a night club afterwards."

32

In a second my mind had raked over everything in my suitcase, had placed me at the dinner table—perhaps not quite at the Senator's right—had moved me on to the little round table on the dance floor.

"I just remembered," I said. "I didn't put in my evening shoes."

"*I* just remembered," said Luke. "I didn't bring a proper tie."

We burst into laughter, "We'll swing round by way of New London," said Luke. "We can get things there."

When we got to the main street of the town, it was crowded, but the clothing stores were closing. Luke rushed into a haberdashery shop and came out with a tie. At the dark end of the shopping district we found a shoe store whose proprietor, counting stock in his dim interior, opened his locked door. I bought a pair of silver, girl-graduate sandals, the first pair he showed me. "Gee, lady," he said, as we whisked out of his shop, "I wish every lady was as quick as you."

Smiling to ourselves, we reentered the car. There was a charm that hung about us then, and we were not insensible of it, even aware that it had more to do with our situation than ourselves. We were still guests in the adult world of "lady" and "gentleman"; lightly we rode anchor in their harbor, partook of its perquisites, and escaped again to our enviable truancy. The rest of the world—we saw it in their faces—would be like us if it could. On the way through Hawthornton, I looked for a florist shop, but we passed too quickly by.

Five miles through the woodland of the Hawthorns' private road brought us to the house. There had been no others along the way. But the house that loomed before us, in a cleared area rather bleak and shrubless after the woods behind us, had no baronial mystery about it. By the lights under its porte-cochere, it looked to be about forty years old—one of those rambling, tasteless houses, half timbered, with thick stone porches, which "comfortably off" people built around the turn of the century, more for summer use, but providently made habitable for all year round. As we came to a stop under the porte-cochere, and the coupe's engine died, I heard the rushing sound of water, and saw that we seemed to be on the tip of a promontory that ended several hundred feet beyond.

"We on a lake?"

"Only the Atlantic," said Luke. "Don't you ever know where you are? We've been driving toward it all afternoon."

"Hardly ever," I said. "But we seem to be fated to meet Mrs. H. on one ocean or another."

A capped maid opened the door. Mrs. Hawthorn stood at the foot of the stairs to greet us. It was the first time I had seen her in black, a very low-cut, smart black, enlivened only by the cuff of bracelets on her right arm. It made her seem less of a "character," placing her almost in my mother's generation, although she may not have been quite that, and a little unsettling me. In my world, the different generations did not much visit each other, at least did not seek each other's company as she had ours.

She made a breezy stir of our welcome, giving us each a hand, directing the houseman as to our bags, referring us to separate corners for a wash. "Drinks in the dining room. See you there."

When we entered, she was seated at the long dining table, alone. Three places were set, not at the head, but down toward the middle, ours opposite hers. There was no evidence that anyone else was to dine, or had.

I remember nothing of the room, except my surprise. As we clicked glasses, were served, I tried to recall her voice as it had come over the wire to New York; certainly her airy chitchat had given me the impression that we were to be members of a house party. Otherwise, considering the gap between us of situation, money, age—how odd it was of her to have singled us out! Her conversation seemed to be newly flecked with slang, a kind of slang she perhaps thought we used. "That way for the johns," she had said, directing us to the bathrooms, and now, speaking of Bermuda, she asked us if we had not thought it "simply terrif." She had found European travel "rather a frost."

"I get more of a boot out of cutting a dash at home," she said, grinning.

A second manservant and maid were serving us. "I keep the estate staffed the way it's always been," she said. "Even though a good bit of the time it's only just me. Of course we've had to draw in our horns in lots of ways, like everyone else. But I've washed enough dishes in Hawthornton, I always say." She smiled down at her bracelets.

34

"Have you always lived in Hawthornton?" said Luke.

She nodded. "The Senator's people have always had the mills here. The Hawthorn Knitting Mills. And my father was the town parson—also the town drunk. But I married the mill-owner's son." She chuckled, and we had to laugh with her, at the picture she drew for us. It was the same with all her allusions to her possessions—allusions which were frequent and childlike. As they ballooned into boasting, she pricked them, careful to show that she claimed no kind of eminence because of them.

What she did claim was the puzzling thing, for I felt that "the estate" meant something to her beyond the ordinary, and that her choice of our company was somehow connected with that meaning. Certainly she was shrewd enough to see that our scale of living was not hers, although for a while I dallied with the idea that a real social ignorance—that of the daughter of the down-at-the-heel parson, suddenly transmuted into the mill-owner's wife—had kept her insensitive to all the economic gradations between, had made her assume that because we were "college people," had been on the Bermuda boat, and had an anonymous East Side address, our jobs and our battered Chevvie were only our way of drawing in our horns. But she did not seem to be really interested in who we were, or what our parents had been. Something about what we had, or were now, had drawn her to us; in her queer little overtures of slang she seemed to be wistfully ranging herself on our side. But I did not know what she imagined "our side" to be.

We took our coffee in what she referred to as "the big room"—at first it was hard to categorize as anything else. Large as a hotel lounge, it had something of the same imperviousness to personality. Sofas and club chairs, stodgy but solid, filled its middle spaces; there was a grand piano at either end, and all along the edges, beneath the irregularly nooked windows, there were many worn wicker-and-chintz settees. But, looking further, I saw the dark bookshelves filled with Elbert Hubbard editions, the burnt-leather cushions, of the kind that last a lifetime, scattering the wicker, the ponderous floor lamps, whose parchment umbrella shades were bound with fringe—and I began to recognize the room for what it was. This was a room from which the stags' heads, the Tiffany glass had been cleared, perhaps, but it was still that room which lurked in albums and memoirs, behind pictures labeled *The Family at* ——. *Summer of 1910. Bottom row my son Ned, later to fall in the Ardennes, daughters Julie and Christine, and their school friend, Mary X, now wife of my son George.*

"I never did much to this room except put in the pianos," said Mrs. Hawthorn. "It's practically the same as when we got married, the year Harry's mother died, and he came back from France. We had some helluva parties here, though. Wonderful!" And now, as I followed her glance, I fancied that I detected in the room a faint, raffish overglaze of the early twenties, when I was too young to go to parties—here and there a hassock, still loudly black-and-white, a few of those ballerina book ends everyone used to have, and yes, there, hung in a corner, a couple of old batiks. Dozens of people could have sprawled here, the young men with their bell-bottomed trousers, the girls with their Tutankhamen eardrops, pointed pumps, and orange-ice-colored silk knees. The weathered wicker would have absorbed the spilled drinks without comment, and cigarette burns would have been hilariously added to the burnt-leather cushions. Yes, it could have been a hell of a room for a party.

Mrs. Hawthorn led us to the windows and pointed out into the dark, staring through it with the sure, commanding eye of the householder. "You can't see, of course, but we're on three bodies of water here—the river, the Sound, and the ocean. There's the end of the dock—the Coast Guard still ties up there once in a while, although we don't keep it up any more. When I was a kid, it used to be fitted out like a summer hotel. I used to swim around the point and watch them." Then, I thought, she would not have been one of the three little girls in the bottom row of the picture—she would never have been in that picture at all.

She closed the curtain. "Let me show you your room, then we'll be off." She led us upstairs, into a comfortable, nondescript bedroom. "That's my door, across the hall. Knock when you're ready."

"Oh, it won't take a minute to change," I said.

"Change? Dear, you don't have to change."

"Oh, but we've brought our evening things," I said. "It'll only take us a minute." There was a slight wail to my voice.

"Really it won't," said Luke. "We're awfully sorry if we've delayed you, but we'll rush."

We continued our protests for a minute, standing there in the hall. She leaned down and patted my shoulder, looking at me with that musing smile older women wore when they leaned over baby carriages. I had encountered that look often that year, among my mother's friends. "No, run along, and never mind," she said. "Nobody else is going to be there."

In front of the mirror in our room, I ran a comb through my curls. "Nobody who *is* anybody, I suppose she meant. I can't imagine why else she picked on us. And when I think of those awful shoes!"

"You can wear them at home," said Luke. "I like women to be flashy around the house. Come on, you look wonderful."

"I'm going to change to them anyway. They'll dance better."

"You'll only have to dance half the dances."

"Luke—" I slid my feet into the shoes and twisted to check my stocking seams. "Do you suppose that little man, Dave, will be there? Do you suppose we're being used as a sort of *cover?*"

He laughed. "I don't know. Come on."

"Don't you think it's funny she doesn't say where the Senator is? At least make his excuses or something?"

"Away on business, probably."

"Well, why isn't she in Washington with him, then? I would be —if it were you."

"Thank *you*," he said. "But how come you got through college? There's no Connecticut senator to Washington named Hawthorn."

"Luke! I knew there was something fishy! Maybe there isn't any Senator. Or maybe he's divorced her, and nobody around here will know her. Or maybe she's a little off, from his being dead, and wants to go on pretending he's alive. With people like us—who wouldn't know."

He put back his head in laughter. "Now I know how you did get through college." He kissed the back of my neck, and pushed me through the door. "State senator, dope," he whispered, as we knocked at Mrs. Hawthorn's.

"Ready?" She opened the door and held it back in such a way that we knew we were to look in. "This is the only room I changed," she said. "I had it done again last year, the same way. I thought the man from Sloane would drop in his tracks when I insisted on the same thing. All that pink. Ninety yards of it in the curtains alone." She laughed, as she had done at the child in Bermuda. "Of course I had no idea back then . . . I thought it was lovely, so help me. And now I'm used to it."

We looked around. All that pink, as she had said. The room, from its shape, must be directly above the big room below; its great windows jutted out like a huge pink prow, overlooking the three bodies of water. Chairs with the sickly sheen of hard candy pursed their Louis Quatorze legs on a rose madder rug, under lamps the tinge of old powder puffs. There were a few glossy prints on the walls—nymphs couched like bonbons in ambiguous verdure. Marble putti held back the curtains, and each morning, between ninety yards of rosy lingerie, there would rise the craggy, seamed face of the sea.

Mrs. Hawthorn put her hand on one of the cherubs, and looked out. "We sailed from there on our honeymoon," she said. "On the old Hawthorns' yacht, right from the end of the dock. I remember thinking it would give, there were so many people on the end of it." She took a fur from a chair, slung it around her shoulders, and walked to the door. At the door, she turned back and surveyed the room. "Ain't it orful!" she said, in her normal voice. "Harry can't bear it."

She had two voices, I thought, as we followed her downstairs and got in the car she referred to as her runabout, that she'd made Harry give her in place of the chauffeur-driven Rolls. One voice for that tranced tale of first possession—when the house, the dock, the boudoir, Harry were new. And one for now—slangy, agnostic, amused.

She drove well, the way she swam, with a crisp, physical intensity. There had been bridle paths through these woods, she told us, but she hadn't really minded giving up the horses; swimming was the only thing she liked to do alone. She swam every day; it kept her weight down to the same as when she married. "You'll be having to pick yourself some exercise now too, honey," she said, sighing. "And stick to it the rest of your days."

We would turn on to the main road soon, I thought, probably to one of those roadhouses full of Saturday night daters such as Luke and I had been the year before, spinning out the evening on the cover charge and a couple of setups, and looking down our noses at the fat middle-agers who didn't have to watch the tab, but were such a nuisance on the floor.

The car veered suddenly to the left, and reduced speed. Now we seemed to be riding on one of the overgrown paths. Twigs whipped through the open window and slurred out again as we passed. Beside me, Luke rolled up the window. We were all in the front seat together. No one spoke.

We stopped. We must be in the heart of the woods, I thought. There was nothing except the blind probe of the headlamps against leaves, the scraping of the November wind.

"Guess the switch from the house doesn't work any more," she said, half to herself. She took a flashlight from the compartment. "Wait here," she said, and got out of the car. After she had gone, I opened the window and leaned across Luke, holding on to his hand. Above me, the stars were enlarged by the pure air. Off somewhere to the right, the flashlight made a weak, disappearing nimbus.

Then, suddenly, the woods were *en fête*. Festoons of lights spattered from tree to tree. Ahead of us, necromanced from the dark wood, the pattern of a house sprang on the air. After a moment our slow eyes saw that strings of lights garlanded its low log-cabin eaves, and twined up the two thick thrusts of chimney at either end. The flashlight wigwagged to us. We got out of the car, and walked toward it. Mrs. Hawthorn was leaning against one of the illuminated trees, looking up at the house. The furs slung back from her shoulders in a conqueror's arc. As we approached, she shook her head, in a swimmer's shake. "Well, ladies and gents," she said, in the cool, the vinaigrette voice, "here it is."

"Is it—is this the night club?" I said.

"This is it, baby," she said, and the way she said it made me feel as if she'd reached down and ruffled my curls. Instead, she reached up, and pressed a fuse box attached to the tree. For a minute, the red dazzle of the sign on the roof of the house made us blink. GINGER AND HARRY's it said. There were one or two gaps in GINGER, and the second R of HARRY's was gone, but the AND was perfect.

"Woods are death on electric lines," she said. Leading the way up the flagged path to the door, she bent down, muttering, and twitched at the weeds that had pushed up between the flags.

She unlocked the door. "We no longer heat it, of course. The pipes are drained. But I had them build fires this afternoon."

It was cold in the vestibule, just as it often was in the boxlike entrances of the roadhouses we knew, and, with its bare wood and plaster, it was just like them too—as if the flash and the jump were reserved for the sure customers inside. To our right was the hat-check stall, with its brass tags hung on hooks, and a white dish for quarters and dimes.

"I never had any servants around here," said Mrs. Hawthorn. "The girls used to take turns in the cloakroom, and the men used to tumble over themselves for a chance to tend bar, or be bouncer. Lord, it was fun. We had a kid from Hollywood here one night, one of the Wampas stars, and we sneaked her in as ladies' matron, before anyone knew who she was. What a stampede there was, when the boys found out!"

I bent down to decipher a tiled plaque in the plaster, with three initials and a date—1918. Mrs. Hawthorn saw me looking at it.

"As my mother used to say," she said. "Never have your picture taken in a hat."

Inside, she showed us the lounges for the men and the women— the men's in red leather, hunting prints, and green baize. In the powder room, done in magenta and blue, with girandoles and ball fringe, with poufs and mirrored dressing tables, someone had hit even more precisely the exact note of the smart public retiring room —every woman a Pompadour, for ten minutes between dances.

"I did this all myself," she said. "From top to bottom. Harry had a bad leg when he came back—he was in an army hospital before we got married. He gave me my wedding present ahead of time— enough to remodel the old place, or build a new one. I surprised him. I built this place instead."

"Is his leg all right now?" I said.

"What?" she said.

"His leg. Is it all right now?"

"Yes, of course. That was donkey's years ago." She was vague, as if about a different person. Behind her, Luke shook his head at me.

"And now . . ." she said. "Now . . . come in where it's warm." And this time my ear picked up that tone of hers as it might a motif—that deep, rubato tone of possession fired by memory. She opened the door for us, but for a scant moment before, with her hand on the knob, she approached it as a curator might pause before his Cellini, or a hostess before the lion of her afternoon.

And here it was. The two fires burned at either end; the sultry

40

hooded sidelights reflected here and there on the pale, unscarred dance floor. The little round tables were neatly stacked at its edge, all but one table that was set for service, as if now that it was 3 A.M. or four, the fat proprietor and his headwaiter might just be sitting down for their morning bowl of soup. On the wall, behind the tables, flickered the eternal mural, elongated bal-masqué figures and vaudeville backdrops, painted dim even when new, and never meant to be really seen. It could be the one of the harlequin-faced young men with top hats and canes, doing a soft-shoe routine against an after-dark sky. Or it might be the one of the tapering Venuses with the not-quite bodies, behind prussian-blue intimations of Versailles. It didn't matter. Here was the "Inn," the "Club," the "Spot," the Glen Island, where one danced to Ozzie Nelson, the Log Cabin at Armonk, the one near Rumson, with the hot guitarist, the innumerable ones where, for an evening or a week of evenings, Vincent Lopez's teeth glinted like piano keys under his mustache. The names would have varied somewhat from these names of the thirties, but here it was, with the orchestra shell waiting—the podium a little toward one end, so that the leader might ride sidesaddle, his suave cheek for the tables, his talented wrist for the band. Only the air was different, pure and still, without the hot, confectionery smell of the crowd. And the twin fires, though they were burning true and red, had fallen in a little, fallen back before the chill advance of the woods.

So, for the second time, we sat down to champagne with Mrs. Hawthorn. There was a big phonograph hidden in a corner; after a while she set it going, and we danced, Luke first with her, then with me. And now, as the champagne went to our heads, it was not the logs, or the chair arms that moved, but we who moved, looping and twirling to the succulent long-phrased music, laughing and excited with the extraordinary freedom of the floor. I thought of Dave, the little man, but Mrs. Hawthorn never mentioned his name. She was warm, gay—"like a young girl"—as I had heard it said now and then of an older woman. I had thought that this could not be so without grotesquerie, but now, with the wisdom of the wine, I imagined that it could—if it came from inside. She had the sudden, firm bloom of those people who really expand only in their own homes. For the first time, we were seeing her there.

Toward the evening's height, she brought out some old jazz records, made specially for her, with the drum and cymbal parts left out, and from the wings back of the podium she drew out the traps, the cymbals, and the snare. In the old days, she told us, everybody who came did a turn. The turn with the drums had been hers. We made her play some of the songs for us, songs I remembered, or thought I remembered, from childhood, things like *Dardanella* and *Jadda Jadda Jing Jing Jing.* She had some almost new ones too— *Melancholy Baby,* and *Those Little White Lies.* We gave her a big hand.

Then, just as we began to speak of tiring, of going to bed because we had to drive back early the next day, she let the drumsticks fall, and put her fingers to her mouth. "Why, I forgot it!" she said. "I almost forgot to show you the best thing of all!" She reached up with the other hand, and turned off the big spotlight over the orchestra shell.

Once more, only the sidelights glowed, behind their tinted shades. Then the center ceiling light began to move. I hadn't noticed it before; it was so much like what one expected of these places. That was the point—that it was. It was one of those fixtures made of several tiers of stained glass, with concealed slots of lights focused in some way, so that as it revolved, and the dancers revolved under it, bubbles of color would slide over their faces, run in chromatic patches over the tables, and dot the far corners of the room.

"Dance under it," she said. "I'll play for you." Obediently, we put our arms around one another, and danced. She played *Good Night, Ladies.* The drums hardly sounded at all. When it was over, she let the sticks rest in her lap. The chandelier turned, silently. Oval blobs of light passed over her face, greening it and flushing it like long, colored tears. Between the lights, I imagined that she was looking at us, as if she knew something about us that we ourselves did not know. "It was lovely," she said. "That first year." And this time I could not have said which of her two voices she had used.

We left early the next morning. By prearrangement, she was to sleep late and not bother about us, and in a sense we did not see her again. But, as we drove down the private road, we stopped for a moment at a gap in the trees, to see the sun shining, great, over the sea. There was a tall, gray matchstick figure on the end of the dock. As we watched, it dove. She could not have seen us; probably she would not have wanted to. She was doing the exercise to keep her weight down, perhaps, or swimming around the dock, as she had done as a child. Or perhaps she was doing the only thing she cared to do alone. It was certainly she. For as the figure came up, we saw its arm—the one mailed arm, flashing in the sun.

During the next few years I often used to tell the story of our visit to Hawthornton. So many casual topics brought it up so naturally—Bermuda, the people one meets when one travels, the magnified eccentricities of the rich. When it became fashionable to see the twenties as the great arterial spurt of the century's youth, I even told it that way, making her seem a symbol, a denizen of that time. I no longer speculated on why she had invited us; I never made that the point of the story. But for some time now I have known why, and now that I do, I know how to tell her story at last. For now that I know why, it is no longer Mrs. Hawthorn's story. It is ours.

It is almost eighteen years since we were at Mrs. Hawthorn's, just as it was then almost eighteen years since Harry had come back from France. I was never to meet anyone who knew them, nor was I ever to see her again. But I know now that there was never any special mystery about her and Harry. Only the ordinary mystery of the distance that seeps between people, even while they live and lie together as close as knives.

Luke is in the garden now. His face passes the window, intent on raking the leaves. Yet he is as far from me now as ever Harry was from Hawthornton, wherever Harry was that day. He and I are not rich; we do not have the externalizations of the rich. Yet, silently, silently, we too have drawn in our horns.

So, sometimes, when I walk in the woods near our house, it is to a night club that I walk. I sit down on a patch of moss, and I am sitting at the little round table on the unscarred floor. I fold my hands. Above me, the glass dome turns. I watch them—the two people, about whom I know something they themselves do not know. This is what I see:

It is a long, umber autumn afternoon. To the left the sun drops slowly, a red disc without penumbra. Along the country roads, the pines and firs are black-green, with the somber deadness of a tyro's painting of Italy. Lights pop up in the soiled gray backs of towns.

43

Inside the chugging little car the heater warms them; they are each with the one necessary person; they have made love the night before. The rest of the world, if it could, would be like them.

Two Colonials

◄§ WHEN YOUNG Alastair Pines came out from Leeds, England, to teach on an exchange fellowship at Pitt, a small college about a hundred miles from Detroit, Michigan, he was the second foreign teacher ever to be in residence there. Pitt, founded in the Eighteen-sixties by a Presbyterian divine, and still under a synod of that church, had kept its missionary flavor well up to the Second World War. Set in Pittston—a bland village of white and cream-colored houses whose green roofs matched, even in summer, dark lawns compelled by lamasery effort (and perhaps a cautious hint of divine favor) from the dry Michigan plain—the school had kept a surface calm even during the war. It was the centripetal calm of those who, living in the sacred framework of morning, noon and evening service and a perfect round of dedicatory suppers, could not help feeling ever so slightly chosen—of people whose plain living and high thinking was not that of poverty, but of ample funds conserved. Some of the college halls had been built as recently as the Thirties (when labor was so cheap) and the organ (though not baroque to the point of Episcopalianism) was first-rate. Salaries had lagged well behind. Since, however, the non-smoking rule was still in effect on campus, and no teacher was supposed to have wine or spirits in his larder, he was officially helped to escape the extravagances of the age, as well as some of its anxieties. True, the table set by most of the younger faculty was somewhat farinaceous, but this might be less Franciscan than Middle Western, since most of the teachers and students came from that region. A glance at the roster showed a global scattering of names which were American, not international; the Kowalskis and Swobodas were Poles and Czechs from Hamtramck in Detroit, the Ragnhilds and Solveigs from Minnesota, and

45

so on. Alone in the catalogue until the advent of Mr. Pines, the name of Hans Weil—philologist and onetime professor of *Linguistik* at Bonn—represented a Europe not once, twice, or further removed.

With Hans Weil's arrival in 1945, there had also come to Pittston the first of certain changes brought by the war. Like so many other scholars in the days of Hitler, Weil had been passed from hand to libertarian hand like a florin stamped "Freedom"— whisked, in his case, to London, via Holland, in 1939, and from London to Rochester, New York, in 1942, after which he was presumed to be on his own. In 1945, at his own behest, or rather at that of his wife, whose sister and brother-in-law, helped by the Weils to America, now had a flourishing but immovable dry-goods shop in Lansing, he had come to nearby Pitt as provisional candidate for a newly established chair in the humanities, and had remained there ever since. There was small need for philology at Pitt, most of whose students were on their way to being music teachers, social workers or ministers, and Weil, lacking new-world versatility, did not find it easy to "double" in related courses. Nevertheless, he had no fears for his job.

On this fine fall morning of the new term, as Weil walked across campus at his short, duck-footed pace, the beret that he wore for his baldness emphasizing Raphael curves of cheek which softened the fact that he was almost as old as the century, and—as he would blithely have admitted—as profane, he well knew that his value to Pitt went subtly beyond its being able to mutter behind him that he had recently refused an offer from Yale. Thirty years ago, he was thinking, if by some unlikely chance he had landed at Pittston, he might at least have had to grow a beard, and, under the old tradition that all German professors were a kind of nursery-uncle emissary from the land of sugared postcards and cuckoo clocks, might also have had to submit to being called "Dr. Hans," or "Papa Weil." But as things were, he was not even under any particular necessity of writing those little monographs that sometimes brought him an Eastern offer. For, since the war, the GI Bill, and an engineering endowment from one of the big labor unions in Detroit, although Pitt's lawns were still clear of cigarette butts and its brains still Protestantly clear of fumes, a complexity had entered its air. Through the windows of the music department's practice rooms, once so liturgically pure with Bach and Buxtehude, he could now hear Bartók, Khatchaturian and even Sauter-Finnegan squawking under official sanction. Opposite, in Knox Hall, although there were still two strong classes in scriptural exegesis and one on missions, called "The Protestant Evangel," a visiting divine from Union Theological was treating of Kierkegaard, Niebuhr and Buber in a course called "Quest"—and all four of these classes were embarrassingly near a group of acolytes studying guided missiles, on the grant from the C.I.O.

For "comparative" thinking—the modern disease, the modern burden—had come to Pittston. And as Hans Weil walked down the main street, on his way for a word with Mrs. Mabie, the wife of the art historian in whose house Mr. Pines, the exchange fellow, was to be quartered, he knew that he owed his tenure to it. He had begun by being Pitt's "refugee professor," and, with certain accretions of prestige and affection, he would end that way. He had merely to wear his beret, pay attention in his own classes in Anglo-Saxon, stubbornly drink his forbidden wines at dinner in full sight of whatever of the faculty, and on their insufflated bosoms abide. He was their prideful little exercise in comparative humanity—he had merely to *be*.

A passing car slowed, and the driver, unknown to him, called out, "Lift?"

"Walking, thanks," said Weil, thinking of how often he would have to say this until the new students got used to his intransigence, born of a youth spent with alpenstocks. For here, this near the automotive Rome, driving a car on the shortest haul had nothing to do with economy or abstinence. Even the poorest student might have his second-hand leviathan; Weil himself had his Pontiac at home.

Passing under McFarland's open windows, he waved up at the president's housekeeper, who was airing the living room against a background of teal-dark wall. A good many of the Pittston parlors had taken on this color in the three years since the president's mother had chosen it for hers. And at the curb, McFarland's new two-tone Buick shone in silver-blu beauty, Rhadamanthine sign that by next year or so, other two-tone jobs, less violent in color of course than some that were floating the highways like zooming banana splits, would be chosen by those of the faculty who were "turning theirs in." He would keep his old one as long as he could. Whether from age, or from that creeping anti-Americanism which so often flawed the recipients of American bounty, he had begun to have a horror of turning things in.

And now, just ahead of him, was Mrs. Mabie's. As Mr. Pines, presently riding undreaming through Pennsylvania or Ohio, might well say, once he got to know her—now he was "for it." Professor Weil's affectionate remembrance of London and the English went deep, deeper than the language lilt and the old gray streets, down to that sudden rest of the heart when he had stepped off the Dutch plane into a ring of their steady, un-Wagnerian faces. Its compound would already have been working in him, at the good thought of young Pines, had he not been all too sure of what was already working in Mrs. Mabie.

Portia-Lou Mabie, a quondam painter known at her own insistence by her maiden-professional name of Potter (and therefore a constant twinge of explanation in the salons of Pittston and in poor old Mabie-Potter), was an unsuccessful faculty wife who was the more annoying because she gave no sign of knowing it. She was not, however, of that familiar sort, objects of pity, who were always twenty-three sour diapers too late for the Inter-Faith Tea. Dr. Mabie had met and been married by her while he was on a field trip to Mexico City, where—in common with others from St. Louis, Stroudsburg, Orlando—she had been leading the stridulant life of Greenwich Village when it hits the *corrida*. A bony *princesse lointaine* of about thirty-five, who wore her hair in a weak-lemonade waterfall down the small of her back, she was to Weil a confirmation of his private opinion that art historians ought never to come that close to art. She had a talent for endorsing the worthiest convictions in a way that made their very holders wish immediately to disavow them. Openly lamenting that she had been born too late to join the Left Bank expatriates of the Twenties, her shrill disparagements of the crass standardization of life in the United States brought a sudden flush of *amor patriae* to the most disaffected cheek. And ever since the Mabies' recent Fulbright year at Oxford, her conversation, fresh with Anglophiliac sighs and knowing locutions, was likely to become especially matey in the presence of Hans

Weil—climaxing on the occasion of the Weils' yearly dinner for the McFarlands, when he had had to explain to the elderly wife of a Kansas divine what Mrs. Mabie had meant when she had left the table with a bright look at Weil, and the remark that she had to go and spend a penny.

Now, on her doorstep, he deplored, for Mr. Pines's sake, the enthusiasm of her offer to house him, but the childless Mabies had two spare bedrooms, and there were not many such in Pittston.

Mrs. Mabie opened the door, chin forward, hair brimming over. "Oh Hans, did you try to ring me? I was out getting in some coal."

"Coal?" He knew the Mabies heated with oil.

"Yes, you know how *they* like a morning fire. And Pattini wouldn't deliver less than half a ton, so I brought some home in the car. Come on in."

"No, no," he said. "I came only to say I cannot go with you to meet him tomorrow; I must go earlier for the language convention in Chicago. So I have here a little note—" He heard his own words, the German juxtaposition, with outrage. He almost never did that any more; the woman acted on him like a solvent, fuddling all his backgrounds together.

She made him come in, and, although he kept out of her sooty clutch the coat his wife, Hertha, had just cleaned for him, he had to follow her up the stairs to see the bedroom.

"Hope he'll like his digs." She flung the door back smartly. "Just finished distempering the walls."

Looking, Weil hoped that Mr. Pines would see nothing more unusual than kindness in the hot-water bottle prominently posed on the turned-down bed, near the radiator, or in the huge, brass scuttle of coal in a steam-heated American room. "Distemper?" he said. He sniffed an odor. "Oh, yes, rubber paint."

"Worst thing about American progress," she said. "Always sure to bring something bloody nasty along with it."

He bent to examine the coal scuttle, thinking that he was not quite enough of an American, although naturalized, to be able to agree with her in comfort. "Didn't know you used this fireplace. Don't you burn wood in the one downstairs?"

Ignoring him, she fingered the hot-water bottle. "Such a naked red, these things look; that's because we only use them for illness.

But of course there wouldn't be a cover for it in all of Michigan. I tried the tea cozy on it, but it was no go."

Weil straightened, and took out the note to the expected guest, placing it on the night table, where, next to the neat pile of towels and soap, he saw a worn packet of Players. "Portia-Lou. They are crazy for our cigarettes, you know. And after all, isn't he here to see us as we are?"

She flung out a hand in an impatience that included Pittston, Michigan, the hemisphere. "Don't worry. He will. He will."

"Well—" he said. "'Wiedersehen," and ground his teeth. He no longer said that, except to Hertha.

On his way downstairs, she called after him. "You and Hertha wouldn't have brought over one of those big sponge-things, would you? Isn't that what they use?"

He turned his head. "You mean possibly a loofah?"

"Oh, is *that* what they call them?"

"I wouldn't know. I never saw one in London. But if my reading is correct he would carry his own with him. In something called a sponge-bag." He clapped his beret firmly on his head. "'Bye now."

"Cheerio," said Mrs. Mabie.

Later that night, at about one-thirty, when Weil could not stay asleep, as often happened, he got up noiselessly and went downstairs to forage in the bookshelves and the icebox until Hertha should miss him and come after him. This, the constant nervous rounding-up of what family was left to her—by telephone, by visit, from room to room—was almost all that remained, after all these years, of the effects of the concentration camp. It was why, as long as her sister Elsa and Sigmund had the store in Lansing, as long as she could talk with Elsa every morning, drive over for the biweekly *Kaffee-klatsch*, and exchange Sunday dinners, he would never take up the offers from Princeton or Yale. It was no use telling himself that they might none of them be here now had he not gone ahead to England; he could not forget where she had been while he had been safe from all but the bombs in London, nor would he forget her eyes, so blue under the grizzled hair, when she had said to him, on the morning the letter came from Pittston, "Only that we should be together, Hans! Only that we should all of us be together."

He was reading when she came to the top of the stairs in her nightgown. "Hans! You will catch cold. *Soll ich* cocoa *machen?*"

"*Nein, nein. Ich hab' ein bischen Wein. Und Schmierkäse. Wilst du?*"

She wrinkled her nose, but came and sat at the table, looking over his shoulder. "You are working?"

"No, I just wanted to look something up, and I found it." He chuckled, thinking that he might tell her of his encounter with Mrs. Mabie, but she had little ear or eye for the nuances of their life here, content to display her cuisine at intervals to these supermarket savages, to wonder whether she could get the fruiterer to stock fennel, and to lament with Elsa that there was no little *Conditorei* in East Lansing.

"Here. Let me read you something." He got up and put an afghan around her shoulders. "What they call a stole, *ja? Sehr schön*, matches the eyes."

"*Schmeichelkatz'*. You just want me to let you stay up." But she liked him to read to her.

"Listen." He read out bits of the passage he had hunted up, smiling to himself, in Max Müller. " 'We do not want to know languages; we want to know what language is, how it can form a vehicle or an organ of thought. . . . The classical scholar uses Greek or Latin, the Oriental scholar Hebrew or Sanskrit, to trace the social, moral progress of the human race.' "

He looked up. "You follow? Now listen." He took a sip of wine. " 'In *comparative philology* the case is totally different. The jargons of savage tribes, the clicks of the Hottentots, and the vocal modulations of the Indo-Chinese, are as important, nay, for the solutions of some of our problems, more important than the poetry of Homer, or the prose of Cicero.' "

He slapped his thigh, and took another sip of wine.

" 'The clicks of the Hottentots.' What you think of that for a title for my little Chicago piece on the Middle West 'r'? Good, hah? In fact, *bloody* good!"

"*Säufer*," she said. "How much wine did you have? Come to bed."

He was still laughing when she got him to go to bed, and the next morning, looking for something to read on the train, he took Max Müller with him.

Meanwhile, on a Greyhound bus approaching Detroit, Alastair

Pines, slumped next to the window he had opened at once on entering, was sleeping off both a night out in New York (paid for with
the difference between the cashed-in train ticket sent from Pittston
and the bus fare) and the eyestrain of hours of digestive gazing at
the country that, unknown to it, he meant to call his own.

The wind, ruffling a blond lock that flopped engagingly over his
forehead even when he was awake, passed without a ripple over his
well-rigged old Aquascutum, over his skis and duffelbag on the rack
above. Travel fitted him like a skin; he voyaged with all the aplomb
of his nation, of school holidays spent in Paris, of walking tours on
the cheap in Yugoslavia. He was that unobtrusive man to be met
everywhere in or out of the sterling area—leaning over the rails of
the small steamers that plied the lesser isles of Greece, knees pressed
together in the third-class carriage going over Domodossola or
through Torremolinos—the Englishman of between twenty and
forty, whose berth in life and appearance is also somewhere adequately middle, who, to Americans, travels disarmingly light in baggage and heavy in experience. To his compatriots, he was recognizable in more detail, as that projectile still spinning with leftover
impetus down the targetless postwar years, that "type" known to
them as "R.A.F."

When he awoke, the bus was nearing downtown Detroit, and he
was surprised to see that there were skyscrapers here too, not on a
stunning pedestal of bridge and harbor, as in New York, but forming upward like some harder fusion of the smoky, after-barrage air.
He leaned forward eagerly, though not romantically; the point about
new places, and the duty, was to grip the *fact* of them. New York's
air, mica-shot, had the fluid chic of big business; this place had the
heavy thunder-shade of industry.

He took out one of their sweets and ate it thoughtfully. With the
two strings that he had to his bow, there was no reason why, during
the year at Pittston, or after, he should not find some post here that
would suit him. He had had three terms reading history at a provincial university, before the war saved him from the likelihood that
he would be sent down. After the war, the government had been
well pleased to send him to an engineering college, where he had
since taught for several years. Browsing over a list of posts abroad,
he had come upon the exchange offer from Pitt; trying for it on the

hunch that they couldn't have the pick of his betters, he had found his divided talents suited them to a T. He would be a Fellow in English, but would also teach a course in mechanics on the side— what luck to find that his education, on the spotty side for home, had shifted about in a way they seemed to admire here. And after his year here, he ought to feel cheeky enough to jump ship, into the wider seas of industry.

To Alastair, third son of a colonial servant who had died in the service before rising in it—but not too soon to see his children reared as they should be, on the strong asses' milk of the imperial habit—it was normal beyond notice to have a brother in Malaya, another in Johannesburg, a married sister in Cyprus and an uncle in Accra. Hitherto, Alastair had been the one who had worried *them*, but now he rather pitied them, dogging along as they did, bewailing the loss of India, toward a half-pay retirement in Kensington—and all for a groundling lack-of-vision that had kept them from seeing the modern world as he had once been used to seeing it from his plane. At twenty thousand feet up, the technical lines of empire erased themselves; one saw that one might descend on the States as in other days one might have sailed to Kenya, but carrying a passport now, instead of a gun. And colonial sacrifices were still to be made; although in the modern way one might have to give up one's citizen- ship instead of one's health. Had to be done, unless one wanted to fizzle out in some corner, still denying that sahibs were passé. For, entering a country already in a high state of cultivation, and one in a certain sense already appropriated, the trick was to play it in reverse, to go native as quickly as possible. Which he was fully resigned to do.

When he was met by his hosts at the end of his journey, they all took to each other at once. Dr. Mabie, stammering a pace behind his wife, expanded on being deferred to as "sir." Mrs. Mabie crim- soned with understanding when Mr. Pines referred to the bus as a charabanc. As for their guest, taking note of the man's jellyfish way with his wife, and the woman—hair right out of the flicks, and such an oddly nasal way of talking—he thought them as American as anything he'd seen yet.

It was close to two weeks before the professor, delaying happily

in conferences and libraries, returned to Pittston alone, having left
Hertha for a visit in Lansing. He spent Saturday night alone by
choice, in one of those reflective lulls of the closely married, and,
noting a card in the collected mail, went on Sunday afternoon to the
McFarlands' opening tea of the academic season.

It was a lovely day, both crisp and smoky with autumn expectancy, and Weil, refreshed in perspective, leaned against Mrs. Mc-
Farland's wall with an enjoyment not yet dampened by the grape-
juice-tea punch, watching the *Les Sylphides* advances between
teacher and student, savoring a familiar, faculty-wife hat heightened
inexplicably by a new feather. Then Mrs. McFarland bore down on
him with a group, muttering names all round in her furry Scots.
"Yeer to stay on, Mr. Pines," she said, tapping one young man on
the shoulder, and passing by Weil, of whose worldliness she disap-
proved.

So this was young Pines. Listening with a pang of remembrance,
Weil docketed the accent: not quite Oxford or B.B.C., but within
the gates—of Knightsbridge say, Kensington, or St. John's Wood.
And could it be, yes, relaxing already into a certain Americanism?
Looking, he saw what he used to think of as one of their *blended*
faces, too browned and water-slapped for a man of intellect, too
veiled for a man of sport.

He approached him, and they exchanged amenities on the wind
and the weather, and on how Pines was settling in; it didn't occur
to Weil that Pines might not have caught his name. Those around
them, all students, melted back in deference to this faculty meeting.
From a group across the room, Portia-Lou waved to Weil and
called out an inquiry about Hertha. The young man included himself in her wave, and signaled back. "Hi!" he said.

To Weil's surprise, Mrs. Mabie's nod seemed sullen. "You are
quite comfortable at the Mabies'?" he asked.

"Oh yes, rather. She's been incredibly, well—very kind really.
Yes!"

"She seems a little—quiet," said the professor.

"Rather hard to take someone in, don't you know. Privacy, and so
on," said Pines. "By the way, you pronounce it pri-vacy here, with
the long 'i'?"

Weil nodded. "The great vowel change. Among others."

"Rather think I may have got her back up a bit, though. You see, I asked her to coach me in American. It was before I knew that she, er well, that she—"

"That she was so very British?" said Weil.

Mr. Pines began to laugh, then thought better of it. "You see—I hadn't the faintest. You see—I offered to *exchange*."

Weil grinned. "Poor Portia-Lou. When I was in London, I always felt one had to be *très bien élevé* to be able to say 'bloody.' "

Mr. Pines smiled, eyes hooded. "There during the war?"

"Yes."

There was a pause, during which Mr. Pines took a frail sip of punch, then set his cup decisively down.

"You drink wine?" asked Weil.

"When I can get it. But I was given to understand that one doesn't do, here."

"*They* don't," said Weil. "But I do." He smiled. "And if you play it right—I should think you could." He saw a clear path to the door. Clapping on his beret, he shook hands in adieu. "We must have a bottle, some night. See you in the department."

When Mr. Pines returned to his quarters at ten in the evening, the Mabies were still up. He passed them with a greeting, and went up the stairs. Mrs. McFarland's deafness had been rather exhausting; they had however established that his own father had once stayed at Dysart, not a stone's throw from her own town of Kirkcaldy on the Firth of Forth, at a time when she might very well still have been there. Curious how people insistently sought out these little fraternities of time and space; at the thought he went back downstairs, carefully making a noise, and stuck his head around the living-room arch. "Sorry to barge in, but would you mind telling me the name of a chap I met this afternoon," he said, looking at Dr. Mabie.

"If it's a student, they're all so *like*," said Mrs. Mabie.

"Oh no, no, no—a don." He thought the term might please her, but her regard remained cold. "Short, round sort of chap. Little Jew, with a beret."

"Why, that's Hans, Hans Weil. He's in your own department."

"Oh, that's Weil, is it? Stupid of me. Thank you very much." He turned to go.

"He may happen to be a Jew," said Mrs. Mabie, rising from her chair. "He's also very distinguished. And a refugee. And our very good friend."

"Charming fellow, very," said Mr. Pines. "Good night."

When he had gone back up the stairs, and she had listened for the sound of his door shutting, she turned back to Ernest. "I knew it. I knew there was something about that guy. All that going on about wonderful America—he's what *they* call smarmy. Maybe what they call a *spiv*—or worse."

"N-now, now," said Ernest.

"Well, if he's so top-drawer, what's he doing over here?"

"He never said anything about what he is," said Ernest, losing his stammer. "It's you. He just wants to be polite. And I think he's very straightforward."

"Oh-h—you. You didn't even have the spirit to stand up for Hans."

Upstairs, Alastair, whose frank estimate of himself would have been no closer to Ernest's than to Portia-Lou's, was looking in a mirror at his tongue. Yes, it had a boil on it, from the food here— not quite what Americans abroad had led him to expect. He touched the spot with iodine, then took out a pocket notebook in which, after chewing his pencil for a minute, he wrote, "Can't refer openly to origins, as we do. Affronts them." He was snoring by the time Mrs. Mabie, nudging Ernest, who had also begun to snore, wanted to know the name of that girl, the earl's daughter, the one who had fallen in love with Hitler.

A few days later, Weil, catching sight of Mr. Pines chatting with the pretty stenographer in the outer office, invited him for lunch.

"Righto. 'Bye, Janice."

" 'Bye, Mr. Pines."

"Ah now, remember," said Pines as they left. "Just call me Al."

They found a table in the cafeteria on the floor below. "Pretty girl," said Mr. Pines. "*She* don't mind teaching me American."

"Careful you don't teach her anything else," said Weil. "This is a pious campus."

"Not likely. Still, women are so much more irreligious than men, don't you think? Shocking, what some of them will do."

"Mm," said Weil. Though still liking Mr. Pines, he was beginning to place him rather more accurately than had the Mabies. "And how are you getting along in your quarters?"

"Oh, that's another cup of tea. Perhaps you can set me right on that, sir. Mrs. Mabie, would she be—a bit on the barmy side?"

"No-o. Just—exaggerated. Why?"

"Well, the last few days she's got very chatty, in a very odd way. I don't mind her wanting me to natter on about myself, where I've been, what I've done, politics and all that, but—it's as if she's trying to catch me out." Pines hesitated. "With what we've been told at home about things here—do you think she's trying to make me out a Communist?"

"Are you?" said Weil.

"No. Labor. But surely that—?"

"Oh no, you are safe. Each visitor here is allowed certain national idiosyncrasies. That one happens to be yours."

"Well then, I wonder, I do," said Alastair. "You see, although I don't like to say this, I'm rather certain she's been going through my things."

Later, sometime after nine that evening, the Mabies and the Weils faced each other over the latter's dining-room table. Portia-Lou, sitting tall in the fullness of confession, had just refused a proffered slice of *Nüsstorte.*

"So," said the professor. "So Mr. Pines has skis from Garmisch, and his camera is an I.K.G.—as mine would be if I still had them. So he has, among souvenirs from Tangier and Castellammare, also some from Nüremberg—and among his billets-doux a bundle calling him Putzi. Ach, Portia! So during the war he flies over the Alps— and during the occupation he skis over them." He flung up his hands. "So that makes this—this R.A.F. *Spitzbub'*—a *Nazi?*" He pushed his cup toward Hertha for more coffee. "Excuse me, I would laugh, if I could yet laugh at that word."

"But Hans, it's not just that—it's . . . other attitudes," said Portia.

"Ah, so, you are still sore at him because he does not act the way you expected. Excuse me again from your attitudes. I know them. *Arrières pensées,* ten or fifteen years behind the times. Like the Paris styles, by the time they come to Posen."

"*Na, na, Hans, halt dein Mund!*" said Hertha.

57

"Ernest," said Weil, "you will understand. We cannot have this gossiped in the college, on no provocation. Hertha and I have talked it over this afternoon. He will come to us, here."

"Oh, no!" said Portia. "Not to you, of all people. Tell them, Ernest."

"N-now, honey," said Ernest. "You're just building something up."

"Well then, I'll tell them. I'd hoped not to have to. But they can't let themselves in for that."

"For what, Portia?" Weil said.

"Your Mr. Pines. He's an anti-Semite."

Weil put a hand over Hertha's, which had just begun to tremble. "You have proof?"

"Something he said. About you."

"Hans," said Hertha. "Hans." Her hands gripped the table.

"*Du wilst gehen, Liebste?*"

"*Nein, nein.* I will stay."

"Repeat it then, Portia," said Weil, holding his wife's hands in his. "Repeat it exactly."

She repeated it.

"So," he said. "So." He got up, tucked the afghan around Hertha, and walked over to Portia. "Look at me." He leaned over her. "I am short, not? I wear now and then a beret?" He extracted two nods from her. "And I am a Jew?" She nodded again, head down.

"Ah," he said, "the muscles are a little stiff. So it is insult then, to be called a Jew." Drumming on the table, he brought his palm down flat. A cup turned on its side, spilling a stream of brown that seeped into the cloth. "*Ja,* the insult is there. Not in his mind. In yours."

He waved aside Ernest, who had moved to mop up the coffee. "The Jew is so sensitive, hah, and you want to be so sensitive too. So you will take special care not to notice what he is." He blotted at the coffee with a napkin. "I like better your Mrs. McFarland. She refuses me her house, because I drink wine. She is not afraid to include me in her prejudices, as she might any other man."

He went to the door. "Excuse me. Ernest. I am sorry. But maybe the evening is over."

When he had seen them out, he came back up the stairs to

Hertha. "T-t-t," he said, *"was für ein Esel bin ich.* I make everybody cry." He sat down beside her. "Come, laugh. You know what she said to me at the door? She said, 'Hans, I wouldn't hurt *you* for the world. *You* of all people.' " He put his arms around her. *"Na, na,* it's all right. We are all here together." He pressed her head on his shoulder. "Come, it was no tragedy, just a little comic opera. Only —me—I still think I am *Heldentenor."* He rocked her back and forth. "I spilled no blood, *hein?"* he said, rocking. "Just a little *Kaffee."*

On the following Sunday, one of those honey-warm fall days that brought out summer habits like chilled bees, the professor and Alastair Pines sat over a bottle of wine in the Weil garden, a small high terrace overlooking the main highway that ran below. Alastair, member of the household for the past week, had already formed a gourmet's alliance with Hertha, who had taken to producing in triumph at dinner the *Wienerschnitzel* or *Knödel* over which Alastair would have reminisced so charmingly the day before. Now Weil uncorked the wine and set the bottle on the table in the middle of the picnic lunch—roast duck and beetroot *Salat,* that Hertha had left with them before going to Lansing.

"We let the wine breathe a little first, it will be better," he said, and sat back, thinking of how long it had been since he had said that to someone, and of how pleasant this was, this pause so male, so European.

Alastair leaned back, stretching his arms. "Soft berth, this," he said, smiling. "Very. You've both been so kind. Perhaps now you wouldn't mind telling me what was at the bottom of that business at the Mabies'. Not, of course, unless you want to."

"Not at all," said Weil. "It is very instructive." He explained some of Mrs. Mabie's suspicions.

"I say!" said Alastair. "How amazing! But I say, she can't be typical."

"Oh, no, no, she's a silly woman. One can't generalize about this big a country. Still, so often these unilateral fantasies about others. After two wars, still such an island."

"Hasn't done *us* all that much good," said Alastair. "To know all about the other fellow's cooking."

59

"Oh, they are very intelligent, very *sensitive*, the natives." Weil smiled, waving a hand vaguely at the highway. "Only sometimes the silly ones say what the smart ones, the nice ones do not even know they feel. She was for instance very hurt because you refer to me as a Jew."

"But, my word—you are, aren't you?"

Weil stretched his arms in a great, yawning arc, and brought his hands down together on the neck of the bottle. "Precisely. Let's have some wine."

He poured the wine and they sipped it.

"Jolly good."

"Moselle. Too light to travel very well. But then, nothing exports the same."

"Suppose I shall find that out, eh," said Pines, twirling his glass.

"You are planning to stay exported?"

Over a second glass of wine, a third, Pines confided his plans, some of his ruminations on the bus.

"Oh, no, no," said Weil. "My dear fellow, you will allow me to tell you something? Take out citizenship, yes, after all, it is owed. But don't study so hard to be American. Stay *echt*—you will have far more success."

"I suppose people do rather resent the expatriate."

"*Natürlich*. But here it is something more. Especially for an Englishman—they like you to stay as you are. They laugh a little but they admire. Maybe because they are not yet so sure of what they are."

"Ahha," said Alastair. "And is it the same for you?"

"With a difference. You see, you would be an *émigré*. I am a refugee—I have perhaps a few special privileges for humanity's sake." Weil laughed suddenly. "You know perhaps Mark Twain's angry essay against missionaries? On 'Extending the Blessings of Civilization to Our Brother Who Sits in Darkness'?" He poured some more wine. "I often think that for them I am a little 'the person sitting in darkness.'" He shrugged. "So, even in Pittston, I have my Moselle."

Alastair raised his glass. "Cheers."

"Cheers."

Suddenly Weil began to laugh again. " 'The clicks of the Hottentots,' " he said. With some difficulty, he stopped laughing, and explained.

Meanwhile Mr. Pines opened the second bottle, and poured. "T'
the Hottentots!" he said.

"To the Hottentots." The professor looked through his glass at
the sun. "Maybe you will marry one, ha?"

"Oh, I've a sort of understanding with a girl at home—nothing re-
strictive. Joyce is very un—understanding. Good thing too, with all
these—is it *drum girls?*"

"Drum majorettes."

"T-t. On the High Street, too. 'Straord'n'ry."

"Mm. But don't fool yourself you are at the Windmill Theatre.
You may be, but they are not."

They drank to the Windmill.

" 'A night out on the tiles,' " said the professor. "Still say that in
London?"

"Mmm."

The professor leaned back and dreamed, thinking obscurely that a
traveler always brought to a foreign place something that wasn't
really there. If he lived there long enough, he found that out. But
luckily he hadn't lived long enough for that in London. So he might
still dream on it. So he might still dream on it in yet another way,
letting it bear the weight of all that he must no longer give to
Dresden, to München, to Köln.

After a while he roused himself and sat forward, looking intently
into the landscape. "Alastair—I may call you that?"

"Mmm. Call me Alastair. Definitely." The young man sat forward also, following Weil's glance, his lock of hair flopping down on
his forehead. The two of them remained so for some minutes, staring at the same median point in the distance.

"Whatever you do, be firm," said the professor suddenly. "Don't
give in. Even when you see the whites of their eyes."

"Oh, definitely."

They clicked glasses with casual aim, and drank. Sitting back,
they mused sternly for a while on their mutual hardness. Raising
their chins like muezzins, they looked easterly, looking into the air,
into what might be assumed to be the direction of Europe, that old
archipelago of ideas and emotions, which would fade and return for
them, fade and return, coming out for them now and then like an
odor reviving on a damp day.

"Still . . ." said Alastair. He leaned forward again, gazing down on the highway. "Still—everything's laid on very nicely."

"*Ja, ja.* Very."

Shoulders touching, they looked down on the highway, down to where the cars were flashing by like toucans, bright red, hot pink and high yellow, under the aboriginal sun.

The Hollow Boy

◄§ W H E N I was in high school, my best friend for almost a year was another boy of about the same age by the name of Werner Hauser, who disappeared from his home one night and never came back. I am reminded of him indirectly sometimes, in a place like Luchow's or Cavanagh's or Hans Jaeger's, when I am waited on by one of those rachitic-looking German waiters with narrow features, faded hair, and bad teeth, who serve one with an omniscience verging on contempt. Then I wonder whether Mr. Hauser, Werner's father, ever got his own restaurant. I am never reminded directly of Werner by anybody, because I haven't the slightest idea what he may have become, wherever he is. As for Mrs. Hauser, Werner's mother—she was in a class by herself. I've never met anybody at all like her, and I don't expect to.

Although Werner and I went to the same high school, like all the boys in the neighborhood except the dummies who had to go to trade school or the smart alecks who were picked for Townsend Harris, we were really friends because both our families had back apartments in the same house on Hamilton Terrace, a street which angled up a hill off Broadway and had nothing else very terrace-like about it, except that its five-story tan apartment buildings had no store fronts on the ground floors. Nowadays that part of Washington Heights is almost all Puerto Rican, but in those days nobody in particular lived around there. My parents had moved there supposedly because it was a little nearer to their jobs in the Seventh Avenue garment district than the Bronx had been—my father worked in the fur district on Twenty-eighth Street, and my mother still got work as a finisher when the season was on—but actually they had come on the insistence of my Aunt Luba, who lived nearby—a sister of my

63

mother's, of whom she was exceptionally fond and could not go a day without seeing.

When Luba talked about the Heights being higher-class than the Bronx, my parents got very annoyed. Like a lot of the garment workers of that day they were members of the Socialist Labor Party, although they no longer worked very hard at it. Occasionally, still, of an evening, after my father had gotten all worked up playing the violin with two or three of his cronies in the chamber music sessions that he loved, there would be a vibrant discussion over the cold cuts, with my mother, flushed and gay, putting in a sharp retort now and then as she handed round the wine; then too my older sister had been named after Ibsen's Nora—which sounded pretty damn funny with a name like Rosenbloom—and of course nobody in the family ever went to a synagogue. That's about all their radicalism had amounted to. My younger sister was named Carol.

The Hausers had been in the building for a month when we moved in on the regular moving day, October first; later a neighbor told my mother that they had gotten September rent-free as a month's concession on a year's lease—a practice which only became common in the next few years of the depression, and, as I heard my mother say, a neater trick than the Rosenblooms would ever think of. Shortly after they came, a sign was put up to the left of the house entrance—Mrs. Hauser had argued down the landlord on this too. The sign said *Erna Hauser. Weddings. Receptions. Parties,* and maybe the landlord was mollified after he saw it. It was black enamel and gold leaf under glass, and about twice the size of the dentist's. When I got to know Werner, at the time of those first frank questions with which boys place one another, he told me that ever since he and his mother had been sent for to come from Germany five years before, the family had been living in Yorkville in a furnished "housekeeping" room slightly larger than the one Mr. Hauser had occupied during the eight years he had been in the United States alone. Now Mrs. Hauser would have her own kitchen and a place to receive her clientele, mostly ladies from the well-to-do Jewish families of the upper West Side, for whom she had hitherto "helped out" at parties and dinners in their homes. From now on she would no longer "help out"—she would cater.

Most of what I learned about Werner, though, I didn't learn from

Werner. He would answer a question readily enough, but very precisely, very much within the limits of the question, and no overtones thrown in. I guess I learned about him because he was my friend, by sucking it out of the air the way kids do, during the times I was in his house before he was forbidden to hang around with me, and during the dozens of times before and after, when he sneaked up to our place. He was at our place as often as he could get away.

Up there, a casual visitor might have taken him for one of the family, since he was blond and short-featured, like my mother and me. He was a head taller than me, though, with a good build on him that was surprising if you had already seen his father's sunken, nutcracker face and bent-kneed waiter's shuffle. It wasn't that he had the special quiet of the very stupid or the very smart, or that he had any language difficulty; he spoke English as well as I did and got mostly nineties at school, where he made no bones about plugging hard and was held up as an example because he had only been in the country five years. It was just that he had almost no informal conversation. Because of this I never felt very close to him, even when we talked sex or smoked on the sly, and sometimes I had an uneasy feeling because I couldn't tell whether he was stupid or smart. I suppose we were friends mostly out of convenience, the way boys in a neighborhood are. Our apartments partly faced each other at opposite sides of the small circular rear court of the building; by opening his bedroom window and our dining-room window we could shout to each other to come over, or to meet out in front. I could, that is, although my mother used to grumble about acting up like riffraff. He was not allowed to; once, even before the edict, I saw the window shut down hard on his shoulders by someone from behind. After the edict we used to raise the windows very slightly and whistle. Even then, I never felt really close to him until the day after he was gone.

Saturday mornings, when I was that age, seemed to have a special glow; surely there must have been rainy ones, but I remember them all in a powerful golden light, spattered with the gabble of the vegetable men as they sparred with women at the open stalls outside their stores, and ringing with the loud, pre-Sunday clang of the ash cans as the garbage collectors hoisted them into the trucks and the trucks moved on in a warm smell of settling ash. It was a Saturday morning when I first went up to the Hausers', to see if Werner could get off to take the Dyckman Ferry with me for a hike along the Palisades. I already knew that he helped his mother with deliveries evenings and afternoons after school, but I had not yet learned how prescribed all his hours were. The hall door of the Hauser apartment was open a crack; through it came a yeasty current as strong as a bakery's. I flicked the bell.

"Come," said a firm, nasal voice. Or perhaps the word was "*Komm.*" I was never to hear Mrs. Hauser speak English except once, when Werner and I, who had not heard her come in, walked through the parlor where she was dealing with a lady who had come about a daughter's wedding. That was the occasion at which I saw her smile—at the lady—a fixed grimace which dusted lightly over the neat surface of her face like the powdered sugar she shook over her coffee cakes.

I walked in, almost directly into the kitchen. It was very like ours, small and badly lighted, but it had two stoves. Rows of copper molds and pans of all shapes hung on the walls. One graduated row was all of *Bund* pans, like one my mother had, but it was the first time I had seen utensils of copper, or seen them hung on walls. Supplies, everything was in rows; nothing wandered or went askew in that kitchen; even its choke-sweet odor had no domestic vagary about it, but clamped the room in a hot, professional pall. Werner and his mother, bent over opposite ends of a cloth-covered table, were carefully stretching at a large plaque of strudel dough which almost covered its surface. Both of them glanced up briefly and bent their heads again; the making of strudel is the most intense and delicate of operations, in which the last stretching of the dough, already rolled and pulled to tissue thinness, is done on the backs of the hands, and balances on an instinctive, feathery tension. I held my breath and watched. Luba and my mother made strudel about once a year, in an atmosphere of confused merriment and operatic anguish when the dough broke. As I watched, red crept up on Werner's face.

Almost opposite me, Mrs. Hauser bent and rose, angularly deft, but without grace. I had expected some meaty-armed *Hausfrau* trundling an ample bosom smeared with flour; here was the virginal

66

silhouette of a governess, black and busked—a dressmaker's form collared in lace. From the side, her face had a thin economy, a handsomeness that had meagered and was further strained by the sparse hair spicked back in a pale bun.

Suddenly she straightened. The paste had reached the edges of the cloth; in a few whisked motions it was dabbed with butter, filled, rolled, cut, and done. She brushed her hands together, blew on the spotless front of her dress, and faced me. She was not handsome at all. Her nose, blunt-ended, came out too far to meet one, her eyes protruded slightly with a lashless, committed stare, and the coin-shaped mouth was too near the nose. She wore no make-up, and her face had the triumphant neatness of the woman who does not; next to it Luba's and my mother's would have looked vital, but messy. Her skin was too bloodless though, and her lips and the nails of her floured hands were tinged with lavender, almost stone-colored, as if she suffered from some attenuation of the heart.

Werner mumbled out my first name, and I mumbled back my errand.

Mrs. Hauser, holding her hands lightly in front of her, still gave me her stare, but it was to Werner that she spoke at last.

"*Sag ihm nein,*" she said, and turning on her heel, she left the room, still holding away from her dress the hands with the stone-colored nails.

After that, I knew enough not to go to Werner's unless he asked me to, usually on evenings when his father was on night duty in the restaurant where he worked, and Mrs. Hauser had an engagement, or on Sundays, when she had an especially fancy wedding and Mr. Hauser, dressed in his waiter's garb, went along to help her serve.

I never got used to the way their apartment looked, compared with the way it smelled. When there was no cooking going on, and the hot fumes had a chance to separate and wander, then it was filled, furnished with enticing suggestions of cinnamon, vanilla, and anise, and the wonderful, warm caraway scent of little pastries stuffed with hot forcemeat—a specialty of Mrs. Hauser's, of which her customers could never get enough. Standing outside the door, I used to think it smelled the way the house in *Hansel and Gretel* looked, in the opera to which my parents had taken me years before

—a house from whose cornices and lintels one might break off a piece and find one's mouth full of marzipan, an aerie promising happy troupes of children feasting within, in a blissful forever of maraschino and Nesselrode.

Actually, the four dim rooms, curtainless except for the blinds which the landlord supplied—one yellow, one dark green to a window—had an almost incredible lack of traces of personal occupancy, even after one knew that the Hausers never thought of the place as anything but temporary. It was furnished with a bleak minimum of tables and chairs like those in hired halls. Mrs. Hauser had procured everything from a restaurant supply house, all except the beds, which were little more than cots, and wore hard white cotton spreads of the kind seen in hotels. Here, in the bedrooms, some of the second-hand surfaces were protected with doilies, on which a few European family photographs had been placed. Years later, when I was staying in the luxurious house of a family which had managed to keep on its servants in the old-fashioned way, stumbling inadvertently into the servants' wing, one morning, I came upon a room that reminded me instantly of the Hausers', although even its dresser had a homely clutter of tawdry jewelry, dime-store boxes, and letters.

Even so, when Werner and I hung around awhile in his room, we never sat on the drill-neat bed. Usually we sat on the floor and leaned back against the bed. Except for the times we did our homework together, we either just talked or exchanged the contents of our pockets, for it was the kind of house in which there was simply nothing to do. Once or twice we smoked cigarettes there, carefully airing the room and chewing soda-mints afterward. I supplied both the cigarettes and the soda-mints, since it was an understood thing that Werner never had any money of his own; the considerable work he did for his mother was "for the business." The rows of cakes, frilled cookies, and tiny *quenelles* that we sometimes passed, going through the kitchen, were for the business too. I never got anything to eat there.

Usually, after we had been there a short while, Werner, wriggling his shoulders sheepishly, would say, "Let's go up to your place," or I would invite him up. I knew why Werner liked to be there, of course, why he could not keep from coming even after Mrs. Hauser had forbidden it. It may sound naïve to say so in this day and age, but we were an awfully happy family. We really were. And I never realized it more strongly than during the times I used to watch Werner Hauser up there.

I guess the best way I can explain the kind of family we were is to say that, although I was the only nonmusical one in a family that practically lived for music, I never felt criticized or left out. My father, although he tired quickly because of a shoulder broken when he was a boy and never properly healed, was the best musician, with faultless pitch and a concertmeister's memory for repertoire. Nora played the cello with a beautiful tone, although she wouldn't work for accuracy, and Carol could already play several wind instruments; it was a sight to watch that stringy kid of ten pursing her lips and worrying prissily about her "embouchure." Both Luba and my mother had had excellent training in piano, and sang even better than they played, although Luba would never concede to my father that she occasionally flatted. My mother, contrarily, tended to sing sharp, which so fitted her mock-acid ways that my father made endless plays on words about it. "Someday," he would add, striking his forehead with his fist, "I am going to find a woman who sings exactly in the middle; then I will steal the company's payroll, and take her to live at The Breakers in Atlantic City!"

"*Mir nix, dir nix,*" my mother would answer. "And what kind of music would be at The Breakers?"

"A string quartet," Luba would shout, "with a visiting accordion for the weekends!" Then the three of them would pound each other in laughter over the latest "visiting accordion" who had been to our house. All kinds of people were attracted to our house, many of whom had no conception of the professional quality of the music they heard there, and were forever introducing a protégé whom they had touted beforehand. Whenever these turned out to be violinists who had never heard of the Beethoven Quartets, or pianists who had progressed as far as a bravura rendition of the *Revolutionary Etude*, our secret name for them was "a visiting accordion." Not even Carol was ever rude to any of these though; the musical part of the evening simply ended rather earlier than usual, and dissolved into that welter of sociable eating and talking which we all loved.

When I say I wasn't musical, I don't mean I didn't know music or love it—no one in that family could help it—I could reproduce it and identify it quite accurately in my head, but I just couldn't make it with my hands or my voice. It had long ago been settled upon that I was the historian, the listener, the critic. "Ask Mr. Huneker here," my father would say, pointing to me with a smile (or Mr. Gilman, or Mr. Downes, according to whatever commentator he had been reading). Sometimes, when in reading new music the group achieved a dissonance that harrowed him, he would turn on me: "We should all be like this one—Paganini today—Hoffman tomorrow—and all safe upstairs in the head." But the teasing took me in; it never left me out. That's what happened to Werner at our house. They took him in too.

We had our bad times of course. Often my father's suppertime accounts of his day on Seventh Avenue, usually reported with a deft, comedian's touch, turned to bitter invective, or were not forthcoming at all. Then we knew that the mood in which he regretted a life spent among values he despised had stolen over him, or else the money question was coming up again, and we ate in silence. Luba and my mother quarreled with the violence of people who differ and cannot live without one another; their cleavages and reunions followed a regular pattern, each stage of which pervaded the house as recognizably as what was simmering on the stove. My sister Nora, eighteen and beautiful, was having trouble with both these contingencies; each month, just before her monthly, she filled the house with a richly alternating brooding and hysteria that set us all to slamming doors and leaving the house. A saint couldn't have lived with it. And Carol and I bickered, and had our pint-size troubles too.

I can see how we must have seemed to Werner though. No matter what was going on, our house had a kind of ruddiness and satisfaction about it. Partly its attraction was because there *was* always something going on. If anyone had asked me about the state of my innards in regard to my family, I guess I would have said that I felt full. Not full of life, or happiness, or riches, or any of those tiddly phrases. Just chock full. I would have said this, most likely, because, as I watched Werner hanging, reticent but dogged, to the edge of our family, watched him being stuffed by my mother, twitted by my father, saw him almost court being ignored by Nora and annoyed by Carol, I had the awful but persistent fancy that he must be absolutely hollow inside. Literally hollow, I mean. I could see them, his insides—as bleak as the apartment where his parents were either oppressively absent or oppressively around, and scattered with a few rag-tag doilies of feeling that had almost no reason to be there. There would be nothing inside him to make a feeling out of, unless it were the strong, tidal perfume of the goodies that were meant for the business.

One evening at the beginning of that summer, Werner was with us when my father scooped us all up and took us to the concert at the Stadium, only a few minutes' walk from home. We went often to those concerts, although, as everyone knows, open-air music can rarely have the finish of the concert hall. But there is something infinitely arresting, almost pathetic, in music heard in the open air. It is not only the sight of thousands of ordinary faces, tranced and quiet in a celebration of the unreal. It is because the music, even while it is clogged and drowned now and then by the rusty noises of the world outside the wall, is not contaminated by them; even while it states that beauty and the world are irreconcilable, it persists in a frail suggestion that the beauty abides.

Werner, at his first concert, sat straight-backed on one of the straw mats my father had rented for us, taking in the fragments of talk milling around us, with the alertness of a person at a dinner who watches how his neighbor selects his silver. During the first half, when an ambulance siren, combined with the grinding of the trolleys on Amsterdam Avenue, clouded over a pianissimo, he winced carefully, like some of those around him. But during the second half, which ended with the Beethoven Fifth, when a dirigible stealing overhead drew a thousand faces cupped upward, Werner, staring straight ahead with a sleepy, drained look, did not join them.

As we all walked down the hill afterward, Carol began whistling the Andante. As she came to that wonderful breakthrough in the sixteenth measure, Werner took it up in a low, hesitant, but pure whistle, and completed it. Carol stopped whistling, her mouth open, and my father turned his head. No one said anything though, and we kept on walking down the hill. Suddenly Werner whistled again, the repetition of that theme, twenty-three bars from the end, when, instead of descending to the A flat, it rises at last to the G.

My father stopped in his tracks. "You play, Werner?"
Werner shook his head.
"Somebody plays at your house?"
"*Nein*," said Werner. I don't think he realized that he had said it in German.
"How is it you know music?"
Werner rubbed his hand across his eyes. When he spoke, he sounded as if he were translating. "I did not know that I know it," he said.

In the next few weeks Werner came with us almost every time we went. I didn't know where he got the money, but he paid his own way. Once, when he hadn't come to go with us, we met him afterward, loitering at the exit we usually took, and he joined us on the walk home. I think he must have been listening from outside the Stadium wall.

He always listened with a ravenous lack of preference. Once he turned to me at the intermission and said with awe, "I could hear them both together. The themes. At the *same* time." When I spoke sophomorically of what I didn't like, he used to look at me with pity, although at the end of a concert which closed with the "Venusberg," he turned to me, bewildered, and said. "It *is* possible not to like it." I laughed, but I did feel pretty comfortable with him just then. I always hated those triangles in the "Venusberg."

Then, one time, he did not come around for over a week, and when I saw him in the street he was definitely avoiding me. I thought of asking why he was sore at me, but then I thought: The hell with it. Anyway, that Sunday morning, as my father and I started out for a walk on Riverside Drive, we met Werner and his mother in the elevator. Mrs. Hauser carried some packages and Werner had two large cartons which he had rested on the floor. It was a tight squeeze, but the two of us got in, and after the door closed my father succeeded in raising his hat to Mrs. Hauser, but got no acknowledgment. My father replaced his hat on his fan-shaped wedge of salt-and-pepper hair. He chewed his lips back and forth thoughtfully under his large, mournful nose, but said nothing. When the door opened, we had to get out first. They passed ahead of us quickly, but not before we heard what Mrs. Hauser muttered to Werner. "*Was hab' ich gesagt?*" she said. "*Sie sind Juden!*"

Anybody who knows Yiddish can understand quite a lot of German too. My father and I walked a long way that day, not on the upper Drive, where the Sunday strollers were, but on those little paths, punctuated with iron street lamps but with a weak hint of country lane about them, where the city petered out into the river. We walked along, not saying much of anything, all the way up to the lighthouse at Inspiration Point. Then we climbed the hill to Broadway, where my father stopped to buy some cold cuts and a cheese cake, and took the subway home. Once, when my father was paying my fare, he let his hand rest on my shoulder before he waved me ahead of him through the turnstile, and once he caught himself whistling something, looked at me quickly, and closed his mouth. I didn't have a chance to recognize what he whistled.

We were at the table eating when the doorbell rang. Carol ran to answer it; she was the kind of kid who was always darting to answer the phone or the door, although it was almost never for her. She came back to the table and flounced into her seat.

"It's Werner. He wants to see you. He won't come in."

I went to the door. He wasn't lounging against the door frame, the way he usually did. He was standing a couple of paces away from it.

"Please come for a walk," he said. He was looking at his shoes.

"Gee, whyn't you come in?" I said. "I'm dead."

"Please," he said, "I want you please to come for a walk."

I was practically finished eating anyway. I went back to the table, grabbed up a hard roll and some pastrami, and followed him downstairs.

Summer in the city affects me the same way as open air music. I guess it's because both of them have such a hard time. Even when the evening breeze smells of nothing but hot brick, you get the feeling that people are carrying around leaves in their hearts. Werner and I walked down to our usual spot on the river, to a low stone wall, which we jumped, over to a little collection of bushes and some grass, on the other side. It was an open enough spot, but it reacted on us more or less like a private cave; we never said much of anything till we got there. This time it was up to Werner to speak. I had the sandwich, so I finished that.

73

The electric signs across the river on the Jersey side were already busy. Werner's face was turned parallel with the river, so that it looked as if the sign that gave the time signal were paying out its letters right out of his mouth. THE TIME IS NOW . . . 8:01 . . . Ordinarily I would have called his attention to this effect and changed seats with him so he could see it happen to me, but I didn't. The sign jazzed out something about salad oil, and then paid out another minute.

Werner turned his head. "You heard . . . this morning in the elevator?"

I nodded.

"Your father heard too?"

I nodded again.

He pressed his knuckles against his teeth. His words came through them with a chewed sound. "It is because they are servants," he said.

"Who do you mean?"

"My father and mother."

"You mean . . . they don't like Jews because they have to work for them sometimes?"

"Maybe," said Werner, "but it is not what I mean."

"It's no disgrace, what anybody works at, over here." I wasn't sure I believed this, but it was what one was told. "Besides, they have the business."

Werner turned his back on me, his shoulders humped up against the Palisades. "Inside them, they are servants."

He turned back to face me, the words tumbling out with the torn confiding of the closemouthed. "They do not care about the *quality* of anything." His voice lingered on the word. He jerked his head at the Mazola sign. "Butter maybe, instead of lard. But only because it is good for the business."

"Everybody has something wrong with his family," I muttered.

Werner folded his arms almost triumphantly and looked at me. "But we are not a family," he said.

I got up and walked around the little grass plot. The way he had spoken the word *quality* stayed with me; it popped into my mind the time in spring when he and I had been sitting near the same old stone wall and two scarlet tanagers lit on it and strutted for a min-

ute against the blue. You aren't supposed to see tanagers in New
York City. Sooner or later, though, you'll see almost everything in
New York. You'll have almost every lousy kind of feeling too.

The river had a dark shine to it now. It smelled like a packing-
house for fish, but it looked like the melted, dark eyes of a million
girls.

"I wish we were going up to the country this year," I said. "I'd
like to be there right now."

"I hate the country!" Werner said. "That's where they're going
to have the restaurant. They have almost enough money now."

Then it all came out—in a rush. "Come on back," he said.
"They're out. I want to show you something."

All the way up the hill he talked: how his mother had worked as
a housekeeper for a rich merchant after his father had left for
America; how he had always been the child in the basement, allowed to play neither with the town children nor the merchant's;
how his mother would not agree to come over until his father had
saved a certain sum, and then required that it be sent to her in dollars before she would sail. Then, in Yorkville, where they had only
taken a larger room because the landlady insisted, they used to walk
the garish streets sometimes, listening to the din from the cafés—
"*Ist das nicht ein . . . ? Ja, das ist ein . . .*"—but never going in
for a snack or a glass of beer. "We breathed quiet," I remember him
saying, "so we would not have to use up too much air."

And always, everything was for the restaurant. At Christmastime
and birthdays they did not give each other presents, but bought
copper pans, cutlery, equipment for the restaurant. They had their
eye on an actual place, on a side road not too far from some of the
fancy towns in Jersey; it was owned by a man whose wife was a
cousin of Mrs. Hauser's. It already had a clientele of connoisseurs
who came to eat slowly, to wait reverently in a waft of roasting
coffee, for the *Perlhuhn* and the *Kaiser-Schmarren*. The cousins were
smart—they knew that Americans would pay the best for the best,
and even wait a little long for it, in order to be thought European.
But they had let the place get seedy; they did not have enough discipline for the long, sluggish day before the customers arrived, and
they had not learned that while the Americans might wait out of
snobbishness, they would not do so because the owners were getting

75

drunk in the kitchen. The Hausers would be smarter still. They would serve everything of the best, at a suitably stately pace for such quality, and they would not get drunk in the kitchen.

He stopped talking when we got to his door. The whole time, he hadn't raised his voice, but had talked on and on in a voice like shavings being rubbed together.

His room was dark and full of the cloying smell. He stood in front of the window, not turning the light on, and I saw that he was looking over at our place. I saw how it looked to him.

That was the summer radios first really came in. Almost everyone had one now. We hadn't got one yet, but one of Nora's boy friends had given her a small table model. There were a couple of them playing now at cross purposes, from different places on the court.

"Thursday nights they are broadcasting the concerts, did you know?" he said softly. "Sometimes someone tunes in on it, and I can hear, if I keep the window open. The echoes are bad . . . and all the other noises. Sometimes, of course, no one tunes it in."

I wondered what he had to show me, and why he did not turn on the light.

"Today was my birthday," he said. "I asked them for a radio, but of course I did not expect it. I am to get working papers. When they leave, I am to leave the high school."

He walked away from the window and turned on the light. The objects on the bed sprang into sharp black and white: the tie disposed on the starched shirt, which lay neatly between the black jacket and pants. That's what it was. It was a waiter's suit.

"Of course I did not expect it," he said. "I did not."

It was after this that Werner, when he whistled across the court, started using themes from here and there. Sometimes it was that last little mocking bit from *Till Eulenspiegel* when Till's feet kick, sometimes it was the Ho-yo-to-ho of the Valkyries, sometimes the horns from the "Waltz of the Flowers." It was always something we had heard at the Stadium, something we had heard together. When my father, to whom I had blabbed most of that evening with Werner, heard the whistle, his face would sometimes change red, as if he were holding his breath in anger against someone; then this would be displaced by the sunk, beaten look he sometimes brought home from Seventh Avenue, and he would shrug and turn away. He never said anything to Werner or to me.

The last night, the night it must have happened, was a Thursday a few weeks later. It was one of those humid nights when the rain just will not come, and even the hair on your head seems too much to carry around with you. We were all sitting in the dining room, brushing limply now and then at our foreheads. Nora was in one of her moods—the boy who had given her the radio had not phoned. She had it turned on and sat glowering in front of it, as if she might evoke him from it.

My father was standing at the window, looking up at the sky. The court had its usual noises, children crying, a couple of other radios, and the rumble from the streets. Once or twice some kid catcalled from a higher floor, and a light bulb exploded on the alley below.

My father leaned forward suddenly, and looked across the court, watching intently. Then he walked slowly over to the radio, stood in front of it a moment, and turned it on loud. We all looked at him in surprise. He didn't think much of the thing, and never monkeyed with it.

I looked across the court at Werner's window. I couldn't see into its shadows, but it was open. I thought of the look on his face when he met us outside the Stadium walls and of his voice saying, "Sometimes no one tunes it in." I would have whistled to him, but I couldn't have been heard over the music—*Scheherazade*, it was—which was sweeping out loud and strong into the uneasy air.

My mother whispered a reproach to my father, then took a side look at his face, and subsided. I glanced around at Carol, Nora, all of us sitting there joined together, and for some reason or other I felt sick. It's the weather, I thought, and wiped my forehead.

Then, in the square across the court, the blackness merged and moved. The window began to grind down. And then we heard Werner's voice, high and desperate, louder even than the plashing waves of the Princess's story—a long, loud wail.

"No! Please! Scheherazade is speaking!"

Then there were two figures at the window, and the window was flung up again. My mother clapped her hand against her face, ran over to the radio and turned it down low, and stood bent over with

77

her back against it, her fist to her mouth. So it was that we heard Werner again, his words squeezed out, hoarse, but clear. *"Bitte, Mutter. Lass mich hören. Scheherazade spricht."*
Then the window came down.

The next evening the house was like a hive with what had happened. The Hausers had gone to the police. There had been one really personal thing in their house after all, and Werner had taken it with him. He had taken the whole of the cache in the wall safe, the whole ten thousand dollars for the restaurant.

The detectives came around to question me—two pleasant enough Dutch uncles who had some idea that Werner might have made a pact with me, or that I could give them some clues as to what had been going on inside him. I couldn't tell them much of use. I wasn't going to tell them to look over at the Stadium, either outside or in, although for years afterward I myself used to scan the crowds there. And I wasn't fool enough to try to explain to them what I had hardly figured out yet myself—that nature abhors the vacuums men shape, and sooner or later pushes the hollow in.

Mr. and Mrs. Hauser stayed on, and as far as anyone could tell, kept on with their usual routine. They were still there when we moved—Luba had decided the air was better in Hollis, Queens. During the months while we were still at Hamilton Terrace though, my father acquired an odd habit. If he happened to pass the open dining room window when our large new radio was playing, he was likely to pause there, and look out across the court. Sometimes he shut the sash down hard, and sometimes he let it be, but he always stood there for a time. I never decided whether the look on his face was guilty or proud. I knew well enough why he stood there though. For it was from our house that the music had come. It was from our window that Scheherazade spoke.

The Rehabilitation of Ginevra Leake

꿹 E v e r s i n c e our State Department published that address of Khrushchev's to the Twentieth Congress of the Communist Party, in which he noted the "posthumous rehabilitation" of a number of Russians who had been executed as enemies of the people, I've been nagged by the thought that I owe it to our bourgeois society to reveal what I know about the life of my friend Ginny Doll—or as she was known to her friends in the Party—Ginevra Leake. If you remember, Mr. Khrushchev's speech was dotted with anecdotes that all wound to the same tender conclusion:

> On February 4th Eihke was shot. It has been definitely established now that Eihke's case was fabricated; he has been posthumously rehabilitated . . . Sentence was passed on Rudzutak in twenty minutes and he was shot. (Indignation in the hall) . . . After careful examination of the case in 1955 it was established that the accusation against Rudzutak was false. He has been rehabilitated posthumously . . . Suffice it to say that from 1954 to the present time, the Military Collegium of the Supreme Court has rehabilitated 7,679 persons, many of whom were rehabilitated posthumously.

Being dead, Ginny Doll would certainly fall into the latter category if anyone chose to rehabilitate her, but since the manner of her death has elevated her, however erroneously, to martyrdom in the American branch of the Party, it's unlikely that any of her crowd will see the need of arousing indignation in the hall. The task therefore devolves on me, not only as a friend of her girlhood, but as her only non-Party friend—kept on because I represented the past, al-

79

ways so sacred to a Southerner, and therefore no more disposable than the rose-painted lamps, walnut commodes and feather-stitched samplers in the midst of which she pursued life on the New York barricades, right to the end. If to no one else, I owe to the rest of us Southrons the rehabilitation of Ginny Doll, even if, as is most likely, it's the last thing she'd want.

I first met Virginia Darley Leake, as she was christened, Ginny Doll as she was called by her mother and aunts, when she and I were about fifteen, both of us daughters of families who had recently emigrated from Virginia to New York, mine from Richmond, hers from Lynchburg the town that, until I grew up, I assumed was spelled "Lenchburg." My father disliked professional Southerners, and would never answer invitations to join their ancestral societies. However, on one summer evening when he was feeling his age and there was absolutely no prospect of anyone dropping in to hear about it, he succumbed to momentary sentiment and went downtown to a meeting of the Sons and Daughters of the Confederacy. He came back snorting that they were nothing but old maids of both sexes, just as he'd expected; he'd been trapped into seeing home a Mrs. Darley Lyon Leake who'd clung to him like a limpet when she'd found they both lived on Madison Avenue, and he warned my mother that he was afraid the woman would call—his actual phrase for Mrs. Leake being "one of those tiny, clinging ones you can't get off your hands—like peach fuzz."

Mrs. Leake—a tiny, coronet-braided woman with a dry, bodiless neatness—did call, but only, as she carefully explained to my mother, for the purpose of securing a Southern, presumably genteel playmate for her daughter. My mother was not Southern, but she shared her caller's opinion of the girls Ginny Doll and I brought home from school. The call was repaid once, by my mother with me in tow, after which it was understood that any *entente* was to be only between us girls; my parents and Mrs. Leake never saw each other again.

On that first call I had been relieved to find how much the Leake household, scantily composed of only three females—Mrs. Leake, Ginny Doll and Ida, the cook—still reminded me of our own crowded one, in its slow rhythm and antediluvian clutter. Three years spent trying to imitate the jumpy ways of my New York girl friends had made me ashamed of our peculiarities; it was comforting to be reminded that these were regional, and that at least there were two of us on Madison Avenue.

With the alchemic snobbery of her kind, Mrs. Leake had decreed that the intimacy must be all one way; Ginny Doll could not come to us. So it was always I who went there, at first I didn't quite know why. For, like many of the children introduced to me by my parents, and as quickly shed, Ginny Doll was a lame duck. It would be unfair to suggest that she and her mother were types indigenous only to the South; nevertheless, anybody down there would have recognized them at once—the small woman whose specious femininity is really one of size and affectation, whose imperious ego always has a socially proper outlet (Mrs. Leake wore her heart trouble on her sleeve), and whose single daughter is always a great lumpy girl with a clayey complexion. At fifteen, Ginny Doll was already extremely tall, stooped, and heavy in a waistless way; only her thin nose was pink, and her curves were neither joyous nor warm; her long hand lay in one's own like a length of suet just out of the icebox and her upper teeth preceded her smile. One glance at mother and daughter predicted their history; by producing a girl of such clearly unmarriageable aspect, the neatly turned Mrs. Leake had assured herself of a well-serviced life until her own death—at a probable eighty. After that, Ginny Doll's fate would have been clearer in Lenchburg, for the South has never lost its gentle, feudal way of absorbing its maiden ladies in one family sinecure or another. But up here in the amorphous North, there was no foretelling what might happen, much less what did.

Ginny Doll also had manners whose archaic elegance I remembered from down home—it was these that my mother had hoped I would reacquire—but unfortunately hers were accompanied by a slippery voice, with a half-gushy catch to it, that gave her a final touch of the ridiculous. Still, I found myself unable to desert her. It appeared that I was her only friend (although her importunities were always so restrained that it took a keen ear to hear the tremor in them), and after I had gone there a few times I felt guilty at not liking her better, because I felt so sorry for her.

For it appeared also that my father had been accorded a signal honor in being allowed past their threshold. Mrs. Leake was not a

widow as we had assumed, but a deserted woman, and it was because of this that nothing more masculine than the old pug, which
she sometimes boarded for a rich sister-in-law, was ever allowed
past her door. According to Ginny Doll, her mother had done nothing to merit desertion, unless it was having committed the *faux pas*
of marrying a Texan. Indeed, her position was so honorable that
conscience money from the sister-in-law, the husband's sister, was
the means by which she was quite adequately supported. Still, there
was a stain upon them—it was the fact that Mr. Leake still lived.
Somehow this fact committed them to an infinite circumspection,
and was responsible for the exhausted, yet virulent femininity of
their ménage. It was also to blame for Mrs. Leake's one perverted
economy, for which Ginny Doll was never to forgive her—her refusal to get Ginny Doll's teeth straightened. When approached by
the sister-in-law, Aunt Tot, on this matter, she would reply that
she wouldn't use conscience money to tamper with the work of
the Lord. When approached by Ginny Doll, her reply came nearer the
truth: "You didn't get them from me." As I came to know the
Leakes better, I concluded that the stain was increased by the fact
that Mr. Leake not only was, but was happy somewhere. Although
Ginny Doll never spoke of him, I saw him clearly—a man still ro-
bust, with the slight coarseness of the too-far-south South, a man
barreling along somewhere careless and carefree, a man who knew
how to get peach fuzz off his hands.

By this time the household had won me, as it was to win so many
—in later years I could well understand Ginny Doll's unique position in the Party. How it must have salved Party spirits, after a hot
day in the trenches of the *Daily Worker*, to enter an authentic version of that Southern parlor inside whose closed circle one sits so
cozened and élite, pleating time's fan! Our famed hospitality con-
sists really of a welcome whose stylized warmth is even more affecting than genuine interest, plus the kind of stately consideration for
the trivial that makes everybody feel importantly human—Ginny
Doll did both to perfection. In my case, it was summertime when I
met the Leakes, and our people do have a genius for hot weather.
Inside their living room the shades were drawn cool and gray, white
dust covers were slippery under bare legs, and a music box was set
purling. No one was ever there long before Ida, a frustrated artist

with only two to feed, came in bearing an enormous, tinkling tea which she replenished at intervals, urging us to keep up our strength. When, during the first of my visits, Ginny Doll happened to remark, "Your father is .truly handsome; with that ahngree hair of his and that pahful nose, I declare he looks just like a sheik!" I took it for more of her Lenchburg manners. It was only later that I saw how the *idée fixe* "Men!" was the pivot from which, in opposite ways, the two Leakes swung.

When I was sixteen, my parents gave me a coming-out dance. After a carefully primed phone call to Mrs. Leake by my father, Ginny Doll was allowed to attend, on the stipulation that he bring her home at the stroke of twelve. At the dance I was too busy to pay her much mind, but later I heard my parents talking in their bedroom.

"She ought to take that girl back to Lenchburg," said my father. "Up here, they don't understand such takin' ways, 'less a pretty face goes with 'em. That girl'll get herself misunderstood—if she gets the chance."

"Taking ways!" said my mother. "Why she followed the boys around as if they were unicorns! As if she'd never seen one before!"

My father's shoes hit the floor. "Reckon not," he said.

The next day, Ginny Doll telephoned, eager for postmortems on the dance, but I'd already been through that with several of my own crowd, and I didn't get to see her until the end of the week. I found that she had spent the interval noting down the names of all the boys she had met at my house—out of a list of forty she had remembered twenty-nine names and some characteristic of each of the others, such as "real short, and serious, kind of like the Little Minister." Opening her leather diary, she revealed that ever since their arrival in New York, she had kept a list of every male she had met; my dance had been a strike of the first magnitude, bringing her total, with the inclusion of two doctors, the landlord and a grocery boy, almost to fifty. And in a special column opposite each name she had recorded the owner's type, much as an anthropologist might note "brachycephalic," except that Ginny Doll's categories were all culled from their "library," that collection of safely post-Augustan classics, bound *Harper's*, Thomas Nelson Page and E. P. Roe which used to be on half the musty bookshelves in the Valley of Virginia.

There was a Charles Brandon, a Henry Esmond (one of the doctors), a Marlborough and a Bonnie Prince Charlie, as well as several other princes and chevaliers I'd never heard of before. A boy named Bobbie Locke, who'd brought a flask and made a general show of himself, was down as D'Artagnan, and my own beau, a nice quiet boy from St. Mark's, was down as Gawain. My father was down as Rasselas, Prince of Abyssinia.

I remember being impressed at first; in Richmond we had been taught to admire "great readers," even when female, and almost every family we knew had, or had had, at least one. But I also felt a faint, squirmy disquiet. Many of the girls I knew kept movie-star books, or had pashes on Gene Tunney or Admiral Byrd, but we never mixed up these legendary figures with the boys who took us to Huyler's. I was uncomfortably reminded of my father's cousin, old Miss Lavalette Buchanan, who still used more rouge than you could buy on Main Street, and wore gilt bows in her hair even to the Busy Bee.

From then on, my intimacy with Ginny Doll dwindled. Now and then I dropped by on a hot summer day when no one else was around and I simply had to talk about a new beau. For on this score she was the perfect confidante, of course, hanging breathless on every detail. After each time, I swore never to go back. It was embarrassing where there was no exchange. Besides, she drove me nuts with that list, bringing it out like an old set of dominoes, teasing me about my fickleness to "Gawain." I couldn't seem to get it through her head that this was New York, not Lenchburg, and that I hadn't seen any of those boys for years.

By the time I'd been away at college for a year, I was finished with her. Ginny Doll hadn't gone—Mrs. Leake thought it made you hard. My mother occasionally met Ginny Doll on the avenue, and reported her as pursuing a round that was awesomely unchanged— errands for Mamma, dinners with the aunts, meetings of the Sons and Daughters—even the pug was the same. The Leakes, my father said once, had brought the art of the status quo to a hyaline perfection that was a rarity in New York, but one not much prized there. Who could have dreamed of the direction from which honor would one day be paid?

The last time I saw her was shortly after my engagement had been announced, when I received a formal note from the Leakes, requesting the pleasure of my and my fiancé's company on an afternoon. I remembered with a shock that long ago, "down South," as we had learned to say now, within that circle of friends whom one did not shuffle but lost only to feud or death, a round of such visits was *de rigueur*. I went alone, unwilling to face the prospect of Ginny Doll studying my future husband for noble analogues, and found the two Leakes behind a loaded tea table.

Mrs. Leake seemed the same, except for a rigidly "at home" manner that she kept between us like a fire screen, as if my coming alliance with a man rendered me incendiary, and she was there to protect her own interests from flame. Ginny Doll's teeth had perhaps a more ivory polish from the constant, vain effort of her lips to close over them, and her dress had already taken a spinster step toward surplice necklines and battleship colors; it was hard to believe that she was, like myself, twenty-three. We were alone together only once, when I went to the bathroom and she followed me in, muttering something about hand towels, of which there were already a dozen or so lace-encrusted ones on the rod.

Once inside, she faced me eagerly, with the tight, held-in smile that always made her look as if she were holding a mashed daisy in her mouth. "It's so exciting," she said. "Tell me all about it!"

"I have," I said, referring to the stingy facts that had been extracted over the tea table—that we were both history instructors and were going to teach in Istanbul next year, that no, I had no picture with me, but he was "medium" and dark, and from "up here."

"I mean—it's been so long," she said. "And Mamma made me dispose of my book." It took me a minute to realize what she meant.

She looked down at the handkerchief she always carried, worrying the shred of cambric with the ball of her thumb, the way one worries a ticket to somewhere. "I wondered," she said. "Is he one of the ones *we* knew?"

The Leakes sent us a Lenox vase for a wedding present, and my thank-you note was followed by one from Ginny Doll saying that I just must come by some afternoon and tell her about the wedding trip; Mamma napped every day at three and it would be just like old times. I never did, of course. I was afraid it would be.

Ten years passed, fifteen. We had long since returned from

abroad and settled in East Hampton. My parents had died. The vase had been broken by the first of the children. I hadn't thought of Ginny Doll in years.

Then, one blinding August afternoon, I was walking along, of all places, Fourteenth Street, cursing the mood that had sent me into the city on such a day, to shop for things I didn't need and wouldn't find. I hadn't found them, but the rising masochism that whelms women at the height of an unsuccessful shopping tour had impelled me down here to check sewing-machine prices at a discount house someone had mentioned a year ago, on whose door I'd just found a sign saying "Closed Month of August." In another moment I would rouse and hail a cab, eager enough for the green routines I had fled that morning. Meanwhile I walked slowly west, the wrong way, still hunting for something, anything, peering into one after the other of the huge glass bays of the cheap shoe stores. Not long since, there had still been a chocolate shop down here, that had survived to serve teas in a cleanliness which was elegance for these parts, but I wouldn't find it either. New York lay flat, pooped, in air the color of sweat, but a slatternly nostalgia rose from it, as happens in the dead end of summer, for those who spent their youth there. This trip was a seasonal purge; it would be unwise to find anything.

"Why, Charlotte Mary! I do declare!"

I think I knew who it was before I turned. It was my youth speaking. Since my parents died, no one had addressed me in that double-barreled way in years.

"Why—why Ginny Doll!" Had she not spoken, I would have passed her; she was dressed in that black, short-sleeved convention which city women were just beginning to use and looked, at first glance, almost like anyone. But at the gaspy catch of that voice I remembered everything about her. Here was the one mortal who must have stayed as much the same as anyone could, preserved in the amber of her status quo.

"Why, believe it or not, I was just thinking of you!" I said. It wasn't strictly true; I had been thinking of Huyler's, of old, expunged summers to which she faintly belonged. But early breeding stays with one, returning at odd times like an accent. I can still tell a half-lie, for the sake of someone else's pleasure, as gracefully as anybody in Virginia.

While she extracted the number and names of my children, I revised my first impression of her. Age had improved her, as it does some unattractive girls—we were both thirty-seven. She still stooped heavily, as if the weight of her bust dragged at the high, thin shoulders, but she was better corseted, and had an arty look of heavy earrings and variegated bracelets, not Greenwich Village modern, but the chains of moonstones set in silver, links of carnelians and cameos that ladies used to bring back from Florence—I remembered Aunt Tot.

Something about her face had changed, however, and at first I thought it was merely the effect of her enormous hat (how had I missed it?)—the wide-brimmed "picture" hat, with an overcomplicated crown, often affected by women who fancied a touch of Mata Hari, or by aging demi-mondaines. Later, I was to find that this hat was Ginny Doll's trademark, made for her in costume colors by the obscure family milliner to whom she still was loyal, whose fumbling, side-street touch saved the model from its own aspirations and kept it the hat of a lady. At the moment I thought only of how much it was just what Ginny Doll grown up would wear—one of those swooping discs under which romantic spinsters could visualize themselves leaning across a restaurant table at the not-impossible man, hats whose subfusc shadows came too heavy on the faces beneath them, and, well, too late. Here was her old aura of the ridiculous, brought to maturity.

"And how is your mother?" I asked, seeing Mrs. Leake as she still must be—tiny, deathless companion fly.

"Mamma?" She smiled, an odd smile, wide and lifted, but closed, and then I saw the real difference in her face. Her teeth had been pulled in. She had had them straightened. "Mamma's *dead*," said Ginny Doll.

"Oh, I'm sorry; I hadn't heard—"

"Six years ago. It was her heart after all, think of it. And then I came into Aunt Tot's money." She smiled on, like a pleased child; until the day of her death, as I was to find, she never tired of the wonder of smiling.

"But don't let's stand here in this awful heat," she said. "Come on up to the house, and Ida'll give us some iced tea. Oh, honey, there's so much to tell you!"

"Ida," I said, enchanted. "Still Ida? Oh I wish I could, but I'm afraid I haven't time to go all the way up there. I'll miss my train."

"But I don't live uptown any more, darlin', I live right down here. Come on." I gave in, and instinctively turned east. Toward Gramercy Park, it would surely be, or Irving Place.

"No, this way." She turned me west. "Right here on Fourteenth."

I followed her, wondering, used as I was to the odd crannies that New Yorkers often seized upon with a gleefully inverted assumption of style. From Union Square just east of us, westward for several long blocks, this was an arid neighborhood even for tenements, an area of cranky shops being superseded by huge bargain chains, of lofts, piano factories, and the blind, shielded windows of textile agents. Nobody, really nobody lived here.

We turned in at the battered doorway of a loft building. Above us, I heard the chattering of machines. To the left, the grimy buff wall held a signboard with a row of company names in smudged gilt. Ginny Doll took out a key and opened a mailbox beneath. I was close enough to read the white calling card on it—*Ginevra Leake.*

At that moment she turned, holding a huge wad of mail. "Honey, I guess I ought to tell you something about me, before you go upstairs," she said. "In case it might make a difference to you."

In a flash I'd tied it all together—the hat, the neighborhood, the flossy new name, my mother's long-gone remark about unicorns. It wouldn't be need of money. She had simply gone one Freudian step past Miss Lavalette Buchanan. She'd become a tart. A tart with Ida in the background to serve iced tea, as a Darley Leake would.

"I—what did you say?" I said.

She looked down tenderly at her clutch of mail. "I've joined the Party," she said.

Familiar as the phrase had become to us all, for the moment I swear I thought she meant the Republican Party. "What's that got—" I said, and then I stopped, understanding.

"Honey love," she said. The moonstones rose, shining, on her breast. "I mean the Communist Party."

"Ginny Doll Leake! You haven't!"

"Cross my heart, I have!" she said, falling, as I had, into the overtones of our teens. "Cross my heart hope to die or kiss a pig!" And taking my silence for consent, she tossed her head gaily and led me up, past the Miller Bodice Lining, past the Apex Art Trays, to the top floor.

Ida opened the door, still in her white uniform, and greeted me warmly, chortling "Miss Charlotte! Miss Charlotte!" over and over before she released me.

I don't know what I expected to find behind her—divans perhaps, and the interchangeable furniture of Utopia built by R. H. Macy— certainly not what confronted me. For what I saw, gazing from the foyer where the abalone-shell lamp and the card tray reposed on the credenza as they had always done, was the old sitting room on Madison Avenue. Royal Doulton nymph vases, Chinese lamps, loveseats, "ladies" chairs, and luster candelabras, it was all there, even to the Bruxelles curtains through which filtered the felt-tasting air of Fourteenth Street. Obviously the place had been a huge loft, reclaimed with much expense and the utmost fidelity, "Lenchburg" Ascendant, wherever it might be. Even the positions of the furniture had been retained, with no mantel, but with the same feeling of orientation toward a nonexistent one. In the bathroom the rod held the same weight of ancestral embroidery. The only change I could discern was in the bedroom, where Ginny Doll's nursery chintz and painted rattan had been replaced by Mrs. Leake's walnut wedding suite and her *point d'esprit* spread.

I returned to the parlor and sat down on the loveseat, where I had always sat, watching, bemused, while Ida bore in the tray as if she had been waiting all that time in the wings. "The music box," I asked. "Do you still have it?" Of course they did, and while it purled, I listened to Ginny Doll's story.

After Mrs. Leake's death, Aunt Tot had intended to take Ginny Doll on a world cruise, but had herself unfortunately died. For a whole year Ginny Doll had sat on in the old place, all Aunt Tot's money waiting in front of her like a Jack Horner pie whose strands she dared not pull. Above all she craved to belong to a "crowd"; she spent hours weakly dreaming of suddenly being asked to join some "set" less deliquescent than the First Families of Virginia, but the active world seemed closed against her, an impenetrable crystal ball. Finally the family doctor insisted on her getting away. She had grasped at the only place she could think of, an orderly mountain retreat run by a neo-spiritualistic group known as Unity, two of whose Town Hall lectures she had attended with an ardently converted Daughter. The old doctor, kindly insisting on taking charge of arrangements, had mistakenly booked her at a "Camp Unity" in the Poconos. It had turned out to be a vacation camp, run, with a transparent disguise to which no one paid any attention, by the Communist Party.

"It was destiny," said Ginny Doll, smiling absently at a wall on which hung, among other relics, a red-white-and-blue embroidered tribute to a distaff uncle who had been mayor of Memphis. "Destiny."

I had to agree with her. From her ingenuous account, and from my own knowledge of the social habits of certain "progressives" at my husband's college, I could see her clearly, expanding like a *Magnolia grandiflora* in that bouncingly dedicated air. In a place where the really eminent were noncommittal and aliases were worn like medals, no one questioned her presence or affiliation; each group, absorbed in the general charivari, assumed her to be part of another. In the end she achieved the *réclame* that was to grow. She was a Southerner, and a moneyed woman. They had few of either, and she delighted them with her vigorous enmity toward the status quo. Meanwhile her heart recognized their romantic use of the bogus; she bloomed in this atmosphere so full of categories, and of men. In the end she had found, if briefly, a categorical man.

"Yes, it must have been destiny," I said. Only kismet could have seen to it that Ginny Doll should meet, in the last, dialectic-dusted rays of a Pocono sunset, a man named Lee. "Lighthorse Harry" or "Robert E.," I wondered, but she never told me whether it was his first name or last, or gave any of the usual details, although in the years to come she often alluded to what he had said, with the tenacious memory of the woman who had once, perhaps only once, been preferred. It was not fantasy; I believed her. It had been one of those summer affairs of tents and flashlights, ending when "Party work" reclaimed him, this kind of work apparently being as useful for such purpose as any other. But it had made her a woman of experience, misunderstood at last, able to participate in female talk with the rueful ease of the star-crossed—and to wear those hats.

"I'm not bitter," she said. He had left her for the Party, and also to it. Her days had become as happily prescribed as a belle's, her mail as full. She had found her "set."

"And then—you know I went through analysis?" she said. She had chanced upon the Party during its great psychiatric era, when everybody was having his property-warped libido rearranged. Hers had resulted in the rearrangement of her teeth.

"The phases I went through!" She had gone through a period of wearing her hair in coronet braids; under her analyst's guidance she cut it. With his approval—he was a Party member—she had changed her name to Ginevra. He would have preferred her to keep the teeth as they were, as a symbol that she no longer hankered after the frivolities of class. But they were the one piece of inherited property for which she had no sentiment. Too impatient for orthodontia, she had had them extracted, and a bridge inserted. "And do you know what I did with them?" she said. "He said I could, if I had to, and I did."

"With the teeth?"

She giggled. "Honey, I put them in a bitty box, and I had the florist put a wreath around it. And I flew down to Lenchburg and put them on Mamma's grave."

Something moved under my feet, and I gave a slight scream. It wasn't because of what she had just said. Down home, many a good family has its Poe touch of the weirdie, my own as well, and I quite understood. But something was looking out at me from under the sofa, with old, rheumy eyes. It was the pug.

"It's Junius! But it can't be!" I said.

"Basket, Junius! Go back to your basket!" she said. "It's not the one you knew, of course. It's that one's child. Let's see, she married her own brother, so I guess this one's her cousin as well." Her tone was rambling and genealogical, the same in which my old aunt still defined a cousinship as once, twice or thrice removed. And I saw that the tip of her nose could still blush. "Old Junius was really a lady, you know," she said.

When I rose to leave, Ida followed us to the hallway. "You come back, Miss Charlotte," she said. "You come back, hear? And bring your family with you. I'll cook 'em a dinner. Be right nice to have you, 'stead all these tacky people Miss Ginny so took up with."

"Now Ida," said Ginny Doll. "Charlotte," she said, "if there's

91

one thing I've learned—" Her moonstones glittered again, in the mirror over the credenza. It was the single time she ever expounded theory. "If there's one thing I've learned—it's that real people *are* tacky."

I did go back of course, and now it was she who gave the social confidences, I who listened with fascination. Once or twice she had me to dinner with some of her "set," not at all to convert me, but rather as a reigning hostess invites the quiet friend of other days to a brief glimpse of her larger orbit, the better to be able to talk about it later. For, as everyone now knows, she had become a great Party hostess. She gave little dinners, huge receptions, the *ton* of which was just as she would have kept it anywhere—excellent food, notable liqueurs and the Edwardian solicitude to which she had been born. As a Daughter and a D.A.R., she had a special exhibit value as well. Visiting dignitaries were brought to her as a matter of course; rising functionaries, when bidden there, knew how far they had risen. Her parlor was the scene of innumerable Young Communist weddings, and dozens of Marxian babies embarked on life with one of her silver spoons. The Party had had its Mother Bloor. Ginny Doll became its Aunt.

Meanwhile we kept each other on as extramural relaxation, the way people do keep the friend who knew them "when." Just because it was so unlikely for either of us (I was teaching again), we sometimes sewed together, took in a matinée. But I had enough glimpses of her other world to know what she ignored in it. No doubt she enjoyed the sense of conspiracy—her hats grew a trifle larger each year. And she did her share of other activities—if always on the entertainment committee. But her heart held no ruse other than the pretty guile of the Virginian, and I never heard her utter a dialectical word. Had she had the luck to achieve a similar success in "Lenchburg" her response would have been the same—here, within a circle somewhat larger but still closed, the julep was minted for all. She lived for her friends, who happened to be carrying cards instead of leaving them.

She did *not*, however, die for her friends. Every newspaper reader, of course, knows how she died. She was blown up in that explosion in a union hall on Nineteenth Street, the one that also wrecked a delicatessen, a launderette and Mr. Kravetz's tailoring shop next door. The union had had fierce anti-pro-Communist troubles for years, with beatings and disappearances for years, and when Ginny Doll's remains, not much but enough, were found, it was taken for granted that she had died in the Party. The Communist press did nothing to deny this. Some maintained that she had been wiped out by the other side; others awarded her a higher martyrdom, claiming that she had gone there equipped like a matronly Kamikaze, having made of herself a living bomb. Memorial services were held, the Ginevra Leake Camp Fund was set going, and she was awarded an Order of Stalin, second class. She is a part of their hagiolatry forever.

But I happen to know otherwise. I happen to know that she was on Nineteenth Street because it was her shopping neighborhood, and because I had spoken to her on the telephone not an hour before. She was just going to drop a blouse by at Mr. Kravetz's, she said, then she'd meet me at 2:30 at McCutcheon's, where we were going to pick out some gros-point she wanted to make for her Flint & Horner chairs.

I remember waiting for her for over an hour, thinking that she must be sweet-talking Mr. Kravetz, who was an indifferent tailor but a real person. Then I phoned Ida, who knew nothing, and finally caught my train. We left on vacation the next day, saw no papers, and I didn't hear of Ginny Doll's death until my return.

When I went down to see Ida, she was already packing for Lynchburg. She had been left all Ginny Doll's worldly goods and an annuity; the rest of Aunt Tot's money must have gone you-know-where.

"Miss Charlotte, you pick yourself a momento," said Ida. We were standing in the bedroom, and I saw Ida's glance stray to the bureau, where two objects reposed in *nature morte*. "I just could'n leave 'em at the morgue, Miss Charlotte," she said. "An' now I can't take 'em, I can't throw 'em out." It was Ginny Doll's hat, floated clear of the blast, and her false teeth.

I knew Ida wanted me to take them. But I'm human. I chose the music box. As I wrapped it, I felt Ida's eye on me. She knew what *noblesse oblige* meant, better than her betters. So I compromised, and popped the teeth in too.

When I got home, I hid them. I knew that the children, scavengers all, would sooner or later come upon them, but it seemed too dreadful to chuck them out. Finally, it came to me. I taped them in a bitty box, masqued with a black chiffon rose, and took them to our local florist, who sent them to a florist in Lynchburg, to be wreathed and set on Mrs. Leake's grave.

Nevertheless, whenever I heard the children playing the music box, I felt guilty. I had somehow failed Ginny Doll, and the children too. Then, when Mr. Khrushchev's speech came along, I knew why. I saw that no one but me could clear Ginny Doll's name, and give her the manifesto she deserves.

Comrades! Fellow members of Bourgeois Society! Let there be indignation in the hall! It is my duty to tell you that Ginevra Leake, alias Virginia Darley, alias Ginny Doll, was never an enemy of Our People at all. She never deserted us, but died properly in the gracious world she was born to, inside whose charmed circle everyone, even the Juniuses, are cousins of one another! She was an arch-individualist, just as much as Stalin. She was a Southern Lady.

And now I can look my children in the eye again. The Russians needn't think themselves the only ones to rehabilitate people posthumously. We Southrons can take care of our own.

The Woman Who Was Everybody

◄§ A T A quarter of eight, young Miss Abel was prodded out of sleep as usual by the harsh clanging of the bell in the church around the corner. It went on for as much as forty or fifty times, each clank plummeting instantly into silence, as if someone were beating iron against a stone. She did not get up at once, but lay there, seeing herself rise with the precision of a somnambulist, go from bathroom to kitchenette in the blind actions which would dissolve the sediment of sleep still in her eyes, in her bones. In her throat, a sick resistance to the day had already begun its familiar mounting, the pulse of a constant ache on which sleep had put only a delusory quietus. Lying there, she wondered which unwitting day of the past had been the one on which she must have exchanged the bright morning dower of childhood, that indolent assurance that the day was a nimbus of possibilities, for this heavy ache that collected in the throat like a catarrhal reminder that as yesterday was dusty, so would be today.

There had been nothing in her childhood, certainly, to warrant that early dowered expectancy, nothing in the girlhood spent in her mother's rooming house near that part of the Delaware River consecrated to the Marcus Hook refineries, where the great fungoid tanks bloomed oppressively over all, draining the frontal streets like theirs, which were neither country lanes nor town blocks, but only in-between passageways where the privet died hardily, without either pavement or neon to console one for its death. In that bland, unimpassioned climate the days had been blurred exhalations of the factories, the river and the people, dragging on into a darkness that was like the fainter, sooted, interchangeable breath of all of these. Perhaps the days had rung with expectancy for her, nevertheless, because from the first, for as long as she could remember, she had been so sure of getting out, away. As, of course, she had.

She swung sideways out of bed and clamped her feet on the floor, rose and trundled to the bathroom, the kitchenette. Boiled coffee was the quickest and most economical; watching the grounds spray and settle on the bubbling water, she took comfort from the small action. Everywhere in New York now toasters clicked, clocks rang, and people rising under the weight of the new day took heart from each little milestone of routine, like children, walking past a strange paling, who touch placatingly every third picket, hoping this will bring them through safe.

Fumbling without choice for one of the two dresses of the daily requisite black, she peered out the window into the alley beyond. The slick gray arms of the dwarfed tree, which grew, anonymous and mineral, from its humus of dust and concrete, were charitably fuzzed with light, and above them the water tanks and girders of the roofs beyond stood out against the fine yellow morning, clarified and glistening. Night could still down the city, absorbing it for all its rhinestone effrontery, but the mornings crept in like applicants for jobs, nuzzling humbly against the masked granite, saying hopefully, "Do you suppose . . . is there anything to be made of me?"

Behind her, except for the unmade bed, the room had the fierce, wooden neatness of the solitary, beginning householder. She turned from the window and made up the bed swiftly so that the immobile room might greet her so, with all its rigid charm of permanence, at nightfall. Now there was nothing out of place except the letter from her mother, read and left crumpled on the table the night before.

None of the rooms in the house at Marcus Hook had ever really belonged to her mother, her sister Pauline or herself. The changing needs of the roomers came first—the workmen who had a wife coming or a wife leaving, the spinsters who made a religion of drafts and the devotional bath, the elderly male and female waifs who had to "retrench" farther and farther back into the cheapest recesses of the house, until the final retrenchment, to the home of a relative, could be delayed no longer.

The family, forever shifting, took what was left over. The best times would have been when the three of them slept in the big front sitting-room together, had not these also been the bad periods when the larger rooms went begging, and they and the most unimportant, delinquent roomer were almost on the same footing. But at all times, mornings the kitchen was never clear of "privilegers," evenings the parlor creaked and sighed with those for whom solitude was the worst of privileges. And late at night when, in no matter what bed or room one might be, there was still the padding in the corridors, the leakage of faucets, then the house rumored its livelihood most plainly of all, having no being other than in the sneaked murmurs, the soft crepitations of strangers.

She sipped the coffee, ate a roll, smoothing out her mother's letter. "Mrs. Tregarthen, she lived in New York once, says you are down in a terrible neighborhood and for the same money you could get into a business girls club. The Tregarthens still have the sitting-room thank God. I am so glad you are fixed in the Section Manager job, all that time you studied was not wasted after all. They say even the elevator girls have to be college now. You must be on your feet a lot too, be sure you have the proper shoes. Will you use the store discount and buy Pauline a white dress for graduation, size 14, something not fancy I can dye later. Let me know how much. I am so glad of the discount."

No use to explain again to her mother that she could only buy dark "employee" clothes for herself on the discount. She would send Pauline the dress and take care of the difference herself. All the four years of her scholarship her mother had worked to help her out, in mingled pride and worry over this queer chick who asked nothing better than to waste her real good looks over the books, after something, God knows what all, except that you could be sure it was something that couldn't be touched or twisted to use, and at best could only be taught. Her mother had been right. The year she was graduated Ph.D.'s were a dime a dozen, and the colleges had still less use for Miss Abel, A.B. She had learned that "getting out" meant, sooner or later, having to "get in" somewhere else. But her mother was pleased, now that she was fixed in her job. And glad of the discount.

Now that she was ready, she stared possessively at the safe shell of the room, all she had been able to salvage of her dream of solitary, inviolate pursuit. Each morning she had to resist the binding urge to stay, nestled in familiarity. She forced herself to put her hand on the knob of the outer door, meanwhile contrarily building up the temptation of the ideal day. Projecting herself into the reassuring feel of the chair, she saw herself settled there for hours, retreated into the subtle stream of a book, hugging emotions siphoned through another's words, immolating herself happily on the altar of a problem, an impasse, which might be dropped as one awakens from a dream, with the closing of the book. She wrenched the door open quickly and shut it behind her, giving it a shake to test the lock.

Once outside, she felt lighthearted, the decision for that day, at least, being over. Down here the neighborhood eased itself into living with the unconstraint of a slattern who has no plans. Across the street, in front of the Olive Tree Inn for Homeless Men, one of the flophouses run by the city, a few rumpled bums lounged like fallen dolls, staring vacantly with their frayed, inoffensive look. They were the safest people in the world to live among, she thought, for one could no more focus on their identities than they on the world around them; in their eyes there was never the shrewd look of the striving, but only the bleared gentleness of humiliation, and their dreams were not of women.

As she walked the long blocks westward to the BMT, the streets filled with people who had the crisp silhouette of destination, but as she neared them, going down the subway stairs, she could see the mouths still swollen with the unreserve of sleep, under the eyes the endearing childish puffs of the rudely awakened. Since she was travelling uptown against the morning rush, she got a seat almost at once and, settling into it, looked at the people opposite, who bobbed up and down with the blank withdrawal of the subwayite. Some mornings, translating them into their animal counterparts, she returned to the lidded stare immured in the bravely rouged, batrachian folds of some old harridan, traced the patient, naglike decline of a nose, watched the gibbon antics of the wizened messengers of the garment district as they pushed their eternally harrying, dwarfing packages. Once inside the store where she worked, exposed to them "on the floor," they all became the customer, the enemy, sauntering along freely in their enviably uncaged day, striking at her with the inimical, demanding shafts of their eyes, but here, until then, she could feel a wave of tenderness, of identifica-

98

tion with them, which possessed her with a pity that included herself.

Thinking of the varied jobs toward which the people in the car were travelling, she remembered the prying regard of Miss Shotwell, the head of the store's "interviewing," and heard again the chill beads of words which had dropped from the deceptive, ductile bloom of her face.

"We can get any number of college graduates these days. We're only interested in those with a real vocation for merchandising." The protuberant eyes scrutinized with a glance which seemed to come from the whole eyeball.

"I worked in a store for a year before I went to college. And all my summer jobs were in department stores." She had sat there quietly, trying to shine with vocation, but thinking of those sweating miserable summers which had helped make possible the long winter hibernations in the libraries, she had wished herself back among the books, feeling the nausea of the displaced.

"H'mmm." The sedulously fluffed hair bent over the folder on the desk between them. "Your extracurricular leadership record was really very good." The head cocked to one side as if deliberating an article of purchase, then bent to the folder again in a gesture either habitual or posed, for the folder was closed. "Philosophy major, fine arts minor. That's not so good. We'd rather have it business administration, let's say, or mathematics."

"Something—more concrete?"

"Exactly," said Miss Shotwell, bringing her head back to center, her face obviously readied for the fulsome courtesies of rejection.

Behind the chic camouflage of her own smart appearance, that slick armor which she had learned to assume with the wiliness of the job-hunter, she had felt shaken with hatred for these people who had the power to let you in, who could annihilate, with a dainty, deprecatory finger, spheres of value which were not their own.

"It does not seem to have impaired my 'leadership,' as you call it," she had said at last, anger forcing the gassy word on to her tongue.

The flickering interest had revived in the fish stare opposite. Miss Shotwell had smiled almost in approval. "Perhaps we can use you after all," she had said. "We like them to be aggressive."

99

Them. In the past year she had indeed become one of "them," learning the caitiff acquiescence, the shiny readiness which would cover the segregation of self, acquiring that whole vocabulary of pretense forced upon those who must make themselves commercially valuable, or die.

She looked around now at the others herded together with her in the car. Perhaps her mistake had been to think that she was alone in this; perhaps each of her neighbors was sitting stiffened in the same intent misery before the deadening span of the day to come, each crouched protectively over the misfit hunch or sore of some disparity which had not fitted in. She looked again, but the set faces looked back at hers stonily, as if not all the prying tentacles of her pity could slip behind the mask which each had assumed for his journey through the ambuscade of the practical. Bending her head over the interlocked hands in her lap, she loosened them, cupped them softly over the unwanted extrusion of her compassion. *Everybody*, she said to herself in tentative kinship, each of them, of *us*, locked up alone with the felony of his private difference.

The car rocked to her station and she pressed out with the others, up the stairs into a brief interlude of sunshine and into the swinging door of the employees' entrance, kept constantly ajar by the procession of batting hands. Inside the olive green locker room she found the number of her own compartment and set her hat and coat away, smelling with a dull sense of recognition the basement's odor of wax and disinfectant, interfused with the vague patchouli of congregated women. One after the other, as they took off the bright spring hats and coats which had differentiated them up to now, they sank into conformity, leveled by the common denominator of their dark dresses as if by the command of some sullen alchemist.

Nodding diffidently to the few she knew by sight, she joined them on the escalator to the main floor, her spirits sinking as she rose. Upstairs in the glove department where she had been assistant section manager for the past two months, the salesgirls lounged negligently behind the counters, waiting for the opening bell to ring and the first trickle of customers.

"Good morning," she said.

" 'Morning, Miss Abel." They were polite but reserved, with the resentment of old stagers who see a neophyte brought in to supervise.

"Miss Baxter in yet?" She asked only to make conversation, but was warned by their suddenly innocent gazes. Baxter must have come in drunk again.

"She's behind—in the cubbyhole," said one of the girls, and bent over, stifling a snicker.

Behind the counter there was a door which led into the cavity under the escalator, a space big enough for two people if one sat in the single chair and the other stood with head bent under the declivity of the ceiling. The girls seldom used it, ducking in for an aspirin, or when a garter had broken and there was not time to go off the floor. Once or twice, when the hysteria of milling people around her had overwhelmed her with a feeling of nakedness, of exposure to too much and too many, she had crept in there herself for a moment of poise. She opened the door and went in, closing it behind her.

Miss Baxter sat erect in the single chair, her angular shoulders squared tensely in one of the severely cut suits she wore daily. Miss Abel had never known her to wear a dress. Her cropped black hair was sleek from the brush, and her starched white shirt lay flat and crisp under one of the ties she affected, the cuffs projecting slightly from the jacket sleeves to show the only touch of vanity she allowed herself, onyx intaglio cuff links which clipped together like a man's. With her firm, pallid profile and small, almost lipless mouth, she had the anomalous attractiveness of a well-groomed boy who is knowing and bitter beyond his years. Reputed to be the best section manager on the floor, she had been recruited temporarily from the enormous book department to cover the glove section during the spring rush. Once or twice Miss Abel, longing for congeniality, had tried to get her to talk about books, of which she was supposed to have considerable knowledge, but had been not so much rebuffed as forestalled by the controlled distance of manner, the look of careful mistrust in the deepset eyes.

Miss Baxter grasped her own chin in one hand and gravely swung her head to one side, then back. "I daren't move it by itself," she said in her husky whiskey voice. Staring straight ahead, she uncurled the other hand in her lap to show a package of Life Savers. "Have one?" she said without moving further, and laughed.

"Can I get you anything?" Miss Abel put out a hand, but somehow she did not dare touch her.

In answer Miss Baxter, still erect, closed her eyes. "What a night!" she said. "Lois' job is folding, so we went on the town." The words came oddly from the closed face, with a kind of bravado perhaps made possible by it. "Know Lois Gow, up in the doctor's office?"

"Oh. Yes, of course." She remembered the girl mainly because of the pliant, hesitant manner which did not go with the nurse's uniform, and the suffused pink of her face, which always looked as if she were about to sneeze or break into tears.

"Think I can go on the floor, Abel?" Miss Baxter had opened her eyes, and was looking straight at her with her thin, slight smile. Except for the closed eyes, she had seemed up to now almost as she had on those other mornings when, rigidly controlled, exuding a powerful perfume of cinnamon, she had managed quite competently, handling both staff and customers with a dispatch which was, if anything, chillier than normal. But now, looking into the opened eyes, Miss Abel saw that the liquor had not glazed them but rather had melted from them some last cornea of reserve, so that, nude and pained, they focused beyond her, askance at some unalterable incubus.

"Look," said Miss Abel, "you've signed in, haven't you? Why don't you go to the rest room? I can cover up for you here."

Miss Baxter shook herself slightly. With that shake, policy shuttered her face and she was again the equilibrist, the authority.

"Quite a gal, aren't you?" she said. "Able Abel." She laughed. Then she put her head in her hands.

Miss Abel went out and closed the door behind her. Hurrying to the high desk behind which she would stand all day, she began needlessly to set its sparse equipment in order. She couldn't have gone on the floor, she said to herself. Not with those eyes.

The rest of the morning she worked steadily to reduce the constantly forming queue of women in front of her. Just before noon, a cool voice said, "I'll take over now. Thanks." Miss Baxter stood beside her, resurrected and remote.

Miss Abel got her purse from the desk, signed out and left the floor. Outside the locker-room windows the day had turned greenish and it had begun to drizzle. She had no heart for battling one of the crowded restaurants outside and turned into the employees' cafeteria, where she ate her way through the flaccid "special plate," flavored for the general and made more tepid by the humid smell from the steam tables. Gratefully she remembered that it was Saturday and, half-reluctantly, she visualized her usual date with Max.

As on many other Saturday nights, she would prepare dinner for him, and they would sit over it in a coy, uncomfortable imitation of the domesticity they could not afford to make actual. If, during the past week, he had been called for part-time work in one of the biological-testing laboratories which allowed him, as a former fellow in chemistry, to make tests of blood and sputum, they would go to one of the movies on Fourteenth Street. Otherwise, while he talked ardently of his ambitions, his hopes, warming his self-confidence with her attention, she would watch the light on the humbled nape of his neck, the abnormal cleanliness of his hands, seeing in them something already intimidated, subdued. Either way, she thought, it would end in the half-fearful, fending love-making of the uninitiate, in that tentative groping, not toward affirmation but only toward escape, in which each caressed and comforted the affrighted, sad replica of himself.

She rose with a counterfeit briskness and went back upstairs. Signing in again, "Abel—12:45," she slipped into her station beside Miss Baxter.

At five o'clock when the two of them, working steadily together, had disposed of the last of the queue, the crowd in the store had thinned. It was raining hard outside now, and most of the customers, wandering along desultory and vacant-faced, were of the brand the clerks called "just looking." Miss Abel and Miss Baxter stood together behind the high pulpit of the desk, careful not to mar with more than fragmentary conversation their air of alert, executive readiness.

Along the aisle a small, nondescript woman teetered aimlessly toward them. She was no different from the scores of women who today—and tomorrow—would filter colorlessly through the store from the cardboard suburbs or the moderately respectable crannies of the city. A coat of some nameless but adequate fur flapped back from a dress which was indistinctly neither fussy nor smart. On her precise, mat hair a small flyaway hat with a veil halfway between coquetry and conservatism perched sharply to one side—denotation that its wearer might have lost touch with her sense of the ridiculous but not with her instinct for what was correct for her station in life. Beloved of some man, she would amble through the stores, coming home with a darling blouse or another pair of stubby, frilled shoes, or perhaps only with a sense of virtue at having viewed and resisted all the temptations of the *bon marché* except the paper bag of caramels from which she was now munching.

She stopped in front of them, just to one side, and stared frankly, curiously at Miss Baxter. Then, with her face screwed up in kittenish perplexity, she backed up, sidestepped, craned over to get a glimpse of Miss Baxter's legs.

"Is there something I can do for you?" There was an edge of insolence in Miss Baxter's tone which made Miss Abel catch her breath with apprehension. Sidling a glance from under the dropped lids of embarrassment, she saw what she had never before seen in Miss Baxter's face—the creeping red of color.

"Well, uh, no." The woman tittered ingratiatingly. "I mean—I just couldn't tell whether—I mean I just wanted to see . . . whether you had *trousers* on," she finished, the words coming out on a cozy gust of confidence. She smiled, and tittered again.

"Want to step around and take a really good look?" Miss Baxter's face was white again.

"Why, you—why, this is *outrageous!*" Rage did not dignify the woman's inadequate features. "Why, I could *report* you!"

"Get out." Miss Baxter's immobility was more offensive than her words.

"I'll report you for this!" Looking around for adherents, the woman met the bright, hushed stare of the clerks. Drawing her coat around her, she stalked off, her face working and mottled, the paper bag crackling convulsively in her hand.

She will, too, thought Miss Abel. She kept her glance carefully apart from Miss Baxter. The clerks, heads bent ostentatiously over their books, returned to their tallying of the day's receipts.

With a thin, releasing sound, the five-thirty bell rang through the store. If I tell Baxter to get out quickly, she won't, thought Miss Abel. She said nothing. After a face-saving moment, Miss Baxter opened the desk drawer slowly and took out her purse.

"My turn to close up," said Miss Abel. "Good night."

" 'Night," said Miss Baxter. She hesitated for a moment as if there were something she wanted to say, then gave a half-smile, as if the concession shamed her, and left.

Methodically Miss Abel set the desk to rights for Monday morning. Baxter had left without signing out. As she signed the chart for both of them with a grim feeling of conspiracy, she saw Mr. Eardley, the floor superintendent, a sandy-haired, middle-aged man with tiredly pleasant manners, being pulled toward her down the aisle by the gesticulating woman. They stopped in front of her.

"She isn't here," said the woman. "This girl will tell you, though. The idea!"

"Yes, Madam." Mr. Eardley looked at Miss Abel, his brows raised over his glasses in weary inquiry.

Miss Abel looked at the woman. She was still babbling angrily to Mr. Eardley and her silly hat, held on by elastic, was cocked awry on her head, far beyond the angle of fashion. Even the exertions of her annoyance had not been able to endow her with individuality, but under stress the details of her person, so dependent on the commonplace, appeared disorderly, even daft.

Miss Abel looked past her at Mr. Eardley. Imperceptibly she shook her head and, raising her hand to her temple, she moved her index finger discreetly in the small circle, the immemorial gesture of derision.

As if he had caught a ball deftly thrown, Mr. Eardley nodded imperceptibly back. Turning quickly toward the woman, he burbled the smooth reassurances of his trade. He took note of her name and address in a voice which was soothing and deferential, and on a wave of practiced apologies he urged the woman inexorably toward the door.

Miss Abel walked down to the basement once more on one of the escalators which had stopped for the day, got her hat and coat and a spare umbrella from her locker and left the store. Under the jaundiced cast of the rain the faces of the people on the street looked froglike and repellent. In the subway she sat numbly in a catalepsy of fatigue, her feet squirming in her soggy, drenched shoes. She walked the long blocks from the station at a blind pace, the umbrella slanted viciously in front of her, her mind fixed on the chair at home.

At last she was there, and the dead, still air of the apartment welcomed her, inspiring a relief close to tears. Dropping off her damp clothes and soaked shoes, she put on a wrapper and mules and set a pot of water to boil. Usually when she came home she had cup after cup of dark coffee, but now the thought of its flavor, hearty and congenial, sickened her. Tea, meliorative and astringent, recalled those childhood convalescences when it had been the first sign of recovery, and half-medicine, half-food, it had settled the stomach and warmed the hands. She set a pot of tea to steep, brought the tray around in front of the chair and sat down. After a moment she kicked off the slippers with a dual thud which was like a signal to thought.

Looking back on the day, she curled her lip at the mawkish sentiments of that morning in the train, at the nascent fellowship which had seemed so plausible. The day seemed now like a labyrinth through which she had followed an infallible, an educative thread— to a monster's door.

Everybody, she thought, shivering. The woman in the store was "everybody." Multipled endlessly, she and her counterparts, varied slightly by the secondary markings of sex, education, money, flowed in and out of the stores, in and out of all the proper stations in life, not touched by the miseries of difference but indomitably chewing the caramel cud of their own self-satisfaction. Escape into the long dream of books, behind the ramparts of your special talent or into some warm coterie of your own ilk, and they could still find you out with a judgment in proportion to the degree of your difference. The Misses Baxter they would pillory at once, with the nerveless teamwork of the dull; the Misses Abel might escape their gray encroaching smutch of averageness for a while, behind some *maquillage* of compromise, only to find one day perhaps that the *maquillage* had become the spirit—that they had conquered after all.

They were even there, latent, in the rumpled letter, simple with love, still lying on her table. In the end they could push everything before them with the nod of their terrible consanguinity.

She moved deeper in the chair. Soon the boy, Max, would come, and in the desperate wrenches, the muffled clingings of love-making they would try again to build up some dark mutual core of inalienable wholeness. For there was no closeness, she thought, no camaraderie so intense, so tempting as that of the rejected for the rejected.

But in the end those others would still be there to be faced; in the end they were to be faced alone. Meanwhile she sat on, shivering a little, over the steaming tea, and making a circle of her body around the hardening nugget of herself, she clasped her chill, blanched feet in her slowly warming hands.

A Christmas Carillon

◄§ A B O U T   F O U R weeks before Christmas, Grorley, in combined shame and panic, began to angle for an invitation to somewhere, anywhere, for Christmas Day. By this time, after six months of living alone in the little Waverly Place flat to which he had gone as soon as he and his wife had decided to separate, he had become all too well reacquainted with his own peculiar mechanism in regard to solitude. It was a mechanism that had its roots in the jumbled lack of privacy of an adolescence spent in the dark, four-room apartment to which his parents had removed themselves and three children after his father's bankruptcy in '29. Prior to that, Grorley's childhood had been what was now commonly referred to as Edwardian—in a house where servants and food smells kept their distance until needed, and there were no neurotic social concerns about the abundance of either—a house where there was always plush under the buttocks, a multiplicity of tureens and napery at table, lace on the pillow, and above all that general expectancy of creature comfort and spiritual order which novelists now relegated to the days before 1914.

That it had lasted considerably later, Grorley knew, since this had been the year of his own birth, but although he had been fifteen when they had moved, it was the substantial years before that had faded to fantasy. Even now, when he read or said the word "reality," his mind reverted to Sunday middays in the apartment house living room, where the smudgy daylight was always diluted by lamps, the cheaply stippled walls menaced the oversized furniture, and he, his father and brother and sister, each a claustrophobe island of irritation, were a constant menace to one another. Only his mother, struggling alone in the kitchen with the conventions of roast chicken and gravy, had perhaps achieved something of the solitude they all had craved. To Grorley even now, the smell of roasting fowl was the smell of a special kind of Sunday death.

Only once before now had he lived alone, and then too it had been in the Village, not far from where he presently was. After his graduation from City College he had worked a year, to save up for a master's in journalism, and then, salving his conscience with the thought that he had at least paid board at home for that period, he had left his family forever. The following year, dividing his time between small-time newspaper job and classes, living in his $27 per month place off Morton Street, he had savored all the wonders of the single doorkey opening on the quiet room, of the mulled book and the purring clock, of the smug decision not to answer the phone or to let even the most delightful invader in. Now that he looked back on it, of course, he recalled that the room had rung pretty steadily with the voices of many such who had been admitted, but half the pleasure had been because it had been at his own behest. That had been a happy time, when he had been a gourmet of loneliness, prowling bachelor-style on the edge of society, dipping inward when he chose. Of all the habitations he had had since, that had been the one whose conformations he remembered best, down to the last, worn dimple of brick. When he had house-hunted, last June, he had returned instinctively to the neighborhood of that time. Only a practicality born of superstition had kept him from hunting up the very street, the very house.

He had had over two years of that earlier freedom, although the last third of it had been rather obscured by his courtship of Eunice. Among the girl students of the Village there had been quite a few who, although they dressed like ballerinas and prattled of art like painters' mistresses, drew both their incomes and their morality from good, solid middle-class families back home. Eunice had been the prettiest and most sought after of these, and part of her attraction for some, and certainly for Grorley, had been that she seemed to be, quite honestly, one of those rare girls who were not particularly eager to marry and settle down. Grorley had been so entranced at finding like feelings in a girl—and in such a beautiful one—that he had quite forgotten that in coaxing her out of her "freedom" he was persuading himself out of his own.

He hadn't realized this with any force until the children came, two within the first four years of the marriage. Before that, in the first fusion of love, it had seemed to Grorley that two could indeed live more delightfully alone than one, and added to this had been that wonderful release from jealousy which requited love brings— half the great comfort of the loved one's presence being that, *ipso facto*, she is with no one else. During this period of happy, though enlarged privacy, Grorley confided to Eunice some, though not all, of his feelings about family life and solitude. He was, he told her, the kind of person who needed to be alone a great deal—although this of course excepted her. But they must never spend their Sundays and holidays frowsting in the house like the rest of the world, sitting there stuffed and droning, with murder in their hearts. They must always have plans laid well in advance, plans which would keep the two of them emotionally limber, so to speak, and *en plein air*. Since these plans were always pleasant—tickets to the Philharmonic, with after-theater suppers, hikes along the Palisades, fishing expeditions to little-known ponds back of the Westchester parkways, whose intricacies Grorley, out of a history of Sunday afternoons, knew as well as certain guides knew Boca Raton— Eunice was quite willing to accede. In time she grew very tactful, almost smug, over Grorley's little idiosyncrasy, and he sometimes heard her on the phone, fending people off. "Not Sunday. Gordon and I have a thing about holidays, you know." By this time, too, they had both decided that, although Grorley would keep his now very respectable desk job at the paper, his real destiny was to "write"; and to Eunice, who respected "imagination" as only the unimaginative can, Grorley's foible was the very proper defect of a noble intelligence.

But with the coming of the children, it was brought home to Grorley that he was face to face with one of those major rearrangements of existence for which mere tact would not suffice. Eunice, during her first pregnancy, was as natural and unassuming about it as a man could wish; she went on their Sunday sorties to the very last, and maintained their gallant privacy right up to the door of the delivery room. But the child of so natural a mother was bound to be natural too. It contracted odd fevers whenever it wished and frequently on Sundays, became passionately endeared to their most expensive sitter or would have none at all, and in general permeated their lives as only the most powerfully frail of responsibilities can. And when the second one arrived, it did so, it seemed to Grorley, only to egg the other one on.

There came a morning, the Christmas morning of the fourth year, when Grorley, sitting in the odor of baked meat, first admitted that his hydra-headed privacy was no longer a privacy at all. He had created, he saw, his own monster; sex and the devil had had their sport with him, and he was, in a sense that no mere woman would understand, all too heavily "in the family way." Looking at Eunice, still neat, still very pretty, but with her lovely mouth pursed with maternity, her gaze sharp enough for *Kinder* and *Küche*, but abstract apparently for him, he saw that she had gone over to the enemy and was no longer his. Eunice had become "the family" too.

It was as a direct consequence of this that Grorley wrote the book which was his making. Right after that fatal morning, he had engaged a room in a cheap downtown hotel (he and Eunice were living out in Astoria at the time), with the intention, as he explained to Eunice, of writing there after he left the paper, and coming home weekends. He had also warned her that, because of the abrasive effects of family life, it would probably be quite some time before "the springs of reverie"—a phrase he had lifted from Ellen Glasgow—would start churning. His real intention was, of course, to prowl, and for some weeks thereafter he joined the company of those men who could be found, night after night, in places where they could enjoy the freedom of not having gone home where they belonged.

To his surprise, he found, all too quickly, that though his intentions were of the worst, he had somehow lost the moral force to pursue them. He had never been much for continuous strong drink, and that crude *savoir-faire* which was needed for the preliminaries to lechery seemed to have grown creaky with the years. He took to spending odd hours in the newspaper morgue, correlating, in a half-hearted way, certain current affairs that interested him. After some months, he suddenly realized that he had enough material for a book. It found a publisher almost immediately. Since he was much more a child of his period than he knew, he had hit upon exactly that note between disaffection and hope which met response in the breasts of those who regarded themselves as permanent political independents. His book was an instant success with those who thought of themselves as thinking for themselves (if they had only had time for it). Quick to capitalize upon this, Grorley's paper gave him a biweekly column, and he developed a considerable talent for telling men of good will, over Wednesday breakfast, the very thing they had been saying to one another at Tuesday night dinner.

Grorley spent the war years doing this, always careful to keep his column, like his readers, one step behind events. With certain minor changes, he kept, too, that scheme of life which had started him writing, changing only, with affluence, to a more comfortable hotel. In time also, that *savoir-faire* whose loss he had mourned returned to him, and his success at his profession erased any guilts he might otherwise have had—a wider experience, he told himself, being not only necessary to a man of his trade, but almost unavoidable in the practice of it. He often congratulated himself at having achieved, in a country which had almost completely domesticated the male, the perfect pattern for a man of temperament, and at times he became almost insufferable to some of his married men friends, when he dilated on the contrast between his "continental" way of life and their own. For by then, Grorley had reversed himself—it was his weekends and holidays that were now spent cozily *en famille*. It was pleasant, coming back to the house in Tarrytown on Friday evenings, coming back from the crusades to find Eunice and the whole household decked out, literally and psychologically, for his return. One grew sentimentally fond of children whom one saw only under such conditions—Grorley's Saturdays were now spent, as he himself boasted, "on all fours," in the rejuvenating air of the skating rinks, the museums, the woods, and the zoos. Sundays and holidays he and Eunice often entertained their relatives, and if, as the turkey browned, he had a momentary twinge of his old *mal de famille*, he had but to remember that his hat was, after all, only hung in the hall.

It was only some years after the war that Eunice began to give trouble. Before that, their double ménage had not been particularly unusual—almost all the households of couples their age had been upset in one way or another, and theirs had been more stable than many. During the war years Eunice had had plenty of company for her midweek evenings; all over America women had been managing bravely behind the scenes. But now that families had long since paired off again, Eunice showed a disquieting tendency to want to be out in front.

"No, you'll have to come home for good," she said to Grorley, at the end of their now frequent battles. "I'm tired of being a short-order wife."

"The trouble with you," said Grorley, "is that you've never adjusted to postwar conditions."

"That was your nineteen-forty-six column," said Eunice. "If you must quote yourself, pick one a little more up-to-date." Removing a jewel-encrusted slipper-toe from the fender, she made a feverish circle of the room, the velvet panniers of her housegown swinging dramatically behind her. She was one of those women who used their charge accounts for retaliation. With each crisis in their deteriorating relationship, Grorley noted gloomily, Eunice's wardrobe had improved.

"Now that the children are getting on," he said, "you ought to have another interest. A hobby."

Eunice made a hissing sound. "Nineteen-forty-seven!" she said.

In the weeks after, she made her position clear. Men, she told him, might have provided the interest he suggested, but when a woman had made a vocation of one, it wasn't easy to start making a hobby of several. It was hardly much use swishing out in clouds of Tabu at seven, if one had to be back to feel Georgie's forehead at eleven. Besides, at their age, the only odd men out were likely to be hypochondriacs, or bachelors still dreaming of mother, or very odd men indeed.

"All the others," she said nastily, "are already on somebody else's hearth rug. Or out making the rounds with you." Worst of all, she seemed to have lost her former reverence for Grorley's work. If he'd been a novelist or a poet, she said (she even made use of the sticky word "creative"), there'd have been more excuse for his need to go off into the silence. As it was, she saw no reason for his having to be so broody over analyzing the day's proceedings at the U.N. If he wanted an office, that should take care of things very adequately. But if he did not wish to live *with* her, then he could not go on *living* with her. "Mentally," she said, "you're still in the Village. Maybe you better go back there."

Things were at this pass when Grorley's paper sent him to London, on an assignment that kept him there for several months. He was put up for membership in one or two exclusively masculine clubs, and in their leonine atmosphere his outraged vanity—("creative" indeed!)—swelled anew. Finally, regrettably near the end of his stay, he met up with a redheaded young woman named Vida, who worked for a junior magazine by day, wrote poetry by night, and had once been in America for three weeks. She and Grorley held hands over the mutual hazards of the "creative" life, and on her lips the word was like a caress. For a woman, too, she was remarkably perceptive about the possessiveness of other women. "Yes, quite," she had said. "Yes, quite."

When she and Grorley made their final adieu in her Chelsea flat, she held him, for just a minute, at arm's length. "I shall be thinking of you over there, in one of those ghastly, what do you call them, *living rooms*, of yours. Everybody matted together, and the floor all over children —like beetles. Poor dear. I should think those living rooms must be the curse of the American family. Poor, poor dear."

On his return home in June, Grorley and Eunice agreed on a six-months trial separation prior to a divorce. Eunice showed a rather unfeeling calm in the lawyer's office, immediately afterward popped the children in camp, and went off to the Gaspé with friends. Grorley took a sublet on the apartment in Waverly Place. It was furnished in a monastic modern admirably suited to the novel he intended to write, that he had promised Vida to write.

He had always liked summers in town, when the real *aficionados* of the city took over, and now this summer seemed to him intoxicating, flowing with the peppery currents of his youth. In the daytime his freedom slouched unshaven; in the evenings the streets echoed and banged with life, and the moon made a hot harlequinade of every alley. He revisited the San Remo, Julius's, Chumley's, Jack Delaney's, and all the little Italian bars with backyard restaurants, his full heart and wallet carrying him quickly into the camaraderie of each. Occasionally he invited home some of the remarkables he met on his rounds—a young Italian bookie, a huge St. Bernard of a woman who drove a taxi and had once lived on a barge on the

East River, an attenuated young couple from Chapel Hill, who were honeymooning at the New School. Now and then a few of his men friends from uptown joined him in a night out. A few of these, in turn, invited him home for the weekend, but although he kept sensibly silent on the subject of their fraternal jaunts, he detected some animus in the hospitality of their wives.

By October, Grorley was having a certain difficulty with his weekends. His list of bids to the country was momentarily exhausted, and his own ideas had begun to flag. The children, home from camp, had aged suddenly into the gang phase; they tore out to movies and jamborees of their own, were weanable from these only by what Grorley could scrape up in the way of rodeos and football games, and assumed, once the afternoon's treat was over, a faraway look of sufferance. Once or twice, when he took them home, he caught himself hoping that Eunice would ask him in for a drink, a chat that might conceivably lead to dinner, but she was always out, and Mrs. Lederer, the housekeeper, always pulled the children in as if they were packages whose delivery had been delayed, gave him a nasty nod, and shut the door.

For a few weekends he held himself to his desk, trying to work up a sense of dedication over the novel, but there was no doubt that it was going badly. Its best juice had been unwisely expended in long, analytic letters to Vida, and now, in her airmail replies, which bounced steadily and enthusiastically over the Atlantic, it began to seem more her novel than his. The Sunday before Thanksgiving, he made himself embark on a ski-train to Pittsfield, working up a comforting sense of urgency over the early rising and the impedimenta to be checked. The crowd on the train was divided between a band of Swiss and German perfectionists who had no conversation, and a horde of young couples, rolling on the slopes like puppies, who had too much. Between them, Grorley's privacy was respected to the point of insult. When he returned that night, he tossed his gear into a corner, where it wilted damply on his landlord's blond rug, made himself a hot toddy—with a spasm of self-pity over his ability to do for himself—and sat down to face his fright. For years, his regular intervals at home had been like the chewed coffee bean that renewed the wine-taster's palate. He had lost the background from which to rebel.

Thanksgiving Day was the worst. The day dawned oyster-pale

and stayed that way. Grorley slept as late as he could, then went out for a walk. The streets were slack, without the twitch of crowds, and the houses had a tight look of inner concentration. He turned toward the streets which held only shops, and walked uptown as far as Rockefeller Center. The rink was open, with its usual cast of characters—ricocheting children, a satiny, professional twirler from the Ice Show, and several solemn old men who skated upright in some Euclidian absorption of their own. Except for a few couples strolling along in the twin featurelessness of love, the crowd around the rink was type-cast too. Here, it told itself, it participated in life; here in this flying spectacle of flag and stone it could not possibly be alone. With set, shy smiles, it glanced sideways at its neighbors, rounded its shoulders to the wind, turned up its collar, and leaned closer to the musical bonfire of the square. Grorley straightened up, turned on his heel, smoothed down his collar, and walked rapidly toward Sixth Avenue. He filled himself full of ham and eggs in one of the quick-order places that had no season, taxied home, downed a drink, swallowed two Seconal tablets, and went to bed.

The next morning, seated at his desk, he took a relieved look at the street. People were hard at their normal grind again; for a while the vacuum was past. But Christmas was not going to catch him alone. He picked up the phone. At the end of the day he was quite heartened. Although he had not yet turned up an invitation for Christmas Day, he had netted himself a cocktail party (which might easily go on to dinner) for two days before, a bid to an eggnog party on New Year's Day, and one weekend toward the middle of December. A lot of people did things impromptu. A phone call now and then would fix him up somehow.

But by Christmas week he was haggard. He had visualized himself as bidden to share, in a pleasantly avuncular capacity, some close friend's family gathering; he had seen himself as indolently and safely centered, but not anchored, in the bright poinsettia of their day. Apparently their vision of him was cast in a harsher mold; they returned his innuendoes with little more than a pointed sympathy. Only two propositions had turned up, one from a group of men, alone like himself for one reason or another, who were forming a party at an inn in the Poconos, and one from a waif-like spinster—"Last Christmas was my last one with dear Mother"—who

A *Christmas Carillon*

offered to cook dinner for him in her apartment. Shuddering, he turned down both of these. The last thing he wanted to do on that day was to ally himself with *waifs* of any description; on that day he very definitely wanted to be safely inside some cozy family cocoon, looking out at *them*.

Finally, the day before Christmas, he thought of the Meechers. Ted was that blue-ribbon bore, the successful account-executive who believed his own slogans, and his wife, a former social worker, matched him in her own field. Out of Ted's sense of what was due his position in the agency and Sybil's sense of duty to the world, they had created a model home in Chappaqua, equipped with four children, two Bedlingtons, a games room, and a part-time pony. Despite this, they were often hard up for company, since most people could seldom be compelled twice to their table, where a guest was the focus of a constant stream of self-congratulation from either end. Moreover, Ted had wormed his way into more than one stag party at Grorley's, and could hardly refuse a touch. And their Christmas, whatever its other drawbacks, would be a four-color job, on the best stock.

But Ted's voice, plum-smooth when he took the phone from his secretary, turned reedy and doubtful when he heard Grorley's inquiry. "Uh-oh! 'Fraid that puts me on the spot, fella. Yeah. Kind of got it in the neck from Sybil, last time I came home from your place. Yeah. Had a real old-fashioned hassle. Guess I better not risk reminding her just yet. But, say! How about coming up here right now, for the office party?"

Grorley declined, and hung up. Off-campus boy this time of year, that's what I am, he thought. He looked at his mantelpiece crowded with its reminders—greetings from Grace and Bill, Jane and Tom, Peg and Jack, Etcetera and Mrs. Etcetera. On top of the pile was another airmail from Vida, received that morning, picture enclosed. Sans the red in the hair, without the thrush tones of the assenting voice, she looked a little long in the teeth. Her hands and feet, he remembered, were always cold. Somehow or other, looking at the picture, he didn't think that central heating would improve them. "The living room is the curse," she'd said. That's it, he thought; that's it. And this, Vida, is the season of the living room.

He looked down into the street. The Village was all right for the summer, he thought. But now the periphery of the season had changed. In summer, the year spins on a youth-charged axis, and a man's muscles have a spurious oil. But this is the end toward which it spins. Only three hundred days to Christmas. Only a month —a week. And then, every year, the damned day itself, catching him with its holly claws, sounding its platitudes like carillons.

Down at the corner, carols bugled steamily from a mission soup-kitchen. There's no escape from it, he thought. Turn on the radio, and its alleluia licks you with tremolo tongue. In every store window flameth housegown, nuzzleth slipper. In all the streets the heavenly shops proclaim. The season has shifted inward, Grorley, and you're on the outside, looking in.

He moved toward the phone, grabbed it, and dialed the number before he remembered that you had to dial the code for Tarrytown. He replaced the receiver. Whatever he had to say, and he wasn't quite sure what, or how, it wasn't for the ears of the kids or the Lederer woman. He jammed on his hat. Better get there first, get inside the door.

Going up to Grand Central in the cab, he pressed his face against the glass. Everything had been taken care of weeks ago—the kids had been sent their two-wheelers, and he had mailed Eunice an extra-large check—one he hadn't sent through the lawyer. But at five o'clock, Fifth Avenue still shone like an enormous blue sugar-plum revolving in a tutti-frutti rain of light. Here was the season in all its questionable glory—the hallmarked joy of giving, the good will *diamanté*. But in the cosmetic air, people raised tinted faces, walked with levitated step.

In the train, he avoided the smoker, and chose an uncrowded car up front. At his station, he waited until all the gleaming car muzzles pointed at the train had picked up their loads and gone, then walked through the main street which led to his part of town. All was lit up here too, with a more intimate, household shine. He passed the pink damp of a butcher's, the bright fuzz of Woolworth's. "Sold out!" said a woman, emerging. " 's try the A & P." He walked on, invisible, his face pressed to the shop window of the world.

At Schlumbohn's Credit Jewelry Corner he paused, feeling for the wallet filled with cash yesterday for the still not impossible yes over the phone. This was the sort of store that he and Eunice, people like them, never thought of entering. It sold watches pinned to cards, zircons, musical powder-boxes, bracelets clasped with fat ten-carat hearts, Rajah pearl necklaces and Truelove blue-white diamonds. Something for Everybody, it said. He opened the door.

Inside, a magnetic salesgirl nipped him toward her like a pin. He had barely stuttered his wants before he acquired an Add-a-Pearl necklace for Sally, two Genuine Pinseal handbags for his mother-in-law and Mrs. Lederer, and a Stag-horn knife with three blades, a nailfile, and a corkscrew, for young George. He had left Eunice until last, but with each purchase, a shabby, telephoning day had dropped from him. Dizzy with participation, he surveyed the mottoed store.

"Something . . . something for the wife," he said.

"Our lovely Lifetime Watch, perhaps? Or Something in Silver, for the House?" The clerk tapped her teeth, gauging him.

He leaned closer, understanding suddenly why housewives, encysted in lonely houses, burbled confidences to the grocer, made an audience of the milkman. "We've had a—Little Tiff."

"Aw-w," said the clerk, adjusting her face. "Now . . . let me see. . . ." She kindled suddenly, raised a sibylline finger, beckoned him further down the counter, and drew out a tray of gold charms. Rummaging among them with a long, opalescent nail, she passed over minute cocktail shakers, bird cages, tennis rackets, a tiny scroll bearing the words, "If you can see this, you're too darn close," and seized a trinket she held up for view. A large gold shamrock, hung on a chain by a swivel through its middle, it bore the letter I. on its upper leaf, on its nether one the letter U. She reversed it. L.O.V.E. was engraved across the diameter of the other side. The clerk spun it with her accomplished nail. "See?" she said. "Spin it! Spin it and it says I. L.O.V.E. U!"

"Hmmm . . ." said Grorley, clearing his throat. "Well . . . guess you can't fob some women off with just a diamond bracelet." She tittered dutifully. But, as she handed it to him with his other packages, and closed the glass door behind him, he saw her shrug something, laughing, to another clerk. She had seen that he was not Schlumbohn's usual, after all.

As he walked up his own street he felt that he was after all hardly anybody's usual, tonight. It was a pretty street, of no particular architectural striving. Not a competitive street, except sometimes in summer, on the subject of gardens. And, of course, now. In every house the tree was up and lit, in the window nearest the passer-by. Here was his own, with the same blue lights that had lasted, with some tinkering on his part, year after year. Eunice must have had a man in to fix them.

He stopped on the path. A man in. She was pretty, scorned, and— he had cavalierly assumed—miserable. He had taken for granted that his family, in his absence, would have remained reasonably static. They always had. He'd been thinking of himself. Silently, he peeled off another layer of self-knowledge. He still was.

He walked up the steps wondering what kind of man might rise to be introduced, perhaps from his own armchair. One of her faded, footballish resurrections from Ohio State U., perhaps: Gordon, this is Jim Jerk, from home. Or would she hand it to him at once? Would it be: *Dear*, this is Gordon.

The door was unlocked. He closed it softly behind him, and stood listening. This was the unmistakable quiet of an empty house—as if the secret respiration of all objects in it had just stopped at his entrance. The only light downstairs was the glowing tree. He went up the stairs.

In the bedroom, the curtains were drawn, the night light on. The bed was piled with an abandoned muddle of silver wrappings, tissue paper, ribbons. He dropped the presents on the bed, tossed his hat after them, let his coat slip down on the familiar chair, and parted the curtains. It had a good view of the river, his house. He stood there, savoring it.

He was still there when a car door slammed and the family came up the path. The Christmas Eve pantomime, of course, held every year at the village hall. Georgie had on one of those white burnooses they always draped the boys in, and Sally, in long dress and coned hat, seemed to be a medieval lady. He saw that this year she had the waist for it. Eunice and Mrs. Lederer walked behind them. He tapped on the glass.

They raised their faces in tableau. The children waved, catcalled, and disappeared through the downstairs door. Mrs. Lederer followed them. Below, Eunice stared upward, in the shine from the tree-window. Behind him, he heard that sound made only by children—the noise of bodies falling up a staircase. As they swarmed in on him, she disappeared.

"You shoulda been to the hall," said Georgie, seizing him. "Christmas at King Arthur's court. I was a knight."

"Was it corny!" said Sally, from a distance. She caught sight of herself in a pier glass. "I was Guinevere."

"Had to do some last-minute shopping," said Grorley.

"I saw my bike!" said Georgie. "It's in the cellar."

"Oh . . . Georgie!" said Sally.

"Well, I couldn't help seeing it."

"Over there are some Christmas Eve presents," said Grorley.

"Open now?" they said. He nodded. They fell upon them.

"Gee," said Georgie, looking down at the knife. "Is that neat!" From his tone it was clear that he, at least, was Schlumbohn's usual.

"Oh, Dad!" Sally had the necklace around her neck. She raised her arms artistically above her head, in the fifth position, minced forward, and placed their slender wreath around Grorley's neck. As she hung on him, sacklike, he felt that she saw them both, a tender picture, in some lurking pier glass of her mind.

The door opened, and Eunice came in. She shut it behind her with a "not before the servants" air, and stood looking at him. Her face was blurred at the edges; she hadn't decked herself out for anybody. She looked the way a tired, pretty woman, of a certain age and responsibilities, might look at the hour before dinner, at the moment when age and prettiness tussle for her face, and age momentarily has won.

"Look what I got!" Georgie brandished the knife.

"And mine!" Sally undulated herself. "Mums! Doesn't it just *go*!" She stopped, looking from father to mother, her face hesitant, but shrewd.

"Open yours, Mums. Go on."

"Later," said Eunice. "Right now I think Mrs. Lederer wants you both to help with the chestnuts."

"No fair, no fair," said Georgie. "You saw ours."

"Do what your mother says," said Grorley. The paternal phrase, how it steadied him, was almost a hearthstone under his feet.

"Oh, well," said Eunice, wilting toward the children, as she invariably did when he was stern with them. Opening the package he indicated, she drew out the bauble. Georgie rushed to look at it, awarded it a quick, classifying disinterest, and returned to his knife.

"Oo—I know how to work those! Margie's sister has one," said Sally. She worked it. "If that isn't corny!" she gurgled. Eunice's head was bent over the gift. Sally straightened up, gave her and Grorley a swift, amending glance. "But cute!" she said. She flushed. Then, with one of the lightning changes that were the bane of her thirteen years, she began to cry. "Honestly, it's sweet!" she said.

Grorley looped an arm around her, gave her a squeeze and a kiss. "Now, shoo," he said. "Both of you."

When he turned back to the room, Eunice was looking out the window, chin up, her face not quite averted. Recognizing the posture, he quailed. It was the stance of the possessor of the stellar role—of the nightingale with her heart against the thorn. It was the stance of the woman who demands her scene.

He sighed, rat-tatted his fingers on a table top. "Well," he said. "Guess this is the season the corn grows tall."

A small movement of her shoulder. The back of her head to him. Now protocol demanded that he talk, into her silence, dredging his self-abasement until he hit upon some remark which made it possible for her to turn, to rend it, to show it up for the heartless, illogical, tawdry remark that it was. He could repeat a list of the game birds of North America, or a passage from the Congressional Record. The effect would be the same.

"Go on," he said, "get it over with. I deserve it. I just want you to know . . . mentally, I'm out of the Village."

She turned, head up, nostrils dilated. Her mouth opened. "Get it ov—!" Breath failed her. But not for long.

Much later, they linked arms in front of the same window. Supper had been eaten, the turkey had been trussed, the children at last persuaded into their beds. That was the consolatory side of family life, Grorley thought—the long, Olympian codas of the emotions were cut short by the niggling detail. Women thought otherwise, of course. In the past, he had himself.

Eunice began clearing off the bed. "What's in those two? Father's and Mother's?"

"Oh Lord. I forgot Father."

"Never mind. I'll look in the white-elephant box." The household phrase—how comfortably it rang. She looked up. "What's in these then?"

"For Mother and Mrs. Lederer. Those leather satchel-things. Pinseal."

"Both the same, I'll bet."

He nodded.

Eunice began to laugh. "Oh, Lord. How they'll hate it." She continued to laugh, fondly, until Grorley smirked response. This, too, was familiar. Masculine gifts: the inappropriateness thereof.

But Eunice continued to laugh, steadily, hysterically, clutching her stomach, collapsing into a chair. "It's that hat," she said. "It's that s-specimen of a hat!"

Grorley's hat lay on the bed, where he had flung it. Brazenly dirty, limp denizen of bars, it reared sideways on a crest of tissue paper, one curling red whorl of ribbon around its crown. "L-like something out of Hogarth," she said. "The R-rounder's Return."

Grorley forced a smile. "You can buy me another."

"Mmmm . . . for Christmas." She stopped laughing. "You know . . . I think that's what convinced me—your coming back tonight. Knowing you—that complex of yours. Suppose I felt if you meant to stand us through the holidays, you meant to stand us for good."

Grorley coughed, bent to stuff some paper into the wastebasket. In fancy, he was stuffing in a picture too, portrait of Vida, woman of imagination, outdistanced forever by the value of a woman who had none.

Eunice yawned. "Oh . . . I forgot to turn out the tree."

"I'll go down."

"Here, take this along." She piled his arms with crushed paper. In grinning afterthought, she clapped the hat on his head.

He went to the kitchen and emptied his arms in the bin. The kitchen was in chaos, the cookery methods of *alt Wien* demanding that each meal rise like a phoenix, from a flaming muddle below-stairs. Tomorrow, as Mrs. Lederer mellowed with wine, they would hear once again of her grandfather's house, where the coffee was not even *roasted* until the guests' carriages appeared in the driveway.

In the dining room, the table was set in state, from damask to silver nut dishes. Father would sit there. He was teetotal, but anecdotalism signs no pledge. His jousts as purchasing agent for the city of his birth now left both narrator and listener with the impression that he had built it as well. They would hear from Mother too. It was unfortunate that her bit of glory—her grandfather had once attended Grover Cleveland—should have crystallized itself in that one sentence so shifty for false teeth—"Yes, my father was a physician, you know."

Grorley sighed, and walked into the living room. He looked out, across the flowing blackness of the river. There to the south, somewhere in that jittering corona of yellow lights, was the apartment. He shuddered pleasurably, thinking of all the waifs in the world tonight. His own safety was too new for altruism; it was only by a paring of luck as thin as this pane of glass that he was safely here—on the inside, looking out.

Behind him, the tree shone—that *trompe-l'oeil* triumphant—yearly symbol of how eternally people had to use the spurious to catch at the real. If there was an angel at the top, then here was the devil at its base—that, at this season, anybody who opened his eyes and ears too wide caught the poor fools, caught himself, hard at it. Home is where the heart . . . the best things in life are . . . spin it and it says I. L.O.V.E. U.

Grorley reached up absently and took off his hat. This is middle age, he thought. Stand still and hear the sound of it, bonging like carillons, the gathering sound of all the platitudes, sternly coming true.

He looked down at the hat in his hand. It was an able hat; not every hat could cock a snook like that one. From now on, he'd need every ally he could muster. Holding it, he bent down and switched off the tree. He was out of the living room and halfway up the stairs, still holding it, before he turned back. Now the house was entirely dark, but he needed no light other than the last red sputter of rebellion in his heart. He crept down, felt along the wall, clasped a remembered hook. Firmly, he hung his hat in the hall. Then he turned, and went back up the stairs.

Il Plœ:r Dã Mõ Kœ:r

•§ I w a s taught to speak French *with* tears. It was not I who wept, or the other girls in my high-school class, but the poet Verlaine—the one who wrote "Il plœ:r dã mõ kœ:r." Inside forty slack American mouths, he wept phonetically for almost a semester. During this time, we were not taught a word of French grammar or meaning—only the International Phonetic Alphabet, the sounds the symbols stood for, and Verlaine translated into them. We could not even pick up the celebrated pen of our aunt. But by the time Verlaine and our teacher Mlle. Girard had finished with us, we were indeed ready to pick it up, and in the most classically passionate accents this side of the Comédie Française.

Mlle. Girard achieved her feat in this way. On the very first morning, she explained to us that French could never be spoken properly by us Anglo-Saxons unless we learned to reanimate those muscles of the face, throat, *poitrine* that we possessed—even as the French—but did not use. Ours, she said, was a speech almost without lilt, spoken on a dead level of intonation, "like a sobway train."

"Like this," she said, letting her jaw loll idiotically and choosing the most American subject she could find: "Ay wahnt sahm ay-iss cream." French, on the other hand, was a language *passionné* and *spirituel*, of vowels struck without pedal, of "l's made with a sprightly tongue tip—a sound altogether unlike our "l," which we made with our tongues plopping in our mouths. By her manner, she implied that all sorts of national differences might be assumed from this, although she could not take the time to pursue them.

She placed a wiry thumb and forefinger, gray with chalk dust, on either side of her mouth. "It is these muscles 'ere I shall teach you to use," she said. (If that early we had been trained to think in phonetic symbols, we would have known that what she had actually said was "mœslz.") When she removed her hand, we saw that she had two little, active, wrinkling pouches, one on either side of her mouth. In the ensuing weeks I often wondered whether all French people had them, and we would get them, too. Perhaps only youthful body tone saved us, as, morning after morning, she went among us pinching and poking our lips into grimaces and compelling sudden ventriloquisms from our astonished sinuses.

As a final coup, she taught us the classic "r." "Demoiselles," she said, "this is an *élégance* almost impossible for Americans, but you are a special class—I think you may do it." By this time, I think she had almost convinced herself that she had effected somatic changes in our Anglo-Saxonism. "*C'est produit,*" she said, imparting the knowledge to us in a whisper, "by vibr-rating the uvula!"

During the next week, we sat there, like forty purring Renaults, vibrating our uvulas.

Enfin came Verlaine, with his tears. As a supreme exercise, we were to learn to declaim a poem by one of the famous harmonists of France, and we were to do it entirely by ear. (At this time, we knew the meaning of not one word except *"ici!"* with which, carefully admonished to chirp "œp, not down!" we had been taught to answer the roll.) Years later, when I could *read* French, I came upon the poem in its natural state. To my surprise, it looked like this:

> *Il pleure dans mon coeur*
> *Comme il pleut sur la ville.*
> *Quelle est cette langueur*
> *Qui pénètre mon coeur?*
>
> *O bruit doux de la pluie*
> *Par terre . . .*

And so on. But the way it is engraved on my heart, my ear, and my uvula is something else again. As hour after hour, palm to breast, wrist to brow, we moaned like a bevy of Ulalumes, making the exquisite distinction between *"pleure"* and *"pleut,"* sounding our "r" like cat women, and dropping "l"s liquid as bulbuls, what we saw in our mind's eye was this:

Il Plœ:r Dã Mõ Kœ:r

il plœ:rə dã mõ kœ:r
kɔm il plø syr la vij
kɛl ɛ setə lãgœ:r
ki penɛtrə mõ kœ:r

o bryi du də la plyi
par te:r . . .

And *so* on.

Late in the term, Mme. Cécile Sorel paid New York a visit, and Mlle. Girard took us to see her in *La Dame aux Camélias*. Sorel's tea gowns and our own romantic sensibilities helped us to get some of her phthisic story. But what we marvelled at most was that she sounded exactly like us.

L'envoi comes somewhat late—twenty years later—but, like the tragic flaw of the Greeks, what Mlle. G. had planted so irrevocably was bound to show up in a last act somewhere. I went to France. During the interim, I had resigned myself to the fact that although I had "had" French so intensively—for Mlle. G. had continued to be just as exacting all the way through grammar, *dictée*, and the rest of it—I still did not seem to "have" it. In college, my accent had earned me a brief eminence, but, of course, we did not spend much time *speaking* French, this being regarded as a frivolous addiction, the pursuit of which had best be left to the Berlitz people, or to tacky parlor groups presided over by stranded foreign widows in need of funds. As for vocabulary or idiom, I stood with Racine on my right hand and Rimbaud on my left—a *cordon-bleu* cook who had never been taught how to boil an egg. Across the water, there was presumably a nation, *obscurcie de miasmes humains*, that used its own speech for purposes of asking the way to the bathroom, paying off porters, and going shopping, but for me the language remained the vehicle of de Vigny, Lamartine, and Hugo, and France a murmurous orchestral country where the *cieux* were full of *clarté*, the oceans sunk in *ombres profondes*, and where the most useful verbs were *souffler* and *gémir*.

On my occasional encounters with French visitors, I would apologize, in a few choicely carved phrases that always brought compliments, for being out of practice, after which I retired—into English if *they* had *it*, into the next room if they hadn't. Still, when I sailed, it was with hope—based on the famous accent—that in France I would somehow speak French. If I had only known, it would have been far better to go, as an underprivileged friend of mine did, armed with the one phrase her husband had taught her—"*Au secours!*"

Arriving at my small hotel in Paris, I was met by the owner, M. Lampacher, who addressed me in arrogantly correct English. When we had finished our arrangements in that language, I took the plunge. "*Merci!*" I said. It came out just lovely, the "r" like treacle, the "ci" not down but œp.

"Ah, Madame!" he said. "You speak French."

I gave him the visitors' routine.

"You mock, Madame. You have the accent *absolument pur.*"

The next morning, I left the hotel early for a walk around Paris. I had not been able to understand the boy who brought me breakfast, but no doubt he was from the provinces. Hoping that I would not encounter too many people from the provinces, I set out. I tramped for miles, afloat upon the first beatific daze of tourism. One by one, to sounds as of northern lights popping and sunken cathedrals emerging, all the postcards were coming true, and it was not until I was returning on the bus from Chaillot that, blinking, I listened for the first time that day.

Two women opposite me were talking; from their glances, directed at my plastic rain boots, they were talking about me. I was piqued at their apparent assumption that I would not understand them. A moment later, listening with closed eyes, I was glad that they could not be aware of the very odd way in which I was not understanding them. For what I was hearing went something like this: "rəgard lameriken se kautʃu sɛkõvnabl sa nɛspa purlɑ̃sɑ̃bl õ pəvwarlesulje"

"a ɛl nəsõpavremɑ̃ ʃik lezameriken ʃakynrəsɑ̃blalotr"

"a wi [Pause] tykonɛ mari la fijœl də mõ dəmi frɛr ɑ̃dre səlwi [or sɛl] avɛk ləbuk tylarɑ̃kõtre ʃemwa alo:r lœdi swa:r ɛl ʃor il] a fɛt yn foskuʃ"

Hours later, in my room, with the help of the dictionary and Mlle. G.'s training in *dictée*, I pieced together what they had said. It seemed to have been roughly this: "*Regarde, l'Américaine, ses caoutchoucs. C'est convenable, ça, n'est-ce-pas, pour l'ensemble. On peut voir les souliers."*

"Ah, elles ne sont pas vraiment chics, les Américaines. Chacune ressemble à l'autre."

"Ah, oui. [Pause] *Tu connais Marie, la filleule de mon demi-frère André—celui* [or *celle*] *avec le bouc. Tu l'as rencontré chez moi. Alors, lundi soir, elle* [or *il*] *a fait une fausse couche!"*

One of them, then, had thought my boots convenient for the ensemble, since one could see the shoes; the other had commented on the lack of real chic among American women, who all resembled one another. Digressing, they had gone on to speak of Marie, the goddaughter of a stepbrother, "the one with the *bouc*. You have met him [or her, since one could not tell from the construction] at my house." Either he or Marie had made a false couch, whatever that was.

The latter I could not find in the dictionary at all. *"Bouc"* I at first recalled as *"banc"*—either André or Marie had some kind of bench, then, or pew. I had just about decided that André had a seat in the Chamber of Deputies and had made some kind of political mistake, when it occurred to me that the word had been *"bouc"*—goatee—which almost certainly meant André. What had he done? Or Marie? What the hell did it mean "to make a false couch"?

I sat for the good part of an hour, freely associating—really, now, the goddaughter of a stepbrother! When I could bear it no longer, I rang up an American friend who had lived in Paris for some years, with whom I was to lunch the next day.

"Oh, yes, how are you?" said Ann.

"Dead tired, actually," I said, "and I've had a slight shock. Listen, it seems I can't speak French after all. Will you translate something?"

"Sure."

"What does to *'faire une fausse couche'* mean?"

"Honey!" said Ann.

"What?"

"Where are you, dear?" she said, in a low voice. "At a doctor's?"

"No, for God's sake, I'm at the hotel. What's the matter with you? You're as bad as the dictionary."

"Nothing's the matter with *me*," said Ann. "The phrase just means 'to have a miscarriage,' that's all."

"Ohhh," I said. "Then it was Marie after all. Poor Marie."

"*Are* you all right?"

"Oh, I'm fine," I said. "Just fine. And thanks. I'll see you to-morrow."

I went to bed early, assuring myself that what I had was merely disembarkation jitters (what would the psychologists call it—trans-literation syndrome?), which would disappear overnight. Otherwise it was going to be very troublesome having to retire from every con-versation to work it out in symbols.

A month went by, and the syndrome had not disappeared. Now and then, it was true, the more familiar nouns and verbs did make their way straight to my brain, by-passing the tangled intermediaries of my ear and the International Phonetic Alphabet. Occasionally, I was able to pick up an unpoetically useful phrase: to buy a brassière you asked for "something to hold up the gorge with"; the French said "Couci-couça" (never "*Comme ci, comme ça*") and, when they wanted to say "I don't know," turned up their palms and said "Schpuh." But meanwhile, my accent, fed by the lilt of true French, altogether outsoared the shadow of my night. When I did dare the phrases prepared carefully in my room for the eventualities of the day, they fell so superbly that any French vis-à-vis immediately dropped all thought of giving me a handicap and addressed me in the native argot, at the native rate—leaving me struck dumb.

New Year's Eve was my last night in Paris. I had planned to fly to London to start the new year with telephones, parties, the wire-less, conversation, in a wild blaze of unrestricted communication. But the airport had informed me that no planes were flying the Channel, or perhaps anywhere, for the next twenty-four hours, New Year's Eve being the one night on which the pilots were tradition-ally "allowed" to get drunk. At least, it *seemed* to me that I had been so informed, but perhaps I libel, for by now my passion for ac-curately understanding what was said to me was dead. All my pockets and purses were full of paper scraps of decoding, set down in vowel-hallucinated corners while my lips moved grotesquely, and it seemed to me that, if left alone here any longer, I would end by having composed at random a phonetic variorum for France. In a small, family-run café around the corner from my hotel, where I had often eaten alone, I ordered dinner, successive *cafés filtres*, and repeated doses of marc. Tonight, at the elegiac opening of the new year, it was "allowed"—for pilots and the warped failures of educational snobbism—to get drunk. Outside, it was raining, or weeping; in my heart, it was doing both.

Presently, I was the only customer at any of the zinc tables. Opposite, in a corner, the *grand-père* of the family of owners lit a Gauloise and regarded me with the privileged stare of the elderly. He was the only one there who seemed aware that I existed; for the others I had the invisibility of the foreigner who cannot "speak"— next door to that of a child, I mused, except for the adult password of money in the pocket. The old man's daughter, or daughter-in-law, a dark woman with a gall-bladder complexion and temperament, had served me obliquely and retired to the kitchen, from which she emerged now and then to speak sourly to her husband, a capped man, better-looking than she, who ignored her, lounging at the bar like a customer. I should have liked to know whether her sourness was in her words as well as her manner, and whether his lordliness was something personal between them or only the authority of the French male, but their harsh gutturals, so far from the sugarplum sounds I had been trained to that they did not even dissolve into phonetics, went by me like the crude blue smoke of the Gauloise. A girl of about fourteen—their daughter, I thought—was tending bar and deflecting the remarks of the customers with a petted, precocious insouciance. Now and then, her parents addressed remarks, either to her or to the men at the bar, that seemed to have the sharpness of reprimand, but I could not be sure; to my eye the gaiety of the men toward the young girl had a certain avuncular decorum that made the scene pleasant and tender to watch. In my own country, I loved to listen at bars, where the human scene was often arrested as it is in those genre paintings whose deceptively simple contours must be approached with all one's knowledge of the period, and it saddened me not to be able to savor those nuances here.

I lit a Gauloise, too, with a flourish that the old man, who nodded stiffly, must have taken for a salute. And why not? Pantomime was all that was left to me. Or money. To hell with my perfectionist urge to understand; I must resign myself to being no different from those summer thousands who jammed the ocean every June, to whom Europe was merely a montage of their own sensations, a glamorous old phoenix that rose seasonally, just for them. On impulse, I mimed an invitation to the old man to join me in a marc. On second thought, I signaled for marc for everybody in the house.

"To the new year!" I said, in French, waving my glass at the old man. Inside my brain, my monitor tapped his worried finger—did "*nouvelle*" come before or after "*année*" in such cases, and wasn't the accent a little "ice cream"? I drowned him, in another marc.

Across the room from me, the old man's smile faded in and out like the Cheshire cat's; I was not at all surprised when it spoke, in words I seemed to understand, inquiring politely as to my purpose in Paris. I was here on a scholarship, I replied. I was a writer. ("*Ecrivain? Romancier?*" asked my monitor faintly.)

"Ah," said the old man. "I am familiar with one of your writers. Père Le Buc."

"Père Le Buc?" I shook my head sadly. "I regret, but it is not known to me, the work of the Father Le Buc."

"*Pas un homme!*" he said. "*Une femme! Une femme qui s'appelle Père Le Buc!*"

My monitor raised his head for one last time. "Pɛrləbyk!" he chirped desperately. "Pɛrləbyk!"

I listened. "Oh, my God," I said then. "Of course. That is how it would be. Pearl Buck!"

"*Mais oui,*" said the old man, beaming and raising his glass. "Pɛrləbyk!"

At the bar, the loungers, thinking we were exchanging some toast, raised their own glasses in courteous imitation. "Pɛrləbyk!" they said, politely. "Pɛrləbyk!"

I raised mine. "*Il pleure,*" I began, "*il pleure dans mon coeur comme il pleut . . .*"

Before the evening was over, I had given them quite a selection: from Verlaine, from Heredia's "Les Trophées," from Baudelaire's poem on a painting by Delacroix, from de Musset's "R-r-ra-ppelle-toi!" As a final tribute, I gave them certain stanzas from Hugo's "L'Expiation"—the ones that begin "*Waterloo! Waterloo! Water-*

loo! Morne plaine!" And in between, raised or lowered by a new faith that was not all brandy, into an air freed of cuneiform at last —I spoke French.

Making my way home afterward, along the dark stretches of the Rue du Bac, I reflected that to learn a language outside its native habitat you must really believe that the other country exists—in its humdrum, its winter self. Could I remember to stay there now— down in that lower-case world in which stairs creaked, cops yelled, in which women bought brassières and sometimes made the false couch?

The door of my hotel was locked. I rang, and M. Lampacher admitted me. He snapped on the stair light, economically timed to go out again in a matter of seconds, and watched me as I mounted the stairs with the aid of the banister.

"Off bright and early, hmm?" he said sleepily, in French. "Well, good night, Madame. Hope you had a good time here."

I turned, wanting to answer him properly, to answer them all. At that moment, the light went off, perhaps to reinforce forever my faith in the mundanity of France.

"Ah, *ça va, ça va!*" I said strongly, into the dark. "Couci-couça. Schpuh."

If You Don't Want to Live I Can't Help You

◆§ MARY PONTHUS stepped outside, into the straw-colored June morning, from the Fifth Avenue entrance of the bank to which, as administratrix of her nephew's trust fund, she had just paid her usual call when in New York. In her size forty-two Liberty lawn and wide ballibuntl hat set firmly on unshorn white hair, she might have just stepped off a veranda in Tuxedo or Newport, from one of those corners where the dowagers affixed themselves. It would be a corner, perhaps, smelling pleasantly of Morny bath soap and littered with playing cards, over which the pairs of blue-veined hands with the buffed, pale nails would pass expertly, pausing to dip now and then into the large Beauvais handbags—hallmarks of Parisian honeymoons of forty years ago—that had outlasted the husbands and were likely to outlast the owners as well.

In fact, Mrs. Ponthus had not been on such a veranda since a morning thirty years ago, when news had been brought to her there of the drowning of her husband and son, while out sailing, in a sudden squall. Her summers, ever since, had been spent in a house on the grounds of the New England college from which she had been married and to which, desperate for occupation, she had returned to teach within a year after the news. Occasionally the summers had varied, with trips abroad to university friends made through correspondence over the slowly published critiques which had earned her a more than scholarly repute during those years when, while teaching, she herself had learned—and had finally brought her the honorary doctorate of letters that she was to be awarded here later in the day.

She walked south on the Avenue, reluctant to complete her errand, to keep her appointment with her nephew and her old acquaintance, the doctor who had once more been summoned to treat him. If she thought, momentarily, of her husband now, it was not of the tall young man standing in the boat in that aura of lost grace and virility with which the youthfully dead surrounded themselves. His influence had survived in other ways—in the money he had left her, which had not only exempted her from that professorial scratching for preferment out of which so many theses were born, but had allowed also her dearest extravagance, the subsidizing, now and then, of some young person of promise. It had survived too in the income siphoned through her to the son of his dead brother—the nephew Paul she was on her way to see. And for him, Paul, it had been, blameless in itself, perhaps the touch of ruin.

She turned down Lexington Avenue toward the old brownstone where Paul and Helen, or rather just Paul now, had the second floor front. Here the street had a nineteenth-century breadth which only pointed up the dullness of the façades on each side, houses without resurrectible charm, that still had escaped the ash-can vibrancy of a slum. Really, Paul had a homing instinct for the vitiated, the in-between. In a city where almost no place was any longer this way depersonalized, he had managed to find a street still as inconclusive as himself, this byway that neither stank nor sparkled but merely had a look of having been turned, like the collar on an old shirt. Here and there the lights of some marginal enterprise glistened indeterminately on a parlor or a basement floor, but in general, if the street had any character at all, it was that of the "small private income." Opposite Paul's corner there was a vestigial hotel with an open-cage, curlicued elevator, potted plants at a few of its bays and a permanent roster of vintage guests. On her last visit she and Paul had breakfasted in its coffee shop in the company of two of these—an elderly theatrical relic in wing collar and Homburg, and a hennaed old woman, fussily ringed and dressed as if for some long-superannuated soirée, leading a dachshund that had settled down to sleep at once in an accustomed spot. The talkative waitress had fed scraps to the dog, provided saccharin for the old man and inquired about Paul's last X rays, performing a function that, in a brisker neighborhood, might have been that of the neighborhood bartender.

She walked up the steps of Paul's house and hunted for the bell in the dimness of the not quite seedy vestibule. It was no wonder that Paul had gravitated here, to the acquiescent company of other pensioners. In an age which demanded that money be accompanied by personal achievement, a young man with a small private income was an anachronism, unless he had other directives or talents that made the money only accessory. And for Paul, with neither, and a pensioner since twenty, it had indeed been the touch of ruin. He had made the grand tour of the talents in a time when the mere possession of the means to do so was already antiquated. He had dabbled in painting in southern Italy, had written for and later supported a magazine in the Village, where he had been pitilessly marked for exploitation by those with greater needs and coarser drives, and all along the way he had dabbled in women and in wine, not so much out of lechery or a compulsion to alcohol as because these were good ways to pass the time—and of time he had so much to pass. Whatever his inner lack, his lack of need had enlarged it, making of him, at thirty-six, a "young man" whose every activity, foredoomed to the dilettante, was tolerated by his elders and suspect to his contemporaries. So finally, as some might say, he had dabbled in disease. And if so, even here he had been lucklessly dilettante too, for tuberculosis, that mordant parlor wound which had once bred so many gallantly ethereal heroines and interesting, smoking-jacketed heroes among the people of his class of another day, had now become, for such people, almost an anachronism too.

Mrs. Ponthus pressed the bell next to the nameplate, which still said "Paul Ponthus—Helen Bonner," although Helen had been gone for months. Helen had been Paul's "girl," as Paul's crowd would have put it, in the way they had of using the catch phrases of juvenility to convince themselves that they had all remained indecorously young. In and out of Paul's life for years, although he had never married her—perhaps because he hadn't—Helen had been one of those girls who yearly assaulted the city with a junior-executive energy, quickly learning to adulterate their wheaten, somewhat craggy good looks with a certain uniformity of style—women who, if they did not conventionally marry or brilliantly succeed, plodded hopefully along at the careers that kept them girls, often with some attachment in the background, some man with a talent to be nourished, a weakness to be supported, who always seemed to be earning less money than they.

Mrs. Ponthus pressed the bell again, with a longer ring. Paul

usually slept late, in the drugged burrowing of a man without pressing appointments. Poor Helen, she thought. To her, at first, Paul's
aimless round would have seemed Bohemian, their affair cosmopolitan. With the pitiable eagerness of those who seek love she
would have mistaken for passion what might never have been much
more than the heightened sexuality of the man without a job; later,
too deeply entangled, she would have refused to face the fact that
Paul's variety of joblessness was for life. With him she had gone
through all the fantastic travail of the woman's end of such an affair,
his rebellions against possessiveness, his ego-driven nights out with
other women, his reluctance to give her any certainty except the
abject one of his return. And her Griselda devotion had had its reward. For even as she became that background against which he
could most serviceably revolt, her lap had become that confessional
in which his head felt most at home. She had become that familiar
woman who stands behind the "artistic" man, patches up his
vagaries and explains him to a misunderstanding world—particularly,
in Paul's case, to those malicious ones who noted that Paul had all
the sufferings of the artistic personality without having anything to
show for it. And finally, now that she had left him—for he had always before done the leaving—she had achieved wifely status at last,
as the person by whom he was most misunderstood. For now that
she had found the will to leave him, they no longer said of her,
"Poor Helen." "Poor Paul," they said now. Poor, poor Paul.

The buzzer rang suddenly, stopping before she had time to press in
the door. Then it rang again, a long, sustained ring. She walked
slowly up the stairs. Remember not to be disarmed this time, she
told herself. Not this one time. He had never let her be the conventional aunt but had wooed her knowingly, as a confrere, drawing
out her own susceptibility to that, attaching her to him with her
own sticky, spidery thread. For, knowing so much about weakness,
he disarmed people with his delicate appreciation of theirs, and
before they knew it, like a child pressing his one grubby treasure
into their hands, he had given them his own weakness to hold.

His hall door was open. She stepped inside and closed it. Dusty
sunlight from the avenue ribbed the empty front room. Back of her,
the high, sliding doors to the bedroom were almost completely
closed.

"Helen!" said a bemused voice from behind the doors. "Helen?" She bit her lip, already disarmed. "No, it's Mary, Paul," she said. "No, it's Mary."

She walked toward the doors, letting him hear her footfalls on the bare floor, waited, then slid the doors back.

He stared at her, raised up on one elbow in bed, the other hand still pressed near the buzzer, against the wall. Then recognition woke him and he dove back under the covers, so that she could only see the back of his head. "Don't look at me," he said, muffled. "Don't look at me for a minute."

She turned her back on him. After an interval she heard him get up and turn on the shower in the bathroom. She walked over to the window and looked out, feeling as if she were collaborating in the byplay of a child. This was his talent perhaps, that one could collaborate with him only on his own basis, drawn in a trice into his world of willful charm and egocentric fears, forgetting that this was a dangerous juggernaut of a child with the body and impulses of a man.

"Sorry, Mary. I had a rough night." He had come from behind her, putting his hands lightly on her shoulders and turning her around. She inclined her cheek, but he shook his head, stepping significantly back with the courtesy of his disease.

"Were you sick again?"

He twisted the towel he held. "No more than usual. As a matter of fact—I broke training. Went on a party."

"Oh. Oh, Paul!" She knew those parties, which he ferreted out with professional desperation, calling up all over town, hoping to catch all the other busy, busy people on the prong of some momentary idleness, persuading them to take time out with an ardor like that of a drunkard who feels better when others are drinking.

He shrugged and sawed the towel back and forth on his wet hair.

"Ought you to get your head wet like that?"

"Now, don't go auntie on me. You women—at bottom you're all nannies."

"So I've heard," she said. "Usually from some man who's looking for one."

"Touché," he said, sitting down rather too quickly in a chair and smiling up at her. Certainly no special weakness appeared,

Lombroso-like, in that face, in the wide brow, firmly jutting nose, the cheekbones joined to the square jaw by the long, concave dimples of his illness. How wrong we are, she thought, to believe that character always sneaks into the lineaments of a face. This is what people would call a strong face, whose strength was only sapped if you knew its age. Then, indeed, it seemed almost criminally young.

"Come on," he said, "take off your hat. Such a nice, sensible hat. Ah, I'm glad to see you, Mary." He stood up and lifted the hat lightly from her head, bent to set it on a table wooled with dust, blew futilely at the table and finally hung the hat on the finial of a chair that held a pile of clothing. "Sit down, if you can find a spot. And don't say I ought to have a woman in. I'm working on that. Hard."

"I've no such intentions, Paul." She felt suddenly weary and sat down.

"I know, I know," he said, hovering above her. "But don't declare them, whatever they are, till I've had coffee. Have you had breakfast?"

"Of course I've had breakfast."

"Of course," he said. "Such a sane, sensible hat!" His voice faded, and he had to sit down on the nearest chair. She started toward him, but he waved her back. "Not what you think. It's just a dirty old hangover."

They looked at each other from chair to chair. "You fool," she said. "You fool!"

"Ah, Mary, you *are* good for me," he said.

Here it comes, she thought. The sweet bait that works on any age, any sex. The terrible, tricksy intimacy of another's need, saved up just for you. Thus is the thread spun—and to any comer. "I'll make you coffee," she said.

She crossed the room and opened the folding shutters of the kitchenette. Its sparse equipment, ranged stiffly, was grimy with disuse. On the drainboard a dishcloth, frozen into a contortion of days back, gave off an odor of mildew.

"Smell it?" he said. "The odor of celibacy. Varied by an occasional woman—and an occasional mouse."

"Spare me the details," she said, her back to him.

"No, that's one of the reasons you are so good for me. You and

Helen. You're the lucky ones. You don't have to be spared."

"We have our limits," she said. "Such as making coffee when there is none." She picked up her bag. "I'll go get some. You better stay to let Jamie in."

"He's not coming. He's washed his hands of me."

"But I spoke to him yesterday! Yesterday morning."

"So did I. Yesterday afternoon, in his office. He wanted me to go back to that magic mountain of his. No, that's not for me. What'll they do? Patch up the lesion in my chest? So I can hang around a little longer, to rot of the one in my head?"

"Paul." She sat down again, heavily. The handbag slid to the floor. "Paul . . . what *is* for you?"

"You tell me." His short laugh turned into a cough. He leaned forward and took her hands in his, staring at her with the mesmeric shine of the devotee. "It's Helen. I know that now. I haven't any shame about it. I'll turn somersaults. I'll lie, I'll be honest, just so she comes back. But she won't see me. I haven't even talked to her in five months. I don't even know where she's living, and when I call her office she's got them primed to say, 'Miss Bonner's not in.' 'Miss Bonner's not at her desk.' I've written, I've had friends badger her . . ." He sat back, closing his eyes. When he opened them again she saw that the shine in them was actually tears. "She let me lean on her for years," he said, in a voice almost without breath. "She got me into this straitjacket. Now she can damn well get me out of it."

For a moment she was rigid with anger, on the part of a woman she had never known well. "Perhaps she has other plans."

"No," he said. "I was her first. I'll be her last. Without me she doesn't feel the need. That's why she's afraid to see me, don't you see that?"

"I'd rather not tell you what I see."

"Oh, go on," he said, "tell me I'm a bastard. I don't know why I have such trouble getting people to believe it."

Because they see the real straitjacket, she thought—and know it in part for their own. Because, locked in yourself, you are to the nth degree that sad monstrosity which we are all in part. "No . . . you're not a bastard."

"No?" he said. "Sometimes my own cleverness sickens me. Your coming today—I was pretty sure Jamie had asked you to stop the money unless I went up to that place. And you know what I thought?" He gave her the intense, open stare of the man who, despairing of gulling one with lies, tries the truth. "I thought, all right, let them turn the house cat into the jungle. Then he'll really touch bottom. Then Helen will take him in." He gripped her hands again. His own were burning hot. "She'll listen to you. Just do that for me. Just get her to see me—see the spot I'm in. I'll take it from there."

She stood up, wrenching her hands away, and walked to the window. One of the shades was uneven. She straightened it without seeing it. "I wish to God the money'd been left to you in one sum. So you could have stood or fallen on it. As it is, I blame myself. For not stopping it. Years ago."

"Oh, let's face it, Mary. No matter what chances I'd have had—something's been left out. I can't manage. The best I can do is to cling to someone who can."

She turned from her view of the meager street in time to see him stand up, take a step toward her and falter with a look of surprise. "As now," he said. His knees buckled and he slid to the floor. She ran toward him. "Blankets . . ." he said through chattering teeth, but by the time she had torn them from the bed and helped him into a chair, the chill had subsided and his pajamas were dark with sweat. She went to the phone and dialed the doctor's number. When she had finished she sat down at Paul's side and put her hand on his forehead.

"He won't come." His whisper held a note of satisfaction. "He's given me up."

"He's coming right away. On his way to the hospital." After a few minutes she looked secretly at her watch, which said two. She was due at the university at three-thirty, robed and in place for the procession.

"What's the time?"

"Two, Paul."

He nodded gravely, as if she had given him a fact of importance. "Helen used to say I watched the clock more than anyone she knew." He moved his head from side to side. His hurried breathing was like a pulse in the room. "You and Helen, most people, you get

141

up in the morning, you go through the day—as if . . . there were a plan. Maybe you don't know what it is either, but you all act . . . *as if* . . ."

She found herself breathing with him as one did leaning over the feverish bodies of children. "Better not talk."

He rolled his head impatiently. "When I was a kid—I used to think grown people had some gimmick that kept them pushing through their days—it was a gimmick they had and I would get it too." He turned his head away from her and was silent. There fell between them that suspended communion of the sickroom, in which conversation was only a recitative against the forces of dark. Street noises crowded into the room, poignant with health. She raised her head and found him looking at her.

"What is it?" he said.

"That—? A car. A truck."

"The gimmick," he said. "I meant the gimmick."

"Sh." She put her finger against her lips, with the tic-like smile with which one cajoled the sick. For if now, in his fever, he brought up truth like phlegm, there was no way to treat it except as fever.

The bell rang curtly, bringing an image of Jamie downstairs, grizzled hair, sandy face lively with impatience, feet shuffling in the way he had of always seeming to be treading water. His was a cathartic presence that comforted, not with calm but with the energy of an annoyance that barked peremptorily at the forces of ill: I won't have this. I simply won't have it. She walked the length of the room and leaned against the buzzer with a sigh of relief.

On her way back Paul caught at her hand. A blue smear of beard on his upper lip and on the round of flesh under his chin gave him the culprit look of a boy long since too old to be told to wash. "Call her," he said. "Promise."

She detached her hand, even flexed her white, wrinkled palm to show that it was still empty, still free. "Yes," she said, "I promise," and went to open the door.

Jamie stumped past her, dropped his bag on the floor near Paul and stood looking down at him. He bent, flipped back Paul's blankets and straightened up, still looking at him. Neither spoke.

She took up her post at the window again. Behind her the small, diagnostic clinkings went on, and she could hear the separate breathings that haunted a room at such times—the heavy intake of the patient, the quiet, judging respiration of the doctor, and her own breath, held. Then Jamie's voice, brusque at the phone, ordered an ambulance. He joined her at the window, lit a cigarette and puffed at it angrily. Behind them Paul seemed to doze. A Good Humor wagon went slowly down the street, pricking at the heat with its feeble icicle of sound, but no children came from the elderly doorways and it puttered on out of sight.

"There it is," said Jamie. He opened the window and motioned to the orderlies, who were drawing the stretcher from the ambulance.

"Pleurisy," said Paul's voice behind them. "Isn't it?" The doctor, shutting his bag, did not answer. "Where you taking me?"

"Lenox Hill. You'll need a tent."

"Is that routine?"

The doctor reddened. "I told you yesterday. Your condition's routine. But you seem to want to distinguish yourself by dying of it."

Paul's eyelids flickered. "I'm just like everyone else. I don't want to die." His voice tremored defiantly, like that of a man presenting doubtful credentials at a bank.

She put her hand on Jamie's arm. He was glowering at Paul as if they were enemies. "Maybe not," he said. "But if you don't want to live I can't help you."

There was a knock and a shuffling at the door. She opened it. "This it?" said one of the men, and with a joint, hard glance at Paul they pointed the litter inside. They moved quickly, two vacant-faced nullities, one that chewed, one that did not, and when they had finished, Paul, neatly cocooned in gray, was a nullity too. But as they swung him toward the door his hand came imperiously out of the gray cowl, and they paused, holding him slung between them, two indifferent caryatids, smelling faintly of dishwater and iodoform.

"Mary!"

"Yes, Paul. Yes, I will. Yes!"

His hand touched his smile, saluted, and let them bear him off. It was the gesture of a hero borne wounded from the field—but on the winning side.

She turned to find Jamie watching her as if he saw something telltale, symptomatic, in her. "Going uptown?" he said. "I'll drop you."

"I better find the key." She found it, in the pocket of the trousers collapsed on a chair. Holding it in her hand, she looked around the room, feeling that she must tidy it, but already its disorder had the subtle, irreparable flavor of desertion. *No one here by that name now. The policy has changed.* "How quick trouble is!" she murmured, and for a moment felt the thirty-year-old shock turn and reverberate in her heart. They left, locking the door behind them.

In the car he offered her a cigarette like a truce. "Will he be all right?" she asked.

He was silent until they had pulled away from the curb and were part of the traffic. "They're hard to kill."

"People with TB?"

He shook his head. "Sometimes I think I could go down the file in my office and tick them off. The ones who want to, and the ones who don't."

"Die, you mean?"

"No. Live."

She ground out her cigarette. "Pretty subtle distinction."

"No!" He kept his eyes on the traffic. "We're all subject to the normal human damnations. We're all 'afraid to die.'" His voice was a faint, savage mimicry of Paul's. "But these people make their whole lives a deathbed—and expect the rest of us to gather round." He flicked her a glance. "And we do. We do."

"I can think of a lot of books, a lot of art, came out of some of them."

"No. Those were the ones who wanted to live most of all. Wasn't Keats a lunger? And still able to make such an expression of interest in the world?" His voice softened. "No—that's the crux of it—when you see that."

"Oh, if Paul had found his talent . . ."

He grunted. "I oughtn't have blown up at Paul yesterday—but the man in before him was an old patient, a graduate of Dachau—and gangrene. Long since turned him over to an orthopedist. Fitted with a hand four years ago. He sells soap—but he wants to go back to being a printer. Barged in full of excitement to show me his new hand. Untied my tie—and tied it again."

He dug down on the gas pedal and they spurted ahead of the parallel traffic. "No, this is pre-Freud, something in the egg. Maybe

144

we'll get so we can calibrate it in the kindergarten. The ones who are willing, and the ones who will have to be dragged. Try it on your friends sometime."

She looked out the window. The day was in full blare now, the air like an agar through which the outlines of people vibrated and doubled. "You're pretty arbitrary."

"No," he said. "The egg is arbitrary."

She was silent until they reached the university. "Anywhere along here."

He let her out at a corner. She thanked him, leaning for a moment on the car door. "And the others, Jamie? What do we do about them?"

He patted her hand and gave it back to her. "What do you do? What do I do?" he shrugged. "Visit as usual," he said, and tipped his hat and drove off.

She walked into a drugstore opposite the main building and ordered a sandwich and coffee. This place was a student haunt well known to her: three years ago she had been a visiting professor at the university. Even this late in the year it was packed with glossy boys and girls, talking and lolling with that combination of urgency and unpremeditated time for which they would be nostalgic the rest of their lives. She ate hurriedly, sitting among them with the sad anonymity of the outsider—a feeling as familiar to her home ground as here. With them, any age past their own was the outsider; any skin that had made its concessions or eye that had veined with memory was both beneath their notice and beyond it. One sat with them, skeletal at their feast, knowing something about them that they would be incapable of believing, that the skeleton, if challenged, would be unable to describe.

An hour later, however, seated on the platform in the immense white daze of the stadium, she felt closer to them than to her colleagues sitting on the dais with her in their annual empurplement of heat and dignity. So many of these were such dry sticks as collected wherever intellectual pursuits went on, kindling to occasions like this one with an inescapable air of having been rejected at better fires. Now the chancellor was making his address, and out into the air floated all the baccalaureate cognates—"war . . . goal

. . . peace . . . aspiration . . . from our failing hands"—in a style that just skirted iambic pentameter, leaving one doubtful as to whether it ran from it or toward it. On his head he wore a little pillow of scarlet plush of whose heraldry she was ignorant, unless it signified an eminence that no longer bent the knee but rather must be protected from the jagged points of the stars. Now he spoke directly to the graduates, telling them, with the easy teleology of the safe, that certain wars were sacred, certain generations—perhaps theirs—divinely lost, and they lifted their faces toward him in a thousandfold ovoid innocence. If some among them saw privately that the emperor had no head but a pillow, ten years from now they would be less sure.

Hearing her own name, she raised her head, but bent it quickly, for her own citation had begun. "For achievement in the world of letters . . . for yeoman service to young candidates for that world . . ." The university had already approached her with a plan for its administering, as scholarships, the money she used for her own scattered benefices, but the citation, laying no indelicate emphasis on these, circled lavishly around her own work. *Timeo Danaos*, she thought, but the praise lapped her with shameful warmth.

At a benedictory signal from the chancellor she went forward, bending to receive the brilliant capelet on her shoulders. He shook her hand, turning it with practiced dismissal, so that for a moment she faced her audience, a speaker who was not to be allowed to speak.

As she returned to her seat, Sweet, the head of the department, shot out a hand as if it had been tapped with a mallet and beamed violently, making a noise like a bubbling kettle, but already his face was angled toward the next to be honored, as were all the young faces before her. Tipped and oval, a thousand eggs of unknown impulse, they waited, dressed in their rented black, as if the old could not quickly enough take the young into the dark seminary of responsibility. If she had been allowed to speak, she thought, what would she have told them? That life gave no baccalaureates? That there was always the visit to be paid as usual, always the telephone call to be made?

At last the ceremony was over. With one final fanfare it smashed and dispersed, scattering its components over the grounds like bright and drab bits of glass from which no further pattern could be expected that day. She walked slowly, through family groupings, toward the Faculty Club, where her presence had been requested at tea and where there was a phone.

In the booth she dialed the number of Helen's office. It was not quite five o'clock.

"Manning and Coe, good afternoon."

"May I speak to Miss Bonner, please?"

She gave her own name, spelling it out. After an interval a second voice spoke. "What is it, please?"

"Helen? Is this Miss Bonner?"

There was a pause, then the voice spoke again. "Miss Bonner is no longer connected with this office."

It was close in the booth but she suddenly found herself shivering. "Can you tell me where I can reach her?"

Again the voice waited. "No," it said finally. "I'm sorry—but I cannot."

She drew a long breath. "If she—gets in touch with you, perhaps you'd give her a message?"

"What is the message." It was less a question than a statement.

"I'm calling for my nephew, Paul Ponthus. He is seriously ill in Lenox Hill Hospital. He would like to get in touch with her."

Over the wire she could hear the breathing of the other woman. She waited. "Yes," the voice said, and its weary inflection made her certain. "I'll see that she gets the message. If she calls. But I doubt if she will call."

When she left the booth she was still shivering. She hadn't seen Helen in over a year. But she was good at voices, good at inflections. The second voice had been Helen's.

In the Faculty Parlor she held herself apart from the chattering groups, drank two cups of hot tea and took a third to a seat in a corner. I caught a chill, she told herself, and knew that she had not. Most of us are such drifters, she thought, leaving our fates to erosion, our amputations to death and accident. When we see someone his own surgeon, we are filled with awe.

Through an open window at her side she heard children playing outside the chapel gates, exchanging the familiar twilight calls: "Where are You?" . . . "I'm anyplace, where are You?" The cries rose gawkily, the sound of viols played by amateurs for whom the opulent instrument was yet too much. For an insistent moment she wished herself back there with them, with the sun going down in a clash of skates. Not to be here in his tea-colored room where the old condescendingly relaxed with the young, and the young were so ruddy and unaware of how powerfully they could condescend to the old. Not to be sitting here, an elderly voyeur, holding in my lap, like knitting, the severed nerve ends of two lives. But not quite yet the voyeur. There is still the visit to be made.

Someone turned on the lights, the dusk at the window snapped to a sharper blue, and people, blinking in the orange brightness, plunged again into the rubble of talk. She looked down the room as one did at funerals, reunions, all the roll calls at which one took stock of the assessments of time. Brewster, that sorry sufferer from the worst of academic diseases, had retired into some cranky shade, taking with him his disappointment in himself. But Baldwin was gone too, the tall, bearded medievalist whose mind had been of such an opaline goodness that, staring into it, one almost saw striations of goodness that were one's own.

"Felicitations! Felicitations!" Sweet teetered on his heels before her, his clasped hands cherishing his tweed belly. "How does it feel, eh? How does it feel?" Having founded a career on repetition, he was not one to desert it for lesser purposes. "But they'll be wanting to meet you," he added. "Come take your turn at the urn. Ha! Turn at the urn."

He led her to the long table and installed her in front of the tea service. "Young chap you must meet," he whispered. "Just back to the graduate school from the Army. Did some brilliant emendations on *The Pearl* before he left. 'S matter of fact—if you should see your way clear—hm—he'd be one of our first candidates. Used to be a protégé of poor Baldwin." She watched him shamble over to a group and detach a young man from it. She had always piqued him with her preference for Baldwin, a man of no great departmental or secular distinction. But the patronage of the dead, if useful, would not offend.

She looked at the boy Sweet was bringing toward her, a nice enough young man with his hair cut in that neat furze they all affected, his face still that printless mask which nature affected for them. For the first time she could not summon the friable tenderness, that perverse sense of her own youth whereby she seemed to herself really only a prisoner, caught in some gargantuan trap of flesh

148

and years. For the first time she felt the great disinterest that was age. They keep coming, she thought, another and another. It's time I stopped running toward them, poking at them for whatever it was I was seeking. Perhaps it's time to admit what that was too—nothing much more than the bawling of an old cow with caked udders, lowing for a calf thirty years gone. I'll let the college have the money, let them handle it any way they wish. I'll take on Paul, for whom nothing can be done, and it will at least be better that the nothing be done by me than by Helen. People like Paul can be looked after quite easily out of duty; the agony comes only when they are looked after with hope.

Sweet intoned a name she didn't catch. "Great fan of yours, this young man. Great fan." He beamed impartially at them and departed.

"You don't have to *say* anything." She smiled up at the young man.

"It's true, though." He spoke with a bluntness past having to be put at its ease. "Charles Baldwin put me on to your work."

"Yes?" she said. She looked down the room. "I miss him here."

He too looked down the room. "I loved Baldwin," he said. "Even if you were only a student, he made you feel that you counted."

She glanced at him more sharply. One seldom heard them use the word "love" in the quiet sense that he had used it—it was contrarily the one four-letter word they still spoke with a sense of shame.

"Yes," she said. "He was a good man."

"They never made too much of him here."

"No," she said. "I guess the good don't dramatize easily."

"That's true!" he said with a rush. "True in books too, isn't it?"

She nodded, smiling. "So then—you're going to specialize in Medieval?"

He grinned at her and, grudgingly, she felt the familiar rictus of interest. Intelligent, of course, she warned herself, but then the room was full of intelligence, beady-eyed with it, full of quick-billed birds, and if the eyes of the younger ones seemed more luminous, it was only because they hadn't quite learned when to drop the secondary lid, the filmy lid of conformism.

"No," he said. "I'm giving up the graduate school. I haven't told anyone yet. I've—I've got some notes for a book."

"Oh?"

He bent his head, flushing. "Actually . . . I wrote a book. While I was in the Army. But I chucked that too. I had just enough sense to see how derivative it was." He brought out the phrase, as they so often did, like a password.

"But we're all that," she said, hearing in her voice a melting note that she decried.

"But this wasn't just style," he said, raising his head. "It was full of the best prime anxiety—and all secondhand. It had everybody's fingerprint on it except mine."

"And your fingerprint?" she said. "What will that be?"

He drooped again. "Oh, I'm still in boot camp. I know that!" But his doldrums were only those of the young, easily routed by the tensing of a muscle, or rain drying on a pane. He reached toward a plate on the table and popped several pallid triangles into his mouth. "This lost-generation stuff we were tossed this aft—you believe that?"

"I'm not sure," she said. "I've never been sure. It's more important whether you believe it. All of you."

"We get so confused," he said. "They've got us staring at their navels, not our own. And we've got nothing to answer them with—yet." He cast her a desperate smile and concentrated on an empty cup and saucer, pushing them back and forth on the table. "Guess I'm a freak or something. But I like being in the world. And if I write, oughtn't it to have some—some of that in it? Oh, I was in the Army—I know there's enough trouble to go around. But I have to earn mine—not inherit it!" He cast her another agonized glance and bent again to his game with the saucer. "Speech, speech," he said.

"No," she said slowly, "you're not a freak," and caught an echo of what she had said to Paul. No, you're not a bastard. But what they are, she thought, I can't tell them.

"Anyway, that's why I'm leaving," he said. "I told myself, okay, I helped mop up a war for them. But I'm damned if I'll write their books for them."

His voice was loud and she looked apprehensively around the room, but it had emptied and they were alone.

"I guess I shouldn't get so angry," he said, averting a cheek that was as mild as a child's.

She leaned forward, peering at him with the habit of a lifetime.

If You Don't Want to Live I Can't Help You

It's just the glow they all have once, she told herself, nothing special. It's like the gaudy light that clings to their first poems; one must always be suspicious of it, for it may be simply the peak of freshness attained at least once by everyone, like the transitory skin bloom on a plain girl.

"I seem to be angry practically all of the time," he said. But his eyes, before he slanted them away again, were proud.

She looked at him. Maybe, she thought. But in any case why do I watch for it, why have I spent my life watching it? The Freudians would say I was still looking for a son. She drew a deep breath and leaned back. And if so, she thought, we are all, at any age past a certain one, hunting hopefully for our sons.

He'll think me odd, she thought, staring at him this way without speaking. But she saw that he stood there dreaming, lost in a dream of his own oddness.

Yes, they keep coming, she thought—another and another. And some of them will be the Pauls, who dramatize so easily, to love whom is the worst dead end of fate—for they will knock at every door and never be able to unlock their own. But these others will be coming too. They'll keep coming, the angry ones, another and another, and when they hold out, they are the bright specks on the retina of the world.

He turned. He had picked up the cup and saucer and was holding them out to her with a tentative smile.

She took them and held them, staring down into the cup. I can't help it, she thought; I'm of the breed that hopes. Maybe this one wants to live, she thought. *Maybe this one wants to live.* And when you see that—that's the crux of it. We are all in the dark together, but those are the ones who humanize the dark.

Pouring the cold tea into the cup, her hands trembled so that the cup clinked against the saucer, but when she held out the cup, staring up at him, her wrist was firm.

A Wreath for Miss Totten

৶ CHILDREN GROWING up in the country take their images of integrity from the land. The land, with its changes, is always about them, a pervasive truth, and their midget foregrounds are crisscrossed with minute dramas which are the animalcules of a larger vision. But children who grow in a city where there is nothing greater than the people brimming up out of subways, rivuleting in the streets—these children must take their archetypes where and if they find them.

In P.S. 146, between periods, when the upper grades were shunted through the halls in that important procedure known as "departmental," although most of the teachers stood about chatting relievedly in couples, Miss Totten always stood at the door of her "home room," watching us straightforwardly, alone. As, straggling and muffled, we lined past the other teachers, we often caught snatches of upstairs gossip which we later perverted and enlarged; passing before Miss Totten we deflected only that austere look, bent solely on us.

Perhaps, with the teachers, as with us, she was neither admired nor loathed but simply ignored. Certainly none of us ever fawned on her as we did on the harshly blond and blue-eyed Miss Steele, who never wooed us with a smile but slanged us delightfully in the gym, giving out the exercises in a voice like scuffed gravel. Neither did she obsess us in the way of the Misses Comstock, two liverish, stunted women who could have had nothing so vivid about them as our hatred for them, and though all of us had a raffish hunger for metaphor, we never dubbed Miss Totten with a nickname.

Miss Totten's figure, as she sat tall at her desk or strode angularly in front of us rolling down the long maps over the blackboard, had

A Wreath for Miss Totten

that instantaneous clarity, one metallic step removed from the real, of the daguerreotype. Her clothes partook of this period too—long, saturnine waists and skirts of a stuff identical with that in a good family umbrella. There was one like it in the umbrella-stand at home—a high black one with a seamed ivory head. The waists enclosed a vestee of dim, but steadfast lace; the skirts grazed narrow boots of that etiolated black leather, venerable with creases, which I knew to be a sign both of respectability and foot trouble. But except for the vestee, all of Miss Totten, too, folded neatly to the dark point of her shoes, and separated from these by her truly extraordinary length, her face presided above, a lined, ocher ellipse. Sometimes, as I watched it on drowsy afternoons, her face floated away altogether and came to rest on the stand at home. Perhaps it was because of this guilty image that I was the only one who noticed Miss Totten's strange preoccupation with "Mooley" Davis.

Most of us in Miss Totten's room had been together as a group since first grade, but we had not seen Mooley since down in second grade, under the elder and more frightening of the two Comstocks. I had forgotten Mooley completely, but when she reappeared I remembered clearly the incident which had given her her name.

That morning, very early in the new term, back in Miss Comstock's, we had lined up on two sides of the classroom for a spelling bee. These were usually a relief to good and bad spellers alike, since it was the only part of our work which resembled a game, and even when one had to miss and sit down, there was a kind of dreamy catharsis in watching the tenseness of those still standing. Miss Comstock always rose for these occasions and came forward between the two lines, standing there in an oppressive close-up in which we could watch the terrifying action of the cords in her spindling gray neck and her slight smile as a boy or a girl was spelled down. As the number of those standing was reduced, the smile grew, exposing the oversize slabs of her teeth, through which the words issued in a voice increasingly unctuous and soft.

On this day the forty of us still shone with the first fall neatness of new clothes, still basked in that delightful anonymity in which neither our names nor our capacities were already part of the dreary foreknowledge of the teacher. The smart and quick had yet to assert themselves with their flying, staccato hands; the uneasy dull,

153

not yet forced into recitations which would make their status clear, still preserved in the small, sinking corners of their hearts a lorn, factitious hope. Both teams were still intact when the word "mule" fell to the lot of a thin colored girl across the room from me, in clothes perky only with starch, her rusty fuzz of hair drawn back in braids so tightly sectioned that her eyes seemed permanently widened.

"Mule," said Miss Comstock, giving out the word. The ranks were still full. She had not yet begun to smile.

The girl looked back at Miss Comstock, soundlessly. All her face seemed drawn backward from the silent, working mouth, as if a strong, pulling hand had taken hold of the braids.

My turn, I calculated, was next. The procedure was to say the word, spell it out, and say it again. I repeated it in my mind: "Mule. M-u-l-e. Mule."

Miss Comstock waited quite a long time. Then she looked around the class, as if asking them to mark well and early this first malfeasance, and her handling of it.

"What's your name?" she said.

"Ull—ee." The word came out in a glottal, molasses voice, hardly articulate, the *l*'s scarcely pronounced.

"Lilly?"

The girl nodded.

"Lilly what?"

"Duh-avis."

"Oh. Lilly Davis. Mmmm. Well, spell 'mule,' Lilly." Miss Comstock trilled out the name beautifully.

The tense brown bladder of the girl's face swelled desperately, then broke at the mouth. "Mool," she said, and stopped. "Mmm—oo—"

The room tittered. Miss Comstock stepped closer.

"*Mule!*"

The girl struggled again. "Mool."

This time we were too near Miss Comstock to dare laughter.

Miss Comstock turned to our side. "Who's next?"

I half raised my hand.

"Go on." She wheeled around on Lilly, who was sinking into her seat. "No. Don't sit down."

A Wreath for Miss Totten

I lowered my eyelids, hiding Lilly from my sight. "Mule," I said. "M-u-l-e. Mule."

The game continued, words crossing the room uneventfully. Some children survived. Others settled, abashed, into their seats, craning around to watch us. Again the turn came around to Lilly.

Miss Comstock cleared her throat. She had begun to smile. "Spell it now, Lilly," she said. "Mule."

The long-chinned brown face swung from side to side in an odd writhing movement. Lilly's eyeballs rolled. Then the thick sound from her mouth was lost in the hooting, uncontrollable laughter of the whole class. For there was no doubt about it: the long, coffee-colored face, the whitish glint of the eyeballs, the bucking motion of the head suggested it to us all—a small brown quadruped, horse or mule, crazily stubborn, or at bay.

"Quiet!" said Miss Comstock. And we hushed, although she had not spoken loudly. For the word had smirked out from a wide, flat smile and on the stringy neck beneath there was a creeping, pleasurable flush which made it pink as a young girl's.

That was how Mooley Davis got her name, although we had a chance to use it only for a few weeks, in a taunting singsong when she hung up her coat in the morning, or as she flicked past the little dust-bin of a store where we shed our pennies for nigger-babies and tasteless, mottoed hearts. For after a few weeks, when it became clear that her cringing, mucoused talk was getting worse, she was transferred to the "ungraded" class. This group, made up of the mute, the shambling, and the oddly tall, some of whom were delivered by bus, was housed in a basement part of the school, with a separate entrance which was forbidden us not only by rule but by a lurking distaste of our own.

The year Mooley reappeared in Miss Totten's room, a dispute in the school system had disbanded all the ungraded classes in the city. Here and there, now, in the back seat of a class, there would be some grown-size boy who read haltingly from a primer, fingering the stubble of his slack jaw. Down in 4-A there was a shiny, petted doll of a girl, all crackling hairbow and nimble wheelchair, over whom the teachers shook their heads feelingly, saying: "Bright as a dollar! Imagine!" as if there were something sinister in the fact that useless legs had not impaired the musculature of a mind. And in

155

our class, in harshly clean, faded dresses which were always a little too infantile for her, her spraying ginger hair cut short now and held by a round comb which circled the back of her head like a snaggle-toothed tiara which had slipped, there was this bony, bug-eyed wraith of a girl who raised her hand instead of saying "Present!" when Miss Totten said "Lilly Davis?" at roll call, and never spoke at all.

It was Juliet Hoffman, the pace-setter among the girls in the class, who spoke Mooley's nickname first. A jeweller's daughter, Juliet had achieved an eminence even beyond that due her curly profile, embroidered dresses, and prancing, leading-lady ways when, the Christmas before, she had brought as her present to teacher a real diamond ring. It had been a modest diamond, to be sure, but undoubtedly real, and set in real gold. Juliet had heralded it for weeks before and we had all seen it—it and the peculiar look on the face of the teacher, a young substitute whom we hardly knew—when she had lifted it from the pile of hankies and fancy notepaper on her desk. The teacher, over the syrupy protests of Mrs. Hoffman, had returned the ring, but its sparkle lingered on, iridescent around Juliet's head.

On our way out at three o'clock that first day with Miss Totten, Juliet nudged at me to wait. Obediently, I waited behind her. Twiddling her bunny muff, she minced over to the clothes closet and confronted the new girl.

"I know you," she said. "Mooley Davis, that's who you are!" A couple of the other children hung back to watch.

"Aren't you? Aren't you Mooley Davis?"

I remember just how Mooley stood there because of the coat she wore. She just stood there holding her coat against her stomach with both hands. It was a coat of some pale, vague tweed, cut the same length as mine. But it wrapped the wrong way over for a girl and the revers, wide ones, came all the way down and ended way below the pressing hands.

"Where you been?" Juliet flipped us all a knowing grin. "You been in ungraded?"

One of Mooley's shoulders inched up so that it almost touched her ear, but beyond that, she did not seem able to move. Her eyes looked at us, wide and fixed. I had the feeling that all of her had retreated far, far back behind the eyes which—large and light, and purposefully empty—had been forced to stay.

My back was to the room, but on the suddenly wooden faces of the others I saw Miss Totten's shadow. Then she loomed thinly over Juliet, her arms, which were crossed at her chest, hiding the one V of white in her garments, so that she looked like an umbrella which had been tightly furled.

"What's *your* name?" she asked, addressing not so much Juliet as the white muff which, I noticed now, was slightly soiled.

"Jooly-ette."

"Hmm. Oh, yes. Juliet Hoffman."

"Jooly-ette, it is." She pouted creamily up at Miss Totten, her glance narrow with the assurance of finger rings to come.

Something flickered in the nexus of yellow wrinkles around Miss Totten's lips. Poking out a bony forefinger, she held it against the muff. "You tell your mother," she said slowly, "that the way she spells it, it's *Juliet*."

Then she dismissed the rest of us but put a delaying hand on Mooley. Turning back to look, I saw that she had knelt down painfully, her skirt-hem graying in the floor dust, and staring absently over Mooley's head she was buttoning up the queerly shaped coat.

After a short, avid flurry of speculation we soon lost interest in Mooley, and in the routine Miss Totten devised for her. At first, during any kind of oral work, Mooley took her place at the blackboard and wrote down her answers, but later, Miss Totten sat her in the front row and gave her a small slate. She grew very quick at answering, particularly in "mental arithmetic" and in the card drills, when Miss Totten held up large Manila cards with significant locations and dates inscribed in her Palmer script, and we went down the rows, snapping back the answers.

Also, Mooley had acquired a protector in Ruby Green, the other Negro girl in the class—a huge, black girl with an arm-flailing, hee-haw way of talking and a rich, contralto singing voice which we had often heard in solo at Assembly. Ruby, boasting of her singing in night clubs on Saturday nights, of a father who had done time, cowed us all with these pungent inklings of the world on the other side of the dividing line of Amsterdam Avenue—that deep, velvet murk of Harlem which she lit for us with the flash of razors, the honky-tonk beat of the "numbahs," and the plangent wails of the mugged. Once, hearing David Hecker, a doctor's son, declare "Mooley has a cleft palate, that's what," Ruby wheeled and put a large hand on his shoulder, holding it there in menacing caress.

"She ain' got no cleff palate, see? She talk sometime, 'roun' home." She glared at us each in turn with such a pug-scowl that we flinched, thinking she was going to spit. Ruby giggled.

"She got no cause to talk, 'roun' here. She just don' need to bother." She lifted her hand from David, spinning him backward, and joined arms with the silent Mooley. "Me neither!" she added, and walked Mooley away, flinging back at us her gaudy, syncopated laugh.

Then one day, lolloping home after three, I suddenly remembered my books and tam, and above all my homework assignment, left in the pocket of my desk at school. I raced back there. The janitor, grumbling, unlocked the side door at which he had been sweeping and let me in. In the mauve, settling light the long maw of the gym held a rank, uneasy stillness. I walked up the spiral metal stairs feeling that I thieved on some part of the school's existence not intended for me. Outside the ambushed quiet of Miss Totten's room I stopped, gathering breath. Then I heard voices, one of them surely Miss Totten's dark, firm tones, the other no more than an arrested gurgle and pause.

I opened the door slowly. Miss Totten and Mooley raised their heads. It was odd, but although Miss Totten sat as usual at her desk, her hands clasped to one side of her hat, lunch-box, and the crinkly boa she wore all spring, and although Mooley was at her own desk in front of a spread copy of our thick reader, I felt the distinct, startled guilt of someone who interrupts an embrace.

"Yes?" said Miss Totten. Her eyes had the drugged look of eyes raised suddenly from close work. I fancied that she reddened slightly, like someone accused.

"I left my books."

Miss Totten nodded, and sat waiting. I walked down the row to my desk and bent over, fumbling for my things, my haunches awkward under the watchfulness behind me. At the door, with my arms full, I stopped, parroting the formula of dismissal.

"Good afternoon, Miss Totten."

A Wreath for Miss Totten

"Good afternoon."
I walked home slowly. Miss Totten, when I spoke to her, had seemed to be watching my mouth, almost with enmity. And in front of Mooley there had been no slate.

In class the next morning, as I collected the homework in my capacity as monitor, I lingered a minute at Mooley's desk, expecting some change, perhaps in her notice of me, but there was none. Her paper was the same as usual, written in a neat script quite legible in itself, but in a spidery backhand which just faintly silvered the page, like a communiqué issued out of necessity, but begrudged.

Once more I had a glimpse of Miss Totten and Mooley together, on a day when I had joined the slangy, athletic Miss Steele who was striding capably along in her Ground Grippers on the route I usually took home. Almost at once I had known I was unwelcome, but I trotted desperately in her wake, not knowing how to relieve her of my company. At last a stitch in my side forced me to stop, in front of a corner fishmongers'.

"Folks who want to walk home with me have to step on it!" said Miss Steele. She allotted me one measuring, stone-blue glance, and moved on.

Disposed on the bald white window-stall of the fish store there was a rigidly mounted eel which looked as if only its stuffing prevented it from growing onward, sinuously, from either impersonal end. Beside it were several tawny shells. A finger would have to avoid the spines on them before being able to touch their rosy, pursed throats. As the pain in my side lessened, I raised my head and saw my own face in the window, egg-shaped and sad. I turned away. Miss Totten and Mooley stood on the corner, their backs to me, waiting to cross. A trolley clanged by, then the street was clear, and Miss Totten, looking down, nodded gently into the black boa and took Mooley by the hand. As they passed down the hill to St. Nicholas Avenue and disappeared, Mooley's face, smoothed out and grave, seemed to me, enviably, like the serene, guided faces of the children I had seen walking securely under the restful duennaship of nuns.

Then came the first day of Visiting Week, during which, according to convention, the normal school day would be on display, but for which we had actually been fortified with rapid-fire recitations which were supposed to erupt from us in sequence, like the somer-saults which climax acrobatic acts. On this morning, just before we were called to order, Dr. Piatt, the principal, walked in. He was a gentle man, keeping to his office like a snail, and we had never succeeded in making a bogey of him, although we tried. Today he shepherded a group of mothers and two men, officiously dignified, all of whom he seated on some chairs up front at Miss Totten's left. Then he sat down too, looking upon us benignly, his head cocked a little to one side in a way he had, as if he hearkened to some unseen arbiter who whispered constantly to him of how bad children could be, but he benevolently, insistently, continued to disagree.

Miss Totten, alone among the teachers, was usually immune to visitors, but today she strode restlessly in front of us and as she pulled down the maps one of them slipped from her hand and snapped back up with a loud, flapping roar. Fumbling for the roll-book, she sat down and began to call the roll from it, something she usually did without looking at the book and favoring each of us, instead, with a warming nod.

"Arnold Ames?"

"Pres-unt!"

"Mary Bates?"

"Pres-unt!"

"Wanda Becovic?"

"Pres-unt!"

"Sidney Cohen?"

"Pres-unt!"

"L—Lilly Davis?"

It took us a minute to realize that Mooley had not raised her hand. A light, impatient groan rippled over the class. But Mooley, her face uplifted in a blank stare, was looking at Miss Totten. Miss Totten's own lips moved. There seemed to be a cord between her lips and Mooley's. Mooley's lips moved, opened.

"Pres-unt!" said Mooley.

The class caught its breath, then righted itself under the sweet, absent smile of the visitors. With flushed, lowered lids, but in a rich full voice, Miss Totten finished calling the roll. Then she rose and came forward with the Manila cards. Each time, she held up the name of a state and we answered with its capital city.

Pennsylvania.
"Harrisburg!" said Arnold Ames.
Illinois.
"Springfield!" said Mary Bates.
Arkansas.
"Little Rock!" said Wanda Becovic.
North Dakota.
"Bismarck!" said Sidney Cohen.
Idaho.
We were afraid to turn our heads.
"Buh . . . Boise!" said Mooley Davis.
After this, we could hardly wait for the turn to come around to
Mooley. When Miss Totten, using a pointer against the map, indi-
cated that Mooley was to "bound" the state of North Carolina, we
focused on one spot with such attention that the visitors, grinning
at each other, shook their heads at such zest. But Dr. Piatt was look-
ing straight at Miss Totten, his lips parted, his head no longer to
one side.

"N-north Cal . . . Callina." Just as the deaf gaze at the speaking, Mooley's eyes never left Miss Totten's. Her voice issued, burred
here, choked there, but unmistakably a voice. "Bounded by Virginia on the north . . . Tennessee on the west . . . South Callina on the south . . . and on the east . . . and on the east . . ."
She bent her head and gripped her desk with her hands. I gripped
my own desk, until I saw that she suffered only from the common
failing—she had only forgotten. She raised her head.

"And on the east," she said joyously, "and on the east by the
Atlannic Ocean."

Later that term Miss Totten died. She had been forty years in the
school system, we heard in the eulogy at Assembly. There was no
immediate family, and any of us who cared to might pay our respects at the chapel. After this, Mr. Moloney, who usually chose
Whispering for the dismissal march, played something slow and
thrumming which forced us to drag our feet until we reached the
door.

Of course none of us went to the chapel, nor did any of us bother
to wonder whether Mooley went. Probably she did not. For now
that the girl withdrawn for so long behind those rigidly empty eyes

161

had stepped forward into them, they flicked about quite normally, as captious as anyone's.

Once or twice in the days that followed we mentioned Miss Totten, but it was really death that we honored, clicking our tongues like our elders. Passing the umbrella-stand at home, I sometimes thought of Miss Totten, furled forever in her coffin. Then I forgot her too, along with the rest of the class. After all this was only reasonable in a class which had achieved Miss Steele.

But memory, after a time, dispenses its own emphasis, making a *feuilleton* of what we once thought most ponderable, laying its wreath on what we never thought to recall. In the country, the children stumble upon the griffin mask of the mangled pheasant, and they learn; they come upon the murderous love-knot of the mantis, and they surmise. But in the city, although no man looms very large against the sky, he is silhouetted all the more sharply against his fellows. And sometimes the children there, who know so little about the natural world, stumble still upon that unsolicited good which is perhaps only a dislocation in the insensitive rhythm of the natural world. And if they are lucky, memory holds it in waiting. For what they have stumbled upon is their own humanity—their aberration, and their glory. That must be why I find myself wanting to say aloud to someone: "I remember . . . a Miss Elizabeth Totten."

II

Time, Gentlemen!

&§ M Y F A T H E R, born in 1862, and old enough to be my grandfather when I entered the world a year after his marriage to a woman twenty-two years younger than he, was by birth therefore a late Victorian. By 1900 he had already been of an age to have emigrated long since from South to North, and to have acquired both a business successful enough to permit him to celebrate the Diamond Jubilee at his usual haunts of Mouquin's and Delmonico's, and a rheumatism fashionable enough to require recuperation at Mount Clemens Spa. But like so many youngest sons of those large families whose fortunes have either declined or not been built, he had from the first shown a precocious, Alger-like energy which—in his case combined with some of the bright fairy-tale luck that comes to the third sons in Grimm—was to keep him all his life younger in appearance and temperament than others of his span, pushing him constantly toward modernity, even while he dragged his feet, protesting. During the nineteen-twenties and thirties, when I knew him best, he was, at the very least, early Edwardian.

Since he was the youngest of a family so long-lived that he and his sisters and brothers, all close to seventy, still had their mother, and one so close-knit that all its branches lived within round-the-corner call of each other in Manhattan, I spent the indoor part of my childhood with old people—people old enough to regard my mother, in her thirties and forties, as a young person of promise who still owed them deference but might now and then be admitted to the family councils in a listening capacity. Her own fluttering efforts, either to freshen the décor of the anciently cluttered household she had married into, or to cling weakly to some of the habits of her contemporaries, were looked upon somewhat as the *art nouveau* bric-a-brac of an incoming bride might be regarded by the chatelaines of a manor house—with the tolerant knowledge that all this nonsense would eventually disappear.

Down at the bottom, a pebble at the roots of this banyan tree, was I, leading a curious double life, half of me in one century, the other half very nearly in the one preceding it. Once out of the house, on my way to school or in the long, spinning afternoons, I had the urchin street-freedom that descends upon the middle-class apartment-dweller's child at the age of seven or eight, when the nursemaid is passed on to the younger ones. As I whizzed around the block, one of a scabby-legged pack of skaters with two-wheelers clamped on their high brown shoes, or tore through forbidden cellars macaronied with steam pipes and elevator cables, leaving behind me shreds of plaid and a trail of bone underwear-buttons, I was as much a child of my sector of the new century as any other. Yet, once the brown metal, fireproof door of our apartment closed behind me and I stood listening in the foyer, whose dark air had a dried-olive smell from the books musting double-rowed on the shelves, and a black-leather tint from the davenport that gloomed in the shadows, I stepped, without ever questioning it, into another element, one not present in the home-worlds of my fellows.

Entering this element, the raw light of the new decade had to humble itself past towering cabinets, through bead-crowded, wood-carved space in order to glint on the round, gold-wired spectacles of elderly people as they sat endlessly over coffee that streamed like a continuous soothing syrup from the kitchen. From there the light had to cool itself against much marble and be strained through many yards of lace, before it might arrive, collected and plain once more, at the calm blue and white of my bedroom. Even then, it might have to rest resignedly on what someone had had the relentless patience to cut, sew and starch—my two weeks' supply of fourteen white organdy sashes.

The "element" itself, however, was composed of much more—of all the ways that people had found to carve intaglio from the smaller moments of their lives, and more significantly, of all the spaces in between, when they found nothing to do at all, and did not seem to notice or mind. Within it, all the violent temperaments in our family, the daily puppet-clashes and doge intrigues, lay swaddled in a fleece of security, where life might recompose itself in the thick texture of those novels whose undemanding dramas flamed at writing desks and petered out in morning rooms. This element was, of course, the Victorian sense of time.

Possibly the best way to describe how it worked, or rather—since there was no sense of anything working—how things were, would be to chronicle the daily phenomenon known in our household as "getting Father off." As a young man, my father had acquired a decorous old business that dealt wholesale in perfumes, soaps, complexion powders, essences and pomatums for the toilette, a trade of enough French frivolity to give his personality that tinge of the panache which it might not have had, had he dealt in staples. Since he was the owner, had long since placed the factory side under the supervision of one brother, the office under another, and had various cousins and brothers-in-law at a straggle of desks in between, he felt himself under no obligation to get downtown at any particular hour. Indeed, since he was a man of the most delicate family feelings and could not have borne to have any of his relatives think that he wished to lord it over them, it was probable that he preferred to schedule his arrival at the office at an hour late enough to keep him from ever knowing the hour of theirs.

My mother, however, although she had never been in the business world, had certain convictions about it which would have done her credit in a later era. She believed that a business run with such unpressurized ease, even enjoyment, must be well on its way to ruin, that one so nepotically staffed could survive only at the price of eternal vigilance, and that even if my father had managed to do very well for years before he met her, he now owed it to her self-respect, to his own Dun & Bradstreet rating, and to their joint children, to give at least the appearance of frenzied toil. She was a woman who would have felt much safer breathing hard and fast in the wake of one of those lunchless men whose race with their calendar ends only with death. And she was never to comprehend the real truth: that people loved to do business with my father because, in an already accelerating age, his dandified air of the coffeehouse, his relaxed and charmingly circuitous tongue—which dwelt much on anecdote but only lightly on orders or due dates—and above all, his trust in the "plenty" of time, made them feel participants in a commercial romance, gentlemen met by chance on the Rialto, who had decided to nurture a little affair.

But since she did *not* understand, each morning at home was a contest, a parable in which Conscientious Practicality, my mother, strove to get Imaginative Indolence, my father, out of the house somewhat nearer nine than noon. Imaginative always won, partly by refusing to notice the strategic lines of force sent out constantly, all morning, by Conscientious, and partly, as I came to believe, because Time itself, elsewhere being made to skip so violently, was coming to lean more and more sympathetically on my father's side.

I awake then, on a certain morning, almost any morning in the nineteen-twenties. Perhaps the milkman's clop-clopping horse has already been replaced by a rubber-tired van, but I hope not, since the horse's reflective, frequently interrupted pace is so much more suitable to what is going to follow. It is somewhere between six and seven o'clock back there; Josie, the maid, is still curled in her central cubicle in the angle of the long, wandering L that is our apartment; my grandmother sleeps, as she will for hours yet, in her separate wing; even my mother and my two-year-old brother, those disciples of *Achtung*, are still fast on their pillows.

But my father, strangely enough, as you might think, for a man who is always reassuring people that he and they have "all the time in the world," is already up and about, puttering in the kitchen for himself, as he loves to do. Not strange at all—he who is at home in Time rises with interest at the prospect of a new stretch of it; only its minions need to bury their heads. And if there is a little of the insomnia of the aging in his early habit, then it is never fretful, but spry and accepting, like a man who has been offered more food than he is hungry for, but will do what he can.

I get up too and go to the kitchen and we look at one another, each in our pajamas. And now a nice thing happens. He says nothing—no probing for the day's beginning or for me, as I re-form myself out of dream—but merely reaches behind him, fumbling in a collection of brown paper bags he brought home last night, brings out a blood orange, of the kind he knows fascinates me, and hands it to me. Were my mother here she would say, "Say Good Morning to Your Father, say Thank You!", not to me really, but to serve notice to the world that she is ready for her obligations, *en garde* for all the swordthrusts of the day.

But she is much younger than we are. Two of a kind, we enter the dining room without saying a word. He is carrying the pot of coffee he has made, a low thing for a man in his position to do, as we both know, and akin to the smelly kippers he will toast for breakfast if not watched, and to that itinerant hobnobbing in delicatessens which produces the brown paper bags.

Saturdays, when my mother returns in a flurry of delivery boys, her beaver toque askew over cheeks fretted rosy from her plundering of the shops, and exclaims, "Done for the week, for the entire week!" my father may reply mildly, "A cuisine should saunter, m'dear. From day to day." He is thinking then perhaps of his old housekeeper in New Orleans, who used to cuddle his pears in tissue paper and reverse his wine bottles of an evening; but he will say nothing, because of the cheese he hid and forgot, that my mother found last week, that waved in a blossom of maggots when she lifted the sweating, china dome—and because she believes that wine makes you drunk. It is difficult, he knows, for a woman to have married an old man so full of comparisons. But it is difficult too—although this he never says—to have married out of one's century.

Now, however, in this hour while the morning freshens at the window, and some of the lamps that are always left burning to chart our household through the night are still on, Time moves for him as it should, like treacle, or even, as in my child's world, not at all.

Then, all at once as it seems, the morning paper thumps outside the hall door, the veteran clock in the hall gives its strangled cluck for the half hour, Josie lets fly the flush handle in her bathroom with a bang that can be heard all over the house, the weakening lamps give up the ghost, my brother roars. My father gives me an untranslatable look that I understand perfectly. The century, this one, has spoken; the contest has begun.

Mrs. Huber, my brother's nurse, who is as much on my mother's side as Josie, if anywhere, can be said to be on ours, passes us, bottle in hand, on her way to the kitchen, giving us a starched, thermometric nod for the tacky pair we are.

"Run, stop the paper boy," my father says to me. "I want to pay him." He ambles after me, and I leave them deep in confab at the hall door. I return to the table, at which I find my mother, in her morning chain-mail of ribbon and lace. She wears a boudoir cap to match, shaped like an upside-down ruffled spittoon, but beneath it, her voice is edged with modernity.

"Whom can he have found to talk to already!" she says.

When my father returns he has some paper greenery that he tries to stuff into the nonexistent pants pocket of his pajamas. Tickets for the Irish Sweepstakes, it develops, that McDonough, the paper boy, has sold him. My mother sits still for a moment, then says in a stifled voice that of all the fifty heads of families in this building, it is probable that only my father has the time to learn the name of every mendicant who plies its halls, and hadn't he got a similar packet of tickets last week?—to which my father incautiously replies that the more coverage the better in any gamble. Gamble is one of the money words which produce a known response in my mother; when it does not come as usual I say it for her, since I have my own reasons for currying her favor this morning, and I know by heart all the public expressions of her private terrors.

"Everything going out," I say, "nothing coming in."

My father's reaction to this is such as requires her telling him not to encourage me, and her commanding me to dress at once, or else I shall be late for school.

"Nonsense!" he says, for secretly he resents the school for daring to impose temporal restrictions on any flesh of his flesh. "She has plenty of time." And such is my faith in his faith that, although he has thus made me late morning after morning, and I am consistently punished in the school world for being also a resident of his, it will be years before I am willing to admit that it was he who was out of step with them.

"What time is it?" says my mother, and in the same instant closes her eyes and puts the back of her hand against her capped brow. For there are at least eight running clocks in our house in addition to broken ones in drawers and antique ones with stopped faces— almost one for every room—and not one agrees with any other. And this is so not only in our house, but in the houses of all the uncles and aunts on my paternal side. They all have something in their blood that slows clocks, my mother claims, but this is not true, for one clock we have breaks into rowdy tarantellas in the night and must be forcibly calmed—it is more probable that they confuse them. I do not mind our eight—it gives one such a choice.

"Oh, do *you* have a headache *too*," I say quickly. At once my father's hand, dry with years, is at my forehead, as I knew it would be, feeling for temperature. I droop cooperatively and let him see that I, nicknamed "hungry Henrietta," have pushed aside my plate. Death is a word never spoken in our family, since there are so many of an age to expect it, but my father, who will thus deny his own mortality, is always hearing its dragon breath snuffing near the heads of his children, as if he fears that Providence will surely snatch from him early what he neglected to take from it until so late.

"Now, Joe," says my mother, "you know as well as I do that she will recover like magic as soon as it's safely ten o'clock!"

"Ah, now, now," he replies, his hand holding safe my cheek, "you know you'd never forgive yourself, if . . ."

My mother throws up her hands, and I see that this will not be one of the mornings when, enraged, she will threaten castor oil or the enema, or when, half convinced, she will suggest citrate of magnesia or Feenamint, or any other of those mild unspecifics she claps down us to warn the dark powers that she is aware. She gives me up, the better to concentrate on him. "Tailor came last night," she says. "He brought back your pearl-gray."

My father accepts the prod with grace, having won the first round, and goes off with a tuneless whistle, although he is not a whistling man. This means that even he does not believe me this morning. It is an expression also of his refusal to truckle to schools on principle, on the grounds that they are coarse instruments for the shaping of such quality material as he sends them. Above all, it means that his day has begun as a proper day should, easing itself so gently into the whorls of circumstance that it can scarcely be said to have moved, and with the first prerequisite of a Victorian household— with *everybody home*.

My mother has barely time enough to dress and to make one rapid round-trip through the apartment, setting higher the fires under everybody's caldron, and there he is back at the table—shaved, spatted, cologne on handkerchief, stickpin in lilac tie. And this provokes her most of all, that while his long view of life is so deliberate, he is not at all dilatory about its detail; it is hardly to be borne that of the thousands of trains he has had to make in his life he has, by not only the neatest but the calmest of margins, never missed one. Time is her enemy, and, she knows, the natural enemy of us all; it is not fair that my father's naïve trust in it works for him as pragmatically as some people's trust in God. She sits at table, thinking of the enviable tohu-bohu of shaving cuts and indigestion in which the other fifty fathers have long since whirled away, and wonders if this morning, just this morning, after the incontestable interval of the *Tribune* and the grapefruit, she might not be able to get him off with a couple of three-minute eggs.

"Fix you some calfs-brains, Misser Joe?" This is Josie, bearing the first cup of coffee, and one of the clocks has just struck ten. My mother flinches—calves' brains have to be poached, and after the poaching, breaded, and after the breading, fried.

"Mmmm," he says, "and with black butter, eh Josie? Black butter, not brown."

Another clock—sometimes they do their best to be helpful—strikes the hour, and my mother murmurs rapidly and bitterly of all the duties before her, including the fact that she must be off to the bank, to which my father says nothing, for he knows that she will not leave the house before him, although he does not know why. It is because she must protect his reputation, since he will not, and she considers it infinitely low-class for a woman to be seen up and abroad when her man is still lounging at home. Forgotten by them, I listen, incognito unless I turn healthy before noon. Nested in the shawls that have been mustered against disease, I mull over which of them is the aristocrat, which the low, over why it is so hard to love the worthy, so warming to be in the presence of one who will allow himself to be deceived. Above all, I wonder which of them is right about Time, not knowing that it is more than my mother and father who do battle here. Contra, contra I hear their dividing voices, as, with an Eurasian aching, I hear them yet.

The doorbell rings and now my father rises, eager, nostrils sniffing the true pursuit of the morning. For the second prerequisite for a Victorian household is that all morning long its doors, front and back, be applied to by processions of those who either bring special services or require them. Before noon we will have had, besides our regular shipment of eggs from coquettishly pastoral places with names like Robin Roost, of French Vichy from the drugstore, and panatela cigars from the little Spaniard in Harlem, also various but unvarying visits from upholsterers, dressmakers, opticians, even a bootlegger whose *ton*, like all the others, so remarkably suits us—a rococo little man, trapped like us, between two eras, who carries a cardcase and deals only in wine. In between come the variables, perhaps a former servant girl with her new baby, or a long-lost cousin with her old debts (both of them aware that petitions will not do as well in the afternoon, which is my mother's dominion), or perhaps an old-clothes man who does not yet know that we never ever sell anything off, we only buy. Even he is detained long enough to learn that he has one commodity for which my father will find some way to reward him—conversation.

"It's the Walker-Gordon man," my mother says, in triumph, and my father sits down. This is the man who delivers the special acidophilus milk for my brother, a routine meant to cease in the first month after birth but prolonged by my father so that the heir may have his traditions too. In other respects it has been a failure—the Walker-Gordon man will not stop to talk.

Providentially, Mrs. Huber enters to say that if my father wishes to pay his usual visit to the nursery, will he kindly do so at once, so that she may get her charge out in the sun "while it is high." As soon as he is gone, my mother puts on her hat, not that he will take the hint, but it makes her feel better, and besides, since there is no routine left to him now except his half hour's reading to my grandmother, and since this has been an exceptionally reasonable morning so far, it is just possible that, if no bells ring, she may get him off by eleven, which is at least a half hour better than par.

I am quite used to seeing her go about her housewifery for hours on end thus hatted; she was wearing one on that extraordinary day when, in a similar period of waiting, she suddenly lifted her petticoats, revealing to my pleased eye that although she had laughed at my yellow satin Christmas garters she sometimes wore them, took three steps back, and kicked the dining-room clock. There is red in her eye now as she looks in on me in passing, but she will kick no more clocks. The subsequent *sal volatile* and sweeping-up provided my father with an hour's valid delay, and the clock returned from repair "same like ever" just as the old watchmaker had promised, that is, running ten minutes later than the one in the hall.

But joy of joys, here he is and it is only eleven, and he has actually

already completed his devoirs to his mother, his matins to his son—
it must be the spring, ding-a-ding, for matters 'gin arise, time's on
the run, and father makes for the hatrack, on which his bowler lies.
. . . And two bells ring.

At the front door. At the back. And now there is no device of wit,
verb or cachinnation by which I can follow the final counterpoint of
my father, the *a cappella* exits and returns by which he halts, circles, hedges, rises to the high C of delay, and ultimately, coda, goes.

Let me try. The ring at the front door belongs to Mr. Krauss the
cabinetmaker, who comes to us once a month, to feed the furniture.
There is nothing *outré* about this; we have masses of elderly wood
and veneer that apartment-house heat withers, and Mr. Krauss
spends an earnest day feeding linseed oil and casauba to our parched
gargoyles, griffons and lion-footed tables, never troubled by any
fantasy that he might do as well by placing his supplies in the center
of the arena and quickly taking his leave. He is a tall, cavernous
German, full of Hegelian pauses through which occasionally climbs
one memorable phrase—the kind of old-fashioned workingman
whose society is always courted by urban men like my father. The
ring at the back door belongs to Cyril, one of the West Indian elevator boys, who can also talk Creole. He has come to borrow my
father's roulette wheel, and this I shall not bother to explain; if by
now it does not seem perfectly natural, there is no more to be done.
No, better to leave them at once, the three of them bogged there
forever, Cyril's winsome causerie on one side, Krauss's silence on the
other, and my father somewhere in between them, with his foot on
the stile.

He goes at last, of course, although I never seem to see him do it,
only hearing his parting, customary cry. It is his one mock-fierce
threat, one so gay, so mild, so aptly like him, yet its *frisson* always
travels up my spine as no threat of the cat-o'-nine-tails could. "Be a
good girl!" he always cries. "Else I'll throw you into the middle of
next week!"

Now my mother is left in her bevy of women, free to chivy us
back into her century. As dusk advances, her siege of him will be
renewed by telephone, and pointed the other way, toward us, as she
begins to doubt that he will ever again come in the door she was at
such pains to get him out of; for an office where there is plenty of

time is just as hard to leave, and all the way up the avenue from the subway station there are cracker-barrels which know Mr. Joe. Now, however, she rests. One more morning has passed without realizing her worst fear—that the dreadful, shiftless day will come when he will still be there for lunch.

But he comes, and evening with him, and all his clan gathered to him from block and cranny, and then his star rises to its full. For in the end he draws us all back with him into his calm antipodes. Supper-talk is slowed, appetites dreamy, now may our griffons protect us, our curtains swaddle. Even my mother has stopped her White Queen running and sinks in her chair, a little muzzy with life, as at those times when she can be persuaded to a single glass of ruby claret. I fall asleep on the davenport, smelling its ageless, mummy leather, hearing the murmur of the elders. The last thing I see is my father, his eyes sweet with triumph. The vital threads of existence are blending, yet endless, the furniture is fed. We are all together with him in the now, rocking in the upholstered moment, in the fur-lined teacup of Time. The lamps are lit for the night, against that death which is change. And tomorrow, *da capo*, it is all to do over again.

And now I am awake on another night, tonight. Thirty years have gone by, and I no longer hear the murmuring of the elders. All around me, as I slept back there, my own century was coming to the fore. Flappers, streaking by me in Stutzes and Auburns, were already disappearing over the edge of their era; each day the stock market climbed like the horses of Apollo, yet at nightfall had not come down. Later would come the false stillness of the thirties when hands hung heavy; then, with a proletarian clanking of machinery we would be off again, into a war, into the self-induced palpitations of the forties, as, pit-a-pat, pit-a-pat, we changed matter into light, outdistanced sound, and came roaring out upon the strait turnpike of the fifties in our new pink cars.

And now there is nothing left to outdistance, except Time. I am awake wherever I am; is it on the rim of the world, the lip of the Time-machine? All around me there is a cold, sublunary glare, the sourceless light of science fiction, that greens the skin, divorces cell from cell.

I know where I am now. If there are any gods in this place I must pray to them, as once one could to the comfortable old evils of Ra or Baal. I must pray to s-s-s, or b-oom. For this place is the middle of next week.

Then, from over the rim of the world, I hear voices, the dividing voices.

"Run! Run!" says my mother. "Can't you run a little faster!"

And then I hear my father's voice, Rhadamanthine, serene.

"You have time," says my father. "All the time in the world."

And from the pinpoint where I stand, I can see it, the old place, lit up bravely as a fish bowl against the dark shadows of eternity, moving slowly while it persuades itself that it stands still—the whole improbable shebang, falling through the clear ether silently, with all its house lights on.

May-ry

~§ M Y F A T H E R , born in Richmond about the time Grant
took it, was a Southerner therefore, but a very kind man. All of us—
children of his sixties, with abolitionist consciences—knew that. The
limits of his malice extended to flies, and to people who hit children
or mistreated the helpless anywhere. His pocket was always to be
picked by any applicant, and no matter how many times my mother,
much more of a grenadier, pointed out where they did him in, he
remained the softest touch in the world.

His manners were persistently tender to everyone, and perhaps
because he looked and dressed somewhat like Mark Twain and
shared a small, redeeming slice of Twain's humor, nobody ever
seemed to find this saccharine. He was, for instance, the only person
I ever knew who could chuck a carriage baby under its chin and goo
at it—"Coo-chee-coo!"—without making anybody gag at the sight,
or doubt for one minute that it was done out of pure spontaneity
and love. Yes, he was the kindest man in the world. Yet, when the
time came, it was my father who was purely unkind to our colored
maid Mary—May-ry.

May-ry, who must have been about thirty at the time I speak of,
was no old family retainer; she had come to work for us, her first job
in New York, through an ad in the *Times* ten years back, when I
was very little. Even then, our family had already been forty years
away from the South. But my father's memories of the first twenty
years of his youth there were deep and final. At bedtime he would
often tell us of Awnt Nell, the mammy who had brought him up,
although he never mentioned her in public—"too many Southern
colonels around already." Awnt Nell had been a freedwoman; even
before the War our grandmother, his mother, would never have

servants of any other description. He was so firmly proud of this that when I found, flattened away in the old Richmond Bible, a receipt made out to my grandfather for insurance on a slave, I slipped it back and never taxed him with it.

In any case, all that our tradition had boiled down to was my father's insistence that my mother always keep colored help. This was hard on her, since, being German, she could never quite manage or understand them. She had an inflexibly either-or attitude toward trust, plus a certain jealousy of other people's hardships, that made her stiff with those who had more of them. Also, without any reason to be, she was always a bit afraid of May-ry, referring to her whenever she could as "Die Schwarze." My father did not like this, and often caught her up on it. And nobody, at any time, ever said "nigger" in our house.

Meanwhile, May-ry and my father kept up their special allegiances. There were of course a thousand ways in which he knew the life she had come from, and she "knew" us. Whenever he would be heard embarking on one of the ritually flamboyant regional anecdotes that my mother couldn't bear, May-ry usually was to be seen edging closer to the company, only as decorous as a uniform could make her, her mouth drawn out like a tulip ready to burst at the familiar denouement—which brought shriek after shriek of her released laughter, followed, under my mother's glance, by a quick retirement. But she and my father also shared more particular sympathy, or professed to, over the rheumatism. As a young man, he had had to take an eighteen-week cure for his at Mount Clemens Spa, and like many diseases contracted early, it had kept him youthful, healthy, and appreciated; on a dull day a loud twinge of it would suddenly announce itself to the house—and to his best audience.

May-ry's rheumatism was of another sort. It was her euphemism for the fact that, periodically, she drank. Whenever she felt a long attack coming on, about every four months or so, she always absented herself from our house on a short trip to Roanoke, where she could lay up in the sun a little. We all were aware of the probable truth—that she was holing up in Harlem with one or the other of the people she had originally come up here with in the wake of the preacher who had brought them all North together. My father knew she drank, and she knew that he knew, but the fiction of

Roanoke was always maintained. She was a child—and he loved all children. Just so long as she kept herself seemly in front of him (and she never did anything else), she was only doing what was expected of her, and he the same. "What you recommend I do for *my* rheumatiz, May-ry?" he might sometimes tease, but this was as far as he ever went.

Once a year, on her paid vacation, May-ry did go to Roanoke. We knew this because just before she was due back, a case of jars of home-canned peaches always arrived. She liked to use them during the year and tell us something about the farm as each jar was opened; these were her anecdotes, and I knew all of the characters in them, from Mooma and Daddy Gobbo down to the cow that always stood with its head over the gate, like a cow in a primer. On rheumatism vacations no jars ever came; only, of a sudden, there would be May-ry back again, scrubbing at the moldings as if these had to be whitened like her sins, cooking up for my father everything she could sink in the brown butter he adored. Between these times, once in a while she failed to come back from her Thursday night off until Monday; when she returned, it would not be she who had been sick, but one of the friends "over on One Hundred Twenny-ninth Street." But someone else there always had to phone for her, so we knew. On these occasions my mother would be furious. She wanted a German girl whose docile allegiance would be to her, whose ins and outs she would know the way my father knew May-ry's. Patiently, he would explain these to her. "They're children, that's all. They can't stand up to us. Never have been able to. Never will. But if you just give them their head a little, they're the best servants in the world. And the loyalest."

Then came Somus. May-ry had always been allowed to entertain her many suitors, evenings and Sundays if she wished, in our kitchen, Father sometimes stopping in to chat with them, to let them know on what terms they were welcome, to have a little Southern cracker-barrel time—and to see that they were the right sort for May-ry. With Somus, this all vanished. Somus was the son of that same preacher of the Abyssinian Church of God who had brought May-ry up here, and he was the real reason (besides us, she said) why she had never married; she'd been in love with him, hopelessly until now, ever since they'd spatted mud pies together down home. Somus had quarreled with his own father almost from the moment they all came up here and had been away studying for a long time. Now he was here to take his civil-service examinations.

Somus turned out to be just as handsome as she'd said he was. Rebel from the church he might be, but I could never see him, black in his black suit, without thinking Biblically, things like "the ram of God" and "His nose is as the tower of Lebanon that looketh forth toward Damascus." There was not an inch of ornament upon him, beyond the strict ivory of his teeth, the white glare of his eye. Not that I saw much of him. When Somus took May-ry out, he did just that, took her *out*, never sat in our kitchen or ate in it; later on we knew that she'd had a bad time getting him to ring at the back door.

Somus. Why he loved May-ry was not hard to tell, quite apart from the fact that she too was handsome, with a shapely mouth, a sweet breadth of brow and eye. She drank—and he didn't approve of that. She dressed high and loud, not even in the New York way but in the bandanna bush colors that antedated Roanoke—and he was forever trying to get her to imitate that sister of his who wore navy blue with round organdy collars. She liked to dance at the Club Savoy—and it pained Somus to find himself still that good at it. Worst of all, she was the staunchest and most literal of Bible beaters, and to an emancipated man, this opium of his people must have been as the devil. So, all told, love between them was fore-ordained.

She adored him, of course. He was just like his father, strong, dour, and, like many ministers' sons before him, with the genes of faith coming up in him just as hot and strong in other ways—in the very form of his unbelief.

I remember just when the trouble came. It could have been the red spring dress that sparked it. "Kah-whew!" I said, when she showed it to me. It was almost purple, and still trying. "Never get to heaven in that!" Heaven was a great topic between us. "Besides, it'll run."

"Sho' will." She stuck out her chin, pushing her smile almost up to her nose, her nostrils taking deep draughts of the dress, as if it, all by itself, were perfume. "And me with it. All the way."

"May-ry, tell us about heaven." It was a dull day.

May-ry

Always willing, she answered me, explicit as if it were Roanoke, as if we had just opened the largest peach jar of all. It was a nice fleshly style of heaven but not rowdy; a touch of the Savoy maybe, but enough pasture for the cow. Triumphant, in the red dress, she entered it.

"Where's Somus? Isn't he there? Where he gonna be?" In these exchanges, exactly like my father, I used to fall into her language.

She cast her head down, furred up her brows under a forehead as smooth as a melon. "He be there," she said after a while, in a low voice. Pushing out her chin again, she asserted it. "You just wait and see. He be!" And in the same moment she whirled around and caught me at the icebox, my hand in the evening dessert. Washing my hand at the tap, she warned me, "You go on like you been doing, you gonna come to no good end."

"If I do—how'm I gonna be up *there*, to see *him!*" She and I loved to crow at each other that way, to cap each other's smart remarks, in the silly sequiturs of childhood. But this day, something else teased at me to tease her. It wasn't my own unbelief; that had already been around for some time. But in other ways I could feel how I was going on, and I didn't like it either. I was growing out of my childhood. Maybe, like somebody else, I envied her the perfection of hers.

"Listen, May-ry," I said, squinting. "Suppose . . . when you get there . . . it isn't at all like you said it was. Suppose they don't let you sashay around in any red dress—suppose they just hump you over your Bible in a plain old white one. No music either, except maybe a harp. Oh, May-ry—what the Sam Hill you gonna do if they give you a harp?"

Once more, she considered. The dignity with which she mulled my cheap dialectic already smote me. She raised up and looked at me. "Then I *wears* my white dress, and I *plays* my harp," she said, her lip trembling, "and I praises the Lord God."

I ran and kissed her. "You'll look beautiful, I bet. You'll look pyorely beautiful, pretty as pie."

"You hush," she said, sharp and starched. "Stop that talking like a nigger, you hear?" Yes, I forgot to mention that. She was the only one who ever said it in our house.

The next night, Thursday, Somus came to call for her. I was

peeping, to see her in the dress, and that was the last time I saw him. Ram of God again, height six cubits and a span. May-ry looked beautiful. But in about an hour she came back alone, then went out again. I was the only one who saw her. We had the phone call the next morning, one of the several voices never identified but familiar. May-ry's Mooma was taken bad. May-ry was already on her way down there.

The Saturday afternoon she returned, nine days later, my mother was out, as May-ry had known she would be. I heard May-ry's voice, talking low to my father, in the parlor. Usually the sight of the place, left to the mercies of the day cleaners from the agencies, would enrage her at once, emboldening her enough to fling off her good clothes for her cleaning smock, bind up her hair, and set to work, meeting no one's eye and loudly scolding the air. But this time, I could see by peeping that she was sitting in the stiffest chair and had not even removed her gloves.

"No, Mr. Joe," she was saying, nervously holding on to her pocket-book. "No, suh—no." No. She had to leave us. Somus say he wouldn't marry her unless she did.

I heard my father "remonstrate" with her, as he always called it. This meant that he was using the same comfort voice that he used on us when delegated by Mother to punish us, the voice with which he helped us toward the first stage of being good again, by mending the amour-propre that we ourselves had injured in being bad.

It was all right, he was saying. Why, it was going to be all right! Whoever expected a girl like her to stay single? Especially when she was being spoken for by a fine boy like Somus. But what was all the fuss about? Mustn't she know that all along we had expected it— that some day or other she was going to want to get married and live out? He put his hands on his spread knees and leaned back, shaking his speckled ruff of hair at her. "Lord, what you women won't do to get a little torment." This too was part of the comfort, to put the offense as quickly as possible in the realm of human nature.

She didn't answer him, although she opened and closed her mouth several times.

"I see," he said after a while, biting at his mustache, "Somus doesn't want you to work at all."

Oh nossuh, it wasn't that. She was able to say this clearly; then she fell to mumbling, her head all the way down. Then she was silent again. He had a hard time getting it out of her. It wasn't that, she said at last. She and Somus would surely have to count on her doing day work. But Somus say what the use of her being up North if she work for *home* folks? Somus say she won't really *be* up North until she stop working for people from home.

And now my father really was nonplussed at first, then angry enough to stomp around the room. "Why, good God in heaven, girl!" (This was just what he always said to me at such times.) What in the name of the Lord had got her into such monkeyshines? Was she going to let that boy sell her down the river? Who was going to treat her better than us—not to mention pay! Didn't she know right well, from talking to the other maids on the roof when she hung out the washing, how some people treated colored folks up here?

Yes, she knew. She said it in a voice like the Victrola's when something was wrong with its insides, her head hanging down. She didn't expect to be as well off, she said. And she would never forget his kindness—us. But Somus.

So, at last, my father played trumps.

He was standing over her by this time, looking down. "Day job or not, you're going to want some kind of steady *family* people, aren't you?" He said "ain't you" really, or close to it. "Don't tell me he wants to make you into one of those pitiful agency creatures working from dawn to dusk, getting somebody else's piled-up dirt every day!"

No suh. For the first time, she looked at the moldings.

"Then—" he said, and hesitated. "Now then, May-ry—" His voice dropped to a conspirator's. He rubbed the red spot left on his nose by his pince-nez, as always when he was embarrassed. "Now then, May-ry, what about . . . what about Roanoke? You know you got to go there, times you get laid up. You know right well not everybody going to give you the time off we do."

Yes, Mr. Joe. She whispered it. And this was the point at which she stood up, stopped her hands from their fooling with each other, and looked straight ahead of her, as if she were going to speak a piece, or were attending a wedding. "Somus say I got to have that out with you too." She spoke quietly, but she could not look at him.

"I never did go there but once a year, on my vacation. And you all knowed it."

He actually put up a hand to ward her off. "Now, now, don't you go and say anything foolish, girl. No need to do what you might regret later on."

"It's true," she said. Even her accent had shifted, hardening toward something like Somus's—who, by some steady effort, had almost none. "I get drunk." Then she turned gray, and started to shiver.

My father stepped back, and he too changed color. It was almost as if she had touched him.

Then a most peculiar scene took place. My father positively refused to consider, to treat, to discuss, to *tolerate* a hint of what she wanted to tell him and he knew as well as she did. That she'd been lying all these years and wanted the dear privilege of saying so. And she followed him around the room in circles after him, snuffling her "Mr. Joe" at him, all the time growing more halfhearted, confused —ever so often looking over her shoulder to see if Somus, that tower of strength, mightn't have appeared there. But he hadn't. He'd told her what she must do, and left her to it. He was a stern man, Somus, and a smart one—and he understood my father right down to the ground.

Finally, she stopped in the middle of the room and screamed it, exactly like a baby repudiating the universe, her face all maw. "I never was down there but once a year, and you know it. I was getting drunk over on One Hun' Twenny-ninth Street. And you know it, and you know it." Rocking back and forth, she beat her foot on the ground. "I'm going there now. And I'm not coming back." But by this time she was crying like a baby too.

When my father took her to the back elevator, she was still weeping. "Now, now, we'll just forget everything you said," he said. "We'll just forget this whole afternoon. Why, getting married is a serious thing, girl—no wonder you all upset." His voice took on the dreaminess with which he told us our goodnights. "Hush now, hush. You just have yourself a good rest down there in Roanoke." By the time he rang the bell for her, she was already nodding.

When the elevator door opened, she turned back to him. "I'd

ruther . . . ruther—" But then she choked up again, and we never did hear what.

"Hush now," he said, patting her into the elevator. "And when you come back . . . it'll be just like always, hear? Meantime, you send us up some of those peach jars." As the door closed, she was still nodding.

In the succeeding weeks, my mother and father kept a bet on. "You'll see," he'd say, even after the time had long since stretched beyond what May-ry had ever been away before. "She'll have her jobs—and she'll lose them. Nobody up here's going to appreciate enough what she does do—and what she can't. And she knows it, she knows it." It was almost as if he were echoing May-ry, in a way. Other times, he just worried it aloud. He loved taking care of people. "Who's going to take care of her like us?"

Then, one morning, the box of jars came—the herald. But when the box was opened, the jars were found to be of grape— grape conserve. Now, grapes were all over the shops right here, at the time—it was October. "Idiots," said my father. "What was the address on the outer wrapping?" But it had already gone down the dumb-waiter with the trash. I think my mother knew, but she never said. She was never much for children really. Except for my father. And after that, as more weeks went by and we began the endless series of German "girls" whom I never quite liked or my father either, he submitted, and spoke no more of colored help, or of May'ry. My mother had won, it appeared—and Somus.

But I still yearned sometimes, and wondered. *Did* she go back to Roanoke? I tried hard as I could to recollect whether there had ever been talk of grape arbors on Fox Road in Roanoke—in the tales that had come out of the peach jars. There had been damson, I knew, and elderberry. Damson too sour for you folks, and all the berries goes to the wine. Had she ever said there were grapes? I couldn't remember, though every now and again for years I tried. Had she sent them from there, or from Harlem? I knew well enough what the box meant, though, same as my father had. It meant pure spontaneity, and love.

Later on, years later when I was teaching in college, there was a girl who looked so much like May-ry—her eyes and that brow—that

I had all I could do not to go up and speak to her, ask her who was her mother. Of course I couldn't. How could I be sure, these days, of terms that would be pleasing to her? Besides, I never knew May-ry's last name—or Somus's. That was the way it was, in those days. So I'll never know for sure whether Somus did marry May-ry and she got emancipated, at least enough to work for Northerners, and send that girl on to college. Or whether, by now, she's only been emancipated as far as heaven. If so, I hope she has the dress she wants, and maybe even a little snifter after dinner—and I'm purely sorry I ever was mean enough to insinuate that heaven might be anything else. People should be able to get freed without having to be perfect for it beforehand. Maybe even Somus knows that now. I'm even big-hearted enough to hope that he's with her, either here or there, and has been all along. She'd never be happy without him, so he must be. For if anything had gone wrong, she'd always know whom to come to. And it's been a long time. It's been thirty years now, and she hasn't come back yet.

The Coreopsis Kid

✺§ O n a n afternoon late in the Indian summer of 1918, on the lawn of the house from which the Elkin family was returning to the city the next day, a garden party was ending, and the talk there was all of the war, which was ending too. But inside the house—in a room called the "music" room because it held chairs in which no one could settle, a piano on which no one played, and a broken guitar slanted in a corner like a stricken figure—the Elkin child, Hester, lay on the floor, wishing that the war would never end and that a little old couple called the Katzes had never come to the party at all.

Outside, in the pink, operatic light, all the town guests, most of them Mr. Elkin's elderly retainers, had just gone, looking almost rakish out of their city serge, in the foulards, pongees, and sere straws they had thought proper to the occasion. Her father, who was the head of the family and of the business which supported it, attracted retainers—as her mother often said—as if he were royalty. Even when they were no kin and useless to the point of impossibility, like old Mr. Katz, they swam knowingly toward him out of the sea of incompetents, and he kept them on, out of sympathy, some vanity, and an utter lack of the executive violence necessary to have off with their heads.

Today, all of them had eaten greedily of cakes whose scarce ingredients had been so happily procured, had partaken reverently of Mr. Elkin's claret—meanwhile chattering thinly of what the end of the war boom might do to such claret-consuming incomes as the one which maintained them—and ancient relatives whom Hester had never before seen out of chairs had sat daringly on the grass. Toward the end of the party, Mr. Katz (thought of by Hester as her Mr.

Katz), who had drunk no claret, had nevertheless been found sitting on the grass too, dazedly preoccupied in wrapping remnants of cake and ice cream, plates and all, in some napkins and a length of string, yards of which projected from a ball in his pants pocket and coiled fecklessly in his lap. He and his wife had just gone, gathered up and reassembled by Miss Lil, Mr. Elkin's forelady, a tall old woman with dead-black hair and a face like a white Jordan almond, who had shepherded them into a taxi, flapped her draperies officiously over their humbled, retreating backs, and climbed in after them with a great show of agility, as one whose competence age had not affected.

Outside the window now, Hester's mother and Mr. Elkin's sisters, Aunt Mamie and Aunt Flora, clinked and murmured over retrospective cups of coffee. The aunts, as per custom, had come out from the city the night before, to "help" in their peculiar way—Flora to check interminably on Mrs. Elkin: "What you have to pay for this chicken, your butter, these berries, Hattie?" and to cap each of her sister-in-law's responses with some triumphantly cawed instance of her own shrewdness in such matters. Mamie would clog the air with vague recipes out of their Southern girlhood, recipes which she seemed to think had an extra and regional delicacy either because these scorned Yankee exactitude for "a pinch" of this and "a piece the size of a walnut" of that, or had some little trick she could never quite recall—"a wild geranium leaf, I think it was"—or had no pertinence whatever to the occasion at hand—like okra soup, when the question was afternoon tea. In addition, both had to squelch any assumption on the part of the maid that they might be poor relations, and this they did by handily assuming any of Mrs. Elkin's duties which were merely verbal, and by their keenly critical acceptance of service at one magpie sit-down snack after another.

"Good coffee," said Flora.

"The last of the Mocha Joe got from his importer friend," said Hester's mother. It was in the nature of things that Flora's remark was tinctured with disapproval, and Mrs. Elkin's with a hint of scarcities to come.

"I mustn't eat another thing," added her mother. "Kozak says I'm not to gain another ounce beforehand. Did you know—I ate a pound and a half of Seckel pears the night before Hester was born!"

"No wonder she's so greenish," said Mamie's pecking voice.

"I know, I know," said her mother. "The summer hasn't done a thing for her. Autointoxication, Kozak says. He thinks I ought to put her on a farm, let her get built up. I thought maybe next spring, when the time comes. Or afterwards."

Hester inched closer to the window. The family had made the transition from Manhattan to White Plains very late this summer, because of that ailing of Mrs. Elkin's which Hester knew to be connected with the impending birth of a baby. She had guessed this, just as she had long ago concluded that what her parents really wanted, and what they must have wanted her to be, was a boy. To the aunts, and Mr. Elkin's brothers, all girls had been born. At fifty, Mr. Elkin had produced Hester, last in a line of six girl first cousins, the other five of whom— Isabelle, Lucille, Jessamine, Gertrude, and Caroline—were sitting in their own group on the lawn now. All of these were flamboyantly handsome young women, to whom the nine-year-old Hester had never once been likened except, ruefully, in the matter of sex. If the women in her family (as, possibly, in the world) seemed to be of peculiarly dominant natures, it might be because they must never admit to a value somewhat lowered because there were so many of them.

"I've set my foot down with Joe," said Mrs. Elkin. A cup rang decisively in a saucer. "We're not going to take on this place another summer, with the war ending, and nobody knowing what business will do. Now he's even talking about a trained nurse, instead of a practical. When we should be cutting down—all along the line."

"My brother's extravagances are never for himself," said Flora.

"No," said Mrs. Elkin. "No, *indeed*."

"The way he lets people run on at the factory!" Mamie put in hastily. "A place that size, without a proper chemist! But he lets that Lil, who I remember when she was nothing but the head girl . . . and now she won't even tell Joe himself the formulas!"

Oakley and Company, as Mr. Elkin's business was known, were wholesale purveyors of finely milled hand soaps, individually wrapped in paper printed with testimonials so genteel, so familiar to the devoted users, and in such fine type, that these were rarely read. In addition they had several lines of talcums and toilet water —old-fashioned essences of lilac, rose, coreopsis, lily of the valley, and violet, favored mostly by that trade which had once been carriage: gentlemen whose tastes had retired with their incomes, and *grandes dames* living in rooms already overheated with the floral essence of the past. As for the company itself—much of its staff was as old as its clientele.

"And Katz!" said Flora. "My God, Hattie, isn't Joe going to do something about Katz? It's a wonder the firm isn't a laughingstock to the trade!"

"I keep telling him," said Mrs. Elkin. "I had it out with him that awful day we came down here."

That day, the trip had been made, as usual, in a touring car hired with driver for the occasion, and as usual it had been a caravan of hampers, floating motor veils, and hindsight ejaculations. At the last minute, the two aunts had arrived uninvited, with a bland coincidence that had overreached itself in their already having donned veils. At that minute which inevitably followed the very last one, "old man Katz," the messenger boy attached to Mr. Elkin's office, had arrived with a folder of money, checks, and notes that he seemed unwilling to surrender, standing there with an amnesia to which he was subject at times so apparent on his bewildered, age-spotted face that they had been afraid to leave him there on the street, and had wedged him in, too. Hester, squeezed in next to him for the long ride, sneaking looks at his shaky, almost luminous hands with the blue veins and the brown cemetery spots, had felt that he and she were kin. He and she were the worthless people, whom the practical people could not forever afford.

With her father, she and Katz were safe. Mr. Elkin, when pressed for an indulgence, might counter, "Money doesn't grow on trees, daughter!" but this was a joke promptly nullified by the indulgence itself, provoking only a delightful image of a tree from which, in ropes and ribbons and spangles, money did somehow hang. But from her mother's arpeggios of background complaint came another portent, tied to the lurking references to the baby, and focused not so much on living expenses as on the particular objects of Mr. Elkin's headstrong altruism—of which Hester felt herself to be one. For with her father, one had only to be. But with Mrs. Elkin, some businesslike reason for being was expected. With her there was a status to be earned, either by a displayable beauty, like that of those cousins to whom Hester was never compared, or by some competence, of which, in company with Katz, Hester had only the lack. Lately, the predicted end of the war and the arrival of the baby had joined in Hester's mind as the probable end of a halcyon time, after which expenses like herself and Katz, unless they could justify themselves in the meantime, might not be rescuable, even by her father, from her mother's measurement of worth. All that uneasy summer she had listened with concern to the fluctuating dinner-table destiny of Katz, appraising it silently, feeling that it involved her own.

Today though, at the party's beginning, Mrs. Elkin had sat in its midst in a peaceful mood that had thickened upon her of late, letting others do the bothering, with a *laissez faire* that was for her, and for them all, the ultimate extravagance. With the most lavish, reassuring touch of all—she had invited Mr. and Mrs. Katz.

Therefore, when Mr. and Mrs. Katz had trotted up the path this afternoon, it had at first seemed an augury of the best for them and Hester also, for expendables everywhere. For, judged by the least worldly of standards, the market value of the Katzes must be doubtful indeed. With matching white wool hair, stunted twin statures of something under five feet each, and flat, cartilaginous faces nodding, blanched and puzzled, over their hard Sunday black, they looked like two elderly lambs, somewhere between full size and mantelpiece. Lambs, moreover, between whom there must be a preliminary agreement that Mr. Katz was to do the gamboling for the family, and Mrs. Katz the baaing. While Mr. Katz, whisking back and forth between the guests, his hands tremulous with cake plates and cups, seemed determined to prove that his rickety legs and understanding were still capable of infinite errands, Mrs. Katz plodded from the edge of one group to another, looking up at the faces of the conversationalists until she caught a declarative sentence, which she would thereupon confirm with a loud, assenting "Annnnh!" Watching them, Hester thought it cheering that two of such small wit had not only found each other, but managed to grow old. Later, watching her mother, as Mr. Katz was uncoiled from his string, wiped, and sped on his way, she had seen that her mother had not been cheered.

Now she stretched out an arm and scuffed the strings of the guitar, which let out a plangent sigh.

"Hester! Come out in the open air!"

191

Outside, clouds of motes gyrated in the lustrous, Indian heat. Her mother bent again over her embroidery hoop. Aunt Mamie was crocheting in nervous jerks, and Aunt Flora was stringing the bronze beads and jet passementerie with which she would later adorn her front. Near them, in a circlet of their own, the five cousins were doing no fancywork, but such was the twiddling of curls by ringed fingers, the fluttering of chiffon kerchiefs drooped from airy wrists, that one had almost an impression that they were.

Behind the casement Hester stuck out a wrist and shook it, but the effect was not the same. She picked up the guitar, hugging it to her like a doll, and walked outside. Standing near the older women, she listened to the ripple of the cousins, the stirred flounces, the round-robin lilt of "the Casino," "the Island," "the Turkey Trot," that went from velvety head to head of those five who so resembled one another in their dark-fanned eyes, fair necks, and cheeks that curved with rose.

"Will you look at that hem line," said her mother. "Half up from her knees again!" Hester sat down, looking at herself. One was to be built up, yet one's hem lines were to stay the same. There was no pleasing them—the practical ones. Yet they had to be pleased.

She looked over at the cousins. They are a wreath, she thought. They are like a rosy wreath. They were as closed to her as if they had locked hands against her, meanwhile interchanging the soft passwords of their pet names—Belle, Cile, Jessy, Trudy, Lina.

"Mother," she said. "Why don't I have a nickname? Why don't I?"

Her mother's needle speared a French knot. "Oh—I don't know." She held her work critically at arm's length. "Daddy and I are just not a nickname family, maybe."

"Nicknames come natural," said Aunt Flora. "Drink more milk. Maybe one'll float up." She looked over at her Belle, her mouth smug.

Hester took a breath. "When the baby comes—will Daddy keep Mr. Katz?"

"Why, whatever put . . . ?" Her mother glanced at the aunts, who looked down in their laps. "Why, that has nothing to. . . ." Mrs. Elkin expelled her breath in a chiding sigh, as if at some unknown transgressor. "There's a limit to what one can do for some people. Sometimes it isn't even a kindness to do it." Reddened, she stared at Hester, with severity, as if some of the unseen offender's guilt had rubbed off on her.

Hester stood up. At the far end of the lawn, her father and the uncles were talking business, ratifying their words with large, blue puffs from their long cigars. She walked toward them.

"What do you know!" said her mother behind her.

"Out of the mouths!" said Mamie. "Out of the mouths."

Hester sat down on the grass near her father's chair. He was lighting a fresh cigar, and absently passed her the band. "Coronas!" her mother had said this morning, watching her father carefully slit a brown box. "Nothing too good for them, I suppose. Coronas!" But during the week her father smoked Garcia Vegas. "Here's a quarter, Hester. Run down and get me three Garcia Vegas."

Bending over, she saw her face in the shiny guitar, sallow, shuttered, and long. It must lack some endearing lineament, against which people and language might cuddle. For it, a nickname was a status to be earned. Leaning against her father's chair, she fell asleep, rocking the guitar. Sometimes, in her doze, it was Mr. Katz she rocked, sometimes it was herself.

During the next days, after the Elkins' return to the city, all New York seemed brimming with more than the autumn season. At school assemblies, teachers rehearsed "The Red Cross Nurse," "There's a Long, Long Trail A-Winding," "In Flanders Field," with a zest that lilted through and contravened even the saddest days. During the day, street corners knotted up with chattering crowds, and at night, Hester, dreaming uneasily of farms, was awakened by the sound of windows upflung to the halloos of newsboys who ran below with indistinct, curdled wails.

On the morning of the Armistice, racing home from school declared off for the day, she was certain that this morning, in her absence, the baby must have been born, too. Her mother however was there as usual in toque and wide, shapeless coat edged in martin, waiting for Hester to eat her creamed carrots and change into her pink crepe. It was dancing-school day, and they were to go, though, because of traffic and people already shoaling the streets, they were to leave early and take a cab.

They were an hour getting to the place, normally a short ride away, for not only were cars and buses creeping bumper to bumper, but people trailed heedlessly between them, poking their grin-split faces into cars, swarming on the platforms and roofs of the buses, as if on this one day bodies were more indestructible than machines. Inside the brownstone which housed the dancing academy there was an air of desertion. The little anterooms where private pupils received coaching in "toe," or young men and women initiated each other into the wicked mysteries of the Turkey Trot, were dark and quiet. In the grand ballroom, the rows of gilt chairs, where the mothers usually knitted and watched, were empty, but a few mothers clustered around Mr. Duryea, a loose-jointed, very tall man whose length seemed the more exaggerated because all significant detail—toupee, dental plate, ribboned eyeglass—was crowded together at the top. Now he detached himself from the twittering group, clapped his hands, and the lesson began. No commotion in the street was to interfere with the verity of the two-step, the waltz. At the end of the lesson, however, Mr. Duryea, pairing off the pupils, presented the girl of each couple with a single American Beauty rose, from the long stem of which dripped streamers of red, white, and blue. As often had been the case before, he had left out Hester to dance with himself. With a nod to the pianist they were off, for chorus after chorus of a bounding, exultant waltz, Mr. Duryea bending low so that Hester might approximate the correct position with her arms, in her fist the rose of peace.

Back in the returning cab, Hester held the bruised rose thoughtfully against her skirt, as one who was not easily to be tricked into believing that pink crepe and roses were her just and personal due. She glanced over at her mother. Sirens and whistles were keening overhead; as they drove slowly past a church they heard the continuous shrike-shrike of its bell. Her mother, holding her coat tightly around her, stared out fearfully at the crowds which caromed in the streets. Hester would not have been surprised if she had said, "Now that this has happened I must see about getting the baby born," but her mother said nothing.

"Is the war really and truly over?" said Hester.

"Indeed it is, indeed it is," said her mother, still looking out the window. Several people had been pushed off the curb nearest the cab. One of them, an elderly man, rose painfully, scrabbling for his hat.

Hester's fingers tightened on the mauled rose. She put her hand on the fur band of her mother's sleeve, then drew it back. There was no use asking her again about Mr. Katz. Just before they got out of the cab at their door, her hand crept out again and touched the sleeve. "Do you suppose . . . do you suppose it's because I'm the *best*—that Mr. Duryea dances with me?"

Her mother, fumbling for change, looked up as if she were looking over the rims of eyeglasses, although she wore none. "Might be," she said, and gave her a pat to hurry her out of the cab. "But it's more likely because you're far and away the tallest."

In the weeks after the Armistice, the city faded slowly through an anticlimactic New Year into the liverish restlessness of off-season. It was now that almost weatherless time when even the sparrows seemed to idle in the trees, and through days the color of flat soda water one saw more clearly the chapped curbstones of the streets. At the Elkins' there was quiet, too; even the number of family visitors had fallen off. A nurse had come to stay, whose only function seemed to be the arranging in the spare room of packages which arrived constantly, or to watch, squinting, while Mrs. Elkin, who spent most of her days in a wrapper, sat nibbling shamefacedly from little plates, or even from paper bags. Mornings Mr. Elkin could hardly be got out of the house, and he came home earlier and earlier, stopping to kiss Hester as she played, for the first time unsupervised, with the gangs of children in the streets.

There, as in the papers read aloud at the Elkin dinner table, the talk was all of a great victory parade with which the city was to greet General O'Ryan and the victorious Twenty-seventh. At Madison Square, statues and pylons of plaster were to form a Court of the Honored Dead. The Washington Arch was to be transformed into an electrified version of the Arc de Triomphe. Fifth Avenue was to have arches hung with glass jewels, in front of the longest continuous grandstand in history. And here, in the matter of the grandstand, history reached out to the Elkins' dinner table. For according to the outcry in the papers, in spite of all that welter of plaster and wood and glass, no seats in the grandstand had been provided for those wounded soldiers who had been returned to their country in a condition which prevented their being honored either as part of the line of march—or in Madison Square. A group of merchants whose places of business fronted on Fifth Avenue had arranged, angrily and proudly, to accommodate these. Oakley and Company had been allotted four.

On the morning of the parade, Hester, waking before it was light, heard the milkman's horse clopping in the street below. By the time she reached the window it had vanished, but she could still pick out the fading tramp of its hoofs and the lurch of the wagon as it stopped far down the block. The growing morning had a glinting change in it; there was a green trickiness in the March air, and paper scraps scuffled high above the streets. She dressed hurriedly, without calling for help in buttoning the backs of her camisole and sailor dress. Dragging a chair to the closet, she took from a high shelf a blue serge cape and a Milan straw hat with a broad band trailing from its rear. With luck, since her mother was not to be of the party watching the parade from the Oakley and Company premises, no one would notice that Hester was not wearing her winter coat and had substituted for woolen knee socks the short, pale silk ones which were always the true demarcation of spring.

At the breakfast table, occupied only by her father and the nurse, no one spoke. The nurse looked at them with that slit-eyed remoteness with which she regarded their family life, as if she were telling herself and them, "My concern, after all, is for my patient." Mr. Elkin ate abstractedly, fidgeting without his newspaper, which had not yet arrived. They were to go in the touring car, for which they had a special permit. The streets were to be closed to all downtown traffic by eight.

Downstairs, the open car was waiting, the two aunts, here this time by invitation, already in the back seat. Hester got in between them, noting with disappointment that, except for the veils, they were dressed much as usual: Flora in the violent stripings and trembling arrays of jet on which hardly any extra would be noticeable, and Mamie in that lofty dowdiness which exempted her from style.

"How's Hattie?" said Flora.

"Wish I didn't have to go," said Mr. Elkin, getting in with the driver, "but the nurse is with her."

"Any time?"

"Any time."

"Isn't this child dressed rather thin?" said Mamie.

196

The car started, drowning out Mamie's remark. Hester squeezed down as far as possible between the aunts. Near her left ear, the tiny percussions of Flora's jet went on and on in a rhythm that aped the car's, then paused.

"What are we stopping for?" said Flora.

Hester, sitting up, saw that they had pulled up in front of one of the tenements on Amsterdam Avenue.

"I thought I better get the Katzes there with us," said Mr. Elkin.

"Oh good God, Joe," said Flora.

"I know, I know," he answered. "Pull down those two extra seats, will you. Hester, you go on in and tell them we're here. It's the ground floor right." He pointed up at a window. "Just knock and tell them. I don't think there's a bell."

Hester went up the stoop and into a vestibule floored with linoleum, in it a great worn hole. The door groaned closed and she was left almost in the dark. Stairs rose sharply in front of her, their risers just visible. Far above, at least four flights higher, a skylight glimmered. There was no definite sound, but the building murmured, nevertheless, with the unseen nearness of people. The riband hanging down her back rustled in a steady, poking draught, and she flipped it quickly forward over her shoulder. A door at the right had a glass pane at the top, over which lozenge-patterned paper had been pasted. She knocked. She heard the tinkle of a plate or a spoon being pushed back, a creak, a tread—all the noises, begging for mystery, which sounded so exciting from behind closed doors.

The door opened and Mrs. Katz stuck her head out on a level with Hester's. Her woolly fringe caught on the brim of the straw hat, and Hester looked for a moment straight through Mrs. Katz's spectacles at eyes which rolled like large blue immies behind them.

"Annnnh!" said Mrs. Katz, clapping her hands. She patted Hester into the room and shut the door. "Katz! Katz, they are here. The child is here. Come, Katz!"

In the room, there was so much, so fantastically much, that at first Hester could not untangle Mr. Katz from the rest. This was not merely the furniture, which seemed to consist of innumerable small mounds, so swagged with throws and coverlets and scarves that tables could not be told from chairs. The walls, the surfaces of the mounds, the ceiling, from which objects hung on strings, the very air was crammed with such a miscellany that Hester's eyes could not take it in, but had to stop, blinking, on one thing, until recognition set in. This thing resolved itself into Mr. Katz, who lay on one of the larger mounds, looking vaguely in front of him. He was dressed as he had been at the garden party, except for a wide collar of flannel which was tied around his neck with two long ears sticking up behind.

"Annnnh," said Mrs. Katz, nodding and smiling at Hester. "He has with the throat." Still nodding, she scuttled to Mr. Katz's side and began pecking at him with little croons and pats. "Up, Katz. Come. Up!"

Hester stared at one of the walls of the corner in which Mr. Katz lay. It was tacked from top to bottom with scraps of lace, colored and plain, pleated and flat, fanned out straight or puffed in bows that quivered with dust. On a shelf above his head, several yards of it were festooned over drapery cards. Between these there was a signed picture of the banquet variety, and a placard which said *Henkel Brothers. Fine Laces and Veilings*. Beneath the shelf, almost touched by one of Mr. Katz's flannel ears, there was a collar and cuff set, tacked in dainty alignment, as if waiting for a neck and two wrists to sprout neatly into place out of the wall.

Hester looked at the other side of the corner. This wall was cross-hatched with narrow shelves, dozens of them, on which there were ranged, almost there tinkled, an army of china trifles: Dutch boys, pagodas, slippers filled with pincushions, tankards and bud vases gilded with the names of towns or painted with simpering girls whose ringlets ended in a curl flowing artlessly over a shoulder. Among these, too, there were pictures, and one large placard—*Weinstein and Gaby. Jobbers to the trade.*

Hester turned on her heel. Here was a far corner devoted to buttons, there, beyond it, objects she could not identify. Each section had its photographs and placards. Even among the things which swung from the ceiling—an assortment of feathers—there was a sizable plume to which a placard had been pinned. On the mantelpiece, arranged as in a showcase, there was something—familiar.

"Katz!" said the crooning voice behind her. "Mr. Elkin is waiting. On you he *depends*, Katz."

At the sound of her father's name, the array on the mantelpiece merged and made sense. Set there, exactly as in the anteroom of Oakley and Company, were samples of all its products. Here were the bottles with their intricate labels: Lilac, Parma Violet, Coreopsis of Japan, and Triple Essence of California Rose. On tripods between them were the "compacts," small rounds of satin centered with moiré rosebuds, each box containing a hard cake of powder, or a flaming oval of orange or purplish rouge. There was even a display of one of Mr. Elkin's transient ventures—tiny vials of rosy or greenish liquid (each with a brass clip at its back), which had been designed to hook onto a lady's corselette or inside the lacy masses of her *décolletage*, there to dispel a mysterious fragrance as she breathed —but which, Hester knew, had somehow or other "not caught on." Set in the center of all this, flanked by many gilded cardboard trademarks, were two pictures.

She moved nearer. One was a picture of the Oakley office. The other was a picture of herself. It was a replica of one on her father's desk downtown—of herself at the age of three, in white corduroy bonnet with lining frilling her solemn face, coat with belt absurdly far below the waist, the hem just touching the kid uppers of her patent boots. Scrawled in her father's fancy hand, on this copy, however, an inscription ran right across the boots: *To Mr. and Mrs. Katz. Regards. From the Coreopsis Kid.*

"Annnnh. Now!" said Mrs. Katz in a failing voice. Hester turned. Mr. Katz was on his feet. He still had a vague look of waiting for instruction, but he was vertical.

"Come," said Mrs. Katz. She stepped nimbly in front of Mr. Katz, as if she were used to shielding him from notice. "You looking samples?" She pointed a knotty paw. "When Katz was in Lace." She pointed again. "When he was Souvenirs."

"What are those?" Hester indicated the far corner.

"Findings," said Mrs. Katz. "Ledder Findings. Was before Buttons." She followed Hester's gaze to the mantel. "Annnnh," said Mrs. Katz, folding her hands. "The *Company*."

Behind her, Mr. Katz jackknifed so suddenly that Hester thought he had fallen over, until she saw that he was tugging at several packages which were piled on the floor under the mantel.

"Nah, nah, Katz." said Mrs. Katz, with a fretful sob. She tweaked at the flannel. "Today is holiday, remember, Katz?"

There was a sharp rat-a-tat at the door.

"Annnnh, *Gott*," Mrs. Katz sighed, and pulled Mr. Katz upright. She pressed her face close to Hester's "Sometimes Katz cannot think how to come any place but home. *Versteh?*" she whispered. "So he brings them here, the bundles, and we go out togedder. Him to carry. Me to show where."

There was another, louder knock at the door. "Like podnership, see?" whispered Mrs. Katz. She put a blunt forefinger against her pleading, wrinkled muzzle. "Sh-h-h. You are good girl, *nu?*" Then she scurried to the door. "Yes, yes! We are ready!" she cried, and flung the door open, bobbing low behind it, almost in a curtsy.

"Well, please come on then," said Mr. Elkin, in a voice more indulgent than his expression. "Or we'll never get there." He looked at Mr. Katz, shook his head, then took Katz by the arm and led him out the door.

Hester and Mrs. Katz waited on the stoop while Mr. Katz was inserted in the front seat of the car, next to the driver. Mrs. Katz put a hand on Hester's upper arm and squeezed it. "Big strong girl," she muttered. She nodded closer, so that Hester again looked through the spectacles at the round, swimming eyes. "Sometimes I carry, too," whispered Mrs. Katz.

Mrs. Katz was to have shared the back seat with the aunts, but with the mulishness of the timid, she pleaded the anxiety of her "podnership" and was finally allowed to get up front. From the back seat only her nodding bonnet was visible, next to the tartan shawl she had wrapped carefully around Katz.

Mr. Elkin got in one of the small seats facing the back, turning around to hand the driver a large engraved card. "Drive down to Washington Square and back up, whichever way they'll let you go," he said. "I think this will get you through." He sat Hester on the little seat next to him and cradled her hand in his lap. "I want Hester to see the Arch."

It was still very early. The car made good headway, creeping along the battered streets near the East River.

"How many boys will you have, Joe?" said Flora.

"Four, they said."

"They say some of them . . ." Mamie said nervously. "*Basket cases.*"

"Oh, no, nothing like that, Mamie." Mr. Elkin gnawed his mustache. "They wouldn't."

Hester saw the soldiers in her mind, baskets over their poor, mad heads, with holes woven for the strange, lucent eyes.

"Joe," Flora's voice cracked, parrotlike, above the motor hum. She motioned with her chin toward the front seat. "Is he always like that?" she said, lowering her voice. "Really, you ought to realize."

"On and off," said her father. "He's not much use around the office any more. Still pretty fair on deliveries, though."

Hester lowered her eyes to the hand held in her father's and counted her breaths. In, out. In, out.

"Couldn't you mail?" said Mamie.

"Oh . . ." said her father, looking vaguely out the window. "There's always something."

"You mean you see to it there's something," said Flora. "That business will collapse of its own dead weight one of these days."

Mr. Elkin looked patiently back at the two who had been part of the dead weight for years. "They haven't a soul. I'm trying to get them into a home."

"Daddy," said Hester, "what is the Corylopsis Kid?"

"The Coreopsis Kid?" Mr. Elkin squeezed her hand with an absent smile. "That's you, m'dear."

"Me?"

Mr. Elkin nodded over her head at the aunts. "Louis Orenstein, wasn't it, who started it with that telegram the day she was born. 'Three cheers for the Coreopsis Kid.' "

"What a fool you were that day, Joe," said Flora, her jet beads quivering with chuckles. "What an old fool."

"Why not?" said Mr. Elkin. "I'd waited a long time for that day."

"And the telegrams *you* sent out later," said Mamie with a pursed smile. "Eight hundred of them. 'Greetings, from Oakley and Company and the Coreopsis Kid.' "

"Well, the line's known from coast to coast," said Mr. Elkin. "And so am I." He looked down at Hester. "And so is Hester. When I'm on the road I get it all the time. 'How's the Coreopsis Kid, Joe?' "

Suddenly, turning a corner, they were at the Arch. It gleamed in front of them like an enormous croquet wicket massed with jewels.

Then it was hidden by the blue bulk of a policeman. When he saw the card, his face cleared. "I'll get you over to the curb, sir. You'll have to wait there a bit, but we'll get you through."

At the curb, the people packed swelling behind the barrier looked enviously into the long car. The two aunts held up their bosoms, looking stiffly ahead with the hauteur of influence. The car edged into a line of others and stopped, pointing straight at the Arch. To the north, south, and west, phalanx after phalanx of waiting uniforms quivered in the early morning sun. Here and there commands sparked suddenly above a continuous surf of sound. To the left of the car, a horse curvetted and was reined in, his nostrils distended but still.

Hester looked at the Arch. Hung with a dazzle of light, it swayed with the sound of thousands of colors chiming softly together. It kept time with the dazzle in her chest, inside of which a music box tintinnabulated over and over, "Coreopsis . . . Coreopsis . . . Coreopsis Kid."

She stood up, and stepped on Mamie's foot. At Mamie's sharp yelp, she sat down again.

"When that baby comes," said Mamie, nursing her foot, "I know someone whose nose is going to be out of joint."

"Mamie," said Mr. Elkin, "sometimes you haven't the sense of a mule."

Hester stared at Mamie. Idly, she noted how well her aunt's triangular mouth suited her sly bird-speech, was perhaps too small for anything more, but her own answer came from far below the stare. "I don't know," she said. "I guess Daddy can afford us all."

A murmur from the crowd drowned out her father's guffaw. The lines of soldiers tautened, each to a single glitter. Waves of brass washed over them, and the glitter moved with the drums. Now everyone in the crowd was throwing something— packs of cigarettes, oranges, paper rosettes, and streamers of *tricolore*. The aunts dug down in a hamper and brought out things to throw, too. From the windows around the Square, confetti flaked and fell through the air. Some of the brilliant bits spiraled onto the car, and Hester, leaning against her father, raised her face to receive them, as she did in winter with the first, slow feathers of snow. Her father held her, as he would uphold them all. And there was no other quite so dashing name in the whole Oakley and Company line.

Then the band converged upon them. Its clangor invaded her chest. She burst into tears.

"What . . . what?" said her father, bending down.

"I loved it," she whispered back. "I loved the war." But her father shook his head, his smile half turning into a frown.

Mrs. Katz leaned over the back seat. Her arms and hands were crammed full, and her muzzle was pleated with glee, with the joy of having things to throw away. She pressed an orange into Hester's hand.

"Throw!" she said, nodding her woolen lamb-curls. "Throw!"

Hester cupped the orange in her hand. It was round, perfect, like the world at this moment. If there was a flaw in it, it could not yet be seen. She held onto it for as long as she could. Then, closing her eyes tight, she threw it.

A Box of Ginger

~§ FIVE STORIES below, the hot white pavements sent the air shimmering upward. From the false dusk of the awning, Kinny, leaning out to watch the iridescent black top of the funeral car, smelled the indeterminate summer smell of freshly ironed linen and dust. Below, he could see his father help the aunts into the car and stumble in after them, and the car roll away to join the others at the cemetery. The winter before, at the funeral of his father's other brother, everything had left from here, hearse and all. The house had been crowded with people who had entered without ringing and had seated themselves soundlessly in the parlor, greeting each other with a nod or a sidewise shake of the head, and for days there had been a straggling procession of long-faced callers, who had clasped hands with his father and mother and had been conducted, after a decent interval, to his grandmother's rooms, where she lived somewhat apart from the rest of the family. They had all come out clucking, "She's a wonderful woman, a won-der-ful old woman!," had been given coffee, and had gone away. Today, there was no one, and the wide glaring street was blank with light.

"Kinny, where are you?"

"I'm in the parlor."

"How many times have I told you to say 'living room'? Parlor!" His mother clicked her tongue as she came into the room. "Why didn't you go to the Park?" She walked toward him and looked at him squarely, something he had noticed grown people almost never seemed to have time to do.

"Listen, Kinny!" Her voice had the conspiratorial tone that made him uncomfortable. "You're not to let on to Grandma anything—anything about the funeral. It's a terrible thing to grow to a great

204

age and see your children go before you." Her gaze had already
shifted back to normal, slightly to the right of him and just above
his head. "Don't lean so far out the window!" She turned and went
into the kitchen to help Josie, the maid. His family never sat down
to a dinner for just themselves; there were always the aunts, or the
innumerable cousins, who came to pay their short devoirs to
Grandma and stayed interminably at her daughter-in-law's table.

He wandered back into the room, dawdling. It *was* a parlor, very
unlike the Frenchy living rooms of his friends. Opposite him, the
wall was half covered by a tremendous needle-point picture, framed
in thick, curdled gilt, of Moses striking the rock and bringing forth
water at Meribah. "And Moses lifted up his hand," it said in the big
Doré Bible, "and with his rod he smote the rock twice: and the
water came out abundantly, and the congregation drank, and their
beasts also." The faces of Moses and the Israelites were done in
such tiny stitches that they looked painted, and there was a little
dog lapping at the gush of water, which had minute, glistening
beads worked into it. Diagonally across the room from the picture,
the wreathed cherubim of a Vernis-Martin cabinet were flanked by
a green marble column, on which poised an anonymous metal girl,
arms outflung against a verdigrised apple tree, which sprouted
electric-light bulbs.

He went over and fingered the Victrola, the only relatively new
thing in the room. Slanting back on its lemon-oiled shelves lay all
the newly acquired Red Seal records: Galli-Curci in the sextet from
"Lucia"; the Flonzaley Quartet, whose sprigged mustachios he
knew well from the Victor catalogue; and Alma Gluck, singing
"From the la-and of the sky-ee blue" and then "wawtah" very
quick. He would have liked to play that one, or "Cohen on the
Telephone," but he was sure that he would not be allowed to today.

Walking into the hot, brassy clutter of the kitchen, he stopped at
the icebox and drew himself a glass of water from a pipe that ran
back into the ice chamber—a fixture in which his mother took pride
but which he thought overrated.

"Can I have some of Dad's French Vichy?" He wasn't even sure
that he liked its flat, mineral taste, but it was something of a feat to
get it.

"No, you can't," said his mother, gingerly taking a tray of prune pockets out of the oven. "I can't be sending to the drugstore all the time. Catering to the fads and fancies of a lot of—A boarding house, that's what I'm running! You'd think they all *lived* here!"

"Mother, what did Uncle Aaron die of?" he said idly.

He already knew the answer. He rarely needed to ask an explicit question about family affairs. By picking up crumbs and overtones at the endless family gatherings, he had amassed his information. His Uncle Aaron had had pneumonia and had been convalescing on an upstate farm all spring. But his mother said, "Of old age, I guess," and gazed past him. Kinny's father, years older than she, was only a decade younger than the dead uncle. The family was getting down. His father had only sisters now. Kinny began to eat a prune pocket.

"You wait till you get to the table. One of these days, you'll burst!"

"Hattie!" a sharp, high voice called. "Hattie!" Then a small bell tinkled insistently.

"Go in and see what Grandma wants," his mother said. "Tell her the optician's man will be in this afternoon. And if she asks about a letter from Aaron, for goodness' sakes don't say anything!" She sighed. "I'm sure I don't know what they're going to tell her *this* time."

He idled slowly down the hall to his grandmother's bedroom, although he knew she had already been helped to her sitting room, where she spent most of the day. Light filtered through the half-drawn shades over the huge bed, with its wide panel of burled Circassian walnut, topped by a two-foot pediment of acanthus leaves. He swung himself onto the broad footboard, high as his shoulder. Up to it swelled the feather bed for which his mother was always wanting to substitute a hair mattress. Everything was big here—the looming wardrobe, where he had sometimes hidden, choking, among the tight-packed camphored clothes; the long chests, with their stretches of cold, fatty-looking brown marble; the towering, grim-latched trunks.

On his confirmation day, just past, when one of the trunks had been opened for the presentation of a gold watch with a remote, scrolled face, he had been allowed to finger a drawerful of Virginia Treasury notes with the serial numbers marked by hand in brown ink, and a miniature envelope, addressed in long-essed script—his grandmother's wedding invitation, dated 1852. Still in her twenties, his grandmother had married a man well past fifty, and her youngest son, Kinny's father, had waited for marriage until he, too, was almost fifty, so if you figured back, here was he, Kinny Elkin, in 1924, with a grandfather, sunken in the ciphers of time, who had been born in the eighteenth century. In his mind, he saw the generations as single people walking a catwalk, each with a hand clutching a long supporting rope that passed from one to another but disappeared into mist at either end.

"Kinny! Grandma wants you!" From the sitting room down the hall he heard the familiar clank-clank of the gadrooned brass handles on the sideboard. Grandma would be standing stiffly with the yellow box of preserved ginger, uglily lettered in black, clutched in one knuckled hand, waiting for the small afternoon ceremony that had been her only apparent notice of him for as long as he could remember. Reluctantly, he opened the door and went down the hall.

She stood there just as he had known she would, a dainty death's head no taller than he, in the black silk uniform of age, one hand wavering on her cane, the other tight on the yellow box. The sparse hair, dressed so closely on the skull, enlarged the effect of the ears and the high nose with its long nostrils; the mouth, a mere boundary line for tributary wrinkles, firmed itself now and again. She was neat as old vellum, and though time had shrunk her to waxwork, it had left her free of the warts and hairs and pendulous dewlaps he saw on other old people. Her admitted age was ninety-three, but the family was of the opinion that she had concealed a few years, out of vanity.

"Here I am, Grandma." He moved toward her.

"Come here, child." Steadying her hand with his, she fumblingly placed in his palm a few tawny sugared slices of ginger. Under her waiting gaze, he placed a slice in his mouth and chewed. There was a small, acrid explosion in his throat; his eyes pinkened, but he swallowed obediently, knowing that she thought she was giving him a confection of which he was fond.

"Thank you, Grandma," he said thickly, his mouth on fire.

"All right, now." It was time for the other part of the ceremony.

Slowly she leaned on his arm and he guided her steps across the room to the wicker armchair, into which she tottered, bearing down heavily on his shoulder and sending the cane in a rasping slide to the floor. Feeling in a pocket at one side of the chair, she brought up her glasses, polished the lenses with a bright-pink cloth, and put them on. Opening a folded afternoon paper, she began to read the headlines with the aid of a handled magnifying glass the size of a small saucer. The ritual was over. After supper, Kinny's father would read her the articles she asked for, or, in his absence, Kinny would declaim them with careful dignity.

Dangling his legs from the dark old couch, he tried to place just what pulled at him so strongly in Grandma's rooms. Here in the sitting room, there were only a few steel engravings of Biblical scenes and a big, dark cloisonné pot stuffed with some brackish moss that never seemed to grow or die. Everything was still, but if he sat long enough, he felt the dim waves of history lapping at him, a moving, continuous stream that culminated in him.

He went restlessly toward the window and mooned out at the river. Maybe he could call for Bert, and they could go out and get some isinglass from the rocks that stuck out all over the ground across Riverside Drive. Bert maintained that if you could peel a whole clear sheet of it, it could be sold, like tinfoil.

"Call Hattie," said his grandmother fretfully. "Ask her if that optician man is coming." He had never heard her speak of the steady contraction of her sight, or of any other physical drawback, but Mr. Goldwasser came once a month and carefully did something —a plucking or trimming of the short, stiff eyelashes that tended to mat in the corners—which she thought beneficial.

"Mother said to tell you he's coming."

In the kitchen, his mother was discarding her apron.

"Here they come," she said. "Kinny, get away from that table." She brushed past him. Under Josie's reproachful, bovine stare, he took another prune pocket and stood at the head of the hall, watching.

Kinny's father, Aunt Flora and Aunt Amy, and his father's cousin Selena, old as the aunts, came in from the foyer. He thought that they looked furtive, as if they'd been doing something they shouldn't and were glad that it was over. Amy's face, wry and puckered now under her great bird's nest of iron-gray hair, was tiny and aquiline, with a short arc of mouth, and was supposed to be very like that of her mother as a young woman, but she had none of her mother's cameo neatness, and was always leaving untidy packages and having to come back for them, so that "something Amy left" had become a byword in the house.

"I think I dropped my gloves at the—" she said tremulously, and stopped. Nobody said the usual "Oh, A-amy!" His father groaned and walked heavily to the sideboard. Rooting in one of the compartments, he brought out the decanter.

"Now, Joe, do you think you'd better?" said his mother. "Come on, everybody. It'll do you good to eat something."

"Oh, leave him alone, Hattie," said Aunt Flora testily, jerking back the white pompadour that reared high over her rouged beak of face. Her inimical glance seemed to concentrate the momentary feeling of the others. Hattie hadn't just been through what they had.

Flora was the first to sit down at the table. Food, poker, and having the last word were her passions, in that order. "Come on, Amy, Selena," she said.

Usually, Selena wore puce or mustard or reseda green, but today she wore muddy brown, underlining the mud tints in her equine face.

Kinny's father sat at the head of the table kneading his gray curls while the others ate, in silence. Kinny stole into the kitchen and got out the bottle of Vichy. Tiptoeing into the dining room, he placed the green bottle at his father's elbow. He heard the doorbell ring and Josie ushering somebody into the parlor. She came to the dining-room door.

"Is here the eye doctor, Mrs. Elkin," she said.

"Take him on back to Grandma, Josie," said his mother.

His father stirred and groaned again. "What in God's name am I going to tell Maw? I haven't the heart. I haven't the heart, so soon after Nat."

"Never thought she should have been told about Nat," said Flora, brushing the crumbs from her black, bugled front.

"What? Maw?" said Amy heatedly. "She seemed to catch on almost as soon as it happened. She sits there half blind and part deaf, and she hasn't been outdoors in ten years, but try and fool her about anything in the family!"

Selena leaned forward with a faint flush. "You've been fooling her about Aaron's letters, haven't you?" she asked. "Hasn't Joe been writing them and mailing them ever since Aaron went into a coma?" She looked around the table avidly.

"Aaron and I write—wrote—a lot alike," his father said. "I just wanted to keep her from worrying at not seeing him. I told her he might have to go out West." He turned down his mouth wryly.

Selena leaned forward again, triumphantly. "Well, why don't you just go on writing them?"

"It's a ghoulish thing to do." He rose and moved to the window. Pulling up the awning, he wound the cord hard around the hooked prong in the casement and stood looking out. It was as if someone had suddenly thrown yards of blue soft stuff into all the corners of the room and veils had settled on the furniture. The white cloth gleamed. Across the wide avenue, the people in the building opposite had already turned on their yellow squares of light.

"She asked me four or five times yesterday," said his mother gently. "The last letter you had mailed from the farm is here, but I didn't know what to do."

The optician's man came to the door and peered at them obsequiously. "Er-hmm. I'm finished now." He held a little black bag in one hand and a round black bowler at his chest.

"Oh, yes, Mr. Goldwasser." His father turned from the window, reaching into his pocket for his wallet. "I'll see you to the door."

"Just a minute, Joe!" said Flora. She pushed back the dish in front of her and swivelled around in her chair. "Mr. Goldwasser."

"Yes?" He blinked at her politely.

"Can you tell us—how much can my mother see?"

"See?" he paused. "Why, she hasn't had an eye test in years, Mrs. Harris. It's hard to say. The lenses she has are the strongest made, and she's had them a good, long time." He shrugged. "She's lucky not to have a cataract, at her years. She sees enough to eat, does she not, and get around a little? What I do for her only makes her more comfortable, you know."

"Could she read, do you think?" Amy faltered, one of her bone hairpins sliding into her lap, where she worked at it nervously.

"Read!" He seemed surprised. "I can hardly think—maybe a block letter or two. You mean she still tries?" He shook his head admiringly. "A wonderful woman. Well!" He bowed and left them, followed by Kinny's father.

"They never will come right out with anything. Doctors!" Flora snapped.

"He's not a doctor, Flora," said Kinny's father wearily, returning to the room. He slumped into a chair. "I'm all worn out."

His mother was at the *secrétaire*. She held an envelope in her hand. "Better to get it over with, Joe, or she'll surely catch on. She complained about Amy and Flora not stopping in today."

Amy looked up vaguely and dabbed at her eyes with a napkin. "I just can't face her without showing something. I know I can't."

"Oh, Amy, be practical," said Flora. "How do you think we all feel? She's too old to suffer another shock like that. We'll have to warn everyone who comes in to see her. Go on, Joe."

"I'm no good at that sort of thing," he said, choking. "Not today, of all days."

"You've always been the one to read to her," said Kinny's mother. "She'd think it strange if any of us—"

Kinny found his voice, with a croak. "I—I read to her sometimes." He looked hastily around the table and then down at his shoes. Selena switched around in her chair and raised her brows at him.

"Why, Kinny!" said his mother in a slow, pleased way.

"I won't embroil the child in this!" said his father angrily.

"Little pitchers have big ears," said Selena with a caustic smile.

"I'm not a child." He hung his head and looked at his father sidewise. "She's used to me. I can do it." His voice trailed off weakly.

"After all, I was the one who had to go in and tell her about Nat," said his mother bitterly. "All of you avoid anything unpleasant."

"Maybe the child *could* do it," said Flora hurriedly.

His mother came around the table and thrust the envelope into his hand. "That's a good idea, Kinny. Just read to her, like you always do."

"All right. All right, all of you," muttered his father, not looking at him. "Just be careful, Kinny."

Now that their collective eyes, raw and ashamed, seemed to be pushing him out of the room, he felt uneasy. Carefully, he straightened the silver on his plate. There were several large crumbs on the floor next to his chair. With a prim show of industry, he picked them up, one by one, and put them on the cloth. Grinding his shoulder blades together, he left the room.

In the hall, he pressed his face against the cold, stippled wall. There were too many dark-angled halls in this apartment. He wished that the family would leave soon for the summer place, and thought with relief of the house, where you could dash straight through from back to front, out into the sunshine, slamming the door behind you. Stacked at a corner of the hall, rolled-up carpets wrapped in tar paper waited to be stored, giving out a drugged, attic smell. He flicked each one as he went by, rattling the paper in drum time.

Outside his grandmother's sitting-room door, there were several pictures that had been taken down and swathed in cheesecloth. He spent some time peering at these, trying to make out which was the one of the old bookshop and which the red-coated dragoon and his bride. Through the half-shut door he could see his grandmother in the unlit room. She was snoring softly, head back.

"Grandma," he said, his voice cutting the cobwebs. "It's me, Kinny." He went up and touched her lightly on the arm.

"Ah—oh. Yes?" The folded newspaper slid off her lap and she blinked up at him. Turning on the lamp beside the old cloisonné bowl, he laid the letter in her hand.

"A letter for you. Shall I read it?" It seemed to him that she hunched into herself like an old bird, listening.

"Where's your father? Where's Amy and Flora?"

"In the—in the dining room." He rocked back and forth on his ankle. "Can I use your paper cutter?"

She nodded, drawing her shawl around her, although the dank heat in the room made his lip bead. He got out the paper cutter, rubbing his thumb against the ivory hair of the girl on the handle, and slit the envelope. In the uninflected drone taught in the grade schools, he began to read his father's high, knotted script.

"My dear Mother: Trust this finds you well and in good spirits. Everything is fine here. The meals are good and the rooms are nice and clean. I miss seeing you and my dear family, but the doctor says that everything is going as well as can be expected, though he still would like to see me go out West this fall. Please God, we will all see each other before then. Keep well and do not worry if I write seldom, as there is very little news here. Your affectionate son, Aaron."

Rubbing the ball of one thumb ceaselessly in the palm of the other hand, his grandmother looked straight through him. He'd never noticed before how her head shook a little, as if blown by a slight, steady current from behind. "Read it again, Kinny," she whispered.

He read it again, more quickly, thinking that its phrases sounded a lot like the letters his father sent home from his travels—"please God" and "trust you are well," and signed always "Yrs. aff., Joe."

"Let me have the letter." Searching shakily in the side pocket of the chair, she brought out the thick, bevelled magnifying glass. Holding it almost under her nose, she inched it slowly along the letter, then the envelope, then back to the letter again. She sat for a long time with the letter in her lap; then a sharp movement of her arm sent the magnifying glass across the room, where it hit the couch and spun to the floor with the dull, rubbling sound of a top but did not break. He pressed his knees together, listening to the echo.

He saw that she was feeling for the cane. Frightened, he thrust it under her hand, but was reassured by the familiar heavy way she rested on him and pulled herself up in three marionette jerks. The two of them made their way to the sideboard. As she bent over the drawer, he saw the moisture from her eyes run six ways down the channels in her cheeks and fall into the drawer. Turning, she let her sticks of fingers brush his face in a dry gesture.

"Thank you," she whispered. "You were good to try." Thrusting the box into his hand, but not releasing it finally, she held her hands cupped around his, and for a moment, they rocked back and forth together, in a movement of complicity and love.

The Pool of Narcissus

⟨§ W H E N T H E Muschenheim limousine slid up to the curb, like a great, rolling onyx, it had hardly stopped before the chauffeur, in broadcloth cerements, leaped out and flourished open the door. Mrs. Muschenheim emerged slowly, her enormous bulk divided and encircled with ruchings, the elegiac balloon of velvet that compressed her black pompadour looking like the knob on the chess queen.

Hester, watching intently from a cramped stone niche in the courtyard entrance, where she had been sitting in Sunday-afternoon stiffness, knew that this arrival was the signal that the birthday party at the Reuters' was about to begin. While Mrs. Muschenheim stared before her with majesty, the chauffeur reverently brought forth several cakeboxes of a whiteness and size that drew awed murmurs from the kids around the entrance, then bore them smartly behind his employer as she lumbered through the courtyard and into the apartment house on her way up to the Reuters', on the ninth floor.

Hester could never decide which attracted her more—the elaborate sweets or the solemn pageantry of the Reuter family life. Sometimes she was given tastes from the boxes of mocha torte or glazed cherries when Clara, the fifteen-year-old granddaughter of the Reuters, descending to Hester's twelve-year level on bored, boyless afternoons, asked her upstairs, and the two of them hovered hopefully on the periphery of the stately orgies of pastry, coffee, and talk.

The Reuters belonged to the solid phalanx of upper-middle-class German burgher families that moved in its own orbit in New York. During the first World War, just past, the women had learned to knit by the jerky American method and had bought Liberty Bonds stolidly, but through this period, as always, they lingered over the coffeepot on smoky winter afternoons, did their hair leaning over rivulets of scalloped dresser scarves made by the daughters of the house, and married off their sons and daughters to one another—not by compulsion but through the graceful pressure of cocoa parties together at the age of ten and dinner parties at the age of twenty.

Hester detached herself painfully from her cold seat, permitted herself one superb glance around at the other kids, who did not share her entrée, and followed Mrs. Muschenheim in, just slowly enough not to catch the same elevator. She went up to her own family's apartment, four floors below the Reuters', and scurried back to her room, sliding off her coat. Because of the inactivity of Sunday afternoon, her new dress was still fresh. Ramming her barrette to a firmer hold on her hair, she burrowed in her bureau drawer for the tissue-wrapped handkerchief that would serve as her ticket of admittance to the birthday party. Holding it by its rosette of ribbon, she slipped out of the apartment, climbed the four flights to the Reuters' floor, and rang the bell. Clara opened the door.

"Oh, h'lo, Hester," said Clara, her eyes on the little package.

" 'S for your mother's birthday," Hester muttered, and thrust the package at her.

"Oh, *thank* you, Hester! She'll be pleased," said Clara with sweet artificiality. Both were aware that a handkerchief was not to be considered a real present but, rather, a kind of party currency. Then Clara dropped her adult tone. "Listen! Guess what!" she said, and hurried Hester along the hall toward her mother's bedroom. Going past the piles of tissue paper and ribbon on the waxed foyer table, turning her head to peer back through the living-room doorway at the people gathered inside, Hester thought there was no place for a party like the Reuters', where all the material panoply of life was treated with such devotion.

Both Mrs. Reuter, the grandmother, and her sister, Mrs. Enke, rivalled Mrs. Muschenheim in size. Their mammoth hips swelled like hoop skirts under their made-to-order dresses. Behind her nose glasses, Mrs. Reuter's enlarged blue eyes melted innocently in the genial arrangement of red pincushions that was her face. From Mrs. Enke's more elegant profile, wan folds draped away sculpturally, as befitted her long-standing widowhood. In this citadel of women, which included Clara and her mother, Mrs. Braggiotti, Mr. Reuter might have felt oppressed had he not been equally large, and likely to find, on his four-o'clock return from the lace business, various Adolphs and Karls, of severe clothes and superb, gold-linked linen, who had already deserted the garlanded cake plates for a bottle of schnapps, over which they would discuss the market. Once, Hester had even seen the German consul there, his domed head rolling and stretching out on his creased neck like a sea lion accepting the deference of the crowd. When, on such occasions, Mrs. Reuter's eyes turned too explicitly to Hester's grubby play dress and battered knees, the two girls played in Clara's room with the frilled doll that had belonged to Clara's mother, or made exploratory tours of the other bedrooms.

All the bedrooms were of such complete neatness that Hester had never been able to imagine the Reuter women as really going to bed at all, but saw them moving serenely through the night ready to meet the first caller of the day, their hair unawry, their watches pinned to their waists. To her, these rooms full of starched bolsters, where every plane was animated with linen and crisped with laces, seemed the ideal toward which any girl would aim her hope chest, but sanctuaries, nevertheless, in which it was improbable that any of the natural functions went on. The closet floors were not cluttered with stray shoes or saved boxes, and in the dresser drawers there were no broken earrings tumbled among cards from the upholsterer, bits of cornice off the mirror, and odd ends of elastic. Each object, useful and needed, reposed in a wash of space and calm. Mrs. Braggiotti's room had, in addition, the aura of the romantically pretty woman.

In this room, Hester and Clara always went to the dresser first, passing from the etched-crystal tray, with its kaleidoscopic row of perfume bottles, whose number and style varied with Mrs. Braggiotti's admirers, to the rosy pincushions, where, among hat daggers and florists' pins, sometimes lay two great dinner rings, with rows of huge diamonds in pavements of smaller ones. These, Clara said, had been the Reuters' gift to her mother on her marriage. Who or what Mr. Braggiotti was or had been, Hester had never been told. If she conceived of him at all, it was as an alien, a kind of slim, Italianate poniard that had once got embedded mistakenly in the firm dough of the Reuter household.

What drew Hester most in this room was the shoes. Clara would ostentatiously swing open the closet door, and there, in the soft cretonne pockets that covered it from base to top, were her mother's thirty pairs of small, high-arched shoes, some in leathers of special kinds—snake or piped kidskin—but most of them dyed in pale costume shades that resembled in their gradations of color the row of sewing silks on a drygoods counter. Looking at them, Hester could see Mrs. Braggiotti, who, with her tilted nose, masses of true-blond hair, and bud mouth, was what every shag-haired girl staring into the Narcissus pools of adolescence hoped to see. Hester thought of her as she had often met her, riding down serenely in the elevator, a pale, wide hat just matching the flowers in her chiffon dress, a long puff of fur held carelessly against the faintly florid hips. Mixed with this image was a more perplexing vision, of Mrs. Braggiotti at the piano, where she played Chopin with much ripple and style but wearing a pince-nez that mercilessly puckered the flesh between her brows, giving her the appearance of a doll that had been asked to cope with human problems. Hester preferred to think of her as endlessly floating from one assignation to another in an endless palette of costumes that matched.

It was toward Mrs. Braggiotti's dresser, then, that Clara pulled Hester, pointing out the huge bottle that stood on the tray, eclipsing all the others. "George gave it to her, just now!" said Clara.

"Who's he?"

"He's *in love* with her."

It was only recently that Hester had learned not to giggle at the term. Now the phrase fell on her ear like something dropping softly, momentously, from a tree.

"Is *she* in love with *him?*"

"How should I know?" Clara stared down her nose at her. Apparently, Hester had again made one of the major errors that were always emphasizing the age gap between them. Obviously, to Clara's way of thinking (which must also be the adult one), the important thing was to *be* loved and to enjoy all the gestures thereof.

Without stopping to inspect the rest of the room, the girls went back along the hall and edged into the overheated living room. Mrs. Reuter was with a group near the door, and on the far side Mrs. Braggiotti, this time without the pince-nez, was playing the piano for a number of gentlemen gathered around her. "How pretty your dress is, my dear! Did your mother make it?" panted Mrs. Reuter, her glance approving Hester's cleanliness, one hand blotting the drops of sweat from her hot face and just preventing them from falling on her gray satin prow.

"She did the flowers." Hester looked down doubtfully at the lavender voile, its color harsh against her olive-brown hands. All over its skirt and sleeves, unsuccessfully tiered to hide her lankness, large bunches of multicolored flowers were worked at careful equidistance. It had been the tenant of her mother's workbasket all the preceding summer.

"My, she does beautiful work!" Mrs. Reuter fingered the dress tenderly. "Did you have some Nesselrode?" She nodded to Hester and left her.

"That's him," Clara whispered, at Hester's elbow.

"Where?"

"By the window," said Clara. She left Hester and went over to her mother.

Looking, Hester saw a man somewhat under middle height standing near Mrs. Enke. Against the Wagnerian proportions of the others, he appeared unobtrusive but not negligible, as if their fleshy tide might flow past but not engulf him. There was something about his pleasant, even-featured face that was as firm and self-contained as a nut. He crossed the room to speak to Mrs. Braggiotti, whose head and neck made a pretty arc as she inclined upward toward him, her circlet of crystal beads shining in the afternoon sun. Clara pranced over to Hester again. "Guess what!" she said. "George is going to take you and me and Mama for a soda!"

"Maybe I better not go."

"Oh, sure. It's just to a drugstore, silly. He *owns* it—a nice one, not like the one downstairs. Over on Madison Avenue. You needn't even tell your family you're going. I'll lend you a coat, and we can take turns on my skates. Come *on!*"

They walked the few blocks over to Madison Avenue, George and Mrs. Braggiotti far ahead, linked as sedately as any married couple. Combined with the cold thrill of the brilliant afternoon Hester felt the lovely unease of wearing someone else's clothes. As they walked, they could glimpse the frozen brown fronds of the park between the tall buildings, on which the hard, white winter sun struck, audible as a gong.

The Pool of Narcissus

Set discreetly into the limestone corner of a block of private houses, Sunday-quiet behind their fretworks of iron, the ruby urns of the Town Pharmacy sent out a message of mystery and warmth. George unlocked the door and let them in to the aromatic smells of the pharmacopoeia and vanilla. Rising from the long expanse of tiled floor, the glass shelves, serried with pomades and panaceas, looked housewifely and knowledgeable, as if filled with the lore of the ages. Clara rushed to the small marble counter near the door and balanced on one of the high, curved metal chairs.

"A sundae, George, with everything."

"I don't open until four, Madam," he said, sliding off his coat and standing revealed in his suspenders and full, white shirtsleeves before he slipped on an alpaca jacket. Hester thought that he looked very intimate, but Mrs. Braggiotti, sitting formally on another chair, one pale-blue heel hooked over the rung, seemed not to notice. She refused a sundae, saying, "Oh, no, George, thanks. You know Mama's dinners!," in her high, untimbred voice.

After the sundaes, Hester and Clara went outside. Clara put on her skates and, promising not to take too long a turn, went grinding down the empty asphalt, rounded a corner, and was gone. Hester grew chilly waiting, and the sundae was cold inside her. Tiptoeing back around the half-open door into the store, she crouched down on a wooden box behind the marble counter and fingered the levers that controlled the soda water and syrups. Warm and hemmed in, she felt that it would be good to spend one's life in this shadowy store, away from the airless routine of an apartment but suspended a step above the rough street—like being on a little island, with faucets for running water and a bathroom at the back. There was a movement at the darker end of the store.

"Etta!" George's voice said pleadingly. "Etta!"

Hester peered out cautiously. Mrs. Braggiotti, hatless now, was pressed back against the prescription counter, leaning away from George, who stood in front of her with his hands against her waist.

"No, George." She reached along the counter to her hat, but he caught at her hand. They looked awkward, as if they were about to begin dancing but were not sure of the steps.

"We're not young enough to go on like this," he said. "Courting, like a couple of kids." Mrs. Braggiotti looked back at him woodenly, between her brows the same perplexed groove that she wore at the piano. She looked stilted, like an actress unsure of her lines. "Sometimes I think that's all you want," George said. "Someone hanging around." His voice sank.

Mrs. Braggiotti worked her blue shoe on the tiled floor, like a child enduring a familiar reproof.

"Why do you always"—he gripped her shoulders—"do you always . . ." He dropped his hands. "You can't go on forever being the pretty Reuter girl. Not even you."

She reached along the counter again, her rings chipping the light, her hand smoothing the hat expertly, assuredly. The hand wandered to the nape of her neck, patting the smooth hair, outlining, reassuring. He seized her with a kiss that grew, his face deep red, his hand kneading around and around on her back, one dark, tailored thigh thrust forward against the watery design of her dress. Inside Hester, a buried pleasure turned over, and vague, ill-gotten rumors and confirmations chased in her head.

Mrs. Braggiotti pushed George away sharply. "My shoe! Oh, you've got dirt all over my shoe!" She bent down to brush it, real distress on her face.

"What is it you *do* want, Etta?"

Mrs. Braggiotti tilted her face up at him, her eyes clear, her forehead unfurrowed. "Why, I don't want anything, George," she said, in the same tone with which she had refused the sundae.

Hester crept out of her niche and slid carefully around the door. Across the street, the other limestone houses were still there, withdrawn, giving out none of their meaning. Behind her, the dim island of the store no longer drew her with its promise of suspension, of retreat. Looking down at her hands, she thought suddenly that they were a good color; it was the lavender voile that was wrong. She wavered against the blind hush of the street, wishing it full of people she could jostle, buffet, and embrace. Down the block she saw Clara coming back, her skates clashing and chiming. She drew a long breath and stepped further out into the seminal sunlight.

The Watchers

◆◆ T H R O U G H T H E aqueous summer night, the shop lights
along the avenue shone confusedly, like confetti raining through fog.
From bench to bench in the narrow strip of park down the center,
voices bumbled softly against one another, as from undersea diver to
diver, through the fuzzy, dark medium of the evening.

Over toward the river, groups of girls and boys in their teens
foraged for mischief and experience in the anonymous blur of the
shadows, but Hester, bound to her mother, sat between her and her
father's elderly cousins on a bench that they kept to themselves,
repairing somewhat, by this separation, the *déclassé* gesture of sitting in the park. Across from them, in the big gray apartment house,
Hester could see the long, lit string of their own windows—at one
end the great, full swags of the Belgian-lace curtains of the living
room, and around the corner the faint glow of her grandmother's
night light.

Outwardly, it was because of her grandmother that their home
swirled continuously with family company, but actually the visitors
spent no more than a token time with the old lady, whom longevity
had made remarkable but unapproachable other than as a household god. In reality, according to Hester's mother's exasperated
comments, the visiting was a holdover from the bland, taken-for-
granted gregariousness of the Southerner, whereby, in a rhythmic
series of "droppings-in," in corner tête-à-têtes of intramural gossip,
they all reaffirmed the identity of the family and of themselves.

Now, after the Sunday-night supper of cold cuts and cheese and
pastry, most of the company had eddied away, and only three were
left here with Hester and her mother—Rose and Martha, who lived

in Newark and came only on Sunday, and Selena, who lived Hester did not quite know where but came most often of them all. Under the incomplete dark of the New York sky, their faces bobbled, uncertain and white, above their sombre, middle-aged dresses, and from time to time they pushed up sporadic remarks through the stifling heat.

"When does Joe get back?" asked Martha.

"Tomorrow morning," said Hester's mother. "This is his last trip for the year."

"Then you go to the country?" said Rose, with her plaintive whine, in which there was a hint of accusation.

"Yes, to White Plains. The same house as last year," said her mother, as if she regretted the disclosure. She would deplore their visits in conversation, behind their backs, but they would all come anyway, sending her into grudging paroxysms of hospitality.

"Not a breath stirring," said Martha, twitching her lip with a movement Hester could not really see but knew was there. Martha was a steady little person, dumpy-legged, with a face as creased and limited as her conversation. A milliner, working at home, she specialized in such oddly assembled trivia that Hester wondered often who bought them. She never went hatless and often appeared in rearrangements of the same materials, so that the lilies of the valley of last week, detached now from their wreath of green leaves, turned up limp but enduring on the orange velvet toque of the week before. Martha's rooms, which Hester had once seen, had the same scattered look, as if her whole life were composed of bits of trimming and selvage that she endlessly, faithfully, turned and made do. On the speckled, polka-dotted, or mustily striped bosoms of her dresses, anchoring her together, there was always the gold brooch lettered "True Sisters," symbol of a Jewish ladies' organization that was her extracurricular glory. To Hester, it seemed that this must have some esoteric significance, about which she never dared inquire, since, in so doing, she would be delving impolitely into the personal springs that must lie under the trivia of Martha, would be asking of that cramped, undreaming little body, "Cousin Martha, to what is it you are True?" Another thing that lifted Martha from the ordinary was her tic, which consisted of a wetting of the lips and a side twitch of the mouth that occurred at regular intervals, whether or not she happened to be talking. At first repelled by it, then fascinated by the way Martha and those around her ignored it, Hester had finally come to watch for it and dwell upon it, for it seemed to her a sign that obscure, eternal forces nudged even at the commonplace Martha, twitching at her, saying, "Even under your polka-dotted bosom, under your bits and stuff, we are working, we are here."

Next to Martha, Rose, her younger sister, whom she intermittently supported, made the muted small sounds that were meant to indicate delicately that her digestion, as usual, was not acting well. Rose was the only one of her father's cousins whom Hester disliked. With the slack shoulders and drooping neck of the invalid, she sloped inward upon herself, as if it were only by an intense concentration on her viscera that their processes might be maintained, as if the fractional huff-huff of her heart would go on only so long as she was there to listen and bid it. About her there was always the cottony, medicinal smell of indefinite ailments which would never be confirmed, Hester felt unsympathetically, except by that astringent confirmer, death.

"Want some soda, Rose?" asked her mother. "We could run across to the drugstore."

"No. I'll be all right," said Rose, satisfied that her distress had been noted. She turned toward Hester, whose stolidity she was always trying to court. "Getting such a big girl!" she said. "Why isn't she at camp, with Kinny?"

"She has to make up her algebra at summer school," said her mother. "Besides, she says fourteen and a half is too old for camp."

"Fourteen years. Imagine!" said Martha, the involuntary spasm flicking over her face, like an oblique comment. "Why I can remember her in her bassinet!"

"Yes," said Hester, in a dreamy urgency to say it before anyone else could. "How time flies!"

"Hester!" said her mother.

From Selena, sitting rigid, unyielding, in the supple currents of the dark, came a stifled snort, whether of amusement or disapproval Hester could not quite tell. Of all the adjuncts to their household, Selena was the most constant and the most silent. Spare and dark-haired, the color of a dried fig, she wore odd off colors, like puce and mustard and reseda green. Although they did not become her, she carried them like an invidious commentary on the drab patterns around her, and her concave chest was heavily looped with the coral residue of some years' stay in Capri as an art student, in her youth. She was the secretive spinster remnant of a branch of the family that had once been rich, so her concealment of her circumstances and her frequent presence at meals provoked occasional discussion as to whether she was still rich but miserly or had lost her money. "Poor Selena," Hester's father had once commented. "She's hungry for *people*." With her face pursed in her habitual contempt for the family of Philistines, she sat at their table nevertheless, partaking voraciously of something more than food.

"Where does Selena live?" Hester had once asked her mother.

"Oh, somewhere in Brooklyn," her mother had answered indifferently. "In the house her mother left her, I think."

"Were you ever there?"

"No-o." Her mother had shaken her head, amused, with the depreciative smile of those for whom Manhattan was New York. "Someone once told your father she'd sold it. No one really knows, though. She keeps very close."

"Did you ever see any of her paintings?"

"She painted me once, holding you, just after you were born. Mother and child." Her mother had laughed slightly.

"What was it like? Can I see it?"

"Oh!" Her mother had thrown up her hands, then brought them together, shaking her head in derision. "I don't know where it went. I suppose she took it back."

It had been Selena's mother, the old grandmother's elder sister, who had sent the grandmother, long ago, from California, the silver service with the pistol-handled knives the family still used at dinner parties. With it had come the large cup and saucer, covered with beaten gold, that Hester and her brother, long used to hearing their father say, "That cup's over a hundred years old!," had taken to calling "the hundred-year cup." Translating this to Selena, Hester privately visualized her as living in the narrow, high rooms of one of the single houses she associated with the very rich—in a house, perhaps, that was a kind of hundred-year cup of treasure, from which the humdrum touch of people would be inscrutably barred.

Leaning forward, Hester almost touched her hand softly to the coral hanging like strips of rosy twigs on Selena's flatness.

"I like it better this way," she said, "than round and smooth, like my baby beads."

"Oh?" said Selena, raising the furry circumflexes of her eyebrows. "And why do you like it better?"

Accustomed to asking why, rather than to being asked, Hester hesitated, startled. "It's more real," she said, finally.

"Real?" echoed Selena, the harsh tang of her voice thrusting the word forward, like a marble, to be felt and examined. Through the dimness, Hester could see her long, saffron face poised on one side, listening, weighing the word and Hester's use of it.

Emboldened by attention, Hester went further. "Where did you get them all—the corals, I mean?" she asked.

"On the island of Capri." There was a sostenuto, heroic pride in her tone, in the lifting of her chin, that stirred the others, Hester thought, to embarrassment and impatience.

"We'd better be going in," said her mother. "It's getting damp."

"What's it like—Capri?" asked Hester, imitating Selena's drawn-out Italian vowel.

"You might see for yourself someday," said Selena.

"Me?" said Hester. "Why, nobody ever travels in our family, except Daddy."

"No?" said Selena. She leaned back on the bench, turning her face away from them, shaking the loops on her chest slightly with her bony fingers, producing the slack sound of imperfect castanets.

"I really think . . ." said Hester's mother.

Across the street, through the sluggish air, there floundered a white, heavy figure, moving in starts and stops. It was Josie, the maid. As she ran, she gesticulated sidewise with her arms, wailing, "Meesis Elkin! Oh, Meesis Elkin!," so that the people on the other benches turned to look at them.

"Oh, that girl!" muttered her mother.

Josie had reached them. "Granma!" panted Josie. "I took in the eggnog and I could not vake her. I think—Come quick!"

"My God!" said Hester's mother. "Joe will never forgive me!"

Like a chorus, the three other women wheeled protectively around her, and, gathering up their long skirts, they all ran stumbling across the street to the entranceway of the apartment house. Catching up as they were entering the elevator, Hester tugged at her mother's elbow.

"Forgive you for what?" she said.

"For letting his mother die while he's away," said her mother, staring ahead. As they entered the apartment, she turned savagely on Hester. "You go in your room and *stay there!*"

The house filled almost magically with people, so no one noticed that Hester remained in the dining room, taking it all in, sitting alone on one of the ring of chairs that were ranged around the table like supernumeraries in a play. First had come the doctor, routed from his Sunday-night card game, on whom her mother and Rose and Martha hung, as if on a priest, as he came out of her grandmother's bedroom now, solemnly nodding his head. Selena followed, a step behind them.

"Selena, phone the others, will you?" said her mother.

"Be glad to," said Selena gruffly.

What perplexed Hester was that she really seemed to be glad to. Sitting straight as an upholstered stick in front of the phone, she handled it with import, calling Flora and Amy—the daughters of the dead one—and all the lesser relatives who would be offended if they were not among the first to be notified. Using the same formula as she got each number, she said not "your mother" or "your grandmother," as the case might be, but "Aunt Bertha." "I'm sorry to tell you," she would say, "but just a little while ago Aunt Bertha . . ."

It was the closest to death Hester had ever been. Seated there alone at the great, round communal plate of the dining table, she felt herself all over, inwardly, for the abrasions that were proper to the circumstance, but found none—nothing except a shameful sense of excitement over an extraordinary drama in which everyone unwontedly exposed himself. Aunt Flora, who had come, in answer to Selena's call, from her apartment a block away, had superseded Selena at the phone, as befitted a daughter of the deceased. With tears ruining the rouge on her aged-soubrette face, under the high white hair, she called number after number, bearing up remarkably until she got her party and identified herself, at which point she quavered, "Oh, Nettie!," "Oh, Walter!," and then burst into what seemed to be welcomed, cathartic tears.

I never cry over anything except myself, thought Hester guiltily, wondering whether, if they noticed her, they would expect her to be crying. Worriedly she tried to think of something that would make

226

her cry, but nothing stirred in her except the neutral, dispassionate awareness, the ignoble spur of interest.

Dispossessed from her post, Selena came and sat down opposite her. She raised her brows in surprise at Hester's still being up but said nothing, and her cheeks were hennaed with an unaccustomed tinge of participation. For a long time, the two of them sat there watching, while between them grew a tenuous thread of communion, as between two who sit at the edge of a party or a dance, sipping the moderate liqueur of observation, while around them swirl the tipsier ones, involved in a drunkenness the watchers do not share.

At last, Hester's mother, who had been busying herself like a distraught hostess, noticed her and, with an enraged whisper, sent her away to bed. Since Hester had always felt that her mother in the presence of others talked to her rather for their benefit than for hers, the scolding rolled off her numbed, sleepy head, and she walked away untouched, undisturbed, down the long hall to her room, past the closed door of her grandmother's bedroom. As she stood tentatively in the darkness of her own doorway, the door of the bedroom opened, and two men came out carrying a long wicker hamper, which they set down, securing the creaking cover, and then swung between them again, with a servile, devotional gait.

Sleepily pulling off her clothes, she was almost too tired to go through her nightly custom. She climbed onto the radiator under the window and stood there splayed out against the pane, feeling the familiar welling triumph of being suspended in space above people. She thought emulously of Selena, who remained apart, uninvolved, in her rich security of far places experienced, of distances apprehended. Bending down, she completed her ritual, sniffing at the jointure of the window, at its dark smell—a mixture of moisture and dust and the sharpening cool of night.

In bed, the last thing Hester remembered was the word "capri," which rolled toward her, in her mind uncapitalized, like a small coral bead, but when the brilliant afternoon sun woke her the following day, and sent her nuzzling down into the bedclothes, with their comfortable odor of orris and of her carelessly washed flesh, it was the hamper she remembered. She saw again the sickening rhythm in which the two men had moved—conspirators, shuffling out between them the surprisingly dowdy appurtenance of death.

She reached under the bed, and, drawing out one of the books she kept secreted there, held it in her hand for a long time, but when her mother opened the door and surveyed her exasperatedly, she still had not opened it.

"I never saw a more indifferent girl!" said her mother. "Your father's home and carrying on terribly. Everything falls on me!" She walked around the room, flipping back the bedclothes, picking up objects with the grim, abstracted compulsion of the housewife, the straightener, the manager. "Get up!" she said fiercely. "The funeral's at four o'clock. Make yourself a little decent, for once. Get that hair out of your eyes!"

"Am I going to the funeral?" asked Hester.

"No," said her mother. "Your father doesn't approve of children being exposed to death." Then she walked to the window and, slowly, measuredly, as if she were moving in time with a conventional elegy prescribed for the occasion, pulled the shade down firmly all the way to the sill and left the room. Chilled, Hester watched her go, wondering, as she dressed herself haphazardly, if the hard little correctnesses—the properness that seemed so difficult to acquire—crept in gradually as one grew, or whether, on some unspecified name day, one came of age, stepped into the finished, hypocritical shell, and was suddenly grown.

Once outside her door, she found the rest of the apartment sequestered and dim, as if some orderly person had just left, after solicitously muting the colors, numbing the sounds, strewing over everything the careful bleach of bereavement. From behind the closed door of her grandmother's sitting room, she heard a low rustle of voices and, centered in them, an indescribable retching sound.

She ran toward the warm neutrality of the kitchen. Josie was flusteredly scrabbling at batches of cookery, for which she had rooted out almost everything from the vast storecloset.

"Don't touch nothing!" Josie said hastily. Then, contrarily, she pushed toward Hester a plateful of *palacsinta*—thin pancakes stuffed with sweetened cottage cheese or melted jelly, which she would never make on command but which would appear suddenly when she had been moved, perhaps, by homesickness for her own country or by a sense of occasion. As Hester ate, Josie hovered over her, sighing.

The Watchers

"T-t-t!" said Josie, rocking back and forth. "Is too bad." Again Hester felt the flicker of guilt, as if someone had twanged a string inside her and had found it slack, without resonance.

She left the kitchen and crossed the hall to the dining room. Peering into the parlor through the French doors, dully masked with net, she made out a corner where chairs had been drawn aside to make room for what must be the coffin. Parting the doors stealthily, she went in, planning to see for herself the thing to which children must not be exposed.

As she entered, a figure seated in front of the coffin moved slightly. Terror of the unimaginable jumped in her, for the figure was tiny, bent, and dressed in spare black, as her grandmother had always been. Expelling her breath, she saw that this was a stranger, whose china teeth and thick, glossy brown wig, rimming her face like a hat, were both too big for her, giving her the appearance of a Punch-and-Judy doll that had been excessively repaired.

Hester drew back, but the woman, misinterpreting her withdrawal, motioned toward her ingratiatingly, with a custodian's pride. Drawing Hester compellingly to the coffin's side, the woman then stood with her hands bunched together at her neckbones, her bright, avian stare cocked sidewise as Hester looked down into the box.

Less wrinkled, whiter than in life, Hester's grandmother extended her short length in the box, with the same finished, miniature look she had always had, with the same natural dignity. At any moment, Hester felt, she might unlock her eyes and say, "But how could you think I would not handle *this* decently, properly, too?" Shrinking from the gross casualness of the woman attitudinized beside her, Hester wavered nearer the box, and when she turned and ran from the room, it was from the live woman that she ran.

In the hallway, she collided with the hatted figure of her mother, and for a moment that soft collision with dim, powdery fragrance, with the half-remembered enveloping warmth of babyhood, clouded the barrier of properness between them.

"Who's that little old woman in there?" Hester whispered.

"Who? Oh, she's a professional watcher," said her mother. She was carefully draping a thick veil over her hat. "Your grandmother was Orthodox, you know," she added with a certain disdain. "Someone has to be with the dead until the burial, the next day."

"Is that her *job*?" Hester whispered.

"It's a volunteer society, I believe. I suppose women who have no other . . . I suppose one gives them *something*," her mother said impatiently, with a final shake of herself. "Go stay with Josie," she added, frowning.

Lingering in the hall, Hester watched her mother listen at the sitting-room door for a minute and then knock.

"Joe," said her mother, "it's almost time."

The door opened and Hester's father came out, surrounded by the hovering women: Flora and Amy—his sisters—and the cousins Rose and Martha. Selena was not among them. Her father looked blindly ahead of him, and half groans, the replica of the awful sound she had heard before, still shook him.

"Joe," said her mother, "get ahold of yourself!"

He raised his head. "Ahold of myself!" he said. He bent his head again, and the women closed around him—the red-eyed, solicitous sisters first, then the border of cousins—and, moving their dark caravan slowly, steadily, they passed through the dim foyer and out the apartment door.

Hester tiptoed to the empty kitchen. Through the half-open door of Josie's room, she saw her sleeping on her bed, openmouthed. Shutting the back door of the apartment softly behind her, Hester ran down the five flights of service stairs into the back court of the apartment house. Making a wide circle, she arrived at the front entrance and unobtrusively joined the audience of children and passersby that flanked it.

All along the street, the line of black cars waited in heavy perfection, closed to the great blond sea of the sun. From both corners, people converged upon them, like a stream of ants,.and were met at the center by a gentleman with a fixed look of gravity, who murmured something to each of them, referred to a list in his hand, and, nodding, conducted them to one or another of the cars.

Next to Hester, a woman nudged another. "The family," she mouthed.

Now the grave man's look deepened, became even more carved, as, with a stooping, comma-like posture, the list disregarded, he handed Hester's parents and the aunts into the central car, bearing them along almost on his arm, as if they were the veritable royalty of grief. Behind them, Martha, in an aspiring headdress poised like an aigrette on a sparrow, and Rose, straighter than usual, were shunted into one of the rear cars by an assistant. By now, the cars were full, and the stragglers who still came were people, unfamiliar to Hester, who did not seem to expect to go with the cortege but passed on, whispering among themselves, into the building. Four men, dressed the same, and of a size, like dummies, emerged, carrying the coffin. At the curb they paused, shifting the weight between them, then slid it neatly into the hearse.

The carved gentleman raised his hand officiously toward his assistant. "All set," he said.

Suddenly, walking alone, came Selena. Even today, she had been unable to resign herself to black and wore a dress the rubbed blue of plumskin, whose texture seemed flattened here and there by years of waiting in a box. Without the insignia of her coral, she looked somehow bereft, but she walked toward the gentleman in austere pride, on her cheeks the henna tinge of the night before.

The gentleman looked discomforted. "Only the immediate family," he said placatingly.

"I am a member of the family," said Selena in a secure contralto, but one hand opened and closed at her chest, seeking the reassurance of the corals, as if she might at any moment add, "The member from Capri."

Bending nearer, the gentleman murmured an inquiry and agitatedly checked her answer against his list. "I am sorry," he said in buttered tones, "but there seems to have been an oversight. Do you wish me to check with a member of . . ." He paused and allowed a delicate insinuation of disapproval to affect his face.

"No," said Selena in a rusty voice. "Never mind."

He bowed. "The family," he said consolingly, "will receive friends of the deceased upstairs when they return." He flicked a nod to his assistant, and with a sinuous deftness they inserted themselves into the hearse, which pulsed into a motion that reverberated sluggishly down the line of cars.

In a few minutes, the street was almost empty of cars and onlookers, except for Hester, who had crept behind one of the ironwork grilles in the courtyard, and Selena, who remained as if held by a need to see the last of the cars inexorably gone. Standing there in the open light of summer, she looked to Hester at once bizarre and dusty, like one of those oddly colored bits of bric-a-brac that seem mysterious and compelling in the back of the store but, when brought to the light by the excited purchaser, are seen to be lurid and unsuccessful. When the last car had gone, Selena stood there for a moment, her hand still nervously groping on her chest; then, slowly, with a ragged, indecisive gait, she turned and walked away.

Hester saw her recede down the long block, until she vanished around the corner. In her mind, like a frieze, she saw the added-up picture of Selena, always watching tentatively, thirstily, on the fringe of other people's happenings, and fear grew in her as she became suddenly aware of her own figure, standing now in the hot sun. It was watching, too.

The Gulf Between

~§ T URNING THEIR backs on the last fanfare of sunset over the river, Hester and Kinny Elkin, side by side, skated laboriously up the hill, toward Broadway. Ordinarily, they would have kept a more cynical distance between elder sister, gone past twelve, and younger brother, but today, in the sprawling ten-room apartment which had always been their home, the shape of things was being dismantled for removal to a sunless five rooms in the rear of the building, on the same floor. Neither was anxious to return to the uneasy place now revealing itself as no longer theirs.

For Hester, it was hard to believe that things back there would not be the same as they always had been at this hour, full of the settled ease of women from both sides of the family, dropped in for their afternoon coffee—white tablecloth, the cake plates with angels painted in their centers, cocoa for the children; to think of all this as not there to return to was like trying to hold in the ear two separate chords. Surely, when Josie, the maid, opened the door, her hectic look, both shaky and starched, would advise that the usual assortment of aunts and cousins was already sitting within, the two clans politely opposed as always, joined only on such topics as their common opinion of the Elkin maid. Silent on the things that mattered, they would be exchanging crumbs of agreement on whatever didn't, across a little neutral sea where innuendo slid like eels; this was what adult "politeness" was. For the half-grown like herself, its counterpart was: to say, and appear to see—nothing. To rest on the yet safer swells of a bottom dark was what it had been to be a child.

Meanwhile, in the exchanges that had gone on above, the women of her father's family, no longer rich or beautiful, older than her mother by the same some twenty years as her father, had always held the upper hand. Allied closest to the household by their dependence on Mr. Elkin, on a business just large enough to be sometimes in important difficulties—and until recently, by their deference to her grandmother, the six-months-dead monarch of them all —something they owned had nevertheless kept them always the winners over her mother, and the family on her mother's side.

Her mother's people, when momentarily left to themselves, to the thriftier gossip of their own smaller businesses, households, smaller everything, could often be heard to cluck a "T-t-t"ing disapproval of this quality, whatever it was, and—in the dead waits between those murmurs—to admire. As later comers to the country from a rural part of Bavaria, after fifty years here the men of her mother's people still had fingers thick at the root, the women a strong village-sense of disaster. The Elkin lot, born in the laziest part of America, sometimes wasted time, and, on occasion, fortune— they knew how to waste. Her mother's people were drawn daily to the comfort of it. Yet, if on those slow afternoons the Elkin women still triumphed, it was by the others' subservience to what could be seen most clearly in the two lots of unframed family pictures, enemies tumbled together in an old breakfront's drawer. For while her mother's aunts and cousins were always taken at their rigid best, in full-length, marble-finish studies by Sarony—within the faultless drape of ballgown or teagown, perhaps gazing at a long dinner-ring on a forefinger, or all unconscious of a high-lighted necklace—the Elkin women (by her mother's comment and Hester's own admission "foolish dressers") were invariably shown to the waist only, emerging from that photographer's mist which gave predominance to the face, these upheld proudly, as if something within, flowering from neck to brain, to hair wild or confined but always luxuriant, said, "We are more than we have. We are."

Ordinarily, Hester held both sides under advisement, and knew too well their estimate of her—on her case, as on Josie's, they were joined. Today, however, she wished against hope that she might find them all there taking their comfort, however divided, as a sign to her that it was still there to take.

"Race you down the new sidewalk," said Kinny.

On Fort Washington Avenue, the top of the hill, they wheeled sideways and rested, wheezing for breath. Before them, seen through the sidestreet, the blinding bronze of the high windows on Broadway flashed like cymbals turning away from light, faded floor by floor, and went out. Here, the pebbly tan stone of the pavement changed to a smooth concrete, more dangerous to skate on, of a kind which slid under wheel silkily with a high, singing sound.

"Ah no. Let's not race." Mostly, she let him win, not minding. It was the contest she minded. "Want to go down holding on, no knee-bend?" This was more dangerous, but a trial against the hill, not between themselves. But Kinny whizzed ahead, crouched over, shouting low insults to that imaginary combatant boys always carried with them, and disappeared around the corner.

Knees straight, Hester, insolently balanced, clasped her hands in front of her and rolled down the hill after him, almost persuading herself that while she was immovable, the houses were being pulled past her on an endless tape. As she flew around the corner, another change in the sidewalk threw her forward, almost on her face, but she saved herself with a few hacking steps and slid down on the stoop of the corner house, pulling at her skate-straps with fingers numbed by the darkening air. During the moment in which she had turned the corner, the dusk had become palpable, in that gradual surge she could never arrest with her eyes.

"Got the key?" Kinny swooped down beside her. She dug in her pocket and handed him the skate-key. From the curls of its broken, grayish string, a nickel fell out and rang on pavement speckled here with particles which would prickle into silver when the streetlights went on.

"Buy us a chocolate bar?" said Kinny.

"Let's get a frank, and divvy." Recently, her greediness had shifted away from the sweet to the sour. Herder's frankfurters were served with a gamboge daub of mustard and a fringe of kraut. She picked up the nickel and spun it on the stone.

"It'll go down the grating," he said.

"We could fish for it with a magnet." Between the dim edges of a pervading sadness, she saw herself looking for the magnet in the topsy-turviness of her room as she had left it this noon, bureaus emptied, bed stacked against the wall. Over her protests, the rattan toy chest had had its contents dumped into a carton, and had been packed with linen.

She kicked off her skates and stood up. Swinging them by the thongs, she walked with him back up the hill on the Broadway side, feeling deflated and set down, her legs wobbling oddly on the suddenly still ground. All the interstices of the city were deepening with a chill color and people were passing quietly, their faces softened and reminiscent. She had a feeling that if she wet her finger and drew it through the air it would return stained with the dye of dusk. Even Mr. Mishnun, the old stationer, emerging from his stunted store to shoo out a small boy who had been snitching candy, paused for a minute, looking upward, abashed by the dumb, violet passage of the city into evening.

Herder's dairy was warm, insulated from the transit of the day by bright, particolored shelves and a smell of breads and peppercorns. She and Kinny ate slowly, served absent-mindedly by Mrs. Herder, who stood behind the counter, talking to a woman customer.

"Ja, that's the way it is," said Mrs. Herder, nodding her head, smoothing together the crumbs and poppyseed on the cutting-board with her raw, boiled-looking hand. "That's the way it is."

"Comes to everybody," said the customer, grasping her bundle stolidly before her.

"Sooner or later," said Mrs. Herder, still nodding. Looking past them all into some mournful middle distance, she let out her breath in a long, confirming sigh. The nodding, like the last effort of a pendulum, quivered into ever shorter arcs, and stopped.

To Hester, reared among so many elderly and middle-aged of both clans, these sad conversational cul-de-sacs of the grown had a sound both familiar and elusive. Though unable to define that central foreboding which, lurking always under the oblique talk, was acknowledged and propitiated by all, she recognized that some hovering bird, whether of time or death or doom, circled over all the grown, and that even while they confirmed its presence with this rallying of voices, each hoped secretly that this would forestall the moment when it would notice *him* in his cranny of safety—and pounce. Each said to himself cannily: "As long as I can speak of it to others, it is not yet here for me."

Kinny had darted out of the store, but Hester, chewing speculatively, stared at Mrs. Herder until the woman looked at her, inquiring.

236

"Th—thank-you," muttered Hester, and left, closing the door behind her with special care. As she stepped outside, the streetlamps went on, with their succinct "Now!" and the night was there.

Far down the block of small old-fashioned shops still bare of neon, Kinny was peering into the weakly shining window of Pachmann's jewelry store on the corner.

"Looka here!" he called.

She ran over and knelt down next to him. Against the darkened inner store, a single bulb in the window burned over rows of square cards spaced on humped-up red velvet, each card holding a single, gleaming nugget of lure. Behind them, a row of clocks told various times of day, all false except the large moving one in the center.

"Keep looking in sideways!" Kinny knelt in front of the window, hooking an arm around its side. She knelt beside him. Through the glass corner she saw, refracted and shimmering, an airy replica of the whole display. Kinny's plump fingers, exaggeratedly curved, poised over a man's watch, dipped recklessly through it and alighted again, this time over a heart-shaped locket with an enameled American flag blowing in its center.

"Want it?" Pinching the image between thumb and forefinger, he tossed it to her. She cupped herself, almost expecting to receive it. The locket remained. If she shifted her head past a certain angle of interception, it blinked out, on. In the window, the real one had a solidity almost disappointing. Outside it, very slightly double-edged, the other bloomed with an added shine. She stretched out her own hand.

"Holy mackerel!" said Kinny. "Will we catch it. Look at the time!"

Grabbing up their skates, they scurried down a sidestreet into the doorway of their own apartment house. Its lobby had the deserted look of dinnertime. Far above them, the elevator hummed dispiritedly in its shaft, and came to a jouncing stop on some upper floor.

"Wish we didn't have to go in." Kinny kicked glumly at the carpet, his ruddy face chapfallen and aggrieved under the jaundiced tan light here. Against the Oriental splendor of the lobby, his rotund figure in its eternally battered clothes caught at her sympathy like a humpty-dumpty version of herself.

"Let's walk up," he said at last.

Toiling up the stairs in front of him, past each hallway, past the closed doors of the Shoemakers, the Levys, the Kings and other residents she didn't know, she visualized each family, unchanged and comfortable at their white-draped tables, behind them the maids serving unhurriedly from massive sideboards on which were ranged, permanent and secure, the tureens, the candlesticks, and the bowls of fruit. Only at the Elkins' was there distortion beyond repair but not yet complete, where one groped absently for the displaced chair, the drawer that had been "there," caught in the painful torsion of contexts not quite yet shelved into retrospect.

"Wish we were leaving here altogether," she said, as they reached their own floor. She put a hesitant hand on the bell.

"Go on. Ring." Kinny goosed her from behind. Swatting back at him, she was almost comforted, half convinced that behind the door everything would be unchanged. At this hour, her father would open it, crying, "Good God in heaven, where have you two been!" and even before they got their jackets off, her mother's honing recitative against dirt would be at them to wash their hands. Hester, once she had slipped into the place at table marked by her own dented napkin ring, could then slip into her childish role of culprit permanently arraigned, in which, comfortably abraded, suspended between her parents' personalities, she could regress into her revery with herself.

Hester's mother opened the door. Against the grotto welter of piled goods looming behind, her head, covered with a white hand-towel pinned at the nape, had an air of heroic resolve, coifed for the worst, like the nurses in the recruiting posters that hung on the walls at school. She snapped on a brighter light, as if to bring their lateness into surer focus.

"No consideration whatsoever—none at all!" she said. She shook her head, but her face had an abstracted look, and her hands, whose usual cleanliness in the midst of the grimiest task was to Hester half an attractive riddle, half a reproof, were dusty, and left a smear on the head-towel as she patted it irritably.

"Daddy home?" asked Kinny.

"Yes," said his mother, looking at him sternly. "He came home early." Kinny slipped past her.

"Where's Josie?" asked Hester.

"You know Josie went to find a room in Yorkville," said her mother. "We won't have room for a sleep-in girl in the new place. Can't you get it through your head that—?" She broke off in the long, exasperated sigh that was almost a reversion to her native *Ach!* To Hester, her mother's face, formed with a beautiful inevitability of bone, much resembled a head of Venus in her Latin book, or would have, had it not had also the lurking contour of a plaintiveness ever-ready for some disaster sure to occur. Tonight, as always in time of crisis, her face had the triumphant look of disaster confirmed.

For a moment she looked at Hester significantly, searching, in a way she had been doing of late, as if the fact of Hester's being a girl, almost a woman, should make her rise to the stature of confidante. Then, as if what she saw only confirmed the impossibility of such an alliance, she threw up her hands and went back toward the kitchen.

Hester went into the dining room. The polished table shone emptily.

" 'Lo, darlin'," said her father. He was bent over the sideboard, tussling ineffectually with the rope bound around its doors in preparation for tomorrow's moving. He patted her absently.

"Where's the sherry, Hattie?" he called.

"Sherry!" Her mother reappeared at the door to the kitchen. Behind her Kinny lounged, already munching a roll. "Table's set in the kitchen!"

They had never before eaten in the kitchen, too small except for scratch lunches or the solitary, clinking meals of the maid.

"Look, Hattie," said her father, frowning, "why don't I take you all out to dinner?"

"Hmmph!" said her mother. "Delmonico's, perhaps?"

"No need to grind it in," said her father, flushing. His teasing account of their engagement dinner—when he, the so much older man of the world, had found himself at Delmonico's with a girl made tipsy by one glass of champagne—was known to all.

Mrs. Elkin sat down at the kitchen table and began to eat. Set out were cheeses still in their cartons, cold sliced meat in butcher's paper, everything haphazard and at odds, as if she, normally a heckler of maidservants on table detail, would forcibly show her family the ugly pattern of tomorrow.

"Get your father some coffee," she said to Hester, pointing to the pot on the stove.

Hester waited, warily. Her mother had a habit of urging her to activity, then stopping Hester's clumsy efforts midway.

"Let the child alone. I'll get my own coffee," said Mr. Elkin, his face red and miserable above a dandified tie and jeweled stickpin which contrasted queerly with the stove, as he bent over it.

"Time they realized their father isn't a millionaire," said Mrs. Elkin. Kinny had already tiptoed away.

"Now look here, Hattie . . ." said her father. He brought his cup to the table and sat down, sighing. Suave after-dinner raconteur, he was completely lacking in the vocabulary of dissension. Time after time, Hester had watched his superior verbal elegancies falter and dry up before the thrust of his wife's homely tongue.

"They've never wanted for anything so far," he said. "And neither have you."

Mrs. Elkin's lips tightened. Large-boned, calmly moving, she had few fussy mannerisms; it was only her voice that fiddled. "Time they realized their father isn't getting any younger."

In the silence, the percolator chortled on the stove. The cup shook in her father's veined hand, and a drop fell on the waxy linen of his cuff, near the lion-headed cuff link. He set the cup carefully down.

Mrs. Elkin's cheekbones and eyelids reddened. It was known that she lived among dreamers who could be educated for the worst only by her savage ability to get under the skins of those she loved and must awaken; this was why she was compelled first to tear down the self-deceptive veils with which they wreathed themselves and only afterwards could poultice up their wounds with love—with the tray of food brought to the banished boy, the party dress ironed to perfection for the girl who had given up going. All this was known, and now contemplated.

"Joe . . ." said Mrs. Elkin.

Raising his head, Mr. Elkin took off his noseglasses and rubbed at the inflamed prints on either side of his nose. The luxuriant up-twirl of his dated moustache looked suddenly too jaunty for his exposed face. He slid the glasses into their case, which popped shut with a snap, and looked at his wife. "For God's sake, Hattie, take that damn *thing* off your head!"

Hester, chewing a soda cracker, heard the sound twice: the dry champing heard by their ears, at the same time magnified in her head. Wishing that she might melt from the room, carrying her dislocation with her, she started to tiptoe from the table.

"Come on back now, and finish your supper," said her father, pleading, anxious as always to deny the ugly breach, to cover it over with the kindness that bled from him steadily, that he could never learn not to expect in return.

"I'm sleepy." With the word, sleep fell on her like a blow. Seeing herself already in a mound of blankets, folded impervious in her own arms until tomorrow, she turned away, down the hall to the haven of her room.

She was halfway into the darkened room before she felt the alteration in it. Thinking that some of the furniture must be ranged along the walls, she moved confidently toward the island of the bed. Her body passed through its image with the ease of fingers passing through a locket. A moving reflection from the headlights of a car going by in the street below traveled up one wall, trembled watery on the ceiling, and swept down the other wall, leaving a scene fanned into an instant's being, and gone. There was nothing in the room.

She turned and ran back down the hall, cracking a knee against chairs stacked one-over-one, as in restaurants in the early morning. Lumpily shrouded barriers extended all along the walls. She felt down them, hunting a cream-colored bed with insets of caning, the surely discoverable scallop-shape of a mirror, the bureau with bow-front swagged in wooden roses, in a pattern that was like a silly friend.

Holding onto the bruised knee, she limped back to the kitchen and confronted her mother. "Where's all my room?" she said.

"What?" asked her father, puzzled.

"Oh, I meant to tell you," answered her mother, composedly. "You're to sleep in Grandma's old room. Your nightgown's there on the bed."

"But where's my furniture?"

"You're to have Grandma's old set. You know that. How many bedrooms do you think we'll have, in the new place!"

"What have you done with the child's things!" Mr. Elkin's face was already shrunken with a warding-off of the answer.

Mrs. Elkin hesitated, but only to trim a note of triumph. "I—sold them."

"I might know you'd start dramatizing," he said. "There's no need to act as if we were down to our last penny."

"Are we?" Hester saw it, copper-bright and final, in the linted seam of his pocket.

For answer, he pulled her onto his lap. She perched there awkwardly, conscious of her gangling legs, but savoring the old position of comfort. "Almost forgot what I brought you from downtown," he said, fumbling in the pocket and bringing out two objects. "New compass for Kinny," he said, laying it on the table. "And this—for you." In his palm, he held a tiny, round vanity-case of translucent, rosy enamel and painted flowers, its cover fitted with a golden latch.

"Fellow brought it in the office," he mumbled.

Mrs. Elkin, for whom the extras of life had a touch of the dissolute, turned her head aside.

Hester, warming the pink gift in her hand, stood up between them, in the gap between her mother, immovable on her plateau of the practical, and her father, wavering curator of intangibles he could assert but not protect. All this was known, yet there was never a way to say it. She aligned her free hand on his shoulder. "I wonder what I would have looked like," she said in a hard voice, "if you had not married her." Without waiting for an answer to what was not after all a question, she left the kitchen again.

In the doorway of her room, she stopped, waiting until she could half-see in the darkness. The nude walls poured from ceiling to floor, regarding her. Refracted in her mind, she saw the room as it had been, its objects spaced with the exact ruler of remembrance but already blurred with the double-edge of the past. Wading carefully into its center, she set the gift down on the bare floor. She knelt over it a moment. Then she walked out and closed the door.

In her grandmother's room, she flipped the light switch on and off just long enough to see the odd note of her own sprigged flannel gown on the huge bed. The room, shrouded in dust-covers since its owner's death, had the reserve of disuse. Ordinarily Hester would have tried the locks of the trunks which held the vestees of *broderie anglaise* and the threadlace shawls, and run a scuttling finger through bureau drawers still full of passementerie rejected by the raiding relatives six months ago. Tonight, she had begun to understand the mechanics of desecration. She stepped out of her clothes and into the nightdress, feeling as strange here as on the one night she had spent in the hospital. Crouched down under the comforter, she gripped her ankles with her hands. Burrowing her head into the blackness between her knees, listening to the purling of her own breath, she slept.

Sometime during the night she woke, her heart hammering up from a dream in which two hands, smooth, anonymous and huge, emerging wrist upward from mist, wrestled with one another, the great fingers twining in silent, marble struggle. From beneath a coverlet of stone, she waited for the mushrooming spaces of the dream to settle and ebb. Through the open door of the bathroom connecting with her parents' bedroom, she heard their voices, locked and vying.

"No!" said her mother, in a whisper as long-drawn as a scream. "I won't let you have it. What should be kept for your own children. To let it go down the family drain, like all the rest."

"By God," said her father's voice, "how would you have it, except for me? How many women are there who can buy ten thousand dollars' worth of stock out of their household allowance?"

"Sixteen years," said her mother, still in that shuddering whisper. "Licking their backsides. Being the *Ausländer*. Being the responsible one. Carrying the bedpans to your mother, so your sisters could visit, and drink cream. . . . And the miles and miles of fine words, of fine *feelings* that the Elkins have such a talent for—as long as someone else underwrites them . . . Someone crass—like me."

"No one asked you to martyr yourself. Who do you think I work for, if not for you and the children?"

"For anyone who gets to you first with a few cheap words to make you feel big Ike. For anyone who will say 'dear Joe.' "

"Now listen, Hattie—"

"You corrupt people," said her mother, her voice rising. "Because you are too weak to refuse them."

"For the last time . . ."

243

"No!" said her mother. "Not this time," the words pulling from her as if she spun them one by one from a pit of resolve. "Not if you go down on your knees."

"God, what kind of woman are you, to make a man abase himself so? Over *money*," said her father, his voice ratchety and breathy.

"Family of leeches, leeches," intoned her mother. "Sister Flora's husband can't get a job in anyone else's business, but dear Joe will give him one. Sister Mamie can't live with her rotter of a husband, but she can talk about his aristocratic Leesburg connections, as long as dear Joe will help her out. And the bookkeeper you won't accuse of stealing from you, because he is your sister-in-law's brother. Even your brother's widow, that low Irish, complaining about the settlement you gave her. What was he but a shoe salesman until he brought her from Chicago, and dear Joe gave him the factory to manage. Fine manager."

"Leave the dead alone!" Her father's voice had an empty sound. There was a pause, in which the edges of silence rubbed together. "Ask the dead for your collateral."

From beneath the stone coverlet, Hester heard that last, faceless word sink into the quiet. After a time, someone shut the connecting door.

In the hollow of the bed, the dream waited to grow again. With an effort, she pushed up the rim of stone, and slipped out of bed. Dragging after her the comforter, suddenly light and threatless in her hand, she felt her way down the corridor to Kinny's room. Always in a state of embattled flux, even packing day had scarcely dislodged it from the norm, and its shadows had the clutter of homeliness.

She sat on the edge of his bed and drew the comforter around her, nestling toward him, feeling him warm and insensate beside her, smelling of boy-sweat and grubbiness, and infinitely removed. From behind them, the moiling quarrel between her parents pierced through her, past her, into the world beyond. All of it had been known, but she could now see, as never before, the exact angle of its interception. On the one side stood her mother, the denying one, the unraveler of other people's façades, but resolute and forceful by her very lack of some dimension; on the other side stood her father, made weak by his awareness of others, carrying like a phy-

244

lactery the burden of his kindliness. And flawed with their difference, she felt herself falling endlessly, soundlessly, in the gulf between.

On Kinny's shoulder, rounded in sleep, a lozenge of light wavered. She put out her hand hopefully, but she had lost the trick of playing with such semblances. She tried to cry, but could not summon that childish scald. Though she could not name the bird now hovering, she knew its nature. Slowly the bird descended, and chose. She began to weep the sparse, grudging tears of the grown.

The Sound of Waiting

~§ SUNDAY WAS the day you hung around listening to the echoes of yourself. In the fat silences after dinner, everyone hovered, holding on to the dwindling thread of yesterday's routine, wretchedly waiting to join it to that of tomorrow. Outside, the soft tearing sound of the traffic rushed people to innumerable delights and conclusions; inside the ticking room anticipation swelled like a bell that was never sounded. Laved, in fresh clothes, the body thudded, poised for its adventure, until the sharp definitive click of the lamps slid the day down from the hope of change into the pigeonhole of reality.

For all, for everyone except his father. For him, Sunday was a kind of justification, whose rest he took in the biblical sense, a patriarch relaxing superbly from converse into the sleep where he lay now, the mock-fierce mustache stirred by the breath from the hidden kindly mouth, the delicately made spatted ankles, out of another era, crossed sideways on the sofa.

If he moved now, his father would stir irritably, muttering "Eh? Where're you going now? Can't you spend a day with your family?" for, to his almost tribal sense of family, outside interests were always to be secondary, and—with the dwindling of his own family contemporaries by death—the attainment of adulthood in his children and their increasing focus outside the home seemed to induce in him a pathetic rage, almost as if over a breach of allegiance.

If wholly awakened now, he would rise to potter testily with his cigar, roughing the newspapers back into coherence with mutterings against the disorderliness of the rest of the family, or, if fate provided an attentive Sunday visitor, settling benignly again into the anecdotes that eructated like bubbles from the ferment of his

246

memory. "Salesman's talk," his mother called it, for to her his father's expansiveness, always a continual social embarrassment to her aloofness, had become even more of a reminder that his father was really an old man now, that the long gap of age between them would never again be bridged. His father was old enough to be his grandfather—had the gap between his father and himself never really been bridged at all because of this alone, he wondered? Or was it because his father belonged to the last outpost of a generation which regarded its children as the final insignia of a full life, perhaps, but always as extensions of its own identity, interposing between them and it a wall of glass, through which the pattern of daily intimacies might be filtered, but through which the self-contained globe of a child's private world was forever inadmissible?

Over and above the flood of real "goods" that his father sold twinklingly, unfailingly, in the backslapping camaraderie of business, his father *was* a salesman, he thought—a salesman of the past. Rootless though the family had long been, in the shifting way of the apartment dweller, because of his father they had continued to live as if they still had attics and cellars, their closets and rooms crammed with the droppings of generations, the yellowed inanimates that had pitilessly survived the transient fingerprints of the flesh. When he, his son, had looked about him at the mass of young men at college with him, he had felt that, compared to his own, their backgrounds were as truncated, as flat, as their tidy one-step-above hire-purchase homes, where a family picture was an anachronism that must not mar the current scheme, where the old and worn must immediately be slip-covered with the new. And it had seemed to him then, that although he had never had the permanence of a homestead, of the landed people, he was rooted, he had been nourished, in the rich compost of his father's reminiscence.

But now, in the taut room, where the silence stretched like a wire vibrating with impulses that were never heard, he felt suddenly that his father had always been as remote to him as a figure in a pageant, or as a storyteller between whose knees he had been gripped, enthralled, but whose recitative backward glance had never bent itself to him. And torn, half by a jealousy for that panoramic experience, that sweep of life that he and his own contemporaries might never duplicate, he looked across at his father with regret, feeling that he, the son, had listened indeed, but had never himself been heard. From all the crooning corners of his childhood he could hear his father's teasing, crowing voice: "Sure, boy. I've been everywhere! I've been to Europe, I-rup, O-rup, and Stir-rup!"

As in the faded primary tints of a lithograph on a thumbed calendar, he could see, he could almost *remember* the dusty provincial streets and lanes of the post-Civil War Richmond of sixty-five years ago, and the little boy with black Fauntleroy curls being dragged along by the gaunt, arrogant Negro woman, past the jeers of the street urchins.

"Plenty of professional Southerners talk about their colored mammies—but Awnt Nell—she was a real woman. Freed woman too, but she would never leave your grandmother. And proud of my curls—as if they were her own boy's! Kept me getting in fights over 'em. Then she took to follering around behind me, 'til I went to Maw and cried to have 'em cut off. Stayed with us too; wouldn't go away even after Paw's business went bad with the rest." . . . The remembered voice went on, like a record he could pluck out from the years at will.

"Guess I should have been a lawyer. Always wanted to be." Yes, his father would have liked that—the poised strut in front of the attentive jury, the poured-out display of the enormous, sometimes inaccurately pronounced vocabulary.

"Left school too early. Heh! The Academy—that's where we went in those days—all religions alike. Academy of St. Joseph. That old harridan there—Miss Atwell—she never did like me. One day she said to me 'Joe! Come up here!' And she had the ruler in her hand. Now your grandmother—she never raised her hand to the eight of us, and she kept us all in line. I wasn't gawn to stand for any ruler rapped on my knuckles. So I walked up there . . . and I stood there . . . and I put out my hand. And when she raised the ruler I took it, and broke it over my knee, and threw it out the window. I left there and I never went back. Never. Only time I ever made my mother cry. Swore I would never make her cry again. I was a good son, and I didn't. But I never went back there again."

Then the first job—the grocery store—almost like the stereotype beginnings of the self-made American, but with the imprint of the fastidious Joe, the *bon vivant*, the *fin de siècle* beau-to-be, already implicit in the tale.

The Sound of Waiting

"That herring barrel! Seemed 's if everybody who came into that store wanted herring. So I'd reach my hand down in that cold slithery mess of stuff and haul up one of those herring. Ugh! Quit that job as quick as I could . . . went into a lawyer's office licking stamps. At the end of a week I went to Mr. Fitzmorris (your grand-mother was married from his house) and I said 'Mr. FitzMorris, I want to leave.'

" 'Why Joe,' he says, 'what's the matter?'

" 'Mr. Fitzmorris,' I said, 'my tongue is sore!'

"He sat back and laughed and laughed. 'Why Joe,' he says, 'we'll give you a sponge!' "

In the stereopticon of his mind he could see his father's hand reaching down into the barrel, but somehow it was not the raw hand of the thirteen-year-old boy, but the elegant knotted hand with the raised blue veins and the brown diamond finger ring, in the graphically illustrative gesture he had seen again and again, the hand he saw now drooping over the sofa, lifted imperceptibly now and again in the current of slumber.

Glancing back into the dimness of the foyer, he could see the huge triple-doored bookcase, its sagging shelves stuffed three-deep with the books that had been his father's education. He thought of his own studies, the slow acquisition of the accepted opinions on the world's literature, sedulously gathered from the squeezings of the compartmented minds of his professors, the easy access to the ponderous libraries with their mountains of ticketed references as available as his daily dinner. Yet it had been years before he could mention a book of which his father had not heard. "Baldassare Castiglione!" his father would say, taking the book from his hand, rolling the syllables on his tongue. "*The Courtier!* My God, it must be nearly fifty years since I saw that!" For a moment a formless eagerness has trembled on his own lips, as if he might say at last "What do you—?—This is what I—Let us exchange . . ." but the book would be handed back, the sighing revelation had not been made, the moment passed.

All during the early years while his father had been selling soap for a Quaker merchant in Philadelphia he had also been studying Italian in the evenings so that he could read Dante in the original, or picking his way through Horace and Ovid with the aid of the "trots" that would have been forbidden to him had he gone to college. On one shelf of the bookcase, *Mademoiselle de Maupin*, the *Mémoires de Ninon de Lenclos*, and a row of Balzac stood as evidence of the years in New Orleans, where, only in his twenties, but already the dashing representative of "Oakley and Co., Manufacturers and Perfumers, Founded 1817," he had, according to his own testimony, spent half his time at Antoine's, and the rest on the pouting bosoms of Creole ladies of good family. On the other shelves *Rasselas, Prince of Abyssinia*, a red-edged set of Thackeray, and some funereally bound Waverley novels were jumbled together; copies of Burns, Mrs. Browning, and the *Heptameron of Marguerite of Navarre* might be interlarded with the Victoriana of Quiller-Couch, Sir Edmund Gosse, and an old copy of Will Carleton's *Farm Legends*. In the brown dusk of the foyer they all melted together, holding under their dusty gilt a repository of his own childhood, for on them he had fed also, and from them had been drawn the innumerable orotund tags of his father's conversation.

Stealthily he rose and went to the window. On one of the nearby tables lay the broken-backed copy of Pope from which his father often quoted, its cover scrolled and illuminated to look like a church window. Published by William P. Nimmo of Edinburgh. He had never realized until he was almost grown that his father's vaunting chant was not literally true; that his father had never actually been out of America. Where had he picked this up? He opened it and read the inscription: "J. Henri Elkin, Mar. 26th, 1882," and beneath that, underlined with flourishes, "sans puer et sans reproche." With a smile for the insouciant motto and the error in spelling, both so typical of his father, he grimaced at his own forgotten inscription underneath, written in the brash pencil of his sophomore year:— "J. H. Elkin, Jr., Jan. 5th, 1929. De gustibus non est disputandum."

"Europe, I-rup, O-rup, and Stir-rup," he thought bitterly. He had believed it of his father; in a way it was his trouble that he still believed, not only for his father, but for himself. The phrase had meant for him all the perilous seas beyond the casement, all the width of the future that lay before the "compleat," the "whole" man, all the roads to Rome. When he heard the foghorns lowing on the river, the phrase sometimes came to him still, with a quickening of inexplicable delight and unease.

Now suddenly its echoes brought to him, with an association he did not understand, the image, sharp and disturbing, of the glass of anise on Anna Guryan's table.

Shutting the image out, he turned his back to the sleeping figure and stared out the window, past the blurred palette of the park with its motley strollers, to the strong blue of the river, which struck through the tentative spring air like a flail. It was not too late to fill the day that was draining away from him with one of those commonplace devices for seeking human warmth, a dinner, a date, a movie—the little second-rate enterprises where there was always the chance, after all, that reality might explode upon one in the exchange of a word, a recognition, an embrace.

He turned over a roster of people in his mind: the earnest young men of his own age, whose conversation would turn inevitably from books and jobs to girls, with the fascinated allusiveness of inexperience, or the gauche young girls tricked out in the bright dresses, shrill patter, and the finger-snapping gestures of allurement that would lead them not too improperly to their goal of a doctor or a dentist.

There was no one, nothing that he could scrape up that would serve as a palliative for the driving sense of alienation, of constriction, that sent him out more and more on his free Saturday afternoons and Sundays, prowling the dim drowsy art galleries, standing before each picture as if it were a window to a world, yet always subtly conscious of the current of people moving behind him, their dress and their speech, and of how he, in his stance before the picture, looked to them. Or he would walk the brilliant mid-town streets briskly, as if he had a destination, savoring the expensive color and movement, glancing at the great carved upheaval of buildings with a pride almost of ownership, until a dusk the color of melancholy blended all the outlines of faces and buildings in a brooding preamble to the great play of light that was to come.

Then he would flee into the haven of some small restaurant, always somehow, the wrong one, where, under the slack gaze of the waiter, he would choose from the menu with an exaggerated sense of the importance of his choice, and eat his dinner slowly, head bent, whetting himself against the knife of his solitude, until home seemed at last the only destination there was, and he would rise and go. Home, exhausted, ready at last for its commonplaces, he would let himself into the dim clogged air of the hall. Nodding over a book, his father would look up to mutter his half-irritated "Where've you been?" and to all the sounds and stimuli singing in his head the remark would be like a shutter, closing down between the halves of himself, and he would reply guiltily, almost as if he had been lying, *"Just around"* . . . or *"Nowhere."*

Tomorrow, delivered once more from the disturbed, uninhabited spaces of the week end, he would sink almost gratefully into the round of his job, that job which was so far from the context of his home that he could never have expected it to be understood at home, had he ever been asked. Along with the hundreds of others spewed out by the colleges the previous summer, into professions that had no room for them, he had found a place in the only employment where there was room, in the vast framework of the city's welfare department. He had been at it almost a year now, toiling up the steps of tenements in neighborhoods he had never before seen, delivering his blue and yellow tickets to existence to his one hundred and forty families.

In the beginning it had been exciting, almost romantic, to penetrate deeper into the unknown capillaries of the city that he loved, finding, in the midst of the decaying East Side tenements, the rococo hoardings on an old theatre that had been the glory of his father's day, seeing a date on the crumbling pink façade of the stables on Cherry Street where the peddlers kept their nags, reading the layered history of the city like a palimpsest. But lately it had seemed more and more as if he were immured in the catacombs of a daily round, from which he would never work himself up into the clear.

He thought of the families he would be visiting tomorrow, each of them like a little aperture into the world that really was. There would be the whine of Mrs. Barnes, born, raised, and married, on some form of aid, but with the steamy smell of comfort somehow always in her kitchen.

"Now there's William," she would whisper, with her sidelong glance. "Poor boy, he's a diabetic, you know. He needs special food." And the boy William would stand there with his over-sharp, delicate Irish face averted, his hunched shoulders straining away from notice. In the next house, Mr. McCue, "brassworker for thirty years," would once more exhume the badge to which he clung, the bank book showing the $4000 savings which had lasted three and a half years until now, and on his broad brick face there would be the usual look of puzzlement at what could happen to a man who had worked and done what was right and proper.

This was Yorkville, but over on 95th, near the river, the stunted inhabitants had seemed to him at first like a race of anthropophagi whose faces he never would be able to distinguish one from the other. Stumbling once through one of these buildings, in search of a family that was about to be evicted, he had passed through room after room in which the varicolored women, sprawling on daybeds, or huddled around tables in shrieking atonal conversation, had paid no more attention to him than if he had been invisible. Passing on into the dark center of the building, he had found himself in a black windowless room where there was no light but the red sparks flying out from under the frying pan in which a girl with wild Hottentot hair was cooking fish. She had looked at him indifferently, as though she would not have been surprised if he had grown from the floor, and had replied hoarsely to his question: "Family? There ain' no *families* here." He had stood there for a moment in the disoriented blackness, feeling himself shrunk to a pinpoint, a clot in time, and it had seemed to him that he had penetrated to the nadir of the world, where personality was at an end.

In the quiet planes of the room behind him, his father's breathing went on, like a gentle, insistent susurrus from a world that had been. Only that morning, the radio, playing Grofé's "Grand Canyon Suite," with its swaying theme of the donkeys, had reminded him, as always, of one of his father's favorite anecdotes, one that, as a boy, he had never heard without an ache of emulation, of desire for the avenues of action that would one day be his.

"That summer I was eighteen, Mr. Oakley sent me out all the way to San Francisco. Some responsibility for a boy, but I'd been working there in New York for him for two years, and he trusted me. Travelling on the Union Pacific, met a man in the dining-car, Colonel Yates, big mine-owner out there. Took a liking to me and invited me to stop off the next day and go down to one of his mines. I thought I shouldn't stop off to do it, but he said 'Listen, boy! You *want to see the world, or not?*' So the next morning I got off with him, but when he saw me he said, 'God, boy! You can't go down a mine in those clothes!' You see, those days, every salesman of any account dressed to look the part, and I had on a three-button cutaway and a top hat.

" 'Colonel,' I said, 'these are the only clothes I have.' And it was true, too. He shook his head, but we went on anyhow, and when I saw that canyon we were going down into I wished I'd stayed home in New York. A drop down into nothing for miles, and the only way to go down it was a narrow little trail not wide enough for a man. What they did, they used these little Kentucky single-footers, mincing from side to side, one foot in front of the other. Well, I looked at that donkey, and he looked at me, and I flipped up my coat-tails and got on. Went all the way down that canyon with my top hat on my head, and my coat-tails hanging down behind!"

The picture of his father, middle-sized, dapper, in the raw West of the eighteen-eighties, brought back momentarily the pride and tenderness which had always been a part of the feeling that he supposed was meant by the term "filial." As a boy he had never minded that his aging father had never joined in the baseball games like other fathers, or taken him swimming, for in his tales of the trotting-races at Saratoga, the fights in which John L. Sullivan had battered round after round bare-knuckled, the cockfights held secretly in a grimy cul-de-sac in New Orleans, had been the heady sense of an apprenticeship to the masculine world. And blending always with that gamy recall of the sporting world of the nineties had been the undercurrent that was implicit in his father's knowing allusion, in the slow spreading smile of reminiscence, in the anecdote lopped off at an unsuitable part—an undercurrent that spread beneath his talk, moving provocatively under the lace of words like a musky perfume —the sense of beautiful women.

Outside he could almost feel the subtle pressing of the sooty spring air, snubbing against the pane like an invitation. In his mind he traversed again the grim woodcut streets of his "district" wondering whether Sunday brought easement there, or whether there too, it was like a vacuum sucking the inhabitants into a realization of despair. He thought again of Anna Guryan, whom he had first visited two days before.

The address had been that of an old tenement off Hester Street, most of the occupants of which were already on his list. On the

The Sound of Waiting

paper-strewn gritty stoop he had met old Mr. Askenasi, evidently on his way to the barber-shop for the pre-Sabbath "shave with hot towels" to which the Jewish men, young and old, clung, throughout the humiliation of being on relief, as to a last shred of independence and manhood, though there might be no cholla for the table, or little tea for the glass.

"Guryan?" The old man had shaken his head. Then he had drawn back, pressing his lips together. "That one? You mean she will get on the relief too?" Throwing up his hands, he had exploded in a torrent of Yiddish. Then he had drawn closer. "Listen!" he had whispered in English, patting the other rhythmically on the shoulder for emphasis. "Since she has been here that door has never been closed. All hours of the night, men going up there. It is a shame for the other people in the house. Listen . . ." But at the other's guardedly professional lack of response he had broken off and gone on down the stoop, turning once to shake his head angrily with a glance that was like an accusation.

He had found the door easily enough, on the ground floor to the left, as one entered the dank focus of smells that was the hall. Most of these apartments led directly into the kitchen from the hall, and his first impression as he entered was that the kitchen was far cleaner than most, partly perhaps because the furniture was so sparse and there was no litter of food, or evidence of where it might be stored. He had been prepared for one of the volubly evasive women who were flocking to the protective disguise of the relief rolls, or who were occasionally referred to him by the probation officers on a promise to "go straight," many of them fat and aging, distinguished from the neighborhood women only by their carefully hammered hair and the clear, aseptic finish of their make-up.

He had found her sitting at the table, a small, deceptively young woman, her figure thin and unexuberant under the dark blue dress. To his first surprised glance she had appeared dated somehow, possibly because of the way she wore her hair, close to her head in the casque effect of the flapper period, with its sharp black wings pointed flatly against the white-powdered oval of her face. As she answered his formal questions in the slurred, unclassified monotone of her speech, her poised hands folded in her lap, he had been reminded of that Egyptian cat in the Museum, which had come through the erosive sands of the centuries and the trembling hands of archaeologists, to sit finally on its chill pedestal in the echoing gallery, regarding the modern world still with its glance of impenetrable dislike. He had found himself avoiding her unreflecting onyx gaze, which slid over him as if she were making some secret assessment of himself. Ruffled, he made a show of scrawling her answers in his notebook, a technique he hated and almost never used, partly because he had always felt too keenly the humiliation of those who were being probed, and partly because he had found soon enough that the intonations of misery were not easily forgotten.

She had just been discharged from the hospital, she said, and had told them she had no means of support. They had told her to go to the relief. The janitor of the building was a friend of hers and had let her have the apartment free until the end of the month, since the rent collector had already made his rounds. The furniture? The janitor had lent her an old bed for the back room, and the kitchen set had been left by the previous occupant.

In this neighborhood, where everything was sold and exchanged down to the very nail-parings of existence, where old men sat in front of stalls formed by their knees and the sidewalk, haggling over used shoestrings, a few screws and bent nails, even a single boot, he had known this could not be true. Even so, the kitchen table stood between them, irrefutably new, its white baked-enamel surface shining like a statement.

Raising his head to confront her with this, he had found that he could not say the bald words, and across the table he had seen a thin film of triumph slide over the opaque slits of her eyes. With a gesture of finality she had risen for the first time and pulled the chain on the light bulb that hung over them. Behind her the two blotches of windows sprang forward onto his sight like two frames holding forth the dark. On one uncurtained sill there was a bottle. Reaching for it, she drew a shot-glass from the table drawer, and poured.

"Anise. You have some."

He had refused, out of a conflict of reasons that were obscure to him, the least of which was that the rules of his job would have forbidden it. Gathering up his pencil and notebook, he retreated to the door, explaining hurriedly that he would let her know the decision of the office.

She had opened the door for him, clasping it close against her to let him by.

"All right. You come back and let me know. Any time." A smile had widened her lips, spreading like oil, and just before the door closed, looking down, he had seen, like a revelation, an intimacy, the pink inner orifice of her mouth.

Hurrying into the half-tones of the evening, all the way home in the swaying push of the subway, even now, as he leaned against the pane, he had retained in his mind, like the central core of an undifferentiated whirl of feeling, the image of the glass of anise waiting on the table, light radiating from its icy viscous white as from a prism.

Behind him on the sofa his father still slept, punctuating with his breath the quiet that pressed on the eardrums like a weight. For one warm moment it seemed almost possible to him that, shaking the slumped shoulders, touching the brown crepe hand, he might awaken his father beyond the present minute, into an awareness of him at last; in some long shared conversation, that backward elegiac glance would for once be forced fully, openly, on him, and he might say, "Father . . . was it so for you? . . . For what is it I wait?" Instantly the fantasy shrank, and he winced at the picture of the clumsy byplay that would really occur, knowing that between them lay the benumbing sleep of the years, a drowse from which it was not possible to awake.

Outside the window there was sound, motion, involvement, even if only in one of his long aimless hegiras through the streets. He turned slowly and left the room. Down the long hall, the first door open on the right was that of his parents' bedroom. Entering, he picked up the hairbrush from his father's chifferobe and began brushing his hair.

Even here, the sense of his father's youth was present to him, like a minimizing mirror in which he saw himself. On the high chifferobe, neatly arranged, as were all his father's accouterments, lay the silver toilette set of which the hairbrush, with a handle, in the old style, like a woman's, was a part. There was a broad clothes-brush, then a narrower hat-brush, and a small stud-box, all with heavy intricately wrought tops of silver repoussé, in the center of each the flat shield with the monogram JHE, and a soap-box, like a huge Easter egg of plain silver, on its top the embossed head of a nymph with twining silver hair. One saw odd pieces of similar sets now, unwanted and forlorn, in the dusty jackdaw windows of Third Avenue junk shops, crowded among the sad statuary and implements of a period that was done but had not quite yet slipped into the cherishable patina of the antique. Holding the brush, he remembered.

"Who do you suppose is in New York?" his father had chuckled from behind the *Times* one morning at breakfast, sitting there easy and fresh, wearing one of the dandified light silk ties and curious scarf-pins from the collection that crowded his dresser drawers, a mode that his wife could never persuade him to discard, that was as much a part of his style as the faint odor of cologne left clinging to the crumpled towels in the bathroom.

"Letty Danvers," said his father. "Arrived on the *Queen Mary*. Stopping at the Great Northern. That's where they all used to stop in the old days."

"Who's Letty Danvers?" he had asked, savoring the graceful English name on his tongue, sensing already, in his mother's stiffness, the possibility of mischief. In the portfolio of family pictures there were several of unidentified women, mostly in profile, in the clear unshaded photographic style of another day, staring large-eyed and proud from under the curled fringe of their bangs. His mother would never confess to a knowledge of who they were. "Ask your father!" she would say, tossing back her head.

"Why she was what they'd call a 'diseuse' now, I guess," his father said reflectively. "The greatest of her day. I knew her, my God—years ago. You know that silver dresser set of mine? She gave me that."

"I always thought Mother gave it to you."

His mother shook her head, tightening her lips.

"Maybe I'll go and see her," said his father. "Talk over old times."

"Kind of an elaborate present, wasn't it?" he had said, watching his mother.

"Not for those days," his father said musingly, from behind the paper. Then, looking up, he had met his son's arch glance, his wife's bridling look.

"Purely platonic!" he had growled. "Purely platonic, I assure you!"

"Hmm," his mother said.

His father had slammed the paper down on the table. "My God, Hattie, it was forty-five years ago. She was years older than I was. Why she must be damn near eighty years old!" He had stamped away from the table in a self-conscious huff, mock-angry, but pleased. For once, vanity had wrung from him the nearest allusion to his exact age that he would ever make. . . .

Like a boy building over and over the same tower from blocks grooved with use, he could reconstruct the times of his father. He watched him living with his young French friend, Louis Housselle, in the Prince Albert Apartments, home of the fancy theatre set of the day and their ardent hangers-on. He saw him, a few tables behind Diamond Jim Brady, betting on that famous marathon of the appetite, or leaning intimately toward women over the small round tables, almost eclipsed by the velvet swoop of their hats. In yachting clothes he leaned back jauntily, legs crossed, the hand with the ring draped easily on the chair; posing for a portrait he held the aquiline medallion of his profile sideways, the black curls cropped almost to the bone, on his shapely upper lip a feather of mustache. . . .

The rough bossing of the brush handle had left a pattern on his own clenched hand. With a conscious, almost defiant gesture, he set the brush down askew in the long neat silver line. Stepping softly down the back hall, he let himself out of the apartment door. Avoiding the elevator, he hurried down the five flights of stairs and out into the street.

As always before, the milling streets gave him back the feeling of action; the air blowing against his face set up an unreasoning tingle of anticipation. Flower shops, pastry shops, and stationery stores were all open; people wove in and out of them on their beelike errands. Down the perspective of the side street he could see the olive-green buses, their open decks crammed with people in vivid spring hats, rocketing by like floats.

He ran down the intervening blocks. Wedging himself onto one of the buses he followed the line of people up the swaying stair. Upstairs the deck held the rows of people like a well-arranged tray, everyone coupled and spruced as a crowd just out of church, varied only by the restless dots of children.

They rolled by the Museum and stopped. Clutching the change in his pocket, he thought of getting off there, but while he wavered between indecision and habit, the bus heaved on. He knew the Museum too well, anyhow, particularly the American Wing, where he had wandered too many desultory afternoons, past the snub, diffused faces of the Cassatts, the small violent Homers, pausing longer at the moon-wracked Ryders, held for minutes before the unfathomable Sargent "Madame X." By now it was too well-defined a theme in his routine of hope and ennui.

At Fifty-seventh Street he got off and walked east. Stopping at the Kraushaar Galleries, he peered in at the blank dark doors. Several weeks ago they had been open one afternoon and he had wandered in. No one had intercepted him, and he had found himself in the midst of an opening show of French paintings, mostly Renoirs. Behind him the silky authoritative murmurs of approval or contempt went on almost unheard, for he had been held in front of the Renoirs by a shock of familiarity, of recognition. They sat there, the women of his father's day, stiffly at their garden tables, under their enormous hats, in spade-shaped bodices, their faces and hair fretted by light and leaf shadow; in the dim blur of their boudoirs they curved over dressing tables their bodies of impermeable lavender and rose.

Today the window held a few Flemish *genre* paintings in overpowering frames, and the interior was lifeless and dark. The plate glass gave him back a dusky astigmatic version of himself. He turned away. No one was coming down the long suave street; held there, gripped again by the drag of time draining away, he felt that no one would ever come. He waited, avoiding the knowledge of where he wanted to go. Time passes, he thought; perhaps one should go toward it. Far down the street, the thin line of the horizon was like a sealed eyelid waiting for him to lift it, to expose the huge wink of the future.

Turning on his heel, he walked slowly eastward down the long street, which grew more squalid with every step, with the inevitability of a declining curve on a graph. At Second Avenue he mounted the rickety stairs of the "El" and caught a train that was just winding its parabola into the station.

The Sound of Waiting

Jigging past the tenements in the settling dusk he watched the window scenes as they flicked by: a woman leaning over a sink, a man stretched out with his feet up, somnolent in a chair. Since childhood he had done this, hanging out from the tops of the buses on Fifth to catch a flash of a paneled drawing-room, a great brown wall of books, or people, muffled and vague behind a shimmering curtain; riding past in the veiled evening he had fondled these glimpses and enlarged upon them.

In this neighborhood he could now, because of his work, fill out the scenes to the last detail of mohair armchairs and cracked, calendared walls. He knew well the sameness of the life that went on behind those window lights that were so sterile and graceless from inside—the endless arias of family quarrels, and the blind grapplings of love. Even so, as he walked or rode along, each appearing lamp stood out like a lighthouse of warmth that drew him in his lonely role of beholder; each was an evocation of possibility.

At home now, their own lamps would be turned on soon for supper, and his father would rise, yawning, to go to the table, happy and complete in his belated role of paterfamilias if the family were all present, grumbling and swearing one of his strange oaths that were like no one else's, if one of them were missing. "*Phantasmagoria!*" he would shout. "Where in God's name does that boy find to go?" In the landscape of his mind he watched the image of his father collapse and dwindle with distance, heard the sonorous echo of his voice trickle and die; in his mind he pursued the image and the echo for a last minute, before he let them go.

At the last station, he got out. It was still a long way to Hester Street, and he walked the odd-angled asymmetric streets with a delaying step, remembering his first experience of them last year, when the heat of summer had been a great blunting hand pushing the people out of doors, the whole area had had the smell of a dying fruit, and his clothes had felt like a cage.

He stopped at last in front of the house. It must have rained recently down here. The carts and hagglers had deserted the block, leaving in the gutters pools that gave back the last light of the sky. A slate-colored breeze from the river blew brinily against the empty, peeling doorway.

He walked inside and put his hand on the doorknob. Over on the river the foghorns spoke, making over and over their slow mysterious statement. He had never been able to decipher it until now. It is the sound of waiting, he thought. *The sound of waiting.*

Cupped in his hand, the oily doorknob spread under his palm as if he were touching a slowly widening smile. He knocked. He heard a light-chain being pulled on in the back room, and the high-heeled sound of footsteps coming toward the door. After the first compromise, he thought, all others follow.

Looking back through the open doorway, he saw the dome of the day melting downward irretrievably into the river. One by one, in the great pitted comb of the city, the evocative lights went on.

Old Stock

⋙ THE TRAIN creaked through the soft, heat-promising morning like an elderly, ambulatory sofa. Nosing along, it pushed its corridor of paper-spattered floors and old plush seats through towns whose names—Crystal Run, Mamakating—were as soft as the morning, and whose dusty little central hearts—all livery stable, freight depot, and yard buildings with bricked-up windows and faded sides that said "Purina Chows"—were as down-at-the-heel as the train that strung them together.

Hester, feeling the rocking stir of the journey between her thighs, hanging her head out of the window with her face snubbed against the hot breeze, tried to seize and fix each picture as it passed. At fifteen, everything she watched and heard seemed like a footprint on the trail of some eventuality she rode to meet, which never resolved but filled her world with a verve of waiting.

Opposite her, her mother sat with the shuttered, conscious look she always assumed in public places. Today there was that added look Hester also knew well, that prim display of extra restraint her mother always wore in the presence of other Jews whose grosser features, voices, manners offended her sense of gentility all the more out of her resentful fear that she might be identified with them. Today the train rang with their mobile gestures, and at each station crowds of them got off—great-breasted, starched mothers trailing mincing children and shopping bags stuffed with food, gawky couples digging each other in the side with their elbows, girls in beach pajamas, already making the farthest use of their smiles and great, effulgent eyes. At each station, they were met by the battered Fords and wagons that serviced the farms which would accommodate them, where for a week or two they would litter the tight Catskill

263

towns with their swooping gaiety and their weary, rapacious hope.

"Wild!" said Mrs. Elkin, sotto voce, pursing her mouth and tucking her chin in her neck. "Your hair and that getup! Always so wild." Hester, injured, understood that the indictment was as much for the rest of the train as for herself. Each summer for the past three years, ever since Mr. Elkin's business had been doing poorly and the family had been unable to afford the summer rental in Westchester, Mrs. Elkin had resisted the idea of Old Corner Farm, and each year she had given in, for they were still of a status which made it unthinkable that they would not leave New York for some part of the season. This year and last, they had not been able to manage it until September, with its lowered rates, but it would have been a confession of defeat for Mr. Elkin had he not been able to say during the week to casual business acquaintances, "Family's up in the country. I go up weekends." Once at the farm—although the guests there were of a somewhat different class from the people in this train, most of them arriving in their own cars and one or two with nursegirls for the children—Mrs. Elkin would hold herself aloof at first, bending over her embroidery hoop on the veranda, receiving the complimentary "What gorgeous work you do!" with a *moue* of distaste for the flamboyant word that was a hallmark of what she hated in her own race, politely refusing proffered rides to the village, finally settling the delicate choice of summer intimacy on some cowed spinster or recessive widow whom life had dampened to the necessary refinement. For Mrs. Elkin walked through the world swinging the twangy words "refined," "refinement," like a purifying censer before her.

Hester, roused momentarily from her dream of the towns, looked idly across at her mother's neat navy-and-white version of the late-summer uniform of the unadventurous and the well bred. Under any hat, in any setting, her mother always looked enviably right, and her face, purged of those youthful exoticisms it once might well have had, had at last attained a welcomed anonymity, so that now it was like a medallion whose blurred handsomeness bore no denomination other than the patent, accessible one of "lady." Recently, Hester had begun to doubt the very gentility of her mother's exorcistic term itself, but she was still afraid to say so, to put a finger on this one of the many ambiguities that confronted her on every side. For nowadays it seemed to her that she was like someone forming a piece of crude statuary which had to be reshaped each day—that it was not her own character which was being formed but that she was putting together, from whatever clues people would let her have, the shifty, elusive character of the world.

"Summitville!" the conductor called, poking his head into the car.

Hester and her mother got off the train with a crowd of others. Their feet crunched in the cinders of the path. The shabby snake of the train moved forward through its rut in the checkerboard hills. Several men who had been leaning on battered Chevvies ran forward, hawking persistently, but Mrs. Elkin shook her head. "There's Mr. Smith!" She waved daintily at an old man standing beside a truck. They were repeat visitors. They were being met.

Mrs. Elkin climbed into the high seat and sat tight-elbowed between Mr. Smith and Hester, denying the dusty indignity of the truck. The Smiths, people with hard faces the color of snuff, made no concession to boarders other than clean lodging and massive food. Mr. Smith, whose conversation and clothing were equally gnarled, drove silently on. At the first sight of him, of old Mr. Smith, with his drooping scythe of mustache, Hester, in one jolt, had remembered everything from the summers before.

The farm they travelled toward lay in a valley off the road from Kerhonkson to Accord. The house, of weatherbeaten stone, was low and thick, like a blockhouse still retreating suspiciously behind a stockade long since gone; upstairs, beaverboard had partitioned it into many molasses-tinted rooms. In front of it would be the covered well, where the summer people made a ceremony of their dilettante thirst, the children forever sawing on the pulley, the grown-ups smacking their lips over the tonic water not drawn from pipes. Mornings, after breakfast, the city children gravitated to the barn with the indecipherable date over its lintel and stood silent watching the cows, hearing their soft droppings, smelling the fecund smell that was like the perspiration the earth made in moving. Afterward, Hester, usually alone, followed the path down to the point where the brown waters of Schoharie Creek, which featherstitched the countryside for miles, ran, darkly overhung, across a great fan of ledges holding in their center one deep, minnow-flecked pool, like a large hazel eye.

"There's Miss Onderdonk's!" Hester said suddenly. They were

passing a small, square house that still preserved the printlike, economical look of order of old red brick houses, although its once-
white window frames were weathered and shutterless, and berry
bushes, advancing from the great thorny bower of them at the back,
scraggled at the first-floor windows and scratched at the three stone
steps that brinked the rough-cut patch of lawn. A collie, red-gold and
white, lay on the top step. "There's Margaret!" she added. "Oh, let's
go see them after lunch!"

A minute before, if asked, Hester could not have told the name of
the dog, but now she remembered everything: Miss Onderdonk,
deaf as her two white cats, which she seemed to prize for their affliction (saying often how it was related in some way to their blue eyes
and stainless fur), and Miss Onderdonk's parlor, with a peculiar,
sooty darkness in its air that Hester had never seen anywhere else, as
if shoe blacking had been mixed with it, or as if the only sources of
light in it were the luminous reflections from the horsehair chairs.
Two portraits faced you as you entered from the bare, poor wood of
the kitchen; in fact, you had only to turn on your heel from the
splintered drainboard or the match-cluttered oilstove to see them—
Miss Onderdonk's "great-greats"—staring nastily from their un-
lashed eyes, their pale faces and hands emerging from their needle-
fine ruffles. The left one, the man, with a face so wide and full it
must surely have been redder in life, kept his sneer directly on you,
but the woman, her long chin resting in the ruffle, one forefinger and
thumb pinching at the lush green velvet of her dress as if to draw it
away, stared past you into the kitchen, at the bare drainboard and
the broken-paned window above it.

Last year, Hester had spent much of her time "helping Miss Onderdonk," partly because there was no one her own age at the farm
with whom to while away the long afternoons, partly because Miss
Onderdonk's tasks were so different from anyone else's, since she
lived, as she said, "offen the land." Miss Onderdonk was one of
those deaf persons who do not chatter; her remarks hung singly, like
aphorisms, in Hester's mind. "All white cats are deaf." "Sugar, salt,
lard—bacon, flour, tea. The rest is offen the land." The articles thus
enumerated lodged firmly in Hester's memory, shaped like the
canisters so marked that contained the only groceries Miss Onderdonk seemed to have. Most of the time, when Hester appeared,

Miss Onderdonk did not spare a greeting but drew her by an ignoring silence into the task at hand—setting out pans of berries to ferment in the hot sun, culling the warty carrots and spotted tomatoes from her dry garden. Once, when she and Hester were picking blackberries from bushes so laden that, turning slowly, they could pick a quart in one spot, Hester, plucking a fat berry, had also plucked a bee on its other side.

"Best go home. Best go home and mud it," Miss Onderdonk had said, and had turned back to the tinny plop of berries in her greedy pail. She had not offered mud. Hester, returning the next day, had not even felt resentment, for there was something about Miss Onderdonk, even if one did not quite like her, that compelled. As she worked at her endless ministrations to herself in her faded kitchen and garden, she was just like any other old maid, city or country, whose cottony hair was prigged tight from nightly crimpings never brushed free, whose figure, boarded up in an arid dress, made Hester gratefully, uneasily aware of her own body, fresh and moist. But when Miss Onderdonk stepped into her parlor, when she sat with her hands at rest on the carved knurls of the rocker or, standing near the open calf-bound book that chronicled the Onderdonk descent from De Witt Clinton, clasped her hands before her on some invisible pommel—then her role changed. When she stepped into her parlor, Miss Onderdonk swelled.

"How *is* Miss Onderdonk, Mr. Smith?" Mrs. Elkin asked lightly.
"The same." Mr. Smith kept his eyes on the road.

They turned in to the narrow dirt road that led off the highway down to the farm. Hester recognized a familiar curve in the sweep of surrounding hills, patch-quilted with crops. "There are hardly any white patches this year," she said.

Mr. Smith flicked a look at her, almost as if she had said something sensible. "People don't eat much buckwheat any more," he said, and brought the truck to a bumpy stop in front of the covered well.

Hester and her mother ran the gauntlet of interested glances on the porch and went up to their room. The room had a mail-order austerity, with nothing in it that was not neutralized for the transient except the dim cross-stitch doily on the dresser. Hester was glad to see their clothing shut away in the tar-paper wardrobe, sorry to see their toilet articles, the beginning of clutter, ranged on the dresser. This was the most exciting moment of all, before the room settled down with your own coloration, before the people you would get to know were explored.

"I saw that Mrs. Garfunkel on the porch," she said.

Her mother said "Yes" as if she had pins in her mouth, and went on putting things in drawers.

Mrs. Garfunkel was one of the ones who said "gorgeous"; it was perhaps her favorite word. A young matron with reddish hair, chunky, snub features, and skin tawnied over with freckles, she had the look of a Teddy bear fresh from the shop. Up here, she dressed very quietly, with an absence of heels and floppy sunwear that, with her pug features, might have satisfied certain requirements in Mrs. Elkin's category of refinement. Neither did she talk with her hands, touch your clothing with them, or openly give the prices of things. But it was with her eyes that she estimated, with her tongue that she preened, and it was not long before you discovered that her admiring comment on some detail of your equipment was really only a springboard for the description of one or the other of her own incomparable possessions. Her satisfaction in these rested in their being not only the best but the best acquired for the least: the furs bought in August, the West Indian nursegirl who would work a year or so before realizing that the passage money Mrs. Garfunkel had advanced was more than underwritten by her inequitable salary, the compliant, self-effacing Mr. Garfunkel, who would probably go on working forever without realizing anything—even the languid, six-year-old Arline, who was so exactly suitable that she might have been acquired, after the canniest negotiation, from someone in that line to whom Mrs. Garfunkel had had a card of introduction. Perhaps, Hester thought now, her mother could better have borne Mrs. Garfunkel and her bargains if all of them had not been so successful.

When Hester and her mother, freshly washed and diffidently late, entered the dining room for dinner, which was in the middle of the day here, Mrs. Garfunkel hailed them, called them over to her table, pressed them to sit there, and introduced them to the others already seated. "Mrs. Elkin's an old-timer, like Mel and me. Meet Mr. and Mrs. Brod, and Mr. Brod's mother. And my brother Wally,

Mrs. Elkin and daughter. What's your name again, dear?" She paid no heed to Hester's muttered response but dug her arm affectionately against the side of the rickety young man with slick hair who sat next to her, doggedly accumulating food on his plate. "Wally ran up here to get away from half the girls in Brooklyn."

The young man gave her a look of brotherly distaste. "Couldn't have come to a better place," he said, and returned to his plate. Great platters of sliced beefsteak tomatoes and fricasseed chicken were passed, nubs of Country Gentleman corn were snatched and snatched again; the table was one flashing activity of reaching arms, although there was much more food upon it than the few of them could possibly eat. This amplitude was what one came for, after all, and this was its high point, after which there would be nothing much to look forward to through the afternoon daze of heat but supper, which was good, though not like this.

Eating busily, Hester, from under the wing of her mother's monosyllabic chilliness, watched Mr. and Mrs. Brod. They were newly married, it developed, but this was not the honeymoon. The honeymoon, as almost every turn in the conversation indicated, had been in California; they were at the farm to visit old Mrs. Brod, a little leathery grandmother of a woman, dressed in a jaunty Roman-stripe jumper and wearing a ribbon tied around hair that had been bobbed and blued. The young Mrs. Brod had a sleepy melon face with a fat mouth, dark-red nails, and black hair cut Buster Brown. Mr. Brod, a bald young man in fawn-colored jacket and knickers, said almost nothing, but every so often he did an extraordinary thing. At intervals, his wife, talking busily, would extend her hand sidewise, palm upward, without even looking at him, and in one convulsive movement that seemed to start somewhere outside him and end at his extremities, as if he were the tip of a smartly cracked whip, a gold case would be miraculously there in his hand, and he would place a cigarette tenderly in her palm. A second but lesser convulsion produced a lighter for the negligently held cigarette. He did not smoke.

The two Mrs. Brods were discussing the dress worn by the younger, evidently a California purchase. "Right away, I said, 'This one I take!'" said the bride. "Definitely a knockout!"

"Vunt vash," said her mother-in-law, munching on an ear of corn.

The bride shrugged. "So I'll give to cleaners."

"Give to clean, give to ket." The mother put down her ear of corn, rolling it over reflectively.

"Don't have a cat, Ma."

Mrs. Brod the elder turned away momentarily from her plate. "Sah yull *buy* ah ket!" she said, and one lean brown arm whipped out and took another ear of corn.

The bride looked miffed, then put out the cigarette-seeking hand. Flex, flash from the solicitous Mr. Brod and the cigarette, lit, was between her lips, smoke curling from her scornful nostrils.

"Sweet, isn't it, the way he does that? And not a smoke for himself," said Mrs. Garfunkel in an aside to Hester's mother. "You better watch out, Syl," she called across the table to the bride. "He forgets to do that, then the honeymoon is over."

Mrs. Elkin smiled, a little rigid but perfectly cordial, unless you knew the signs, and stood up, reaching around for her big knitting bag, which was hung on the back of her chair. "Come, dear," she said to Hester, in accents at which no purist could cavil. "Suppose you and I go out on the porch."

On the empty porch, Mrs. Elkin selected a chair far down at the end. "Those people!" she said, and blew her breath sharply between set teeth. "I told your father this place was getting rundown."

"Sah yull *buy* ah ket," said Hester dreamily, and chuckled. It was the illogic of the remark that charmed.

"Must you *imitate?*" said her mother.

"But it's funny, Mother."

"Oh, you're just like your father. Absolutely without discrimination."

Hester found nothing to answer. "I think I'll walk down to the creek," she said.

"Take a towel."

Hester ran upstairs. Suddenly it was urgent that she get down to the creek alone, before the others, digestion accomplished, went there to bathe. Upstairs, she shed her clothes swiftly and crammed herself into last year's bathing suit—tight and faded, but it would not matter here. She ran downstairs, crossed the porch without looking at her mother, and ran across the lawn into the safety of the path, which had a wall of weeds on either side. Once there, she walked on, slow and happy. The wire tangle of weeds was alive with stalks and pods and beadlets of bright green whose shapes she knew well but could not, need not, name. Above all, it was the same.

She pushed through the bushes that fringed the creek. It, too, was the same. In the past year, it must have gone through all the calendar changes. She imagined each of them—the freeze, the thaw, the spring running, like conventionalized paper pictures torn off one by one—but they were as unreal as the imagined private dishabille of a friend. Even the bushes that ran for miles along its edge were at the same stage of their bloom, their small, cone-shaped orange flowers dotted along the leaves for as far as she could see. The people around the farm called them "scarlet runners," although their flowers were as orange as a color could be.

She trod carefully across the slippery ledges out to the wide, flat slab that rose in the middle of the stream, and stretched out on her stomach on its broad, moss-slimed back. She lay there for a long time looking into the eye of the pool. One need not have an appointment with minnows, she thought. They are always the same, too.

At a crackling sound in the brush, she looked up. Mrs. Garfunkel's head appeared above the greenery, which ended in a ruff at her neck, like the painted backdrops behind which people pose at amusement parks. "Your mother says to tell you she's gone on down to Miss Onderdonk's." She waited while Hester picked her way back to shore. Until Hester gained the high weeds of the path, she felt the Teddy-bear eyes watching idly, calculating and squint.

In her room once more, Hester changed to a paper-dry cotton dress, then hurried out again, down the dirt road this time, and onto the state highway, slowing down only when she was in sight of Miss Onderdonk's house, and saw her mother and Miss Onderdonk sitting facing one another, one on each of the two butterfly-winged wooden benches built on the top step at either side of the door, forming the only porch there was.

"Why that dress?" asked her mother, with fair reason, for it was Hester's best. "You remember Hester, Miss Onderdonk?" she added.

Miss Onderdonk looked briefly at Hester with her watery, time-eclipsing stare. There was no indication that she knew Hester's name, or ever had. One of the white cats lay resiliently on her lap, with the warning look of toleration common to cats when held. Miss Onderdonk, like the creek, might have lived suspended from last September to this, untouched by the flowing year, every crimp in her hair the same. And the parlor? It would have to be seen, for certain.

Hester sat down quietly next to her mother, whose sewing went on and on, a mild substitute for conversation. For a while, Hester watched the long, important-looking shadows that encroached upon the hills, like enigmas stated every afternoon but never fully solved. Then she leaned carefully toward Miss Onderdonk. "May I go see your parlor?" she asked.

Miss Onderdonk gave no sign that she had heard. It might have been merely the uncanny luck of the partly deaf that prompted her remark. "People come by here this morning," she said. "From down to your place. Walk right into the parlor, no by-your-leave. Want to buy my antiques!"

Mrs. Elkin, needle uplifted, shook her head, commiserating, gave a quick, consolatory mew of understanding, and plunged the needle into the next stitch.

"Two women—and a man all ninnied out for town," said Miss Onderdonk. "Old woman had doctored hair. Grape-colored! Hollers at me as if I'm the foreign one. Picks up my Leather-Bound Onderdonk History!" Her explosive breath capitalized the words. The cat, squirting suddenly from her twitching hand, settled itself, an aggrieved white tippet, at a safe distance on the lawn. " 'Put that down,' I said," said Miss Onderdonk, her eyes as narrow as the cat's. " 'I don't have no antiques,' I said. 'These here are my belongings.' "

Mrs. Elkin put down her sewing. Her broad hands, with the silver-and-gold thimble on one middle finger, moved uncertainly, unlike Miss Onderdonk's hands, which were pressed flat, in triumph, on her faded, flour-sack lap.

"I told Elizabeth Smith," Miss Onderdonk said. "I told her she'd rue the day she ever started taking in Jews."

The short word soared in an arc across Hester's vision and hit the remembered, stereopticon picture of the parlor. The parlor sank and disappeared, a view in an album snapped shut. Now her stare was for her mother's face, which was pink but inconclusive.

Mrs. Elkin, raising her brows, made a helpless face at Hester, as if to say, "After all, the vagaries of the deaf . . ." She permitted herself a minimal shrug, even a slight spreading of palms. Under Hester's stare, she lowered her eyes and turned toward Miss Onderdonk again.

"I thought you knew, Miss Onderdonk," said her mother. "I thought you knew that we were—Hebrews." The word, the ultimate refinement, slid out of her mother's soft voice as if it were on runners.

"Eh?" said Miss Onderdonk.

Say it, Hester prayed. She had never before felt the sensation of prayer. Please say it, Mother. *Say "Jew."* She heard the word in her own mind, double-voiced, like the ram's horn at Yom Kippur, with an ugly present bray but with a long, urgent echo as time-spanning as Roland's horn.

Her mother leaned forward. Perhaps she had heard it, too—the echo. "But we are Jewish," she said in a stronger voice. "Mr. Elkin and I are Jewish."

Miss Onderdonk shook her head, with the smirk of one who knew better. "Never seen the Mister. The girl here has the look, maybe. But not you."

"But—" Mrs. Elkin, her lower lip caught by her teeth, made a sound like a stifled, chiding sigh. "Oh, yes," she said, and nodded, smiling, as if she had been caught out in a fault.

"Does you credit," said Miss Onderdonk. "Don't say it don't. Make your bed, lie on it. Don't have to pretend with me, though."

With another baffled sigh, Mrs. Elkin gave up, flumping her hands down on her sewing. She was pinker, not with anger but, somehow, as if she had been cajoled.

"Had your reasons, maybe." Miss Onderdonk tittered, high and henlike. "Ain't no Jew, though. Good blood shows, any day."

Hester stood up. "We're in a book at home, too," she said loudly. " 'The History of the Jews of Richmond, 1769–1917.' " Then she turned her back on Miss Onderdonk, who might or might not have heard, on her mother, who had, and stomped down the steps.

At the foot of the lawn, she stopped behind a bush that hid her from the steps, feeling sick and let-down. She had somehow used Miss Onderdonk's language. She hadn't said what she meant at all. She heard her father's words, amused and sad, as she had heard them once, over her shoulder, when he had come upon her poring over the red-bound book, counting up the references to her grandfather. "That Herbert Ezekiel's book?" He had looked over her shoulder, twirling the gold cigar-clipper on his watch chain. "Well, guess it won't hurt the sons of Moses any if they want to tally up some newer ancestors now and then."

Miss Onderdonk's voice, with its little, cut-off chicken laugh, travelled down to her from the steps. "Can't say it didn't cross my mind, though, that the girl does have the look."

Hester went out into the highway and walked quickly back to the farmhouse. Skirting the porch, she tiptoed around to one side, over to an old fringed hammock slung between two trees whose broad bottom fronds almost hid it. She swung herself into it, covered herself over with the side flaps, and held herself stiff until the hammock was almost motionless.

Mrs. Garfunkel and Arline could be heard on the porch, evidently alone, for now and then Mrs. Garfunkel made one of the fretful, absent remarks mothers make to children when no one else is around. Arline had some kind of wooden toy that rumbled back and forth across the porch. Now and then, a bell on it went "ping."

After a while, someone came along the path and up on the porch. Hester lay still, the hammock fringe tickling her face. "Almost time for supper," she heard Mrs. Garfunkel say.

"Yes," said her mother's voice. "Did Hester come back this way?"

"I was laying down for a while. Arline, dear, did you see Hester?"

"No, Mummy." Ping, ping went Arline's voice.

" 'Mummy'!" said Mrs. Garfunkel. "That's that school she goes to—you know the Kemp-Willard School, on Eighty-sixth?"

"Oh, yes," said Mrs. Elkin. "Quite good, I've heard."

"Good!" Mrs. Garfunkel sighed, on a sleek note of outrage. "What they soak you, they ought to be."

Arline's toy rumbled across the porch again and was still.

"She'll come back when she's hungry, I suppose," said Mrs. Elkin. "There was a rather unfortunate little—incident, down the road."

"Shush, Arline. You don't say?"

Chairs scraped confidentially closer. Mrs. Elkin's voice dropped to the low, *gemütlich* whisper reserved for obstetrics, cancer, and the peculations of servant girls. Once or twice, the whisper, flurrying higher, shook out a gaily audible phrase. "Absolutely wouldn't believe—" "Can you imagine anything so silly?" Then, in her normal voice, "Of course, she's part deaf, and probably a little crazy from being alone so much."

"Scratch any of them and you're sure to find it," said Mrs. Garfunkel.

"Ah, well," said Mrs. Elkin. "But it certainly was funny," she added, in a voice velveted over now with a certain savor of reminiscence, "the way she kept *insisting*."

"Uh-huh," said Mrs. Garfunkel rather flatly. "Yeah. Sure."

Someone came out on the back porch and vigorously swung the big bell that meant supper in fifteen minutes.

"Care for a little drive in the Buick after supper?" asked Mrs. Garfunkel.

"Why—why, yes," said Mrs. Elkin, her tones warmer now with the generosity of one whose equipment went beyond the realm of bargains. "Why, I think that would be very nice."

"Any time," said Mrs. Garfunkel. "Any time you want stamps or anything. Thought you might enjoy a little ride. Not having the use of a car."

The chairs scraped back, the screen door creaked, and the two voices, linked in their sudden, dubious rapprochement, went inside. The scuffling toy followed them.

Hester rolled herself out of the hammock and stood up. She looked for comfort at the reasonable hills, whose pattern changed only according to what people ate; at the path, down which there was nothing more ambiguous than the hazel-eyed water or the flower that should be scarlet but was orange. While she had been in the hammock, the dusk had covered them over. It had settled over everything with its rapt, misleading veil.

She walked around to the foot of the front steps. A thin, emery edge of autumn was in the air now. Inside, they must all be at supper; no one else had come by. When she walked into the dining room, they would all lift their heads for a moment, the way they always did when someone walked in late, all of them regarding her for just a minute with their equivocal adult eyes. Something would rise from them all like a warning odor, confusing and corrupt, and she knew now what it was. Miss Onderdonk sat at their table, too. Wherever any of them sat publicly at table, Miss Onderdonk sat at his side. Only, some of them set a place for her and some of them did not.

The Rabbi's Daughter

✍§ THEY ALL came along with Eleanor and her baby in the cab to Grand Central, her father and mother on either side of her, her father holding the wicker bassinet on his carefully creased trousers. Rosalie and Helene, her cousins, smart in their fall ensembles, just right for the tingling October dusk, sat in the two little seats opposite them. Aunt Ruth, Dr. Ruth Brinn, her father's sister and no kin to the elegant distaff cousins, had insisted on sitting in front with the cabman. Eleanor could see her now, through the glass, in animated talk, her hat tilted piratically on her iron-gray braids.

Leaning forward, Eleanor studied the dim, above-eye-level picture of the driver. A sullen-faced young man, with a lock of black hair belligerent over his familiar nondescript face: "Manny Kaufman." What did Manny Kaufman think of Dr. Brinn? In ten minutes she would drag his life history from him, answering his unwilling statements with the snapping glance, the terse nods which showed that she got it all, at once, understood him down to the bone. At the end of her cross-questioning she would be quite capable of saying, "Young man, you are too pale! Get another job!"

"I certainly don't know why you wanted to wear that get-up," said Eleanor's mother, as the cab turned off the Drive toward Broadway. "On a train. And with the baby to handle, all alone." She brushed imaginary dust from her lap, scattering disapproval with it. She had never had to handle her babies alone.

Eleanor bent over the basket before she answered. She was a thin fair girl whom motherhood had hollowed, rather than enhanced. Tucking the bottle-bag further in, feeling the wad of diapers at the bottom, she envied the baby blinking solemnly up at her, safe in its surely serviced world.

276

"Oh, I don't know," she said. "It just felt gala. New Yorkish. Some people dress down for a trip. Others dress up—like me." Staring at her own lap, though, at the bronze velveteen which had been her wedding dress, sensing the fur blob of hat insecure on her unprofessionally waved hair, shifting the shoes, faintly scuffed, which had been serving her for best for two years, she felt the sickening qualm, the frightful inner blush of the inappropriately dressed.

In front of her, half-turned toward her, the two cousins swayed neatly in unison, two high-nostriled gazelles, one in black, one in brown, both in pearls, wearing their propriety, their utter rightness, like skin. She had known her own excess when she had dressed for the trip yesterday morning, in the bare rooms, after the van had left, but her suits were worn, stretched with wearing during pregnancy, and nothing went with anything any more. Tired of house dresses, of the spotted habiliments of maternity, depressed with her three months' solitude in the country waiting out the lease after Dan went on to the new job, she had reached for the wedding clothes, seeing herself cleansed and queenly once more, mysterious traveler whose appearance might signify anything, approaching the pyrrhic towers of New York, its effervescent terminals, with her old brilliance, her old style.

Her father sighed. "Wish that boy could find a job nearer New York."

"You know an engineer has to go where the plants are," she said, weary of the old argument. "It's not like you—with your own business and everything. Don't you think I'd like . . . ?" She stopped, under Rosalie's bright, tallying stare.

"I know, I know." He leaned over the baby, doting.

"What's your new house like?" said Rosalie.

"You know," she said gaily, "after all Dan's letters, I'm not just sure, except that it's part of a two-family. They divide houses every which way in those towns. He's written about 'Bostons,' and 'flats,' and 'duplexes.' All I really know is it has automatic heat, thank goodness, and room for the piano." She clamped her lips suddenly on the hectic, chattering voice. Why had she had to mention the piano, especially since they were just passing Fifty-seventh Street, past Carnegie with all its clustering satellites—the Pharmacy, the Playhouse, the Russian restaurant—and in the distance, the brindled windows of the galleries, the little chiffoned store fronts, spitting garnet and saffron light? All her old life smoked out toward her from these buildings, from this parrot-gay, music-scored street.

"Have you been able to keep up with your piano?" Helene's head cocked, her eyes screened.

"Not—not recently. But I'm planning a schedule. After we're settled." In the baby's nap time, she thought. When I'm not boiling formulas or wash. In the evenings, while Dan reads, if I'm only—just not too tired. With a constriction, almost of fear, she realized that she and Dan had not even discussed whether the family on the other side of the house would mind the practicing. That's how far I've come away from it, she thought, sickened.

"All that time spent." Her father stroked his chin with a scraping sound and shook his head, then moved his hand down to brace the basket as the cab swung forward on the green light.

My time, she thought, my life—your money, knowing her unfairness in the same moment, knowing it was only his devotion, wanting the best for her, which deplored. Or, like her mother, did he mourn too the preening pride in the accomplished daughter, the long build-up, Juilliard, the feverish, relative-ridden Sunday afternoon recitals in Stengel's studio, the program at Town Hall, finally, with her name, no longer Eleanor Goldman, but Elly Gold, truncated hopefully, euphoniously for the professional life to come, that had already begun to be, thereafter, in the first small jobs, warm notices?

As the cab rounded the corner of Fifth, she saw two ballerinas walking together, unmistakable with their dark Psyche knots over their fichus, their sandaled feet angled outwards, the peculiar compensating tilt of their little strutting behinds. In that moment it was as if she had taken them all in at once, seen deep into their lives. There was a studio of them around the hall from Stengel's, and under the superficial differences the atmosphere in the two studios had been much the same: two tight, concentric worlds whose *aficionados* bickered and endlessly discussed in their separate argots, whose students, glowing with the serious work of creation, were like trajectories meeting at the burning curve of interest.

She looked at the cousins with a dislike close to envy, because they neither burned nor were consumed. They would never throw down the fixed cards. Conformity would protect them. They would marry for love if they could; if not, they would pick, prudently, a candidate who would never remove them from the life to which they were accustomed. Mentally they would never even leave Eighty-sixth Street, and their homes would be like their mothers', like her mother's, *bibelots* suave on the coffee tables, bonbon dishes full, but babies postponed until they could afford to have them born at Doctors Hospital. "After all the money Uncle Harry spent on her, too," they would say later in mutually confirming gossip. For to them she would simply have missed out on the putative glory of the prima donna; that it was the work she missed would be out of their ken.

The cab swung into the line of cars at the side entrance to Grand Central. Eleanor bent over the basket and took out the baby. "You take the basket, Dad." Then, as if forced by the motion of the cab, she reached over and thrust the bundle of baby onto Helene's narrow brown crepe lap, and held it there until Helene grasped it diffidently with her suede gloves.

"She isn't—she won't wet, will she?" said Helene.

A porter opened the door. Eleanor followed her mother and father out and then reached back into the cab. "I'll take her now." She stood there hugging the bundle, feeling it close, a round comforting cyst of love and possession.

Making her way through the snarled mess of traffic on the curb, Aunt Ruth came and stood beside her. "Remember what I told you!" she called to the departing driver, wagging her finger at him.

"What did you tell him?" said Eleanor.

"Huh! What I told him!" Her aunt shrugged, the blunt Russian shrug of inevitability, her shrewd eyes ruminant over the outthrust chin, the spread hands. "Can I fix life? Life in Brooklyn on sixty dollars a week? I'm only a medical doctor!" She pushed her hat forward on her braids. "Here! Give me that baby!" She whipped the baby from Eleanor's grasp and held it with authority, looking speculatively at Eleanor. "Go on! Walk ahead with them!" She grinned. "Don't I make a fine nurse? Expensive, too!"

Down at the train, Eleanor stood at the door of the roomette while the other women, jammed inside, divided their ardor for the miniature between the baby and the telescoped comforts of the cubicle. At the end of the corridor, money and a pantomime of cordiality passed between her father and the car porter. Her father came back down the aisle, solid gray man, refuge of childhood, grown shorter than she. She stared down at his shoulder, rigid, her eyes unfocused, restraining herself from laying her head upon it.

"All taken care of," he said. "He's got the formula in the icebox and he'll take care of getting you off in the morning. Wish you could have stayed longer, darling." He pressed an envelope into her hand. "Buy yourself something. Or the baby." He patted her shoulder. "No . . . now never mind now. This is between you and me."

"Guess we better say good-bye, dear," said her mother, emerging from the roomette with the others. Doors slammed, passengers swirled around them. They kissed in a circle, nibbling and diffident.

Aunt Ruth did not kiss her, but took Eleanor's hands and looked at her, holding on to them. She felt her aunt's hands moving softly on her own. The cousins watched brightly.

"What's this, what's this?" said her aunt. She raised Eleanor's hands, first one, then the other, as if weighing them in a scale, rubbed her own strong, diagnostic thumb back and forth over Eleanor's right hand, looking down at it. They all looked down at it. It was noticeably more spatulate, coarser-skinned than the left, and the middle knuckles were thickened.

"So . . . ," said her aunt. "So-o . . . ," and her enveloping stare had in it that warmth, tinged with resignation, which she offered indiscriminately to cabmen, to nieces, to life. "So . . . , the 'rabbi's daughter' is washing dishes!" And she nodded, in requiem.

"Prescription?" said Eleanor, smiling wryly back.

"No prescription!" said her aunt. "In my office I see hundreds of girls like you. And there is no little pink pill to fit." She shrugged, and then whirled on the others. "Come. Come on." They were gone, in a last-minute flurry of ejaculations. As the train began to wheel past the platform, Eleanor caught a blurred glimpse of their faces, her parents and aunt in anxious trio, the two cousins neatly together.

People were still passing by the door of the roomette, and a woman in one group paused to admire the baby, frilly in the delicately lined basket, "Ah, look!" she cooed. "Sweet! How old is she?"

"Three months."

"It *is* a she?"

Eleanor nodded.

"Sweet!" the woman said again, shaking her head admiringly, and went on down the aisle. Now the picture was madonna-perfect, Eleanor knew—the harsh, tintype lighting centraled down on her and the child, glowing in the viscous paneling that was grained to look like wood, highlighted in the absurd plush-cum-metal fixtures of this sedulously planned manger. She shut the door.

The baby began to whimper. She made it comfortable for the night, diapering it quickly, clipping the pins in the square folds, raising the joined ankles in a routine that was like a jigging ballet of the fingers. Only after she had made herself ready for the night, hanging the dress quickly behind a curtain, after she had slipped the last prewarmed bottle out of its case and was holding the baby close as it fed, watching the three-cornered pulse of the soft spot winking in and out on the downy head—only then did she let herself look closely at her two hands.

The difference between them was not enough to attract casual notice, but enough, when once pointed out, for anyone to see. She remembered Stengel's strictures on practicing with the less able left one. "Don't think you can gloss over, Miss. It shows!" But that the scrubbing hand, the working hand, would really "show" was her first intimation that the daily makeshift could become cumulative, could leave its imprint on the flesh with a crude symbolism as dully real, as conventionally laughable, as the first wrinkle, the first gray hair.

She turned out the light and stared into the rushing dark. The physical change was nothing, she told herself, was easily repaired; what she feared almost to phrase was the death by postponement, the slow uneventful death of impulse. "Hundreds of girls like you," she thought, fearing for the first time the compromises that could arrive upon one unaware, not in the heroic renunciations, but erosive, gradual, in the slow chip-chipping of circumstance. Outside the window the hills of the Hudson Valley loomed and receded, rose up, piled, and slunk again into foothills. For a long time before she fell asleep she probed the dark for their withdrawing shapes, as if drama and purpose receded with them.

In the morning the porter roused her at six, returning an iced bottle of formula, and one warmed and made ready. She rose with a granular sense of return to the real, which lightened as she attended to the baby and dressed. Energized, she saw herself conquering whatever niche Dan had found for them, revitalizing the unknown house as she had other houses, with all the artifices of her New York chic, squeezing ragouts from the tiny salary spent cagily at the A & P, enjoying the baby instead of seeing her in the groggy focus of a thousand tasks. She saw herself caught up at odd hours in the old exaltation of practice, even if they had to hire a mute piano, line a room with cork. Nothing was impossible to the young, bogey-dispersing morning.

The station ran past the window, such a long one, sliding through the greasy lemon-colored lights, that she was almost afraid they were not going to stop, or that it was the wrong one, until she saw Dan's instantly known contour, jointed, thin, and his face, raised anxiously to the train windows with the vulnerability of people who do not know they are observed. She saw him for a minute as other passengers, brushing their teeth hastily in the washrooms, might look out and see him, a young man, interesting because he was alone on the platform, a nice young man in a thick jacket and heavy work pants, with a face full of willingness and anticipation. Who would get off for him?

As she waited in the jumble of baggage at the car's end, she warned herself that emotion was forever contriving toward moments which, when achieved, were not single and high as they ought to have been, but often splintered slowly—just walked away on the little centrifugal feet of detail. She remembered how she had mulled before their wedding night, how she had been unable to see beyond the single devouring picture of their two figures turning, turning toward one another. It had all happened, it had all been there, but memory could not recall it so, retaining instead, with the pedantic fidelity of some poet whose interminable listings recorded obliquely the face of the beloved but never invoked it, a whole rosary of irrelevancies, in the telling of which the two figures merged and were lost. Again she had the sense of life pushing her on by minute, imperceptible steps whose trend would not be discerned until it was too late, as the tide might encroach upon the late swimmer, making a sea of the sand he left behind.

"Dan!" she called. "Dan!"

He ran toward her. She wanted to run too, to leap out of the hemming baggage and fall against him, rejoined. Instead, she and the bags and the basket were jockeyed off the platform by the obsequious porter, and she found herself on the gray boards of the station, her feet still rocking with the leftover rhythm of the train, holding the basket clumsily between her and Dan, while the train washed off hoarsely behind them. He took the basket from her, set it down, and they clung and kissed, but in all that ragged movement, the moment subdivided and dispersed.

"Good Lord, how big she is!" he said, poking at the baby with a shy, awkward hand.

"Mmm. Tremendous!" They laughed together, looking down.

"Your shoes—what on earth?" she said. They were huge, laced to the ankle, the square tips inches high, like blocks of wood on the narrow clerkly feet she remembered.

"Safety shoes. You have to wear them around a foundry. Pretty handy if a casting drops on your toe."

"Very swagger." She smiled up at him, her throat full of all there was to tell—how, in the country, she had spoken to no one but the groceryman for so long that she had begun to monologue to the baby; how she had built up the first furnace fire piece by piece, crouching before it in awe and a sort of pride, hoping, as she shifted the damper chains, that she was pulling the right one; how the boy who was to mow the lawn had never come, and how at last she had taken a scythe to the knee-deep, insistent grass and then grimly, jaggedly, had mown. But now, seeing his face dented with fatigue, she saw too his grilling neophyte's day at the foundry, the evenings when he must have dragged hopefully through ads and houses, subjecting his worn wallet and male ingenuousness to the soiled witcheries of how many landlords, of how many narrow-faced householders tipping back in their porch chairs, patting tenderly at their bellies, who would suck at their teeth and look him over. "You permanent here, mister?" Ashamed of her city-bred heroisms, she said nothing.

"You look wonderful," he said. "Wonderful."

"Oh." She looked down. "A far cry from."

"I borrowed a car from one of the men, so we can go over in style." He swung the basket gaily under one arm. "Let's have breakfast first, though."

"Yes, let's." She was not eager to get to the house.

They breakfasted in a quick-lunch place on the pallid, smudged street where the car was parked, and she waited, drinking a second cup of coffee from a grainy white mug while Dan went back to the station to get the trunk. The mug had an indistinct blue V on it in the middle of a faded blue line running around the rim; it had probably come secondhand from somewhere else. The fork she had used had a faint brassiness showing through its nickel-colored tines and was marked "Hotel Ten Eyck, Albany," although this was not Albany. Even the restaurant, on whose white, baked look the people made gray transient blurs which slid and departed, had the familiar melancholy which pervaded such places because they were composed everywhere, in a hundred towns, of the same elements, but were never lingered in or personally known. This town would be like that too; one would be able to stand in the whirling center of the five-and-dime and fancy oneself in a score of other places where the streets had angled perhaps a little differently and the bank had been not opposite the post office, but a block down. There would not even be a need for fancy because, irretrievably here, one was still in all the resembling towns, and going along these streets one would catch oneself nodding to faces known surely, plumbed at a glance, since these were overtones of faces in all the other towns that had been and were to be.

They drove through the streets, which raised an expectation she knew to be doomed, but cherished until it should be dampened by knowledge. Small houses succeeded one another, gray, coffee-colored, a few white ones, many with two doors and two sets of steps.

"Marlborough Road," she said. "My God."

"Ours is Ravenswood Avenue."

"No!"

"Slicker!" he said. "Ah, darling, I can't believe you're here." His free arm tightened and she slid down on his shoulder. The car made a few more turns, stopped in the middle of a block, and was still.

The house, one of the white ones, had two close-set doors, but the two flights of steps were set at opposite ends of the ledge of porch, as if some craving for a privacy but doubtfully maintained within had leaked outside. Hereabouts, in houses with the cramped deadness of diagrams, was the special ugliness created by people who

would keep themselves a toehold above the slums by the exercise of
a terrible, ardent neatness which had erupted into the foolish or the
grotesque—the two niggling paths in the common driveway, the
large trellis arching pompously over nothing. On Sundays they
would emerge, the fathers and mothers, dressed soberly, even thread-
bare, but dragging children outfitted like angelic visitants from the
country of the rich, in poke bonnets and suitees of pink and mauve,
larded triumphantly with fur.

As Dan bent over the lock of one of the doors, he seemed to her
like a man warding off a blow.

"Is the gas on?" she said hurriedly. "I've got one more bottle."

He nodded. "It heats with gas, you know. That's why I took it.
They have cheap natural gas up here." He pushed the door open,
and the alien, anti-people smell of an empty house came out toward
them.

"I know. You said. Wait till I tell you about me and the furnace
in the other place." Her voice died away as, finally, they were inside.

He put the basket on the floor beside him. "Well," he said, "this
am it."

"Why, there's the sofa!" she said. "It's so funny to see everything
—just two days ago in Erie, and now here." Her hand delayed on the
familiar pillows, as if on the shoulder of a friend. Then, although a
glance had told her that no festoonings of the imagination were
going to change this place, there was nothing to do but look.

The door-cluttered box in which they stood predicated a three-
piece "suite" and no more. In the center of its mustard woodwork
and a wallpaper like cold cereal, two contorted pedestals supported
less the ceiling than the status of the room. Wedged in without
hope of rearrangement, her own furniture had an air of outrage, like
social workers who had come to rescue a hovel and had been confronted, instead, with the proud glare of mediocrity.

She returned the room's stare with an enmity of her own. Soon I
will get to know you the way a woman gets to know a house—where
the baseboards are roughest, and in which corners the dust drifts—
the way a person knows the blemishes of his own skin. But just now
I am still free of you—still a visitor.

"Best I could do." The heavy shoes clumped, shifting.

"It'll be all right," she said. "You wait and see." She put her palms on his shoulders. "It just looked queer for a minute, with windows only on one side." She heard her own failing voice with dislike, quirked it up for him. "Half chick. That's what it is. Half-chick house!"

"Crazy!" But some of the strain left his face.

"Uh-huh, *Das Ewig Weibliche*, that's me!" She half pirouetted. "Dan!" she said. "Dan, where's the piano?"

"Back of you. We had to put it in the dinette. I thought we could eat in the living room anyway."

She opened the door. There it was, filling the box room, one corner jutting into the entry to the kitchenette. Tinny light, whitening down from a meager casement, was recorded feebly on its lustrous flanks. Morning and evening she would edge past it, with the gummy dishes and the clean. Immobile, in its cage, it faced her, a great dark harp lying on its side.

"Play something, for luck." Dan came up behind her, the baby bobbing on his shoulder.

She shook her head.

"Ah, come on." His free arm cinched the three of them in a circle, so that the baby participated in their kiss. The baby began to cry.

"See," she said. "We better feed her."

"I'll warm the bottle. Have to brush up on being a father." He nudged his way through the opening. She heard him rummaging in a carton, then the clinking of a pot.

She opened the lid of the piano and struck the A, waiting until the tone had died away inside her, then struck a few more notes. The middle register had flattened first, as it always did. Sitting down on the stool, she looked into her lap as if it belonged to someone else. What was the piano doing here, this opulent shape of sound, five hundred miles from where it was the day before yesterday; what was she doing here, sitting in the lopped-off house, in the dress that had been her wedding dress, listening to the tinkle of a bottle against a pan? What was the mystery of distance—that it was not only geographical but clove through the map, into the heart?

She began to play, barely flexing her fingers, hearing the nails she had let grow slip and click on the keys. Then, thinking of the entities on the other side of the wall, she began to play softly, placating, as if she would woo them, the town, providence. She played a

Beethoven andante with variations, then an adagio, seeing the Von Bülow footnotes before her: ". . . the ascending diminished fifth may be phrased, as it were, like a question, to which the succeeding bass figure may be regarded as the answer."

The movement finished but she did not go on to the scherzo. Closing the lid, she put her head down on her crossed arms. Often, on the fringes of concerts, there were little haunting crones of women who ran up afterward to horn in on the congratulatory shop-talk of the players. She could see one of them now, batting her stiff claws together among her fluttering draperies, nodding eagerly for notice: "I studied . . . I played too, you know . . . years ago . . . with De Pachmann!"

So many variants of the same theme, she thought, so many of them—the shriveled, talented women. Distance has nothing to do with it; be honest—they are everywhere. Fifty-seventh Street is full of them. The women who were once "at the League," who cannot keep themselves from hanging the paintings, the promising *juvenilia*, on their walls, but who flinch, deprecating, when one notices. The quondam writers, chary of ridicule, who sometimes, over wine, let themselves be persuaded into bringing out a faded typescript, and to whom there is never anything to say, because it is so surprisingly good, so fragmentary, and was written—how long ago? She could still hear the light insistent note of the A, thrumming unresolved, for herself, and for all the other girls. A man, she thought jealously, can be reasonably certain it was his talent which failed him, but the women, for whom there are still so many excuses, can never be so sure.

"You're tired." Dan returned, stood behind her.

She shook her head, staring into the shining case of the piano, wishing that she could retreat into it somehow and stay there hud-dled over its strings, like those recalcitrant nymphs whom legend im-mured in their native wood or water, but saved.

"I have to be back at the plant at eleven." He was smiling un-certainly, balancing the baby and the bottle.

She put a finger against his cheek, traced the hollows under his eyes. "I'll soon fatten you up," she murmured, and held out her arms to receive the baby and the long, coping day.

"Won't you crush your dress? I can wait till you change."

"No." She heard her own voice, sugared viciously with wistfulness. "Once I change I'll be settled. As long as I keep it on . . . I'm still a visitor."

Silenced, he passed her the baby and the bottle.

This will have to stop, she thought. Or will the denied half of me persist, venomously arranging for the ruin of the other? She wanted to warn him standing there, trusting, in the devious shadow of her resentment.

The baby began to pedal its feet and cry, a long nagging ululation. She sprinkled a few warm drops of milk from the bottle on the back of her own hand. It was just right, the milk, but she sat on, holding the baby in her lap, while the drops cooled. Flexing the hand, she suddenly held it out gracefully, airily, regarding it.

"This one is still 'the rabbi's daughter,'" she said. Dan looked down at her, puzzled. She shook her head, smiling back at him, quizzical and false, and bending, pushed the nipple in the baby's mouth. At once it began to suck greedily, gazing back at her with the intent, agate eyes of satisfaction.

The Middle Drawer

◆§ THE DRAWER was always kept locked. In a household where
the tangled rubbish of existence had collected on surfaces like a scurf,
which was forever being cleared away by her mother and the maid,
then by her mother, and, finally, hardly at all, it had been a permanent cell—rather like, Hester thought wryly, the gene that is carried over from one generation to the other. Now, holding the small,
square, indelibly known key in her hand, she shrank before it, reluctant to perform the blasphemy that the living must inevitably per-
petrate on the possessions of the dead. There were no revelations to
be expected when she opened the drawer, only the painful reitera-
tion of her mother's personality and the power it had held over her
own, which would rise—an emanation, a mist, that she herself had
long since shredded away, parted, and escaped.

She repeated to herself, like an incantation, "I am married. I have
a child of my own, a home of my own five hundred miles away. I
have not even lived in this house—my parents' house—for over seven
years." Stepping back, she sat on the bed where her mother had died
the week before, slowly, from cancer, where Hester had held the
large, long-fingered, competent hand for a whole night, watching
the asphyxiating action of the fluid mounting in the lungs until it
had extinguished the breath. She sat facing the drawer.

It had taken her all her own lifetime to get to know its full contents, starting from the first glimpses, when she was just able to lean
her chin on the side and have her hand pushed away from the
packets and japanned boxes, to the last weeks, when she had made a
careful show of not noticing while she got out the necessary bank-
books and safe-deposit keys. Many times during her childhood, when
she had lain blandly ill herself, elevated to the honor of the parental

bed while she suffered from the "autointoxication" that must have been 1918's euphemism for plain piggishness, the drawer had been opened. Then she had been allowed to play with the two pairs of pearled opera glasses or the long string of graduated white china beads, each with its oval sides flushed like cheeks. Over these she had sometimes spent the whole afternoon, pencilling two eyes and a pursed mouth on each bead, until she had achieved an incredible string of minute, doll-like heads that made even her mother laugh.

Once while Hester was in college, the drawer had been opened for the replacement of her grandmother's great sunburst pin, which she had never before seen and which had been in pawn, and doggedly reclaimed over a long period by her mother. And for Hester's wedding her mother had taken out the delicate diamond chain—the "lavaliere" of the Gibson-girl era—that had been her father's wedding gift to her mother, and the ugly, expensive bar pin that had been his gift to his wife on the birth of her son. Hester had never before seen either of them, for the fashion of wearing diamonds indiscriminately had never been her mother's, who was contemptuous of other women's display, although she might spend minutes in front of the mirror debating a choice between two relatively gimcrack pieces of costume jewelry. Hester had never known why this was until recently, when the separation of the last few years had relaxed the tension between her mother and herself—not enough to prevent explosions when they met but enough for her to see obscurely, the long motivations of her mother's life. In the European sense, family jewelry was Property, and with all her faultless English and New World poise, her mother had never exorcised her European core.

In the back of the middle drawer, there was a small square of brown-toned photograph that had never escaped into the large, ramshackle portfolio of family pictures kept in the drawer of the old break-front bookcase, open to any hand. Seated on a bench, Hedwig Licht, aged two, brows knitted under ragged hair, stared mournfully into the camera with the huge, heavy-lidded eyes that had continued to brood in her face as a woman, the eyes that she had transmitted to Hester, along with the high cheekbones that she had deplored. Fat, wrinkled stockings were bowed into arcs that almost met at the high-stretched boots, which did not touch the floor; to hold up the stockings, strips of calico matching the dumpy little dress were bound around the knees.

Long ago, Hester, in her teens, staring tenaciously into the drawer under her mother's impatient glance, had found the little square and exclaimed over it, and her mother, snatching it away from her, had muttered, "If that isn't Dutchy!" But she had looked at it long and ruefully before she had pushed it back into a corner. Hester had added the picture to the legend of her mother's childhood built up from the bitter little anecdotes that her mother had let drop casually over the years.

She saw the small Hedwig, as clearly as if it had been herself, haunting the stiff rooms of the house in the townlet of Oberelsbach, motherless since birth and almost immediately stepmothered by a woman who had been unloving, if not unkind, and had soon borne the stern, *Haustyrann* father a son. The small figure she saw had no connection with the all-powerful figure of her mother but, rather, seemed akin to the legion of lonely children who were a constant motif in the literature that had been her own drug—the Sara Crewes and Little Dorrits, all those children who inhabited the familiar terror-struck dark that crouched under the lash of the adult. She saw Hedwig receiving from her dead mother's mother—the Grandmother Rosenberg, warm and loving but, alas, too far away to be of help—the beautiful, satin-incrusted bisque doll, and she saw the bad stepmother taking it away from Hedwig and putting it in the drawing room, because "it is too beautiful for a child to play with." She saw all this as if it had happened to her and she had never forgotten.

Years later, when this woman, Hester's step-grandmother, had come to the United States in the long train of refugees from Hitler, her mother had urged the grown Hester to visit her, and she had refused, knowing her own childishness but feeling the resentment rise in her as if she were six, saying, "I won't go. She wouldn't let you have your doll." Her mother had smiled at her sadly and had shrugged her shoulders resignedly. "You wouldn't say that if you could see her. She's an old woman. She has no teeth." Looking at her mother, Hester had wondered what her feelings were after forty years, but her mother, private as always in her emotions, had given no sign.

There had been no sign for Hester—never an open demonstration of love or an appeal—until the telephone call of a few months before, when she had heard her mother say quietly, over the distance, "I think you'd better come," and she had turned away from the phone saying bitterly, almost in awe, "If she *asks me* to come, she must be dying!"

Turning the key over in 'her hand, Hester looked back at the composite figure of her mother—that far-off figure of the legendary child, the nearer object of her own dependence, love, and hate—looked at it from behind the safe, dry wall of her own "American" education. We are told, she thought, that people who do not experience love in their earliest years cannot open up; they cannot give it to others; but by the time we have learned this from books or dredged it out of reminiscence, they have long since left upon us their chill, irremediable stain.

If Hester searched in her memory for moments of animal maternal warmth, like those she self-consciously gave her own child (as if her own childhood prodded her from behind), she thought always of the blue-shot twilight of one New York evening, the winter she was eight, when she and her mother were returning from a shopping expedition, gay and united in the shared guilt of being late for supper. In her mind, now, their arrested figures stood like two silhouettes caught in the spotlight of time. They had paused under the brightly agitated bulbs of a movie-theatre marquee, behind them the broad, rose-red sign of a Happiness candy store. Her mother, suddenly leaning down to her, had encircled her with her arm and nuzzled her, saying almost anxiously, "We do have fun together, don't we?" Hester had stared back stolidly, almost suspiciously, into the looming, pleading eyes, but she had rested against the encircling arm, and warmth had trickled through her as from a closed wound reopening.

After this, her mother's part in the years that followed seemed blurred with the recriminations from which Hester had retreated ever farther, always seeking the remote corners of the household—the sofa-fortressed alcoves, the store closet, the servants' bathroom—always bearing her amulet, a book. It seemed to her now, wincing, that the barrier of her mother's dissatisfaction with her had risen imperceptibly, like a coral cliff built inexorably from the slow accretion of carelessly ejaculated criticisms that had grown into solid being in the heavy fullness of time. Meanwhile, her father's uncritical affection, his open caresses, had been steadiness under her feet after the shifting waters of her mother's personality, but he had been away from home on business for long periods, and when at home he, too, was increasingly a target for her mother's deep-burning rage against life. Adored member of a large family that was almost tribal in its affections and unity, he could not cope with this smoldering force and never tried to understand it, but the shield of his adulthood gave him a protection that Hester did not have. He stood on equal ground.

Hester's parents had met at Saratoga, at the races. So dissimilar were their backgrounds that it was improbable that they would ever have met elsewhere than in the somewhat easy social flux of a spa, although their brownstone homes in New York were not many blocks apart, his in the gentility of upper Madison Avenue, hers in the solid, Germanic comfort of Yorkville. By this time, Hedwig had been in America ten years.

All Hester knew of her mother's coming to America was that she had arrived when she was sixteen. Now that she knew how old her mother had been at death, knew the birth date so zealously guarded during a lifetime of evasion and so quickly exposed by the noncommittal nakedness of funeral routine, she realized that her mother must have arrived in 1900. She had come to the home of an aunt, a sister of her own dead mother. What family drama had preceded her coming, whose decision it had been, Hester did not know. Her mother's one reply to a direct question had been a shrugging "There was nothing for me there."

Hester had a vivid picture of her mother's arrival and first years in New York, although this was drawn from only two clues. Her great-aunt, remarking once on Hester's looks in the dispassionate way of near relations, had nodded over Hester's head to her mother. "She is dark, like the father, no? Not like you were." And Hester, with a naïve glance of surprise at her mother's sedate pompadour, had eagerly interposed, "What was she like, Tante?"

"*Ach,* when she came off the boat, *war sie hübsch!*" Tante had said, lapsing into German with unusual warmth, "Such a color! Pink and cream!"

"Yes, a real Bavarian *Mädchen*," said her mother with a trace of contempt. "Too pink for the fashion here. I guess they thought it wasn't real."

Another time, her mother had said, in one of her rare bursts of anecdote, "When I came, I brought enough linen and underclothing to supply two brides. At the convent school where I was sent, the nuns didn't teach you much besides embroidery, so I had plenty to bring, plenty. They were nice, though. Good, simple women. Kind. I remember I brought four dozen handkerchiefs, beautiful heavy linen that you don't get in America. But they were large, bigger than the size of a man's handkerchief over here, and the first time I unfolded one, everybody laughed, so I threw them away." She had sighed, perhaps for the linen. "And underdrawers! Long red flannel, and I had spent months embroidering them with yards of white eyelet work on the ruffles. I remember Tante's maid came in from the back yard quite angry and refused to hang them on the line any more. She said the other maids, from the houses around, teased her for belonging to a family who would wear things like that."

Until Hester was in her teens, her mother had always employed young German or Czech girls fresh from "the other side"—Teenies and Josies of long braided hair, broad cotton ankles and queer, blunt shoes, who had clacked deferentially to her mother in German and had gone off to marry their waiter's and baker's apprentices at just about the time they learned to wear silk stockings and "just as soon as you've taught them how to serve a dinner," returning regularly to show off their square, acrid babies. "Greenhorns!" her mother had always called them, a veil of something indefinable about her lips. But in the middle drawer there was a long rope of blond hair, sacrificed, like the handkerchiefs, but not wholly discarded.

There was no passport in the drawer. Perhaps it had been destroyed during the years of the first World War, when her mother, long since a citizen by virtue of her marriage, had felt the contemporary pressure to excise everything Teutonic. "If that nosy Mrs. Cahn asks you when I came over, just say I came over as a child," she had said to Hester. And how easy it had been to nettle her by pretending that one could discern a trace of accent in her speech! Once, when the family had teased her by affecting to hear an echo of "public" in her pronunciation of "public," Hester had come upon her, hours after, standing before a mirror, color and nose high, watching herself say, over and over again, "Public! Public!"

Was it this, thought Hester, her straining toward perfection, that made her so intolerant of me, almost as if she were castigating in her child the imperfections that were her own? "Big feet, big hands, like mine," her mother had grumbled. "Why? Why? When every woman in your father's family wears size one! But their nice, large ears—you must have *those!*" And dressing Hester for Sunday school she would withdraw a few feet to look at the finished product, saying slowly, with dreamy cruelty, "I don't know why I let you wear those white gloves. They make your hands look clumsy, just like a policeman's."

It was over books that the rift between Hester and her mother had become complete. To her mother, marrying into a family whose bookish traditions she had never ceased trying to undermine with the sneer of the practical, it was as if the stigmata of that tradition, appearing upon the girl, had forever made them alien to one another.

"Your eyes don't look like a girl's, they look like an old woman's! Reading! Forever reading!" she had stormed, chasing Hester from room to room, flushing her out of doors, and on one remote, terrible afternoon, whipping the book out of Hester's hand, she had leaned over her, glaring, and had torn the book in two.

Hester shivered now, remembering the cold sense of triumph that had welled up in her as she had faced her mother, rejoicing in the enormity of what her mother had done.

Her mother had faltered before her. "Do you want to be a dreamer all your life?" she had muttered.

Hester had been unable to think of anything to say for a moment. Then she had stuttered, "All you think of in life is money!", and had made her grand exit. But huddling miserably in her room afterward she had known even then that it was not as simple as that, that her mother, too, was whipped and driven by some ungovernable dream she could not express, which had left her, like the book, torn in two.

Was it this, perhaps, that had sent her across an ocean, that had impelled her to perfect her dress and manner, and to reject the humdrum suitors of her aunt's circle for a Virginia bachelor twenty-two years older than herself? Had she, perhaps, married him not only for his money and his seasoned male charm but also for his standards and traditions, against which her railings had been a confession of envy and defeat?

So Hester and her mother had continued to pit their implacable difference against each other in a struggle that was complicated out of all reason by their undeniable likeness—each pursuing in her own orbit the warmth that had been denied. Gauche and surly as Hester was in her mother's presence, away from it she had striven successfully for the very falsities of standard that she despised in her mother, and it was her misery that she was forever impelled to earn her mother's approval at the expense of her own. Always, she knew now, there had been the lurking, buried wish that someday she would find the final barb, the homing shaft, that would maim her mother once and for all, as she felt herself to have been maimed.

A few months before, the barb had been placed in her hand. In answer to the telephone call, she had come to visit the family a short time after her mother's sudden operation for cancer of the breast. She had found her father and brother in an anguish of helplessness, fear, and male distaste at the thought of the illness, and her mother a prima donna of fortitude, moving unbowed toward the unspoken idea of her death but with the signs on her face of a pitiful tension that went beyond the disease. She had taken to using separate utensils and to sleeping alone, although the medical opinion that cancer was not transferable by contact was well known to her. It was clear that she was suffering from a horror of what had been done to her and from a fear of the revulsion of others. It was clear to Hester, also, that her father and brother had such a revulsion and had not been wholly successful in concealing it.

One night she and her mother had been together in her mother's bedroom. Hester, in a shabby housegown, stretched out on the bed luxuriously, thinking of how there was always a certain equivocal ease, a letting down of pretense, an illusory return to the irresponsibility of childhood, in the house of one's birth. Her mother, back turned, had been standing unnecessarily long at the bureau, fumbling with the articles upon it. She turned slowly.

"They've been giving me X-ray twice a week," she said, not looking at Hester, "to stop any involvement of the glands."

"Oh," said Hester, carefully smoothing down a wrinkle on the bedspread. "It's very wise to have that done."

Suddenly, her mother had put out her hand in a gesture almost of appeal. Half in a whisper, she asked, "Would you like to see it? No one has seen it since I left the hospital."

"Yes," Hester said, keeping her tone cool, even, full only of polite interest. "I'd like very much to see it." Frozen there on the bed, she had reverted to childhood in reality, remembering, as if they had all been crammed into one slot in time, the thousands of incidents when she had been the one to stand before her mother, vulnerable and bare, helplessly awaiting the cruel exactitude of her displeasure. "I know how she feels as if I were standing there myself," thought Hester. "How well she taught me to know!"

Slowly her mother undid her housegown and bared her breast. She stood there for a long moment, on her face the looming, pleading look of twenty years before, the look it had once shown under the theatre marquee.

Hester half rose from the bed. There was a hurt in her own breast that she did not recognize. She spoke with difficulty.

"Why . . . it's a beautiful job, Mother," she said, distilling the carefully natural tone of her voice. "Neat as can be. I had no idea . . . I thought it would be ugly." With a step toward her mother, she looked, as if casually, at the dreadful neatness of the cicatrix, at the twisted, foreshortened tendon of the upper arm.

"I can't raise my arm yet," whispered her mother. "They had to cut deep. . . . Your father won't look at it."

In an eternity of slowness, Hester stretched out her hand. Trembling, she touched a tentative finger to her mother's chest, where the breast had been. Then, with rising sureness, with infinite delicacy, she drew her fingertips along the length of the scar in a light, affirmative caress, and they stood eye to eye for an immeasurable second, on equal ground at last.

In the cold, darkening room, Hester unclenched herself from remembrance. She was always vulnerable, Hester thought. As we all are. What she bequeathed me unwittingly, ironically, was fortitude —the fortitude of those who have had to live under the blow. But pity—that I found for myself.

She knew now that the tangents of her mother and herself would never have fully met, even if her mother had lived. Holding her mother's hand through the long night as she retreated over the border line of narcosis and coma into death, she had felt the giddy sense of conquering, the heady euphoria of being still alive, which comes to the watcher in the night. Nevertheless, she had known with sureness, even then, that she would go on all her life trying to "show" her mother, in an unsatisfied effort to earn her approval—and unconditional love.

As a child, she had slapped at her mother once in a frenzy of rebellion, and her mother, in reproof, had told her the tale of the peasant girl who had struck her mother and had later fallen ill and died and been buried in the village cemetery. When the mourners came to tend the mound, they found that the corpse's offending hand had grown out of the grave. They cut it off and reburied it, but when they came again in the morning, the hand had grown again. So, too, thought Hester, even though I might learn—have learned in some ways—to escape my mother's hand, all my life I will have to push it down; all my life my mother's hand will grow again out of the unquiet grave of the past.

It was her own life that was in the middle drawer. She was the person she was not only because of her mother but because, fifty-eight years before, in the little town of Oberelsbach, another woman, whose qualities she would never know, had died too soon. Death, she thought, absolves equally the bungler, the evildoer, the unloving, and the unloved—but never the living. In the end, the cicatrix that she had, in the smallest of ways, helped her mother to bear had eaten its way in and killed. The living carry, she thought, perhaps not one tangible wound but the burden of the innumerable small cicatrices imposed on us by our beginnings; we carry them with us always, and from these, from this agony, we are not absolved.

She turned the key and opened the drawer.

III

The Summer Rebellion

◆§ THE SINISTER thing about Hillsborough, since I come back, is that the soda parlors are gone. You have to know the place why. Since I *came* back—O.K. I could talk that way even before I left for the Agricultural; why else did my Aunt Mary bring me up to read every old book in the shop, and hang my junior excellence medal in the parlor—though she never hung the one for sharpshooting—and sell off, to the summer people to build a house of, that last old cypress-colored barn we had at the edge of where the acreage once was? They were going to use it to build a house. But if I like to talk that way at my convenience, it's like putting on jeans again after Sunday dinner and church—or it used to be. The whole trouble must have begun, I think, when the summer people started wearing our jeans. But that was way back; I don't go that far back personally. Our family goes eight generations in Hillsborough, but I only go as far back as when it began for us, when those two come to buy the barn. That's as far back as I like to go.

"Cedar," says the man, and the woman whispers *Did you ever see such weathering!*, and I'm standing by, about fourteen years old, and I start to say, "Why, that ain't cedar, it's bir—," when my aunt's fingers, steelhard from sanding old trestle tables to the pine again and emerying off the chipped places on flint glass, grabs me at the neck. "Don't say 'ain't,' Johnny One—you know how to talk right!" So I do; isn't she always jabbing at me "Talk like the summer people—you don't have to pay any attention to what they *say!*"

She's still holding me. "This boy has got hisself a medal," she says. She can say "himself" just as well, too. But this way, the pair will think the old shack—which isn't birch but isn't cedar either—is just what they want for front trim.

301

"Why do you call him Johnny One?" the woman says, curious.

This is the first time I date too that my aunt speaks the way she then does—vague—even for all that energy she's putting out, getting rid of all our junk first and then all she can find in the neighborhood. And how she looks; I notice that too. Faded. "Why do I call him Johnny One?" she says, the way people do, bidding for time, and when they've never noticed themselves before. "Why, my sister —what was her name?—she only left one." She smartened then— why she used to be so smart, smarter than me! "Why, I guess I call him Johnny One cause I haven't got two!" And then she and I, my neck free now, looked back triumphantly; from our ways lately, that explanation seemed clear enough.

They bought the barn—which wasn't a barn. But on their way off, I snaked through the woods alongside of the path they took back to their car—I used to like to watch summer people the way any boy, all of us children liked to watch the doings of ghosts who never intended or did anything mean to us except bring gifts and then in the fall fade away again—and I heard them talking, different than they talk to us, the way they talk to each other. " 'My sister, what was her name?' " said the woman. "Can you imagine!" When I went off to the A., I found out of course what she meant. Our town sure had been dragging its feet—though it wasn't the only hill town in New Hampshire to do it, not by a longshot, I found.

But at the moment I was more interested in what the man said. "You pipe the boy?" They don't always talk so fine themselves.

"Did I!" she said. "Whew."

"Quite an Apollo, wasn't he."

"If there were two," she said giggling, "who could bear it?" She sighed. "What a waste. Such a beautiful kid."

"Think that barn *is* birch?" said the man.

"Of course not. Let her think she's putting something over on us, poor thing, if she wants. But you and I know what it would cost at a lumberman's, aside from the *color*. To buy all that oak."

That was the way it always turned out between Hillsborough and the summer people, from the very first, when we sold off the land by the lakeshore that was no good for farmland if they only knew, and woods that didn't have nothing in them, anything in them but birch. Until I came home this June, I didn't know who was to blame. I found that out at the college. Let me tell you about Hills-borough, first.

When you come north by the state road, on your way to the White Mountains, the road goes straight for a while, past a few houses; then all of a sudden it humps up very sharp, through a few stores at the hilltop, with a side road going east over the hill and down out of sight. If you continue on, there's a garage and some empty stores at the bottom again, then whoosh, the town is gone. If you park your car at the top and stay a while—that's us. Or if you've been there forever.

In the summertime, with the summer people all here, used to be such a big bottleneck in that ring of stores, on a Friday shopping especially, that the town board had the hump all divided in those slanted, white-painted parking lines. Still is a bottleneck, but if you look hard and knowing enough, it's mostly all tourists, of a bright summer afternoon. As they drive up the hill, on their left side, first comes a few old mashed-together buildings every town here has, no-body knows much what they were, then comes the closed-up church, then the store where the number one soda parlor always was, and then the supermarket, once the barbershop and the corner shoe. It came the last few years ago, for the summer people, but it may be too late for them. Has a coke machine out front. Next to it is The Service Shop, still there. That's for sewing wools and stuffs, the kind of thing women call "notions," and seems to last, no matter what. Or old Mrs. Hupper who keeps it does. "Shut up shop, or hang her-self," she says, before she'll go to selling junk as antiques. Still has a few customer ladies from the lakeshore, so old and pinkfaded they still look to us like all the lakeside houses and inhabitants used to, just a summer vision that would soon fade.

On the other side of the crest of our hill, hung over the steep road that goes off it down and east, is a numb little grocery, just the sort you'd think we'd shop in ourselves—washed-out cardboard signs in windows under the old house eaves, and packaged bread. But in the fall, you'd be surprised how bright it is, when the fishing talk is over, and the gun talk begins. Fellow who owns it, used to have his gun collection hung on the wall right over the milk-and-cheese counter, until he sold it, all but one deer rifle, last year. And nowadays he stocks frozen food and all that, like for the summer people, and we eat it, hoping for health. But it may be too late for that too.

Next to him, just before you get to the crest, used to be the second soda place, just a home restaurant but where we kids could go for ice cream; now it sells sandwiches in booths meant for tourists, but it has no beer and looks like it would have the crummy coffee we do have, so they don't go in. And neither do we. And back down the hill, next to that, used to be a stationery and male notions sort of place; he had a malted-milk machine we could hang around too—but he was no Hupper, he's gone too, though not far. Most any afternoon until dusk, you can see him sitting there on his front lawn behind the tables with anything from hubcaps to kitchenware to framed saints'-pictures on them; often he's there with a light, after dark. Or in the morning, if he's not, the tables are, and anybody takes the trouble to knock, he's out in a jiffy. "Just shavin'. What vase? Be one dollar, that vase." Anybody takes the trouble to go down any of our side roads, will find any of us with our things all set out, sitting back of the tables, or in a rocking chair if we're old, or inside. We're a town on a hill, so we can't stretch the business out straight like some can, and catch it all in one trough. And we haven't got the knowhow like FitzWilliam, where the professionals are. Or the houses and granges and live churches to look at, like Hancock. Houses and hardware both, we run closer to junk than antiques. But you'll find us. Behind that hillside everywhere, is us. We're still there.

On the grocery's eave, pointing down the east road, there's a marker says Aunt Marietta's Antiques. That's us in particular, I and Aunt Mary, and her husband, my uncle Andy—in our family there's only one of each of us. Before you come to our house, there's the mill—the standard, red brick, New England, New Hampshire knitting mill, with its sluices and iron gone to rust, and what seems like a hundred gross of spidered windowpanes, not half enough of them knocked in. Those Victorian windowpanes stay orderly looking until the end, and good red brick don't ever seem to fall, or get haunted. Those greenery things, sumac and ailanthus, that always take over, look feathery nice around it. It could start up again in a minute, you think, passing by. Opposite it though, is what, after the church of course, used to be our real pride.

It's a chocolate-and-tan frame structure of some seven stories high, built in the seventies, with balconies and fretwork running even and complete around every story; if it leaned just a little, or was skinny and not square, it would look like a monument. As it is, it is supposed to be one of the last specimens of that architecture, and when we first had Aunt Mary's shop, she used to take picture postcards of it, which sold very well. I don't know why she hasn't the get-up to, anymore. Or I'm beginning to think I do. Anyway, the Geracis, who now own it, you sometimes hear one of them tell a tourist it was a hotel, but it never was; it was a kind of high-class rabbit warren for the mill workers to live in, with enough railing and banisters to match those factory windows across the way. To give the Geracis credit, they keep it painted. They're Italians, Hillsborough's only, and they still have the energy for a place like that, and the relatives; Italians can always take in each other's washing from all the other onlies in the towns roundabout, and keep separate that way; in the basement they even have a store none of us sets foot in, unless ours runs out of something and we haven't got the gall to sneak in opposite to the supermarket, which is what we would like best. The Geraci children still have separate names, too—saints' names, but separate.

And after Geraci's, down the road that leads straight to the lake shore and to all the summer people, that's us in particular. Our house is one of the larger old white ones, an old Apollo of a house, you might say, and we are accustomed to hearing, in summer, how beautiful it —could become. In winter we are inclined to think how comfortable it could be—to keep. But we still have it, and we're the only house out that way, with our back garden—or that once was—on a little rise too, and pointed straight toward the lake that is really a huge, circular "pond" as we call it—Willard's Pond—and toward them. We're the only family on the way to them, and that is our peculiar distinction—though we have another. Between them and us, is our woods, or what used to be ours, where, last year, I used to make out with one of their Barbaras. From our back windows we can see them, in all their homes they've made out of our houses and our barns—stretching on and on in a half-circle, but even bright with upkeep though they are, a mirage.

In summer, what with boats and docks and waterskiers this year and all that gradual growth of plastic, they tend to seem brighter, and it's true every year they seem healthier, staying on longer each year. They like to keep up what they call their relationship with us;

that helps to keep them healthy too. "That's *their* upkeep," my aunt once said tartly. Truth was, she thought some of their ladies liked to keep it up with my uncle, who at thirty-nine years old is blonder and taller than I am, a retired Marine with muscles that last year he used to maintain, too, with a set of barbells my aunt swapped somewhere.

The swap shop was no distinction, only what my aunt got into years ago out of sheer energy and not liking to embroider, starting it out as a gift shop with a line of dollclothes, and those new gilt memento cups—none stamped for Hillsborough, we were too small for that, but Portsmouth and so forth—when the new people came. If they started her on the antiques, always being so wistful after our chipped buttercrocks and old end-of-day vases, who was to blame? Meanwhile, it didn't say we weren't just as healthy as ever, only rightfully lazier—if now and then we swapped a bit of land. Or woods that were mostly only birch. White birch is good sure enough for those new-style kitchen cabinets. But the sawmill over at Nubanusit is all ailanthus too.

And meanwhile, there they were, only the summer people, that mirage across Willard Pond. We took care of their houses, shut off their waterpipes and promised to turn them on again come "the season," and to mow their first lawn. Come Labor Day, they began to go. Come October, they were gone. With their extra keys jingled away in our dresser drawer, we forgot them, or sometimes, just to check up of course, in the performance of duty, we toured their houses and habits from top to bottom, fingered their linen and the quilts they'd bought from us, laughed at that other junk, the cobalt glass bottles and a Stafford pitcher in the window and somebody from Antrim's greatgranny on the wall—and remembered to remind ourselves how faded, like the new owners, all this was. Come November, when gun talk was all over the grocery, bright as apples and the huntsmen's china teeth, we had forgotten them altogether. Mrs. Hupper took the needlepoint wool out of her window and hung there a glorious pink-and-purple afghan, with a sign saying it was to be raffled for the church, and chances could be bought right there. The church itself came open, with a visiting preacher every third Sunday. And then at last, our real mirages took over again all the way, from the woman in white you could see on one of the balconies at Geraci's on a moonlit evening, to the sea monster that was supposed to be in the Pond.

This was all the change I noticed until I went away and came home from college, but that's supposed to be natural, isn't it?—even though college wasn't the real state university I like to say. It was a state-run one, sure enough, but the old two-year Agricultural and Manual-training unit, switched off now from Guernseys, and onto economics and business courses—gone to that kind of grass. There were a lot of dopes there who would do well at these, plus a few hopelessly smart ones, still on the agriculture, like me. We quickly discovered who we were—there was usually about one of us from a particular town.

We were the aristocrats of the upkeepers, all of us, and many of us were the Apollos, too, who some summer person had stuck the idea of a scholarship in the mind of, or had even written away for to help him, all the way back from "Ooo, Aunt Mary, what a beautiful little boy you have, and so smart." And keep him away from my Barbara. We knew who we were, and began pooling our information right away. We were the elite.

And we were the ones (though we learned to hide it except among one another) who came from the towns where people's names had gone back to grass too. The way we found out about each other was—there were so many Johnnies. There are always a lot of people named John anywhere, I understand that. But were there ever so many boys who answered—unless they were quick enough—to the names of Johnny One, Johnny Two, Johnny Three and so on? We even had one Johnny Ten, but he was unusual. Our families weren't so big anymore.

"Sometimes even the summer people do better," said the boy in whose room we were, a skinny Johnny One from over to Contoocook, but still with a lot of tawny gumption in his cheek—he didn't eat their frozen, and his folk had a pig littered every spring; wouldn't let them eat *her*, wouldn't let them sell her either.

"Over our way," another said proudly, "we've still got Buddy names as well; my best friend is a Buddy Four"—but he wasn't much. And there were a few other reports of the old original names, the tombstone ones—Lukes and Patiences and so forth—though there would still be only two names to a family, for the girls and for the boys. But mostly, the families were running to Mary One, Two, and Three and so forth for the girls, and Johnnies of the same.

"Why is it do you suppose it's happening?" said Johnny Ten, not the brightest of us, only there because if a Ten wasn't eligible, who was?

Nobody liked to say, even among us though there wasn't a boy didn't have an inkling.

"But I can tell you why we've still got our different last names," said the boy from Contoocook. "Otherwise, it would be too confusing to them—even though they don't much use those. And too noticeable. This way, we can just fade quietly. And they can keep tally on us, like they like to do of the oldest stones in the graveyard."

Well, we didn't do much but form the club, that year. Freshmen do that. Then we came home, and I suspect that ordinarily the same thing would have happened to the boys from those other towns as to me; clubs fade too, like winter seasons. But now it was summer again. And I was shocked to the gills when I saw my uncle and aunt. People not forty years old yet don't just all of a sudden look like that, not when they've both always been lively as a barn dance— not unless they have a mortal disease. And it wasn't as if they just suddenly looked older in any healthy way, or even downright old, the way some people's hair turns gray overnight. He was still blond as could be; she was still brown. Morning early, and evening late, that is. In the strongest noon light, you couldn't quite tell. What's sucking them?—I thought, but we are a reserved family and I knew even if I could bring myself to ask, they wouldn't say. They moved lightly these days, and vaguely—my uncle, with tattoos half the length of his burly forearm, and his machinist's shoes and his heavy fingernails powerful as old yellow horn!—and their thoughts seemed to come from a long way back.

"Look at *him!*" cried my aunt when she saw me, "Oh, Johnny One." Her face puckered up, not much, just faintly, and then she stepped back, and put her hand to her hair in an absentminded way, and said in a thin voice, almost cold, and to my uncle, "Maybe he shouldn't of come back at all!" She hadn't the energy you see, to feel more.

But I was just inside the door and I hadn't tipped to any of it yet; I was waiting as usual for her to fall all over me and my growth like when I'd been to scout camp—in the winters, I'd used to hear her whispering at him in bed, "We've got to manage it for him another year, Andy, we've got to—we can't let him stay here all summer long." I was waiting for my uncle to thump me and kid around, and even for my aunt to say with a toss of her head that over at Willard Pond, they'd better look after their Barbaras, whereupon I would have to look both wise and innocent—for it was already too late to prevent that, too.

Instead, my aunt came up to me and timidly touched me on the sleeve. And passed her finger like a dandelion-fluff over my cheek. "You're so red," she said. "And your eyes, so blue. Don't tell me they feed *you* packaged stuff." And I said, bewildered, "No, the college has got its own farm—part of the program is we have to work it." And before I could say any more, she burst out, "Oh Johnny One, Johnny One, maybe you should go away for good *now*."

"What are you talking about?" I said. "This is our place." And it is too, though it's only free and clear because they won't give *us* a mortgage on it, and there isn't much to it except the windows and walls, still thick and healthy, and the bit of furniture we swapped to keep. We were lucky in some ways, some said. Some have waited until the place is so slatted to the roof, there's nothing of it to sell at all.

"You're not going to *sell*," I said. "Why, I could paint it up here in no time—if you could get the paint. And the roof too—I see where the water's come through."

My aunt looked crafty—I'd never seen her look like that before. Even when she was cheating them a little, not with any outright lie; she'd look merry. "Not on your tintype," she said—when you haven't the energy, you sound hard and mean when you only intend to sound strong. "Catch me doing up what they'd only tear away. This place won't tumble, not in our time. But I'll make them pay the higher for every fence hole, inside and out. They like it better that way—don't I know from the shop? They like to start from *scratch*."

Brrr. How that word sounded when she said it, half snake, half claw. I looked around me more carefully. The shop was gone of course—that went last year, no great decision, just weaseled away with the last load of goods. They could start up again, any time they had the gumption, and could fix the car. In the old farmland, it used to be when the cow died; now the cow is the car. But they still had their jobs surely.

"How're the Blazers?" I said. The Blazers are *our* summer people. My uncle clicked a thumbnail. "Mr. Blazer is thinking of doing his own garden. He was telling me only the other day how healthy it makes him, not only to eat. 'The old customs, Andy; we should all go back to them.' He's learning to do it all quicker than me. Got a lot of energy, that man. He showed me. Only thing he don't do good yet is all that boxwood he just put in, front of the house. He's no hand with the clipping shears yet. But he learns fast."

I looked over at my aunt. She hung her head, then looked at me sideways and through her hair, like those moron-children in our local family of the same. O my darling chubby, freckle-tan aunt, where had she got to?

"Aunt Marietta!" I said. That was her full name, sunk away somehow. And do you know, she straightened a little, and the color came back to one cheek.

"That's it!" said my uncle. Usually he didn't do the thinking for the family. He took a step forward, stamping as hard as if it was a resolution all in itself. But he was all excited. "We'll go back to the old customs. I'll be Andrew again." Not Mr. Blazer's Andy, is what he meant. "And he'll be our John, or our Johnny. But not Johnny One. That way it won't touch him, he'll stay healthy. That way, he can stay."

"And I'll make a garden!" I said. "I could do it out on the—" And then I looked outside, and remembered. What wasn't all dock and burr, and those good New Hampshire boulders which take block-and-tackle to move where it doesn't take eight generations of wall-building—was gone to wood. We'd let our old woods, sold to them, creep up on us. They hadn't seemed to mind. But there was worse than that. The trouble really didn't begin when they started wearing our jeans. When the old tools began to go, that was the beginning—from when we couldn't tell, even ourselves, was a tool to stay in the barn or go to be sold in the shop?

My aunt hung her head down again. But my uncle's idea, poor Andy muscleman, had really bolstered him. "Marietta, our John is home," he said, all dignity. "I'm going to shave."

I watched him while he did it. His great weightlifter's arm, molded in biceps, always did look funny handling that delicate razor, but now it looked foreshortened too, like all the rest of him, as if something underneath the muscles was shrunk. He looked all shrunk and contorted, like those woodenheaded character dolls we used to find in a bunch of goods now and then, old shepherds and bent-over wives marked Nuremberg and Tyrol. That's the way it took him, not like my aunt; it doesn't take everybody the same. Funny thing too, I saw that though his beard and hair were still as blond as mine, the leavings in the bowl were different. I walked over to see for sure. He'd had a week's beard on him. Yes, the scrapings in the bowl were gray. Or you could call it a dim green.

All this time, my aunt, still peering at me now and then from under her hair, was fixing supper. And as the dusk came on, and before the lamps were lit, they began to look better to me. Maybe the green from outside, pressing in at the back window, rosied them a little; as we were told in art course, the complementary color to green is red. Oh I hadn't gone without learning that year; as well as the grammar and the art and the regular animal husbandry, we'd had a course in plant ecology too.

"What about that boxwood, what's that for?" I said idly, only wanting to make conversation. Soon's I got home, that's all I seemed to want to do, and not too much of it. I just wanted to sit, really. I felt tired, down to the hair on my limbs.

"Blazer wants to keep his privacy," said my uncle Andrew. "Oh, not from us." He gave a little snort—a weak one. "Not on the Pond and wood side. Round on the front side of the house. Seems the kids on their road are puttin' up a neighborhood affair to keep them out of mischief, center of that common lawn they have, used to be the old green. Oh he approves of it, helped to do that. Just don't want to see it, that's all, from the house. Band stand, or suthin'."

"Bandstand? They don't have any band," I said. Neither do we, anymore. We younger ones used to, mellaphone and xylophone. But all that beating and blowing takes it out of you. And over there, why should they bother with that stuff, summers?

"Close the window," said my aunt. "Don't look out." She went and closed the shutters, moving slow, like her own shawl. I'd never known her to wear a shawl before. And there was a line of dark on her upper lip. I never did like dark on the upper lips of ladies. Then she came and sat down again.

But I'd already seen the outside green, pressing in on us. Funny thing. Our own woods never seemed to close us in before—or out. But that was when they were our own.

"Think I'll go up the hill after supper," I said. "See what's doing at the soda parlor." It didn't have a name anymore, but they knew where I meant, the place next to the supermarket—where we young ones all make tracks for first. The number one Soda Parlor. Not such a bad dump that the Barbaras from over Willard Pond can't come looking for us.

"But it's gone," said my aunt.

I'd come in at night, hitching with a couple of salesmen kept me yapping and dropped me over the hill. But I'm quick to rally, at least in winter weather, or fresh from the Agricultural.

"Well, then, guess I'll have to go to the greasy spoon." The coffee-and-sandwich tourist place. No ice cream, but soda parlor number two, in a pinch. That's where they'd all be, if they couldn't the other.

"Closes at six, when it's open. Not open during the week."

Something in her tone put me wise. I hadn't been back all year. "And Schlock's malted?"

"He's been junking since spring." My aunt began a kind of sing-song. "Kelley One, Kelley Two, up the Niansit Road, they're junking, doing the best of any, they've got Irish blood keeps them going, and they never even knew what was in that barn of theirs from thirty years ago when they bought the place, many's the time I tried to tell them. And Anderson, the real estate, of course they've been at it always, near far back as me, and they only do to dealers, but now the mother-in-law too. And Cargill at the Souhegan crossroads, and back of the Monadnock Road, and Pack Monadnock—" That's a mountain. "When they're not at the tables, they're digging for bottles. Bottles are very good this year. There's tables out everywhere. Up and down the Pack."

"Bottles" means old "hand-blown" medicine bottles, from bitters to what can be only bromo-seltzers, or old commemoration bottles and so forth—I've dug those often, at the town dump, to sell back to *them*.

"But where do we hang out now?" I said.

My uncle meanwhile was rocking. Takes practice in our old Boston—he was going at it like a master. "I know what those kids—must be a grange. Saw all these colored lampshades going in, like we once had, the dining-room table. Kelleys sold them two. That's what it is. A grange."

Wasn't any reason my aunt should snap at him, more than at me. But she went for him, almost with her old spunk. "No it isn't," she said. "You know right well what it is and must be. It'll be like the woods, not to hunt in—for you. And not to swim in—for him. Like the Pond." Then she turned to me."It's to be what they call a teen-age hangout," she said.

So then I was so tired. I didn't say anything, didn't say nothing. Either way—I didn't. Supper was fixed; you'd never believe what. I ate it, but I won't talk about it, even now.

And the next morning, I was up early to go up over the hill and see for myself, about the town. At least I meant to, but somehow I slept until noon. When I got there, it looked lively enough, cram-jam with tourists. They didn't stay on the hilltop long; just parked their cars in the white lines—and everywhere else—and spread out by foot. They have some idea that coming up to a table, if you don't see their license, you won't know they're not local and soak 'em for it. But they look so healthy, you can always tell. They're not a mirage, summer *or* winter. They're just passing through, so you can say it. They're real.

And I thought, not seeing anybody who was anybody—my age that is—that maybe the Agricultural gets out earlier than their schools would, from the old days when the farm boys had to get home. But there was none of our town kids around either; few as there are left, there wasn't a Johnny or Mary of any denomination, in sight. Later on, I knew where they were; if they weren't digging bottles, they were rocking in their junior-size rockers, to guard the tables, or just hanging on the front steps, looking sideways through their hair. But just then I had to walk up and down the whole street a dozen times, to convince myself. There wasn't a one of us kids, either from Willard Pond or our side, in town.

I hung around until after suppertime, not being over anxious for it, and at the grocery steps—ours of course. After supper would be the time, if any. Not much custom came by—two. One was a great, strapping beauty of a girl we older boys had been warned away from ever since she went to live by herself, even before the school shut down for good. Other was her sister. Beautiful as sin they still were, even yet. Fading had even helped them; their hair was a cooler color, and it rippled, rippled down their backs. Going in and coming out, they made a sign of interest in me, but they couldn't maintain it. I could see they didn't know who I was anymore, but I wasn't only glad, as I watched them away, I was scared, past any connection with them alone. We always had some moustached old ladies in the town, and some of the Geracis have like a pencil smear, but this, on these girls' upper lips, above the pretty pucker, was different—a green mold. And I knew it didn't have anything to do with their sinfulness—on account of my aunt.

When they were gone, I got up and went inside the shop. The owner was sitting there, just like an album leftover of last year. Only thing shining was his china teeth; I never knew why the old hunting men around there always either had them, or else none. Maybe because only the old ones still knew how to hunt. I could see he didn't know me either, or try, though he was once the one first let me have a shot at the target. But they always have a big calendar, and there it was, hung right under the big long-barreled gun they never used but said was for deer.

"I just want to see the date," I said. "The day of the month. I just want to see for sure what day it is in June." For though I was sure I'd been home long enough for any school to be out by now, I couldn't remember.

He didn't move any more than a wooden Indian. He let me lean right over him. I saw that the calendar page was still at October. Had an Audubon picture above the empty days, a mother woodcock with her brood nice and quiet and ready, in a field. I started to lift the page.

"Leave that be." He didn't move. His eyes were pink, from staring ahead.

"I just wanted to—"

He raised his hand to the gun. The hand was shaking, but kind of an old brown-pink too, almost healthy. And by God, the gun barrel was shining too, more than anything else in sight in Hillsborough. I had to admire his energy.

"It's always October here," he said, as I left the shop.

But being the age I am, the soda parlors seemed to me the most sinister. "Sinister" is a word our plant-and-forestry instructor begins the hour with almost every morning; it's his first year too, and he comes from one of the fancy places, Cornell. He's only teacher-in-training to us, before he goes off to the job he's going to get after the summer, in research. "Be seated, gentlemen," he always says, "and let me impart to you another sinister fact about the ecology of our world." Then he flashes a grin at us, to show us we can be at our ease, but if he gave the command, he could keep some of us straight in our chairs for double the time. Talk about D.D.T., that's only the beginning; he can tell you a hundred different ways, from detergents to depth-bombs, how the natural balance of the world is being upset. And another hundred brave ways of how nature plans to keep it. About the rise and fall of all plants, and how certain plants, even trees, have to have other trees near by them, little numbly ones you would never look at for themselves, in order to survive. "Survive" is another word he's always at, when he isn't at the other. Boy, has he ever given it to us. Even Johnny Ten knows what Ecology is. It's our favorite course. "Even about the Dutch elm, boys, don't be so quick to blame it all on that beetle, or even that aphid they're blaming now. Look for some tree, maybe the commonest genus in the world, that isn't standing by any more, and once used to be."

It was about eight o'clock or less when I left the grocery, still to be light for an hour or so, and I decided to go to the woods and think about making out. How else was I going to meet her, otherwise? I could go through our old wood and up to the rim of Willard Pond, just one open place on it, but I couldn't go round the rim to their side, that's all theirs, and we younger ones never do—did. They always used to come here. And that's how it happened between her and me last year. I just went and sat at the edge of our woods, in the high, flat, mossy place I'd known forever, where you could lie and be seen or not seen, as you chose. I used to sit there regularly, day and evening, always at the same times, so that anybody saw me from over there, they'd begin to know. I used to just sit there, and think about making out with girls. And one day, parting the birches, from where she'd come around the rim, there she was. Of course we'd seen each other at the soda parlor, before.

Usually they come in twos, if they come at all. But she came alone; that's what interested me. I like things interesting in that style. And she felt the same. We found that out quick enough about each other. But in fact, what with her family owning her place for four years now and our summer staring at each other across the soda parlor for two of those, we already knew. There are sides to a soda parlor too of course, or were—ours and theirs. But sometimes, like a wood, it can be crossed.

"Why don't you ever come and swim," she said, sitting down as graceful on my moss as if it were her own—which it partly was. She knew why of course. The Pond is private. But they like to ask. To hear us answer. Especially if we're handsome.

But I wasn't going to give her that satisfaction.

"Because of the leeches," I said.

The leeches in the pond—we'd never told any of them, when we sold off a patch of shoreline, that these were in the pond thick as seeds at the edge, or how to avoid them—by flat-diving and swimming out quick—or how to get one off if it fastened on you. Let them find out for themselves. But wouldn't you know, just as with the land and the shack that wasn't any good to us, after a while the leeches went away—the summer people's blood wasn't rich enough yet. "All goes into their money," my aunt said. We did used to swim some of course, sneaking it in early or after they'd gone. But I hadn't seen a leech in years.

"Why, I've never seen one, what do they look like?" she said.

Well, no use going over all of it. It wasn't a large conversation. She never did like to hear me talk much, and all this last year through we didn't write, didn't either of us plan any mention of that. And we'd each made out with other persons before.

But she did say that one thing.

"I'd never make out with any other one of you," she said. "Only you."

And I thought the same, or even better. It's like when the one tree knows that the other tree is in the forest, standing by. And I thought to myself that there ought to be a better word for it, than—making out.

So that evening, I went back through the woods, to our joint-owned mossy place, that evening and many more, and daytimes, too. All through what must have been the rest of June, and then July and part of August, I sat there; I hunted up a calendar at home, and counted it out. Except to creep into a store for my aunt—and then I'd sneak into Geraci's when I could on credit, for it was healthier— I never went up the hill to town at all.

And as I sat there, high in my open eyrie, I could see well enough what they were building. My, it was sharp and bright, as shining as anything on the state highway, with a baby-sized turret, orange-sherbet colored with a rod waiting for the weathercock to be fixed on it, and a plateglass entrance you could see in through, just like the state liquor store. I have excellent sight. I could see it all, like an anthill milling, at all hours of the day and late on into the evening, when they kept worklamps burning. That's why it went on for so long; they were doing it themselves, as they had learned more and more to do. I could see the boys and girls bending to their jobs, but could not always tell one girl from the other, because of that long hair style falling over their faces, and their same halters and jeans. Sometimes I could. My, how bright and particular and blooming it had gotten to be over there on the lakeshore, and not all with plastic either! Browning that way in their gardens, putting up their preserves in our old Mason jars, even hoisting lumber as if they saw a block-and-tackle every day in the week—they're getting healthier. I could see well enough what they were up to. I clenched my hands in the moss, and thought about it. It wasn't so far to across there; it only had always seemed to be.

Then, one day just at the end of summer, she came. It had taken a long devotion of my sitting there, but I had always known she would. And if it had taken longer than last year, this was because back then I'd just been dreaming on it generally, on making out with any girl. I hadn't been thinking of it with Barbara Blazer.

That's who it was of course. After all, even after another summer, if it is known where to look, the tree can see the tree.

When she parted the birches and came in, I wondered how I could ever have confused her with the others, even at a distance. Her hair was the longest, long and straight as any sin. A gold hoop hung in the ear I could see. The lobe was red, where the hoop of light pinched it. Her mouth matched the ear. Above, the sun was just going down, ahead of the dusk. My, I said to myself—she looks strange for a member of that mirage. So rosy and separate.

She came and sat down beside me, graceful as ever, on the moss. I dug my fingers in it, but I couldn't make it just mine any more. It's too late for it.

"Late this year," I said. "Aren't you."

She tossed back her hair. The other ear had a hoop in it too, and a pulse of red. "Oh, we're *very* late—we meant to have it ready by midsummer." She flicked a look at me, and away, and sighed. "Like father says, you have to work hard to know how hard work *is*."

For a minute I didn't answer. Then I said, "Well, you'll have long enough to use it. If you're going to stay on longer this year."

Or all year round. That's what I'd been telling myself. That's what my aunt had been telling me. When able.

While the sun went down, she didn't answer. Then she said low—I will say she speaks low, not screech-owl like some of them—"It was you, wasn't it, put that pine-pillow heart under my bed pillow, up at the house? After the house was closed?" We were neither looking at the other, but she felt my nod. "You dope," she said, "wouldn't you know my mother'd find it before I did. But we were lucky. 'How sentimental of her,' my mother said. 'Guess she wants to show us how much she likes us, to stay on.' She thought it was your aunt."

"It was sentimental," I said. But the thing had been around our family a long time. I thought they liked that. I'd even had to mend it. "I thought you'd like it." And it was all I had.

"A Pillow of Pine for a Sweetheart of Mine," she said. "You dope." But she smiled. "It was pretty grundgy by the time I got it. You must have put it there way last fall."

"I've been away since then."

"I know." We still weren't looking at each other. "But we know you all go through the house when we're not there and look us over. We've always known. We can tell." And then, maybe even not conscious of it, just as I looked at her, she wrinkled her nose.

Anger makes for strength. "I was at *college*, all year."

"I heard. We're very proud of you—the only one in town. And that's why I came over." Her hair hid her face. She spoke through it. "I thought maybe you could do something with your aunt and uncle. Mainly with your aunt. Before my mother has to tell her. She's gotten so—careless with herself—not even worth her pay, my mother says. The house was a sight, when we walked in. All spidery. And your uncle remembered to turn the water back on, but left the sump-pump going. Oh that's all right, we're sentimental too, my father says—to a point. But—"

I thought she would never be done, and the funny thing was it almost didn't seem to matter. When it's too late altogether, what can it matter—once you know that?

"But we've had a new baby," she said. "And around a new baby, you simply can't have somebody like that. Could you somehow—jack her up?"

It's all in the balance of it. They don't intend to be mean.

Laughing helps too. I rolled back against one of the birches, laughing as hard as I could, and then sat up again. "Why she must be forty years old. Your mother." She's forty-two; we know everything about them. And how dare she, with her skinny little bikini figure and dyed red curls? When there hadn't been a baby in our family since me—and my mother'd died of it.

She giggled. "Oh, the country's great for us. Even the doctor said it. Or maybe it's the moons."

"Going to be one tonight," I said.

Say a thing like that, and it shakes you with it. My hand walked across the ground and took hers.

"Oh golly, don't say it," she said. "We've got to open the place by the full moon, we've promised ourselves. Lanterns and all." But her voice was false; she wasn't listening to it half as much as to her hand. She let me keep it. And then at last, she looked up.

It was dusk by now, but I tried to see myself in her eyes like in a mirror; we don't have a good one at home any more.

"What's the baby?" I said. "Boy or girl?"

"Girl." Her hand was still in mine. "You're so pale," she said. "Whatever makes you look so pale?"

Must be the hair on my head, I thought; with no barbershop on the hill, I hadn't had a trim all summer; how do their heads support all that hair?

"How many Barbaras does that make in your family?" For I knew she had at least one sister; couldn't remember if more. "Will that make her Barbara Three or Four?"

"Her name's *Anne*," she said. "What do you mean." But she knew. Her hand had come away from mine. "That's moron stuff," she said. "That's that awful family with the whiteheaded, pink-eyed children. Down back of the factory. They say that." Her lip shivered, and she held it with her teeth. They aren't china. "You were always just Johnny."

My hand felt lonely. I made like sweeping a cap off my head to my knee. I was standing up by now, braced against the birch. "Let me introduce you. To Johnny One."

Her hand went to her mouth. She was still on the ground, at my feet. "You were still so handsome," she said. "Just a little while ago, when you first came back." She looked about to cry. "What's the matter with you people?"

"You were watching," I said. "All the time?"

"Yes—I was watching." It sounded as if she hated it.

"Can you really see us that well, over there? I always wondered." I leaned against the birch, which helped. Some of the full grown birches have one high fork, like a giraffe face up there on its long, scribbled bark neck. But this one is just a sapling, with the crotch still low enough to rest an elbow in.

"Not really. But I can always see you."

It was like our last year's promise. I dropped back to the ground. That was a relief. I was about to kiss her. Two can suck strength together. Then I saw the black spot on her leg.

"What's that! Barbara Blazer—you've got a leech there."

"Oh golly, have I? They're in the lake in droves this year."

It was on the calf of her right leg. Both of us stared down. I for one never saw anything like it, on us. The little black thing wasn't deep in yet. But it was already fat and red too. Rich.

"You wait right here," I said. "I'll go back for matches. You know what we have to do." If it's not too far in, it'll shrivel. "Or you could come back with me—" I hadn't meant to say that. But maybe if she saw us at home, with everything still there that couldn't be sold— the fanlight, and the banister like a turned ribbon, and the floors— maybe they'd see us better. "If it's in too deep, my aunt has a special knife." Or did once. "She's very good at it."

"Don't be sil—" Though we had our arms round each other, her voice had turned silvery again. "Don't be archai-ic. We've had them all summer. Daddy's got a compound you just touch them with— they drop right off. And I wouldn't want your aunt—" In spite of herself, she shivered. I saw the nostril again. But she didn't mean to. It's their strength.

"Won't it suck your strength?" I said. "Hadn't you better—?" But I knew she could wait. I touched the hoop in her ear—the thinnest wire.

"I'll go home in a minute," she said, snuggling deep into my shoulder. "Then I'll come back." The voice was last year's voice. And my mouth was already on her mouth, taking strength.

How did she spring away? They're like electric, these people. Their feet these days must scarcely touch the ground. There she was, arms spread out against another young birch, yards away. "What's that awful thing on your lip?"

The moon was up. We could see each other clearly. But I knew she wouldn't let me move back close, to see myself in her eye-mirror. And I knew what it was. My hand went to my upper lip, rubbing. At first I couldn't feel anything; then it was there, cool as down under my forefinger. "It's—my moustache." But I knew I was looking at her sideways.

"Green?" She whispered it. "Green?"

"It's the moon. It must be." I whispered back. Funny though, how you fade all the faster. Once you know.

For she made a sound in her throat like a squirrel. "Johnny. Look at your *hands*."

It was the nails, really. There was a line of green around each of them. I suppose it takes each person according to his substance. "It's only our moss," I said.

But I could only stand there, hands hanging, glad even that I could stand. Even if at first it takes you according to your own nature, in the end, won't it be all the same? I could feel the down on my lip now without touching it. Growing slow, like a shawl. Like the two girls at the grocery, like my aunt and uncle—I was going back to the green, to the grass, to the ground.

It was then she shrieked; I've never heard screech-owl worse. "You've got a disease! A mortal disease!" She bent over to the thing on her leg, and brushed at it as if it were me. Her head down low and forward, like a dog covering me, she breathed deep and growling, all the voices of the Blazers, hardened into one. "Keep away. Keep away. Don't you ever come near us again, any of you." She shrank back behind the birch tree. "Don't you ever even let us *remember* you." And then she ran off, low to the ground and bawling, her hand clapped to her leg.

But she had a long way to go, around *our* pond or *their* lake—anyway you look at it, and I could hear her for a considerable time, crashing her way—the sound of the mirage, going back where it belonged.

And the moon through the trees helped me find my echo. The moon was riding higher now, like a sign of how much time I had.

I called after her. "Why am I Johnny One?" I called, "Johnnnn-nny Onn-ne? Because there aren't two." And I knew she heard me. All her way back, my echo would carry it.

Then I went home, to see how much time I and the other boys

would have to gather, home to look it up on my aunt's calendar, which is a large one, turned regularly to the last days of summer, and with many almanac directions, including moons. The strength her kiss hadn't given me, her scream had.

On the night of the full moon to be, we were ready for them. For almost a week past, never in our house had there been such lights and noises and creepings, such a stamping and a brawling and a *blazing*—not in my time. I'd gathered them in by every marathon way I could think of, by bikes stole at evening and then passed on, by notes sent on by the diesel gas trucks—their drivers were the decentest, by tokens jammed in the pay telephone and then a message to the firehouse, where a town had one, by everything but drumbeat— and a little of that too it almost seemed, as the call got nosed about stronger—and always by our best chariot, shank's mare. It was always hard to believe that something so modern as the Agricultural was only thirty miles away and most of the boys in near the same radius, but now that fact was gold to us. And I had done it, I and my best deputy, the skinny Johnny from Contoocook, who I'd remembered was a Johnny One too. If we had more get-up-and-go than the rest of them, it was because the onlies, like with some plants, fade slower than the rest. And we'd done it. We'd gathered in the club. Once I'd got them collected, I wondered why I hadn't saved my strength by just staring at the sky and calling them in by mental telepathy. For funny thing, I didn't hardly have to open my mouth, to tell them what they were here for.

And now here they were, lolling knees up, or on elbow and stomach, draped around like any boys you might see around a roaring fireplace, though the golden flames made them seem a mite rosier than they were. Gold of any other sort, we didn't have much of. And now, though it was only five o'clock in the afternoon and the moon not to be up for several hours yet, we could tell by our blood that it was going to be one of those Hampshire early in September nights with scarcely a nip in it. The last of the locust-nights; that's what it was. This was the way men in the wilderness used to tell the hours for fires and club-gatherings—by the blood.

And lolling with them, staring to the flames, I was almost happy, in thinking of the gathering business itself, and knowing they were too. I hadn't yet told them everything. They didn't know we were to gather at our side of Willard Pond earlier than they thought; but I'd about decided we weren't to wait for the moon. But they knew all the rest of it, learning it as they brought in the wood from here and there—because for a long time at home there hadn't been axe or arm for it—and bringing in the food by raid, like a cat with a chipmunk, or from some overlooked last pocket of rightful ownership. Bringing in the tools—that gathers people, like proudflesh to a wound. And even bringing in money if you happen to have any; it was Johnny Ten who brought in a sack, that first night we were up to score—a full dozen of us—and showed us old pennies like beans in it, and took one out, an Indian head, and then another, and said, "What's it say? Read it out." It was an old one too. "E Pluribus," I said. Anyone knew that—if you've had my aunt.

Even she and my uncle had helped me as they could, bringing out things from the attic like ideas we hadn't known we had. The old pine-needle mattresses came from the spare rooms we never went into. Like pine pillows they were, though without any inscription. My uncle'd brought out a sackful of bottles to sell, dug from the quarry once, and in ten minutes and four different directions we'd sold them, to buy the steakmeat I'd gone bold as a bear into the supermarket to buy for our strength—and we'd just now eaten, for the early supper I'd insisted on. Even my aunt said every morning "I'll make you a flag"—though she didn't quite know what for, and by evening had forgotten it. I lay there thinking of all this, from that first minute of the week, when John of Contoocook came up the heaved stones of the front walk, just as I was thinking on him, thinking on him—and I said to him, grinning. "How's that pig of yours?" And laying down the sack he was carrying, he answered me, grinning. "Here."

Gathering is the gold. They knew that now as well as I. But I lay there wondering, as any leader must, whether it wasn't all the gold we needed, whether the gathering itself mightn't be enough. But there wouldn't be time to go back to school, to find out.

"We'll train in that barn," I'd said, that first morning we were all here. Plus a peewee little Johnny from the morons; we didn't know what was his count and neither did he. He kept running in and out of our ranks, more trouble to shoo him than to let him stay. And we had to conserve our energy.

"As soon as we get the tools," I said, "we'll train. Go round to all the woodpiles and tight barns, there still are some on our side—and get the axes. Drag 'em, if you can't heft. Go round to all the antique tables after dark—hook anything sharp, or that looks like a tool. There's a thing called a sausage-grinder down in Kelley Two's barn, you'll surely have to drag that." I hadn't made definite plans yet, but that would come. "Scythes," I said.

"Will crocks be useful?" said Johnny from Contoocook. I could tell he was puzzled for a plan of action too.

"No, I don't think . . . pitchforks . . . no, there's no time for *torture* . . . it's too serious for that." I found I'd decided. "Permanent useful tools only." That way, whatever we made use of for training purposes would come in handy later also, if there was to be a later time. Would that depend on the training? And then the thought came to me, though I hadn't since told any of them, even my deputy—guns. Or at least one gun. I knew who had a sharpshooter's medal—before it was sold. Guns would be best.

You have to understand about the training. Wasn't anything we could plan to do with any weapon—tool, that is—before we could lift. That's what our training was. Over-the-summer had come to be like a hibernation time for our kind, and if we let ourselves get any weaker, this summer would likely be our last. When we could lift again, and swing and grind and mow and reap, each man alone, and not staggering onto the next one or cooling his temple against any wall that was left him to do it on, then maybe we could start to talk about action—or more of it than just a gathering on the night of the moon when their building was to be done, to make a great clatter to scare them with, over there on the opposite shore.

"Or going all the way round to their side to get our message across," said Johnny from Contoocook. "If we are able."

"Carrying the tools, of course," I said.

He looked at me over the others, stern and thoughtful as always. "Oh yes," he said, nudging me to note a Johnny Three from Nelson, who could almost lift a log singlehanded now, and a Four from West Wilton, who could handle the smallest axe. We had a couple of those Buddy names too, the one kid back at school had been so proud of—and what do you know, they turned out to be the weakest of all. "Oh yes. Carrying the tools."

And here we were, on the very night, and almost able, if that steakmeat could be trusted—and I still had no plan of action. But I had the gun.

I'd hooked it from the store maybe easier than I could handle it. Couldn't even call it a steal. He never even moved a shoulder, when I reached up above him and took it from the wall, up above the calendar. Had all I could do not to drop it; I don't know what kind of game he and his china-teeth friends ever thought they'd need a gun like that for, this part of the country. It's a high-powered rifle all right—a thirty-ought-six. With a telescopic lens. I was halfway out the screendoor dragging it in the gunnysack I'd brought, when he opened his mouth and said one word.

"Cartridges."

They were in a tin box on the counter in front of him. So I had to go back in.

And so I practiced in secret with the gun, the way they all were doing with their implements, their tools. I didn't worry about marksmanship. Once I could heft the gun, steadying my arm maybe in the crotch of a convenient tree, I knew I could fire it. And they all watched me, my army, and never said any more to me about our plan of action, just left it to me. But one thing more, I said to them. I was the leader. "We've got numbers to our names, can't help that, it's too late for it." I happened to glance over at Johnny Ten, the highest of us in number and in brain the lowest; his big round face with the silly smile on it looked just like the hubcaps he'd chosen to carry but I wouldn't let him. "But we won't say Johnny any more; that's how they weaken us too." I took a look at my uncle, snoring there in the rocker. "We'll at least say 'John.'" And my dear deputy, who worried me so, he was getting thinner every day—John of Contoocook—grinned at that too. So that's the way that was. Only one we couldn't get to understand it was the little peewee, the moron, and he didn't count; he'd be a Johnny until the end.

Otherwise, it worked fine. We'd had some trouble at first making Johnny Ten understand that our plan of action couldn't be motorcycles. "Get those snazzy foreign ones!" he'd say every day, at training-time. "Wear those black-and-white crash helmets! Then—*zoom*." And he'd raise the pick-axe with a hubcap on it, almost high. No use telling him that we had as much chance of motorcycles as of getting boats to cross the lake with, like from England to France.

There's never been any boats *between* them and us, only the boats on their side.

"What would that do for us, Ten?" my deputy would answer. His fingers were so dreamy-thin, looked as if they went round the scythe-handle twice. "No, it would just mean that we'd be the ones to move away."

Watching us try to shoulder arms—nobody would exactly see twelve high-class buck-privates. Sometimes I wondered if, even with the training, anybody could see us at all—we were so faded. My own eyesight is still so damn good. But I consoled myself with seeing how at least getting into some action must have helped our circulation. And thinking forward to being Johns again seemed to satisfy everybody, and to improve our complexion too. For the mold that had spotted everyone of us, sometimes in places you wouldn't like to think it—was gone.

One thing we talked out loud about, in those last evenings as we fed the fire before sleeping—was our ecology. We talked a lot about that, and what our summer rebellion could mean to the world. I wished I could ask the instructor. Sometimes we talked about him too, laughing at our secret nickname for him—Mr. Wilderness. For the funniest thing about him, what with all his talk about going to do research work or get him a job as a government forester in one of those high, wild tower overlooks where you can't even have a wife—was that right out in front of the classroom, where we could all see it, he had the brightest, fastest, hottest little bug of a new red two-seater sport car.

And while we talked, I sometimes watched my aunt and uncle, him barefoot now in his rocker, her in her shawl. Soon he would be only ten yellow fingernails and ten toenails—he was going back to the horn. She was dozing, my tawny aunt, with her mouth open; soon she would be only a lost freckle on the air. Was this only the way it always should be, for the other generation? But then, what about us young? I wished I could ask the instructor—even *him*. I hadn't ever told for sure whether his eyes, always so blind with teaching, hadn't seen more about us than we thought he knew. Maybe he could be our control-group, I decided; he'd taught us that in any experiment where you're matching one group of specimens against the other, in the best testing there ought to be still a third. One group, something gets done to it to produce *its* condition; to the second group, you do the opposite. The control doesn't get anything done to it at all to narrow down its condition; that's what it already is. He could be that.

So, two nights ago, I had written him a letter. He could listen to what we had in mind, I thought. Better still, I thought, as I was writing, he could come to be a witness; it was nothing to that red car, only thirty miles. So I wrote giving him directions where to come and when, and what to look for, and mailed it myself and according to what I knew the distribution time for the mail was out there—so he'd get it just in time to decide to come along for the show or not to; after all that effort I didn't want us prevented. "We're having a summer rebellion," I wrote. "It's to be a test. Not a battle." For I knew it couldn't be that. "It can't be that," I said, "even with the gun. Will you be our witness?" I wrote in the best grammar I had, deciding to use that from now on too, for the other only made me weaker. And I signed it "John," without any number at all. What I'd wanted to do was to put my full last name after it, like one of their signatures—but I didn't feel up to that, yet. Besides, he'd know by the postmark and the handwriting. And he always took the trouble to talk to me specially. He'd know.

So here we were, me and my deputy and all twelve of us, not counting that little thirteenth peewee with his white albino head and pink eyes held away from the firelight. Here we are, I said to myself, in our house that hasn't caved in yet, in our flesh that isn't mold yet, and with our tools we've rescued. And over there, on the other side of Willard Pond, their work is done. Turret on the outside—waiting for the weathercock, but that they'll hang at the ceremony—and on the inside, hammered brass and hanging lanterns, and tables and chairs like a soda parlor's, and a milk bar like a counter— and a fireplace, for winter. They couldn't have an outside sign, not with their zoning rules, but just for today they had a great poster up on a tripod, with one of our iron kettles hanging on a chain beneath it. "Dedication ceremony. Everybody come and see us hang the weathercock. Six o'clock." But inside, through the glass door, I'd seen that they had a sign saying The Pancake Palace. So that's where our soda parlor number one, the old sign once on it, had gone. So there they are. Hadn't I seen it all in the storekeeper's binoculars, which on the way out his screen door the second time, he'd let me hock too? They had finished their job in time.

I went outside though, to look again for sure. Yes. It was now only a little past five o'clock, but small as the woods were, I'd better give us three quarters of an hour to get through it, even with the steak. A leader has got to plan. And I hoped I'd thought of everything, except what would have to be left to the last minute—my gun and its target. I'd half wanted to ask him that in the letter, but finally had let it be. For if I have a gun, but don't know my own target—what do I have a gun for at all?

Outside, there was even a kind of double omen. The sun was still shining in that fool's gold way it has at five o'clock. But on the other side of the world, not in any fair balance yet but trying, there was the palest full moon I'd ever seen in a sky. Even my keen sight could barely see it. Couldn't see how it would ever have the energy to rise, except that moons do.

I went back inside, slamming the housedoor so that it shuddered back, wide-open. That was to be our signal. We don't waste our energy. "Here we are," I said. "And it's time."

One by one, we got each other up from the pine mattresses, and began helping the others fit themselves to their tools. Yes, we still had to do that—we'd only had a week. We still were twelve in number and made an honorable display. We'd kept the pitchforks after all, they handle so easy, and even if you aren't going to use them in any other way, still their outline is so plain. I'd turned the house out, looking for my uncle's clipping-shears, then found out he'd been using Blazer's. So, after two of the forks, and counting my deputy's scythe, we had four axes, large and small according to which could best carry the weight of them, two long butcher knives, one queer-angled iron earthtiller so antique we didn't know what it was for but judged we ought to have it for that reason alone—and a hoe. Ten had let the little peewee have his hubcaps to clash.

I myself helped John of Contoocook with his scythe. We had to strap it on him; this was the only way he could manage it, and I'd have been doubtful of that except for his grin, which was still there. "Know you'll do it," I whispered to him. "After all, we don't have to do anything after we get there but stand. But stand *by!*" It was the first time I'd used that expression out loud, and his eyes flickered at it. And you have the gun, he could have said to me, but didn't. He's like me in a way, with the difference that I'd hung on

328

to more energy. Matter of fact, he was worse off than any of us. I couldn't forbear asking him why. "Why do you suppose it is?" I whispered, as I buckled the strap. His grin was like the moon, just barely there, and like the sun, getting ready to set. "It was the pig," he answered. "She was my ecology." He's hopelessly smart.

At the door then, I addressed my men at large as they went by me, both of us in a manner not to waste breath—in silence. My eyes keen upon them, I called their ghostly roll. "Johns of Four and Five —pitchforks. Johns Two and Three, Buddy Two—axes. A John Two and a Buddy One—knives." Him with the tiller. Him with the hoe. And the rear guard. "John of Contoocook. Scythe."

To make sure that none would fall by the wayside unless all did, I roped us all together. At the last minute, one of the knives broke down and couldn't make it—one of the Buddies, wouldn't you know? So to fill up the dozen, we had to count the peewee in anyway. Then they were all ready, weaponed and gathered at the door in the formation I'd decided on—a half circle which could at need fall into line. "You of Hillsborough," I said to them. "Of Jaffrey and Hancock, of Dublin and Antrim, of Rindge and of Nelson, and even of Keene. You of the Monadnock Region. And of the winter time. Get ready. Get Set. G—"

And then my uncle got up from his rocking chair.

He faltered over to me, clickety-click. He was even able to dig his sharp fingers into my chest; he's been a strong man in his day. "The old customs," he said, in his wooden-doll voice. "We'll go back to them. But first, we ought to know who we are, son, oughtn't we." He drew himself up straight as he could. "I'm Andrew. And that is Marietta, my wife." Hearing that name, my aunt woke, looked around bewildered, at this battalion in her old sitting room, and then smiled straight at me, too, from her shawl. "And I know you're John," said my uncle. "I *know* you're John. But son—" I felt his nails through my sweatshirt. "Son, remind me. What's our last name? Our *sur*name, as people used to say. I rock and I rock, but I can't remember it."

I smiled back at them, for love and for leaving, both. For who could know what would be, when and if we came back? And I had an awful temptation to say—"It's Wilderness." That little red bug-on-wheels maybe even now skipping toward us—he would like that.

But that is not my style of interest. I know who we are. We're not that faded, not to me. And I know who I am. I've always known. It's our *other* distinction.

"It's Willard," I said. "For the Pond."

And then we filed out the door, and made up our formation again, outside it. I hadn't even had to say Go. But as we closed ranks, shouldering each as we could, with one hand, and ready to help his neighbor with the other, I heard my aunt's voice. "I'm going to make you a flag."

Then we were on the march. Marching is useful too; some say that all by itself it's as useful to the spirit as gathering is, but in our state it wasn't gold to us; it was simply what we had to do. Funny thing though, the woods, pine to maple to birch, were in perfect order for it. Even the underbrush lay quiet, as if somebody had swept. Yet I knew that although they across there had got as far as browning in the gardens and on the water, they hadn't been much to the woods yet, for health. And they hadn't paid to clear here; who would they pay that was left? Sometimes, toward autumn but before the leaves start twirling down, woods look like that, in perfect order for—something one can't say. From tree to tree, these ragged woods of my forefathers let us by now, not putting out a root to trip us, passing us on, tree to tree. They stood by us. And we walked.

And we walked. Some might have called our pace a stumble. Or only a dragging, with a rope. But it was our pace. And we did it in silence. We had no extra breath for songs. Even the peewee's hub-caps, heavy enough in his tiny hands scaled with skin rash like a lizard's, were still.

Only my gun talked, braced on my shoulder. And only I heard it; it had such a soft voice. "Blazer, Blazer, go away," it said. "Come again some other day." But that was for rain, not people. I knew that, though my own head seemed now and then about to twirl and fall. Then it said, "Hickory, dickory, your son John, took our Barbara with his britches on." Only a nursery rhyme, and wrong at that, but marching was not my true rhythm, and the air at this hour of the day was hot and cold by turns, shiver and blister both. I prayed to the steak in my stomach. I thought I could see the others were too; behind the iron and steel, their lips were moving. But for me, there was worse to come. That gun tried everything. And by the last yard of it—the whole woods isn't half a mile—that gun and I had fallen in rhythm together. "Bar-bar-a *Blazer*," it said, "is beautiful." And my feet answered, "Beautiful"—treading on moss now, for we were there.

We were on the shoreline of my forefathers' pond. We were on the peculiarly mossy and stony patch of it that I could call at least jointly mine, and I turned round to look at my men. They had formed their half-circle again, almost without command from me— my army, my posse, my eleven other Johns and one Buddy. And one whiteheaded peewee. But this was all they could manage. Everything had stopped, but my anger. Above our heads, the sun and moon had stopped too. Or were in perfect balance.

"At ease, men," I said. In silence, their weapons slid to the ground. One voice slid after them. "Hadn't ought to do that, John One. We'll never be able to get them up again."

"Don't worry," I said. "Anger is slow, eight generations slow. But it never stops." And trusting I was right, I inspected my ranks, as must be done before battle—or before testing, to the specimen.

Under that sky of double omen, my friends seemed to me only a step mistier than myself. Their heads were bowl-cut or longhaired like mine, but not in the new style, and their jeans and shirts were ragged, but not ragged new. They were ragged in the old style. They were a strange, weak sight, my winter Apollos, and when their arsenal was raised against that sky, they would be odder still. But maybe the people over there would see them the better for it. That's what specimens are. And they were standing by. In spite of all suffered or lazed or blamed away, they had not utterly gone down yet—into the grass, the ground.

I addressed them.

"We're a little late," I said. "It's past six o'clock." We'd taken a little longer than estimated, to go that half mile. "But I see that over across there, they are late too." I raised the binoculars, to hearten the men behind me, though I could see perfectly well without. And faithfully, my men looked heartened, though as they stared sideways under their weedy fringes of hair, I could tell that they saw across the water just as well as me. "We and they are late together," I said. "Maybe that's an omen, too."

None of my men had been with me to the shoreline before, only me and my deputy, to scout. And now, in their faces I saw all the sight before us across the water—its glass doors open to the shining games inside, and all the tanned people streaming in, or sitting without caution on the green itself. In the face of my Johnny Three, John Three—I saw a pair over there, going in through the door in their waterskis and goggles. Inside the new soda parlor, its hanging lamps were already lit to pale taffy against all that fresh white; I saw their sign, Pancake Palace, in the face of a John Two. One of our Buddies, the one left to us, was seeing that there were even red paper flames in the cookpot under the poster—the Buddy with the knife. Every man and his implement was seeing a detail of it, of that milling, laughing group of sports and silk-headed grandmothers bobbing like cotton—the whole foolish, rosy, expensive Blazer-crowd. On a bench out in front, sat a fat man, no not fat, burly, in bow tie and a flower in his jacket buttonhole—Blazer himself. There were babies scattered like plants all over the place, all with the round, superior look of babies whose mothers were not going to die. I could see it all in my men's faces. Wasn't it the way we had always seen the summer people, in the pale, expensive orange-light of the health-money they were always making? In the dream-face next to one's own, isn't that the way one always sees the mirage?

No, said the gun. This time you are seeing by yourself.

Against that joyous little turret, flipped up in paint-glow to the sun, they were now raising a black, lacy ladder. A band began to play; they had the breath for it. And to each ladder of the song, a golden-legged couple was climbing a step gracefully, hand over hand to the platform at the top. He had on cut-off jeans only, carefully sawtoothed off at the knees, the way they do, and his water-streaked hair had been cut with a scissors. The female of a genus, we had been taught, often has more protective coloration. She had on an orange and white swimsuit, sunset-colored as her limbs, and her hair floated, leafing out along the wind. When the two reached the platform, they stepped up on it, then turned and waved—two shadows, two golden statues, waving to one side and then to another, but not to over here. And I saw that the place for the weathercock was still bare. What were they going to raise there—the sun and moon both?

Down below them, Blazer was speaking. On that side of the water, the whole world was orange with the healthy glow of them. Blazer had a nasturtium in his buttonhole.

"Get ready," I said. "Get set."

All the better for their light, I told myself. We will make better shadow.

"The test is—will they see us?" I said. "That is the battle."

I had never revealed this to my men before, and I turned to them now, to see how they would take it. I saw that they already knew.

"When I give the command," I said, "raise your weapons. They cannot fail to see us—four axes, a scythe, a knife and a tiller, two pitchforks, and a hoe."

My deputy spoke softly. "And a gun."

I turned my back on him.

Across the way, they had raised the weathercock. It was in place. In the old days the style was often a flying horse or a golden rooster; we had sold them in the shop many a time, whenever we could find an old weathercock to sell. I'd expected it would be one of those; they wouldn't buy new. There are other shapes, of course, including our own from the house, gone so long ago, that I'd forgotten what it was. The shape of this one was new to me, or so at first I thought. It was a double pennant, flying to the breeze from where it was fixed to its rod, fixed there by a heartshape over on its side, pierced by an arrow. Then I recognized it. It was exactly the same in shape as the one high on the Meetinghouse at Hancock, hard by Norway Pond. Had they dared to lift it from there? They were so powerful. And the shoreline at Norway Pond is off-limits for some of us, too. Even if nobody but a country is named after it.

The shape of that weathercock troubled me. In the flame of the wind, it looked like a man on his side, blowing in the wind, blowing, his head a heart on its side, and an arrow in his head. Maybe they got it from a closed-up church.

Behind me, I heard a murmur. My men were troubled too. And I had brought them here, over a week and a wood, to this shoreline. What else could I do?

"Shoulder arms," I said.

I turned to watch them, proud. They were tall, all except the Buddy knife and the peewee, and they helped one another until all their artillery was up, shining its broadside against the evening clouds and the woods behind. I went from one to the other, straightening them. The scythe was the highest. And the hill we were on was higher than any rise of theirs, and the couple on the platform was still turning and waving, waving and turning. They couldn't help but see us, I thought. We stood there, a thin rank of us, but sightable surely, black and separate, but gathered too. Even the Pond, rising to the last sun, sent off a sheet of light like a thunderflash, to encourage us.

"Steady," I said. "Stand like the trees."

We waited. *Stand by*, I said to myself. I was the only one of us without a weapon to his shoulder. I don't want to be a John One either, I prayed to them across the water. I only want to be John Willard. See us, standing by.

And the peewee was the one to say it, in his scratchy, dead-white voice. "They don't see us."

Then the Buddy. Then all of them. "They don't see us. We are nothing to them." They murmured it like the leaves. This was all the breath they had.

All except John, my deputy, who swung his weapon high. How could they not see him, even if, all bone as he now was, they only saw the scythe? "If I had a good New Hampshire boulder to ring it on, instead of these old slates!" he cried, and buried the tip in the ground. It made no sound. The others did the same, but a tiller is not made to speak loud against slate, or even granite. The peewee's hubcaps, clashed together, made a faint cry. We had chosen our place too well, or had they chosen it for us? We were moss to the ankles, like the stones in the graveyard those across the water love so well.

"All right," I said. "Stand back." And I bent to the gun. "You can talk," I said. And without any help, bracing myself against a birch tree that presented itself like an aide-de-camp, I shouldered the thirty-ought-six.

Across the water, the couple on the platform each held up a little flag, while the crowd applauded. I could hear them, see them, clear as clear, as pond water. Did the men from Valley Forge, crossing the Delaware, have a flag? They had a boat.

Through the telescopic lens, on the crosshair, I could see the weathercock; slowly it turned in the evening wind, a double pennant, a man on his side, blowing in the wind. I shifted the gun past the boy in his sawed-off jeans. He was a Blazer too, but only her brother. Shaking under the weight of the gun like a body on my shoulder, I brought her slowly to center, on the crosshairs. And there she was, my summer Venus, shining to the wind like the weathercock of a country I had never seen to the full before, her arms spread to its birches. Would she be the rosier without us, without me?

"Shall I shoot our weathercock?" I whispered to my deputy. "Or the weathercock girl." But nobody answered behind me, nobody at all. And the gun bore down. But the birch bore up, lifting me like a brother. This was why it took so long to decide.

Caught on the crosshair with her, was all her new countryside. I could see it well. The horses were returning to fill the barns again. In time, as the summer people lingered, there might even be cows. I couldn't see Blazer in the old grocery store for all the teeth in China, but if I studied it with care I could see the son; I could see it well. And what of us? Would we go to the city in our turn, hoping to be seen again by someone? Or back to the freckle on the air, the horn. And is all this just the balance again, blowing like the wind?

They don't need to see you, Johnny One. Or not much. No more than a mirage of upkeepers, holding up the summertime. All that's needed now, is what already is. *You* see *them.*

So spoke the gun.

How gray your skies will be without them. They were what drew you through the woods—the biggest mirage of all; you couldn't have done it without them.

So spoke the birch.

My eyes were burning with the choice, and I couldn't last the weight much longer—what did they ever plan to kill with a gun like this, the old-timers?

I centered the gun, holding aim. They would see me across there this time. I shoot to kill.

Was it the birch, holding me? Stand by, John Willard, all of you. It's not just a summer rebellion. Stand by.

Or the last minute, did my foot twitch, saying—"beautiful?"

No. I aimed higher than either, high between the sun and the moon. To shoot a mirage, you have to shoot that high. And I aimed to kill us both.

I fired.

They saw me then.

Everything stopped over there, too. And I could see they saw me, milling and talking among themselves. Some had already scattered, on their way around the rim of the Pond, to this side. One took a boat—still carrying her flag. Others got into it. As they all scattered toward me, I could even see what they had in their mind's-eye. Now that I had put down the gun, or fired it high, I could be a hero if I wanted—for a day. I have excellent sight.

I turned to my companions behind me. Their final effort had been too much for them. They could gather for a week, to help a friend with his summer. They could stumble through his wood, behind him on a string—he was their control. But now they were done for. Except for their implements, they were now so faded that nobody but me would see them at all.

Just then the bushes parted, back where the woods begin—and what do you know? I never expected him to come, even though I wrote. But here he was—nobody could miss him!—in a jumping red shirt that matched the car. He was panting. "Don't shoot!" he called. "Don't shoot." And he panted up to me.

"I couldn't lift it again," I said, "if I tried."

"I had to leave the car at the edge of the woods, that's why I'm late. I had to *walk*."

"We're all a little late," I said. And I could see he was still walking round me in his mind.

"How are your researches?" I said.

"Fine, just fine." He was looking at the people just beginning to straggle up the rim of the hill from below on this side—they would have to climb a bit to get here. "And how are you, Johnny—you see I got your letter."

"Oh, everything's stopped," I said. "For the moment." Down below, a boat was pulling into shore. There wasn't much time. "There's something I want to ask you though," I said. "You're the instructor." Then I looked over at my army, so quiet there without any acknowledgment, almost like the trees. "But first—let me introduce my—assistants," I said. "Axe, Hoe, Tiller, Pitchfork, Knife. One Buddy. The rest—Johns. Too late to do anything about that. They all look as dead as stones in a graveyard, I know, but they'll revive shortly, once they remember their last names. All except him, my deputy, there under the scythe." I was watching my new arrival sharply.

He was watching me too, but he strolled nonchalantly to the edge of that mossy precipice. "So this is Willard Pond," he said, staring over the water. "What a great natural oval. I wouldn't mind being buried here myself."

"It belongs to us," I said. Who can sell a grave?

He nodded. "All yours?"

"All ours," I said. "All mine." But I faltered. The boat had docked.

"And those?" he said, half-smiling, pointing to my weapons, which were standing up bravely to the evening, planted one to a mound.

"Those are my forefathers," I said, half-smiling.

"Both?" he said, looking at each mound with its implement.

"Both."

I drew him to the mound under the scythe. "John of Contoocook is his name." I like to say it; it brings back the rivers and the towns, the woods and the ponds. "He was earlier than any of the others. He needed animals, it's said, the way we others only need the winter weather. He'd have been all right if we could have got a pig to him in time."

He stood there, looking down. "We had a boy from Contoocook in class too, didn't we."

"Don't confuse me," I put my hand on the scythe—so thin. "He had no last name," I said. "He was the earliest." And could not survive.

He stood there thinking. "Johnny—" he said. "You were my smartest boy." Then why did he look so miserable.

What can you answer, when you know your own condition exactly?

"Is there—a question you wanted to ask me?" he said.

I looked over the rim. They were out of the boat now and on the land on this side—her and her brother, and even her mother with the curls, and burly Blazer too. And on either side of us I could hear the crowd which had gone round by way of the shore, crashing through the underbrush. They don't know how to walk in a wood yet. And the woods are not yet on their side. They were closing in, from all directions except the woods in back of me.

I nodded at him. "About them—and us. I wanted to ask you. Is it just the balance again, like the elms, like the aphids? Will they ever see us for more than a minute? Can you answer me that? You're the instructor. Can't you teach us which tree is which to the other? Is a rifle across the water the only way? Can't we *both* stand by?"

It was some dose of a question, of course. Though I waited politely, I'd already seen by his shirt he couldn't answer it; he was only Mr. Wilderness.

And when I looked away from him, I saw them all now in their half-circle around me. They thought they had me closed in.

"I see you," I said. Mildly, for after all the gun was still at my feet. "And you see me. Don't you." Even though I could tell from their eye-mirrors how they saw me, it was a satisfaction. And their misery wouldn't last.

But I don't intend meanness either. It's my weakness does it.

"Oh, don't you take all the blame," I said. I cast back a farewell glance at my fallen ones, behind me. "Who can sell a grave? *Us.*"

And then, what do you know, there was a great, windy sob from the middle of them. "Ohhhh Johnny, Johnny One!" It was Barbara the weathercock, with sentiment streaming down her face.

"Don't be so proud," I said. "I didn't dip the gun for you. I raised it. I did it for the birch."

"Oh, Johnny."

She crept nearer me.

"How's your leg?" I said.

She showed me a patch on it I hadn't seen from across the water. She reached out to touch me. "Let me—"

"Let you what?"

"Take you—home with us. To rest."

"Don't come any nearer," I said. "Don't even—remember me. The way you look at me, so proud, I might have shot *myself*." And what would I do with a flag?

Just then, down at the edge of it all, I felt a tugging at my elbow. It was the peewee. I had forgotten him. "Interduce *me*," he said. He's a moron, but he can't help it.

I took his scaly hand. "This is one of my friends also," I said. "He's the one you can see."

But he wasn't satisfied. Still tugging, he sent up a scratch of a question, like the voice of the moss itself. "Did we do it, Johnny? Did we do it? Is it over?"

He was only a moron, but I had to tell someone. "Yes—we did it," I said. "But it's over. The summer people are real."

IV

What a Thing, to Keep a Wolf in a Cage!

◆§ MRS. BOWMAN, the small, dark American woman walking up the Via Aurelia Antica in the sauterne Roman sunlight, was glad that she had worn the good brown pumps with the low French heels. "Take the Monteverdi bus from the Piazza Fiume," Mrs. Wigham, the British journalist resident in Rome, had said on the phone. "After that, it's a twenty-minute walk." But of course it was turning out to be a very British twenty-minute walk, as the American had suspected it might.

Visiting Italian villas, if one had no car and must watch long cab fares, had a technique of its own. One had to be dressed to cope with the crammed *filobus*, the dodging between motorcycles on the steep walk afterward, the long, cobbled approaches to the houses themselves. But once there the *amour-propre* might have to cope with a room full of signoras dressed with their usual black and white graffito perfection or, worse still, with those of one's own countrywomen who traveled preserved in some mysterious, transportable amber of their own native conveniences. Well, the new coat and the brown shoes would about do. She smiled to herself, remembering that she had read somewhere that a lady always traveled in brown.

The road was walled on each side, so that the sun scarcely glinted on the occasional green Vespa, red Lambretta or on herself, the only pedestrian. Here was a door set tight in the wall—number four, and number three had been minutes back. Number twenty-two might well be another mile away. Well, time is not *time* in Italy, she reminded herself. "My time is your time," she sang under her breath, and walked on. After a while she came to the top of a hill and saw four priests approaching from the opposite direction, walking along in their inevitably coupled way. From above, the four black discs of their hats, with the round, center hubs of crown, looked like the flattened-out wheels of some ancient bas-relief vehicle. The wheels of the church, she thought, and crossed the road.

"*Per favore,*" she faltered. "*Il numero ventidue—é lontano?*" In a flood of smiles and gestures they waved her on. High above her head the embankments hid the greenery, making the way seem endless. From the dust of the road came the deciduous, stony smell of antiquity. Her lowered eyes caught sight of a pebble, smooth and egg-shaped, rather like the white jelly-bean stones her younger boy at home in the States had in his collection. She passed it, hesitated, and went back for it. I found it on the Via Aurelia Antica, she would tell him. On Easter Sunday afternoon.

At home it would still be morning. Her boys, released from the school chapel, would be at dinner in the commons or horsing in the yard. It was a habit she had not been able to break, these six months away—this counting back to what time it was over there. She hadn't wanted to go, she hadn't. But "Go!" all the others of the faculty had said. After all—a sabbatical. Once in seven years. "And four of those a widow," they must have whispered behind her. "Perhaps . . . over there . . ." Well, they would find her the same as before her sea change. At forty, forty-one, to range the world like a honing girl, the eye liquid, the breast a cave, was no more decent abroad than it would have been at home. One learned to be alone over here, as one had back there. It was like baggage. She slipped the stone into her pocket and went on.

At last she came to the high iron gates of number twenty-two. They swung open, released by the invisible keeper in the hut at the side, and at the end of a driveway shorter than most she came to the house—nothing of museum grandeur about it, like others she had visited, but low, extended in a comfortable way and about the size of her house at home. No one was about. "*Ciao!*" she would have liked to have called, but did not. "Hello?" she said, and waited. "Hell-lo-o."

Mrs. Wigham came round the corner of her house, neatly gray-haired, sweatered and skirted in dun, a sensible Englishwoman at home in her garden, in whatever country that garden might be. "Ah, Mrs. Bowman, so happy to meet you," she said. "The Maywoods wrote me about you. On leave from your post, they tell me." They shook hands. "Sociology, is it not?" said Mrs. Wigham. "Are you going to be studying us for a book?"

"No," said the American, laughing. "I tell myself I'm seeing and being."

"Oh, well. No one ever does much work in Rome." Mrs. Wigham led the way, past potting sheds, up a brief staircase, into the house and out again. "Two of your compatriots are here this afternoon," she said. "A lady from Hollywood, perhaps you know her? Her husband owns a film company, something like that." She mentioned a name, one of the pioneer, supercolossal names.

"Oh, yes, of course. No—I don't know her," said Mrs. Bowman.

"She's here with a friend of hers sent me by our film man in London. A lady who writes for the films, I believe." Mrs. Wigham, correspondent for a London daily, had that pale, weathered glance which was perhaps *de rigueur* for middle-aged British lady journalists. It had never seen mascara perhaps but, in a quietly topographical way, it had seen almost everything else. It rested thoughtfully now on Jane Bowman. "You know of *her*, possibly? A Miss Francine Moon?"

"No," said Jane Bowman. "I, er—I've never been to Hollywood." There, she thought. Was that snobbery or modesty? Have I established myself as sufficiently Eastern seaboard and impecunious? When abroad alone, particularly on one's first trip, one had constantly to stifle this terrible desire to establish oneself, knowing full well that, with the British, any overtness about that would establish one all too well. She stared at Mrs. Wigham's back as it led the way to the terrace. The most map-conscious people in the world, they were, yet they still alluded to the States as once they might have to Kenya—as to one of those vast but cozy terrae incognitae where certainly everybody knew everybody else.

But when they came out on the terrace and she was presented to the three ladies seated there in the magnificent light that made paintable even the debris of afternoon tea, she was less certain that "the States" was not the intimate terrain that her hostess had presumed it. On their left, the pleasant-faced elderly woman who had answered to the name of Miss Hulme with a brisk "Dew!" was surely English—hatted and caned and wrapped in woollens whose lines one was not meant to pursue. But it was the nearer of the two hatless American women opposite who caught her eye, who was limned in the light with a precision that defeated any tenderizing chiaroscuro of Roman air.

But of course, I do in a way know her, thought Jane. If I were sleepwalking in Arabia deserta and I opened my eyes on her image, I would know her. Gray tailleur, a "Ford" as Seventh Avenue calls it, lapel pin so expensively junk that it does not have to be real. Enormous alligator bag—for this is one of the things that must not be counterfeited—and yes, there are the matching shoes. Gold of bangled wrist, flint of ageless figure, perhaps forty, hair irrefragably gold and coiffed not ten minutes before, butterfly glasses with this year's line of twisted gold at the bridge. How should I not know her —this artifact of North America, authentic in its way as the pebble I picked up back there on the road?

"Francine Moon," said this person, reinforcing their hostess's hummed introduction. One felt her to be a person who established herself immediately.

"Mrs. Bowman has been living in London for the past six months," said Mrs. Wigham. She looked from one American to the other with the bright teatime glance of those for whom conversation was still an accredited pursuit.

"London!" said Miss Moon, attaching the word to herself as she might hook another trinket to the polyglot baubles at her wrist. She was still leaning forward, partially screening the second Californian, a sullenly handsome woman of about the same age, who had acknowledged Jane with a single dead-pan, dark blink, returning to brood behind a lean brown hand afire with one astounding jewel. "Where did you live when you were in London? I had the loveliest flat—on Hay Hill."

"Oh, Pimlico, Chelsea," said Jane. "But most of the time with friends in the Middle Temple," she added demurely. Miss Moon looked doubtfully, then shrewdly at the two British women, suspecting that her own Mayfair-tempered armor might have been pierced in some recondite way.

"In the Law Courts!" said Miss Hulme. "But how—how delightful!" But "How amazing" was what she had begun to say. She and Mrs. Wigham exchanged glances. The Americans; they are everywhere. One has grown used, in the last fifty years, to their heiresses unlocking our dukedoms. But now, even into our sanctuaries they fall, topside up on their incredibly neat, unlineaged legs. Even into the Middle Temple have they fallen, blunt and indiscriminate as the bombs.

"You've just come down from Florence, have you not?" said Mrs. Wigham.

"Ah . . . Florence. I shall not manage it this time," said Miss Hulme. Over her simple, elderly-sweet profile there passed that basking glaze which, at the mention of Florence, crept over the faces of all Londoners old enough to remember the days before the pound-sterling travel restrictions—a moment's Zoroastrian magic, sluicing through fog.

"Florence!" said Miss Moon. "I've been up there for two weeks. Doing some research. Historical stuff. They're all mad for Italy on the Coast, you know."

"The Coast?" said Miss Hulme.

"The West Coast of America, Enid," said Mrs. Wigham.

"Well," said Miss Moon. "I was getting some simply marvelous stuff for my people when Mira here wired me from Garmisch, insisting that I come and stand by her in Rome. She gets so bored, you know—where there's no skiing."

Mira, impassive, blinked once, an animal pricking slightly to the mention of its name. It was enough of a movement to refract the stone that studded her hand like a king's seal. This then was the wife of that California magnate who perhaps had caught an imported starlet as she rose, or had been caught by her as she faded. Under its wiry, black karakul hair, this was a face that had never been personal enough for real beauty perhaps and was now a little too worn for lushness. But, short-nosed and impenetrably planed, it had been that central European cat-face which did well with pictures and with men, which one saw now and then framed in marabou on little girls sitting like spoiled goddesses next to their mothers on the East Bronx train. She wore a coat clipped by couturier scissors but dusty, even dirty, and her scuffed sandals showed a split in one sole. Visiting people of no importance to her, she had abjured even conventional grooming, but the seedlets that hung from her ears had an ineffable grape-bloom and were, Jane saw suddenly, black pearls. It was a pity that Mrs. Wigham, obviously not one for the nuances of dress, might not know how subtly she was being insulted. For this woman was dressed, in a way that the Miss Moons would never dare, with the down-at-the-heel effrontery of the woman who, even in her bath, wears a diamond as big as the Ritz.

"Rome has its attractions," said Mrs. Wigham. "But I fear skiing is not one of them."

"Rome!" said Miss Moon. "I have to keep telling Mira now it's got it all over poor Paris. Sixteen times she's crossed, and this is the first time anybody's been able to drag her here."

"More tea?" said Mrs. Wigham to Mira.

"She hates tea," said Miss Moon. Again Mira blinked, and this time it was as if she had twitched a ridge of skin to remove a fly. "When she's skiing she won't even smoke. She's marvelous at it. Dedicated." She turned to shake her head at Mira, to look enviously at the body, still good, still lithe, that moved now, with the humility of the admired, in its rattan chair. Suddenly Mira took out a mirror and stared at it intensely, moving one hand around her eye sockets. Her face pursed in a spasm of regret. She put the mirror away.

"Tarrible for the skin," she said.

"What . . . tea?" said Miss Hulme.

"The wind and the sun on the slopes, you know," said Miss Moon. "But she will do it." And leaning forward, they could all see the white mask left by the goggles and, radiating through it, the lines of strain, flash burns from the agony of sport.

"But faces are more interesting as they gather life-lines, don't you think?" said Miss Hulme.

Mira stared, unflickering, into space. Then she stood up, flinging out a hip, in a voiceless sex-contempt for women whom nature had not permitted to know what else a face may gather. She spoke, apparently to Miss Moon. "They have ordered that cab yet? You know I have a date at six-thirty."

From Mrs. Wigham's flush it was clear that "they" had been "she," but her face retained its smile with only a slight shift, as if she had quickly substituted a spare. "Giuseppe is ringing about now, I should imagine. One doesn't order anything ahead here, don't you see. Italians don't have our sense of promptness. Miss Moon will have found all this out, I fancy." The rapid flutter of her tongue was meant to imply that she had perceived rudeness and risen above it, but now it was she, Jane thought, who wasted a nuance.

"I alwess like to rest before a date," said Mira. The word "date" seemed to stir her to an anticipatory sleekness. She stretched a long leg in front of her, reared her chin and bosom. Then, uneasily, her fingers returned to explore her eye sockets, as if she were learning an unwelcome Braille. Not once had she looked at anyone directly. Jane had never seen a woman whom it was possible to observe so indiscreetly, without danger of the counterglance, the sudden swerve of rapport.

"Mira's husband phones her every night," said Miss Moon. "Think of it!" Behind the great, clear wings of her glasses she appraised the other women, their dowdy innocence, with marmoset eyes. "Every single night she's been away! All the way from Beverly Hills!"

"Indeed!" said Mrs. Wigham, who was the friend of more than one dexterous marchesa and had looked on Mussolini's paramour hanging wry-mouthed in the public square. She rose. "Let us take a look at the garden until the cab arrives," she said firmly. "I must show you our irrigation system. It's quite unique."

"Ah yes, how lovely," said Miss Hulme, rising also. "I hope to persuade your Giuseppe to sell me an oleander. I must have a present for my little Signorina Necci before I leave for home."

"No!" said Mira. She kicked one shoe against a chair leg, dislodging some gravel from the sole. "I must be back at the hotel at six!"

But Mrs. Wigham had already handed Miss Hulme her cane. "Oh, yes," she murmured. "Giuseppe has developed a very good nursery business on his own." And somehow, between the vague smoke of her chitchat and a guerrilla flanking of Miss Hulme's cane, the three Americans found themselves maneuvered off the terrace, onto a path that meandered far and bournless into the flat surrounding field.

It was a narrow path, hardly more than a rut in the yellow earth, hedged by currant bushes hair-do high and by low clouds of European daisies, their delicate nets set at nylon level, their perfect, flock-pattern faces, scratchier than in Botticelli, tipped ingenuously toward the sun. Miss Hulme headed the line, and her progress was slow. Her cane probed; her enthusiasm, inflected with the remorseless lilt of *solfège*, paused at each planting. Behind her, Mira stumped, taking a step from the hip, when she was able. Miss Moon followed, placing each spike heel with safari decision, turning to flash encouragement to Mrs. Wigham and Jane.

Moving thus crabwise, she was still able to give them a précis of

347

herself. Hearing Jane tell Mrs. Wigham that she had two boys in school, Miss Moon remarked that she had once been a housewife herself. "Married to a script-writer," she said. "Years and years of never using my mind!" Then she had chanced to make some suggestions on a script and it had turned out that she was a born natural. "Ah, then you are one of those writer-teams," said Mrs. Wigham. But it seemed that Miss Moon had ditched the husband—who had not been a natural. She had been in pictures ever since. The work she was doing now was really a luxury of the intellect that she had had to allow herself at last. For, said Miss Moon, whacking viciously at an artichoke plant that had caught her skirt on a spire, her mind was having its revenge for all those fallow years. It had become an instrument that gave her no rest.

"Take Mira," she said. Ahead Mira, face lowered as if to butt, breathed mutinously near Miss Hulme. "There's a girl who knows four languages. And one of those real low singing voices. But all she wants to do is ski like mad and dance all night. Never reads a book or uses her mind."

Mrs. Wigham peered watchfully at Mira, so very near, so extremely close to Miss Hulme. "Sounds frightfully nice," she said. "Don't you think so, Mrs. Bowman?"

"Yes, indeed I do," said Jane.

"Well, of course, she goes in for domesticity like mad at home." Miss Moon's tone was huffy. "Her husband's a great stickler for maturity. Everybody is, with us."

Suddenly the path ended abruptly and they found themselves in front of a large, dirty green pool, the path having led them to the front of the house.

"Dear me," said Mrs. Wigham. "You have left *us* so far behind." She hurried toward the two women ahead at the brink of the pool, and it was thus impossible to say to whom she had addressed this last. Slipping neatly between Mira and Miss Hulme, she embarked on an explanation of the pool as a vestige of the great hydraulic systems of antiquity; waving a brisk hand, she displayed the horizon, on whose line one might just see, or imagine, the worn arches of the aqueducts, marching with ruined step toward classical Rome.

Mira gazed morosely at a stone faun that reared from the center of the pool and made a modest return of water to it on a basic principle. She inhaled ominously in her throat, so that one saw the fine, black ciliar fur of her nostrils. "Francine. Here is not yet that cab."

A white-jacketed servingman came from the house, a Maltese cat nosing between his legs. Mrs. Wigham questioned him in Italian. He spread his hands. Mrs. Wigham sighed and took out a handkerchief. Dabbing her lips with it, as if to blot them free of the hopelessly sweet jelly of Italian, she turned to Mira. "It will take a little time. Meanwhile . . . perhaps you'd like to see the house."

"Yes, may we?" said Jane, with the smoothness of the tourist who knows the rates of exchange. She wondered whether the others knew that they were being asked if they wished to wash their hands.

At that moment the cat, rubbing against Mrs. Wigham's legs, slid also against Mira's. With an electric recoil, Mira screamed and kicked it. The cat, flung several paces, humped and spat. Giuseppe, his mouth open, ran forward and picked it up in his arms.

Mrs. Wigham, immobile, used the handkerchief again to press her lips together. But it was too much for Miss Hulme, who rose telescopic in her suddenly military woollens, her hat a shako, her cheeks a murderous pink. "Really," she said, "but really this cannot be b—!" Her fist rose, the fist with the cane. Ah, thought Jane. She is. She is going to. The cane came down, an inch into the ground, missing Mira's foot by a hair.

There was a moment's silence. For Jane it was a moment of the deepest overtone, that ecstasy of the traveler who realizes that for once he is looking at what he came for. In a moment of almost alcoholic percipience she saw all the inward threads of the *mise en scène*; she saw the Reuters world of Mrs. Wigham, with a fringe of Vatican red; she saw the metro-golden shine of California knocked against the Bayswater Road; down at the bottom she saw even her own little East Coast eye.

And now, it seemed almost as if Mira were going to make apology. Her head dropped to one side, her shoulder moved circularly, as if it wished to rub against Mrs. Wigham as had the cat. "I hate them," she said. "On the plane a woman have one in a box, and it claw me from hip to thigh." She bent and peeled her skirt upward to the waist, extending the thigh as a queen might her hand at levee. "On the United Air Lines," she said.

Behind Mrs. Wigham, Giuseppe stared with interest over the

head of the cat. Mrs. Wigham moved indefinably, and Giuseppe retired in haste, leaving the door open behind him. Since she had not turned her head, her manner too had its touch of the royal. "Do let us go in," she said. "Cyril and James will have got back from their walk. They will be so delighted to meet you. And perhaps you would sing for us. Your friend tells us you have a charming voice."

Mira dropped her skirt down.

"Do," said Miss Hulme, rallying, although her hat retained its outrage. She paused to right it, to make amends. "A little Purcell, perhaps. I do so love the old madrigals. Or a ballad?"

Mira swung her head suspiciously to one side. She thinks she is being chivied, thought Jane. Or like an animal that must be persuaded it has not behaved badly.

Mrs. Wigham moved the door in invitation. Through it Jane saw the room beyond, recognizing the tone of the afternoon that might have been had she and Mrs. Wigham been alone. Tables confused under books, worn couches blotted with pillows and stained with periodicals, all the familiar droppings of the intellect, in the international sitting room of the mind. From an unseen corner came the sounds of gentlemen.

Mira stirred unexpectedly. "All right, I will sing." Her head rose, in the diva's pause. "I will sing—Bhramss' Lullaby." She advanced for entry, and Mrs. Wigham and Miss Hulme moved politely aside. She bent her head. "It is not needful," she said, almost jovial, and it seemed she was awkwardly attempting a joke. "It is not needful to wait for me because I am the star." And, as mutely, they all turned to follow her in, there at last was the cab.

Mira crossed to it without ceremony, leaving their farewells to Miss Moon. "Yes, perhaps so," said Mrs. Wigham to Jane, who thought it wise to share the cab. "We must have our chat another time." As the cab door closed, she leaned across Jane, to the others. "Cyril will be *desolate* not to have met you. And I have *so* enjoyed our afternoon." And from her smile, wide as a salmon's, as the cab drove off, it appeared that he would, that she had.

They rode down through Trastevere in silence. A darkness invested the cab, as if they rode through the white, siesta-stricken streets on the black, plangent core of Mira's impatience. As they

crossed the Tiber she muttered, "I like to *rest* before a date!" and Miss Moon replied, "Well, you are resting. In the cab," in that reasonable tone, half-toady, half-governess, which made Jane wonder at the exact terms of her standing by Mira in Rome. As they rounded the immense white sugar loaf of the Victor Emmanuel monument, Miss Moon remarked that they were not far from where the Roman wolf was kept in its cage. Because of Romulus and Remus—of course, they knew that story? Mira shook her head, intent on twisting her ring in time to the wheels. Miss Moon told the story of Romulus and Remus. "And so, ever since," she concluded, "they keep a wolf, a female wolf, in a cage in the middle of Rome."

"What you mean a wolf!" Mira turned from the window. She stopped twisting the ring. That's what gives her such a queer intentness, thought Jane. She only does one thing at a time.

"What I said, dear. A real she-wolf, just like the one Romulus and Remus had. In a cage in the heart of Rome."

Mira grunted. "What hearts, these people! She does not give suck now, yes?"

"Well, of course not!" said Miss Moon. "It's just a symbol, dear. And they only keep one."

"Fine people!" said Mira. "What a thing!"

"Mira has the dearest little girl at home," said Miss Moon, as if to explain this tenderness on the part of one who had just kicked a cat. "The dearest little four-and-a-half-year-old girl. Just crazy for her mummy. Just pining for her mummy to come home."

Well, no six-o'clock cab will get her *there*, thought Jane. She rubbed the stone in her pocket with a secret, appeasing touch.

Mira ignored this, bristling with some dark, libertarian sympathy that was as powerful as had been her impatience. "Crazy people!" she said. "What a thing!" When the cab drew up at the entrance of the Excelsior, she stood by unheeding while Miss Moon, over Jane's protest and with the alertness of a lady in waiting, paid the very large fare. As they stood on the steps twilight fawned upon them, tangling their lashes with yellow, and from inside the hotel they heard, like a finger drawn across the backbone, the fine tinkle of evening pursuits. Mira blinked, breathing hard. "What a thing!" she said, deep in her throat, before she turned and went inside. "What a thing, to keep a wolf in a cage!"

Left together on the steps of the gleaming entrance, Miss Moon and Jane each turned, hand held out, ready to make off. For there was nothing, each said to herself with an oblique inward glance, certainly nothing that they had in common.

"Well—" said Miss Moon.

"So pleased—" said Jane.

But it was that perilously soft hour of all great cities in the spring, when the evening rises to a sound like the tearing of silk and it is better not to be alone, to have some plan.

"Care to join me in a drink?" said Miss Moon.

"Well—perhaps just one," said Jane. I can't refuse, she told herself. I must buy her a drink, because of that fare. After that it will be time for the eight o'clock sitting at the *pensione*. And after that I can sit on the balcony, on the pretty side, the Pincio side, and write letters home. Or I can ask that nice girl at the next table to have a *granita di caffè* at Doney's. "Shall we go next door to the Flore?" she said. "Or if you'd like a walk—perhaps the Café Greco?" She was faintly proud of knowing both.

"Oh, no, let's go in here," said Miss Moon. As they entered the Excelsior her face brightened. "All California's here on spring location," she said, sotto voce, as she led Jane to a table near the door of the huge lounge, and they sat down. "And this is the bar that gets the play."

At the bar itself there was only a solitary young man, his tall legs wrapped around the bar stool, his blond, "clean-cut American" good looks bent in moody profile over his glass, his tweed back turned away from the groups settled here and there in cushioned niches, as if he uncomfortably knew none of them. It was clear that these others all knew, or knew of, each other. Not that everyone talked to everyone else. But as new people entered conversations were arrested: foursomes spoke deeply among themselves but their glances were asymmetric, and as couples rose, scattering nods, and strode from the arena, a buzz formed behind them. And to the careful watcher, there was still another unity. The women—the wives, that is, for most left hands bore a shock of light—were not all young, but they were younger. The men were beautifully textured as puddings in their minimizing pin-stripe cases, and their cheeks were flanks freshly pummeled by the steam bath, but their wives were their daughters. Opposite them the women sat narrow in luminous

352

sheaths, their shoulders soft explosions of fur, their faces unclench-
ing and closing, automatic as fans.

"Look! There's Sylvia Fairchild!" Miss Moon spoke out of the
side of her mouth. She raised her sharp chin with a brilliant smile
that faded as it was doubtfully returned. Quickly she redistributed
the smile to one far corner, waved briefly to another. She took a
vengeful sip of her Martini. "Believe it or not—she used to do my
nails at Marshall Field's." The Martini sank farther, and she leaned
back with a sigh. "Pretty soon I'll have to go upstairs and pound
that typewriter. I simply have to lock myself in."

"Oh, you're staying here?" said Jane.

"Well, no, but I have a place to work in Mira's suite. She gets in
a dreadful state when there's no—when she gets bored. And I like to
be where the play is, you never know." One of the chattering groups
strolled by, and Miss Moon leaned brightly toward Jane, speaking
very distinctly. "For instance, I was just going to do a book, when I
meet Mat Zipp, of Decca. Why do a book, he says, there's money
in lyrics, and they're shorter. So I do, and it turns out I'm a natural."
The group passed. She waved to the waiter for another drink. "So
then," she said in a lower tone, "so then what does he do but go and
die on me, in a cab on the way to work. With my stuff in his briefcase, right there in the cab."

"Oh, my," said Jane. In her childhood she had been much at the
mercy of a little girl who was always wanting to play house. Now
you just be old Mrs. Brown, Jane, and I'll be Elise Harper, just married, and come to tea.

"So I do a narrative, weave all the stuff together, and almost sell
Dolin and Markova on the idea of a ballet." She took a sip of the
second Martini. "Then they split up."

"Oh, dear," said Jane. It struck her that she was still not a very
good Mrs. Brown.

Behind Miss Moon, at some distance, there was a mirror in which
Jane could just see herself—rather unvarnished, tailored and small
against all this princely down. Not quite plain Jane though, she told
herself, and not quite yet, she thought, looking her age. At home,
when she put on a bare-necked summer cotton and served gin-and-
tonic to the sprightlier clique of the faculty, it was often hardly
credited that she was the mother of those two enormous boys.

"So then," said Miss Moon heavily, "I'm at the Park Lane, and who do I bump into but Grofé. Get him for music and you're set for the Festival Hall, everybody says. The English are suckers for Americana."

Behind her own image in the mirror, Jane saw the bent head of the young man. He bit his lip and recrossed his legs, still staring into his drink. Alone and out of place here, she thought, like me. It would be nice to talk to him, although the idea was, of course, absurd. That was the worst of being on one's own too long in a strange country, so far from the base of affections that steadied one at home. One dried up without some personal emotion; that was all it was. One could not forever be a lens. And at certain hours of the day one found oneself lingering with anyone, as she lingered here.

"Surely you know who Grofé is," said Miss Moon.

"Oh, yes, of course," said Jane. "Philip Morris. I mean the commercial. And isn't he Vladimir Dukelsky for classical—oh, no, of course not—that's Vernon Duke." She thinks me an idiot, she thought, and I am to sit on here, waiting to hear how it was they didn't get Grofé. For from the grim, antiphonal way Miss Moon drew on her glass, it was clear that they hadn't.

"So then," said Miss Moon, but she interrupted herself to twinkle a hand at someone who passed, to murmur an indistinct name.

I'll grab the check and go now, thought Jane. For it was no longer funny to watch Miss Moon. It was like seeing those women who hovered secretly at other women's dressing tables, to spray themselves avidly and cheaply with another person's scent.

I'll take the check and go now. She glanced at her watch. It was seven, that hour here when even the windows of *pensione* bedrooms were violet frames that turned one inside to say Look! to the empty room, to lie face downward, ears stopped against the bell-shake of evening, and say Listen! to the vacant bed. The hour when an experienced traveler knows better than to corner himself there. The hour when the lens turns upon oneself.

"And . . . so then?" said Jane.

But Miss Moon was looking elsewhere again, and this time with such a different, such an unrehearsed expression that Jane looked around too. It was Mira, standing at the entrance. Groomed now for people of importance, she had made herself, as women did, to be as like them as possible. Her dress was luminous too, cut with pale cleverness to conceal where it could no longer insist, and she stood encircled in a huge riband of fur. She looked sleeker and, in a powdery way, older. Perhaps she had seen this in some mirror before leaving, for now she reached up uncertainly and rumpled her tamed hair, as if to declare the girl she had been against the woman she was. She walked forward with a mannequin's glide, her smile full for the room, then turned her back to it and, with an eager, a crescent leaning, slipped her hand through the arm of the young man at the bar.

He looked up, then stood up, and on his face, handsomer even than in profile, one saw the snow marks of the goggles on the brown skin. But where the white circles on Mira's face were fretted like rose windows, his were still smooth. He was about thirty, that age when, with Americans, one often glimpses the young man looking through the palings of the man, and in his look, lightened with relief but somehow hangdog, one caught this now. As he and Mira left the bar, Mira saw the two women, Jane and Miss Moon. For the first time she really saw them. She looked directly into their eyes and she smiled. Then she and the young man passed by them, walking slowly down the long room, and although Mira, nodding here and there with narrowed eyes, clung softly and proudly to the crook of his arm, it seemed almost that he was paraded on hers. A buzz formed behind them.

"She's a fool." Miss Moon breathed this to herself. Behind her glasses her eyes were bright and fixed. "It'll be all over the Coast in twenty-four hours."

Now the couple neared them again, in their return passage down the room. The young man's face was warm. Mira was still faintly smiling, and although this time the smile, fixed on the door, was for neither of the two women, to Jane, trembling suddenly in her tailored suit with a shock that was bitter and sororal, it came as if it was. Almost a grimace, it showed its teeth to an invisible mirror, denying with the lips the secret lines that a body must gather—the crow's feet of the armpit, the dented apple of the belly, the mapped crease, fine leather too long folded, that forms between the breasts. As Mira passed her on the arm of the young man, her scent remained for a moment behind. It rested on Jane as if it were her own.

355

At the door, Mira and the young man paused. A rush of lilac came to them from the outside, and Mira's fur slid from shoulder to waist, a dropped calyx. The young man replaced it carefully. Her lips parted, watching him. It was a beautiful fur, manipulable as smoke. Before the arts of the furrier had dappled it, it might have been just the color of wolf.

Left together by the flicking of the door, the two women stared at one another.

"Traveling alone?" said Miss Moon.

Jane nodded.

"Divorced too?"

"No," said Jane. "I'm a widow." Her head lifted. "I have two boys."

Miss Moon seemed not to have heard this last. "Care to—join forces for dinner?"

No, thought Jane. Don't settle for anybody's company. As she does. As she has. Not yet. She gazed past Miss Moon, saw herself in the mirror, and looked quickly away. "Thanks," she said, and her voice was kind. "I'm afraid . . . I have work to do too."

"Oh, you work," said Miss Moon eagerly. "What do *you* do?"

"I teach," said Jane. "In a university." I teach, an echo said inside her, and of course at home I have the two boys. And suddenly the echo, her breath, something, rammed itself hard against her chest, inside. Not enough, it said, beating behind the mapped crease between her breasts. Not enough. What a thing, it said, crying. What a thing!

"Well, back to the salt mines for us, eh?" said Miss Moon. Her voice was matey, unbearable. Just as if she too had smelled the scent, had heard the thing crying. As if she knew too that Jane, staring into the big, winged glasses, could see the two poor eyes beating against the glass.

And now they stood up quickly, gathered their purses and signaled for the waiter. When he came, they paid him with a dispatch unusual to women, and the lire notes left lying in his saucer were large enough for anybody here. For now they could not part quickly enough. For now, each said to herself, the other's company was no longer to be borne. No, it was not to be borne. Not now. Now that they both knew what it was they had in common.

Songs My Mother Taught Me

❧ S O M E T E N years ago when I was for the first time in London—when, as a rather elderly innocent abroad, I was for the first time *any*where outside New York City except Rochester, Elmira, Binghamton, the Eastern Shore, a few summer resorts in New England and, at the age of twelve, Asbury Park, New Jersey—I attended a semi-diplomatic dinner party at which, after we had all drunk considerable amounts of several delightful wines, one of the ladies present suddenly peeled off her blouse.

Since the other guests, though moist and perfervid, were still upright in their chairs and conversation, the incident caused, even in that imperturbable company, a certain silence. Chitchat, suddenly quenched, faded off into one of those pauses where isolated sentences stand out sharply. The man on my left, whom I had placed tentatively as either a connoisseur of heraldry or a baiter of Americans, had been lecturing me on the purity of lineage maintained by German nobility up to the last war. "Where else," he had just inquired, "can one find, even now, a person whose line shows sixteen quarterings?" Then he stopped short, as if contradicted by circumstance. Headily I reassured myself that quite without knowing it—and in the first week too—I must have scaled one of those dizzily international heights of society so often promised the provincial: a set so patrician that queens had no legs, emperors might be clothed exactly as they said they were, and ladies appeared in their quarterings without shame.

She was an exceedingly pretty young woman of about twenty-five with masses of blond hair arranged ingénue, and a pair of truly enormous blue eyes swimming in some Venus-lymph, clear natural nacre in which a man, or indeed any onlooker, might well sink.

Words like "truly" came inevitably to mind as one regarded them. As I did so, they spilled over pellucidly. Casting a reproachful look at her partner (later it was understood that he had dared her), turning down the corners of a lovely mouth rosied with wine and—though one hated to think it—stupidity, she gazed at us, clutching the discarded portion of her costume, then hung her head and let fall on her lavishly ruffled *broderie anglaise* corselet two neatly schooled tears.

"Why, Lady Catherine!" our host said at once, and rising, he went round the table to her and poured her more wine, murmuring what I thought to be "How very sporting!" and capping it with—as he raised his own glass—"Bravo!"

Other gentlemen took up the plaudit. Lady Catherine, shyly consoled, raised her head, and I remembered her patronymic, ducally familiar even to me: one of her ancestresses, whom she was said to resemble, had been a wife of Henry the Eighth. From her round eyes two more pearls dropped, but this time surely with retrospective art —I wondered whether Henry, watching her ancestress' head fall, might not have thought to himself, "None of my other wives looked that good upside down."

What happened next I can only recount, not explain. It is true that, while we were only fourteen at table, the number of empty bottles ranged testimonially behind us must have totaled more than twice that. I have a vague impression that the male applause may have attained an ethnic intensity. Also that our host, bending over Lady Catherine, was assuring her that she looked smashing, and rather more respectable than the portrait of his grandmother as lady in waiting to Queen Alexandra. And that she, though retaining a disconsolate posture, was looking smug. What I know for sure is that when I next glanced at our hostess—a bishop's daughter—she too had peeled.

"She's upset the gravy boat, Mother!" I murmured delightedly, but of course no one paid any attention to me, or would have understood the reference if they had. No one there was likely to have heard of Mrs. Potter Palmer, much less of my mother. I shall shortly explain—for the benefit of readers who, although they may have caught the allusion to American social history, cannot possibly know anything of mine. But first let me complete the *mise en scène* of a moment in which were to be brought home to me all the old saws of my girlhood—a moment of truth in which, across so much water and over the ten years of my mother's sojourn in Mrs. Grundy's heaven, I could at last exclaim to her, "Mother, you were right!"

Of the seven women at table, six, including myself, were wearing the version of the currently fashionable (and easily doffable) "separates" known as "evening sweaters." There was nothing coincidental about this; the best houses were cold, even for London; rationing was still on and the English were burning an ineffectual sludge called, with their usual talent, "nutty slack." The one exception to the sweaters was also the only one of the others who was neither chic nor pretty, a vast, untidy woman opposite me—Frau Ewig, a noted anthropologist, recently returned from Sierra Leone—whose dress, showing so many possible means of separation that the eye was unable to choose the probable, looked somewhat as if, in order to appear in it at the party, she had first chopped several natives up. She, like the rest of us, had forgotten Lady Catherine in the sight of our hostess, who sat revealed, with the air of a prioress who had removed her wimple, in a rock-pink, ten-guinea model by Berlé.

In the silence that followed I heard the clink of crystal—the gentlemen, according to their needs and natures, were either taking another drink or putting down the one they had. A muted cry of protest was heard—from Lady Catherine. I could have seconded it —for another reason. For glancing round at the other ladies, I sensed something infinitely feminine glissade from eye to eye. In prescience I closed mine. When I opened them, what I saw confirmed it. Every remaining lady—except the anthropologist and the American—had the upper part of her costume in her hand.

Now there was nothing essentially risky in the tableau before us: a number of ladies sitting, modestly swan-necked, in their foundations, is a sight familiar to every window-shopper. Besides, the temperature being what it was, I thought I could discern, between various lacy interstices, the fuzzier-than-flesh-tone of what Debenham & Freebody's (where I bought one the next morning) called a vest. No, the riskiness is often in the eye of the beholder. And this composite eye, twelve times magnified and stern as that of a nudist group eyeing the indecency of a visitor's clothing, was now fixed on my pied vis-à-vis and on me. Leave me there now, while we make our way back—by gravy boat and a sneaky trail of safety pins—to my mother. We shall return.

Moral instruction by moral illustration has long since disappeared from the training of the young. Metaphor itself is considered untrustworthy—likely to weaken the facts of what already is a pretty slippery reality—and every good parent knows that the parable is too "punitive" by far. My childhood was full of them, from boogieman to Bunyan, my parents belonging to a generation still very sure of its facts. And my mother's specialty was what might be called the "social" allegory. Obvious in design, single in target, it was part of the process by which she hoped to transform the unpromising grub at that very moment scratching its knee-scabs in front of her into something pretty and marriageable, designed to preside, with some of her own graces and others she aspired to, at a table even more elaborate than her own.

Under a codex possibly marked "Accidents, Dinner"—for, as will be seen, a good proportion of my mother's tales revolved on accident—reposed Mrs. Potter Palmer. Famous arbiter of bygone Chicago society, she may be the model for performances slightly more rarefied than the one I know her for—as for me, I see her only in the attitude of one. Eternally she presides at her exalted dinner table, from whose foot, in the worm's-eye view of my mother's imagination, she is all but obscured by the gravy boat suited to her station—to my mind about twice the size of our largest tureen. In her historic moment she knows nothing of us, but all is open to posterity—hovering above her now like helicopters, like damsel flies, we see all. Then it happens. Far down the length of the gilt-encrusted table—exactly center I make it for drama—a guest jars a servingman's wrist. A great gout of gravy erupts on the cloth.

My mother pauses; I return her look of high seriousness. Extrasensory perception or what you will, with not a word said between us, our images of that cloth are the same. As a superb embroiderer, my mother's chef d'oeuvre is her banquet cloth. Loaded with eyelet, scallop, punchwork, Valenciennes, fringe and insertion, lying even now on its cardboard cylinder between sheets of preservative blue paper, five years in the making, never used and none like it in the world—yet there on that august table, with a terrible brown blot on its middle, lies its twin.

The guest hangs his head, and no wonder. In unavoidable *frisson* the other guests, well-bred as they are, avert theirs. We gloat over the dreadful moment, knowing rescue is nigh. Mrs. Palmer, whose eagle eye—exactly like my mother's at her half-yearly dinner parties— sees everything while appearing to register nothing, pauses for a fraction in her elegant conversation. Then she makes her gesture—irreparable and immortal. I see her elbow, plump, white and shapely, a noble *fin-de-siècle* elbow suited to its duty, not covered with chicken-skin like mine. Carefully careless as Réjane, no doubt chatting gaily the while, she has swept it outward. Hail Mrs. Palmer, heroic hostess, who, in the imitation that is the ultimate of good manners, is seen now to have overturned, on that cloth, the tureen!

With years of reflection, this tale of my mother's, like another even more pertinent, came to have as many holes in it as the cloth had eyelets. Was it quite the thing to be so exemplary so publicly? Wouldn't the real acme of taste have been not to notice—had the guest felt better, or worse? It came to me that Mrs. Palmer's manner might someday merit the same comment as her money: too much of it. As a matter of fact, if they were being served by footmen, what was the tureen doing in front of her at all?

But at eleven or so, yes, moral illustration, when taken literally, can be dangerous. We were a family of many guests and many, though infrequently regal, dinners at which, since our household was small, I was often allowed up. Time went by while I waited for someone to have his accident, so that I might pridefully watch my mother's aristocratic amends. For months we seemed to feed no one but aunts and uncles; I knew my mother too well to think she would waste that sort of high style on them. But at last one of our guests obliged. He was a Dr. Nettel, fresh from a twenty-year stint in Egypt, who had once been one of my mother's suitors—perhaps it was my father's still sardonic eye on him that caused him to drop a fork into a vegetable dish that splattered wide.

To me, seated at my mother's left, all augured well; the cloth was damask only, but the vegetable was beet. I looked at my mother expectantly; when she did nothing I nudged her, pointing to the service dish of beets which, since it was maid's night out and we were short of footmen, reposed, family-style, in front of her. "Don't be ridiculous," she whispered, her lips sealed, her gaze on the horizon.

I had just been through my eighth-grade graduation—"Into thy hands we give the torch"—the noblesse of our house it would seem, rested with me. I crooked my sharp elbow, bending my hand backward from the wrist as if it held a little pinch of something, meanwhile elegantly averting my head, as if to chitchat, toward Dr. Nettel, but since I could think of nothing to say I remained thus, basrelief—perhaps he thought I was assuming an Egyptian pose just for him. "Stiff neck?" said my father. My mother, knowing better, grabbed for the elbow; absorbed in the mental picture, profile, of myself, I jumped at the touch; between us we upset the ice pitcher. Diversion was thus created, though not as symmetrically as it would have been via beet. Later, before I went to bed, I was whacked. "Because you are so smart," said my mother between whacks, "and because you are absolutely unteachable." She was wrong. I had just learned for sure what I had always suspected—that we were irretrievably middle-class.

Meanwhile, allegory still pursued me, though from another corner. Other girls my age were becoming women, flirts, sirens—at least girls —without trouble, and some avidly; it was my mother's cross that I had to be nagged there inch by recalcitrant inch. Daintiness, my mother said, was its essence; once a woman's daintiness got through to a man, all consummations devoutly to be wished for—such as a trousseau of one's own triple-monogrammed tea napkins—soon followed. To me the word was "daindee," as our German cook crooned it—"Oooh, so daindee!" over anything fancy—and as she looked on her day off, a clumsy veil of white obscuring everything human, excess of starch in the blouse, powder on the neck, fish-net gloves on her honest, corned-beef hands. To me even a bath was an assault on one's boundaries. Cleanliness was hypocrisy, dirt "sincere." Still the other ethic followed me, ruthlessly inserted in my ear along with the morning and evening soapings, and always with some elaboration peculiar to my mother—witness her *divertissement* on the Safety Pin.

I belong to the tail end of the button-traumaed generation. The embarrassments of the zipper-reared are quite otherwise—gaps in the memory or the metal, a fear of being locked in. We lived in the opposite fear of—the very words still have a blush and a hush to them—things "dropping down." Camisoles, panties and petticoats, even when snapped or hook-and-eyed, still required ceaseless vigilance with the needle—and thread was fallible, not nylon. Hence the reign of the safety pin, now used only by cleaners and babies. But the protocol of its use was strict. Emergency supply was always in the purse—in my mother's a chain of small gold ones. In case of "accident" one retired somewhere—to the washroom at Wanamaker's for instance—pinned "things up" and rushed home in a pink state of guilt, praying all the while that one would not be knocked down by a car on the way. For the core of the ethic—known, as I found later, to almost every girl of the era—was: "What if you are rushed suddenly to the hospital, and *there they discover* . . . ?" Dream sequences often finished the line, sung above our shrinking forms by hosts of angelic interns forever lost to us: "She has a safety pin in her corset cover!" The worst offense, of course, against sense as well as neatness, was to start the day or the journey already pinned. Hence my mother's variation, known to me always as The Gentleman from Philadelphia.

There was once a girl who was being courted by such a gentleman. Whether there was any significance in his origin, I don't know; perhaps—this being the unsolicited detail with which my mother often fleshed a fable—he just was. *She* was one of those girls (not unknown to me) who were hastily groomed on the surface, at the cost of squalor below. For a while, said my mother, the girl was able to string him along. But, said she, you can't string them along forever —tangentially I tag this as the single allusion she ever made to sex. There came a day when he arrived with intent to propose. It was a warm occasion; the girl was wearing a peekaboo blouse. Perhaps it was warm enough, say, for him to take off his driving goggles and lean closer. Anyway, just as he was about to declare . . . he saw that her shoulder strap was attached with—you've got it. The gentleman went back where he came from. And the girl is single yet.

It has since struck me that she was well shet of him. But at the time—"*Now* do you see?" said my mother, and I mumbled back, "Yerse."

In time of course, through vanity and the sly connivance of the lingerie-makers, I became as "insincere" as any other "nice" woman, although I never quite convinced my mother of it—or myself. "Fine feathers, *on top*," she would greet a new costume of mine, and sure enough, within minutes, some detail of my toilette would mysteriously unravel. I scrubbed my wedding ring until some of the stones fell out, because she had a habit of murmuring, "Dirty diamonds," whenever she saw an overdressed woman, and I primped for hospital visits as courtesans once may have for their levées. Wanamaker's was torn down, but I sometimes still dreamed myself in its washroom, standing there with the top button gone from my skirt waistband, holding one gaunt safety pin the size of a salmon's skeleton. And I never was able to look a real safety pin straight in its fishy, faintly libidinous eye.

But now—let us return to that table in London. There sit the ladies, swan-necked and squinting—what does the slightly piscine shape of their squint remind me of?—at me. And there, somewhat blue-lawed about the jowl at the very plurality of the situation, sit the men. And me—what I am thinking? As any woman would be, of course, of what I have on underneath. Being me, I am also thinking that I am after all the child, at last the Good Child of my mother, and that the scene before me—although of course she could not possibly countenance it—is the accident we have both been waiting for all my life.

For what I happen to have on underneath—nothing more of course, or less, than what thousands of Rockefeller Center secretaries, window mannequins and ladies out for the evening in Rochester, Elmira and Binghamton are wearing—is a La Belle Hélène Walzette, Model 11A56, Merrie Widowe Waiste Pincher, nyl. lce. blk., size 36 B. Edwardian it may be, but not in execution; no amount of wine will unravel me—Seventh Avenue expertise has machine-tooled me into it and only the hotel chambermaid will get me out. And its modesty is unimpeachable—is, in fact, Mail Order. This, indeed, is the accident. For what I had ordered, in the rush before sailing, was the nyl. lce. wht.—in the catalogue very daindee, with the usual sprig of mashed ribbon rosebuds in the décolletage. But what I have got on—sent me by one of the Eumenides brooding

darkly in Best's warehouse—is the blk. And the blk. is not with rosebuds. Blissfully I feel, beneath my sweater, what it *is* with—something to end traumas forever. There, centered where once button or
pin might have resided, now lies, locking me in by patents pending,
a round red cabochon glass jewel about the size of a nickel, La Belle
Hélène's star ruby clasp, my order of merit, winking rosy and waiting
for the light.

Or is it? Dare I? I look heavenward, seeing at first only a dim,
brackish ceiling in St. John's Wood. But in dreams one does not
always rehearse only one's anxieties. Sometimes one dreams that one
is walking downtown in one's Walzette, and wakes to find—that one
is. And better yet—that Mother is watching. Here I am then, I say
upwards. See me now, met with my accident just as you warned me,
but in what aristocratic company! There sits Lady Catherine, who
began it, surrounded by several others who may well count sixteen
quarterings, whatever that is, among them—if not all in one. There
indeed sits Mrs. Potter Palmer modern version, with her sweater-
tureen in her hand. Mother, you were right. And now, if I do what it
appears I must, aren't I?

And immediately I am answered. Nothing supernatural about it—
if there is any moral to this fable it is that, unbecoming as we at first
may seem to our parents, in the end we become them. At the moment, however, I prefer to think that the suggestion comes via the
grate, where a piece of nutty slack slides down, *sotto voce. Ask the
lady across from you.*

I do so. I tip Frau Ewig a wink toward the others, signaling,
"Shall we join them?" She seems larger and redder in the face than
when I last noticed her. Not to my entire surprise, she shakes her
head imperceptibly. Under my stare her face empurples further.
"Kann nicht!" she murmurs at last, her lips unmoving; and as her
seams stretch with her breathing, I see why—underneath each of her
vast arms, a baleful, metallic winking-back. I look the other way.
More's the pity! Anthropologist or no, Frau Ewig was reared in
Vienna, and I think I know how. Like me. But I don't see how I
can help her. Still, a pity that in every apotheosis of the Good Child,
there must be, clinging to the bottom of the ladder and gazing upward, a Bad.

My mother's face, up there like a decal through which I can still see the ceiling, is of course seen by no one but me. She has her eyes closed, knowing, as usual, just what I am about to do, and she cannot quite approve this modern ending to her fable. But she also cannot help smiling. Listen to them, the heavenly host, not of angels but of interns, as leaning down with her in the center of the circle they sing it to me *a cappella, con amore* . . . "and now we discover . . . she has got . . ." (soft Gilbertian surprise) "No! She has not! . . . Yes she has, yes she *has*, she has got . . ." (*pianissimo, ma non troppo*) "a roo-oo-ooo-ooooby . . . yes, a ruby, ruby, ruby, ruby, ruby . . . a Star Ruby in her corset cover!"

And as, with my hand bent a little at the wrist, I make my gesture, all the company, leaning forward with interest—and perhaps even my mother—may see that I have.

So Many Rings to the Show

ᴥ§ HE AND Esther walked out of the marriage clerk's office, past the other waiting couples and the wedding parties, out into the open air. Down here, the air had a remembered municipal grayness, as if its natural color had long since been gritted over with a light statistical dust. Surely he and Marie had gone to a different place to be married—or else this one had been remodeled. Jim recalled a dirty brownish cubicle stained with the tobacco-juice whiff of small-time political stews, and a clerk with a whine and a conniving eye. This afternoon, the office had shone with a kind of cleanly bureaucracy, and the clerk, cool and dentifriced, had refused Jim's large tip with a grave, ritual shake of the head.

Jim took Esther's elbow and guided her through the corridors, down the steps to the pavement, where still more couples stood about in uncertain tableaux. Dingily new, the city edifices pressed too near, as if seen gigantically close in an opera glass, and looking at one façade, one felt another at the small of one's back. Built in the hope of a Roman dignity, they had managed only a republican durability. They're too close together, he thought—that's it. There's not enough space between them for majesty.

He hailed a cab, and got in after her. The driver looked inquiringly over a shoulder. "Drive uptown—up Fifth," Jim said. The driver shrugged and started off.

Jim settled back and felt for Esther's hand. As soon as they were away, out of that neighborhood, he would be released from his compulsion to compare, to remember. From here on, it would all be new. He was half aware that his unwilling memories were the more painful because his first marriage had been embarked upon in the same golden warmth and faith, the same sense of inevitability. It

367

had been an October day, that day full of scudding cloud and changeableness, and this day, more than twelve years later, was all moist and May, with a muffled vibrato of approaching summer. But in essence each day held the same fixed dream of rightness, of an incredibly lucky voyage with the one person without whom the world dulled. In essence, one day had been, and one day was, the happiest day of his life. It was as if, carefully putting away a freshly inked guaranty in a drawer, he had come upon another, gilt-scrolled and bright and ridiculously voided by time.

He looked at Esther, her serenely musing profile nodding faintly up and down with the movement of the cab. He was beyond seeing her, he knew, in any literal terms as a tall, good-looking girl with dark-blond hair, with features whose imbalance, stopping just short of strangeness, struck one on further scrutiny with their curiously personal beauty. For four years now, from the very beginning of the affair, she had seemed to him a medal struck once, and superbly, for him. Now she looked, as always, fresh and lovely. She always dressed, with wise chic, for the second glance, but today, in a gray dress he had seen once before, and a small spray of veil, she had been perhaps especially careful to avoid the flowery smirk of the bride. Neither of them had brought any huge emphasis to bear on today's ceremony, held as they had been by an unspoken agreement that for two who had so long been lovers this would be silly, perhaps gross. On their way downtown, stopping around the corner from her place to buy her a camellia at the florist shop they always went to, he had found a pleasing element of continuity, almost a safety, in the benedictory smile of the Greek, in the way he handed the flower, as usual, to Jim, and watched, bowing a little, while Jim handed the flower to Esther. She was wearing it pinned not on her shoulder but on her belt.

She looked around at him now with a smile, a slight pressure of the hand in his, then returned to her wide-eyed contemplation of the driver's back, and he saw with a rush of warmth that she was surrounded by her own dream of rightness. If she was thinking of her own first wedding—that phlox-and-roses still life of a Connecticut lawn more than ten years back—he did not begrudge her this. Framed in black, it could lie in her memory only with the finality of a mourning card. The house and lawn of her parents had long since been sold; the boy, with whom she had never shared a house with, dead within two months in Korea, could only tug importunately now and then at the rim of her remembrance. In a frightening way, he envied her this cameo of a memory, which must have for her the perfect finish given only by death. For her, there was no Marie, no young Jimmie, standing forever wounded, forever suppliant, on the fringe of conscience.

He opened his mouth to speak, because one of them must soon speak, and closed it again, in fear of the random significance of the first thing to be said. It was a feeling like that on the birthdays of his boyhood, when he had hesitated, wary, at the childish chant "If you do it on your birthday, you do it all year around—if you cry on your birthday, you cry the whole year round." The long affair had been an idyll, hardly shaken by the long divorce, so sure had they been of themselves and of the deep morality of the end in view. Now that they had it, he wanted to touch wood. He had never been more sure of the end; only the beginning troubled him a little.

"Decided where to, Mister?" the driver asked.

Jim looked over at Esther. She turned the palms of her hands upward, then clasped them lightly in her lap. "Where to . . ." she said, smiling, certain. He gave the driver the address of her apartment and leaned back, stretching his legs.

The cab turned down her street—still hers, even though he had come there for years and his things were there now. "Maybe we should have gone off to the country somewhere," he said. "Would you have liked that?"

"No." She shook her head slowly. "I like us just as we are."

He kissed her and let his face rest for a moment on her shoulder, lazily breathing her perfume, watching the sun and shade dapple her lap. When he had paid off the cab, he followed her down the steps to the dark-blue door, flanked with potted shrubs, through which one entered her building, and they stood in the areaway for a minute, looking down the two streets that converged before it. Spaced along the sidewalks, small, wire-bracketed trees had put out every straining leaf, each trunk holding its rosette of branches like a child's head too heavy for the delicate stalk of neck. "What a day!" she said. "Isn't it a lovely day!" She spun on her heel, and put her hands in his.

"Lovely!" he said. It was the kind of day when the season, poised for the summer plunge, enclosed the city in a golden bubble whose faintly rounded walls distorted everything into a curve of beauty. Down the far distance, where the stores were, windows dazzled into cataracts, signs flew like pennants.

"Spring's the nearsighted season," Esther said softly, and it was true that although he had his glasses on, everything did look blurred, merged, as if he might just have taken them off, except for the door, on whose knob she had put her hand. Over the years of evenings when he had walked toward it in light-footed, sensuous quickening, the door had become the image that had halved his life, first as a rendezvous, with all the giddy charade the word implied, later with urgency and conflict, and finally as a symbol of what he wanted to walk toward forever. During the business days before the nights when he was to see her, it had always been this he had gone toward in his mind, so much so that if anyone had casually asked, "You know Esther King, don't you?" he would have been able to answer indifferently, but if anyone had said, "Do you know a house with a blue door?" he would have been left stammering and undone. Until the very last, when they had had to wrench themselves out into the open, once he had closed it behind him no one else had known where he was, nothing had been able to reach him, shuttered there in secrecy and love.

"Well?" She smiled and twisted her hand on the knob, and again he was back in a forgotten birthday, standing in a clutter of wrapping paper, looking, choked and prayerful, at the largest and most beautiful box of all.

"Too nice to go up yet," he said. "What do you say we have a drink at Rolo's?"

"Yes, let's," she said. "Let's go get a drink at Rolo's," she said singsong, tucking her hand under his arm, urging him back up the steps, as if this had been her idea, almost as if his thought had been hers.

"Strange, isn't it?" she said. She was sauntering along, eyes half closed, smiling. "Not to see you for a month, and then all of a sudden—this. I can't believe it. I can't believe you're not going to have to—go."

He squeezed the arm with her hand in it against his side. During the last weeks, they had kept apart; she had gone out of town while the decree became final and he went through the series of small obsequies—dreadful because they were so small—that had attended his final rupture with the house in New Canaan. Esther had wanted them to start clear, she had said, obsessed by a sudden, wistful grasp at propriety, and they had done so. On his last visit to the house, to get his summer clothes out of the attic and back to the hotel where he was staying, he had come down the attic stairs with his arms full, thinking, Was it only last summer—was it only *last* summer—that he had been living here? And he had run straight into Marie, who had always been carefully absent when he came before, on similar forays or for an appointed outing with young Jim. She had turned quickly into a room, shutting the door behind her, but not before he felt the same oddly monogamous twinge of guilt that had made his continued life there impossible. For it had been guilt, and a monogamous one—but its allegiance had been to Esther.

"Down this way. Remember?" Esther said, and stopped him from continuing past Second Avenue. The bar, Rolo's, was halfway down the block. It was a place they had first gone to one afternoon years before, out of a deep need to show their love in the company of someone. Little by little, as it became the one spot where they let themselves be seen, the magic comfort of such places gathered in its grimy red shadows, for here they were known to belong together. Here they had their own corner and their special drink; and their status, though never commented upon, had been well surmised and appraised—and this, too, made them happy. Finally, even the "characters" in the bar became dear to them, for in the eyes of these, they themselves were characters in their own romance.

At the door of the bar, Jim hesitated. Perhaps she would be hurt, after all, if there were not some celebration, some tiny bursting of the rose, even if only among the supernumeraries here. "As we were?" he asked.

"As we were." She touched a finger to her lips, and the smile was still upon them.

As we still are, he thought, following her in. He nodded to Tom, the bartender, raised two fingers, pulled out Esther's chair, sat down in his own, and nodded again, this time to Lydia Matthews, a white-haired beauty of fifty, who returned the nod with the dainty, spectral

smile of her five-o'clock Martini swoon. The bartender, coming over
to their table to set down their vermouth-cassis, glanced back at her
with a pitying shrug.

Jim clinked his glass against Esther's. "To things as they are," he
said. With a forefinger, he stroked the back of her hand. Over the
raised rim of her glass, her eyes filled with tears.

They sat there for a long time; they had supper there while
the window behind them turned into a great ox eye of blue. When
the bar was crowded, the place full, Lydia left, as she always did.
They watched her thread her way out, a hostess speeding her guests,
pausing here and there to lean over a table and drop the same muted
phrases from the wry, aging dimple of her mouth. She stopped to
speak to a couple at the table next to theirs. "Found your boy?" she
asked the woman. "That's right, darling. That's everything there is."
The woman laughed.

Lydia leaned over Esther. "Found your boy," she said, nodding
like a pink, ruined, grandmotherly girl.

She drew herself up, her head queenly, her purse clasped tight in
front of her. "Night, ducks," she said, her voice round and warm,
and walked past them, out the door, treading lightly on the civet
flow of the Martinis, her head held high in the regency of drink.

Glancing at each other, they rose, too, with intuitive rhythm, and
left the place, walking silently through the blue element of the
evening. And now he caught her around the hip and urged her,
laughing, running, to the corner of their street. There they slackened,
breathless, and again he urged her forward. On the brink of the
steps, they teetered, then ran down them in unison; he flung the
door open, pushed her inside, and caught her in his arms, listening
with satisfaction to the door soothing shut behind them.

"Oh, Lord!" she said, laughing, picking the spray of veil from her
hair and hanging its circlet on her wrist, falling silent as he still held
her. Together they looked through the lozenge of window set high in
the door, thick glass through which the world outside appeared tiny,
distorted, clever—a world in a bull's-eye mirror. The young trees
were holding their brave rosettes cleverly on high, the day was ending in an extraordinary gentleness, as if someone were pouring over
it a knowing wash of dark, and he and she, standing close in its
lambent shadow, were the cleverest of all.

"I'll just get the mail." She darted a quick kiss at him and bent to fumble in her purse for the mailbox key. He felt in a pocket for his key to the inside door, opened it, and, when she had got the mail, pushed her childishly up the stairs in front of him, hearing, with another flicker of satisfaction, the inner door click closed below.

Once inside the familiar oval of her one room, he sank down into a chair, winded and replete, watching her as she went about the room, turned a lamp on, then off, put her hands idly to her hair, flung open the casement, and leaned there, looking out. It was a room that he had never once returned to without feeling grateful that he was there again, another lap won. Now he sat there dizzy with gratitude, assessing each familiar symbol—the ashtray with the two deer beneath the glaze, the copper pot in which she made *espresso* coffee for them, the jar that variously held rhododendron and chrysanthemum, and now had willow in it. He almost resented the willow, because it was new, placed there in his absence, until he remembered that he would never have to resent change in this room again; he would always know what was in the jar.

"Smell it," she said, leaning out. "How can it smell like that— almost like the country? It's like syringa, or honeysuckle."

"It's the spring-blooming neons," he said. "The lovely neon smell."

"A little dusty." She stood up and brushed her hands together, then came and put her head down on him for a moment before she sat down across from him and looked through the mail. He sat watching, in his wonderful sloth of anticipation, thinking of what a remarkable rhythm women had for situation, and how they moved best, to some delicate inner pulse, in the situation of love. He found a moment of pity for the crude young couples they had seen at the marriage bureau, the visionary girls, the red, stammering boys, staring not at each other but past each other at some rigid pantomime of sex. This room was burned into his mind, and now that he sat in its center, it was lit from behind by all the banked hours that started up, once he set foot here, percussive as drums.

She raised her head from an open letter on the pile in her lap. "From my brother. All good wishes—and they want us down for a weekend next month. The twentieth."

Jim took the letter she passed him, only skimming the welcoming words in his relief that now, and so easily, the strands were beginning to knit—all the good, associative strands of dinner with these, Sundays with those. *We look for you two on the twentieth.*

"Why, and here's one for you," she said. "Forwarded from the hotel." She handed it to him with a little flourish that said it was his first letter here, that she, too, had her satisfactions.

One glance at the large, smudged envelope told him that it was from Jimmie. Thin at the crease, worn, with an old business address of his own in the upper corner, it was one of a stock of leftover letterheads that had been kept in the desk at New Canaan. The inscription was printed in purple indelible pencil. *Mr. James Nevis,* it said, then Esther's address, in ink, above the canceled address of the hotel, and then: *New York City. The United States. The World. The Universe.*

"The World, The Universe," she said, leaning over him. "Ah, I used to do that, didn't you?"

"He always signs himself 'your favorite child,'" Jim said. "Joke. Because he's the only one." He heard his tone, the careful deprecation with which parents boast to strangers of their heart's blood.

"His pictures are so like—" she said. "I want so much to—Jim, now we can have him visit here, can't we?"

"Yes," Jim said. "We can have him." He slit the letter open. *Dear Jim,* it said. *This is to remine you the last time Ringling Brothers Barnum and Bailey, the circus, the last time is Sunday May 10. Hoping to here from you. Your favorite child. James R. Nevis.* A clipping of a circus ad was attached, stuck on with Scotch tape.

"But that was yesterday," he said. "Oh, God damn! That was yesterday."

"What, dear?"

He handed her the letter. A final sinking of the light outside the window sent prisms into the room, touching the wall, the jar, her bent head.

"Oh, Jim!" she looked up, clutching the letter, then patted it tenderly straight and handed it back to him. "Oh, the poor—I wouldn't have had it happen for the—"

"Neither would I."

"Had you promised?" she asked.

He nodded. "When I was up there last time," he said. "I came downstairs and found him playing outside, but I'd bumped into

Marie upstairs, and I just wanted to get out of there. Later on, it must have slipped my mind."

He had come down the path, heavy with the unreasoning irritation the house always forced upon him lately, his arms clumsy with the clothes he was carrying, and Jimmie, dropping his ball, had rushed him, butting him in the stomach and uttering one of those comic-book noises that are the Esperanto of eight-year-olds: "Boinng!" Jim had replied feebly, "Playing ball?"

Jimmie had followed him to the car, talking excitedly. Jim had stuffed the clothes hurriedly into the car, promised, and driven away.

"I could have taken him yesterday," Jim said. "I just hung around the hotel. It rained yesterday, though. Didn't it rain yesterday?"

"Yes. But they have it in the Garden."

"Oh, sure," he said. "Sure, that's right."

Last year, Marie and the boy had been in Reno, but the spring before that Jim had taken him for the first time, not to a circus like the cheap-Jack traveling tents of his boyhood but to Madison Square Garden, where the big top was so far up that it was not there at all, and there were no cracks to admit the sky. He had been amused to find how girly the show had grown, but there had still been the all-powerful smell of horse. There had been so many rings in that circus that the most loving gaze could not do them all justice. He had given up, content to watch Jimmie, his head turning like a thatched brown bun, on the rack of delight.

"Call him," Esther said. "Why don't you call him now?"

"What could I say? No, I'll call him tomorrow. I'll think of something." He weighed the letter on his palm. "Besides, he'll be asleep by now." Surely he would be asleep by now, deaf to The World and The Universe, his vigil over. "No. I'll call him tomorrow," Jim said.

She sighed and stood up, looking down at him, her mouth rueful and soft. "Think I'll take a shower," she said. "Unless you want one first."

"No, go ahead."

The bathroom door closed behind her. He reached for his pipe, then chose a cigarette from a table. He turned on a lamp, and the room sprang up, limned and clear. Yes, they would have him come here. Marriage is a small room, too, Jim thought. She does not know that yet. And I have just begun to remember.

When she padded out of the bathroom, flushed and lovely, she had on a housecoat he had never seen. She sat down opposite him for his notice, folding her hands in her lap, childishly hiding her feet under the stiff silk. He lit a cigarette and passed it to her. After a while, she leaned toward him, drew the letter from his fingers, and tucked it out of sight behind the jar of willows. She sat back, her lids lowered, her chin cupped in her hands. Her hair was loose on her shoulders and her face had the vulnerable look this gives to women. So many rings to the show now, he thought. And the loving heart must do each justice.

He knelt and put his head in her lap, kneading his face against her knees. Once, he raised it, as if he heard something waning in the distance. She stretched out a draped arm then, and turned out the lamp. But in the darkness his eyes retained the room in perfect memory, with that finish given only by death. So, in the darkness, he clung to her for a moment not as a lover but as he might cling to some foolish crony who had once been there together with him in the Arcady of the past.

One of the Chosen

⊷ T H E N I G H T before the fall reunion of his college class, Spanner had come home a little ashamed of his easy acceptance of the prod-
ding special invitation over the phone that day from Banks, a man
whose face he could not even remember. For years he had ignored
the printed notices that came to him now and then, even though he
lived in the city where the college was, but this time, Banks had said,
there was to be a private conclave of all the members of the crew
who had won the regatta for the college over twenty years before.
Half reluctant to include himself in the picture of the old grads
redundantly deploying the terrain of dead triumphs, he had found
himself saying that he would come. He had been coxswain of that
crew.

Thinking it over idly in bed later on, in those random images just
before sleep, which carried with them unexpected prickings of realization that lay just below the surface of expressed thought, he had
found himself dwelling, not on the members of the crew, but on all
those odd ones, the campus characters who had existed, hardly
acknowledged, on the penumbra of his own sunlit, multiform activities of those days. Why should he now think suddenly of De
Jong, the spastic, who, jerking and shambling his way one day into
the office of the college literary magazine of which he, Spanner, had
been a staff member, had thrust upon the group there a sheaf of
manuscript, and gargling incomprehensibly, had left before their
gauche heartiness could detain him? The sheaf had contained a
group of poems clearly derivative from the unfashionable Housman,
and therefore unusable, but marked by a discipline of language, a
limpidity, almost a purity of organization—as if in them De Jong had
tried to repudiate his disjointed idiot face, the coarse clayey skin,

377

the wide slobbering mouth, thickened with effort. They had avoided discussing him, until Black, the psychology student, had remarked, with his clinician's air, "I saw him once in Phipps' lecture class, way at the top, you know, in one of those high gallery seats. My God— there he was—twitching away at some lecture of his own—oblivious!" One of the others had sniggered nervously. The talk had passed on, and later that year, because of a lack of copy, one of the poems had been printed after all.

He thought now, with a belated guilt, of the grim separation that must have been De Jong's, and whether there would have been anything that the rest of them, if less swaddled with their own crude successes, could have done. He'd never heard the man mentioned again, or seen a reference to him in the alumni magazine.

Why now, in this context, should he remember George Shipley, the Negro basketball star of their era, certainly handsome enough, with straight, clipped features so completely lacking the prognathous bulges commonly associated with his race that this, no doubt, had some effect on his acceptance on certain levels by the student body. Smiling, quiet, he had often sat near Spanner in the rotunda of the law library; Spanner had heard that he was a professor of law now in one of the good Southern colleges for Negroes. Why, burning now with something like shame, should he remember him at the dances to which he brought always the same prim-faced mulatto girl; why should he see him, wide shoulders bent in the *dégagé* dance fashion of that day, black features impassive, slowly circling with the girl, always in a small radius of their own?

Spanner was fully awake now and, raised up on his elbow, his eyes gradually following the familiar outlines of the furniture as they grew more perceptible in the darkness, he forced himself to probe in the archives of recall for others who, like Shipley, like De Jong, seemed bound together in his memory only by the mark of that rejection by the group, which now, in pitying retrospect, it seemed to him, had he then been less grossly unaware, less young, he, by some friendly overture, might have partially repaired.

There was the Burmese princeling who had lived at International House, who had treated a group of them to several awkwardly accepted dinners at Oriental restaurants of his choosing, whose foreignness and wealth had at first had a certain cachet, but from whom they had shortly retreated in ridicule, in gruff embarrassment at the hand, sliding as silk, the emotional waver of the voice. At that, they had never been sure what he was really—that it hadn't been just a form of Eastern cajolery, or a misbegotten sense of acceptance which had elicited the moist look, the overheated hand. Afterward, when they had met him on campus in a few curt scenes of mis-shapen talk in which it was evident that camaraderie had flown, his gestures had been restrained enough, Lord knows, his eyes suffi-ciently flat and dull, with reserve enough to satisfy the most conven-tional of them.

Of course, there had been that group of those others, pariahs with-out question, who convened always in that little Greek restaurant, the Cosmos, through the door of which they sometimes glanced out at you with the hauteur of tropical birds in a zoo, jangling con-sciously into conversation as you passed, with their tense, dulcet exuberance. Toleration of these had been more than one could expect of boys suffused with their own raw reactions to adulthood, which they covered up with a passionate adherence to the norm, with apprehensive jeerings at the un-average in its lightest forms, so that even displaying too good, too undulate a French accent, in class, was likely to incur for one the horse-laugh from behind. But could they have helped, with some small glow of receptivity, young Schwiller, that model young German from the cleanly swabbed villa in North Jersey, with too little money, background, or ability—too little of everything except a straining, unhumorous will to belong— who, after some covert, abortive incident on a group camping trip, had hanged himself to a tree?

Ah well, Spanner thought, fumbling in the dark for a cigarette, and lighting it in a thankful momentary absorption with the ordi-nary—these had been the extreme cases. But what of the others, less vividly obvious to memory because they had been more usual, or because they had perhaps already achieved their secret dikes of resignation? He remembered, for instance, all the little Jewish boys, with their overexpressive eyes, their thickets of hair whose Egyptian luxuriousness no barber could tame, and most revelatory of all, the forced vying, the self-conscious crackle of their conversation.

As a Jew himself, he had been helped, he knew, by his fair-skinned, freckled, almost "mick" exterior, by the generations of

379

serene cosmopolitan living that were evident, implicit in the atmosphere of his family's sprawling apartment on the park, and frankly, he supposed, by the unrevealing name of Spanner, which his greatgrandfather had brought over from England, and had come by honestly, as far as the family knew. His family had belonged among those lucky Jews, less rare than was commonly realized, who had scarcely felt the flick of injustice expressed socially, much less in any of its harsher forms. Still, despite this, it had been unusual, he knew, to remain so untouched, so free from apprehension of the lurking innuendo, the consciousness of schism—for in addition to his race, he had carried, too, that dark bruise of intellectuality, the bearers of which the group flings ever into the periphery, if it can.

That was where the luck he had had in being coxswain had come in. Because of it, although he had done well, almost brilliantly in his law classes, all his possibly troublesome differences had remained hidden, inconspicuous under the brash intimacy of the training session, under the hearty accolade of his name on the sporting page —because of it he had been hail fellow in the boat house and on the campus—he had been their gallant "little guy." So, he thought, he had ridden through it all in a trance of security which, he realized now, had been given only to the favored few, while all around them, if he and the others had not been so insensible of it, had been the hurts, the twistings, that might have been allayed. The image of the spastic crossed before him again, a distortion to the extreme of that singularity from which many others must have suffered less visibly, from which he himself had been accountably, blessedly safe. He lay back again, and turning, blotted his face against the dispassionate pillow and slept.

The next morning he awoke late. It was Saturday. Taking his coffee at the dining-room table deserted by his wife and children some hours before, he was half-annoyed at the emotionalism of the previous night. "Who the hell do I think I am—Tolstoy?" he thought, wincing. Rejecting the unwonted self-analysis that had preceded sleep, he finished his coffee offhandedly, master of himself once more. He got the car out of the garage and swung slowly down the parkway, thinking that if he delayed his arrival until well after twelve he would miss the worst of the speechifying.

As he approached the college-dominated midtown neighborhood, idling the car slowly along, he passed some of the brownstone houses, shoddier now with the indefinable sag of the rooming house, which had been the glossier fraternity houses of his day. He had heard that many of them, even the wealthier ones which had survived depression times, subsidized to plush draperies and pine paneling by some well-heeled brother, had gone down finally during the war years just past, when the college had become a training center for the Navy. Then, he supposed, those accelerated waves of young men passing through had not only not had time for such amenities, but, trapped together in a more urgent unity, had had no need for the more superficial paradings of Brotherhood.

Although he had had his fair share of indiscriminate rushing during his freshman year, he himself had had no particular desire to join a house, comfortably ensconced, as he had been, in his family's nearby home, already sated with the herded confinement of prep school. In his sophomore year, he remembered, after he had joined the magazine, and it was evident that he would have a place on the varsity crew, the best Jewish fraternity had been very pressing, then annoyed at his tepid refusal, and there had been overtures from one or two of the Christian fraternities whose social position was so solid that they could afford, now and then, to ignore the dividing lines in favor of a man whose campus prominence or money would add lustre to the house, but by this time he had already been focusing on his law career. Still, he thought now, he had always had the comfortable sense of acceptance; he had, for instance, never felt that deep racial unease with the Gentile to which his most apparently assimilated Jewish friends sometimes confessed. To be free from the tortuous doubt, the thin-skinned expectancy of slight—it had helped. He had been lucky.

In front of one of the brownstones not too far from Jefferson Hall, the old residence hall in one of whose rooms the luncheon was to be held, he found a place to park the car, and got out. He hadn't been near here in years; his life was a well-conducted bee-line from suburb to downtown office, and most of his associations were on the East Side anyway. He walked past the familiar architectural hodgepodge of the buildings, noting with pleasure that the rough red cobbles of the walks had been preserved, glancing with disapproval at the new library which had been begun in his time, on the field where they used to play tennis. Half utilitarian, but with reticent touches of bastard Greek on its lean, flat façade, it stretched out, two-dimensional and unassimilable, a compromise of tastes which had led to none. The vulgarization of taste in a place which should have been a repository of the best still had power to shock him; he was pleased at having retained this naïveté, this latent souvenir of youth. Around him and past him, male and female, hurrying or sauntering, or enthusiastically standing still, was that year's crop of imperishable young, on their faces that which the college had not yet vulgarized—the look of horizons that were sure, boundaries that were limitless—the look of the unreconciled.

Already, he twitted himself, he was developing the spots of the returning alumnus. The secret conviction that inwardly, outer decay to the contrary, one had preserved a personal ebullience better than most, the benignant surveying glance with its flavor of *"si la jeunesse savait"*—he had them all. Smiling to himself he turned in at the doorway of Jefferson Hall, and making another turn to the reception room on the right, met the slightly worn facsimiles of his youth full on.

They were gathered around the mantel, most of them, talking in voices at once hearty and tentative, glasses in hand. Drinks to melt the integument of twenty years and more—of course. From the group a man detached himself to come forward and pump his hand.

"Davy! Why, Davy Spanner!" The lost face of Banks coalesced at once in his recognition, fatally undistinguished, except for the insistent, hortatory manner that had battened on the years. He had been business manager of the crew.

Banks conveyed him toward the others like a trophy.

"Look who's here!" he crowed. "Our little coxie!"

Grinning a little stiffly, Spanner acknowledged, not without pleasure, the nickname paternally bestowed on him long ago by these men who had all been so much bigger than he, who had chaffingly, unmaliciously treated him as their mascot perhaps, because of his size, but had unswervingly followed his direction. As a group they were still physically impressive, carrying extra weight fairly well on their long bones.

They gathered around to greet him. With the unfortunate sobriety of the latecomer, he noted, accepting a drink, that they were all, although not yet tipsy, a little relaxed, a trifle suffused, with the larger-than-life voices and gestures of men who had had a few. A table set buffet style in a corner, and a coffee urn, had apparently not yet been touched. Downing his first drink, he took another, and plunged into the babble of expected questions, the "where you been all these years?"—the "what're you doing now?"—the "whereabouts you living?" One by one he remembered them all, even to the little personal tricks and ways they had had in the locker-room. Bates, whose enormous sweaty feet had been a loud joke with them all, was almost completely bald now, as was Goetschius, the polite quiet boy from upstate, who, politely as ever, bent his tonsure over Banks' pictures of his house, his family.

Reassuringly, they all looked pretty good, as he thought he did himself, but he wondered if they knew any better than he did what had impelled them to come. "Horse" Chernowski, who stood nearest him, had driven up from Pennsylvania, beckoned on, Spanner wondered, by what urge to reasseverate the past? In his ill-cut, too thick tweeds, his great shoulders swollen needlessly by shoulder pads, the hocklike wrist bones projecting from the cuffs—his nickname fitted him still. He had been their dumb baby, stronger than any of the others, but dull of reaction; once they had lost a race because of his slowness in going over the side when he had jammed his slide.

"Ah, my God, Davy," said Chernowski delightedly, "do you remember the cops picking us up for speeding after the big day— the night we drove back from Poughkeepsie?"

"Yes. Sure I remember," said Spanner, but he hadn't, until then. From across the room he saw Anderson, the stroke, nursing his drink at the mantel, staring at him ruefully, almost comprehendingly; encountering that blue gaze which had faced him steadily, in the inarticulate intimacy of three years of gruelling practice, faraway incident, and triumph, there was much that he did remember.

Handsome, intelligent son of a family which had contributed both money and achievement to the college for more than one generation, Anderson had more perfectly straddled the continuum of campus approval that stretched between "grind" and "hero" than anyone Spanner had known. Spanner remembered him, effortlessly debonair and assured, burnished hair spotlighted over the satin knee breeches of his costume as Archer in *The Beaux' Stratagem,* or stripped and white-lipped, holding Spanner's gaze with his own as the water seared past the shell. Although he had been as perilously near the prototype of campus hero as one could be without stuffiness or lampoonery, there had never been any of the glib sheen of the fair-haired boy about him, nothing in the just courtesy of his manner except the measurable flow of a certain *noblesse oblige*.

He crossed now to Spanner, and took, rather than shook, Spanner's hand.

"Davy!" he said. "Well, Davy!"

The crisp intonation had the same ease, the ruddy hair had merely faded to tan, the eyes stared down at him now straight as ever, but from between lids with the faint, flawed pink of the steady drinker, and Spanner saw now that there was in his posture the controlled waver, the scarcely perceptible imbalance of the man who is always quietly, competently drunk.

"You look fine, Davy," he said, smiling.

"You look fine too, Bob."

"Sure. Oh sure," he said, with a wry, self-derisive grimace. He indicated with his drink. "Look at us. Everyone looks fine. Householders all. Hard to believe we were the gents who took it full in the belly—depression, social consciousness." His accent was a little slurred now. "And wars and pestilence," he said more firmly. "Even if we were a little late for that." He downed his drink.

"You in the war, Bob?" said Spanner, somewhat lamely.

"Me? Not me," he said. "My kids were. Lost one—over Germany." He walked over to the buffet, poured himself a drink, and was back, swiftly. "Sounds antiquated already, doesn't it? Over Germany. We're back to saying 'in Germany' now." He went on quickly, as if he had a speech in mind that he would hold back if he thought it over.

"Remember the house I used to belong to? 'Bleak House,' they used to call it, sometimes, remember? The one that got into the news in the thirties because they hung a swastika over the door. Or maybe somebody hung it on *them*." He drank again. "Could have been either way," he said.

Spanner nodded. He had begun to be sick of the word "remember"; it seemed as if everyone, including his self of the night before, was intent on poking up through the golden unsplit waters of his youth the sudden sharp fin of some submerged reality, undefined, but about to become clear.

"They were a nice bunch of fellows in our time," said Spanner.

"You know . . . Davy . . ." Anderson said. His voice trailed off. The fellow was apologetic; in his straight blue look there was a hint of guilt, of shame, as if he too, the previous night, had half dreamed and pondered, but unlike Spanner had met the dark occupant of his dreamings face to face.

"I wanted them to take you in," Anderson said. "A few of us together could have pushed it through—but all the others made such a God-damned stink about it, we gave in. I suppose you heard." He looked at Spanner, mistaking the latter's unresponsiveness for accusation perhaps, and went on.

"If we hadn't all been so damned unseeing, so sure of ourselves in those days . . ." He broke off. "Ah well," he said, "that's water over the dam." And grasping Spanner's shoulders, he looked down at him in an unsteady bid for forgiveness, just before he released him with a brotherly slap on the back, and turned away, embarrassed. Standing there, it was as if Spanner felt the flat of it, not between his shoulder blades, but stinging on his suddenly hot cheek—that sharp slap of revelation.

Point of Departure

⋅⋅§ AFTERWARD, LEANING their elbows on the mantel, they lit cigarettes and stared at each other warily. The late afternoon, seeping into the small apartment, pushed back its boundaries, melted them into shadow, intruding into the comfortably trivial box the long finger of space.

They were, she thought, like two people holding on to the opposite ends of a string, each anxious to let go first, or at least soon, without offending the other, yet each reluctant to drop the curling, lapsing bond between them. Always, afterward, there was the sense of a dialectic, a question not concluded; after the blind engulfment the two separate egos collected themselves painfully, slowly donned their bits of protective armor, and maneuvered once more for place.

It would be easy, good, she thought, to talk long and intimately afterward, to meet on close ground, divested of all pretense. But they never want this; they never do. The long, probing conversations that women tried to force upon them, getting closer to the nerve of personality—how they hated them, retreating from them brusquely into silence, sheepishly into the commonplace of the consolatory pat! Or, after the aura of wanting had ebbed, did they too feel a little bereft, bare, in front of the speculative, now disenchanted eyes opposite them; did they too conceal a fumbling need to linger a little longer in the dark recesses of emotion, to examine, to assess what had been separate, had blended, and now was separate again?

Doubting this, she could see him, so quickly, so expertly casual, leaving in a few minutes, gathering up his hat and his briefcase with a delicate assumption of reluctance, exhaling a last relieved whiff of tenderness into her ear. Out of some obscure pride she never went to the door with him; he never remarked on this but always closed the

386

door very gently, like someone leaving a sickroom. She could imagine him standing on the doorstep downstairs, squaring his shoulders and making straight for a bar, eager to immerse himself quickly in the swapping masculine talk of baseball scores and prize fights, blow by blow—all the vicarious jaunty brag that sat upon him as inappropriately as a cockaded paper party hat, but that was indulged in alike, she knew, by the simple male and the clever.

Opposite, already a little absent, he stared at her a trifle wryly, pulling gratefully at his cigarette. Now, he knew, would begin the gentle process of disengagement that he had learned long ago, defensively, to perform so well. Now it would be like a game of gesture in which he excelled, in which it would be as if, smiling the tolerant smile of experience, he divested himself one by one of a series of clinging hands, until he stood again remote, inaccessible, free. Only later, when the warmth and almost all the conquest had worn away, would the slow rise of irritation with self and women begin, then the slight guilt of satiety that would enable the resolve to be made, and finally the shrug and the forgetfulness.

Regretfully, as if taking leave of a landscape that had pleased, he broke his glance from the eyes opposite him, looked down at the hand that lay perhaps intentionally near his on the mantel, curved upward, open. Warned, he had felt all afternoon the too recognizable air of intensity, of special pleading, that had surrounded her; in a woman of less taste it would have taken the form of a dress too tight, or a flock of bows in the hair. Intelligent women stimulated rather than repelled him, if they had the other attraction too; their withdrawals and defenses were heightened by subtleties that it was a challenge to explore and subdue. But in the end it was all the same —gazing up at you afterward with their liquid pained stare, detecting the coil of softness in you that half appreciated, half understood, they all pleaded for an avowal—of what?

The hand on the mantel brushed his, and was withdrawn.

"It's pathetic, isn't it," she whispered, "the spectacle of people trying to reach one another? By any means. Everywhere." There was a rush, a grating of honesty, in her tone that she deprecated immediately with a quick covering smile.

The remark hung too nakedly on the air. He nodded ruefully, and allowing his hand to touch hers for a moment, he stared into their palms, and they stood together for a moment, joined over the body of their failure.

Patting her shoulder in a light rhythm, one, two, three, he grasped her chin tight in his hand and looked down at her for quite a time.

"See you," he said. "Better run for my train." As he took up his hat and briefcase half embarrassedly, leaning against the mantel she was watching him silently, and it was so that he caught the last image of her as he let himself out the door, easing the knob to.

Blinking in the light of the outdoors, which was a lot stronger than one would suspect after that dim apartment of hers, he brought that image with him, but, shielding him, his mind shifted, rioting pleasurably among the warmer images of the early afternoon. All the way down the avenue from the park he carried these with him, until at Forty-second Street, sauntering toward Grand Central, he joined the streams of women carrying their light pastel packages of hose, ribbons, blouses—all the paraphernalia of women at the turn of a season. He was used to seeing them in the train, haggard after the day-long scavenger hunt for the hat to go with the shoes that went with the dress—riding home for the long ritual of unguents that would arm them once more. From his wife, and his sisters before her, he knew it well—the ritual that would transform the kimonoed, the oiled, the bepinned one into the handsome, curled, confident woman waiting at the door, Venus risen triumphant on a shell of empty boxes.

For a while now, out of a sense of the just, the cautious moment, he would be free, but inevitably he would be alert again to the puff of organdie at a throat, a mouth so richly, redly drawn over the scanter curve of lip beneath, a look, plaintive or ripe—the whole froth of femininity that they all put out like entangling scarves. They would be drawn to him too, often out of an awareness of his sensitivity to them, only to be confused by the proffered warmth for warmth of a relationship that ended, not in the conventional brutalities of a rejection they might have understood, but in the firm, knowing refusal to be involved in the abject spiritual surrender which they always ended up by demanding, for which they all longed.

Either they caught you young and eager, as he had been, and—nailed down by their allies, time and habit—incredibly, swiftly, you were a member of the country club, with a mortgage, while across the room, herded together with the others, in their unblushing, blatant discussions of the idiosyncrasies of husbands, they proclaimed your indenture to them—or else, in the byways of *sub rosa* relationships, there too, sooner or later, they strangled calm with their demoniacal need for finality, possession, grown all the stronger because it could not be socially displayed. Perhaps, he thought, it is the riddled period in which we live, in which people are driven endlessly upon one another, hoping to find, in the person of another one of the bewildered, the a priori love, the certainty, the touchstone.

He had reached Grand Central and the long sloping entrance to the suburban trains. Across the way his usual stop-in place beckoned with its promise of a muted jumble of light, noise, and clinking glassware in which feeling could be drowned. Perhaps it is worse for the women, he thought, but they *are* the worst—all of them Penelopes, trying to weave you into the fabric of their lives, building on you in one way or the other until you have to get out from under. Squaring his shoulders, he shifted his briefcase, and walked on toward the sure nepenthe, the comfortable glaze of the bar.

In the apartment, she stood still at the mantel, reluctant to acknowledge the gap in the room, to close it over finally with movement, change. At last she walked over to the sofa and sat down, shrinking into the cushion for its warmth. The room was always like this afterward, like a deserted theatre, and, half actress, half spectator, she sat and mulled over what had gone before, forming, as if into a stylized ballet, the whole interchange of responses that had been their meeting, forestalling, by this means, the sure humming rise of depression.

Her last exclamation, which had been as alienating to him, she knew, as the shock of a cry for help thrust suddenly into the most casual of conversations, had come from the heart, the heart that she knew, by unspoken agreement with him, with all of them perhaps, must always be held behind one. Only among the very young might it be otherwise, possibly . . . before they had acquired the destroying talent for compromise that eased—as it more and more deflated —the drama of experience.

Perhaps, she thought, curvetting so lightly, so "modernly," as we have been taught to do, over the sharp stick of emotion, never daring the banal, the stark word, it is our reticences that trap us after all. It happened everywhere: behind the tidy doors of marriage, in the dark bed of adventure, or in the social bumpings against one another in the crowded rooms where people massed together protectively in frenetic gaiety, hiding stubbornly—"I am alone"—using liquor, music, sex, to say—"You, too?" It happened, sometimes, in rooms at the end of the day, after the scratch of gossip, the long political sighs, were done, and there was a lull, with people staring reflectively into their glasses, twirling the stems, that the lull deepened, a sentence died on the air, and it was as if everyone had plunged his arm into a deep well, searching, seeking—but no hands met and clasped.

She walked into the kitchen and poured herself a drink. Toward her through the window over the sink the stunted city trees stretched in the soft, mottled weather, all along their weak, cramped boughs, the sure, recrudescent leaves. It would be better if it were autumn now, she thought drearily, when people huddling together at concerts, at parties, in front of fires, can persuade themselves that they are huddled there together against the cold.

Tonight there were people coming in to talk. She knew beforehand how she would sit there, in the anodyne of company, cradling the warmth of what had been, while every so often, half savored because it gave a meaning to the hour, half pushed down lest it rise to the surface and become real hurt, there would come, like water washing over a sunken buoy, the little knell of sadness for something that had been, that had never quite been, that now had almost certainly ceased to be.

Letitia, Emeritus

◆§ H O L D I N G T H E small white card so as not to bend it, Letitia
Reynolds Whyte, aged twenty-four, looked cautiously up and down
the main hallway of the school. Only the Senior girls were left in the
school now, and most of them were in their rooms, lying on the beds
in their underwear, talking dreamily of what they were going to do
after graduation, the ones who were not getting married, who were
only going to Europe with their parents, or just back to Locust
Valley, or Silver Spring, or Charleston, listening enviously to the
fluttery, conscious plans of those who were. Through the closed
door of the Green Room down at the end of the hall she heard the
laughter of the girls closeted there, rehearsing the skits for the
Senior Banquet that evening. Tomorrow, hordes of parents would
descend on the school for the graduation exercises, but today, the
empty lawns outside—carefully shaven to a final unusual neatness
that morning by Norval, the gardener—the echoing halls inside, all
had had a hush over them, a left behind hush of desertions and de-
partures, of feverish routines suspended, of another school year gone,
and another deadened summer begun, in which only Miss Sopes—
the Head—the colored cook, and Norval would be left to wait for
fall. And, of course, Letitia.

She looked up and down the hall again. All the teachers' cubbyhole private offices were closed and locked, even the larger one at
the very end, a former parlor, which was rated by "Papa Davis," Professor Walter Wallace Davis, because he was the oldest, the most
distinguished looking, and the only one who was a real professor,
having come to Hyacinth Hall after the close of a career in Latin
and Greek at the State University. Usually, long after the others had
locked up and gone he could be found lingering in the musty brown

391

room with the shabby davenport and the bronze lamp with the purple frosted grapes. "This is my real home, girls. My real home," he would say, leaning forward and smiling expansively, rubbing the grapes with a restless, worrying hand. But today even he had gone home to his palsied sister in their dark old house across the bridge in Minetteville, although he would return tomorrow to address the parents, as he did every year at graduation.

Satisfied that no one was around, Letitia crossed the hall to the large Student Mail box which hung on the wall in its very center. Ordinarily the box was a plain drab, lettered "Hyacinth Hall" in white, a smart, monogram-like inscription which the elder, dead Miss Sopes, *the* Miss Sopes, in some fierce spinsterish urge, thwarted possibly as to bedspreads and guest towels, had always had imprinted on every wastebasket, towel, door, and object that attached to the Hall. This tradition, like every one which stemmed from the mourned competence of her sister, the present tremulous Miss Rosanna had of course carried on.

Today, in accordance with still another tradition, the box was covered, except for the slit for envelopes, with a large, fanned-out frill of stiff white paper, and stuck above it, a fancily inked sign said "Announcements." All week long Senior girls had been surreptitiously seeking out the box and dropping in their white cards, or slips of pink or blue notepaper, when no one was looking. On Banquet night, the box, lifted from its hooks, would be set in the middle of the draped head table where the class officers sat, and after the jerkily rhymed class history had been read and the class prophecies for each girl had sent them all into gales of merriment, the class president, standing solemnly above the box, would dip her hand into it slowly, teasingly, and read off, one by one, the names and announcements of all the girls who were leaving Hyacinth Hall "engaged." Each girl stood, was clapped for, walked forward smiling and reddened to the head table and was handed a long-stemmed rose, which she pinned to her shoulder and wore mincingly the rest of the evening. A girl could not just put any name, or even the name of her "steady" in the box. She had to be really, seriously engaged. Letitia knew, for Senior Banquet, since there were never any boys present, was one of the school functions she was allowed to attend. She had been to two of them already. Tonight's would be the third.

After one more hesitant look around, she bent over the card in her hand, scrutinized it lovingly, tabbing each letter with a slow fore-finger. Some of the girls even got themselves engaged just so they could announce it on Banquet night; just so they would not have to be one of the others barred from the flushed group of those who had been tapped, anointed, by love's mysterious rose. Just a few nights ago, Letitia, leaning pressed against the locked connecting side door of her room, the door which led to Willa Mae Fordyce's room on the other side, but was never opened, had heard Willa pro-claiming to other murmurous visiting voices: "Why I'd count it a disgrace not to announce on Banquet night, really I would. I just wouldn't feel *graduated*, honest!" And Willa had given a low, satis-fied laugh. She had meant it too, for just this morning, Letitia, steal-ing breathlessly into Willa's empty room through the unlocked regu-lar door, had seen the slip readied on Willa's desk. "Engaged. Wilhelmina Mary Fordyce and Homer Watson Ames."

Letitia gave her own card a last admiring look. It was beautifully printed—the best she had ever done. In art class, Miss Tolliver would often pause, leaning over Letitia's shoulder, and knitting to-gether tenderly her gray, mock-fierce eyebrows, she would say, extra-loud: " 'Titia, your copy-work is certainly real nice, dear. Truly lovely." And shaking her head at some imaginary crony in the air, she would make a kind of soft sad sigh and pass on to the desk of the girl in front.

Almost reluctantly, Letitia raised the hand with the card in it, held it poised near the paper frill for a second, then quickly pushed the card through the slit in the box. She heard the slight sound it made, not the sharp tap of paper falling into empty metal, but a slithery rustle which meant that it had fallen on others like it. She gave her flat, tuneless giggle, which always sounded as if it needed finishing, and turning away in the dogged, laborious way she had, she walked down the marble steps, out onto the lawn, and across it to the pretty gabled dormitory on the other side.

From behind, with her pale blond hair swinging over the pink cashmere sweater and the dyed-to-match tweed skirt, with her loafers and pink socks, Letitia looked like any one of a dozen others. Even better groomed, even a little too carefully matched, perhaps—as she had been ever since that day, six years ago, when she had walked into her first class at the school, her mouth, which peaked way up in the center like a baby's, widened in a grin, on her head, perched clumsily there, the glittering gold sequin and seedpearl cap which an inept uncle, knowing her fondness for shiny gauds, had given her for Christmas. Ever since then, Delia, the light-colored upstairs girl, who had seen service as a personal maid on some of the big estates near the school, had been detailed to go to Miss Letitia's room each morning and set out the proper clothes for the weather and the day. Sometimes, if there was a special occasion, although there seldom was, Delia came in the evening, too. In the summer, when Delia worked elsewhere, Miss Rosanna came herself, and would stand there clucking a little to herself, her unassertive manner sharpened with impatience, although once in a while she spent a little extra time handling greedily the beautiful quality underwear and clothes Letitia's family bought and sent down to her, with never any trouble about sizes or ideas, for the girl had stayed the same and looked the same as when she first came.

Even when people saw her from the front, saw the domed childish forehead, the eyes, large with a painful attention, the peaked fledgling mouth always open as if waiting for someone to push into it the blessed worm of enlightenment—even then they were not sure. Feature by feature the face was a pretty one. It was only as people waited covertly for reflection to shadow the eyes, for a self to assemble and animate the face, that the doubt stole over them. The creeping realization began to form only as, shrinking, they became aware of the presence of that same straining of a blocked sense which they felt in the presence of the deaf who leaned to listen, the blind who stretched to feel. But when they heard the light, singsong rote of the voice, the sentence that petered into a laugh, the laugh that was like a pitch-pipe whose single note was query—then they were sure.

Then it was that, at a tea where Mrs. Reese Reynolds Whyte poured, or at a meeting of which she was inevitably chairman, one or the other of the women would purr in the ear of her neighbor: "You've seen that youngest daughter of Gratia Whyte's . . . is she quite . . . ?" and the other would answer: "All right . . . you mean? . . ." covering the words with a disclaiming shrug.

"Borderline?" This, avidly, from the inquirer.

"Well . . . you know Gratia . . ." might come the discreet answer. "She can face up to anything. . . . Look at how they drag the father with them . . . lectures, everywhere!"

It was through the means of Hyacinth Hall that Mrs. Whyte had faced up to Letitia. The Whytes belonged to those quiet rich who managed to imply, by their abstention from show, their endorsement of the proper, noncontroversial causes, such as Poetry and Peace, that wealth could be noble and remain fruitfully in the hands of its rightful inheritors. Summer and winter, their homes had a serene dowdiness possible only to those who could afford to be contemptuous of fashion. Their limousines were the heaviest, but dark, their servants and appurtenances of the most durable best, and none of these was changed too often. Mrs. Whyte had not only "attended" but graduated from one of the severer colleges long before it became commonplace for debutantes to do so, and from the list of benefactions which offered opportunities for conspicuous waste in an altruistic form, she had long since dropped the sponsorship of day nurseries and fallen women, leaving this to the less intellectual members of Society. It was in the poetry leagues and the English-speaking unions that she could be found, and in those spontaneous, pacifist groups of women which were most fervid and vocal just before a war, were as swiftly transmuted into "Bundles for Something" during the war's course, and were once again transformed by victory into Leagues for a Proper Peace. It was related of her, and justly, that she had downed in debate (at a benefit) a Justice of the Supreme Court (retired). Her three daughters before Letitia, had been sent, not to Miss Hewitt's Classes, or various "Halls" in America or Lausanne, but to Radcliffe, Bryn Mawr, and in one case, Oxford, after which, their doughy faces veiled by Venus-nets of trust funds, they had achieved marriage, and settled down to inheriting their mother's committeeships.

Therefore, when Hyacinth Hall, in straits after the death of its founder, had circulated an appeal to "its friends" to rally and save it, it had not been likely that Mrs. Whyte would appear in that category, since the school was superannuated, of a type she deplored, and located beyond the Eastern seaboard, in a part of America in whose pretenses she did not acquiesce. As for Letitia, she had long since been taught at home by elderly women whose need made them tactful, whose chief function was to maintain the tacit assumption that she was being taught at all.

On the very day, however, that Mrs. Whyte received the letter from the Hall in her morning mail, the housekeeper had appeared in her sitting-room, red-faced, almost in tears, with the tale that Miss Letitia was bothering the houseman again.

After the housekeeper had been reassured, halted just short of a bosomy, sisterly commiseration Mrs. Whyte could not have tolerated either as a woman or as an employer, Letitia's mother sat over her dilemma for a long time, contemplating the pitiful mauraudings of her innocent. Then, with one of those masterly inspirations which had made her such a jewel among committeewomen, she had riffled hastily through her correspondence for the letter from the Hall. The school, she recalled, was situated in fox-hunting country; its girls spent a good part of their time in riding clothes. And Letitia could ride, had even appeared unobtrusively, years ago, at one or two shows, in the children's class. She had proved unequal to jumping, or anything fancy; she required a gentle mount, but she loved horses, and she could ride. Her sole other talent, that for "art work," would certainly find a place in the rudimentary classes of such a school, or else one of those special arrangements, of which she had already had so many in her life, could always be made. And what better place for protection, for segregation without emphasis, than a girls' school, especially one where, its highest aim being to equip its young ladies with all the attractions and accoutrements of the belle, the value of protection was understood better than any other?

Therefore, on the list of the influential few who had rallied to the support of the Hall, none had rallied harder than Mrs. Whyte. And at the end of that summer six years before, the newspaper of the little Hudson River town where the Whytes had their bracketed gothic summer place, had reported: "Mr. and Mrs. Reese Reynolds Whyte and their daughter, Miss Letitia Reynolds Whyte, have left for an extended motor tour of the South, their destination Hyacinth Hall, the well-known finishing school, where Miss Whyte will enroll as an art student. Accompanying them is their house guest, Dame Alice Mellish, formerly honored by His Majesty, the King of England, for her studies in Anglo-American semantics."

It had been a queer entourage which had descended upon the

school in those last deciduous days of summer. The few teachers and students already there, waiting out the close, inert days before the beginning of the term, were energized and impressed by the visitors, whose confident eccentricity had as surely betokened superiority. Flanked by Mrs. Whyte, a type instantly recognizable and acceptable, and by Dame Alice, whose skirts were uneven to the point of vagary, but whose title had preceded her through the school like an odor, had come Letitia, not so instantly recognizable, but soon to be. And wheeled out, in dark finale, from the capacious back of the car, had come the chair bearing Mr. Whyte, a beautifully groomed old man in lawyer's black and a stiff collar, his very clean hands nerveless on his knees, the fixed upward twist of one side of his mouth lending him a demeanor of unchangeable pleasure. He did not talk, and apparently could not, but his lack, appearing at the end of life rather than at the beginning, was an honorable one which needed not to be hidden, and he was wheeled in and out of every conversation. From time to time, the chauffeur who attended him leaned over and removed or replaced the silky black beaver hat on the silver head at the proper intervals, and this, seeming to be done according to some prescribed rhythm of etiquette, not only lent the old man a verisimilitude of activity, but created, also, an atmosphere of the most recherché good taste. And when Mrs. Whyte, pointing her arches carefully before her, trailing the confused and conquered Miss Rosanna behind her, had clacked down the marble steps of the main building, she had sailed right up to the wheel chair, which had not attempted the steps, as to a reviewing stand, and with nods and becks and the most wreathed of smiles, had apparently recounted the whole transaction to the unchangeable benevolence of Father.

The Whytes did not stay the night at the school. They departed that same evening, leaving behind them a legend, that had faded, and Letitia, who had stayed the same.

So it was that Letitia, entering her hot, still room on this particular day, entered the only permanent room in the dormitory, a room from which she yearned, each expectant June, to be delivered, and to which she was, each disappointed June, remanded. Most of the other rooms had a littered, bird-of-passage look which suggested that the girl in each was only sojourning on her way to wider fields which Letitia, while she craved them, could not have described. Letitia's room, however, had the same supervised neatness as her person, and with its pictures of her family hanging on the wall in circular silver frames, its chiming clock near the bed, and its large calendar with the block numbers marked off crosswise, looked as if it had long ago made its concessions to forever. During one or two of the early years, the accident of a friendly girl neighbor next door had permitted the unlocking of the connecting door between the rooms, as was done everywhere else in the school, but with the coming of Willa Mae, all this had changed, and little by little, Letitia's almost tolerated, almost earned place in the humming, cozy undercurrents of the dormitory, had slipped away.

"Honestly, Mum," Willa had reported at home, "it would give you the creeps! Really it would!" And at the very next Parents' Day, Mrs. Fordyce, not having trusted herself among the delicacies of correspondence, had actually broached the subject, gaspingly, to Miss Rosanna, but had found her, under her cloud of faltering re-assurances, unexpectedly immovable. For the special arrangement for Letitia was large.

Nevertheless, the last four years had come to have a painful weight of their own, had come to be known, in her sharded thoughts, as "the locked-door years." But now, as she closed the door behind her, excitement twitched at her mouth, gave almost a complexity to the clear glass of her eyes. For a minute she stood in the room like a stranger to it, as if waiting for someone to tell her what to do next. Then she went to the dresser and pulled out a drawer. Behind a pile of tailored slips, all alike, which she moved to one side with patient tidiness, she found what she wanted. With a crow of pleasure, she drew out the sequinned cap and held it in her hand. Straightening up, she walked over to the window, hung the cap on the hooked ornament at the end of the window-shade cord, and stood there dazzled, watching it.

Until now, there had been no occasion important enough for it since the fiasco of its first wearing. Early in her first year at the school Letitia had been permitted to attend the initial one of the highly chaperoned dances which occurred there several times a year in co-operation with a nearby military academy. Halfway through the evening, an affrighted young man, flying incontinently from the coat room, and an incredulous wave of gossip, rippling through the dancers, had made it all too apparent that either Mrs. Whyte's strictures to Miss Rosanna had been too reserved, or Miss Rosanna's interpretation of them insufficiently literal. Ever since then, on such evenings, Letitia, accompanied by Delia, had been sent to the movies in Minetteville, where they stayed right through the double feature, and often even sat over a sundae at Whalen's afterwards, although Delia, admitted there in her capacity as duenna, never ate anything, but sat stiffly, referring quietly from time to time to the watch the Whytes had sent her after the first year.

Now, twisting and turning with a purposeful motion of its own, the cap dangled and reversed itself, glittering in the sun. A prism of light, deflected from it, kindled the silver frames of the pictures, where they hung on the wall, disregarded by Letitia's glance, as their originals hung, neglected, in the dusty galleries of her remembrance. Twice a year she saw her family briefly, but so briefly, so remotely across the hedge to another world, that they had all but receded into symbols of that larger existence into which one was accepted, to which one acceded only after the mystical rite of graduation.

All the signposts, all the clues, had brought Letitia around to this conclusion, and helped by circumstance, to her contrivance for escape. On the door of Papa Davis' office, a yellowed card, pinned to the aged door frame, said in gothicked lettering: "Walter Wallace Davis. Professor, Emeritus," and only yesterday, straying in there in answer to his eager, scooping glance, she had stopped to peer closer, almost professionally, at the lettering on the card, and with a delaying finger on the last queer word, had asked its meaning. Papa Davis had risen from his armchair and bent closer to her over the card, as if he too had had to ponder its meaning. Then, tossing back his head so that she had seen the waggle-tuft of beard on his chin pointing straight out, he had laughed in his neighing voice.

"Graduated!" he had said, smiling at her, nodding like a pendulum. "It means 'graduated,' " he had added, frowning. "Leaving a place forever." In the silence that fell between them he had kept on speculatively nodding. He had stretched an arm past her, then, to grasp the door, had leaned out to stare fretfully up and down the empty corridor, and stepping back into the room, had softly closed the door and locked it.

Even when he had come closer, very close, she had been unalarmed. Each year the school put on a Roman Festival, and Papa Davis had been present at rehearsals to hear the Latin declamations, and pass on the authenticity of the home-draped togas. If she had seen the girls exploding into silent laughter in a corner, if she had heard one whispering to another "Papa Davis has to feel you to see if you're Roman!" it had meant to her, perhaps, one more cryptic notion of authority, or perhaps nothing at all. And so, if at first she had watched his overtures with a docility heightened only with curiosity, then later she had received them with eager warmth, even though he was nothing like the young men to whom she had once put out a questing hand. For the force of his words, just said, hung around him like a clue, a means to an end. Then, too, she had heard him say so often in his peevish, solitary voice, that the school was his real, his only home, and this, interpreted as a complaint, had harped on a reality she understood, which made them kin. And finally, gazing up at him from the cracked leather davenport, she had seen that, with his avid lip drawn back over the long yellow teeth, he had looked unintimidating, familiar, like an old, begging horse.

Now she lifted the cap away from the window, twirled it several times over in her fingers, and walked over to the mirror. With a single uncalculated movement she put the cap on her head and looked into the mirror with a pleased smile. Then she walked over to her desk. Strewn over its surface were a number of small white cards, discarded trial copies of that final, faultless one she had put in the school mail-box.

Still holding the sparkling cap awkwardly to her head with one hand, she bent over the desk and picked up one of the cards. Beautifully printed and shaded in India ink, it seemed unmarred, and in truth, working delightedly all that morning over her inscriptions, she had been almost reluctant to settle on one as perfect enough for her vivid purpose. She had copied the first word secretly from the slip on Willa Mae's desk. Her own name she knew how to do. The last of the legend she had transcribed lovingly from the yellowed card rifled from Professor Davis' office door. Only, here, with this last, making a single change which for her amounted to an act of creation, almost of intelligence, she had inverted the sequence, so that the little card she held in her hand now, copy of that still more perfect one she had slipped into the box, read:

"Engaged. Professor Walter Wallace Davis. And Letitia Reynolds Whyte, Emeritus."

The Seacoast of Bohemia

₰ THROUGH THE carnival loops of the beginning of the bridge the cars, shining suddenly, crept slowly on their way to Manhattan. Back of their packed lines, the dark smear of Jersey, pricked with itinerant sparkles, gained mystery as it was left behind, but never enough to challenge the great swag of coastline that hung on the blackness opposite.

In front of Sam Boardman's car the lines inched forward and stopped.

"Look at that!" he said. He leaned on his motionless wheel and stared south. "Will you look at that!"

Bee's nearer earring, tiny, hard and excellent, flexed with light.

"There she is," he said. "Just past your earring. One of the wonders of the world. If I live to be a hundred, I'll never get tired of it."

Or of knowing I have a piece of it, he thought. The city was his hero, the only one he had ever had or would have. Born into it, funneled through its schools and its cynical, enchanting streets, he was still as tranced by it as all the boys and girls from out of town who ate it up with their eyes and hearts and were themselves eaten in the hunt for a piece of it. There it was, he thought, the seacoast of Bohemia, moving always a little forward as you went toward it, so that even now, when he saw his listing in the telephone directory, *Samuel Boardman atty 351 5 Av, Residence 75 Cent Pk W*, he could hardly believe that he was an accredited citizen of the mirage.

"Give thanks you don't have to look at it from Englewood," she said. She lit a cigarette and blew vigorously on her furs. "How Irv and Dolly—of all people. . . ."

Because of the kids, he thought, as they moved forward a few feet. We know damn well it was because of the kids. All the New

401

Yorkers who grew up there as tough as weeds were convincing themselves that their children couldn't have sound teeth or sound psyches
unless they moved them to the country. Perhaps it was the last
gesture, the final axing of the cocktail hour and the theater-ticket
agency, by those who didn't want to stay in town unless they could
go on being on the town. Or perhaps it *was* decentralization—not of
cities, but the last, the final decentralization—of the ego. At least
they said it was because of the kids, and you didn't say this aloud to
a woman who had been trying to have one for ten years. You took
pleasure, instead, in the quietly serviced apartment with the ex-
pansible dining nook and the contractible servant; and you were
careful to voice this on occasion, perhaps at the little evening ritual
when you were proffered the faultless drink from the crumbless
table, and you reached around to pat the behind, flat as a ghost's, of
the woman who had not let herself go.

Ahead of him, the lines melted slightly; he eased into a better lane
and picked up some speed as they neared the city side. Through the
surge of Irv's after-dinner highballs, he shied away from the image
of Bee, her platformed shoes tucked stiffly to one side on the toy-
strewn rug, her blond wool lap held politely defenseless against the
sticky advances of Irv's twins. After all, there was a certain phoni-
ness in the people who tweeded up and donned couturier brogues
just because they were visiting the country; Bee's bravura Saturday
night chic was more honest. And she had patted the twins' round
fists and held on to them, if a little away from the lap, and had referred to herself as Aunt Bee.

"Talk about wonders," she said. "To see Irv and Dolly Miller
knee-deep in paint and dirt is one of them. Two months out of Sutton Place. And that gem of an apartment."

"You realize they're the fourth in a year?" he said. "The Kauf-
mans, in Stamford. Bill and Chick, in Roslyn. And the Baileys, in
Pound Ridge."

"Oh, it's the same difference," she said. "A perpetual stew of wall-
papering."

He slowed up for the traffic on the New York side. It was true, he
thought; it was about the same difference. Country coy, all of
them, as soon as they hit a mortgage—they made a morality of
acreage and a virtue of inconvenience. In Stamford and Roslyn the
"doing it over" might be less obsessively home-grown, perhaps, and
at the Baileys' there would be brandy instead of highballs after din-

ner—the glasses thinning appropriately with the neighborhoods, all along the way.

Even in the city though, the conversations of their friends were more and more loaded with the impedimenta of the parent. "That's just like my Bobby" and "If you can just remember it's a phase" floated above the bridge tables, and when the men coagulated in a corner afterward, even there, the inverted boasting of the successful male was likely to be expressed in terms of what it had been necessary to pay the orthodontist. When he and Bee met downtown for dinner these days, it was more and more often in a foursome with some couple older than they, some pair admiringly ticked off by others as "so devoted to one another" or "very close"—with only the faintest of innuendoes that this might be because there had been nothing else to come between.

Of a sudden, he turned away from the entrance to the express highway and wheeled up the entrance marked LOCAL TRAFFIC.

"Aren't you going down the highway?"

"Just thought I'd like to go by the old neighborhood."

In front of them, Broadway jigged like a peddler's market. Tonight, Saturday, it would be streaming with the hot, seeking current of young couples walking hand in hand, as Bee and he had once done, picking their futures on the cheap from the glassed-in cornucopias of the stores. He felt an immediate throb of intimacy with these buildings, their fronts pocked with bright store-cubicles, their gray, nameless stone comfortably sooted over with living. From the ocher and malachite entrance of the building where Bee and he lived now, one walked, every pore revealed, into a fluorescent sea of light tolerable only to those who had in some manner arrived—the man jingling pocket change he would never dream of counting, the woman swinging lightly from her shoulders the stole of success. Most of the houses here would have small, bleared hallways with an alcove under the stairs, and on each of the five or six flights above there would be a landing where a boy and a girl, scuffling apart or leaning together, could smell, from their paint-rank corner, the indescribable attar of what might be.

He touched the hydromatic foot pedal as they reached a stop light.

"Not bad for a couple of kids from around here," he said, slapping his free hand on the duvetyn seat.

"Not bad." She smiled up at him eagerly, two lines on either side of her mouth slightly frogging her cheeks. Her almost gross hunger for compliment always touched him nevertheless; she seemed to need to amass his every approving remark—either personal or marginal—as evidence that their life together was what he wanted it to be. He watched her as she looked out the window and squinted slightly for lack of the glasses she would never wear except at home. If you had put the Bee of tonight in a red dress with too much braid on it and had substituted a hairdresser's springy weekend curls for her present casually planed coiffure, she would be very like the girl who had ridden uptown from City College with him, with whom he had walked these streets on countless Saturday nights. Still, with the years, a woman had a choice of either spreading or withering, and behind her quick, compulsive smile he sometimes caught a glimpse of what she might be at fifty. It was less frightening to see only age in the face of someone you loved, than to see the kind of aging it could be. He saw her at fifty—one of those women like shrunken nymphs, all slenderness and simulacrum from the rear, who, turning, met your glance with faces like crushed valentines.

"Where on earth are you going?" she asked.

They had left the vivid, delicatessen reek of the main street, and were traveling slowly down a street that dead-ended on the Harlem River. He stopped the car on a street with a few furtive secondhand stores on the west and a murky fuzz of unregenerated park on the east. None of it had changed with the years.

"There's High Bridge," he said. "And there's the water tower." He was only half aware of her moving sharply to the far end of the seat.

He could just see the water tower, a dun cylinder that had never been much more than a neighborhood mark in the city's proliferating stone. There it was though, a dingy minaret above the brush of the park. Any one of a number of paths led to its base, at the foot of which Bee and he had slept together one night, the first time for each, the only time before they had married. He could scarcely remember the innocence of that urban hedgerow lovemaking. Its details were lost forever, buried under hundreds of superimposed nights in bed. What he remembered was the imperative sense of "now," which had been shuffled off somewhere along the way. And he remembered the city, assisting like a third presence—the river steaming softly behind them in the mosquito-bitten night, and the occasional start of the tugs.

It was early November now, but the air had a delayed softness, the doomed, uneasy gentleness of fall. He put a hand on her lap and found her gloved hand.

"Want to take a walk?"

"No."

"Just for a minute. There's an entrance down there."

"Don't be silly."

"Come on."

"Sam . . . you tight?"

"Look," he said, "I meant a *walk*." He pressed her glove back on her lap and left it there.

Two capped men passed by, looking sideways at the car from vaguely identical foreign faces, and continued down the block, their feet slapping echoes on the dead street.

She watched them through her window, huddling into her furs. "I want to go home."

"You didn't used to be afraid of—neighborhoods," he said.

She sat still for a minute. "Took you twelve years. To throw that at me."

"Oh, look," he said, "I just want to talk to you. Before we get back to that damned apartment."

"I thought you liked the apartment."

"We're not so old we always have to be—inside places," he said.

"God in heaven. Is this what comes of going to Englewood?"

He pulled out a cigarette and pressed the lighter on the dash. Through the windshield, as he leaned forward, he could sense the special outdoors of the city, its compound of peculiar, incessant harvestings from parks muted with dust and pavements oscillating with power.

He lit the cigarette. "I spoke to that woman in Tennessee yesterday. The agency woman."

"You called Tennessee!"

"I figured, cut through the red tape. Look, Bee—we've had all the pictures and stuff. She can come in two weeks. She can bring either the four-month-old girl, or the nine months boy."

"But I told you I wouldn't . . . not from down there. It isn't safe!"

"What's *safe?*" he said. "Ten years ago it was the war. Before that —the depression. But the streets are still full of them."

"That happens to be a different thing." She averted her chin, in a way familiar to him. For the first time, he noted how familiar it was.

"It's no one's fault we had to rule that out," he said gently.

"You can cut the chivalry," she said. "And start the car."

"Ahhh . . . damn," he said.

"Sam—"

"Look," he said, "are we people who want a kid, or—or comparison shoppers? We've gone along on all the proper lists in town for three years, and every year older we go down the list—not up. We're thirty-six years old. We need one now—before it has to wheel us around."

She sat up straight. "Need? Or want?"

"Take your choice," he muttered.

"Maybe I will," she said. "But not from the Ozarks."

He started the car then, and they swept away from the curb in a dangerous arc and an ooze of gas, only to be stopped at the next corner by a red light.

"For your information," he said, "they're all born without shoes."

He let her out in silence at their entrance, drove the car to the garage off Amsterdam, and slowly walked his way back. Even now, he was excited, as he never failed to be by those violent shifts of neighborhood which succeeded one another without warning everywhere in the city. Instruction lurked these streets, and in the end, evaded.

As he walked into his own building, he turned down the collar of his coat. The place was a decorator's cave, so effectively contrived to deny the elements that not to cooperate seemed coarse. Like the apartment upstairs, to which Bee gave so much concentration, it made cunning use of all the sensuous affirmations of safety. In front of the elevator, which was actually self-service, a uniformed attendant lounged nevertheless, reduced to the level of that accessory given to people who had everything. Above the man's head a SHELTER sign pointed, like a rude thumb.

He let himself into the apartment. In the long living room whose every possession schemed toward its perfect one—a casement fram-

406

ing Central Park—a few lamps glowed, but not too many, and the table in the bay held a plate of sandwiches, glasses, a decanter, a bottle of beer and an opener, as if Bee were saying to him: "This is my talent . . . don't despise it . . . don't be angry." Long draperies, in a nervous pattern of darts and runs that he had once dubbed "thrills and chills," and thereafter always referred to thus, had been slid across the window. People like themselves had so many pet names for things, so many terrible mutual coynesses. He pulled the draperies back. There it was—the diorama that never switched off. As he took off his coat, still looking at it, the hem caught the beer bottle, which slipped to the rug unbroken. Bending to pick it up from the soft pile, he saw that the bedroom door was open a crack, shedding light into the hall off the far end of the room.

"Bee. Come in here."

She came in, almost at once. With her, to be caught disheveled was to be caught out; even when ill, she managed it with patient artistry, covering up, under a feverish flow of perfumes and bed-jackets, the less savory fevers of the body. Now, in her pink robe, she looked as if she had put their quarrel under a hot shower, and had powdered over it. She picked up his hat and coat from the sofa where he had tossed them and hung them away in the quilted closet. He watched her until she came and sat down across the table from him, as they had sat together in the oval of thousands of evenings.

"O.K.," he said. "Now we're—inside."

They sat on, in silence.

"You going to make me do it all, Bee?" he said.

"I want you just to see that woman," he said. "See those kids. I'll get her to bring both, if you want. I'll get Parker to check them, test them." His voice trailed off.

"God in heaven!" he said. "It's not usually the *man*. . . ."

She got up from the table then and leaned against the window, her back to him.

"So it's a risk," he said. "Look out there. The whole world has a shelter sign on it. It always has. Some kind of a one.

"Bee." He went over to her and put an arm around her. "It's why people have kids." He rocked her gently back and forth. "Their own gamble."

"But it wouldn't be ours!" she said, and stiffened away from him. "It would never be ours!"

His arm, still on the shape of her, dropped to his side.

"Sit with them in the park sometime," she said. "All those women. Like I do with Lil. They lean over the carriage and say, 'Who does it take after?' And I wouldn't know."

In the black and gold pane, her image, vague and beveled, looked back at him. "I'd get to love it—and all the time I'd be thinking . . . where's the woman who had it . . . who's the father? Even if we knew.

"Sure I'd love it," she said, "but I'd always be *watching* it. Because it wasn't mine."

"Turn around," he said. *"Turn around."*

She turned.

"Those lists," he said. "All those lists!"

She put out her hand, a short wheedling distance.

"Suppose we'd gotten to the top of one of those?" he said.

"You want the truth?"

He looked at her face unrefracted by glass. "If you happen to have some with you."

Under the rosy cast of the lamps and her robe, the tears that immediately crumpled her eyes would be pink too, if he neared them. "I kept telling myself I could—that it would all iron out . . . when I got there."

She reached into the pocket of the robe. It would be there—the handkerchief. It was there. "When you know you can't handle something—isn't it better to know beforehand?"

"Sure," he said, "if you only want what you're sure you can handle."

"All right then. I'm sorry. Then I'm not big enough." She put the handkerchief to her mouth. "Either way!" she said, and ran past him to the bedroom door. He watched her turn there.

"Sam. It's not as if we weren't close. Closer than most people."

He looked at her, across the aisle of wood and leather and arranged cloth that was hers. "Give us time," he said. "A few years—and nobody'll be able to tell us apart. Just give us time."

In the interval before the door closed there was no shading, nothing, between him and what he saw. Not even air.

After a time, he opened the door and walked down the hall. As he stood there, he could hear the tub running in the bathroom off the bedroom. Her remedy for everything, he thought. A washing away. A change of clothes, a lift of heart. His eyes felt hot. What had she done, what had she managed, all these years?

Stop it, he thought. It wasn't so. Even without the endless roster of doctors, he knew that it wasn't. If he was tempted to believe anything of her now, it was only because up to now he had believed everything. There was a raw, terminal sadness in it for them both, in that she had had to be the one to point out to him what her real limits were. And she had not so much concealed these as, briefly and pitiably, risen to an awareness of them—as a marionette might, for one extraordinary instant, see the strings that held it and achieve, in that same mourning instant, the moment when it stood alone.

He walked into the dining nook and poured himself a stiff drink from a cellarette in a corner. Carrying the drink with him, he walked the length of the living room, turning out lamps as he went. With each lamp that went out the city advanced toward him, until, with the last, it stood in the room—a presence—brilliant, and third.

He drank, watching it. It neither extorted nor gave. It was one of the wonders of the world, and had merely to be there. If its Bohemia had, after all, no seacoasts, this would hardly be noticed now, in a world that had all but deserted the horizontal laziness of ships. One could hanker there all one's days and hardly notice that the piece of it earned had come out of oneself.

It was a vertical place for people like them, in which the only way out was up. He watched the two of them, a couple named Sam and Bee, climbing from tower to tower, in a gilt-edged monkeydom of closeness, to the spheric music of the brandy glasses that would get thinner along the climb.

He drank, watching them. Opposite him, against a sky humbled to a perpetual nude, the towers waited, like slowly fizzing rockets that never went out—or soared away.

Mrs. Fay Dines on Zebra

◄§ ARIETTA MINOT FAY, at thirty-seven, still lived in the house in which she, her father and all their known male forebears but the first had been born, a white, Hudson River–bracketed house, much winged and gabled but with a Revolutionary cottage at its core, set in a tiny village, once only a road, on the west shore of the Hudson River, about twenty-five miles from New York. Arietta's first forebear, Yves Minot, had come to the States in the entourage of Lafayette (some said as a body-servant, although this had never been proved) and had managed to stay near the general's person throughout all the general's campaigns except Valley Forge. In 1779, when the general had gone back briefly to France, Yves had stayed behind, first to marry one of the local Dutch girls (receiving the cottage and a large parcel of land as her dowry) and later to leave her at home while he ventured into battle or other forays, whenever he was so minded. In 1824, when Lafayette returned to America for a final visit, Yves was still there, flourishing in all but sons (because of land inheritance, the Minot line usually ran carefully to one) and had accompanied the general on his famous triumphal tour, again in some capacity typical of the Minots, something unidentifiable, profitable and without a doubt enjoyable.

Arietta, if asked to hazard a guess as to what this might have been, usually replied, with the family talent for presenting itself accurately, that Yves's function probably had something to do with a cap and bells. For, all the Minots took for granted what they had been, were, and hoped to go on being. They were jesters, *fonctionnaires* attending the private person only, quartermasters supplying the ego, minor affections and spirits of those who were rich enough to keep living standards equal to their own *bon viveur* tastes, had the intelligence to relish the thrusts of which they were wisely capable, and above all were important enough to enable the Minots to admire them. This was the Minot vanity and their backbone through the years: that managing always to attach themselves to the most honorable patrons, they had meanwhile restricted their own knavish tricks to the surface diablerie required of their profession— that is, to entertainment only. Beneath the skin they were not knaves, beyond a certain French clarity as to the main chance, which in turn had instructed them that a supernormal honesty, shrewdly displayed, was invaluable to him who lived on perquisites.

For no Minot had ever had a salary, or had gone, as phrase is, "to work." Every male Minot had attended a university as a matter of course, to be refined for his trade, and occasionally to pick up there some symbiotic relationship that had lasted him for life. Arietta's father, of the first generation to have no sons, had done his best by sending her to Vassar, where three members of the Rensselaer (an old dining-club of which he was secretary) had sent their girls that same year—the three men representing respectively money with family, money with politics, and—since the Minots had had to lower their standards along with the rest of the world, though belatedly— money with money. For until her father's time—and he, poor man, was in no way responsible for the monstrous change in the world— all had gone marvelously well with the Minots in both comfort and reputation. And deservedly, for all had worked hard. Although their perquisites had often been extraordinarily vague, ranging from small properties given them to manage and subsequently inherited either in part or in toto, from careers as retainers (they retained so gracefully) or as incumbents of benefices that never had to be explained to them or by them, all the way down to the latter-day vulgarities of stockmarket tips—no Minot had ever boondoggled at the earning of what he received. Until well past the First World War, one could imagine two important men murmuring of a third, as in another context they might mention that his chef was the great-nephew of Brillat-Savarin—"Lucky man, he has a Minot."

Even in the non-Venetian world of post-'29, the world that had begun to be so hard on those useful types for which there never seemed to be any but foreign names: the *cavalière servante*, the *fidus Achates*, the *condottiere*, the . . . Minot—the family had still managed, amiably using its talents where there was still scope for them, but for the first time dangerously using its resources when there was not. Over a hundred years in this country had weakened their French pith, making them less antipathetic than they should have been to eating their capital and selling their land. Marrying by inclination had been an even earlier symptom to appear, but here perhaps they had been lucky, for like so many reared nobly, their inclinations had always been a little bit coarse—and this had kept the line remarkably healthy. This meant that Arietta, when she came on the market, did so from a long line of non-idiots, non-hemophiliacs with a minimum life-expectancy of eighty. It also meant that, with one thing and another, she hadn't much expectancy of anything else except the uses to which she might put her share of Minot temperament—that merriment spiked with truth-telling, suppleness just short of servility, and love of ease combined with a wonderfully circuitous energy for pursuing it. Like so many of her ancestors, Arietta was willing to burn any number of ergs in the process, as long as neither dishonor nor the usual channels of attainment were involved.

On this particular summer Saturday evening at about seven o'clock, Arietta, dressed to go out in her one still respectable cocktail dress, sat in the dimming upstairs parlor of the house that had been hers since the death a year ago, within a few months of each other, of her father and her husband, and gazed out on the river, musing, moodily for her, on the narrow area of play offered that temperament by the modern world. Saturday was shopping day for the week, and this morning, hold back as she might on things like paper napkins—they would use the linen ones—she had not been able to avoid spending eighteen dollars on food. Her nine-year-old son Roger, away for the night at a friend's house, would consume that almost unaided during the school week. One of the sweet-voiced robot-ladies from the telephone company had phoned twice during the past few days, and even the Light & Power, usually so kindly, had begun to press her about last winter's heating bill. This week, to the bewilderment of her friends, she had taken to answering the phone in French, ready to aver that "Madame" was away. There had been no cleaning-woman for a year. Behind her, the rooms, receding wing on wing into the hillside with the depressed elegance of a miniature château, showed, besides the distinguished stainings of a hundred and fifty years, the thin, gradual grime of amateur care. The house, free and clear for a century until the thirties, was hers thanks to her father's single quirk of hereditary thrift, hidden from them until the otherwise worthless will was read—mortgage insurance. It was worth about twenty thousand dollars, possibly a little more to one of that new race of antiquarians who had debouched upon these hills aching to "restore" some old place electrically, and able to—viz. the Lampeys, where she was going that evening. But its sale, if she could bring herself to sell, would be slow. Here she sat in it then, in the richest country in the world. In addition to the house, she had a few marketable "old pieces," small ones to be culled from among the massive bedsteads and armoires, but nothing on which to rear a nine-year-old boy. She was sitting at Great-grandmother Marie-Claire's tambour desk; Roger could eat it in two months. She had the pawn tickets for Marie-Claire's rose-diamonds, and for Marie-Claire's daughter-in-law's epergne. And she had $126.35 in the bank.

And in addition she had, of course, herself. It had been her only dowry, and until some six months ago she had never seriously attempted to draw upon it. "What a pity," her golden-haired Uncle Victor—elder brother of her father and the last successful one of his generation—had remarked of her when she was eight, what a pity that Arietta wasn't male, for she seemed to have all the Minot talents, including a marked facial resemblance to the founder of the line. Victor had died, from an overdose of his patron's pheasant and Lafitte, at the minimal age of eighty, spared from knowing that it was even more of a pity that she wasn't a nineteenth-century male. But here she was, and she was neither. The room where she sat now was the *petit salon* that held the conglomeration of family pictures, and without turning to look at that descending gallery of honorable rogues, she could trace in them not only the decline of the private patron—of which all the world was aware—but of his factotum—small, tragic, subdominant theme that the world had ignored.

Above the mantel was Yves, done on ivory, full-length too, which was unusual for the medium. Legend had it that he had insisted on this because, knee-breeched to the end of his life, he had declared a man to be incomplete without a show of calf; certainly their japing angle went with the face above. It was a triangular face in which all the lines went up, a minstrel face whose nose, long for its tilt, must have moved, as hers did, with speech. The enamelist had even managed to indicate in *couleur-de-rose* those same crab-apple bumps of cheek she had when she smiled. Next to him was the Dutch wife, shown in conventional oval to the waist, of which there was much, a great blonde, serene in all but her stays. Beneath the two, depending on lengths of velvet ribbon in the tree of life, were their heirs direct and collateral, daguerreotype to Brownie, spilling from the mantel to the side walls. As a curious phenomenon, one could see one or the other of the two progenitors always recurring, often with such fidelity that there had long been family slang for the two types—"the beefies" for the Dutch ones, and *"les maigres"* for those *mince* creatures who were true Minots. Although there had been no intermarrying, one type had usually managed to marry the other, and his children tended to be his opposites as well.

Yes, it is all very interesting, thought Arietta—we are a fascinating lot, rather like the green and yellow peas in Mendel—and her father had often dined out on that story. In time, if there was time, she might dine out on it too. Meanwhile, brooding on the three pictures between Yves and the wedding portrait of herself and Carolingus Fay, deceased, she traced a history much more in Gibbon's line.

Beneath Yves came his Claude, a "beefy," of whom it might have been said (as Henry Adams had said of himself) that "as far as he had a function in life, it was as a stable-companion to statesmen, whether they liked it or not." In Claude's case they had. Next came Louis, her grandfather, who had switched to railroad barons— a light sprig of a man who had passed on, full in years and benefices, while accompanying home the equally aged body of his baron, on the Union Pacific somewhere between Ogden and Omaha, in a private car. Under him, in the sepia gloss of the eighties, were his sons, beefies again: her father in his teens, in the deerstalker's cap so prophetic of his later years, and Victor, already a man with a beautiful Flemish jowl. Victor had already been with "munitions" at the time. At the minimal age of eighty he had died (her father used to joke) not of pheasant but of pique, because his patron's son, seduced by the increasingly corporate air of Delaware, had entered Victor's exquisitely intangible services on a tax sheet, had actually tried to incorporate *him*. If so, it had still been death in the high style, and of it. But with her father, the long descent, gradual as the grime on her bric-a-brac, was clear. He had still had the hereditary talent, but he had been fifteen years younger than Victor. Patrons herded in groups now instead of carrying on singly, and preferred the distressingly plebeian admiration of the many to the fine, patrician allegiance of the one. And gaiety, the mark of the personal, was suspect in a sociological world. Ergo her father. When a Minot was stripped of his devotion and of the truth-telling that was its honorable underside, when he was reduced to picking up crumbs of "contact" wherever he could, to making public show of his charms like anyone else, then he did so in the only way he knew. Her father had become a diner-out. It was some consolation that, under many lambent chandeliers and between many long-stemmed rows of pink and tawny glasses, he had dined so well.

She glanced at her wrist, remembered that she no longer had a watch, and looked at the river, estimating the seasonal angle of light on the opposite shore. Still too early to walk the short distance to the Lampeys, who, much as they adored her company, touted it, still preferred their guests to arrive, sharply gala, at eight. And these days Arietta aimed to please, had in fact aimed so steadily these past months and so far from her usual haunts, the shabby Saturday night parties of the real denizens of these hills, that it was no wonder if these were already remarking how unexpected it was of Arietta —slated one would have said for years yet to the memory of Carolingus—to be openly hunting a husband, and in such circles as the Lampeys, too. How surprised they would be if they knew that all she was hunting was a job. A job, to be sure, for a Minot—a sinecure not for sloth, but for the spirit. With, of course, perks enough to feed a healthy nine-year-old boy.

She rose and went to the mantel, staring up at Yves—one *"maigre"* looking at another. She was four velvet ribbons removed from him, and—except for Roger, who would be nothing for years yet—the last hope of his line. If from his vantage point he could have approved the resemblance, would he have expected her, a female, nevertheless to do something in his line? Being female, what she had done was, twelve years ago, to marry Carolingus Fay. After Vassar had come a year in Italy with one of the daughters of her father's three friends; the girl had married there, and Arietta, after attending her in a horsehair hat, had returned home. Next, the second girl, married to an Englishman who farmed in Nigeria, had invited her there. Against her father's wishes—it was not cautious for a woman to become too *déracinée*—she had gone, and in her lightsome way had enjoyed it, but marooned there, she had missed much of the war and most of the eligible men. In any case, esprit, or whatever it was she had, was difficult in a woman if it wasn't so much accompanied by looks as contributed to by them. Returning home, with her laugh-lines baked deeper than they should have been for her age, and with some knowledge of cacao and palm oil added to the magpie lore of her clan, she had vegetated in the Hudson Valley for a few restless months—her father's profession so seldom left him home to be cooked for—and then had gone to Baltimore to visit an old cousin.

And there she had met Carolingus. Eighteen years older than she, he had still seemed a man whom many might be glad to marry—a very fine "beefy" with proconsular manners and profile, and all his curls. Actually he had been a cliché, poor dear Carolingus—old Baltimore French, old poor, old hat—and he had been very glad to marry her. For, by heredity, and unfortunately nothing else, he was a patron—an even sadder case than hers. They had recognized each other, or loved—in time it seemed the same thing—at once. The only way he could afford to retain her was to come live in her house, which he did, to her father's delight—their mutual recognition too was a touching affair. Carolingus had been too shy to dine out (he had only the dispensing talent), and in time, with her and her father's full acquiescence, the house and what it held might have been taken by any casual guest to be his. At eighty her father retired, and the two men could not have been happier, jogging along in a life of aristocratic pattern gone native, shooting over their two acres for rabbit instead of grouse, and serving up the game with an excellent dandelion wine. And in their contentment Arietta had been happy too. It was so difficult for a Minot not to be happy, not to see, in whatever dried facts and kernels of incident the day provided, the possibility of a soufflé. Even when Carolingus had not long survived her father, she could not avoid thinking that he was better so, just as she could not help seeing, as the long, curlicued, taupe coffin went down the front steps, that it looked exactly like the éclairs of which he had always been so fond.

And then of course, it had become her turn—to dine out. She had let no one know her real situation; she would have been plied with all usually offered an untrained widow—"rent your lovely rooms to teachers; become a nursery school aide"—all the genteel solutions that would trap her forever. No, she was still child enough of her race to risk all on its chimera: that somewhere there was a post where one might exercise an airy, impalpable training which could never be put down on any resumé, somewhere even in this taxable world.

So far, her efforts to renew her father's contacts in New York had shown her only how faded they were, and how even those old and well-bred enough to remember the breed she sprang from, its always delicate aims, tended to misinterpret when the diner-out was female, however plain. These last months she had been looking about her in the Valley, among people like the Lampeys, whose kindness had the practicality which went with money still fresh in the till. Tonight, for instance, they were having her in to meet a Miss Bissle from Delaware, who was devoting to a state-wide program of hedge roses and bird sanctuaries her one-twenty-fifth share in a great-grandfather's fortune in explosives, and whose secretary-companion had just died. The Lampeys, drawing Arietta out for Miss Bissle's benefit, would no doubt ask her to repeat the story they particularly loved—about the time a zebra, a real zebra, had appeared in her garden—although she had other anecdotes she herself preferred. A humanist, she liked stories about people, and the zebra one was bad art besides, having no ending really, and an explanation that was sadly mundane. She would much rather tell about Claude and Henry Clay, about one of the Great Compromiser's compromises that had never reached the historians. Or about Louis's patron, a philanthropist who gave in kind only, and who, on being approached at his door by a pan-handler who wanted money for a glass eye, was able to invite him into a *cabinet de travail* where he had a box of them. But considering the roses and birds, possibly the zebra was more in line.

Across the river, the last evening light shone on the silver roof of a New York Central streamliner; she had a few minutes' walk and it was time. Courage, she said to herself, thinking of Roger. You are learning your trade a little late, that is all. You still have $126.35 worth of time. And maybe Miss Bissle would be a jolly hedonist who wanted a "good companion," although this was not often the conclusion one drew from watching people who watched birds. Remember, in any case, that when the artist is good, it is still the patron who is on trial. Reaching up toward Yves, she blew the dust from his frame. Why should our art, she thought, the art of happiness, be such a drug on the market these days? On that note, she tilted her head and went out, swinging the skirt of her dress, luckily so dateless, and tapping sharply, almost as if she scolded it, the tambour desk.

Meanwhile, a few minutes away, the Lampeys and their house-guests, Miss Bissle and her second cousin Robert, were speaking of Arietta. Parker and Helen Lampey, a white-haired couple in their sixties, had started life together at Christian College, Missouri, but long since, owing to Parker's rise to the extreme altitudes of inter-national law, had accustomed themselves to the ponderous social mixture to be found there—Swiss bankers, German industrialists, American judge advocates and solid rich like the Bissles. Thirty years of moving intercontinentally had not made them raffish—so far as was known they had never felt an expatriate tingle. What it had done was to give them the eternally pink-cheeked, good-tempered look of summer people; they had in fact been summer people all over the world. By native standards they should have been suffering from all the ills of cosmopolitan riches and ease; actually money, comfort and change had kept them amiable, enabling them to be as kindly as they looked, though considerably more worldly. Parker held several directorships adjacent to Robert, whose share in the family fortune was much larger than Miss Bissle's, and it was through him they had heard of her needs. And had at once thought of Arietta.

"I made Robert come with me," said Miss Bissle, "because Mary Thrace, the last one, you know—drank." She was a large, gray pachyderm of a woman whose eyes blinked slowly. "And I don't at all. You would think that would make it easier to notice in others, wouldn't you? But it doesn't. So I brought Robert."

"Well, I do," said her cousin, looking at his drink through the lower half of his bifocals. "Steadily. So you did just right."

Parker smiled. He knew Robert, a quiet, abstemious sort, widowed early and childless, devoted to rather *sec* philanthropies since. One of those mild, almost expunged men for whom second or third gen-eration fortune was a conscience, not a release.

"Why do men always make themselves out more colorful than they are?" said Miss Bissle, for whom Robert, past fifty, was still a younger cousin.

Helen Lampey glanced at Miss Bissle's shoes, the flat, self-assured feet of a woman who would never know why. Her cousin looked the way most people who wore glasses like that did—round and tame.

"Is this Mrs. Fay outdoorsy?" said Miss Bissle. "Mary Thrace wasn't."

"I don't know that one thinks of her as 'out' or 'in,' " said Helen slowly. "What would you say, Parker?"

"Delightful either place. In Arietta's company, where you are always seems just where you want to be. The father was just the same."

Helen could see Miss Bissle thinking that this was not the way one got things *done*. "She had a year in Africa," she said hastily. "I should think one would have to be . . . outdoorsy . . . there. And of course she grew up right here in the Hudson Valley—why, they caught a copperhead on their place only last year."

"Still has the old place. Old family hereabouts, the Minots," said Parker, rising to replenish the drinks.

"Minot!" Robert said softly. "Did you say—Minot?"

"Yes, ever know any of them? Understand they were quite a family at one time." Busy with the drinks, he did not note Robert's lack of response, covered in any case by Miss Bissle.

"*Trigonocephalous contortrix*," she said. "They don't eat birds."

Robert sat back in his chair. Yes, I knew a Minot, he thought. I knew Victor. Probably isn't the same family; chances are it couldn't be. Still, what Lampey had just said about the woman they were expecting—that was just the way Victor had been, turning life rosy and immediate wherever he was, and for adults too, as could be seen in the aureole that went round a room with him—not merely for Robert, the small boy on whom he had occasionally shone his great face, fair, hot and flame-colored as Falstaff's sun. Looking back on Victor now from the modern distance, it seemed to Robert that he must have dreamed him—that day on the Brandywine for instance, 1912 it must have been, when Victor had taken him fishing, the same day he had insisted on letting Robert join the men lunching at Robert's grandfather's table before the stockholders' meeting, and had fed the boy wine. Robert could see him now, jutting like a Rubens from even that portly group, the starched ears of the napkin he had tied around his cravat shining blue in the water-light reflected from walls that were white instead of walnut because of his choice, the napkin flecked, as lunch went on, with sauces Victor had conspired with the cook, the heavy company meanwhile tasting him with the same negligent appreciation they gave the food, as now and then he sent a sally rolling down the table like a prism, or bent over Robert, saying, "A little more claret with the water, Robert? . . . And now, if you please—a little more water with the claret." After lunch, Robert had seen him give his grandfather a sheaf of papers, saying, "Here they are, Bi—Robert and I are going out after turtle." As they left, one of the men said, "Bi—where do you get your cigars?"—it was Victor who had started people calling Robert's grandfather "Bi." "Victor gets them for me in Philadelphia." At the man's murmured envy, his grandfather had taken a careful puff, gently guarding the long, firm ash, and had smiled.

And that afternoon on the dock, sitting over the lines that the caramel-colored Negroes in the shack behind them had lent them, had been a time he had remembered always, like a recurrent dream —a day on which absolutely nothing had happened except sun, water and the lax blush of the wine in his limbs. And Victor—doing nothing all afternoon except what he did everywhere, making one feel that whatever you and he were doing at the moment was "it," that where you were was "here." They had caught, Robert recalled, two turtles; he remembered being warned of their bite, and informed, lovingly, of their soup. "Victor," he had asked suddenly, "what are you in?"—meaning chemicals, cotton, tin, this being the way men in those days, at that table, had spoken of what they did. "Oh I'm not 'in,'" had been the laughing answer. "You might say I'm—with." Breathing hard, Victor had been peering in at the hamper that held the turtles. Robert had looked down at him. "So shall I be," he had said. "Oh no you won't. You're already stuck with it, like these chaps. You're already in." Victor had risen, puffing. "Best you'll be able to do is to have somebody around like me—way Bi does." Robert had considered. "I'll have you then if I may," he had said.

Victor's face had been in shadow, the sun behind him, but after more than forty years Robert could still sense in him the unnameable quality that had sent him fishing in his cravat. "Mmm. If your father doesn't get to you first," he said. And Robert's father had got to him first, as, in Victor's old age, he had got to Victor. Not a hard man, his father, but a dull one, of the powerful new breed that cherished its dullness for its safety, and meant to impose that, along with the rest of its worldly goods, on its sons. "Like that brew we had at lunch?" Victor had said, as they trotted the hamper along the shore. "And well you might," he said, mentioning a name, a year. "Pity I've only daughters," he sighed. "Women've no palate. Perfume kills it." Above them, atop the green dunes of lawn that swept to the water's edge, a small figure waved at them, his grandfather, guests sped, sauntering the veranda alone. "Will I have one, d'ya think?" asked Robert. "Mmm, can't tell yet." Robert considered. His grandfather, colorless and quiet, seemed to him much like his father, who drank only Saratoga water. "Does Bi?" he said with interest. Victor smiled, waving back. "He's got me," he said.

And Grandfather was like me really, not like Father, Robert thought, returning to the Lampeys', where conversation, as so often happened elsewhere, had rippled on without him. He was a dull man too, as I am, but like me with the different and often painful dimension of not valuing it, of knowing that somewhere, sometimes in the same room, conversation twinkled past him like a prism, a rosier life went by. Grandfather was like me. But Grandfather had Victor.

And looking at the door through which Emily's possibility was to come, telling himself that it was midsummer madness—of Victor's daughters one was dead and the other last heard of years ago in a nursing order in Louisiana—he still told himself that he would not be surprised, not at all, if the woman who came through the door were to be huge and serenely fair, a great Flemish barmaid of a woman, with Victor's florid curls.

When Arietta walked through the door, he was surprised, at the depth of his disappointment. For what he saw was a slight woman, almost tiny, whose hair, sugared now like preserved ginger, might once, at youth's best, have been russet, a small creature whose oddly tweaked face—one of those pulled noses, cheeks that looked as if each held the secret cherry of some joke—was the farthest possible from the classic sun-face he remembered. Even if she were some relation, she was nothing like. There was no point in asking, in opening a private memory to future rakings over whenever he paid a duty call on Emily. For what he was looking at, he reminded himself, all he was looking at was Emily's future companion.

As the evening progressed, he was not so sure. For the Lampeys' protégée remained dumb. From their baffled glances he judged that this was not usual; he himself would have guessed that Mrs. Fay's ordinary manner, if she had any, was more mobile. But for whatever reason, her eyes remained veiled, her hands folded in the lap of her pale, somewhat archaic skirt. A certain stubborn aura spread from her, but nothing else, certainly nothing of the subtle emanation they had been promised, and but rarely a word. Only Emily, impervious to this as she was to so much, noticed nothing, intent on numbering the occasional sips Mrs. Fay took of her wine.

Nor could Arietta have explained. She could have said only that almost at once she had felt Miss Bissle to be a person she could never admire. Or tell the truth to, the truth about Miss Bissle being what it was. Not because Miss Bissle was dull—the best patrons necessarily had almost as much dullness as money—but that she did not suffer from it, whereas the real patrons, all the great ones, had a sweetening tremor of self-doubt at the core. If dullness was what had made them keep Minots, then this human (and useful) sweetening was what had made Minots keep them. But I must, thought Arietta. Roger, she said to herself. $126.35. Nevertheless, when Parker deftly introduced Nigeria, on which he had often heard her entertain, she heard herself furnish him three sentences on the cultivation of the cocoa nib, then fall still. It must be stage fright, her first professional engagement. Her father should have told her that the artist's very piety and scruples were a considerable hindrance when the artist came down to dining out. In desperation she gulped the rest of her wine. Opposite her Miss Bissle blinked slowly at Robert, as if to say "I count on you."

"Arietta!" said Helen Lampey. It was half command, half plea. "Do tell us the story about your zebra."

"Zebra?" said Robert. "Have you hunted them, Mrs. Fay?"

"No." Mrs. Fay addressed her small, clenched hands. "That's equatorial Africa." She heard Helen sigh. "Have you?"

Now, what none of them, what no one knew about Robert Bissle was that once in a while, under certain conditions, he lied. Not on the Exchange of course, or in any real situation. It was his only valve, his sole vice, and it escaped him, with the wistful sound of steam from an air-locked radiator, only when, as tonight, he deemed himself in the safe company of those even duller than he. He leaned back—on these occasions he always did. "Zebras are very beautiful creatures. I never molested them save to procure specimens for the museums, or food for the porters, who liked their rather rank flesh."

Mrs. Fay, for almost the first time, raised her eyes and looked closely at him. "Yes?" she said. Her nose, he observed, moved with speech. "Do go on."

"The hartebeest," he said slowly. "Coke's hartebeest, known locally by the Swahili name of kongoni—were at least as plentiful and almost as tame."

"Why Robert!" said Miss Bissle. "I never knew you were in Africa."

"Oh yes," he said, still looking at his neighbor, in whose odd face —he had not noticed until now—all the lines went up. "One year when your back was turned." He plunged on. "A few months before my arrival, a mixed herd of zebra and hartebeest rushed through the streets of Nairobi, several being killed by the inhabitants, and one of the victims falling just outside the Episcopal church."

"Handy," said Helen Lampey, in spite of having been informed that the Episcopal was Miss Bissle's own. She was watching Arietta and Robert—Arietta *with* Robert, smiling her pawkiest smile at him, and saying, "Yes, yes, do go on."

Robert took off his glasses. No, there was no resemblance, not even if he imagined a napkin tied round her neck, although for a moment there he had almost fancied an echo saying, "and now, a little more claret." He shook his head. The company, whatever it was, was not as safe as he had thought. "Your turn," he said. "Your zebra."

Arietta unfolded her hands. They trembled slightly. Miss Bissle's cousin, and even richer one had heard—and even more. One of the old breed, she was sure of it—and she had almost missed him. "My zebra?" she said. "Mine was—" She had been about to say *real*. But one let people see one knew the truth about them only after one had won them, sometimes long after. And particularly these people. "Mine was—here," she said. "Right here in the Hudson Valley. In our garden."

"So help me it was," said Parker. "I saw it. Go on, Arietta."

So she did. It had been a Saturday morning, she said, and she had been sitting in her bath, when Roger, seven then, had knocked at the door and said there were policemen in the garden and she had called back, "Tell Daddy." Minutes later, Roger had knocked again and said, "Mum, there's a zebra in the garden," and she had replied —"Tell Daddy." "Now," said Arietta, "Roger is not a fey child. I should have known." She knew every periphrasis of this story, every calculated inflection and aside; this was the point where everyone always began to smile expectantly, and pausing, she saw that they had. "I've never been able to afford to disbelieve him since." For then Carolingus had come up the stairs. "He looked," said Mrs. Fay, delaying softly, expertly, "well—like a man who has just seen a zebra in his garden." As, according to him, he had. She went downstairs— and so had he. She made them see the scene just as she had, the two policemen, Mack Sennett characters both of them, yelling "Stand back there!" from a point well behind Carolingus, and there, cornered in a cul-de-sac near the carriage house, flashing and snorting, the zebra, ribanded in the rhododendrons like a beast out of the *douanier* Rousseau.

"The policemen," she said, "had had no breakfast, so there I found myself, carrying a tray with sugar and cream and my best coffee cake—luckily I had baked on Friday—to two policemen and a zebra, in a back yard twenty-five miles from New York." She rose, circled the room, holding the scene with her hands pressed lightly together, and as if absent-mindedly, poured Parker some coffee out of the Lampeys' silver pot. Outside, in the Lampeys' garden, a barn owl hooted—it was the atmosphere, conspiring gently with her as usual. She waited. At this point someone always asked, "But how?"

"But *how?*" said Miss Bissle.

"Ah, now," said Mrs. Fay, "I have to double back. I have to tell you that across from us, in one of those very modern houses with the kitchen set just under the crown of the road, the family gets up very early. They garden, and the mother-in-law is a past president of the Audubon Society of Atlanta, Georgia." Still circling the room, a diseuse gently fabricating her own spotlight, Mrs. Fay rested one hand, a brief wand, on Miss Bissle's shoulder as she passed her. Robert watched, enthralled. There was nothing to it, yet she held them all. They sat like marionettes whom she was awakening slowly to a mild, quizzical sensation like the pleasure-pain in a sleeping foot. "And at about six o'clock that morning, the head of the County Police picked up the phone and heard a cultivated Southern voice say, 'Ah should like to repo't that jus' now, as we wuh setten at breakfas', we saw a zebra payss bah on the Rivuh Road.'" Parker laughed, and Mrs. Fay picked it up, wove him in quickly. "Ah yes," she said, "can't you hear her? And the chief thought to himself that the River Road is rather the bohemian part of his parish, and that

Saturday morning comes, well—after Friday night. So he calls our policeman and says, 'George, people down your neck of the woods seeing zebras.' George decides to wait until, well, two or more people see it. Then Joe Zucca, the old caretaker at Fagan's, telephones, babbling that a striped horse is crashing around his conservatory. And the chase is on. And they bring it to bay in our garden."

Parker guffawed. "There are zebras at the bottom of my garden."

Arietta, reaching her own chair, sat down in it. Someone always said that too. She looked round their faces. Yes, she had them, particularly one. Quickly, quickly now, wind it up. And in a long, virtuoso breath, she wound it all up—how the village had filled the yard, a gold mine if she'd just had the lollipop concession, how her smart-aleck neighbor had stopped by the front gate, offering a drive to town, and when she'd said, "Wait a bit, Tom, we've got a zebra in the back yard," had smirked and said "Yeah, I heard that one at Armando's—and the horse said, 'I've been trying to get it to take its pajamas off all night.' " And how it had been one of the great satisfactions in life to be able to lead him round to the carriage house. And how the cops had finally got hold of the Hudson River Cowboys Association—yes there was one, those kids in white satin chaps and ten-gallon hats who always rode palominos in the Independence Day Parade—and how they'd come, out of costume alas, but with their horse trailer, and how Carolingus and the cops had finally jockeyed the beast in, using a three-man lasso. And how, at the height of it—children screaming, yokels gaping, three heated men hanging on ropes, the whole garden spiraling like a circus suddenly descended from the sky, and in the center of it all, the *louche* and striped, the incredible—how Arietta's eighty-five-year-old Cousin Beck from Port Washington, a once-a-year and always unheralded visitor, had steamed up the driveway in her ancient Lincoln, into the center of it all. "Oh, Cousine Beck," she'd stammered—in French, she never knew why—"you find us a little *en deshabille*, we have us *un zèbre*." And how Beck, taking one look, had eased her old limbs out of the car and grunted, "Arietta, you *are* dependable. Just bring me a chair."

Mrs. Fay folded her hands. Now someone would ask the other question. She gave a sigh. Next to her, her neighbor marveled. No, she was nothing like—no aureole. This one whisked herself in and out, like a conjuror's pocket handkerchief. But the effect was the same. Small sensations, usually ignored, made themselves known, piped like a brigade of mice from their holes. There was a confused keenness in the ear . . . nose . . . air? One saw the draperies, peach-fleshed velour, and waited for their smell. The chandelier tinkled, an owl hooted, and a man could hear his own breath. The present, drawn from all its crevices, was here.

"But where did the beast come from?" said Miss Bissle.

Yes, it would be she, thought Arietta. The cousin, his glasses still off, was staring at her with eyes that were bright and vague. "A runaway," she said in a cross voice. It always made her sulky to have to end the fun this way, with no punch line but fact. "There's an animal importer up the mountain; we found out later. He buys them for zoos." She turned pertly to the cousin. "Perhaps it was one of yours."

"I can't think when, Robert," said Miss Bissle. "I've always known exactly where you were."

Robert, before he replaced his glasses, had a vague impression that Mrs. Fay looked guilty, but she spoke so quickly that he must have been wrong.

"Parker," she said, "did you and Helen ever hear about Great-grandfather Claude, and Mr. Henry Clay?"

They hadn't. Nor had they heard about Louis's patron's glass eye. Robert, saved, sank deeper in his chair. He was his father's son after all, trained to fear the sycophant, and he brooded now on whether Mrs. Fay wanted something of him. Look how she had got round the Lampeys. Was she honest? Victor's tonic honesty, he remembered, had spared no one; he never flattered individually but merely opened to dullards the gross, fine flattery of life alone. And what did he, Robert, want of her? If he closed his eyes, prisms of laughter floated past him, flick-flack, down the long cloth of another table; he could feel, there and here, the lax blush of the present in his limbs. He slouched in it, while Arietta told how, when Carolingus spoke for her, her father had said, "You know she has no *dot*." And how Carolingus, who was slightly deaf, had replied, "I've no dough either." And how in after years, both always amiably purported to be unsure of who had said which.

And then Robert sat up in his chair. For Arietta was telling the story of the "beefies" and "*les maigres*."

So that's it, he thought. I knew it, I knew it all the time. And in

the recesses of his mind he felt that same rare satisfaction which
came to him whenever he was able to add to a small fund he had
kept in a downtown savings bank almost since boyhood, money
separate from inheritance, made by his own acumen, on his own. I
recognized her, he thought, and the feeling grew on him, as it had
been growing all evening, that in the right company he was not such
a dullard after all. He leaned back now and watched her—quiet now
after her sally, unobtrusive whenever she chose. It was not wit she
pretended to; her materials were as simple as a child's. What was the
quality she shared with Victor, born to it as the Bissles were born
to money, that the others here felt too, for there was Lampey, murmuring ingenuously into his brandy-cup "Wonderful stuff this, isn't
it?"—quite oblivious of the fact that it was his own—and there even
was Emily, her broad feet lifted from the floor? Whatever Mrs. Fay
did, its effect was as Victor's had been, to peel some secondary skin
from the ordinary, making wherever one was—if one was with her—
loom like an object under a magnifying glass—large, majestic and
there. She made one live in the now, as, time out of mind it seemed,
he had once done for himself. But he did not know how she did it.
Or whether she did. Watching her rise from her chair, begin to
make her adieu, the thought came to him that he would not mind
spending a lifetime finding out.

"Let me go with you," he said, standing up. "Let me drive you
home."

But Emily had arisen too. "Mrs. Fay," she said, her blinking
fluttered, "have you had any experience with birds?"

Arietta smiled between them. How lucky she had recognized him,
the real thing, poor dear, even if his sad little blague—out of *African
Game Trails* of course, old Teddy Roosevelt, on half the bookshelves in Nigeria—was not.

"Do," she said to him, "but let's walk." She turned to Miss
Bissle, and let the truth escape from her with gusto. After all it was
her own. "No, not really. Of course—I've shot them."

On the short way home, the river, lapping blandly, made conversation. Robert spoke once. "I don't really think Emily would have
suited you," he said, and Mrs. Fay replied that it was nice of him to
put it that way round.

At Arietta's doorway, they paused. But it was imperative that she
find out what was on his mind. Or put something there.

427

"I'd ask you in," she said, "but I've nothing but dandelion wine."

"I've never had any," said Robert. "I'd like to try it."

She led him through the hall, past the rack where Carolingus's leather jacket hung, and her father's, and the squirrel-skin weskit they had cured for Roger, then through the softly ruined downstairs rooms, up the stairs and into the little salon. It was an educative tour; it told him a great deal. And this was the family room; he sensed the intimate patchouli that always clung to the center of a house, even before he looked up and saw them all above the mantel, hanging on their velvet tree. While Arietta went for the wine, he moved forward to examine them. What a higgler's collection they were, in their grim descent from ivory to pasteboard to Kodak, yet a firm insouciance went from face to face, as if each knew that its small idiom was an indispensable footnote to history, to the Sargents, Laverys, de Lászlós that people like him had at home. And *there*, in that small brown-tone. Yes, there.

"Take me round the portraits," he said when she returned, and here too, since she also was on the wall, he learned. He saw that Carolingus must have been of an age near his own. "And who are they?" he said. "You missed that one." They were sitting at a small escritoire on which she had placed the wine, and if he stretched a hand he could touch the faded browntone.

"That's my father as a boy, and his older brother, Victor."

What an absurd feeling happiness was. That must be its name. To feel as if such a sum, such a round sum had been deposited in that bank that he need never go there again. Not if he stayed here. As, in time, he thought, he could arrange.

Opposite him, Arietta fingered a drawer inside which the name of the desk's first owner was inscribed—Marie-Claire, who had married for inclination but had got the rose-diamonds too. She stole a glance at her vis-à-vis. After all, she had recognized him, and in time, as she did remember, this and inclination could come to be almost the same. It was strange that he was no "beefy," but she had already had one—and no doubt her tribe, along with the rest of the world, must move on. And he was very responsive. In time, she thought, the house would come to seem to him like his own.

"Wonderful stuff," he was saying, holding up to the light one of the old green bottles into which Carolingus and her father had put the wine.

"Is it really?" said Arietta. "I was never any help to them on it."

"What it wants," he said, "is to be decanted, for the sediment. One does it against a candle flame. I was thinking—I might come by tomorrow. And show you."

"Do—for company," said Mrs. Fay. "Actually, one wine seems to me much like any other. I've got no palate for it. Women don't, my father always used to say."

"No, they don't." He was looking at her so deeply that she was startled. "Perfume kills it," he said, and so intensely that, odd averral as it was, it hung over them both like an avowal of love.

Downstairs, she led him out the front door, and watched him to the end of the lane. Roger's spaniel yipped, and over the hill another dog set up an answering cry. In the darkness, as she closed the door, she smiled, one of old Teddy's sentences lumbering through her mind. "The hunter who wanders these lands sees the monstrous river-horse snorting, the snarling leopard and the coiled python, the zebras barking in the moonlight." As she went back up the stairs, she wondered whether she would ever tell him. Some truths, as an honest companion, one spoke in jest; others, as a woman, one kept to oneself. At the moment it didn't matter. Standing in the doorway of the little salon, she stretched her arms. "I've dined out!" she said to the pictures, to herself. "I've dined on zebra, and on hartebeest, and yes, I think, on . . . husband. I've dined well."

Outside the hedge at the end of the lane, Robert watched the door close. He knew just how it would begin tomorrow; he would begin by asking her, as he had never asked anyone, to call him "Bi." There would always be a temptation to say more—who, for instance, would understand about that day on the Brandywine better than she? But he must remember; with all she was—she was also a woman. They liked to be chosen for themselves. He must always be as mindful of that as of his incredible luck. And what utter luck it was! He swelled with the urge to tell someone about it. But there were not many in the world today who could appreciate precisely its nature. It was even possible that he himself was the last one extant of all those who once had. Standing in the shadow of the hedge, he whispered it to himself, as once a man had whispered it to his grandfather, over the cigar. "Lucky man," he said to himself, "you have a Minot!"

Saturday Night

❧ T H A T S A T U R D A Y afternoon, after he had left the analyst's office for what might be the last time, he stopped in at the elegant little Viennese bakery in the same block, and bought a mocha cake for his wife. Although, even five years ago, Dorothy had been one of those out-of-towners who slipped into the ways of the city with only a little more emphasis than was natural, she had never lost her glee over the complicated, alien tidbits which were such a contrast to the pies and hefty layer cakes of her native Utica. The huge new "housing development" in which they had been lucky enough to get an apartment quartered only several glittering chain shops, which she had long since learned to snub.

Waiting absently at the counter for his change, he found that actually he could not fully realign Dorothy's face in his memory. Although he could summon a hundred images of their life together, before and now—the curve of her back as she offered the spoon to the child, the tilt of her head as she slumped, reading, in a chair—in full focus her face evaded him, remaining always in the rear, or to one side. A common enough occurrence, he knew. Nevertheless it left a curious hollow in his new-found assurance.

As he left the store, he turned a last look on the block to which he had been coming for almost three years now. Although, when away from it, he could not have told between which two of the line of houses the one he visited was precisely located, the whole of the block reared itself in his mind like a composition, an entity whose significance had become the foreground of his life. Up three steps, in at the gray entrance, into one of those self-service elevators within whose clicking, measured suspension one rode always with a sense of doom, no matter to what event. Then the anonymous room, whose stepped-down colors and noncommittal furniture offered only the neuter comfort of no stimulus to either approval or dislike. Then, finally, another installment in the long, delicate auscultation of himself, during which, sometimes clamped in resistance, sometimes irrigated with relief, he had been free to pursue the quality of his fear.

Turning away, he walked down to the corner and joined the vague group waiting for a bus. Wherever you went, at almost any time, on almost every corner, there would be such a group assembled. It was a deceptively impressive fact which, when elaborated on, he had long since learned, led nowhere. It was part of the provocative pulse of a city, of a world in which, if you did not learn to deflect the thousand casual contacts strewn at you, without attempting to seize upon them, to weld them into some philosophy of destination, you were lost indeed.

He wedged himself onto the bus, carefully protecting the cake. Looking down at the white box, he thought tiredly of what a funny symbol it was of that daily switch-off in which, laying aside the engrossing thread of himself, he bought a cake, he took a bus, and—rapped smartly back into the secondary—he deserted for another day the re-creation of himself as a working being. As a working being, he cautioned himself, he heard himself being cautioned by the dry voice from behind him in the anonymous room. For if the whole process had not helped him to hold himself untremulously at last in a world where others managed, what had it been but an infinitely seductive excursion into ego, after which, as cut off from others as he had been in the beginning, he would find himself twice alone, holding together the explored corners of himself?

Clutching the box in his cramped hand, he got off the bus at his stop. Less than a year ago, down here, there had been nothing but the great cylindrical gas tanks, nuzzled by tenements, slotted shops, and the exhausted outbuildings natural to the wharflike streets near an old river. Now the "housing development" loomed upward before him, an incredible collage pasted against the sky. Even remembering the excavations and the swarmed signs of contractors, even forcibly recalling the scores of families who were inside it going through their daily paces like tidy, trotting simulacra of each other, it was hard to believe that the whole organism had not been stroked from a lamp. Looking at it, the eye seemed always to be trying to wipe it away.

He and Dorothy had already been drawn into the imitatively suburban life of the young couples who lived there. Dorothy, of course, he thought, much more than he—since whatever time he had away from his university job was already so prescribed. Again he strove for a better picture of her, brushing aside the recurrent blankness. In the mornings, waving to her as he passed the playground on the way to his classes, he had seen her sitting talking or reading or sewing with the other mothers, watching Libby as she played with the other beplaided and corduroyed toddlers in the austerely planned sandpit, already cluttered with buried rakes and spoons and lost tin fish. All of the mothers, still slender and attractive, looked like thirty-year-old versions of the college girls they once had been. Many of them had had careers or talents that marriage and children had interrupted or aborted, and to the memory of these they paid insistent and bitter homage, constantly totting up the frustrations of housewifery in remarks which were like a kind of bleak, allusive shorthand understood by them all. For now that they were women of the home, they felt an inferiority to their former selves, and so, too, they had constructed a technical patter full of words like "preschool" and "security" and references to "Gesell-and-Ilg," as if by this subaqueous jargon they would return motherhood, with all its inconvenient secretions and scullion duties, to the status of a profession.

With Dorothy, however, he thought thankfully, this defeated prattling never had been more than part of her half naïve acceptance of the New York "line." She had been reared in a town where people, particularly the women, expected that life would deal with them according to those archaic truisms which, if no longer so hallowed as once, came to them, at least, without the friction of disappointment. It had been this certainty in her which had drawn him as much as her mild blond good looks, whose exact lineaments so curiously evaded him now; it had been to this sureness that he, already deeply flawed with irresolution, had clung and married himself, in the sick hope of transference.

How was he to have foreseen, he thought now, that this very ability of hers to cope, this health, would become formidable between them, sending him further into his cowl of preoccupation, leaving her beached on normality, so that, strangers now, too far apart even for conflict, they had gone on sharing the terrible binding familiarities of the joint board, the joint child, and, less and less often, the graceless despair of the common bed?

For in the world of the normal, he knew now—he heard the dry voice say—to those whose qualms were always based on the tangible, the active, the real, how could he have seemed otherwise than intransigent, when he had insisted that in his world there was a basic, roiling chaos, over which the footage was never more than a series of staircases that dissolved as one trod them, in the midst of which alternatives faced one like knives—and people were the only alternatives?

He walked on through the circuitous approaches to his own building. Light skittered, noise faceted from the hived buildings about him, lazily compounding a day, redolent of livelier Saturdays and more expectant springs, which was like a percussive recall to health. Fear was all right, it said to him, as long as one could bring it out into the light and give it a name. He was almost up out of the ditch now, almost up on the other, the safe side, with Dorothy and all the people who knew where they were going, and could manage.

He turned in at Number 6 Village Drive, noting, as always, the cozy term applied to the massive clinical building whose entrance halls, all of nude beige marble enlivened only by buttons, held the etherized silence of a museum. It was difficult to believe that on its upper floors hundreds of doors opened on interiors rumpled with living and the intimate sediment of people, on kitchens checkered with the aftermath of meals, bathrooms clotted with diapers and cream pots, at whose windows stockings hung swinging in the dust motes and the sun.

The door opened to his key and he stepped into the apartment, receiving the familiar impingement of the pictures, the chairs, the books serried just as he had left them. Everything waited for him like a box full of stale attitudes, old grooves in which he both fitted and chafed. As always on Saturdays, the room had a cleanliness almost pitiable in view of the way Sunday's lax living jarred and crumbled it—almost as if Dorothy expected someone—or something. He hoped she was not going to expect too much of him at first. He hadn't really thought, he hadn't had time to think of it during these years, visualizing her, when at all, as a man in a ward visualizes the ordinary ones, cumbered with health, who wait patiently in the anterooms of hospitals.

In the bedroom, Libby lay on his bed, her face locked fast in the upturned purity of sleep. Dorothy, face down on her own bed, turned her head toward him as he came in. Her mouth, drawn down at the corners at first, in the half-drugged enmity of the dreamer coarsely awakened, quivered faintly in greeting.

Of course, he thought, feeling foolishly relieved. This is she. This is the way she is.

"Hi," he said softly, because of Libby.

"Hi."

He looked down at Libby, who was in pajamas. "She in for the night?"

She nodded. "I gave her an early supper. You know how it is otherwise." She raised herself up on her elbow and pushed back her hair.

"Mmm," he said. He knew how it was. In her voice, her attitude, he heard the echoing plaint of the other women: "If you don't let them nap then they're cranky, and if you do then they never want to go to bed later on—and you have them on your hands till nine!" Nobody seems to enjoy or glory in his children any more, he thought. We're always plotting, calculating how to have a personal life in spite of them.

"Thought you might want to go shopping or something," he said, trying on a smile. In his mood, composed half of his release, half of the infectious rhythm of Saturday expectancy, he found himself thinking of the Saturday afternoons she used to love—in the early days of their marriage, or when Libby had been a woollen-wrapped bundle carried jauntily on his shoulder—when they had been part of all the other families idling through the stores, trekking through Sears, perhaps—and coming out of that array of rose trellises and tires with a pair of curtains or a kitchen tool, they had returned home heartened and gay and somehow conquerors, through that device so feminine, so American—the purchase.

"I've done the shopping," she said, with a faint look of surprise. "The Ewarts asked us upstairs for the usual. I thought we would come down once in a while to check. It's too late for a sitter."

"Mmm." He put the cake-box down on the night table, stretching his cramped hand. "Mocha," he said.

"Thanks." She awarded it a brief, listless smile.

He sat down carefully on the side of her bed. His hand, braced on the bed, was near her waist. She edged away politely, careful not to interpret affection into the casual gesture. For both of them it had become a matter of pride not to admit, to solicit for the shaming need that was no longer closeness. Nightly, the tense waiting for the hand which did not come had sagged more and more often into sleep; in the infinitesimal edgings away they had built the routine of remoteness.

He put his hand in his lap, inspected it. "I'm through," he said. "At the doctor's." He gave her a quick, guilty look, and concentrated again on the hand. Except for the first of the month, when the bills came in, it had been a matter of rigid convention never to mention the doctor.

"For good?" she said.

"He thinks. I hope."

She swung her legs down to the floor on the other side of the bed. After a minute, she padded around in front of him and sat down at the dressing table with her back to him, opened a drawer, took out a hairbrush, ran a finger over the bristles. He waited for her to speak, turn at least, but she began brushing her hair, slapping the brush against her head with a tired halfhearted stroke.

He gave a self-conscious laugh, and again, the surreptitious look. "Ring out, wild bells," he said.

"I'm sorry—" She turned. He waited, he told himself, for her to drop the damn brush.

"I'm sorry," she repeated, "sorry I can't be more . . . oh well—" She looked down at the brush. "I know you expected me to be . . . well . . . waiting." Then she put down the brush and the words came with a rush, a bitterness. "At the door. Or a street corner, maybe. With a lei, or something."

The quick acid of the words surprised him. She was slow and honest in all she did, with no deft talent either with the paring knife or the tongue.

"Forget it," he said, the dread of a scene opening like a funnel before him.

"No," she said, laboring now. "I suppose . . . in a way I *was* waiting." She raised her head. "Did you ever ask your doctor that . . . ask him what happens to people waiting on the sidelines for people like you to—" She stopped.

"To what?"

"To get over their love affair—with themselves."

"Love affair!"

"Ah, you know you loved it," she said. "Spinning out yourself. Because meanwhile you didn't have to do anything—about anything or anybody."

"Would it have been better if I'd had T.B.? Something that showed?"

She put her hand out toward him, almost touching his knee, then drew it back. "I kept thinking of them all the time—all the wives, and husbands, and parents of the people going to your doctor. On the outside all the time, smoothing things over, picking up the pieces—holding their breath. What are we supposed to do? Stop living?"

"If you felt like that, why didn't you say some—"

"Oh no," she said quickly. "I wasn't supposed to interrupt—or intrude!"

It was true, he thought. What she had represented these three years had been the damaging real—which he had avoided even as he fought his way toward it.

"I know it hasn't been easy for you," he said humbly. "Perhaps that was part of my trouble . . . that I didn't think enough about that. But now—"

"What's 'now'?" She looked down at her clenched hands. "People like me will always be on the outside . . . with people like you."

He got up heavily from the bed and crossed to the window. God save us, he thought, us—the equivocal ones—from the ones who see life steadily, and see it whole. From those who can't bury or evade the truth, but have to drag it out and beat it like a carpet. Who can say the raw, the open thing, that can never be glozed over again.

He stared out the window, twisting one hand around and around in his pants pocket. "Come on," he said. "Let's go up to the Ewarts'."

"No. I don't want to go after all."

"Well, for God's sake," he said, sore with his new effort, "you're always the one who's trying to drag me!"

"Because it was better than being alone together." She shrugged, smiling crookedly up at him. "Besides . . . Saturday night . . . one always hopes for the best."

"Come on then." He met the smile with a placating one of his own.

"No, It's just more of the same."

"The same?"

"You know," she said. "Like a record we all play once a week. Jim, hanging around, waiting for Esther to get drunk enough so she'll go home, and Karen watching Lou for her reasons, and me watching you for mine. I just don't want any part of it any more."

He watched it almost jealously, that soft, flexible look of hers, which concealed the enviable certitude, the stubborn strength to reject, to decide.

"Well, what do you want to do?"

She looked away from him consciously. "I thought I'd go back home for a while. If you're really on your feet now."

"For a while? Or for good?" he said. For good, he thought. That's what she asked, only a little while ago.

She was silent.

"What makes you think Utica, or any other place, isn't more of the same, these days?" he said.

"It doesn't matter where. I just can't go on being an adjunct—any more!"

"And Libby?" He softened his voice suddenly, as if their joint concern might wake her, where their forgetfulness had not.

She put her head down in her hands, rubbing her concealed face back and forth. She'll cry now, he thought, although he could not remember when he had last seen her cry, and he waited, almost with relief, for with women, the lucky women, this meant the dissolving of an issue, the haggled end of emotion—but she went on defeatedly rocking.

"Come on," he said, after a moment. "I'll fix us a drink." He waited, and then put a hand on her shoulder. "We'll have a party by ourselves."

In the kitchen, his hands took over the mixing of the Martinis, picking out and combining the gin, the vermouth, the lemon peel, with disembodied competence. "This is real enough for you!" he thought. "Isn't it? Isn't it?" he said defensively to the dry voice in the anonymous room.

He thought of the crowd upstairs now at the Ewarts', in the

pattern, as Dorothy had said, pooling all their uncertainties of the week, drowning them in the fabricated bonhomie of Saturday night. The Ewarts, Syl and Harry, were a few years older than the average couple in the building and were both "in business"; perhaps it was a combination of these facts which led them into great spurts of energy, in which droves of people must be enlisted to help them kill the weekend's frightening acreage of time. To their coarse-grained parties there came, patronizingly, the fledgling physicists, the writers on their way to a foothold, the confused but verbose young men with their foetally promising jobs in the government, in the State Department, or, like himself, in the universities. They came because they were at loose ends, or at odds with themselves or the wife, or roughened with the loneliness of the city, or, let it be said, because the Ewarts could serve the liquor they themselves could infrequently afford. And with each of them came the wife, in the new hair-do, the primary colored dress with its attempted primary appeal —all the intelligent, frustrated girls, fleeing from the diapers toward an evening in which they could forget their altered conceptions of themselves.

He held the Martini mixer up to the light, and stirred, forestalling the thought of Dorothy and himself with critical thoughts of the others. It's true, what she said, he thought. Esther, having to drink herself into insensibility more and more often, with Jim doggedly watching, and Karen, flitting grimly, unobtrusively into the kitchen now and then to see that Lou's reflex skirt-chasing doesn't get him in more trouble than he can handle. And me, wrapped up in a corner. "For once let's not think about me!" he said defiantly to the voice in the repudiated room. And through it all the Ewarts hurried like high-class orderlies, bright with reassurances to the sufferers, administering glasses, plates of food, or winks in the direction of the bathroom.

The sufferers, he thought. The prowlers in retreat from themselves. He put two glasses on a tray and looked at the light through the mixer for a last delaying time. It stared back at him like an unanswerable, viscous, lemon-watery eye.

He walked back with it into the bedroom. Dorothy was stretched out on the bed again, staring into the pillow.

"Want to go in the other room, or stay here?"

"Oh leave me be. Leave me be."

He put the tray on the dressing table and sat down beside her with a brisk, overemphasized resolve.

"Come on," he said, urging her up to a sitting position. "This'll fix you up. We'll rustle up some dinner later."

They sat on the side of the bed together, sipping, not saying anything, as if they both sucked desperately at some potion of last resource. After a while he put a drink-loosened arm around her, using his other arm to refill the glasses, and they sat on in the growing dark, finishing the second drink, the third, watching with careful fixity the lambent points of their cigarettes. Outside the window, the light-studded evening converged, ramified, without them.

A tremor in her shoulder made him know, suddenly, that she was crying, and trying to conceal it. He was cleft with pity, and even a kind of possessive pride because she was the sort of woman who did not cry for show.

"Ah don't," he said. "Ah don't."

She gave her head an angry, backward shake. "I'm not trying to . . . oh you know!" she said, in a strangled whisper.

"I know." He tightened the arm that was around her, and put his other hand blindly toward her. It met her face. She moved her face back and forth in his palm, and he felt the hot sidle of tears through his fingers.

"I'm afraid," she said. "That's all it is."

"Afraid?" he said, delicately handling the sharp tool of the word. "What are you afraid of?"

"That's it. I don't know. I never used to be."

He held her as she sobbed, knowing that for this, on which of all things he should have been most knowledgeable, there was no answer that he could give. But it seemed to him that the edged word, coming through the sweetish, gin-fogged air, came like a bond, a link which slit through the cocoon around himself. He began to kiss her with a kind of heavy sympathy for them both. Turning, they stretched out on the bed and made use of one another in a final spasm of escape.

Long after she slept he lay awake in the dark, which had a pallid incompleteness from the deflected street lights outside. After a while he got up noiselessly and looked at the glowing disc of the clock. It was only nine o'clock. He crossed to the other bed, his own, near the window, and picked up the sleeping child. Holding her, on his way to the crib in her own room, her warm, inert weight seemed to him like a burden he was inadequate to carry. "Parents like us!" he thought. This must be why we avoid them, the children, because they are the mirror we make for ourselves. They are the alternative of no evasion, on whose knife we are impaled. He put her down, tucking the light blanket carefully around her, and went back into the other room.

Through the window he saw and heard it—the Saturday night pattern—its neon blotted by haze, its multiplying, loose roar jingled into softness by the tricky distances of spring. It seemed to him that he heard in it, in that heightened blend of the hundreds of gurgling, cheeping noises of daily living, some of which were quickened for him by memories of aspiration or love, but now never more than quickened—that he heard all around him the endless echolalia of his time, his world, his trap. They were all down in the ditch with him, the prowlers, and the weak alarums of their malaise lacked even the dignity of the old ecclesiastical cry: "Father, what are we? And whither do we go?" For, in our cleverness, he thought, we know what we are, and in the sadness of no mystery, we know where we are going.

He looked down at the other sleeping figure, wondering what there was in the construction, the being of a face, that had once made it his vital necessity, and that now, by some combination of circumstance and familiarity as brutal as it was quiet, had been attenuated past recall. He looked down, waiting, wishing for a sense of ruin. For ruin implied salvage; it implied the loss of something dear. Where there was a sense of ruin, there might also be a sense of hope.

Little Did I Know

૭ৠ AT NIGHT, Florence has no tourists. All along the tables dotted in front of this particularly famous café, people sat close to-gether in the half-light, musing, chatting—though it was midnight—in little infernos of talk that celebrated the hour. On the pavement before the tables an unending line of strollers repeated its themes; how many times, for instance, had there not seemed to pass the same pair of high-stepping, black-crepe-and-honey women—or were they girls?—the pout of their calves and pompadours drawn by the same dusky brush, between shoulder and chin always the same long, half-agonized line of throat? Both sitters and promenaders were alike in that each line thought itself audience to the other; for each, its side was the land of the living, the other side the stage.

"I must have been about your age, about nineteen"—the woman speaking, hidden in the shadows beyond the high-backed chair of her invisible vis-à-vis, either thought them both concealed, or did not care who saw or heard—"maybe nineteen and a half, for we were still counting our years in halves then. That gorgeous spring I spent whirling through first love with a boy named Ben. And planning to murder a professor named Tyng. You ever notice, incidentally, that 'gorgeous' has quite dropped out of the language? Must have gone during the depression; we all came out of those years so very stripped and staccato, cleansed of everything from fake Renaissance furniture to the acting style of Sir Henry Irving. And slang had to be just like the plays—short words, full of compassion.

"Anyway . . . it was the spring of my junior or senior year. I'm not good about dates and time, and that goes for geography too; facts of when or where don't interest me. A person like me's mem-ory is likely to be long, but schoolbook accuracy is seldom its forte.

441

Right in the middle of a conversation, an experience, it goes on selecting, exaggerating, and what we're doomed to remember—believe me, *doomed*—is . . . Oh, well, not so much the facts as the *feeling*. . . .

"But that's just the sort of thing you have to keep in mind about people like us, about me . . . in what I seem to be going to tell you. Yes, I know you're interested, or you wouldn't have looked me up. Just remember, though, that even when we're at our quietest—and we can be quiet—words are our reflex. We spend our lives putting things into words."

Contrarily, before the voice began again—not with a sigh, for there seemed no sighs in this clear-thinking reed—there was a silence. And then the voice again.

"For instance, I'm willing to bet when you go back home you'll have a far better idea of where this terrace was in Florence, and of what we saw today at the galleries, than I—and I've been here before. How I'll remember, dunno—not till I sit down someday to write about it. And then maybe it'll turn into a dialogue between two women of different ages, sitting here watching the other unaccompanied women go by, and wondering which of the well-dressed ones are—see that ladylike one; she's a very well-known one—and pinning us all down in our separate terms."

The occupant of the chair opposite the speaker must have leaned forward, uncurling feet that had been tucked under, for there was now visible one pale slipper of uncertain color, of the kind known as "ballerinas"—a tentative, young shoe.

"Or," said the voice, "I might use *you* discovering Italy, turning you round and round, seeing you with Italy at your edges, or Italy vice versa—though I won't necessarily use what you told me happened between you and the boy in Stamford. . . . Hmm? No, of course I won't. If I'm lucky, you'll be true to life, that's all. Not necessarily true to yours. And I shan't apologize; the odds are I'll be in there too somewhere, on just as sharp a pin.

"Notice I'm not the least interested in what you'll remember. My way of talking's a habit I can't shake. Keep that in mind, won't you, that I warned you? For I've reached an age, you see, where I notice people try to undazzle the young. . . .

"Thank you, you're very sweet, but I'm almost forty-one. There are women who falsify their age and women who ask you to guess; I'm too old to be the first sort and not old enough to be the other. And if you think *that* remark has been made before—well, it has! Oh well, thanks. The hair's a tint of course, but at least I started out a real blonde. And we small-boned types wear better than average; I'll live till ninety and die of a broken hip. And of course nobody who *is* anybody fattens anymore. A social comment, that—maybe you'll use it someday when you use *me.*

"Anyway, there are at least a half dozen of us who might be me. All of us have done enough to be looked up, the way you looked me up, all about forty, forty-five. All with at least two husbands too, although mine were better than most. A painter so handsome you wouldn't believe his work could deserve such success—until you saw it—and a banker of such charm that nobody minded his money. Too good to have let go, both of them. And of course *I* didn't, though they let me think so, right up to the end. Absolute opposites, those two men were, never even met; yet when they left, it was with the same parting words. . . .

"Don't flinch. You said you wanted to be one of us, didn't you? From the pieces you showed me, maybe you will be. That's why I'm telling you this. Get it straight, though—I loved them, and they me. My first used to say he'd *never* seen a woman as pretty and sexy as I was who was so tough to paint. Maybe you're thinking that's because one can't paint a verbal shimmer. But I don't talk very much with men actually, and I never talked at all in bed; I knew enough not to do that, even before I'd read about it. And I suppose it's not surprising they both made the same remark when they left—after all, they were both expressing the same thought. Of course, it wasn't my intelligence that bothered my husbands, though I'm grateful people think so. When asked, I take the line that the painter wouldn't cope—engage—with it, and I couldn't stand that. And that the banker wanted to promote it—and of course I couldn't stand *that* either. That's the line I take."

In the chair opposite, the one pale slipper, twisting, was joined in its movement by the other; then both were set flat, suggesting that the chair's occupant was nervously in thrall.

"So," said the voice quickly, "at last, back to that spring. Couldn't do without the preamble, though; you'll see why, if you haven't begun to already. In fact, because you're so smart—so much smarter than I was at your age—I'll even give you the key to it all, though I expect it'll sound like kitchen-maid stuff to your collegiate ear. *That spring was the last spring she really lived.* Sorry, this is one of those. What I call 'little did I know' stories. Anyway—in case I made you uneasy back there—I still haven't *quite* murdered Professor Tyng.

"William Tenney Tyng. He was a tall, monk-skulled Anglophile, who opened his Daily Theme course every year by reciting 'The policeman's lot is not a happy one.' In private life he was known to be writing an epic poem. He hated to see the student eye in a fine frenzy rolling, and his highest accolade—I never got it—was to put 'Neat but not gaudy' on modest little themes about cats. I suppose his real trouble was he wanted to be teaching young Oxonians, not second-generation American girls who were floundering in a tumescent passion for the language and spoke it mostly in the accents of the Midwest or the Bronx. And I suppose I should feel sorry for him, now that I know he directed his irony at us only because he didn't dare direct it at the sublime. But I can't. Oh, I've used him, now and then, as people like me will use, over and over, those who have humiliated them, and I once said he didn't 'teach the young idea how to shoot,' as the quote says; he *shot* it, wherever, green and trembling, it arose. Let that stand.

"For you see, I'd set myself to handing in poems as themes. Five a week we had to hand in—and almost always I was his target. And I was drunk on language, the way kids used to get on jazz at Birdland. I ran all over the pasture, wondering how I could ever eat all the books there were; I was out of my mind with delight at what some people had been able to do to the world with words. And the words! I collected them in all shapes and sizes, and hung them like bangles in my mind. To this day I've never seen a snaffle, but I remember sitting for hours once wondering what made it twinkle—twinkle—on the page; a lot of those double-consonant words do it. Lots of times I never even knew how the words sounded out loud, and I rarely looked up the meanings—the words simply hung up there, waiting. It wasn't a bad way, really; you don't have much of value to say at that age; what can anybody do but hang up the words and wait?

"So, of course, I was a setup for Tyng. If he hated, as he did, the

exotic in Sir Thomas Browne, De Quincey, Coleridge, what couldn't
he do with me! 'Now, let us see what our young wallower in the
beauties of English literature has for us today! Hmm, a sonnet: "Let
me touch the terrace of the dream, /Soft set foot upon the fragile
stair . . ." Hmm. I'm rather a stupid man. Perhaps the author will
explain this to me. Most of the terraces I'm familiar with happen to
be in Scarsdale.'

"I might have cut his classes—we had free cuts—but I found I
couldn't; I had to sit there, in defense of I didn't quite know what.
He wasn't just preaching against excess; I knew that. He was saying
that all ardor, aspiration, was a disgrace.

"When I was most sunk, I started reading detective stories. Dos-
toevski and Baudelaire were too much for me; in their company I
didn't need Tyng to tell me I was a serf. I don't know how the idea
of writing a theme in which a professor was safely murdered merged
with the idea of murdering a professor—maybe because the plot was
so close to hand. During vacations Tyng had us mail themes to him
with a self-addressed envelope enclosed for their return. He was a
bachelor with no secretary, and the themes always came back
marked in his own crabbed script. If one could find a strong poison
to put under the flap of the return envelope—a delaying poison, of
course, which wouldn't be fatal until the envelope was safely away
in the mail—then 'twere done. Of course, one would have to gamble
that Tyng didn't use a sponge.

"You laugh; I don't blame you. I would too, if I didn't know how
close I came to the deed. I scared myself, because I knew the intense
way I brooded on it wasn't normal. And I had a girl friend whose
father ran an untidy, neglected drugstore; we often stopped by of an
afternoon and made sodas for ourselves. I found myself one day
looking up poisons in the pharmacopoeia, and I tried to reassure
myself by recalling that, no matter how many times I'd read *Crime
and Punishment*, I'd always hoped that Raskolnikov *wouldn't*. Still,
why had I avoided the school library and gone to the city one downtown?

"Then, one day when Tyng stood up to dismiss me after having
been particularly vicious to me in the conference hour, he said:
'Easter vacation coming up. Such a strain on poets. Perhaps you
might curb your *élan* a little, during the Lenten season. Try not to
drink quite so deep of the Pierian spring. Otherwise——' Then he

445

shook his head, licked the flap of an envelope he'd been fiddling with, and set it on the desk, as if for me to see. REPORTS, it said. RETURN to REGISTRAR.

"I walked out of there holding my breath, but not because I was worried about the mark. I'd done the work, and for all its spotty precocity it wasn't the kind he could openly give an F or D; what he'd do would be to purge me with mediocrity as he'd done last term, cupping my overheated blood with a C.

"No, what made me shiver, even as I passed girls in light jerseys on the tennis courts, was that licked envelope, falling to my lot as the knowledge that the old woman would be alone fell to Raskolnikov's. Dozens of times I'd heard someone say, as we left Tyng's course in Room 242: 'Couldn't you *kill* him?' Now I realized that what I'd been saying to myself was 'I *could* kill him.' I don't know what I'd have gone on to do if Ben Bijur hadn't been waiting for me at the dorm—as he usually was, in spite of his best resolutions, almost every other day. He was waiting, though, in one of those chintzy cubicles they made boys wait in. In a way it was like being saved from jumping out the bedroom window by happening to be in the center of the room, thinking about it, when the plaster falls.

"I suppose I was in love with Ben Bijur because he was the first man who'd ever touched me. In later years I've seen words swarm about an idea just the way my spongy dreams clustered about Ben Bijur's head the minute he put a hand on me and I let it stay. At home, in Ontario, I'd been a day student at a convent in a small town; the few local boys I'd known had been as fair and corn-fed as myself. This boy was enticingly swart and world-weary; he had splendid teeth and a fine baritone, but at twenty-two he was already losing his hair—a fact that he and I both looked upon, at the time, as an effect of character—and he was fond of saying quietly that he had been born old.

"The sad truth was that he had; his was one of those temperaments that never, even in senility, take the form of youth. At twenty-two, he was already a disappointed man, sulking at authority instead of flying at its eyes, carrying his hypersensitivity around with him the way a would-be suicide carries a knife—hoping to hurt himself. Even his frustrations seemed secondhand, as if he'd got them only through reading of Prufrock and Leopold Bloom. But at the time I was much impressed by the experiences at which Ben hinted—

446

though he was, no doubt, as virginal as I—and when he repeated his fantasies of affairs with older women, I smoothed his poor, shedding scalp in awe. He was a word collector too, and used to tell me mournfully that he was afraid he was already putting life into footnotes without ever having enjoyed the text. Whereas, he used to say, there was something about me, young as I was, which marked me for the success that would pass him by. Sometimes he drew little word pictures of how, when ten years had passed, I would open the door of my penthouse and find him fainting on the doorstep, his feet wrapped up in burlap bags.

"Ben called me four or five times a week and dropped by during the day, but he would never make a date ahead, and he had a way of not phoning on Saturday night—this was to preserve his freedom and keep me from knowing where I stood. Marriage was never mentioned, of course—he was getting his Ph.D. on an allowance from his father—but neither of us saw anybody else. Nights when he hadn't called, I hung near the phone in agony; when he did call and we went somewhere to neck, it often ended with me crying like mad on his shoulder—I didn't know why. Sadness interested him, and he treated mine with great deference, kissing me with a kind of scientific respect and muttering words like *Sehnsucht* into my ear. The farthest he'd ever gone was to lean against my blouse and quote into it, but this seemed to me very far.

"I'd never told Ben about Tyng, and I didn't this time; I was in such a high state of dejection I hardly noticed him. He'd got me out of the cubicle, bought us both hot dogs, and walked me to our favorite stretch along the river, before I realized that he was hanging on to my arm and looking at me with a humility I'd seen on the faces of young husbands walking their pregnant wives.

"I wasn't noticing *him*, you see; it must have been clear to him that I was swept up in some powerful emotion that was bigger than I. And for people like—well, like Ben—the sight of another person in the throes, divorced from reason, offering a breast for the eagles to pick at and so on, has an attraction just as strong as sex. That's why lots of times you'll see a weak man or an ugly woman with an entourage otherwise hard to explain; it's because they have this talent for letting life blow through them, for seeming to be swept away. And the people who hang around them don't even hope to get into the act; all they ask is to get close enough to be shaken a little themselves—something like kissing the Pope's ring, or being touched by the king for pox.

"Of course, there's another, simpler explanation for the way Ben acted—that he thought I was thinking of some other boy. Whichever it was, between it and the evening, he was done for.

"It *was* a gorgeous evening, one of those butterfly-blue ones. Every once in a while the river gave a little shantung wrinkle and then lay still; there was one sailboat low in the foreground, like Whistler's signature. Behind us, the windows of the Alpha Delt house were open, but there was nobody in them; everybody was off for the Easter holidays. Ben knew the grad student who acted as janitor in exchange for an apartment in the basement, an older man who was doing some kind of endless project on the Risorgimento and went off now and then with the merchant marine, until he had enough funds for another go at research. His door was always unlocked, and we'd been there once or twice alone. That evening there was a note tacked to the door: 'Back next Wednesday at eighteen hours.'

"Ben led me inside, murmuring, 'Say something, darling; you look so sad. I've never seen you look so sad!' By this time I wasn't, of course—he'd never called me darling before, and I knew that for him words spoke much louder than action—but I had the sense to hold my tongue and keep my sad expression, and on a young skin I suppose the wish to murder and the wish to love look much the same.

"He took off my dress, and the sight of me in my long cotton slip sent him down on one knee, his arms flung wide; it was a pose like the gallants in those slightly shady, illustrated editions of *Mademoiselle de Maupin* or the *Heptameron*—both of which Ben had. I was in an odd rig for seduction; there was a fashion on then for Oxford glasses, silver-rimmed ones that snapped open like lorgnettes, and mine hung down over my chest on a chain. My shoes were much too sedate for me too—terribly long, pointed ones, like dachshunds' muzzles—and my stockings, heavy gun-metal silk, were rolled. Despite all this, we were able to lose our heads. Or at least we thought we had—this generation can have no idea of the innocence of mine. When we left the apartment, I was under the confused impression that I had been seduced—an assumption that wasn't corrected until two years later, when I was. Ben must have been under the same misapprehension, because he insisted on taking me back to the dorm, ten blocks away, in a cab. And on the way he asked me for a date—for Saturday night.

"And when Saturday night came, he surprised me by taking me to the Baxter. Unlike the campus joints where we'd always gone for Coke or coffee, the Hotel Baxter was downtown, dull and semi-official; couples went there dutifully the minute they got engaged, for a splurge à la carte. Poor Ben! It was his only way of saying that if necessary he'd do right by me, but I was as insulted as if he'd bought the ring without asking me. It seemed humiliating that only sin had got me to the Baxter—and besides, I wasn't dressed for it.

"To this day those starlight-roof places always make me think of babies born out of wedlock, for of course that's what was on Ben's mind. He ordered Alexanders—in those days that's what you started girls drinking on—and when I said mine made me feel positively sick he turned white, not knowing I'd said it only because at home in Ontario my grandfather had taught us early to disdain anything but Scotch. 'What—what about *Banjo?*' he said.

"Banjo was one of those terrible whimsies that lovers have, like those letters beginning 'Dear Poodles . . .' that stockbrokers always seem to get held up for; you and your Stamford boy probably shared something of the same. Ben was always plying me with anecdotes I didn't yet know were clichés, and once—after he'd told me how Isadora Duncan wrote Bernard Shaw suggesting what a paragon any child of theirs would be—we'd spent an afternoon concocting a paragon of our own. It was to have Ben's teeth, *my* hair, and—since this was also a very feminist era—*both* our brains. We'd dubbed it Ben-Jo, corrupted in time to Banjo.

"And for some reason that wasn't clear to me at the Baxter, his choosing that way to ask me infuriated me. Why did he always have to remove himself from everything, from the most important things, by putting them into quotes!

" 'Oh you!' I said. 'You're so literary you make me spit!' Then I stood up, burst into tears, and we went home.

"Extraordinary, isn't it? There it was, a warning out of my own mouth, and I passed it by, the way you can speed to your death right past a warning from Burma-Shave.

"During the next few weeks Ben scarcely left my side. Vacation was well under way, but by this time I was glad I hadn't had the money to go home; I couldn't have borne being at home feeling like Hardy's Tess. Day after day went by and—it must have been nervous strain or self-hypnosis—I still couldn't assure Ben we weren't going to have a baby. Luckily I had term papers to do, and Ben had his thesis; we spent most of our time in the library or walking by the river, holding hands numbly but not kissing. I was finding out how the world both heightens and darkens under a single, consuming anxiety; normality goes on rattling around you, and your trouble is like a goiter in your gullet that no one else can see. Ben and I couldn't bear to be out of each other's sight; it was such a relief to be with someone who *knew*. At the same time, I couldn't help feeling a certain excitement at being one with several heroines of history. Once, when we were down by the river, I referred darkly to *An American Tragedy* and, to my surprise, Ben gave me a dreadful look and dropped my hand. It hadn't occurred to me until then that he might be having heroic feelings of his own. I wasn't afraid of them, but I was rather miffed at the idea of his enjoying them, and for the first time I wondered whether it would be a bore to marry someone whose reference books were the same as mine.

"Meanwhile, I'd forgotten all about Professor Tyng. Then, the last night before school began again, I remembered I hadn't sent him my ration of themes. I'd enough back poems to choose from, and after Ben and I had parted, I sat up until three retyping them. As I slugged them out I kept thinking of how I might never have been in the situation I was in, if it hadn't been for Tyng. When I'd finished, I went down the hall to wash out some underwear, and in the bathroom I saw the bottle of stuff the maids used for the drains. It was marked POISON in large, navy-blue letters.

"I picked it up and read the fine print on the label: *Antidote: Drink teaspoon or more of magnesia, chalk, whiting or simple wall plaster—or small pieces of soap softened in water—in milk, or raw egg.* Quite a rhythm the first phrases had, each with its feminine ending, then that nice little dactyl: *or raw egg.* Neat, but not gaudy. I went back for the envelope I'd addressed to myself, carefully used an old toothbrush to paint some of the stuff from the bottle onto the underside of the flap, carried the envelope back to my room, and set it on the blotter to dry. I never once thought of using the poison on myself. Indeed, I had never felt more surgingly alive, and for the first time in days I fell asleep like a lamb.

"And the next morning I discovered I wasn't going to have Banjo after all. The world immediately lost that intent, outlined look and went back to being its usual astigmatic blur; I'd never before felt how glorious the ordinary was. Ben had a nine-o'clock in philosophy; I raced over there to tell him.

"The elevator in Philosophy Hall was one of those old-fashioned wire-cage ones that held only about six people. I'd squeezed in and faced the door before I saw that Professor Tyng was one of the six, his height looming over us all. I must have looked wild. My hair was tousled, and I'd just remembered the envelope on my blotter in my room.

" 'Ah, good morning, Miss—er,' he said. He had a very commanding voice. And you know that conscious stillness people have in elevators. 'Tell me,' he said. 'Have you quite deserted poetry?'

"The elevator girl, an old university hand, closed the door softly and waited; she knew as well as I did that he hadn't finished. I lowered my eyes, but I could feel the mass smile all around me.

" 'Ah, well,' said Tyng, 'I always say that one's poetry is a solace to oneself and a nuisance to one's friends.'

"That elevator must have been the slowest in the city; it rose in exact time with the blood in my ears. I didn't answer Tyng and I didn't look him in the face. I just stared at the cords in his neck. Someday I'll murder you, I thought, but not with poison. No, I'll remember what you taught me, that only irony is safe. Just you go on talking, and someday I'll murder you—with words. Some day I'll hang you by the neck with them, until you are *alive*.

"Classes were already on, but I got Ben out of his; he was an awful color and kept saying, 'What is it? What is it?' out of the side of his mouth as we went down the hall. When we got outside on the steps, I told him. At that moment, all I felt was a horrible, female embarrassment at having to tell him.

" 'It's Banjo,' I said. 'He isn't.'

"The most peculiar expression crossed his face. There was relief there first, of course, but then something else took its place. Regret after catharsis is the only way I can describe it—the way people's faces sometimes look when they come out of the theater after a wonderfully harrowing play.

"I didn't understand it until later that afternoon, when we were sitting quietly together over a Coke, in the rear of the soda parlor.

" 'You know,' Ben said, 'when we were so worried, back there
. . . Nevertheless that was *living*, though, wasn't it? That was real.'

"I knew what he meant, of course; I'd seen the world shift that
morning too. But to *say* it, to put it into . . . maybe even while it
was all going on . . . or even before! Poor footnoter, I thought,
poor self-murderer. At the same time I shrank back from the table,
from him—the way one leans away from someone with a bad cold.

" '*I'm* alive!' I said. 'I'm *still* alive.' I stood up. 'Afraid I've got to
run,' I said. And I ran.

"The minute I got back to my room I sat down and wrote him a
letter saying I didn't want to see him again. I didn't understand
quite why yet myself, so I lied and said I was in love with another
man.

"Two weeks later, Ben came to see me; I suppose he thought it
just another dodge to bring him to his knees. Anyway, that's just
what he did—went down on his knees again, without even saying
hello first, and asked me to marry him. Later he told a friend of
mine that from the way I'd refused him—I *knew* I hadn't been sad
enough—it was clear I'd never be a woman of the world. I haven't
seen him since, but now and then I hear he's around somewhere,
technically alive. I sure don't want to see him. Little does he know
the very particular way he could crow over me—fainting on my doorstep or not, with or without his feet in those burlap bags. . . .' "

An intensity of silence reigned now, a contest of quiet in which
the speaker herself must have been wondering if she was to be allowed to get away with it like that—or whether the girl across from
her was going to let her know that she was not.

We can be quiet too, the silence said now. People like us . . .

"What?" Was the voice relieved at not being let off? "Don't
mumble so. . . . Ah, you want to know what it was—what both my
husbands said when they left. Now, really! The listener ought to do
some of the work. I've been telling you, actually, all the way along.
OK, guess, then. Don't be shy; go on, try.

"Oh. You think it was more or less what I said to Ben—just before I ran? That's very clever of you; you're a very clever girl. That
would be a twist, wouldn't it? You've *got* talent, no doubt about it.
Well, I shan't say, but you listen now. You listen very carefully.

"After I'd sealed that letter to Ben and put it into the mail slot in
the hall, I came back to my room. The envelope for Tyng, stained

brown and shriveled, was lying where I'd left it. I picked it up, rolled it in some tissue from an old stocking box, and threw it into the basket. Then I went to the window and leaned on the sill. It was the holy time, a beautiful evening. A dusky wind was blowing, and the west was the color of a peach. I could feel the cold touch of the pearls at my throat, the warm cuddle of the jersey I'd just thrust my arms into; I thought I could even feel the lovely tickle of the blood running in my veins. It was spring, and my whole future was opening up again, full of oysters, music, lovers. A few foghorns were sounding on the river, and I wondered idly whether I would ever be able to set down exactly the emotion that sound always called up in me—as I had tried and failed to do so many times before.

"And after a while, as I leaned there, the words came, began to shimmer and hang in the air about me. There they were, armies of them, ready to be made into ropes for necks, ready for lovers to be put into, husbands, life. They danced in my mind like wild ponies that moved only to my command, with hooves sharp enough to kill, but forelocks meek enough to me.

"It had been a day. All in one day I'd found out I wasn't going to have Banjo, marry Ben, poison Tyng. It had been a day full enough for anyone. Except me—and perhaps you. . . ."

Was she leaning forward? The voice was low now, farther back in its own mists than it had ever been, yet near enough for the quick of any ear.

"So I sat down at the desk again—what I wrote was published the next year. The world stretched all before me that evening, in profuse strains of unpremeditated—life. But I left the window, and began to write about it. . . ."

No, it was the girl, leaning back, away, now stealthily rising. For a moment the figure stayed, a series of soft, dark ellipses lapsing to that poised, no longer tentative shoe. Then it ran. On the edge of the promenade it halted; then the wind, or a gesture of its own, tossed back the free-swinging hair and it was gone.

Did the voice know it was alone now? Had it planned it that way —to be left addressing that perfect, illimitable audience of one? For it was still speaking.

"So I left the window," it said, "and began to write about it. Beginning with the word 'I.' "

Night Riders of Northville

⌇ O n s m o k y spring evenings, from the windows of the com-
muter's train which rides through the lowlands of Jersey, the little
bars, which are seldom more than a block or so from the stations,
look like hot coals burning in the thin dusk. Spotted over the countryside, they send up their signal flares, promising the fought-off
moment of excitement before you open the door—when it seems as
if someone may just this minute have said: "Here is the place—*the
place*," and the flat, sold feeling after the door is open, and you see
that this is just about like any such place anywhere.

If, having missed your usual train perhaps, you stop off at the
particular hole-in-a-corner which clings to your station—Joe's Place,
or Morelli's, or the Rainbow Tavern—and you sit there over your
glass, after your phone call, waiting for the taxi or the wife with the
car—then you may find, after the quick rash of one-shot commuters
is over, that you are alone, or almost alone, with perhaps a solitary,
leather-jacketed baggageman musing over his beer on his stool down
at the other end. And you wonder what keeps a joint like this alive.

Down in the thriving center of town, or settled here and there on
its skirting streets, are places, certainly, which cater more specially
to a man's sudden convivial needs, or to his malaises. Out on the
highway which is never far from such a town, the roadhouses, each
evening, corral the people who want steak, pizza, chicken-in-the-
basket. There is a "good place to take the family and still get a
drink," a haunt for the juke-box babies, a daytime spot which draws
the lawyers from the courthouse over at the county seat, even a
swank little box of a place where certain rich women of the town
gather to sip away time from the huge carafe of it that confronts
them each day between breakfast and the arrival of the evening

train. And because no man or woman lives his life in just one context, sooner or later you may see a person who more properly belongs in a particular one of these places, seated, explicably or not, in another.

But the nondescript place where you are sitting now—could it be said to have a category? To whom or what could it cater, other than to the casual, modestly sated thirsts of its portion of two trainfuls a day of men homeward bound toward the snow shovel or the garden, or toward the less seasonal dictates of the television, the wife, and the children with egg on their chins? And as you rise, relievedly, to the toot of a horn outside, and exchange diffident nods with the owner, you decide that his reserve with you on this and other occasions is the case, not because you are not a regular, but because there are no regulars here. As you go out the door, you wonder idly how he hangs on here at all, and you imagine him of a Sunday, when the trains are all but stilled, totting up his supplier's bills and his receipts, and worrying about a better spot for trade.

Should you sit on there for a sufficient number of evenings, however, you might learn how wrong you were. For that place is one of a circuit of such places which certain men of the town ride ceaselessly, for reasons which neither appear to be simple nor are.

Take, for instance, the Rainbow Tavern at Northville, and four of its regulars—James De Vries, Dicky English, Jack Burdette, and Henry Lister. If you get to know the habits of these four, who are sure to appear there singly or in varying combinations almost every night of the week—and if you also happen to learn of a minor tragedy which befell one of them—then in the course of time you may also sense, although you may never quite be able to put your finger on it, the nature of that *spécialité de la maison* which is served by the Rainbow Tavern.

James De Vries, who is always called "the judge," out of deference to the fact that he was once, for several years, a justice of the peace, is the only one of the four who was born in Northville—and perhaps some of the deference is to this fact too. In a town where most of the men make their living elsewhere, he is one of those vanishing few who subsist on their inherited knowledge of the place and the "connections" in it—a little banking, some law, a few real estate transactions, and a little politicking. He can tell you the real legend

455

of the old Viner place, and what went on there in the old days, can search a title in his mind before he has to refer to county records, and lives in the ground-floor apartment of the cupolaed house in which he was born—the house bought by his grandfather, who was a minor henchman of Boss Tweed. Although there has never been any suggestion of financial hanky-panky about his own reputation, there still clings to him, somehow, the equivocal aura of the man who turns a dollar because he is in the know. As he stands at the bar, with his hat brim turned low over his long, swart face, so that if you are near him and fairly tall you cannot glimpse anything but his mouth (for the judge is quite short, and in the manner of many short men, affects hats a little too high in the crown and wide of brim), he keeps a silence weighted faintly with an indication that silence is what he has come here for. If he is addressed, however, on a question of local affairs, he likes to pronounce the answers in a measured, monotonous voice, although he will never keep the conversational ball rolling with the added fillip of a question or an opinion. He is at the bar briefly at five, at seven-thirty, and at ten, so precisely that Denis, the owner, often may answer a time query from one of the regulars: "Almost time for the judge's last round." He has two drinks at five, three at seven-thirty, and three at ten, always of straight bourbon with a dash of bitters, and always set before him by Denis as soon as he appears. He has probably not ordered out loud for years, never buys or is bought a drink, and has long since managed to convey, by this routine, that for him, liquor—something to be accomplished, as it were, as is a meal by a man not interested in the table—is never in any case a specific for some disreputable need. It is ironic, therefore, that in a place where casualness and haphazard spontaneity are part of the mores, the very carefulness of the judge's behavior has made him the oddity he imagines he is not.

For, often, when a man is to be found night after night in the same place, swaying deep in drink, progressing through the stereotype stages of the drunk—from the painful interest in each newcomer, the mumbled revelation to the bartender, down to the final, locked communion with the glass—often a common thing to be heard in the pitying undertones behind him is: "Nice guy though. They say his wife is a bitch." But in the Rainbow Tavern this is most commonly said of the judge. Not by any of the other three regulars, incidentally, for all the regulars share a solidarity of reticence about their affairs outside, one even stronger than is usual among men, perhaps, and peculiarly noticeable, since it suggests that, with them, home may be really the outside, and "inside" is here. No one knows the origin of this rumor about the judge, or any verification for it, for although the other three know each other in another context, the social life of the town—have visited each other in their homes, and even, by prearrangement, have brought their wives here, after the manner of men who twice a year tolerate ladies' night at the club—the judge does not know any of these people socially, and never brings his "outside" here. The rumor arises, possibly, because there is no worse place to hide than among the heightened awarenesses of others who are hiding too.

When a man walks into the Rainbow Tavern, it is often possible to tell his mood, at what stage in the circuit he is, or how full he is or intends to be, from the angle at which he wears his hat. Dicky English's hat is always tipped toward the back of his head. This is true of him wherever he is making an entrance, whether to the Rainbow or others of its ilk, to a party, to a meeting of one of the dozens of committees on which he is a prime mover, or to the smoker of the morning train. A buzzing, bustling, smart dresser of a man, in whose freshly barbered face, above his bow-tie, the slightly juvenile features are only healthfully obscured by a faintly moony, fortyish fat, Dicky, if not exactly a dream of fair women, is conceivably that of a number of fair typists in the office of which he is manager. Only longer acquaintance with him suggests that in his very trueness to form there is something much too credible. Watching Dicky at first, one is bored or amused by the larger-than-life verisimilitude of the man; later one wonders how, under such a bewildering collection of verisimilitudes, there can be a man at all. Here, one says, as he struts chestily into a conversation, or, his backside waggling in jaunty efficiency, is seen disappearing round the bend in the center of two or three cronies he has marshaled on an errand of pleasure—here is the eternal seller of tickets to raffles, the organizer of poker games and pig roasts; here is the life-of-the-party, in whom, as with so many such, there is just enough of the clown, the simpleton, the butt—so that by his very *bêtises* he breaks down the united ice of others, warming them, even at the cost of ridicule, to that sense of occasion he craves.

To his intimates at the Rainbow, where his invariable greeting is

"You're planning to go, aren't you?" his invariable adieu "Be sure to be there, now," Dicky passes for a joiner, a mixer, a man whose compulsion barely escapes buffoonery, but is invaluable to those whose gregariousness is more wistful, less competent. He is sensitive to the needs of the company, too—a Rotarian in Rotary, a father among fathers, a fornicator among fornicators—always so long as he can go on talking. Even his drinking is versatile and somehow controlled; he is good for an elegiac, gossipy chat in a corner or for an all-night spree with the boys, but even in the midst of the spree he never seems *personally* drunk. Only when you see him at home, a paterfamilias outdoing all others, or at a roadhouse, perhaps, this time with the wife, to whom he is playing the uxoriously gallant part of the husband on his girl's night out, or in the morning smoker, where he persists in reading tidbits of news to men whose issues of the same paper are already slack and crumpled in their hands—only then may you realize that Dicky is more than a man who lives for the occasion—he is a man who cannot live without it, however small. Like those little mechanical toy men with the keys in their split, metal backs, he will scuttle around and around only as long as the original impetus lasts—one begins to imagine, behind the truckling rounds of his talk, a gasping prescience that, when he slackens, he will topple over on his side forever. He is a man who convinces himself into humanity only by the ululating sound of his own voice. And because one can imagine him en route to an experience, or possibly from it, but never actually in the middle of it, one can form conclusions as to Dicky's reasons for stopping so often at a place like the Rainbow, which is essentially, after all, en route.

As for Jack Burdette and Henry Lister, there is no need to take up separately two who are almost always together. They roomed together at college, went into business and married at about the same time, bought houses on adjoining streets in that fancy modern development in Northville before it was too evident that their wives would never get along, and refugees now, each from the disapproval of two wives, are ever more closely united in the deep beatitudes of the bottle. Jack is a great beef of a man with a fine nose only just beginning to vein, and an extraordinarily sweet smile which, with the cleft in the first of his chins, forms a solitary fleur-de-lys above the others. He is one of those large, deceptively solid men who melt in drink: as the evening advances, the smile grows fixed on a face which recedes behind it like a huge, fair egg, the bottom outline of which has been drawn several times over by a wavering artist.

Seen over his shoulder, in that rich, Rembrandt-colored air of the Rainbow, which is half submerged smell, half expunged light, Henry Lister's face, mouse-sharp and precise, does not change at all. There is no mystery about Henry unless it is the absence of one. He is a neutral, common denominator of a man, whose only departure from the ordinary is his drinking; even the latter seems an effort to fill up the uncomfortable reservoir of his averageness. He is never out of place in any company he keeps, and never quite of it; he is a man who is always seen over someone else's shoulder—in this case Jack's.

Over the years, the association of these two has effected a likeness quite apart from looks—the kind of dual semblance which occurs in a long, uneventful marriage. Jack, who is an investment counselor, often surprises his business acquaintances with quite a bookish allusion, and Henry, who is in the trade department of a publishing house, is considered by his colleagues to be pretty sharp on the market. During the business day, Jack's eye is remarkably clear and shrewd, notwithstanding the night before, and Henry's manner may be a little on the vague side, but at closing time in the Rainbow, after the long, matched session of glass for glass, it is Henry who gently leads the faltering Jack away from the bar and drives him home.

One might think that their wives—both childless, both graduates of the stern discipline of the evasive phone call, the mummified supper, the endless evening in the empty living room, of which there happens to be a counterpart not half a block away—one would think that they might pool their grievances in a sort of friendship too. Such is not the case, however. They hate each other—oddly enough each of the women saves her invective not for her rival, but for his wife. It is simpler that way perhaps. Or possibly it is easier to bear the onus of a rival than the presence of someone whose grievances are the same.

Once or twice Henry and Jack have been known to josh each other over this quirk of Alice's and Mary Lou's, but only in the clichés with which men refer to women at the Rainbow, where it is generally conceded that the ladies, all of them sphinxes, are worth the solving at times, but blessedly not here and now. Mostly, however, the two men sit on in silence, accumulating on the abacus of their bar bill an ever huger total of hours they have spent thus together, two eunuchs sitting in a quietude from which trouble has been castrated, at a comfortable, derisive distance from the harem.

This, then, was the way things stood with the four regulars, when Mrs. Henry Lister, on a pink May evening which contrasted, who knows how fiercely, with her sallow day, cut her wrists.

On this particular Monday night, when the phone rang in the booth at the Rainbow, the four men had the bar to themselves. This is often the case on Mondays, for at the Rainbow there is a discernible, taken-for-granted rhythm to the evenings of the week. Sunday is the big night; Denis is rarely able to close the place until four. Tuesdays and Wednesdays are slow; even Henry and Jack may not appear until after ten or perhaps not at all, presumably having gone home for a token dinner and been prevailed upon to stay. Thursdays are pretty normal, and Fridays the bar begins to expand again, with men who drink in a certain propriety, duty-bound, as it were, to honor the inception of the weekend. Saturday is a poor night for the regulars, who are shunted out of their niche by celebrants who come (as the four indicate to each other with faint shrugs) apparently from nowhere, and Denis is kept busy shooing minors out of the place. But on Sunday nights the bar really hums, with an added group of familiars who arrive gratefully after the dearth of the day. Meeting on the station platform the morning after, the three regulars (for the judge, of course, does not commute) greet each other with reminiscent shakes of the head, eying each other's gray gills and red, granular eyelids, and sit at an understanding distance from each other in the smoker, retiring glumly behind their papers. If a man just makes the train by the skin of his teeth, this is the one morning on which he is not chaffed. Even Dicky English has learned to shut his face on Monday mornings.

During this particular first day of the business week, the city streets had been stroked with summer. When the evening train set down its passengers in Northville, it could be seen that the leaves, although still new against the sky, were no longer single and choice. The air had a beautiful, clear expectancy about it, like the inside of a glass bell that was about to be rung. The door of the Rainbow, though not yet screened, had been ajar.

Now, with the bar to themselves, the four were settled restfully on their stools like convalescents from a mutual illness, just able to savor the malted dimness of the place in the safely muted company of their kind. Henry and Jack had been here since train time, the judge was in the middle of his second round, and Dicky had just breezed in.

"Some night last night, eh Denis?" said Dicky.

Denis nodded. He was a profound listener, with a repertoire of silent assent which ranged from the nod to a look of alert, pained sympathy which came, actually, from varicosed veins, but was a great help to his business.

Dicky tipped his hat further back on his head. "Hear Patterson's still on the town. They say he never did get home."

"In here about four o'clock for a minute," said Denis, polishing a glass.

"Better watch himself lately." Dicky clapped his hands together, raised one to readjust his hat, looked about him minutely as if to search the possibilities of the hour, and let his arm sink around Jack's neck. "Howja do at the office today pal?"

Jack turned his head carefully within the crook of the encircling arm, and smiled his sweet, ponderous smile. "I died," he said.

"How about Henry, there? He looks able to sit up and take nourishment?"

Henry screwed his eyes shut appreciatively, but made no answer. Down at the left end of the bar, the judge looked owlishly into an empty glass, Denis moved quickly to replace it with the third and last of his round. And the telephone rang.

No one at the bar flinched in notice, although the telephone rings infrequently at the Rainbow. The phone knew better than to call for any of the men here.

Denis shuffled through the archway into the alcove which held the phone booth and the pinball machine. After a minute he returned, gestured at Henry, and returned to his polishing. Henry pointed at himself with raised eyebrows, shrugged, and walked out of the booth. He was there for some time.

"Da-te-da, da-te-da, da-te-da," said Dicky, falsetto.

Jack hunched himself over the bar, lit a cigarette, dropped the match on the floor before it was quite dead, and rubbed it out with his shoe.

"Jesus Henry what's wrong?" said Dicky.

Henry stood in the archway, his face white, his arms dangling uncertainly at his sides. "The police. They took Alice to the hospital."

Jack lurched to his feet. "Something with the car, Hen?"

"She tried to . . ." Henry turned his head from side to side. "She acted all right this morning," he said on a high note. "She acted perfectly O.K."

"Drive you down, fella?" said Dicky.

Henry seemed not to have heard him. He reached out and touched the bar surface, moving his hand along as if he expected to find a tab there. "They want to type my blood they said." He moved toward the door.

"I'll go with you, Hen." Jack went toward him, weaving a little.

"No," said Henry. His eyes returned to focus. He shivered. "No. Don't do that, Jack." He went out the door.

"Call me here. Call me if you need me." There was no answer except the current of air from the swinging door. They heard the splutter of a motor, its outraged whine and diminuendo. Through the door, which remained ajar, came the dark, stealing scents of May. After a minute, Denis walked over and closed it.

"She have a miss, you think?" whispered Dicky. No one answered him.

The judge coughed, and spoke. "Sold them that house they have. Over on Summit. Nine years ago, just before the rise. Nice little property." He shook his head, as if he could not be responsible for the way people mishandled the lives to which he had helped them attach a property of value. Then, glancing at the clock, he saw that it was time. Pulling his hat brim lower, he nodded and left.

"Well, guess I'm on my way too," said Dicky. "Drop you, Jack? Well, see you in the morning then." He eased himself halfway out the door, then poked his head back in. "Chilly," he said, shaking his head solemnly, and shut the door behind him.

It can be awkward, drinking alone at a bar. Is the man behind it wholly a servitor at such times, or must recognition be made of the fact that two human beings are together in an otherwise empty room? At such times it is good to be where one is known. Denis sat reading his newspaper, his shell-rims far down on his nose, his presence as sane and reassuring as a night nurse. It was a racing final he read; occasionally he made a mark on it with a pencil, or rose to freshen Jack's glass. There were no other demands on his attention either from his customer or from the phone. Gradually the room, although it had no fireplace, took on the gutted look of a room in which a fire had died down. When the late freight chuffed by on her way to Newburgh, Denis went to the booth, called a cabby with whom he had an arrangement, shook Jack by the shoulder, and sent him home.

The next day, Dicky English, purveying the news to the smoker, had the field to himself. Henry, of course, was absent, and Jack did not appear for several days. On the second of these, the smoker heard, as the town had already heard, that Mrs. Henry Lister had muffed it. She would survive. This was received as such news is. The suicide attempt which is successful has an awesome achievement about it, before which we quail, but bow. It is a terrible epitaph, but it is one, and its headstone will sooner or later be obscured like any other. But the incompetent who has botched, who has been retrieved against his will, has committed an indecency. He has brought his nakedness not to the tomb, but to the tea table. Later, his existence will fret us like that of the invalid whose ailment death refuses to dignify.

On the morning when Jack returned to the train, it was observed that he had the drained, pearly look of dedication of the man who is on the wagon. No comments were made, since it was known how close Jack had been to Henry—too close, it was assumed, for comfort. Not a few of the other men who had been riding the circuit a little too steadily were, over that weekend, unwontedly solicitous of their wives and gardens. But, the following week, when Henry, too, returned to the train, it was plain that the shaft which Mrs. Lister had aimed at her husband, had not only struck glancingly at his friend but had also sheared between the two. Their steps no longer joined naturally with each other's, when they greeted, it was with the creaking tact of constraint, and although they both were avoiding the Rainbow, they did not do so together.

When Henry, taking his month off early, took his wife down to Atlantic City, both the town and the smoker were relieved. It was felt that he had done the proper thing not only for his wife, but for the community. At present, for instance, it was neither natural to inquire after her, or to neglect to. But for a long time, even after things blew over, Henry would be a constriction on any company he kept—precisely because he had suffered no conventional loss.

Had he done so, however unusually, one could still have offered him the normal currency of condolence. One could have demonstrated one's fealty at the funeral parlor, or, meeting him at a later date, extended to him, according to the degrees of delicacy and acquaintance, either the mute clasp of the hand, or one of those basso-timbred remarks with which we acknowledge to one another that we are all as dust. Still later, after his sorrow was a little out of its black, one could have propelled him tenderly toward drink, as one propels a widow toward tears. As things were, however, Mrs. Lister, and death, in their brief affair together, had cuckolded Henry, had made of him, moreover, a man whose cuckoldry is known.

During the weeks of Henry's absence, Jack returned, little by little, to the Rainbow. Each evening he walked in earlier and stayed on later, until, rosy once more, he was back at the old routine. On those evenings when Denis judged him unfit to drive himself home the cabman was called. Or sometimes the cabby checked for himself, in a friendly sort of way.

On one of these evenings, just after Denis had made the call, Jack brought his glass down on the bar with a rap that raised Denis' startled glance from his paper, and leaned intently over the bar.

"Not the same around here, is it Denis?" he muttered. "Not the same." He looked into his glass, which he was swiveling in his hand. After a moment he looked up again. "It never will be the same," he said, in a voice suddenly free of rheum.

Denis, who, in his trade, witnessed few of the soaring denouements of drama, but often administered to its tag-ends and dispersals, kept his own counsel.

On another Monday night, this time late in June, Dicky, the judge, and Jack once more had the bar to themselves. It was again the time of the judge's second round, and Dicky, again, had just breezed in. There was nothing oddly Aristotelian about this unity of time, space, and character; as must be clear by now, the very predictability of the Rainbow, the very reassurance of the way in which evenings spent there tend to blur into one long, continuous evening, is a part of its stock in trade. This night, however was the one on which Henry Lister chose to return.

When he walked through the door, which was screened now, and had been closed against the humming insect tide of summer, his manner in no way admitted that this was a return, or that there had been, at any time, a choice to be made. Denis, alone of the men there, was not surprised. On the faces of the other friends there was a momentary flash, like that on a mirror turned once against the light and laid flat.

To the right of Jack, who was farthest down the bar, there were three empty stools. Henry sat down on the middle one of these.

"Evening," said Henry. "Judge . . . Jack . . . Dicky . . . evening."

From the quiet chorus of greetings, Dicky's rose with verve. "Well look who's here! If he isn't a sight for sore eyes!" He walked over and pumped Henry's hand with unction. "Looking fit, boy," he added, in the low, secret tones of allegiance. "Real fit."

Behind him, the others stared into their drinks, but on Henry's face there was a singular look of gratitude. It was as if Dicky, in doing what might be expected of Dicky, had shown him that whatever he had returned for was likely to be here too.

Now the other men began to talk, each punctuating his remarks with the helpful arc of his glass. They said little of local affairs, of all that can happen in a town, or a bar, while some one is away. They talked rather of things in the tenor of the times, of the National League and the American, of the price of government, and the probabilities of war. They spoke of the things people have to keep up to date on, no matter what has happened to them or where they have been.

Time passed, enough for the judge to leave and return for his final call. When the judge was on his last drink of the evening, Henry bought a drink for the crowd, sliding down a stool to the one next to Jack's. "How about you, judge?" he said. "Break down and have an extra?"

This was an old gambit, and the judge made his accustomed response. "Oh no," he said, frowning, made for the door, as if frightened, and left. Behind him, the men smiled at each other, taking pleasure in the foibles of their kind. On Henry's face there was again the look of gratitude.

After a while Dicky went into the alcove to play the pinball game.

When the cabman poked his head with an inquiring look, Jack looked down at the floor. "Tell him never mind," said Henry's voice over his shoulder. "I'll drive you home."

It grew late, but the tawny light in the Rainbow deepened and mellowed, as if it, not the whiskey, had the power to turn men rubicund or gray. The silence purred, that silence of the Rainbow which is like the purring of a great tom resting from the rat cries of reality, from the quest for cream, and the squeaky, flagellant voices of women. From time to time came the ratchety-slat of the pinball machine, than which there is no more aimless sound in the world. And after a while, it was the same.

In the Absence of Angels

♪♪ BEFORE COCKCROW tomorrow morning, I must remember everything I can about Hilda Kantrowitz. It is not at all strange that I should use the word "cockcrow," for, like most of the others here, I have only a literary knowledge of prisons. If someone among us were to take a poll—that lax, almost laughable device of a world now past—we would all come up with about the same stereotypes: Dickens' Newgate, no doubt, full of those dropsical grotesques of his, under which the sharp shape of liberty was almost lost; or, from the limp-leather books of our teens, "The Ballad of Reading Gaol," that period piece of a time when imprisonment could still be such a personal affair. I myself recall, from a grade-school reader of thirty years ago, a piece named "Piccola," called so after a flower that pushed its way up through a crevice in a stone courtyard and solaced the man immured there—a general, of God knows what political coloration.

Outside the window here, the only hedge is a long line of hydrangeas, their swollen cones still the burnt, turned pink of autumn, still at the stage when the housewives used to pick them and stand them to dry on mantels, on pianos, to crisp and gather dust until they were pushed, crackling, into the garbage, in the first, diluted sun of spring.

We here, women all of us, are in what until recently was a fashionable private school, located, I am fairly certain, somewhere in Westchester County. There was no business about blindfolds from the guards on the trucks that brought us; rather, they let us sit and watch the flowing countryside, even comment upon it, looking at us with an indifference more chilling than if they had been on the alert, indicating as it did that a break from a particular truck into

467

particular environs was of no import in a countryside that had become a cage. I recognized the Saw Mill River Parkway, its white marker lines a little the worse for lack of upkeep, but its banks still neat, since they came in November, after the grass had stopped growing. Occasionally—at a reservoir, for instance—signposts in their language had been added, and there were concentrations of other trucks like ours. They keep the trains for troops.

This room was the kindergarten; it has been cleared, and the painted walls show clean squares where pictures used to be, for they have not yet covered them with their special brand of posters, full of fists and flags. Opposite me is their terse, typed bulletin, at which I have been looking for a long time. Built into the floor just beneath it, there is a small aquarium of colored tile, with a spigot for the water in which goldfish must have been kept, and beyond is the door that leads to our "latrine"—a little corridor of miniature basins and pygmy toilets and hooks about three and a half feet from the floor. In this room, which has been lined with full-size cots and stripped of everything but a certain innocent odor of crayon and chalk, it is possible to avoid imagining the flick of short braids, the brief toddle of a skirt. It is not possible in the latrine.

They ring the school bell to mark off the hours for us; it has exactly the same naïve, releasing trill (probably operated electrically by some thumb in what was the principal's office) as the bell that used to cue the end of Latin period and the beginning of math in the city high school where Hilda Kantrowitz and I were among the freshmen, twenty-five years ago. Within that school, Hilda and I, I see now, were from the first slated to fall into two covertly opposed groups of girls.

On the application we had all filled out for entrance, there was a line that said "Father's Business." On it I had put the word "manufacturer," which was what my father always called himself—which, stretching it only a little, is what I suppose he was. He had a small, staid leather-goods business that occupied two floors of an untidy building far downtown. When my mother and I went there after a shopping tour, the workers upstairs on the factory floor, who had banded together to give me a silver cup at my birth, would lean their stained hands on barrels and tease me jocularly about my growth; the new young girls at the cutting tables would not stop the astonish-

ingly rapid, reflex routine of their hands but would smile at me
diffidently, with inquisitive, sidelong glances. Downstairs, on the
office-and-sales floor, where there was a staff of about ten, one or the
other of my uncles would try to take me on his lap, groaning loudly,
or Harry Davidson, the thin, henpecked cousin-by-marriage who was
the bookkeeper, would come out of the supply room, his paper cuffs
scraping against a new, hard-covered ledger, which he would present
to me with a mock show of furtiveness, for me to use for my poems,
which were already a family joke.

The girls I went with, with whom I sat at lunch, or whom I rushed
to meet after hours in the Greek soda parlor we favored, might too
have been called, quite appositely, manufacturers' daughters, although not all of their fathers were in precisely that category.
Helen's father was an insurance broker in an office as narrow as a
knife blade, on a high floor of the most recent skyscraper; Flora's
father (of whom she was ashamed, in spite of his faultless clothes
and handsome head, because he spoke bad English in his velvety
Armenian voice) was a rug dealer; and Lotte's father, a German
"banker," who did not seem to be connected with any bank, went
off in his heavy Homburg to indefinite places downtown, where he
"promoted," and made deals, coming home earlier than any of the
others, in time for thick afternoon teas. What drew us together was
a quality in our homes, all of which subscribed to exactly the same
ideals of comfort.

We went home on the trolley or bus, Helen, Flora, Lotte, and I,
to apartments or houses where the quality and taste of the bric-a-brac
might vary but the linen closets were uniformly full, where the furniture covers sometimes went almost to the point of shabbiness but
never beyond. Our mothers, often as not, were to be found in the
kitchen, but though their hands kneaded dough, their knees rarely
knew floors. Mostly, they were pleasantly favored women who had
never worked before marriage, or tended to conceal it if they had,
whose minds were not so much stupid as unaroused—women at
whom the menopause or the defection of growing children struck
suddenly in the soft depths of their inarticulateness, leaving them
distraught, melancholy, even deranged, to make the rounds of the
doctors until age came blessedly, turning them leathery but safe.
And on us, their intransigent daughters, who wished to be poets,

actresses, dancers, doctors—anything but merely teachers or wives—
they looked with antagonism, secret pride, or dubious assent, as the
case might be, but all of them nursing the sly prescience that
marriage would almost certainly do for us, before we had quite done
for ourselves.

This, then, was the group with which I began; in a curious way
which I must make clear to myself, as one makes a will, it is the
group with which, perhaps tomorrow, somewhere outside this fading,
posthumous room, I choose to end. Not because, as we clustered, by
turns giggling, indecisive, and impassioned, in our soda parlors, we
bore already that sad consanguinity of those women who were to
refuse to stay in their traditional places either as wives, whom we
identified with our mothers, or as teachers, whom we identified with
lemon-faced aunts, lonely gas rings, and sexual despair. Hindsight
gives us a more terrifying resemblance. Not as women but as people.
Neither rich nor poor, we were among the last people to be—either
by birth or, later, by conviction—in the middle.

For the rich, even while they spun in their baroque hysterias of
possession, lived most intimately with the spectre of debacle. Like
the poor, they were bred to the assumption that a man's thought
does not go beyond his hunger, and, like them, their images of ruin
were absolute. When the spectre of violent change arose in our century, as it had in every century, this time with two mouths, one of
which said "Need is common!," the other of which answered
"Therefore let thought be common!," it was the very rich and the
very poor who subscribed first—the rich transfixed in their fear, the
poor transfixed in their hope. Curious (and yet not so curious, I see
now) that from us in the middle, swinging insecurely in our little
median troughs of satisfaction, never too sure of what we were or
what we believed, was to rise that saving, gradient doubt that has
shepherded us together, in entrenchments, in ambush, and in rooms
like these.

Two cots away from mine sits a small, black-haired woman of the
type the French call mignonne; one would never associate her with
the strangely scored, unmelodic music, yawping but compelling, for
which she was known. She is here for an odd reason, but we are all
here for odd reasons. She is here because she will not write melody,
as they conceive melody. Or, to be honest—and there is no time left
here for anything but honesty—as most of us here would conceive

melody. But we here, who do not understand her music, understand her reasons.

Down at the far end of the room, there is a gray, shadowy spinster who knows little of heresies concerning the diatonic scale. She is here because she believes in the probity of mice. All day long now, she sits on her bed in a trance of fear, but the story is that when they came to the college laboratory where for forty years she had bred mice and conclusions, she stood at first with her arm behind her, her hand, in its white sleeve, shaking a little on the knob of the closed door. Then she backed up against the door to push it inward, to invite them in, their committee, with the statement she was to sign. Past all the cages she led them, stopping at each to explain the lineage of the generation inside, until, tired of the interminable recital, they waved the paper under her nose. Then she led them to the filing cabinets, unlocked the drawers, and persuaded them to pore over page after page of her crisscrossed references, meanwhile intoning the monotonous record of her historic rodent dead. Not until then, until the paper had appeared a third time, did she say to them, with the queer cogency of those whose virtue is not usually in talk, "No. Perhaps I will end by lying for you. But the mice will not."

She, the shadowy, weak-voiced woman, and I are alike in one thing, although I am not here after any action such as hers. They came quite conventionally to my suburban cottage, flung open the door, and loaded me on the truck without a word, as they had previously come to another poet, Volk, on his island off the coast of Maine, to Peterson, the novelist, in his neat brick box at the far end of Queens, to all the other writers who were alive because of being away from the city on the day it went down. Quite simply, they, too, have read Plato, and they know that the writer is dangerous to them because he cannot help celebrating the uncommonness of people. For, no matter what epithalamiums they may extort from us, sooner or later the individuality will reappear. In the very poems we might carpenter for them to march to, in the midst of the sanitized theses, the decontaminate novels, sooner or later we will infect their pages with the subversive singularity of men.

She—the biologist—and I are alike because we are the only ones here who do not cry at night. Not because we are heroic but because we have no more hostages for which to weep. Her mice are scattered, or already docilely breeding new dogma under the careful guidance of one of the trainees brought over here from their closed, incredible, pragmatic world—someone born after 1917, perhaps, who, reared among the bent probities of hungry men, will not trouble himself about the subornation of mice.

And I, who would give anything if my son were with me here, even to be suborned, as they do already with children, can afford to sit and dream of old integrities only because I, too, no longer have a hostage—not since the day when, using a missile whose rhythm they had learned from us, they cracked the city to the reactive dirt from which it had sprung—the day when the third-grade class from the grammar school of a suburban town went on a field trip to the natural-history museum.

Anyone born in a city like that one, as I was, is a street urchin to the end of his days, whether he grew behind its plate glass and granite or in its ancient, urinous slums. And that last year, when it was said they were coming, I visited my city often, walking in the violet light that seeped between the buildings of its unearthly dusk, watching the multiform refractions of the crowd, telling myself "I do not care to survive this." But on the way up here, when, as if by intention, they routed our trucks through streets of fused slag and quagmire (which their men, tapping with divining rods, had declared safe), I sat there in one of the line of trucks, looking dry-eyed at the dust of stone. Was it when the class was looking at the dinosaur, the *Archaeopteryx*, that the moment came? Was it while a voice, in soft, short syllables suited to his shortness, was telling him how a snake grew wings and became a bird, how a primate straightened its spine and became a man?

The room is quiet now, and dark, except for the moonlight that shows faintly outside on the hedge, faintly inside on the blurred harlequin tiles of the aquarium. Almost everyone is asleep here; even the person who rings the bell must be asleep, somewhere in one of the rooms in the wing they reserve for themselves. The little composer was one of the last who fell asleep; she cried for hours over the letter they brought her from her husband, also a musician, who wrote that he was working for them, that there could be glory in it, that if she would only recant and work with him, they would release his mother, and the daughter, and the son. The letter was couched in their orotund, professional phrases, phrases that in their mouths

472

have given the great words like "freedom" and "unity" a sick, blood-sour sound. But tomorrow she will agree, and there is no one here who will blame her. Only the gray woman at the other end of the room and I sit hunched, awake, on our cots—taking the long view, who have no other. I sit here trying to remember everything I can about Hilda Kantrowitz, who was my age, my generation, but who, according to their paper on the wall, will not be here with us. Perhaps the last justification for people like me is to remember people like Hilda, even now, with justice.

What I see clearest about Hilda now is her wrists. I am looking back, with some trouble, at a girl who was never, except once, very important to me, and with some effort I can see thick braids of a dullish, unwashed blond, stray wisps from the top of them falling over her forehead, as if she had slept so and had not taken time for a combing. I cannot see her face from the side at all, but from the front her nostrils are long and drawn upward, making the tip of her nose seem too close to the flat mouth, which looks larger than it is because its lines are not definite but fade into the face. The eyes I cannot see at all as yet. She is standing for recitation, holding the Latin book, and her wrists are painfully sharp and clear, as if they were in the center of a lens. They are red—chapped, I suppose—and their flat bones protrude a long way from the middy cuffs. She does not know the recitation—she almost never does—but she does not titter or flush or look smart-alecky, the way the rest of us do when this happens. She just stands there, her eyelids blinking rapidly, her long nostrils moving, and says nothing, swaying a little, like a dog who is about to fall asleep. Then she sits down. Later on, I learn that it may be true—she may never get enough sleep.

We find this out by inference, Lotte and I, when the two of us are walking home together on a winter afternoon. That day, Lotte and I, who live near one another, have made a pact to spend our carfare on eatables and walk all the way home together. We have nearly reached 110th Street and Cathedral Parkway, having dribbled pennies in a store here, a store there, amiably debating each piece of candy, each sack of Indian nuts. In the west, as we walk toward it, there is a great well of dying light fading to apple-green over the river, which we cannot as yet see. The faces of the people hurrying past us have something flowerlike and open about them as they bloom toward us and recede. We are tiring, feeling mournful and waif-like, with a delightful sadness that we breathe upon and foster, secure in the warm thought of home.

Down the block, there is a last, curving oasis of stores before the blank apartment houses begin. After that comes the long hill, with the church park and the hospital on the other side. Lotte has a last nickel. We walk slowly, peering into the stores. Next to a grill whose blind front is stenciled with lines of tangerine and false-blue light, there is one more store with a weak bulb shining. We press our faces against the glass of its door. It is a strange grocery store, if it is one, with no bakers' and bottlers' cardboard blurbs set in the window, no cherry brightness inside. Against its right-hand wall, galled wooden shelves hold a dark rummage of canned goods, with long, empty gaps between the brands. From a single line of cartons near the door on the lowest shelf, there is one hard, red glint of newness; these are packages of salt. Sprawled on the counter to the left, with her arms outflung between some box bottoms holding penny candy, there is a girl asleep. Her face, turned toward us, rests on a book whose thick, blunt shape we recognize almost as we do her. It is Hilda. Behind her, seen through the pane and the thin gruel of light, is the dim blotch of what looks like another room.

We confer, Lotte and I, in nudges, and finally Lotte pushes in ahead of me, her smothered giggle sounding above the rasp of a bell on the door. For a moment, it seems warmer inside—then not. A light is turned on in the back of the store, and we see that the second room is actually only a space that has been curtained off. The curtains are open. A woman comes forward and shakes Hilda angrily by the shoulder, with a flood of foreign words, then turns to us, speaking in a cringing voice. Candy? Crackers? How much money we got? Her face has a strong look to it, with good teeth and a mouth limned in blackish hair. In the half room behind her, on one of two day beds, a boy sits up, huddling in a man's thick sweater whose sleeves cover his hands. A smaller child clambers down from the other bed and runs to stand next to his mother. He is too young to have much hair, and the sight of his naked head, his meagre cotton shirt, and his wet diaper drooping between his legs makes me feel colder.

It becomes evident that Hilda and we know each other. I remember Hilda's cheekbones—sharp, and slowly red. The woman, all smiles now, moves toward us and lightly strokes Lotte's collar. That year, Lotte and I have made a fetish of dressing alike; we have on navy serge dresses with white collars pinned with identical silver bars.

"Little teachers!" the woman says. "Like little teachers!" She hovers over the counter a minute, then thrusts a small box of crackers, the kind with marshmallow, into Lotte's hand. The baby sets up a cry and is pushed behind the woman's skirt. The boy on the bed stares at the box but says nothing. Confused, Lotte holds out her nickel. The woman hesitates, then shakes her head, refusing. Two fingers hover again over Lotte's collar but do not touch it. "Hilda will be teacher," the woman says. She makes a kind of genuflection of despair toward the place behind her, and we see that on a shelf there, in the midst of jumbled crockery and pans, is a man's picture, dark-bordered, in front of which a flame flickers, burning deep in a thick glass. She makes another gesture, as if she were pulling a cowl over her head, lets her hand fall against her skirt, and edges after us as we sidle toward the door. She bends over us. "Your mamas have what for me to sew, maybe? Or to clean?"

Hilda speaks, a short, guttural phrase in the language we do not understand. It is the only time she speaks. The woman steps back. Lotte still has the nickel in her open hand. Now Hilda is at the door. And now I see her mouth, the long lips pressed tight, turned down at the corners. She reaches out and takes Lotte's nickel. Then we are outside the door.

I do not remember anything about the rest of the walk home. But I remember that as I round the corner to my own street, alone, and am suddenly out of the wind, the air is like blue powder, and from the entrance to my house, as the doorman opens it and murmurs a greeting, the clean light scours the pavement. In the elevator, to my wind-smarting eyes the people look warmly blurry and gilded, and the elevator, rising perfectly, hums.

Lotte and I do not ever go back, of course, and we quickly forget the whole thing, for as the school year advances, the gap widens permanently between girls like us and those other unilluminated ones who are grinding seriously toward becoming teachers, for many of whose families the possession of a teacher daughter will be one of the bootstraps by which they will lift themselves to a feeling of security—that trust in education which is the dominant security in a country that prides itself on offering no other.

Then a bad time comes for me. My mother, after the birth of another child, late in life, is very ill and is sent away—to hunt for a warmer climate, it is said, although long afterward I know that it is a climate of the spirit for which she hunts. Once or twice during that time, she is brought home, able only to stand helplessly at the window, holding on to me, the tears running down her face. Then she is taken away again, for our windows are five flights up.

Business is bad, too, everywhere, and my father makes longer and longer sales trips away from home. We have a housekeeper, Mrs. Gallagher, who is really the baby's nurse, since we cannot afford a cook and a nurse, too. She does not wash my hair regularly or bother about my habits, and I grow dirty and unkempt. She is always whining after me to give up my favorite dresses to her own daughter, "a poor widow's child in a convent," after which, applying to my father for money, she buys me new dresses, probably with the daughter in mind, and my clothes become oddly tight and loud. Months later, after she is gone, it is found that she has drunk up a good part of my father's hoarded wines, but now no one knows this, and she is a good nurse, crooning, starched and fierce, over the basket that holds the baby, whom she possessively loves. Standing behind her, looking at the basket, which she keeps cloudy with dotted swiss and wreathed in rosy ribbon, I think to myself that the baby nestled there looks like a pink heart. Perhaps I think secretly, too, that I am the displaced heart.

So I begin to steal. Not at home, but at school. There I am now one of the lowest scholars. I have altogether lost track in Latin, and when I am sent to the board in geometry, I stand there desperately in front of the mazy diagram, the chalk in my slack hand, watching the teacher's long neck, in which the red impatience rises until it looks like a crane's leg. "Next!" she says, finally, and I walk back to my seat. At test time, I try frantically to copy, but the smart, safe ones ignore my pleading signal. And once the visiting nurse sends me home because there are nits in my bushy, tangled hair. Thereafter, when I follow on the heels of the crowd to the soda parlor— my hand guarding several days' saved-up carfare, in the hope of finding someone to treat—the sorority is closed.

So, day after day, I treat myself. For by now, although there is plenty of food at home and Mrs. Gallagher packs me thick sandwiches (mostly of cheese, which she buys conveniently in a big slab to last the week)—by now I am really hungry only and constantly for sweets. I live on the thought of them, for the suspended moment when the nugget is warm in my mouth or crammed, waiting, in my hidden hand. And the sweets that comfort me most are those bought secretly and eaten alone. It never occurs to me to ask Mrs. Gallagher for spending money. At noontime, habitually now, I slip into the dark coatroom, where the girls' coats are hung, one on top of another, and, sliding a hand from pocket to pocket, one can pretend to be looking for one's own. And there, once again, I meet Hilda.

We meet face to face in the lumpy shadows of the coatroom, each of us with a hand in the pocket of a coat that is not her own. We know this on the instant, recognition clamoring between us, two animals who touch each other's scent in the prowling dark. I inch my hand out of the gritty pocket and let it fall at my side. I do not see what Hilda does with her hand. But in that moment before we move, in the furry dusk of that windowless room, I see what is in her eyes. I do not give it a name. But I am the first to leave.

Even now, I cannot give it a name. It eludes me, as do the names of those whom, for layered reason upon reason, we cannot bear to remember. I have remembered as best I can.

The rest belongs to that amalgam called growing up, during which, like everyone else, I learn to stumble along somehow between truth and compromise. Shortly after that day, I fall ill of jaundice, and I am ill for a long while. During that time, my mother returns home, restored—or perhaps my illness is in part her restorative. Her housewifely shock at what she finds blows through our home like a cleansing wind, and her tonic scolding, severe and rational as of old, is like the bromide that disperses horror. When I go back to school, after months of absence, I have the transient prestige of one who has been seriously ill, and with my rehabilitated appearance this is almost enough to reinstate me. Then an English teacher discovers my poems, and although I am never again a sound student in any other class, I attain a certain eminence in hers, and I rise, with each display coaxed out of me, rung by rung, until I am safe. Meanwhile, Hilda has dropped out of school. I never ask, but she is gone, and I do not see her there again.

Once, some ten years later, I think I see her. During the year after

I am married, but not yet a mother, or yet a widow, a friend takes me to a meeting for the Spanish resistance, at which a well-known woman poet speaks. On the fringes of the departing crowd outside the shabby hall, young men and women are distributing pamphlets, shaking canisters for contributions. I catch sight of one of them, a girl in a brown leather jacket, with cropped blond hair, a smudge of lipstick that conceals the shape of the mouth, but a smudge of excitement on cheekbones that are the same. I strain to look at her, to decide, but the crowd is pressing, the night is rainy, and I lose sight of her before I am sure. But now I have reason to be sure. Yes, it was she.

It was she—and I have remembered as best I can. While I have sat here, the moonlight, falling white on the cast-down figure of the other waker, slumped now in sleep, showing up each brilliant, signal detail of the room in a last, proffered perspective, has flooded in and waned. I hear the first crepitations of morning. I am alone with my life, and with the long view.

They will tell us this morning that we must come down off our pin point into the arena. But a pin point can become an arena.

They will tell us that while we, in our easy compassion, have carried the hunger of others in our minds, they have carried it on their backs. And this is true. For this, even when they say it corruptly, is their strength—and our indefensible shame.

They will tell us that we have been able to cherish values beyond hunger only because we have never known basic hunger ourselves— and this will be true also. But this is our paradox—and this is our stronghold, too.

They will tell us, finally, that there is no place for people like us, that the middle ground is for angels, not for men. But there is a place. For in the absence of angels and arbiters from a world of light, men and women must take their place.

Therefore, I am here, sitting opposite the white bulletin on the wall. For the last justification for people like us is to remember people like Hilda with justice. Therefore, in this room where there is no cockcrow except of conscience, I have remembered everything I can about Hilda Kantrowitz, who, this morning, is to be our prosecutor.

I will need to close my eyes when I have to enter the little latrine.

The Scream on Fifty-seventh Street

◆§ WHEN THE scream came, from downstairs in the street five flights below her bedroom window, Mrs. Hazlitt, who in her month's tenancy of the flat had become the lightest of sleepers, stumbled up, groped her way past the empty second twin bed that stood nearer the window, and looked out. There was nothing to be seen of course —the apartment house she was in, though smartly kept up to the standards of the neighborhood, dated from the era of front fire escapes, and the sound, if it had come at all, had come from directly beneath them. From other half-insomniac nights she knew that the hour must be somewhere between three and four in the morning. The "all-night" doorman who guarded the huge façade of the apartment house opposite had retired, per custom, to some region behind its canopy; the one down the block at the corner of First, who blew his taxi-whistle so incessantly that she had for some nights mistaken it for a traffic policeman's, had been quiet for a long time. Even the white-shaded lamp that burned all day and most of the night on the floor of the little gray townhouse sandwiched between the tall buildings across the way—an invalid's light perhaps—had been quenched. At this hour the wide expanse of the avenue, Fifty-seventh Street at its easternmost end, looked calm, reassuring and amazingly silent for one of the main arteries of the city. The cross-town bus service had long since ceased; the truck traffic over on First made only an occasional dim rumble. If she went into the next room, where there was a French window opening like a double door, and leaned out, absurd idea, in her nightgown, she would see, far down to the right, the lamps of a portion of the Queensboro Bridge, quietly necklaced on the night. In the blur beneath them, out of range but comfortable to imagine, the beautiful cul-de-sac of Sutton Square must be musing, Edwardian in the starlight, its one antique

479

bow-front jutting over the river shimmering below. And in the façades opposite her, lights were still spotted here and there, as was always the case, even in the small hours, in New York. Other consciousnesses were awake, a vigil of anonymous neighbors whom she would never know, that still gave one the hive-sense of never being utterly alone.

All was silent. No, she must have dreamed it, reinterpreted in her doze some routine sound, perhaps the siren of the police car that often keened through this street but never stopped, no doubt on its way to the more tumultuous West Side. Until the death of her husband, companion of twenty years, eight months ago, her ability to sleep had always been healthy and immediate; since then it had gradually, not unnaturally deteriorated, but this was the worst; she had never done this before. For she could still hear very clearly the character of the sound, or rather its lack of one—a long, oddly sustained note, then a shorter one, both perfectly even, not discernible as a man's or a woman's, and without—yes, without the color of any emotion—surely the sound that one heard in dreams. Never a woman of small midnight fears in either city or country, as a girl she had done settlement work on some of this city's blackest streets, as a mining engineer's wife had nestled peacefully within the shrieking velvet of an Andes night. Not to give herself special marks for this, it was still all the more reason why what she had heard, or thought she had heard, must have been hallucinatory. A harsh word, but she must be stern with herself at the very beginnings of any such, of what could presage the sort of disintegrated widowhood, full of the mouse-fears and softening self-indulgences of the manless, that she could not, would not abide. Scarcely a second or two could have elapsed between that long—yes, that was it, soulless—cry, and her arrival at the window. And look, down there on the street and upward, everything remained motionless. Not a soul, in answer, had erupted from a doorway. All the fanlights of the lobbies shone serenely. Up above, no one leaned, not a window had flapped wide. After twenty years of living outside of the city, she could still flatter herself that she knew New York down to the ground—she had been born here, and raised. Secretly mourning it, missing it through all the happiest suburban years, she had kept up with it like a scholar, building a red-book of it for herself even through all its savage, incontinent rebuilding. She still knew all its neighborhoods. She knew. And this was one in which such a sound would be policed at once, such a cry serviced at once, if only by doormen running. No, the fault, the disturbance, must be hers.

Reaching into the pretty, built-in wardrobe on her right—the flat, with so many features that made it more like a house, fireplace, high ceilings, had attracted her from the first for this reason—she took out a warm dressing gown and sat down on the bed to put on her slippers. The window was wide open and she meant to leave it that way; country living had made unbearable the steam heat of her youth. There was no point to winter otherwise, and she—she and Sam—had always been ones to enjoy the weather as it came. Perhaps she had been unwise to give up the dog, excuse for walks early and late, outlet for talking aloud—the city was full of them. Unwise too, in the self-denuding impulse of loss, to have made herself that solitary in readiness for a city where she would have to remake friends, and no longer had kin. And charming as this flat was, wooed as she increasingly was by the delicately winning personality of its unknown, absent owner, Mrs. Berry, by her bric-a-brac, her cookbooks, even by her widowhood, almost as recent as Mrs. Hazlitt's own—perhaps it would be best to do something about getting the empty second twin bed removed from this room. No doubt Mrs. Berry, fled to London, possibly even residing in the rooms of yet a third woman in search of recommended change, would understand. Mrs. Hazlitt stretched her arms, able to smile at this imagined procession of women inhabiting each other's rooms, fallen one against the other like a pack of playing cards. How could she have forgotten what anyone who had reached middle age through the normal amount of trouble should know, that the very horizontal position itself of sleep, when one could not, laid one open to every attack from within, on a couch with no psychiatrist to listen but oneself. The best way to meet the horrors was on two feet, vertical. What she meant to do now was to fix herself a sensible hot drink, not coffee, reminiscent of shared midnight snacks, not even tea, but a nursery drink, cocoa. In a lifetime, she thought, there are probably two eras of the sleep that is utterly sound: the nursery sleep (if one had the lucky kind of childhood I did) and the sleep next or near the heart and body of the one permanently loved and loving, if one has been lucky enough for that too. I must learn from within, as well as without, that both are over. She stood up, tying her sash more firmly. And at that the moment the scream came again.

She listened, rigid. It came exactly as remembered, one shrilled long note, then the shorter second, like a cut-off Amen to the first and of the same timbre, dreadful in its cool, a madness expended almost with calm, near the edge of joy. No wonder she had thought of the siren; this had the same note of terror controlled. One could not tell whether it sped toward a victim or from one. As before, it seemed to come from directly below.

Shaking, she leaned out, could see nothing because of the high sill, ran into the next room, opened the French window and all but stood on the fire escape. As she did so, the sound, certainly human, had just ceased; at the same moment a cab, going slowly down the middle of the avenue, its toplight up, veered directly toward her, as if the driver too had heard, poised there beneath her with its nose pointed toward the curb, then veered sharply back to the center of the street, gathered speed, and drove on. Immediately behind it another cab, toplight off, slowed up, performed exactly the same orbit, then it too, with a hasty squeal of brakes, made for the center street and sped away. In the confusion of noises she thought she heard the grind of a window-sash coming down, then a slam—perhaps the downstairs door of the adjoining set of flats, or of this one. Dropping to her knees, she leaned both palms on the floor-level lintel of the window and peered down through the iron slats of her fire escape and the successive ones below. Crouched that way, she could see straight back to the building line. To the left, a streetlamp cast a pale, even glow on empty sidewalk and the free space of curb either side of a hydrant; to the right, the shadows were obscure, but motionless. She saw nothing to conjure into a half-expected human bundle lying still, heard no footfall staggering or slipping away. Not more than a minute or two could have elapsed since she had heard the cry. Tilting her head up at the façade opposite, she saw that their simple pattern of lit windows seemed the same. While she stared, one of the squares blotted out, then another, both on floors not too high to have heard. Would no one, having heard, attend? Would she?

Standing up, her hand on the hasp of the French window, she felt herself still shaking, not with fear, but with the effort to keep herself from in some way heeding that cry. Again she told herself that she had been born here, knew the city's ways, had not the

auslander's incredulity about some of them. These ways had
hardened since her day, people had warned her, to an indifference
beyond that of any civilized city; there were no "good" neighborhoods now, none of any kind really, except the half-hostile enclosure
that each family must build for itself. She had discounted this,
knowing unsentimentally what city life was; even in the tender
version of it that was her childhood there had been noises, human
ones, that the most responsible people, the kindest, had shrugged
away, saying, "Nothing, dear. Something outside." What she had
not taken into account was her own twenty years of living elsewhere,
where such a cry in the night would be succored at once if only for
gossip's sake, if only because one gave up privacy—anonymity—forever, when one went to live in a house on a road. If only, she
thought, holding herself rigid to stop her trembling, because it
would be the cry of someone one knew. Nevertheless, it took all her
strength not to rush downstairs, to hang on to the handle, while in
her mind's eye she ran out of her apartment door, remembering to
take the key, pressed the elevator button and waited, went down at
the car's deliberate pace. After that there would be the inner, buzzer
door to open, then at last the door to the outside. No, it would take
too long, and it was already too late for the phone; by the time
police could come or she could find the number of the superintendent in his back basement—and when either answered—what would
she say? She looked at the fire escape. Not counting hers, there must
be three others between herself and the street. Whether there was a
ladder extending from the lowest one she could not remember; possibly one hung by one's hands and dropped to the ground. Years ago
there had been more of them, even the better houses had had them
in their rear areaways, but she had never in her life seen one used.
And this one fronted direct on the avenue. It was this that brought
her to her senses—the vision of herself in her blue robe creeping
down the front of a building on Fifty-seventh Street, hanging by
her hands until she dropped to the ground. She shut the long window quickly, leaning her weight against it to help the slightly swollen frame into place, and turned the handle counterclockwise,
shooting the long vertical bolt. The bolt fell into place with a thump
she had never noticed before but already seemed familiar. Probably,
she thought, sighing, it was the kind of sound—old hardware on old
wood—that more often went with a house.

In the kitchen, over her cocoa, she shook herself with a reminiscent tremble, in the way one did after a narrow escape. It was a gesture made more often to a companion, an auditor. Easy enough to make the larger gestures involved in cutting down one's life to the pattern of the single: the selling of a house, the arranging of income or new occupation. Even the abnegation of sex had a drama that lent one strength, made one hold up one's head as one saw oneself traveling a clear, melancholy line. It was the small gestures for which there was no possible sublimation, the sudden phrase, posture —to no auditor, the constant clueing of identity in another's—its cessation. "Dear me," she would have said—they would have come to town for the winter months as they had often planned, and he would have just returned from an overnight business trip—"what do you suppose I'd have done, Sam, if I'd gone all the way, in my housecoat, really found myself outside? Funny how the distinction between outdoors and in breaks down in the country. I'd forgotten how absolute it is here—with so many barriers between." Of course, she thought, that's the simple reason why here, in the city, the sense of responsibility has to weaken. Who could maintain it, through a door, an elevator, a door and a door, toward everyone, anyone, who screamed? Perhaps that was the real reason she had come here, she thought, washing the cup under the faucet. Where the walls are sound-proofed there are no more "people next door" with their ready "casserole" pity, at worst with the harbored glow of their own family life peering from their averted eyelids like the lamplight from under their eaves. Perhaps she had known all along that the best way to learn how to live alone was to come to the place where people really were.

She set the cup out for the morning and added a plate and a spoon. It was wiser not to let herself deteriorate to the utterly casual; besides, the sight of them always gave her a certain pleasure, like a greeting, if only from herself of the night before. Tomorrow she had a meeting, of one of the two hospital boards on which, luckily for now, she had served for years. There was plenty more of that kind of useful occupation available and no one would care a hoot whether what once she had done for conscience' sake she now did for her own. The meeting was not scheduled until two. Before that she would manage to inquire very discreetly, careful not to appear either eccentric or too friendly, both of which made city people uneasy, as to whether anyone else in the building had heard what she had. This too she would do for discipline's sake. There was no longer any doubt that the sound had been real.

The next morning at eight-thirty, dressed to go out except for her coat, she waited just inside her door for one or the other of the tenants on her floor to emerge. Her heart pounded at the very queerness of what she was doing, but she overruled it; if she did feel somewhat too interested, too much as if she were embarking on a chase, then let her get it out of her system at once, and have done. How to do so was precisely what she had considered while dressing. The problem was not to make too many inquiries, too earnest ones, and not to seem to be making any personal overture, from which people would naturally withdraw. One did not make inconvenient, hothouse friendships in the place one lived in, here. Therefore she had decided to limit her approaches to three—the first to the girl who lived in the adjacent apartment, who could usually be encountered at this hour and was the only tenant she knew for sure lived in the front of the building—back tenants were less likely to have heard. For the rest, she must trust to luck. And whatever the outcome, she would not let herself pursue the matter beyond today.

She opened the door a crack and listened. Still too early. Actually the place, being small—six floors of four or five flats each—had a more intimate feeling than most. According to the super's wife, Mrs. Stump, with whom she had had a chat or two in the hall, many of the tenants, clinging to ceiling rents in what had become a fancier district, had been here for years, a few for the thirty since the place had been built. This would account for so many middle-aged and elderly, seemingly either single or the remnants of families—besides various quiet, well-mannered women who, like herself, did not work, she had noticed at times two men who were obviously father and son, two others who, from their ages and nameplate, noticed at mailtime, might be brothers, and a mother with the only child in the place—a subdued little girl of about eight. As soon as a tenant of long standing vacated or died, Mrs. Stump had added, the larger units were converted to smaller, and this would account for the substratum of slightly showier or younger occupants: two modish blondes, a couple of homburged "decorator" types—all more in keeping with the newly sub-theatrical, antique-shop character of the neighborhood—as well as for the "career girl" on her floor. Mrs.

Berry, who from evidences in the flat should be something past forty like herself, belonged to the first group, having been here, with her husband of course until recently, since just after the war. A pity that she, Mrs. Berry, who from her books, her one charming letter, her own situation, might have been just the person to understand, even share Mrs. Hazlitt's reaction to the event of last night, was not here. But this was nonsense; if she were, then she, Mrs. Hazlitt, would not be. She thought again of the chain of women, sighed, and immediately chid herself for this new habit of sighing, as well as for this alarming mound of gratuitous information she seemed to have acquired, in less than a month, about people with whom she was in no way concerned. At that moment she heard the door next hers creak open. Quickly she put on her coat, opened her door and bent to pick up the morning paper. The girl coming out stepped back, dropping one of a pile of boxes she was carrying. Mrs. Hazlitt returned it to her, pressed the button for the elevator, and when it came, held the door. It was the girl she had seen twice before; for the first time they had a nice exchange of smiles.

"Whoops, I'm late," said the girl, craning to look at her watch.

"Me too," said Mrs. Hazlitt, as the cage slid slowly down. She drew breath. "Overslept, once I did get to sleep. Rather a noisy night outside—did you hear all that fuss, must have been around three or four?" She waited hopefully for the answer: Why yes indeed, what on earth was it, did you?

"Uh-uh," said the girl, shaking her head serenely. " 'Fraid the three of us sleep like a log, that's the trouble. My roommates are still at it, lucky stiffs." She checked her watch again, was first out of the elevator, nodded her thanks when Mrs. Hazlitt hurried to hold the buzzer door for her because of the boxes, managed the outer door herself, and departed.

Mrs. Hazlitt walked briskly around the corner to the bakery, came back with her bag of two brioches, and reentered. Imagine, there are three of them, she thought, and I never knew. Well, I envy them their log. The inner door, usually locked, was propped open. Mrs. Stump.was on her knees just behind it, washing the marble floor, as she did every day. It was certainly a tidy house, not luxurious but up to a firmly well-bred standard, just the sort a woman like Mrs. Berry would have, that she herself, when the sublease was over, would like to find. Nodding to Mrs. Stump, she went past her to the row of brass mail slots, pretending to search her own although she knew it was too early, weighing whether she ought to risk wasting one of her three chances on her.

"Mail don't come till ten," said Mrs. Stump from behind her.

"Yes, I know," said Mrs. Hazlitt, recalling suddenly that they had had this exchange before. "But I forgot to check yesterday."

"Yesterday vass holiday."

"Oh, so it was." Guiltily Mrs. Hazlitt entered the elevator and faced the door, relieved when it closed. The truth was that she had known yesterday was a holiday and had checked the mail anyway. The truth was that she often did this even on Sundays here, often even more than once. It made an errand in the long expanse of a day when she either flinched from the daily walk that was too dreary to do alone on Sunday, or had not provided herself with a ticket to something. One had to tidy one's hair, spruce a bit for the possible regard of someone in the hall, and when she did see some-one, although of course they never spoke, she always returned feeling refreshed, reaffirmed.

Upstairs again, she felt that way now; her day had begun in the eyes of others, as a day should. She made a few phone calls to laundry and bank, and felt even better. Curious how, when one lived alone, one began to feel that only one's own consciousness held up the world, and at the very same time that only an incursion into the world, or a recognition from it, made one continue to exist at all. There was another phone call she might make, to a friend up in the country, who had broken an ankle, but she would save that for a time when she needed it more. This was yet another discipline—not to become a phone bore. The era when she herself had been a victim of such, had often thought of the phone as a nuisance, now seemed as distant as China. She looked at the clock—time enough to make another pot of coffee. With it she ate a brioche slowly, then with the pleasant sense of hurry she now had so seldom, another.

At ten sharp she went downstairs again, resolving to take her chance with whoever might be there. As she emerged from the ele-vator she saw that she was in luck; the owner of a big brown poodle —a tall, well set up man of sixty or so—was bent over his mail slot while the dog stood by. It was the simplest of matters to make an overture to the poodle, who was already politely nosing the palm she offered him, to expose her own love of the breed, remarking on this one's exceptional manners, to skip lightly on from the question of barking to noise in general, to a particular noise.

"Ah well, Coco's had stage training," said his owner, in answer to her compliments. She guessed that his owner might have had the same; he had that fine, bravura face which aging actors of another generation often had, a trifle shallow for its years perhaps but very fine, and he inclined toward her with the same majestic politeness as his dog, looking into her face very intently as she spoke, answering her in the slender, semi-British accent she recalled from matinee idols of her youth. She had to repeat her question on the noise. This time she firmly gave the sound its name—a scream, really rather an unusual scream.

"A scream?" The man straightened. She thought that for a moment he looked dismayed. Then he pursed his lips very judiciously, in almost an acting-out of that kind of response. "Come to think of it, ye-es, I may have heard something." He squared his shoulders. "But no doubt I just turned over. And Coco's a city dog, very blasé fellow. Rather imagine he did too." He tipped his excellent homburg. "Good morning," he added, with sudden reserve, and turned away, giving a flick to the dog's leash that started the animal off with his master behind him.

"Good morning," she called after them, "and thanks for the tip on where to get one like Coco." Coco looked back at her, but his master, back turned, disentangling the leash from the doorknob, did not, and went out without answering.

So I've done it after all, she thought. Too friendly. Especially too friendly since I'm a woman. Her face grew hot at this probable estimate of her—gushy woman chattering over-brightly, lingering in the hall. Bore of a woman who heard things at night, no doubt looked under the bed before she got into it. No, she thought, there was something—when I mentioned the scream. At the aural memory of that latter, still clear, she felt her resolve stiffen. Also—what a dunce she was being—there were the taxis. Taxis, one of them occupied, did not veer, one after the other, on an empty street, without reason. Emboldened, she bent to look at the man's mailbox. The name, Reginald Warwick, certainly fitted her imaginary dossier, but that was not what gave her pause. Apartment 3A. Hers was 5A. He lived in the front, two floors beneath her, where he must have heard.

As she inserted the key in her apartment door, she heard the telephone ringing, fumbled the key and dropped it, then had to open the double lock above. All part of the city picture, she thought resentfully, remembering their four doors, never locked, in the country —utterly foolhardy, never to be dreamed of here. Even if she had, there were Mrs. Berry's possessions to be considered, nothing extraordinary, but rather like the modest crotchety bits of treasure she had inherited or acquired herself—in the matter of bric-a-brac alone there was really quite a kinship between them. The phone was still ringing as she entered. She raced toward it eagerly. It was the secretary of the hospital board, telling her that this afternoon's meeting, was put off.

"Oh . . . oh dear," said Mrs. Hazlitt. "I mean—I'm so sorry to hear about Mrs. Levin. Hope it's nothing serious."

"I really couldn't say," said the secretary. "But we've enough for a quorum the week after." She rang off.

Mrs. Hazlitt put down the phone, alarmed at the sudden sinking of her heart over such a minor reversal. She had looked forward to seeing people of course, but particularly to spending an afternoon in the brightly capable impersonality of the boardroom, among men and women who brought with them a sense of indefinable swathes of well-being extending behind them, of such a superfluity of it, from lives as full as their checkbooks, that they were met in that efficient room to dispense what overflowed. The meeting would have been an antidote to that dark, anarchic version of the city which had been obsessing her; it would have been a reminder that everywhere, on flight after flight of the city's high, brilliant floors, similar groups of the responsible were convening, could always be applied to, were in command. The phone gave a reminiscent tinkle as she pushed it aside, and she waited, but there was no further ring. She looked at her calendar, scribbled with domestic markings—the hairdresser on Tuesday, a fitting for her spring suit, the date when she must appear at the lawyer's for the closing on the sale of the house. Beyond that she had a dinner party with old acquaintances on the following Thursday, tickets with a woman friend for the Philharmonic on Saturday week. Certainly she was not destitute of either company or activity. But the facts were that within the next two weeks, she could look forward to only two occasions when she would be communicating on any terms of intimacy with people who, within limits, knew "who" she was. A default on either would be felt keenly—much more than the collapse of this afternoon's little—prop. Absently she twiddled the dial back and forth. Proportion was what went first "in solitary"; circling one's own small platform in space, the need for speech mute in one's own throat, one developed an abnormal concern over the night-cries of others. No, she thought, remembering the board meeting, those high convocations of the responsible, I've promised—Lord knows who, myself, somebody. She stood up and gave herself a smart slap on the buttock. "Come on, Millie," she said, using the nickname her husband always had. "Get on with it." She started to leave the room, then remained in its center, hand at mouth, wondering. Talking aloud to oneself was more common than admitted; almost everyone did. It was merely that she could not decide whether or not she had.

Around eleven o'clock, making up a bundle of lingerie, she went down to the basement where there was a community washing machine, set the machine's cycle, and went back upstairs. Forty minutes later she went through the same routine, shifting the wet clothes to the dryer. At one o'clock she returned for the finished clothes and carried them up. This made six trips in all, but at no time had she met anyone en route; it was Saturday afternoon, perhaps a bad time. At two she went out to do her weekend shopping. The streets were buzzing, the women in the supermarket evidently laying in enough stores for a visitation of giants. Outside the market, a few kids from Third Avenue always waited in hope of tips for carrying, and on impulse, although her load was small, she engaged a boy of about ten. On the way home, promising him extra for waiting, she stopped at the patisserie where she always lingered for the sheer gilt-and-chocolate gaiety of the place, bought her brioches for the morning, and, again on impulse, an éclair for the boy. Going up in the elevator they encountered the mother and small girl, but she had never found any pretext for addressing that glum pair, the mother engaged as usual in a low, toneless tongue-lashing of the child. Divorcée, Mrs. Hazlitt fancied, and no man in the offing, an inconvenient child. In the kitchen, she tipped the boy and offered him the pastry. After an astonished glance, he wolfed it with a practical air, peering at her furtively between bites, and darted off at once, looking askance over his shoulder at her "See you next Saturday, maybe." Obviously he had been brought up to believe that only witches dispensed free gingerbread. In front of the bathroom mirror,

Mrs. Hazlitt, tidying up before her walk, almost ritual now, to Sutton Square, regarded her image, not yet a witch's but certainly a fool's, a country-cookie-jar fool's. "Oh, well, you're company," she said, quite consciously aloud this time, and for some reason this cheered her. Before leaving, she went over face and costume with the laborious attention she always gave them nowadays before going anywhere outside.

Again, when she rode down, she met no one, but she walked with bracing step, making herself take a circuitous route for health's sake, all the way to Bloomingdale's, then on to Park and around again, along the Fifty-eighth Street bridge pass, the dejectedly frivolous shops that lurked near it, before she let herself approach the house with the niche with the little statue of Dante in it, then the Square. Sitting in the Square, the air rapidly blueing now, lapping her like reverie, she wondered whether any of the residents of the windows surrounding her had noticed her almost daily presence, half hoped they had. Before it became too much of a habit, of course, she would stop coming. Meanwhile, if she took off her distance glasses, the scene before her, seen through the tender, Whistlerian blur of myopia—misted gray bridge, blue and green lights of a barge going at its tranced pace downriver—was the very likeness of a corner of the Chelsea embankment, glimpsed throughout a winter of happy teatime windows seven years ago, from a certain angle below Battersea Bridge. Surely it was blameless to remember past happiness if one did so without self-pity, better still, of course, to be able to speak of it to someone in an even, healing voice. Idly she wondered where Mrs. Berry was living in London. The flat in Cheyne Walk would just have suited her. "Just the thing for you," she would have said to her had she known her. "The Sebrings still let it every season. We always meant to go back." Her watch said five and the air was chilling. She walked rapidly home through the evening scurry, the hour of appointments, catching its excitement as she too hurried, half-persuaded of her own appointment, mythical but still possible, with someone as yet unknown. Outside her own building she paused. All day long she had been entering it from the westerly side. Now, approaching from the east, she saw that the fire escape on this side did end in a ladder, about four feet above her. Anyone moderately tall, like herself, would have had an easy drop of it, as she would have done last night. Shaking her head at that crazy image, she looked up at the brilliant hives all around her. Lights were cramming in, crowding on, but she knew too much now about their nighttime progression, their gradual decline to a single indifferent string on that rising, insomniac silence in which she might lie until morning, dreading to hear again what no one else would appear to have heard. Scaring myself to death, she thought (or muttered?), and in the same instant resolved to drop all limits, go down to the basement and interrogate the Stumps, sit on the bench in the lobby and accost anyone who came in, ring doorbells if necessary, until she had confirmation—and not go upstairs until she had. "Excuse me," said someone. She turned. A small, frail, elderly woman, smiling timidly, waited to get past her through the outer door.

"Oh—sorry," said Mrs. Hazlitt. "Why—good evening!" she added with a rush, an enormous rush of relief. "Here—let me," she said more quietly, opening the door with a numb sense of gratitude for having been tugged back from the brink of what she saw now, at the touch of a voice, had been panic. For here was a tenant, unaccountably forgotten, with whom she was almost on speaking terms, a gentle old sort, badly crippled with arthritis, for whom Mrs. Hazlitt had once or twice unlocked the inner door. She did so now.

"Thank you, my dear—my hands are that knobbly." There was the trace of brogue that Mrs. Hazlitt had noticed before. The old woman, her gray hair sparse from the disease but freshly done in the artfully messy arrangements used to conceal the skulls of old ladies, her broadtail coat not new but excellently maintained, gave off the comfortable essence, pleasing as rosewater, of one who had been serenely protected all her life. Unmarried, for she had that strangely deducible aura about her even before one noted the lack of ring, she had also a certain simpleness, now almost bygone, of those household women who had never gone to business—Mrs. Hazlitt had put her down as perhaps the relict sister of a contractor, or of a school superintendent of the days when the system had been Irish from top to bottom, at the top, of Irish of just this class. The old lady fumbled now with the minute key to her mailbox.

"May I?"

"Ah, if you would now. Couldn't manage it when I came down. The fingers don't seem to warm up until evening. It's 2B."

Mrs. Hazlitt, inserting the key, barely noticed the name—Finan. 2B would be a front apartment also, in the line adjacent to the A's.

"And you would be the lady in Mrs. Berry's. Such a nicely spoken woman, she was."

"Oh yes, isn't she," said Mrs. Hazlitt. "I mean . . . I just came through the agent. But when you live in a person's house—do you know her?"

"Just to speak. Half as long as me, they'd lived here. Fifteen years." The old lady took the one letter Mrs. Hazlitt passed her, the yellow-fronted rent bill whose duplicate she herself had received this morning. "Ah well, we're always sure of this one, aren't we?" Nodding her thanks, she shuffled toward the elevator on built-up shoes shaped like hods. "Still, it's a nice, quiet building, and lucky we are to be in it these days."

There was such a rickety bravery about her, of neat habits long overborne by the imprecisions of age, of dowager hat set slightly askew by fingers unable to deal with a key yet living alone, that Mrs. Hazlitt, reluctant to shake the poor, tottery dear further, had to remind herself of the moment before their encounter.

"Last night?" The old blue eyes looked blank, then brightened. "Ah no, I must have taken one of my Seconals. Otherwise I'd have heard it surely. 'Auntie,' my niece always says—'what if there should be a fire, and you there sleeping away?' Do what she says, I do sometimes, only to hear every pin drop till morning." She shook her head, entering the elevator. "Going up?"

"N-no," said Mrs. Hazlitt. "I—have to wait here for a minute." She sat down on the bench, the token bench that she had never seen anybody sitting on, and watched the car door close on the little figure still shaking its head, borne upward like a fairy godmother, willing but unable to oblige. The car's hum stopped, then its light glowed on again. Someone else was coming down. No, this is the nadir, Mrs. Hazlitt thought. Whether I heard it or not, I'm obviously no longer myself. Sleeping pills for me too, though I've never —and no more nonsense. And no more questioning, no matter who.

The car door opened. "Wssht!" said Mrs. Finan, scuttling out again. "I've just remembered. Not last night, but two weeks ago. And once before that. A scream, you said?"

Mrs. Hazlitt stood up. Almost unable to speak, for the tears that suddenly wrenched her throat, she described it.

"That's it, just what I told my niece on the phone next morning. Like nothing human, and yet it was. I'd taken my Seconal too early,

493

so there I was wide awake again, lying there just thinking, when it came. 'Auntie,' she tried to tell me, 'it was just one of the sireens. Or hoodlums maybe.' " Miss Finan reached up very slowly and settled her hat. "The city's gone down, you know. Not what it was," she said in a reduced voice, casting a glance over her shoulder, as if whatever the city now was loomed behind her. "But I've laid awake on this street too many years, I said, not to know what I hear." She leaned forward. "But—she . . . they think I'm getting old, you know," she said, in the whisper used to confide the unimaginable. "So . . . well . . . when I heard it again I just didn't tell her."

Mrs. Hazlitt grubbed for her handkerchief, found it and blew her nose. Breaking down, she thought—I never knew what a literal phrase it is. For she felt as if all the muscles that usually held her up, knee to ankle, had slipped their knots and were melting her, unless she could stop them, to the floor. "I'm not normally such a nervous woman," she managed to say. "But it was just that no one else seemed to—why, there were people with lights on, but they just seemed to ignore."

The old lady nodded absently. "Well, thank God my hearing's as good as ever. Hmm. Wait till I tell Jennie that!" She began making her painful way back to the car.

Mrs. Hazlitt put out a hand to delay her. "In case it—I mean, in case somebody ought to be notified—do you have any idea what it was?"

"Oh, I don't know. And what could we—?" Miss Finan shrugged, eager to get along. Still, gossip was tempting. "I did think—" She paused, lowering her voice uneasily. "Like somebody in a fit, it was. We'd a sexton at church taken that way with epilepsy once. And it stopped short like that, just as if somebody'd clapped a hand over its mouth, poor devil. Then the next time I thought—no, more like a signal, like somebody calling. You know the things you'll think at night." She turned, clearly eager to get away.

"But, oughtn't we to inquire?" Mrs. Hazlitt thought of the taxis. "In case it came from this building?"

"This build—" For a moment Miss Finan looked scared, her chin trembling, eyes rounded in the misty, affronted stare that the old gave, not to physical danger, but to a new idea swum too late into their ken. Then she drew herself up, all five feet of her bowed backbone. "Not from here it wouldn't. Across from that big place, may-

494

be. Lots of riffraff there, not used to their money. Or from Third Avenue, maybe. There's always been tenements there." She looked at Mrs. Hazlitt with an obtuse patronage that reminded her of an old nurse who had first instructed her on the social order, blandly mixing up all first causes—disease, money, poverty, snobbery—with a firm illogic that had still seemed somehow in possession—far more firmly so than her own good-hearted parents—of the crude facts. "New to the city, are you," she said, more kindly. "It takes a while."

This time they rode up together. "Now you remember," Miss Finan said, on leaving. "You've two locks on your door, one downstairs. Get a telephone put in by your bed. Snug as a bug in a rug you are then. Nothing to get at you but what's there already. That's what I always tell myself when I'm wakeful. Nothing to get at you then but the Old Nick."

The door closed on her. Watching her go, Mrs. Hazlitt envied her the simplicity, even the spinsterhood that had barred her from imagination as it had from experience. Even the narrowing-in of age would have its compensations, tenderly constricting the horizon as it cramped the fingers, adding the best of locks to Miss Finan's snugness, on her way by now to the triumphant phone call to Jennie.

But that was sinful, to wish for that too soon, what's more it was sentimental, in just the way she had vowed to avoid. Mrs. Hazlitt pushed the button for Down. Emerging from the building, she looked back at it from the corner, back at her day of contrived exits and entrances, abortive conversations. People were hurrying in and out now at a great rate. An invisible glass separated her from them; she was no longer in the fold.

Later that night, Mrs. Hazlitt, once more preparing for bed, peered down at the streets through the slats of the Venetian blind. Catching herself in the attitude of peering made her uneasy. Darkening the room behind her, she raised the blind. After dinner in one of the good French restaurants on Third Avenue and a Tati movie afterwards—the French were such competent dispensers of gaiety—she could review her day more as a convalescent does his delirium—"Did I really say—do—that?" And even here she was addressing a vis-à-vis, so deeply was the habit ingrained. But she could see her self-imposed project now for what it was—only a hysterical seeking after conversation, the final breaking-point, like the old-fashioned "crisis" in pneumonia, of the long, low fever of loneliness unexpressed. Even the city, gazed at squarely, was really no anarchy, only a huge diffuseness that returned to the eye of the beholder, to the walker in its streets, even to the closed dream of its sleeper, his own mood, dark or light. Dozens of the solitary must be looking down at it with her, most of them with some *modus vivendi*, many of them booking themselves into life with the same painful intentness, the way the middle-aged sometimes set themselves to learning the tango. And a queer booking you gave yourself today, she told herself, the words lilting with Miss Finan's Irish, this being the last exchange of speech she had had. Testing the words aloud, she found her way with accents, always such a delight to Sam, as good as ever. Well, she had heard a scream, had discovered someone else who had heard it. And now to forget it as promised; the day was done. Prowling the room a bit, she took up her robe, draped it over her shoulders, still more providently put it on. "Oh Millie," she said, tossing the dark mirror a look of scorn as she passed it "you're such a *sensible* woman."

Wear out Mrs. Berry's carpet you will, Millie, she thought, twenty minutes later by the bedroom clock, but the accent, adulterated now by Sam's, had escaped her. Had the scream had an accent? The trouble was that the mind had its own discipline; one could remember, even with a smile, the story of the man promised all the gold in the world if he could but go for two minutes thinking of the word "hippopotamus." She stopped in front of the mirror, seeking her smile, but it too had escaped. "Hippopotamus," she said, to her dark image. The knuckles of one hand rose, somnambulist, as she watched, and pressed against her teeth. She forced the hand, hers, down again. I will say it again, aloud, she thought, and while I am saying it I will be sure to say to myself that I am saying it aloud. She did so. "Hippopotamus." For a long moment she remained there, staring into the mirror. Then she turned and snapped on every light in the room.

Across from her, in another mirror, the full-length one, herself regarded her. She went forward to it, to that image so irritatingly familiar, so constant as life changed it, so necessarily dear. Fair hair, if maintained too late in life, too brightly, always made the most sensible of women look foolish. There was hers, allowed to gray gently, disordered no more than was natural in the boudoir, framing a face still rational, if strained. "Dear me," she said to it. "All you

need is somebody to talk to, get it out of your system. Somebody like
yourself." As if prodded, she turned and surveyed the room.

Even in the glare of the lights, the naked black projected from
the window, the room sent out to her, in half a dozen pleasant little
touches, the same sense of its compatible owner that she had had
from the beginning. There, flung down, was Mrs. Berry's copy of *The
Eustace Diamonds*, a book that she had always meant to read and
had been delighted to find here, along with many others of its ilk
and still others she herself owned. How many people knew good
bisque and how cheaply it might still be collected, or could let it
hobnob so amiably with grandmotherly bits of Tiffanyware, even
with the chipped Quimper ashtrays that Mrs. Berry, like Mrs. Hazlitt at the time of her own marriage, must once have thought the
cutest in the world. There were the white walls, with the silly, straw-
berry-mouthed Marie Laurencin just above the Beerbohm, the presence of good faded colors, the absence of the new or fauve. On the
night table were the scissors, placed, like everything in the house,
where Mrs. Hazlitt would have had them, near them a relic that
winked of her own childhood—and kept on, she would wager, for the
same reason—a magnifying glass exactly like her father's. Above
them, the only floor lamp in the house, least offensive of its kind,
towered above all the table ones, sign of a struggle between practicality and grace that she knew well, whose end she could applaud.
Everywhere indeed there were the same signs of the struggles toward taste, the decline of taste into the prejudices of comfort, that
went with a whole milieu and a generation—both hers. And over
there was, even more personally, the second bed.

Mrs. Hazlitt sat down on it. If it were moved, into the study say,
a few things out of storage with it, how sympathetically this flat
might be shared. Nonsense, sheer fantasy to go on like this, to fancy
herself embarking on the pitiable twin-life of leftover women, much
less with a stranger. But was a woman a stranger if you happened to
know that on her twelfth birthday she had received a copy of *Dr.
Dolittle*, inscribed to Helena Nelson from her loving father, if you
knew the secret, packrat place in the linen closet where she stuffed
the neglected mending, of another, in a kitchen drawer, full of
broken Mexican terrines and clipped recipes as shamefully grimy as
your own cherished ones, if you knew that on 2/11/58 and on
7/25/57 a Dr. Burke had prescribed what looked to be sulfa pills,

never used, that must have cured her at the point of purchase, as had embarrassingly happened time and again to yourself? If, in short, you knew almost every endearing thing about her, except her face?

Mrs. Hazlitt, blinking in the excessive light, looked sideways. She knew where there was a photograph album, tumbled once by accident from its shunted place in the bookshelf, and at once honorably replaced. She had seen enough to know that the snapshots, not pasted in separately, would have to be exhumed, one by one, from their packets. No, she told herself, she already knew more than enough of Mrs. Berry from all that had been so trustfully exposed here—enough to know that this was the sort of prying to which Mrs. Berry, like herself, would never stoop. Somehow this clinched it—their understanding. She could see them exchanging notes at some future meeting, Mrs. Berry saying, "Why, do you know—one night, when I was in London—"—herself, the vis-à-vis, nodding, their perfect rapprochement. Then what would be wrong in using, when so handily provided, so graciously awaiting her, such a comforting vis-à-vis, now?

Mrs. Hazlitt found herself standing, the room's glare pressing on her as if she were arraigned in a police line-up, as if, she reminded herself irritably, it were not self-imposed. She forced herself to make a circuit of the room, turning out each lamp with the crisp, no-nonsense flick of the wrist that nurses employed. At the one lamp still burning she hesitated, reluctant to cross over that last shadow-line. Then, with a shrug, she turned it out and sat down in the darkness, in one of the two opposing boudoir chairs. For long minutes she sat there. Once or twice she trembled on the verge of speech, covered it with a swallow. The conventions that guarded the mind in its strict relationship with the tongue were the hardest to flaunt. But this was the century of talk, of the long talk, in which all were healthily urged to confide. Even the children were encouraged toward, praised for, the imaginary companion. Why should the grown person, who for circumstance beyond his control had no other, be denied? As she watched the window, the light in the small gray house was extinguished. Some minutes later the doorman across the way disappeared. Without looking at the luminous dial of the clock, she could feel the silence aging, ripening. At last she bent forward to the opposite chair.

"Helena?" she said.

Her voice, clear-cut, surprised her. There was nothing so strange about it. The walls remained walls. No one could hear her, or cared to, and now, tucking her feet up, she could remember how cozy this could be, with someone opposite. "Helena," she said. "Wait till I tell you what happened while you were away."

She told her everything. At first she stumbled, went back, as if she were rehearsing in front of a mirror. Several times she froze, unsure whether a sentence had been spoken aloud entirely, or had begun, or terminated, unspoken, in the mind. But as she went on, this wavering borderline seemed only to resemble the clued conversation, meshed with silences, between two people who knew each other well. By the time she had finished her account she was almost at ease, settling back into the comfortably shared midnight post-mortem that always restored balance to the world—so nearly could she imagine the face, not unlike her own, in the chair opposite, smiling ruefully at her over the boy and his gingerbread fears, wondering mischievously with her as to in which of the shapes of temptation the Old Nick visited Miss Finan.

"That girl and her *log!*" said Mrs. Hazlitt. "You know how, when they're that young, you want to smash in the smugness. And yet, when you think of all they've got to go through, you feel so maternal. Even if—" Even if, came the nod, imperceptibly—you've never had children, like us.

For a while they were silent. "Warwick!" said Mrs. Hazlitt then. "Years ago there was an actor—Robert Warwick. I was in love with him—at about the age of eight." Then she smiled, bridling slightly, at the dark chair opposite, whose occupant would know her age. "Oh, all right then—twelve. But what is it, do you suppose, always makes old actors look seedy, even when they're not? Daylight maybe. Or all the pretenses." She ruminated. "Why . . . do you know," she said slowly, "I think I've got it. The way he looked in my face when I was speaking, and the way the dog turned back and he didn't. He was lip-reading. Why, the poor old boy is deaf!" She settled back, dropping her slippers one by one to the floor. "Of course, that's it. And he wouldn't want to admit that he couldn't have heard it. Probably doesn't dare wear an aid. Poor old boy, pretty dreary for him if he is an actor, and I'll bet he is." She sighed, a luxury permitted now. "Ah, well. Frail reed—Miss Finan. Lucky for me, though, that I stumbled on her." And on you.

A police siren sounded, muffled less and less by distance, approaching. She was at the window in time to see the car's red dome light streak by as it always did, its alarum dying behind it. Nothing else was on the road "And there were the taxis," she said, looking down. "I don't know why I keep forgetting them. Veering to the side like that, one right after the other, and one had his light out, so it wasn't for a fare. Nothing on the curb either. Then they both shot away, almost as if they'd caught sight of something up here. And wanted no part of it—the way people do in this town. Wish you could've seen them—it was eerie." There was no response from behind her.

She sat down again. Yes, there was a response, for the first time faintly contrary.

"No," she said. "It certainly was *not* the siren. I was up in a flash. I'd have seen it." She found herself clenching the arms of the chair. "Besides," she said, in a quieter voice, "don't you remember? I heard it twice."

There was no answer. Glancing sideways, she saw the string of lights opposite, not quite of last night's pattern. But the silence was the same, opened to its perfect hour like a century plant, multiple-rooted, that came of age every night. The silence was in full bloom, and it had its own sound. Hark hark, no dogs do bark. And there is nobody in the chair.

Never was, never had been. It was sad to be up at this hour and sane. For now is the hour, now is the hour when all good men are asleep. Her hand smoothed the rim of the wastebasket, about the height from the floor of a dog's collar. Get one tomorrow. But how to manage until then, with all this silence speaking?

She made herself stretch out on the bed, close her eyes. "Sam," she said at last, as she had sworn never to do in thought or word, "I'm lonely." Listening vainly, she thought how wise her resolve had been. Too late, now she had tested his loss to the full, knew him for the void he was—far more of a one than Mrs. Berry, who, though unknown, was still somewhere. By using the name of love, when she had been ready to settle for anybody, she had sent him into the void forever. Opening her eyes, adjusted now to the sourceless city light that never ceased trickling on ceiling, lancing from mirrors, she turned her head right to left, left to right on the pillow, in a gesture to the one auditor who remained.

"No," she said, in the dry voice of correction. "I'm not lonely. I'm alone."

Almost at once she raised herself on her elbow, her head cocked. No, she had heard nothing from outside. But in her mind's ear she could hear the sound of the word she had just spoken, its final syllable twanging like a tuning fork, infinitely receding to octaves above itself, infinitely returning. In what seemed scarcely a stride, she was in the next room, at the French window, brought there by that thin, directional vibration which not necessarily even the blind would hear. For she had recognized it. She had identified the accent of the scream.

The long window frame, its swollen wood shoved tight by her the night before, at first would not budge; then, as she put both hands on the hasp and braced her knees, it gave slowly, grinding inward, the heavy man-high bolt thumping down. Both sounds, too, fell into their proper places. That's what I heard before, she thought, the noise of a window opening or closing, exactly like mine. Two lines of them, down the six floors of the building, made twelve possibles. But that was of no importance now. Stepping up on the lintel, she spread the casements wide.

Yes, there was the bridge, one small arc of it, sheering off into the mist, beautiful against the night, as all bridges were. Now that she was outside, past all barriers, she could hear, with her ordinary ear, faint nickings that marred the silence, but these were only the surface scratches on a record that still revolved one low, continuous tone. No dogs do bark. That was the key to it, that her own hand, smoothing a remembered dog-collar, had been trying to give her. There were certain dog-whistles, to be bought anywhere—one had hung, with the unused leash, on a hook near a door in the country— which blew a summons so high above the human range that only a dog could hear it. What had summoned her last night would have been that much higher, audible only to those tuned in by necessity —the thin, soaring decibel of those who were no longer in the fold. Alone-oh. Alone-oh. That would have been the shape of it, of silence expelled from the mouth in one long relieving note, cool, irrepressible, the second one clapped short by the hand. No dog would have heard it. No animal but one was ever that alone.

She stepped out onto the fire escape. There must be legions of them, of us, she thought, in the dim alleyways, the high, flashing terraces—each one of them come to the end of his bookings, circling his small platform in space. And who would hear such a person? Not the log-girls, not for years and years. None of any age who, body to body, bed to bed, either in love or in the mutual pluck-pluck of hate—like the little girl and her mother—were still nested down. Reginald Warwick, stoppered in his special quiet, might hear it, turn to his Coco for confirmation which did not come, and persuade himself once again that it was only his affliction. Others lying awake snug as a bug, listening for that Old Nick, death, would hear the thin, sororal signal and not know what they had heard. But an endless assemblage of others all over the city would be waiting for it— all those sitting in the dark void of the one lamp quenched, the one syllable spoken—who would start up, some from sleep, to their windows . . . or were already there.

A car passed below. Instinctively, she flattened against the casement, but the car traveled on. Last night someone, man or woman, would have been standing in one of the line of niches above and beneath hers—perhaps even a woman in a blue robe like her own. But literal distance or person would not matter; in that audience all would be the same. Looking up, she could see the tired, heated lavender of the midtown sky, behind which lay that real imperial into which some men were already hurling their exquisitely signaling spheres. But this sound would come from breast to breast, at an altitude higher than any of those. She brought her fist to her mouth, in savage pride at having heard it, at belonging to a race some of whom could never adapt to any range less than that. *Some of us,* she thought, *are still responsible.*

Stepping forward, she leaned on the iron railing. At that moment, another car, traveling slowly by, hesitated opposite, its red dome light blinking. Mrs. Hazlitt stood very still. She watched until the police car went on again, inching ahead slowly, as if somebody inside were looking back. The two men inside there would never understand what she was waiting for. Hand clapped to her mouth, she herself had just understood. She was waiting for it—for its company. She was waiting for a second chance—to answer it. She was waiting for the scream to come again.